ATANA
and the
FIREBIRD

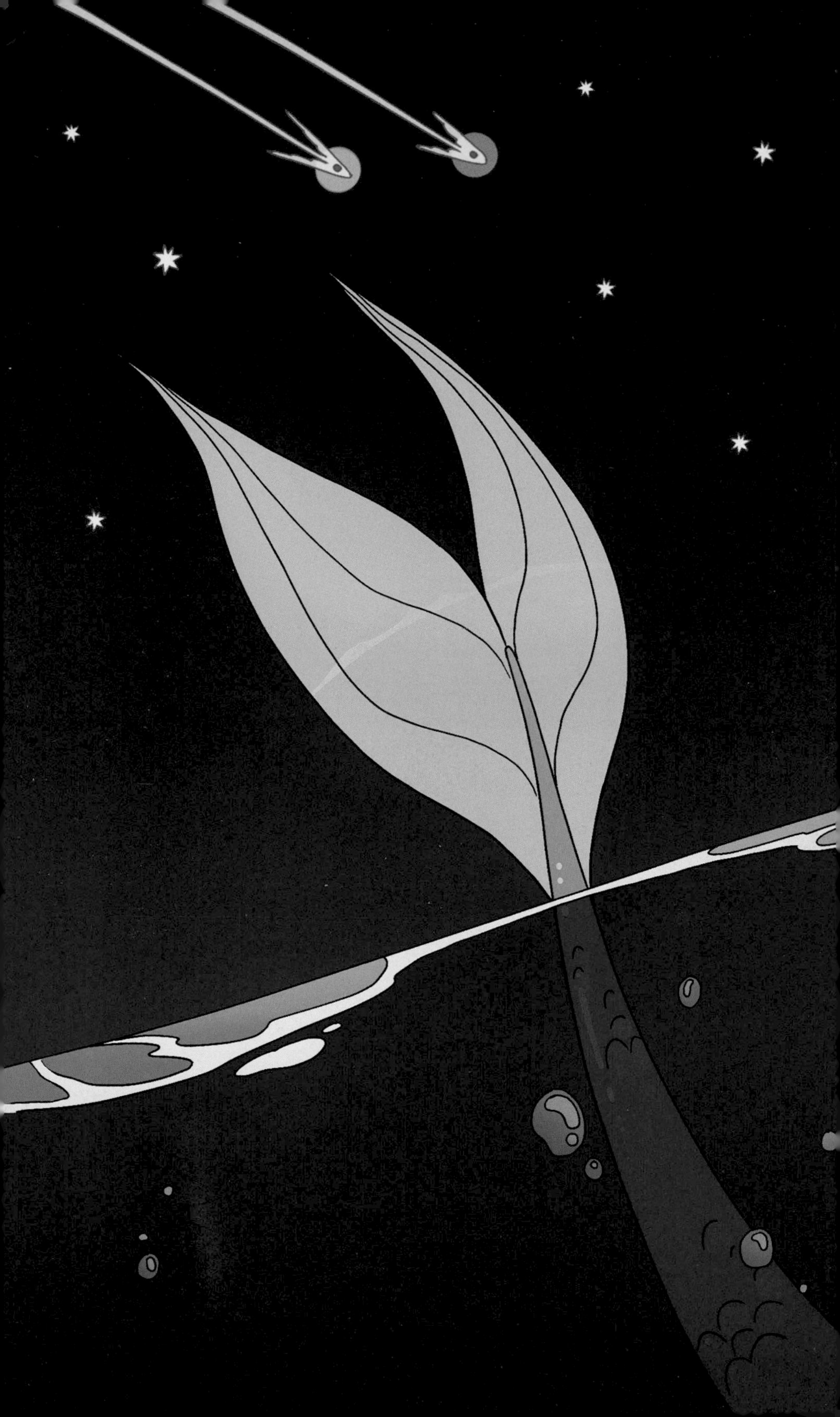

ATANA
and the
FIREBIRD

By Vivian Zhou

An Imprint of HarperCollinsPublishers

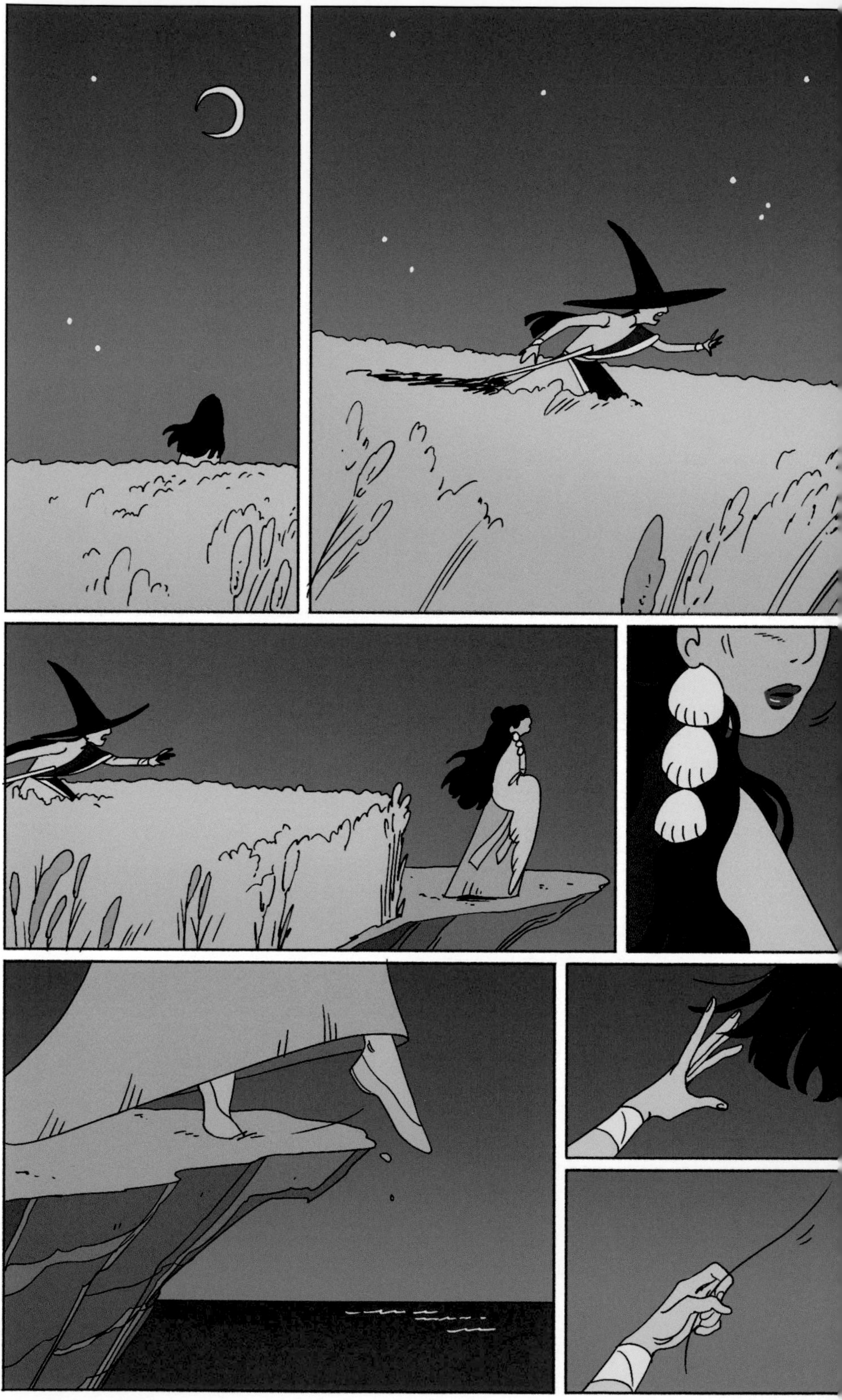

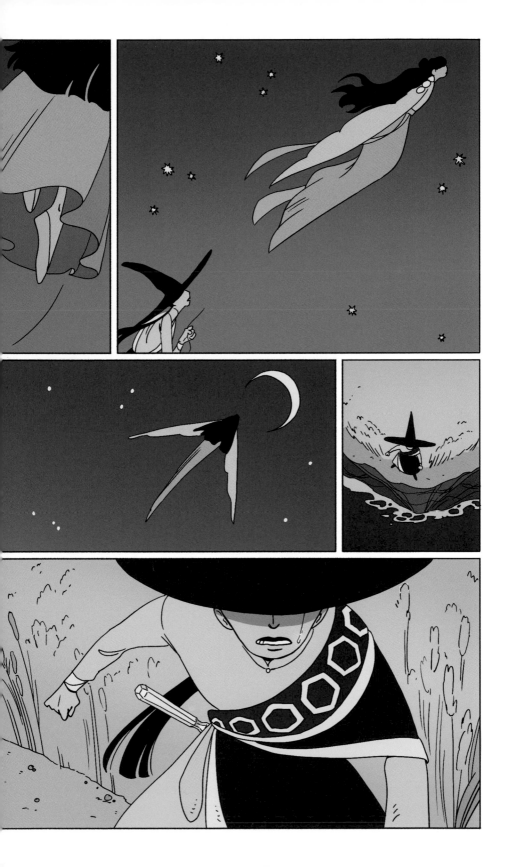

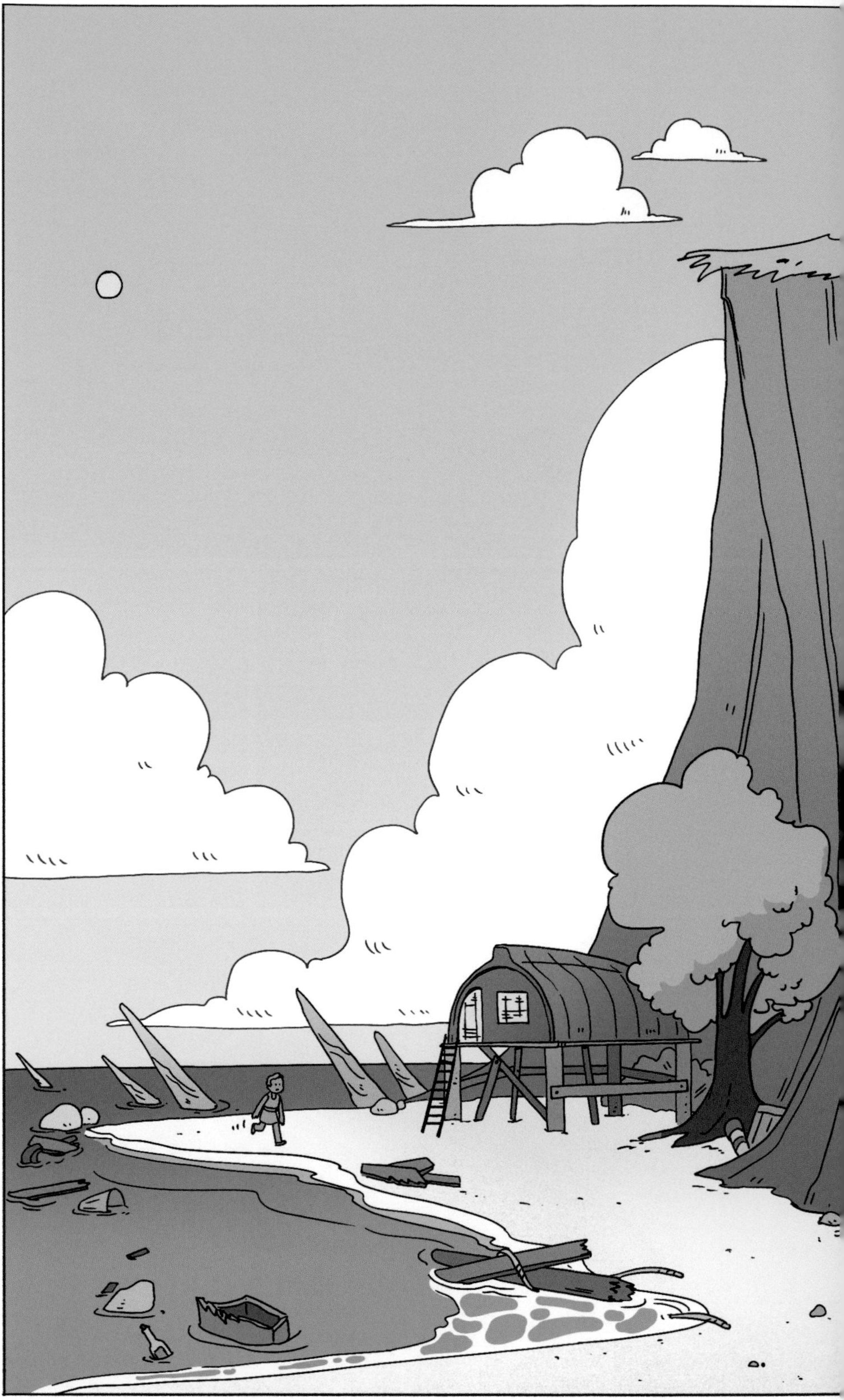

CHAPTER 1

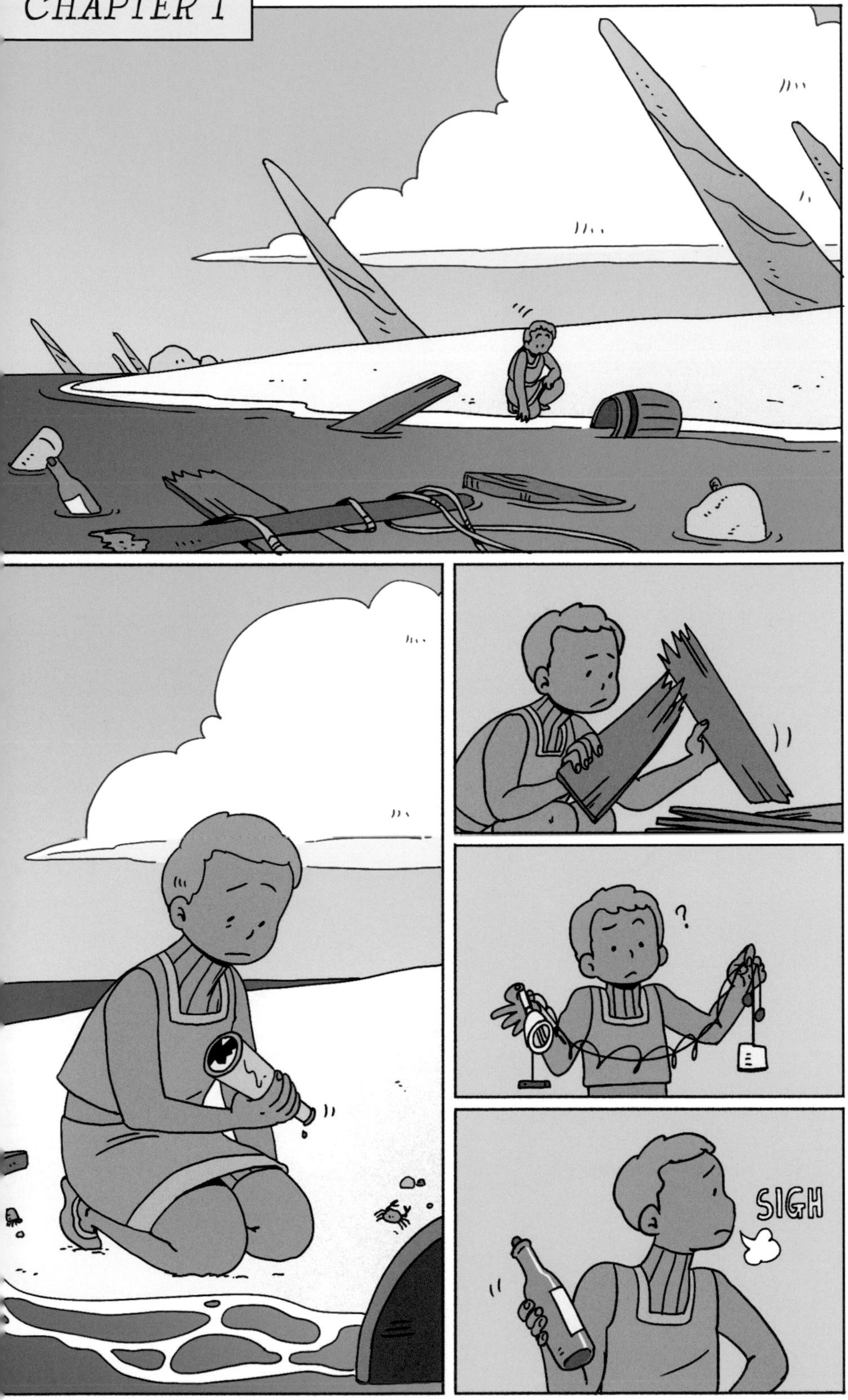
?
SIGH

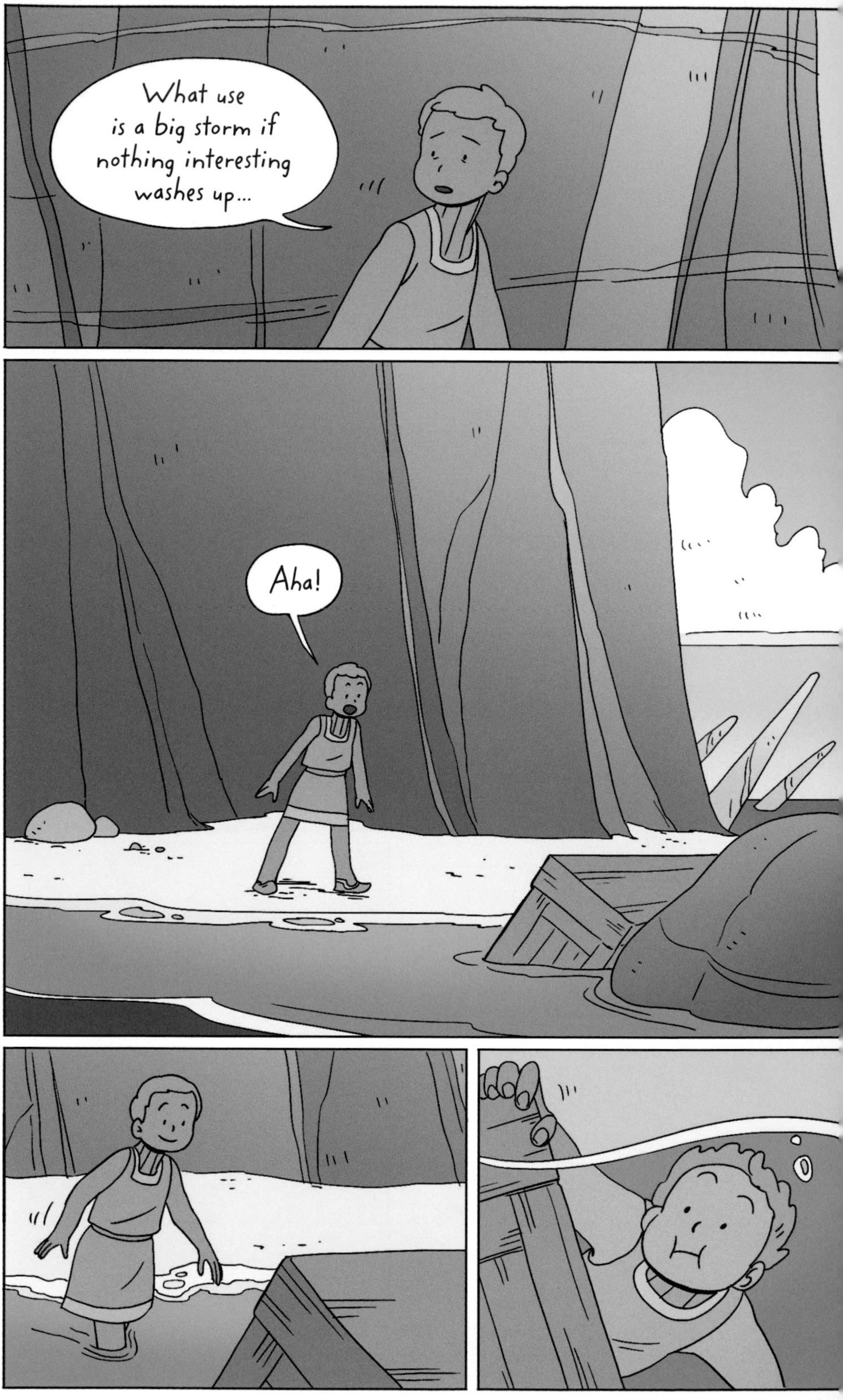
What use is a big storm if nothing interesting washes up...
Aha!

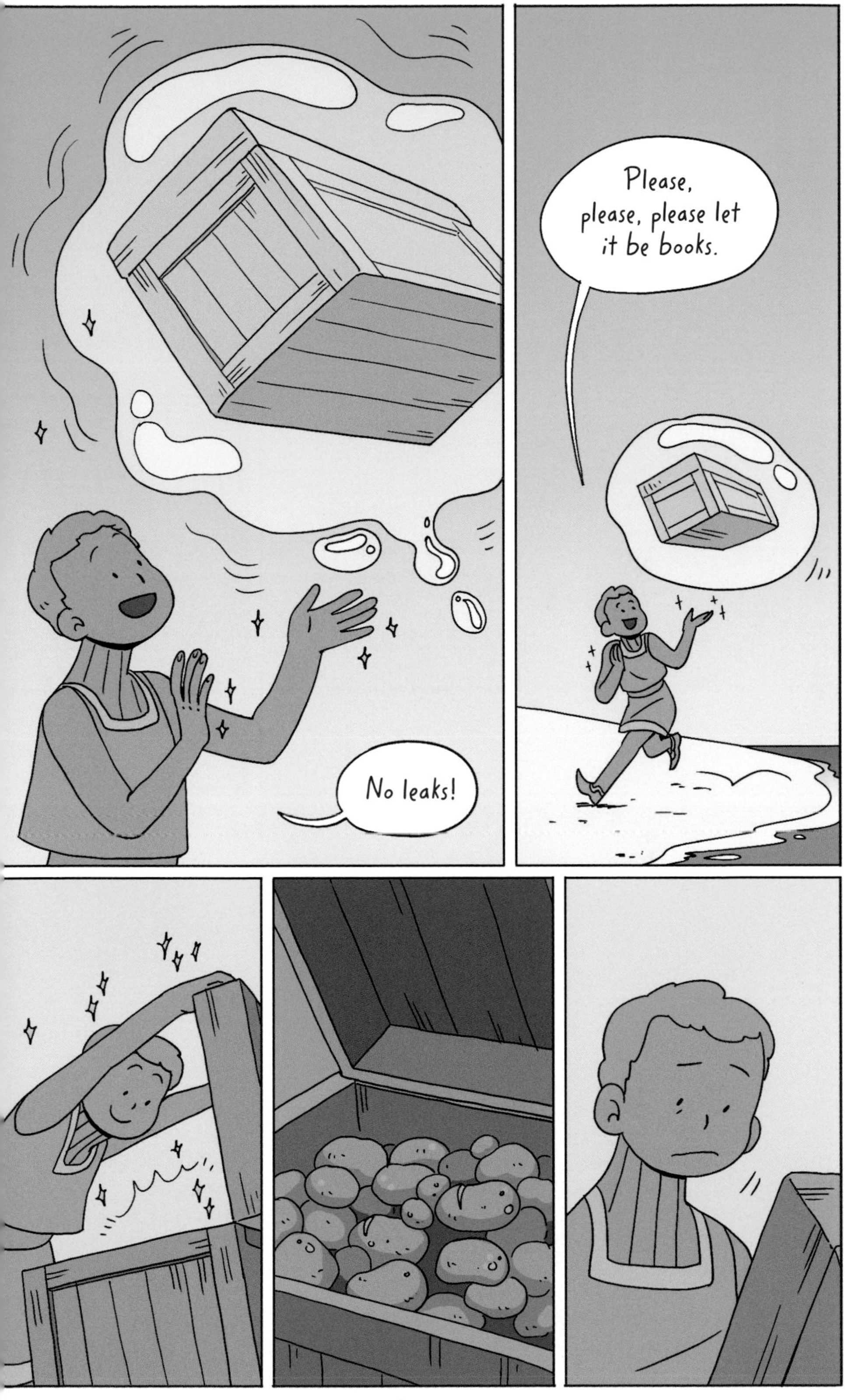
No leaks!
Please, please, please let it be books.

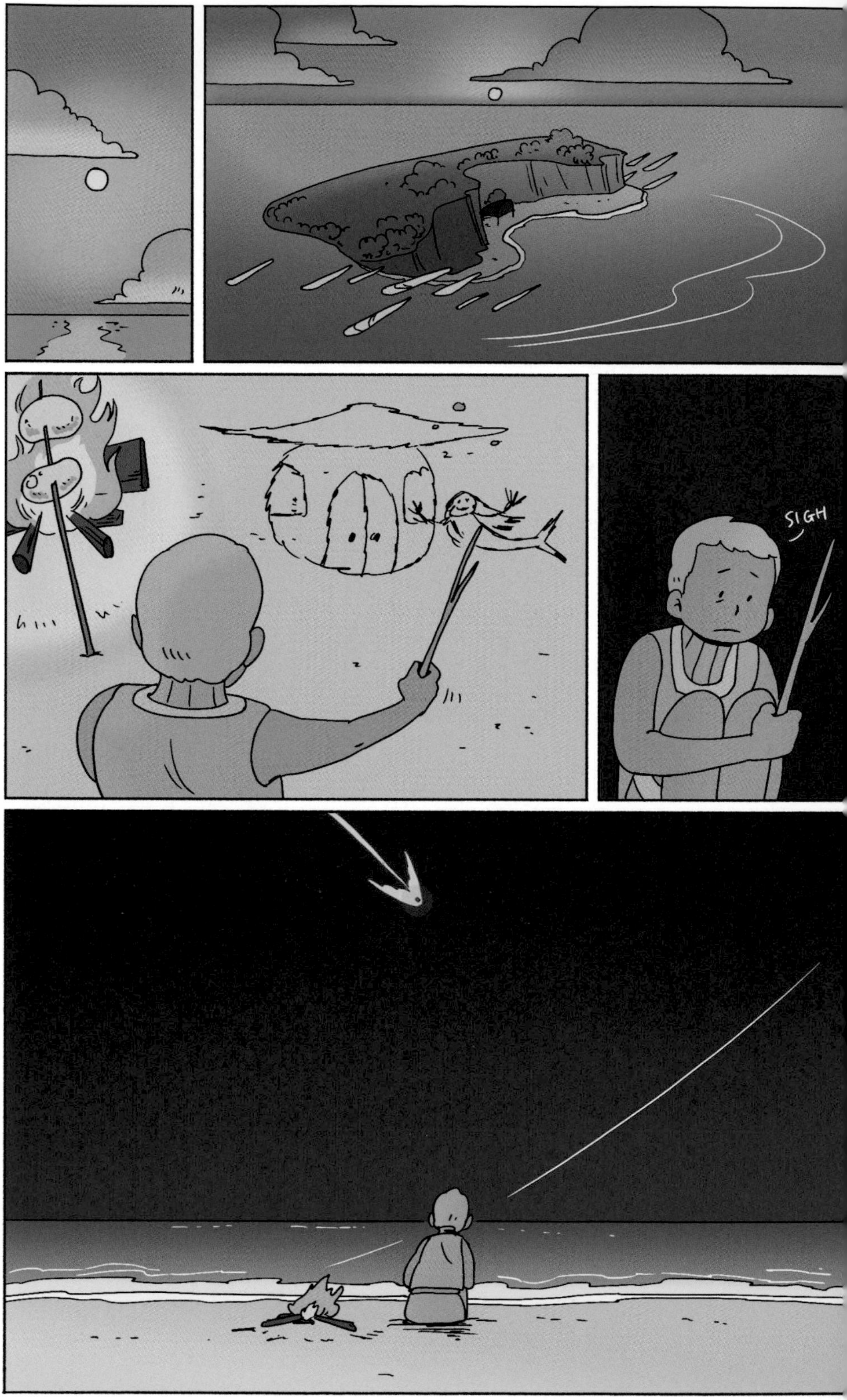
SIGH

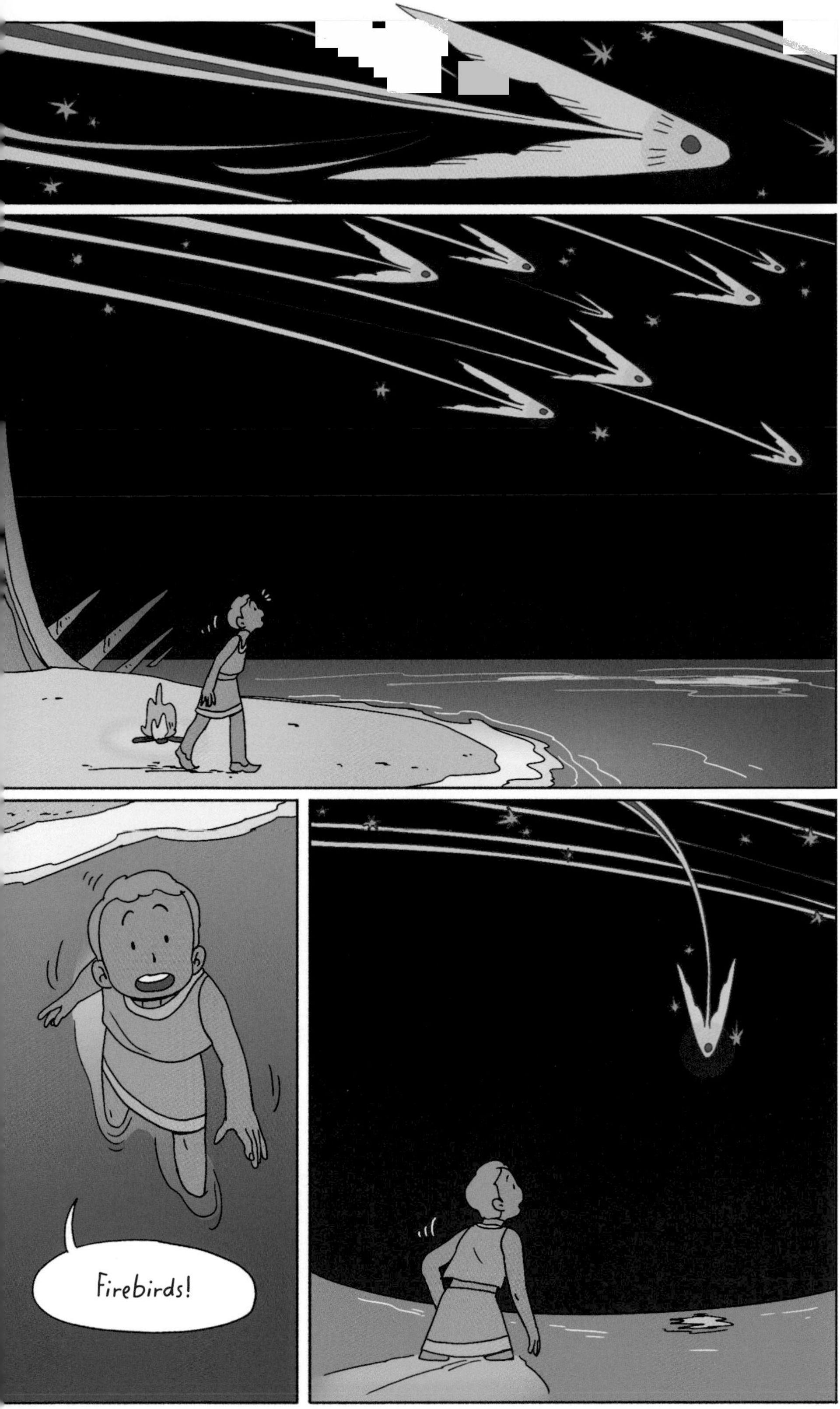
Firebirds!

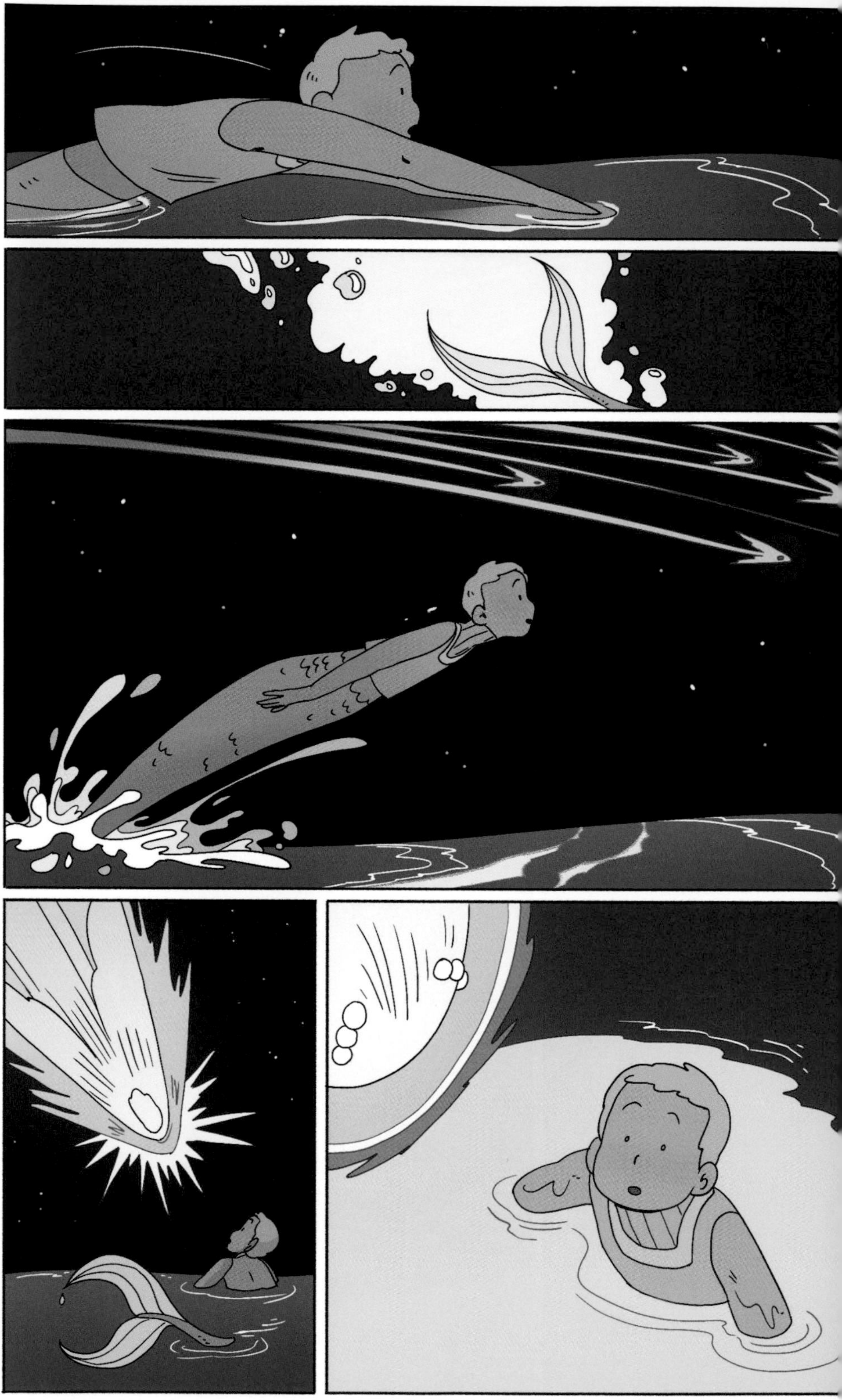

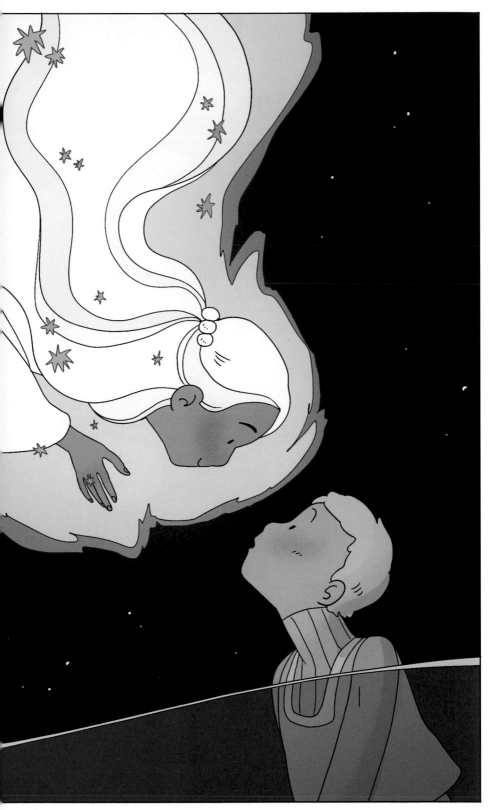

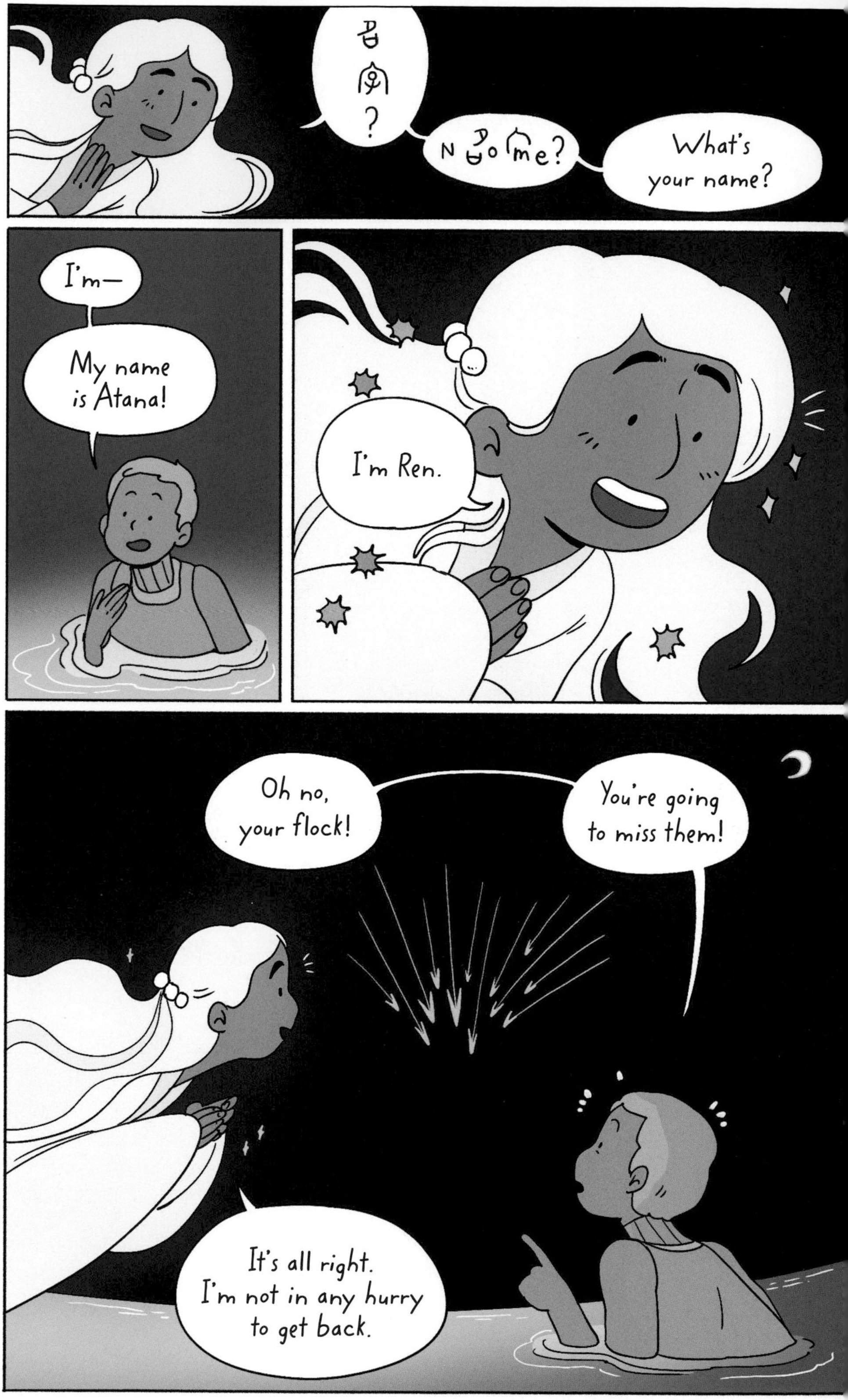
What's your name?
I'm—
My name is Atana!
I'm Ren.
Oh no, your flock!
You're going to miss them!
It's all right. I'm not in any hurry to get back.

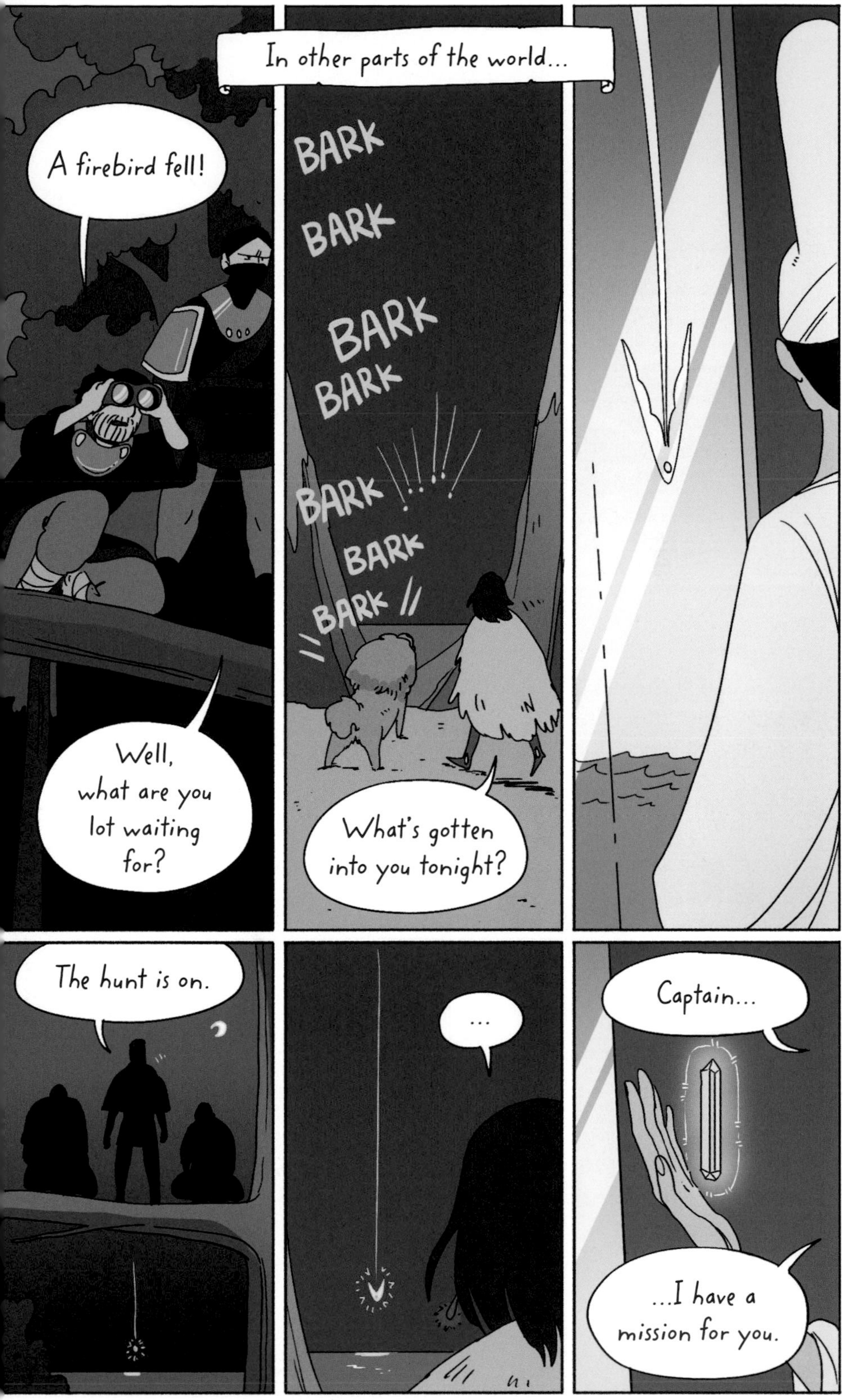
In other parts of the world...
A firebird fell!
Well, what are you lot waiting for?
BARK
BARK
BARK
BARK
BARK
BARK
BARK
What's gotten into you tonight?
The hunt is on.
...
Captain...
...I have a mission for you.

CHAPTER 2

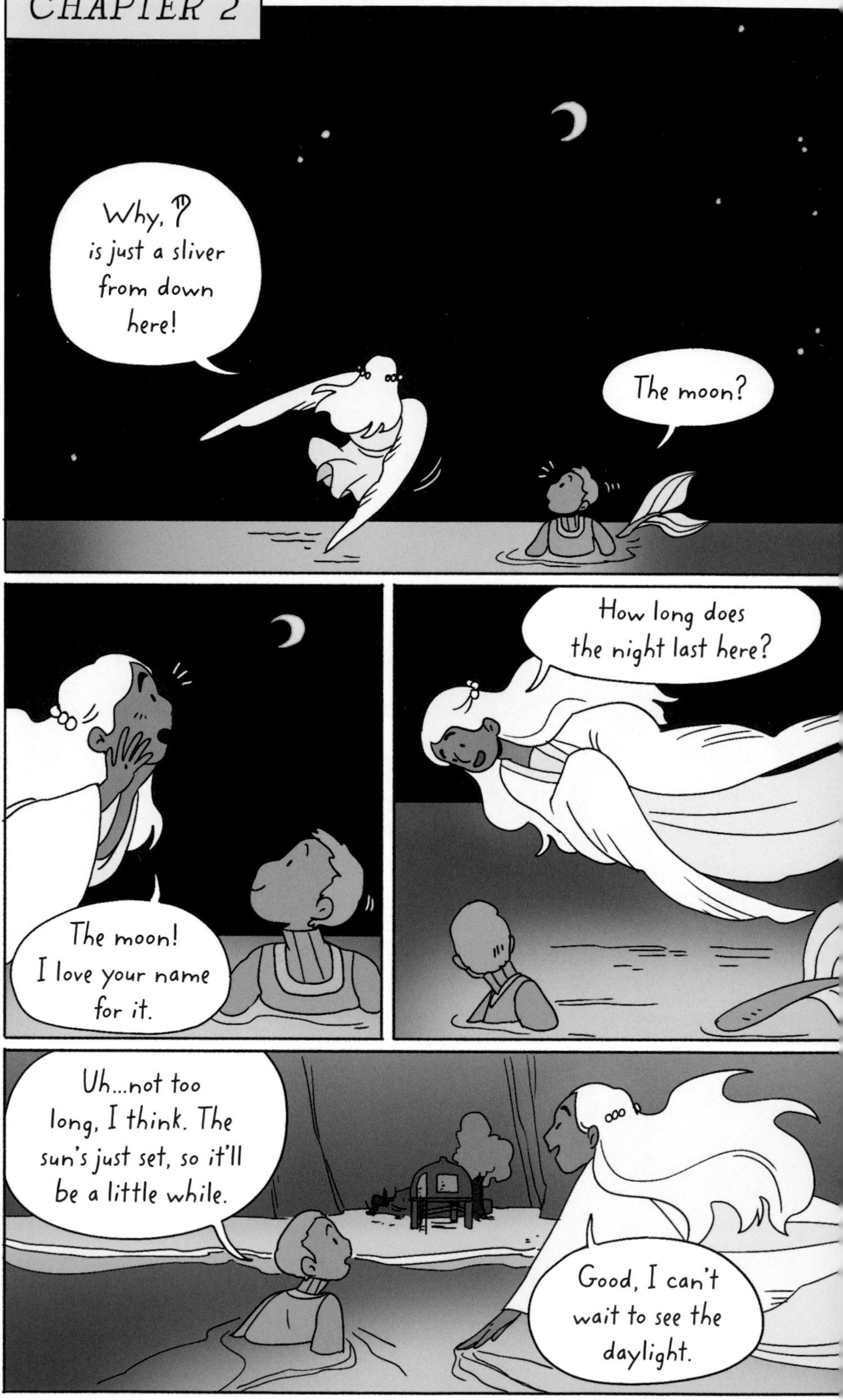
Why,
is just a sliver from down here!
The moon?
The moon! I love your name for it.
How long does the night last here?
Uh...not too long, I think. The sun's just set, so it'll be a little while.
Good, I can't wait to see the daylight.

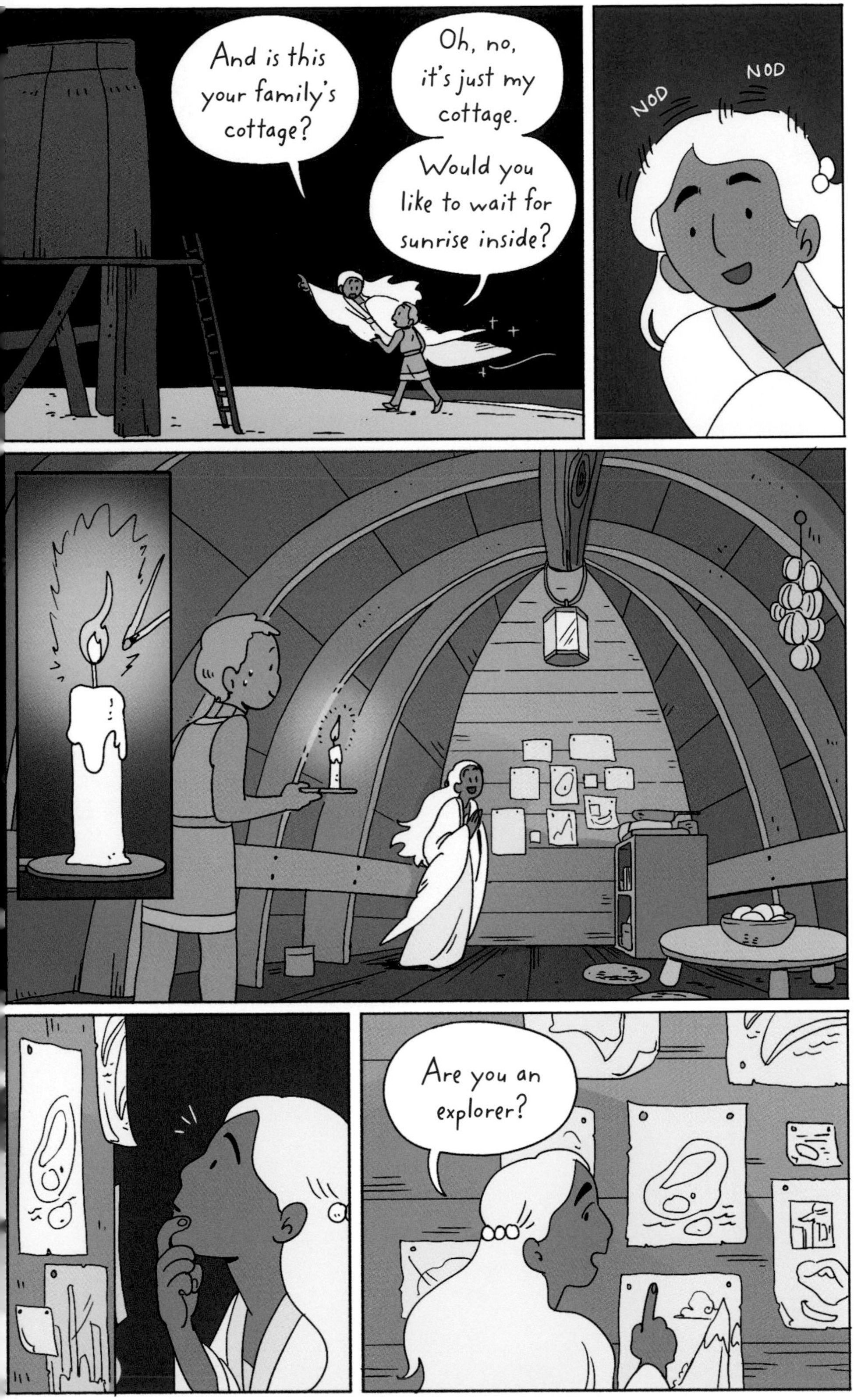
And is this your family's cottage?
Oh, no, it's just my cottage.
Would you like to wait for sunrise inside?
NOD
NOD
Are you an explorer?

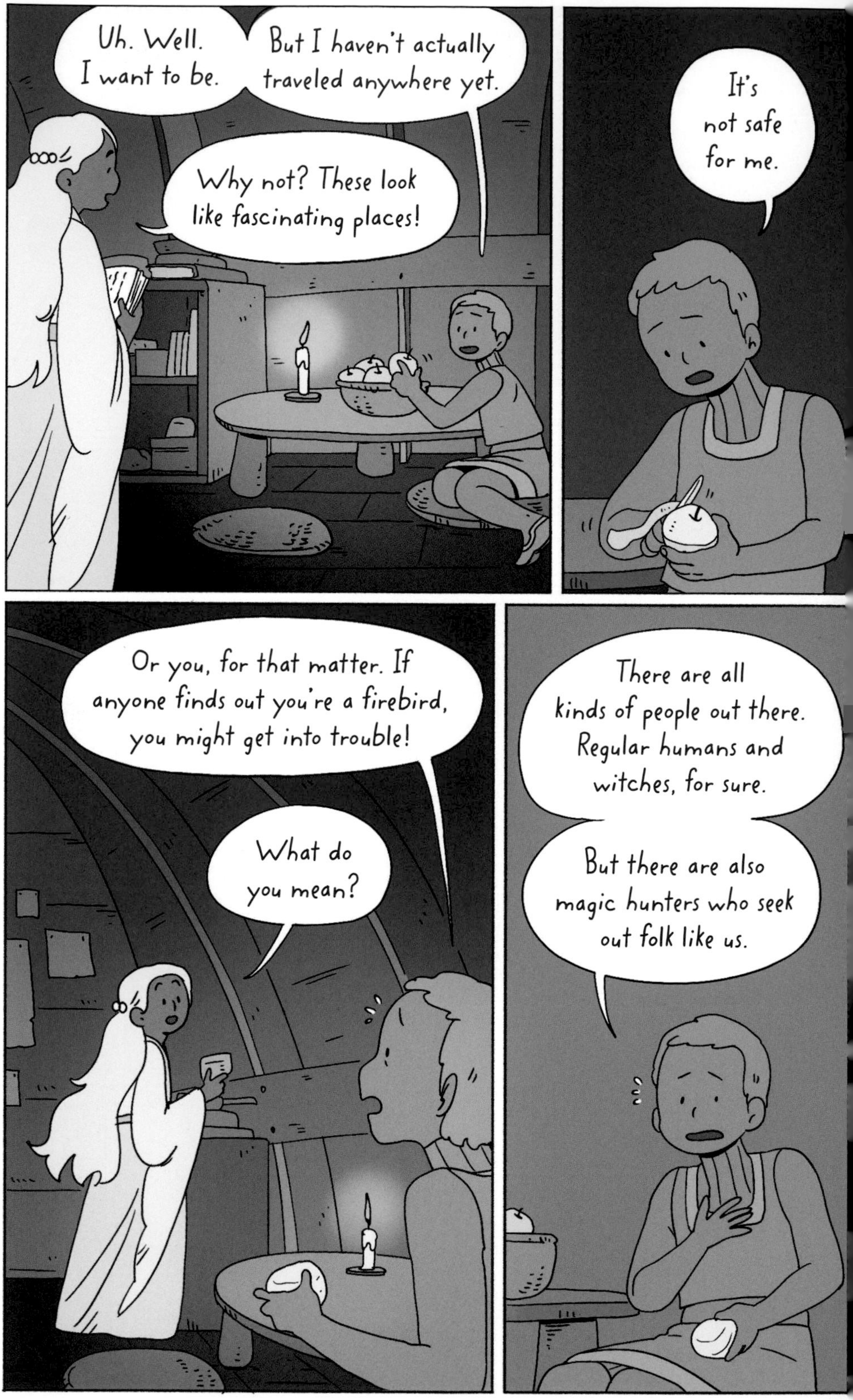
Uh. Well. I want to be.
But I haven't actually traveled anywhere yet.
Why not? These look like fascinating places!
It's not safe for me.
Or you, for that matter. If anyone finds out you're a firebird, you might get into trouble!
What do you mean?
There are all kinds of people out there. Regular humans and witches, for sure.
But there are also magic hunters who seek out folk like us.

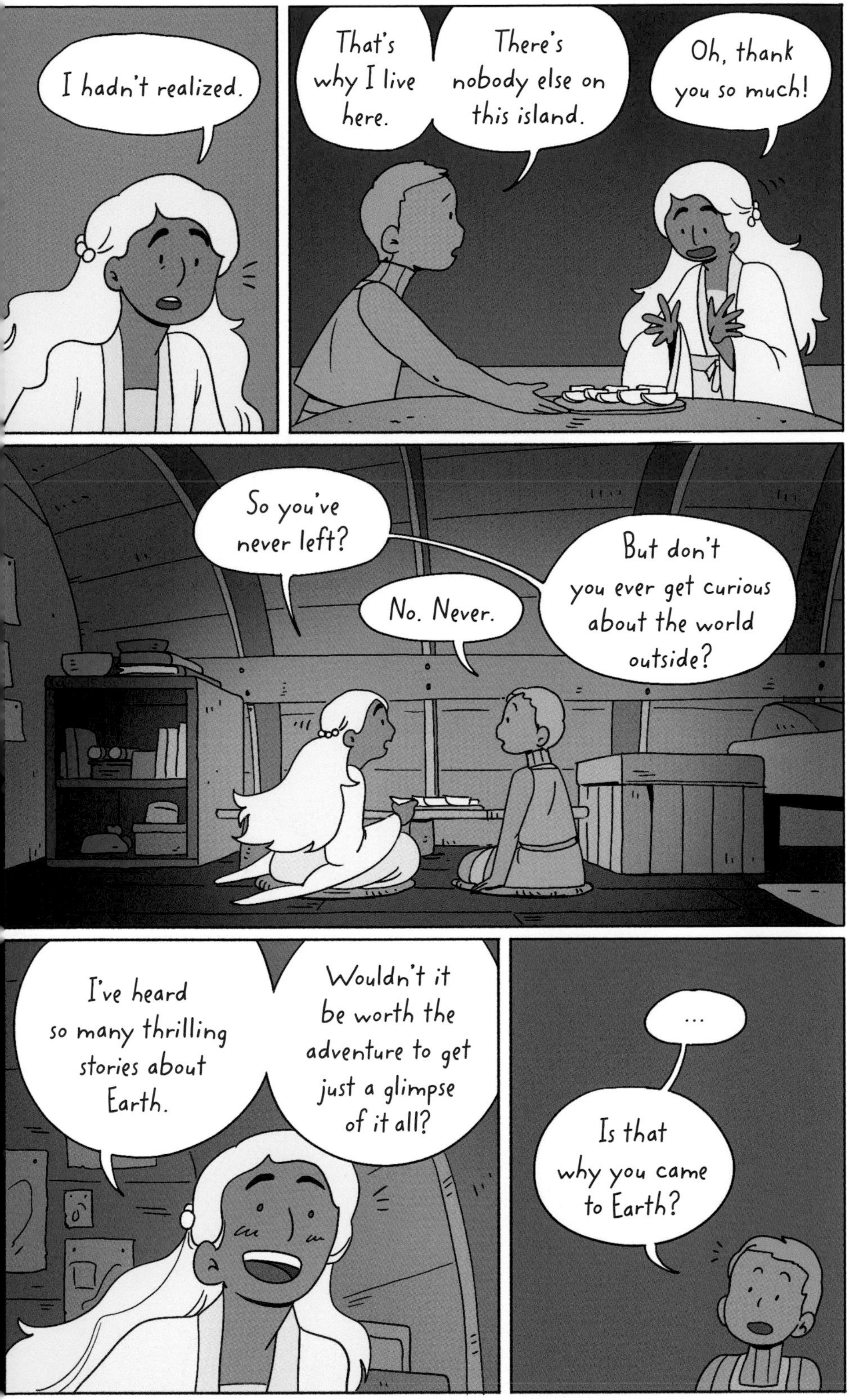
I hadn't realized.
That's why I live here.
There's nobody else on this island.
Oh, thank you so much!
So you've never left?
But don't you ever get curious about the world outside?
No. Never.
I've heard so many thrilling stories about Earth.
Wouldn't it be worth the adventure to get just a glimpse of it all?
...
Is that why you came to Earth?

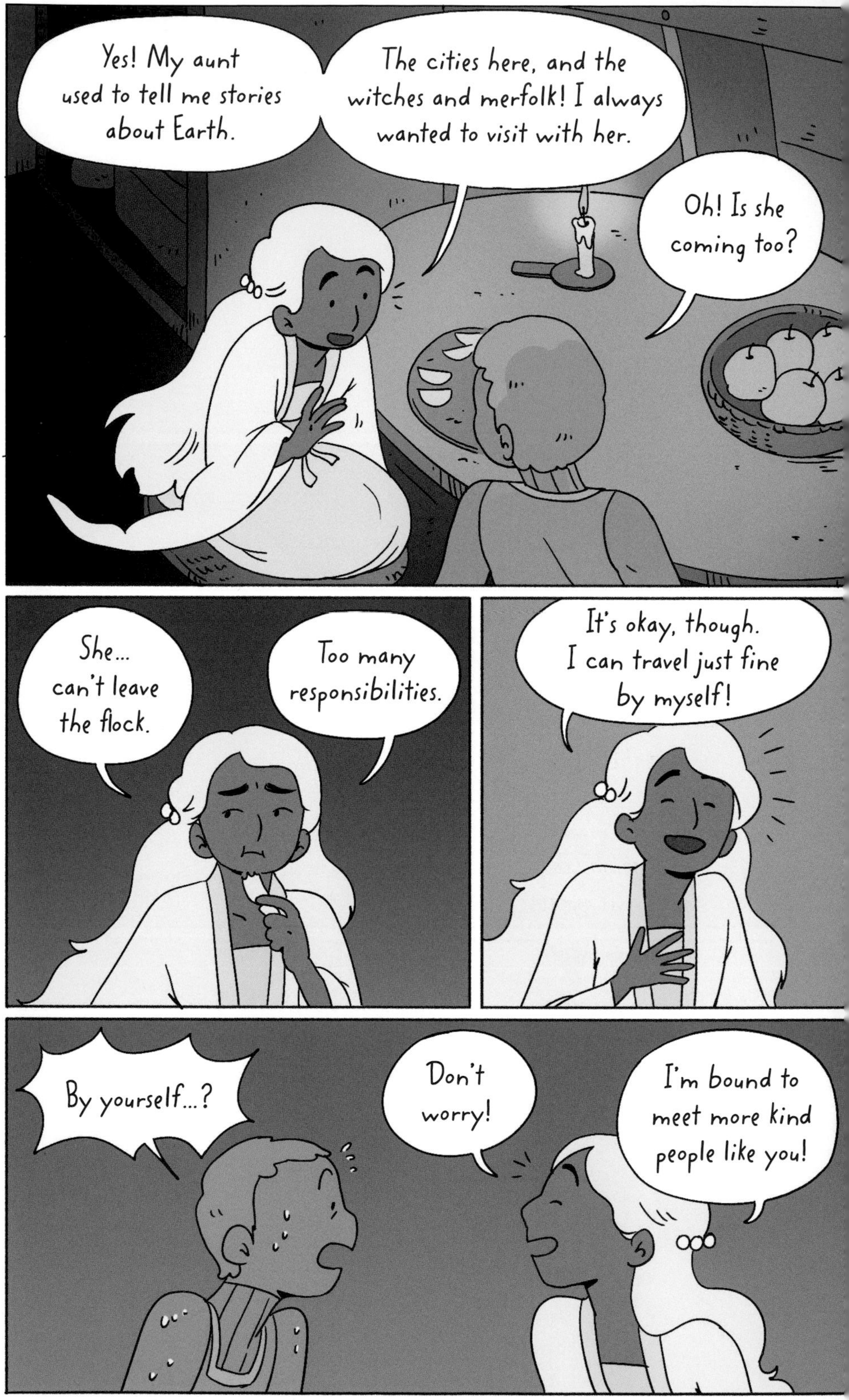
Yes! My aunt used to tell me stories about Earth.
The cities here, and the witches and merfolk! I always wanted to visit with her.
Oh! Is she coming too?
She... can't leave the flock.
Too many responsibilities.
It's okay, though. I can travel just fine by myself!
By yourself...?
Don't worry!
I'm bound to meet more kind people like you!

CHAPTER 3

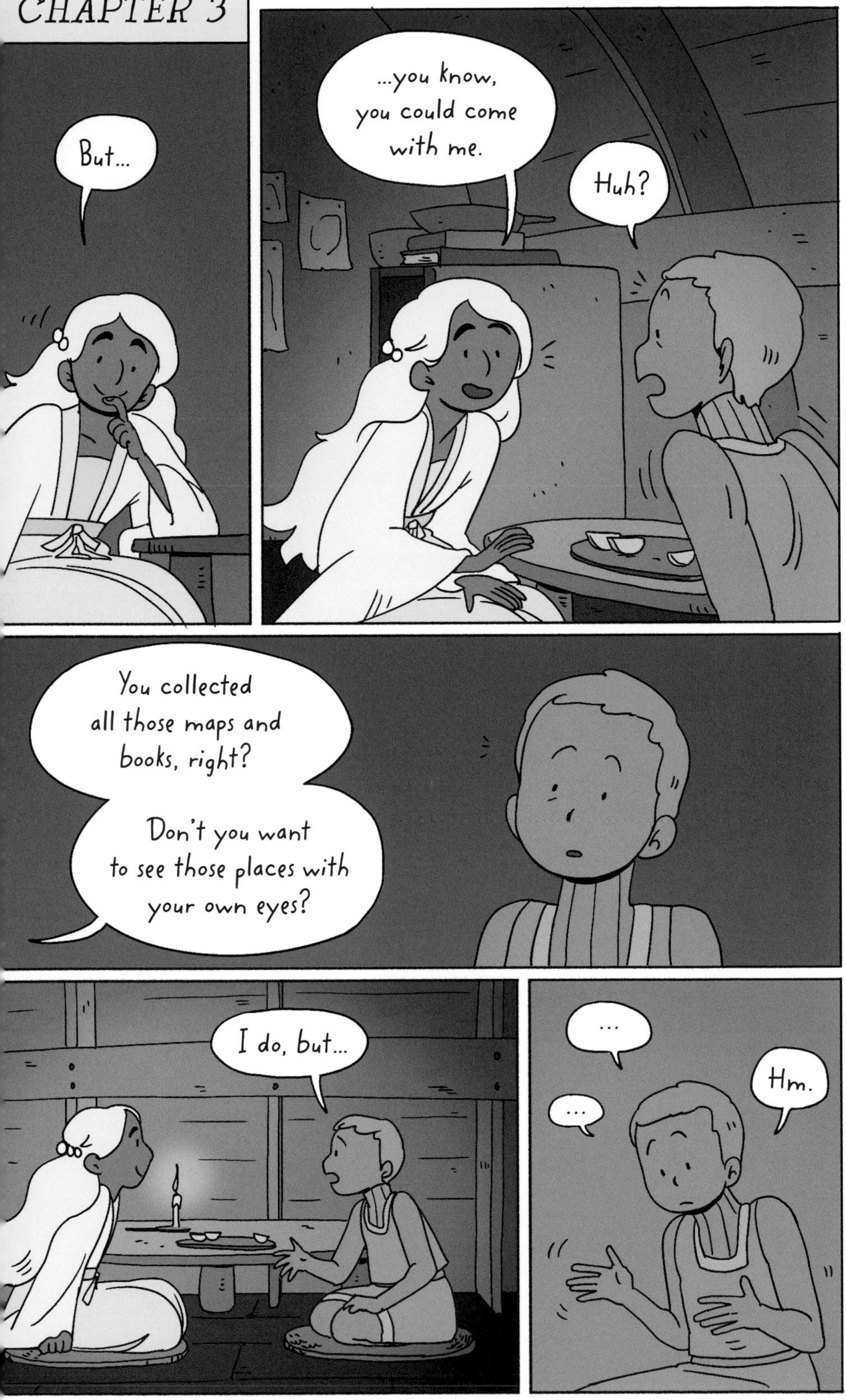

But...
...you know, you could come with me.
Huh?
You collected all those maps and books, right?
Don't you want to see those places with your own eyes?
I do, but...
...
...
Hm.

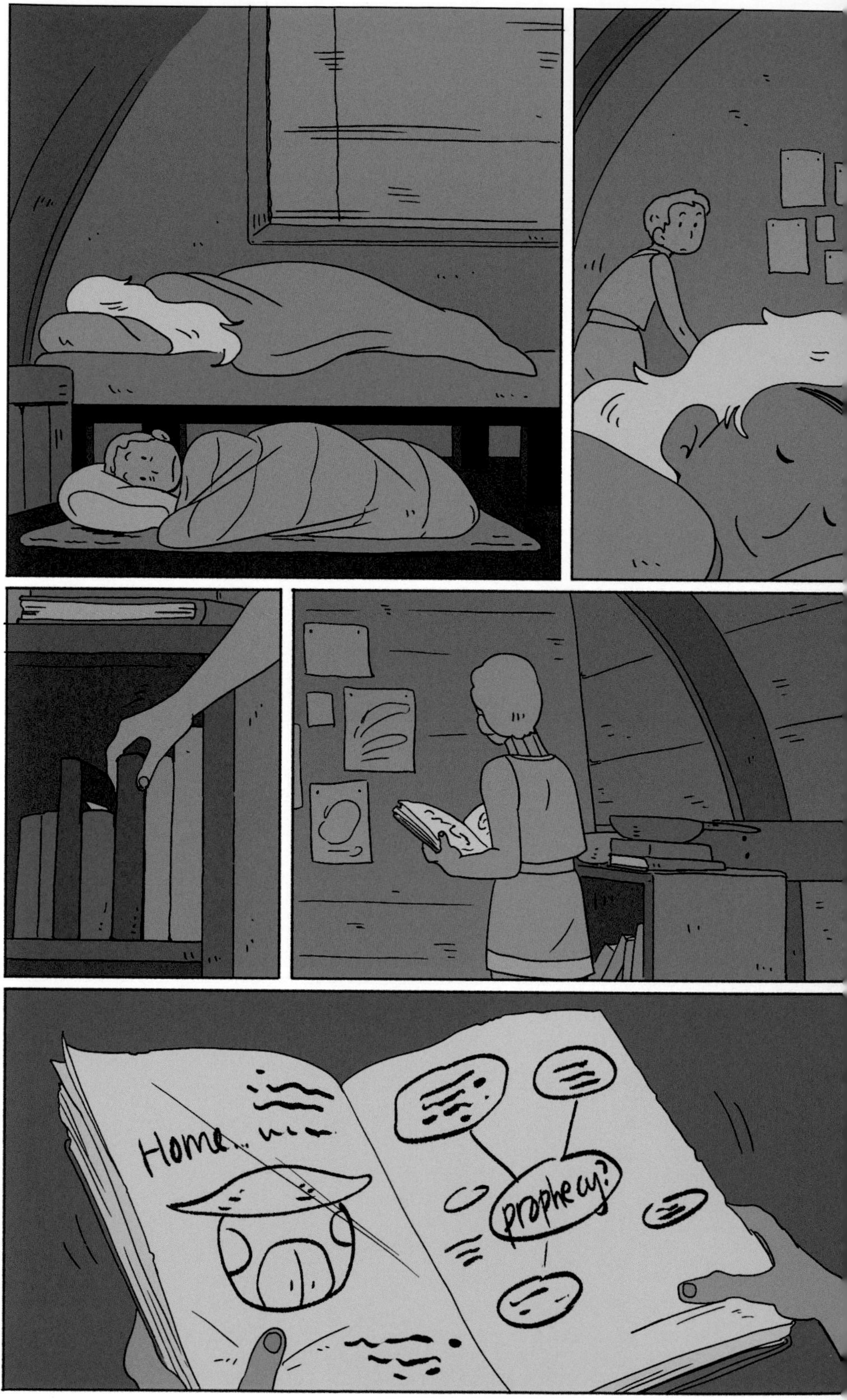
Home...
prophecy?

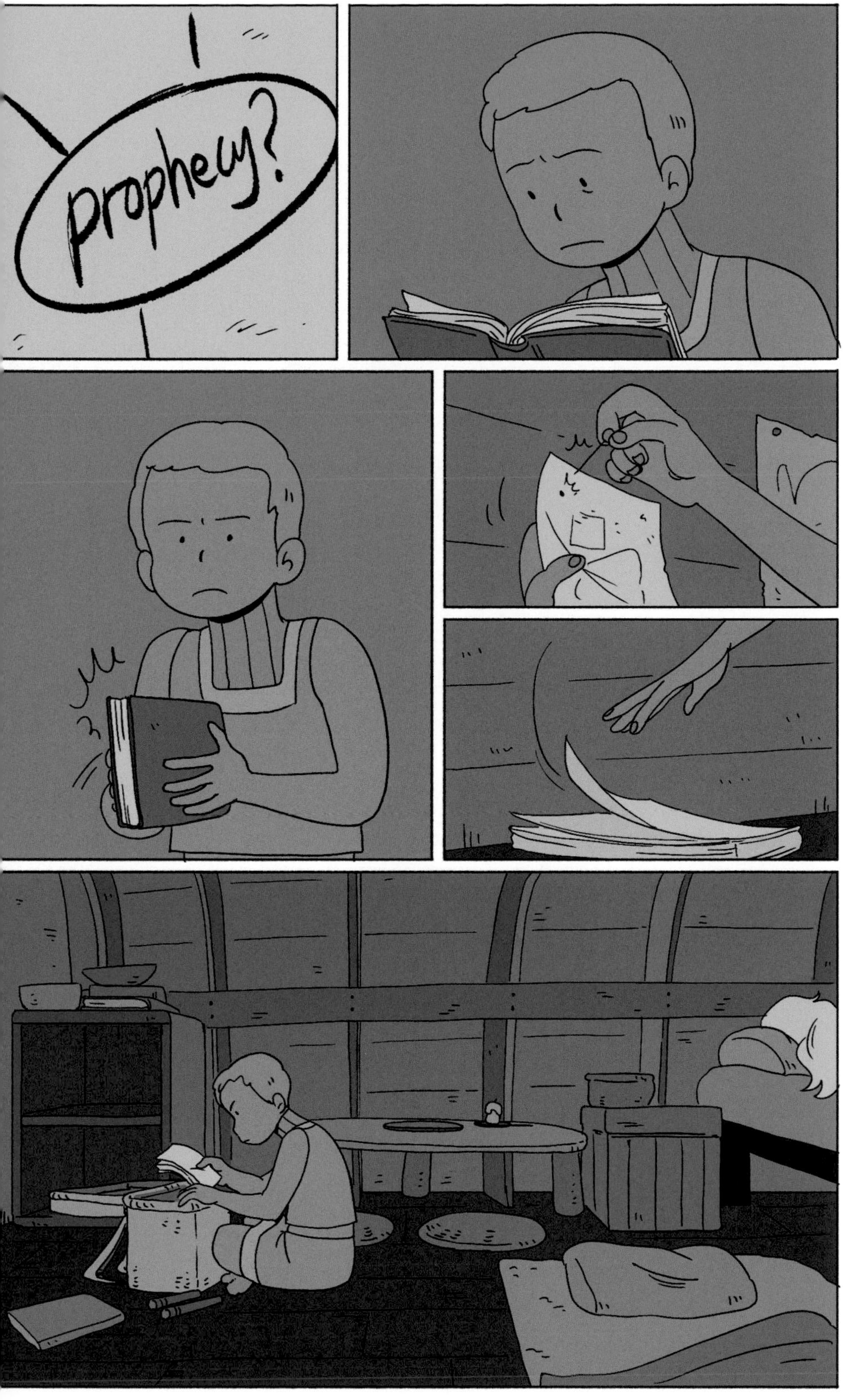
prophecy?

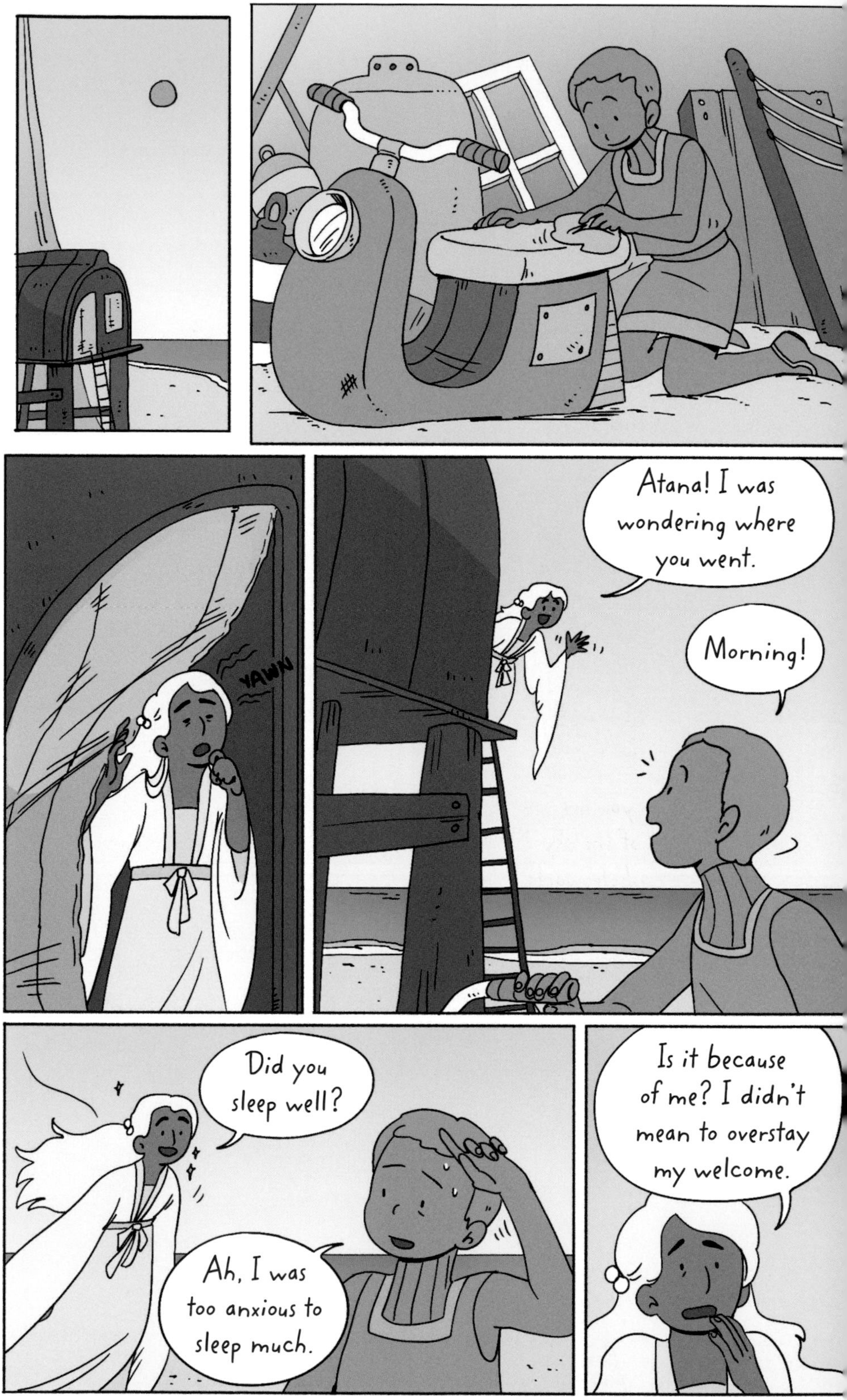
YAWN
Atana! I was wondering where you went.
Morning!
Did you sleep well?
Ah, I was too anxious to sleep much.
Is it because of me? I didn't mean to overstay my welcome.

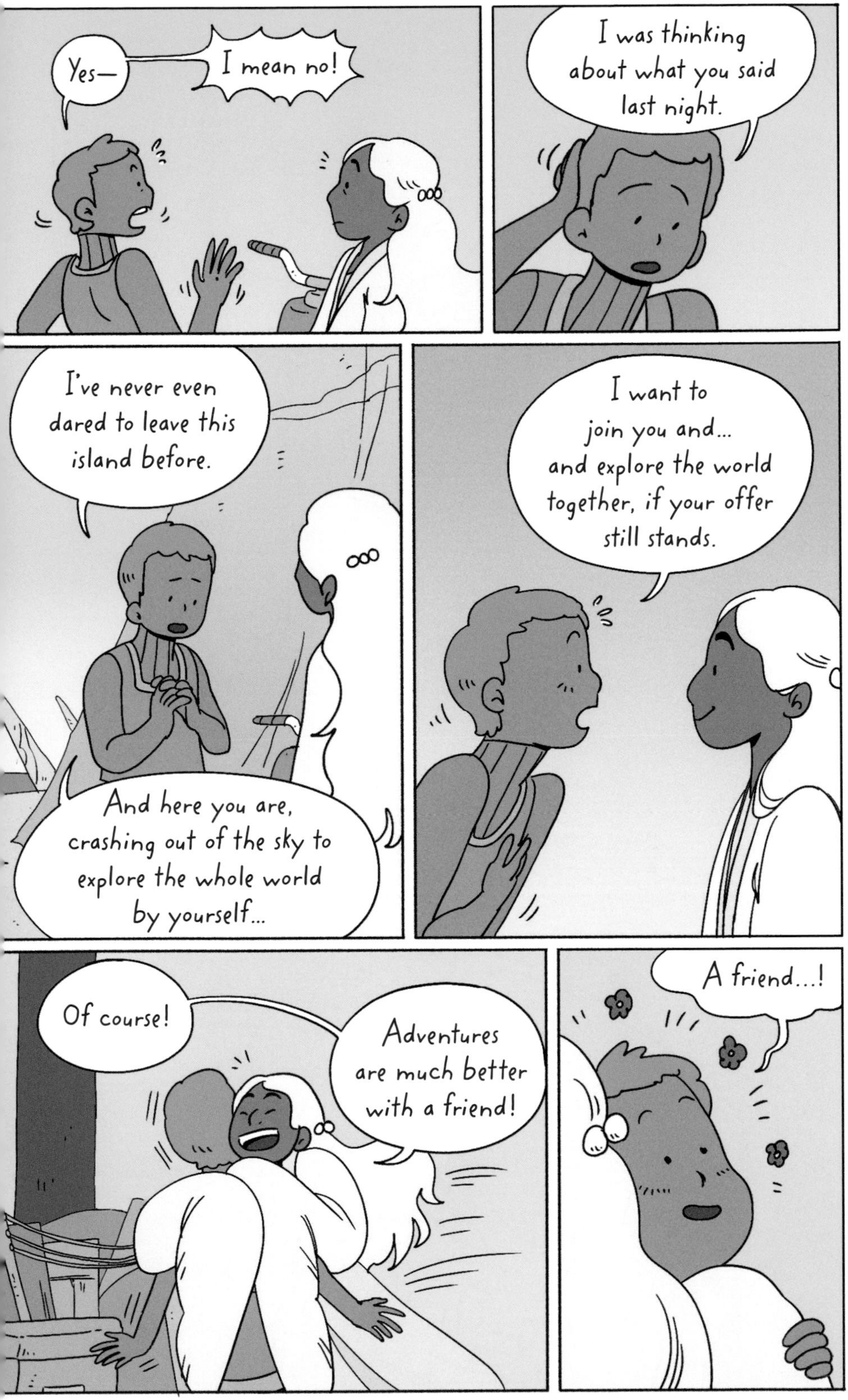
Yes—
I mean no!
I was thinking about what you said last night.
I've never even dared to leave this island before.
And here you are, crashing out of the sky to explore the whole world by yourself...
I want to join you and... and explore the world together, if your offer still stands.
Of course!
Adventures are much better with a friend!
A friend...!

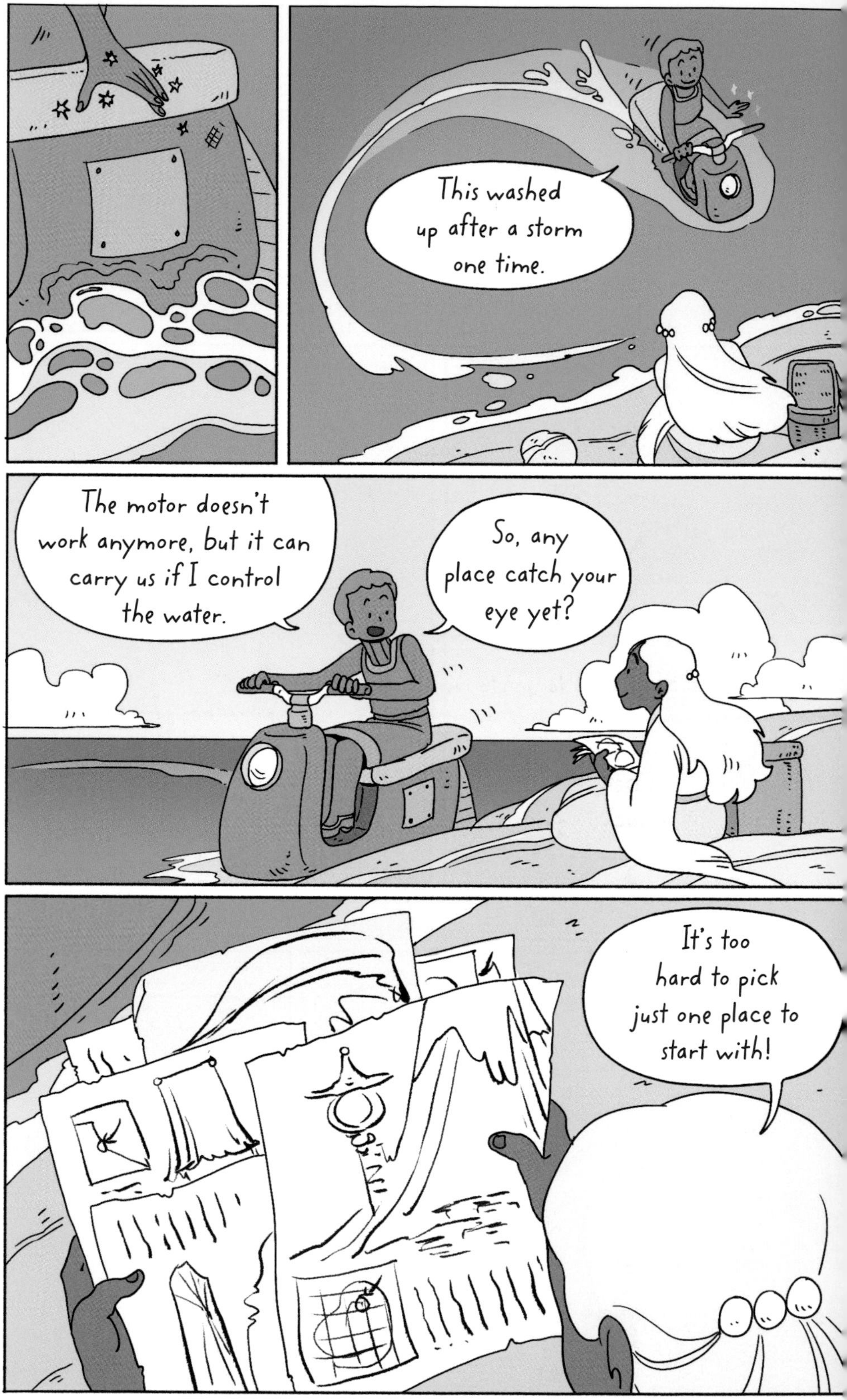
This washed up after a storm one time.
The motor doesn't work anymore, but it can carry us if I control the water.
So, any place catch your eye yet?
It's too hard to pick just one place to start with!

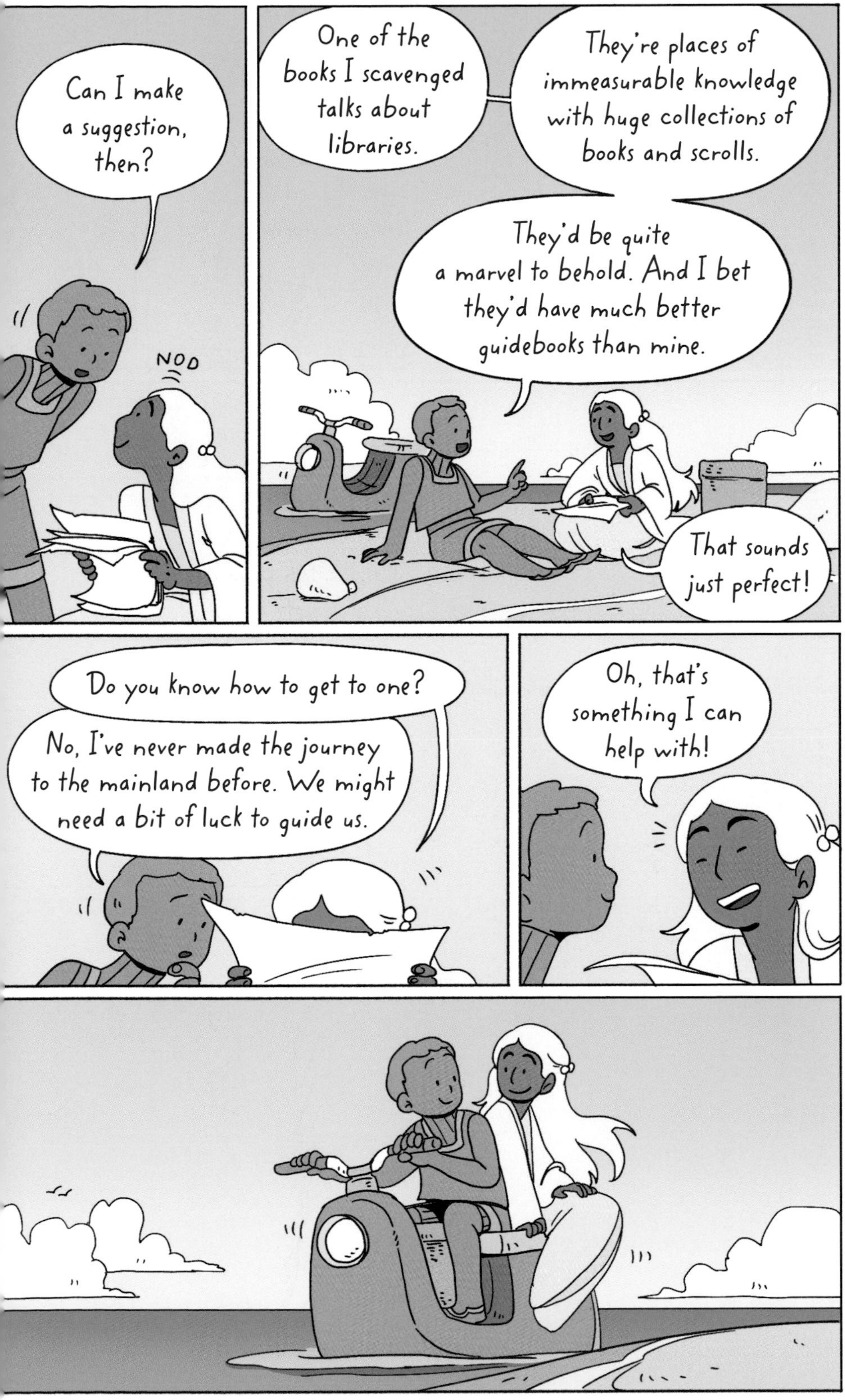

Can I make a suggestion, then?
NOD
One of the books I scavenged talks about libraries.
They're places of immeasurable knowledge with huge collections of books and scrolls.
They'd be quite a marvel to behold. And I bet they'd have much better guidebooks than mine.
That sounds just perfect!
Do you know how to get to one?
No, I've never made the journey to the mainland before. We might need a bit of luck to guide us.
Oh, that's something I can help with!

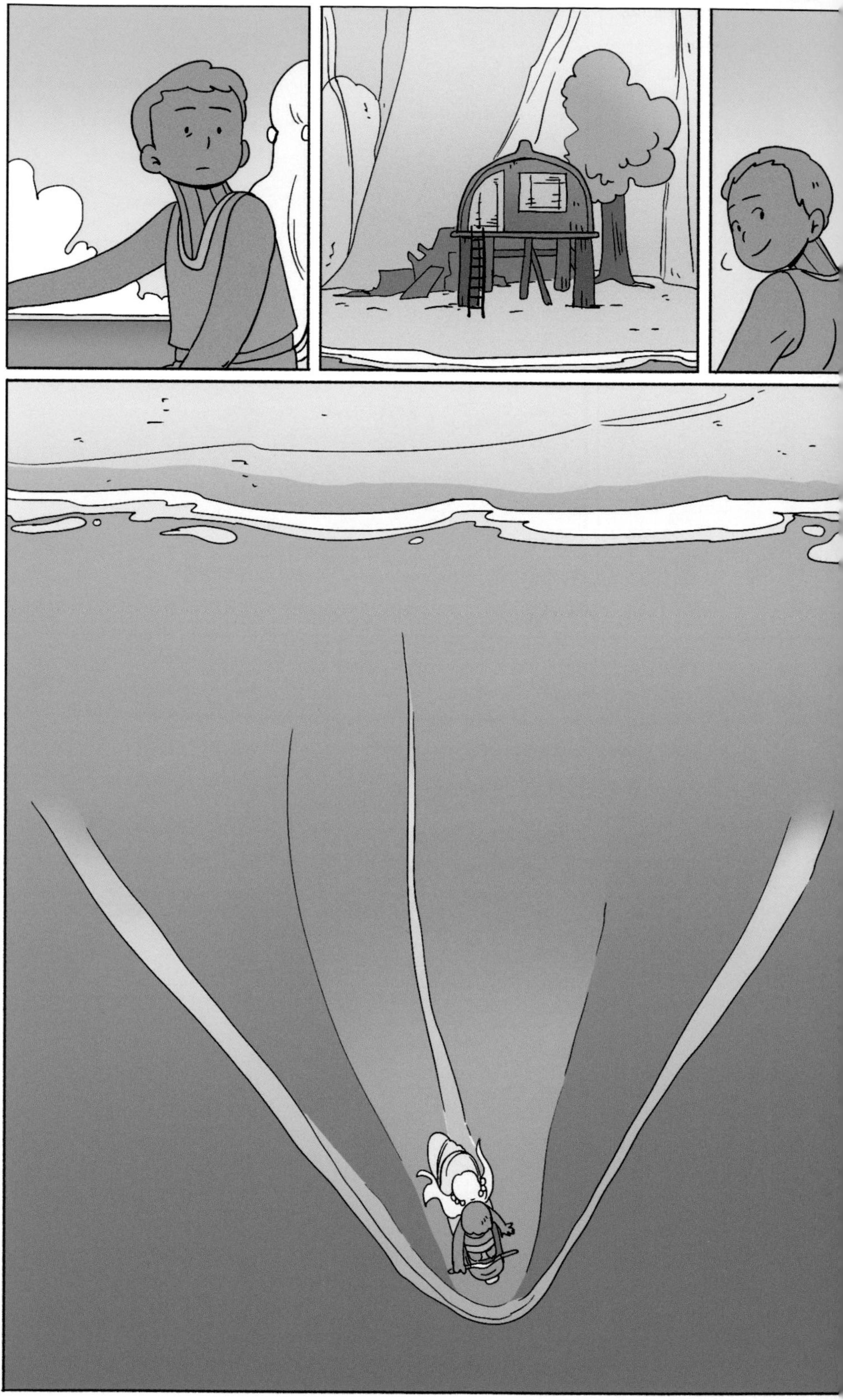

CHAPTER 4

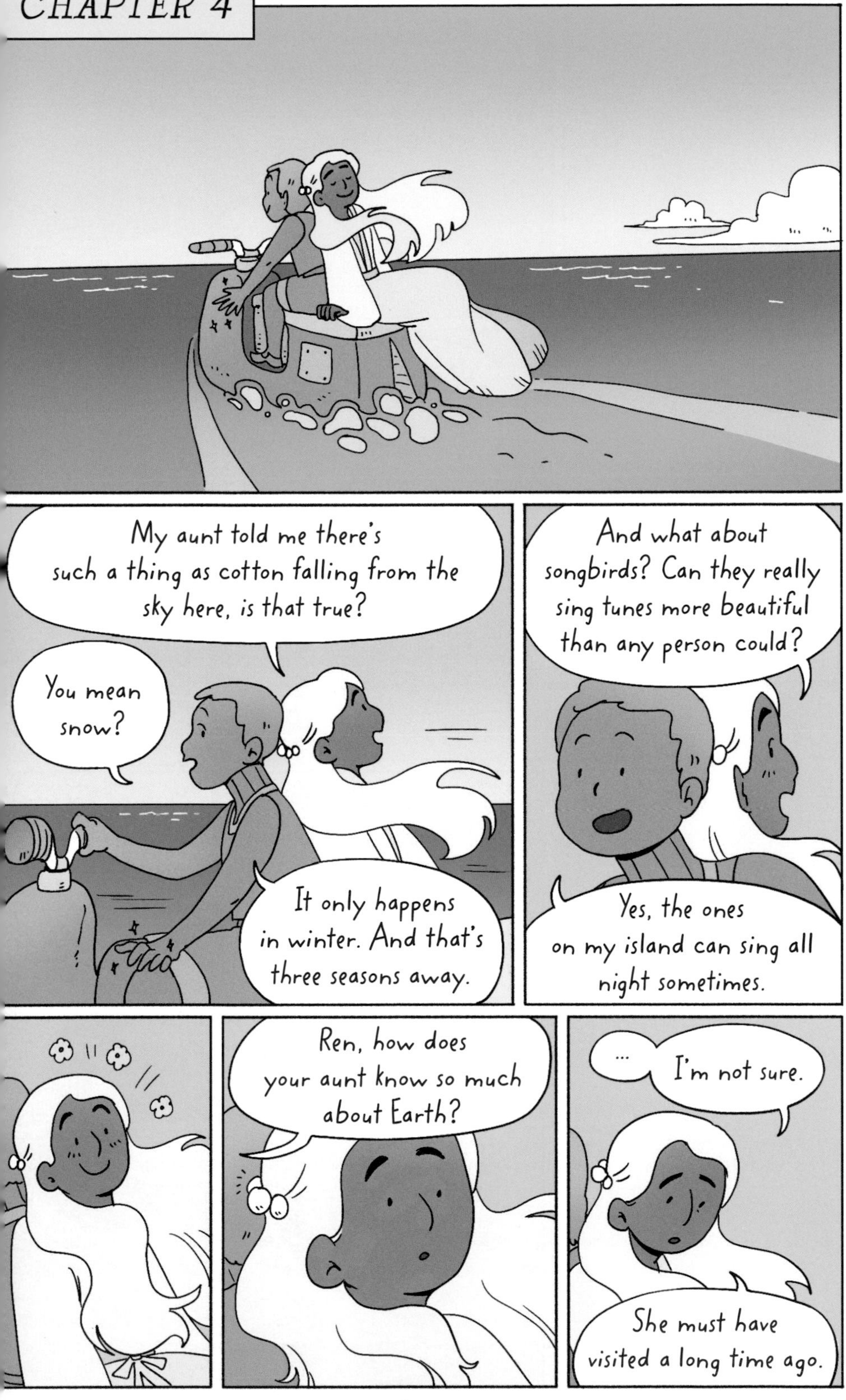

My aunt told me there's such a thing as cotton falling from the sky here, is that true?
You mean snow?
It only happens in winter. And that's three seasons away.
And what about songbirds? Can they really sing tunes more beautiful than any person could?
Yes, the ones on my island can sing all night sometimes.
Ren, how does your aunt know so much about Earth?
...
I'm not sure.
She must have visited a long time ago.

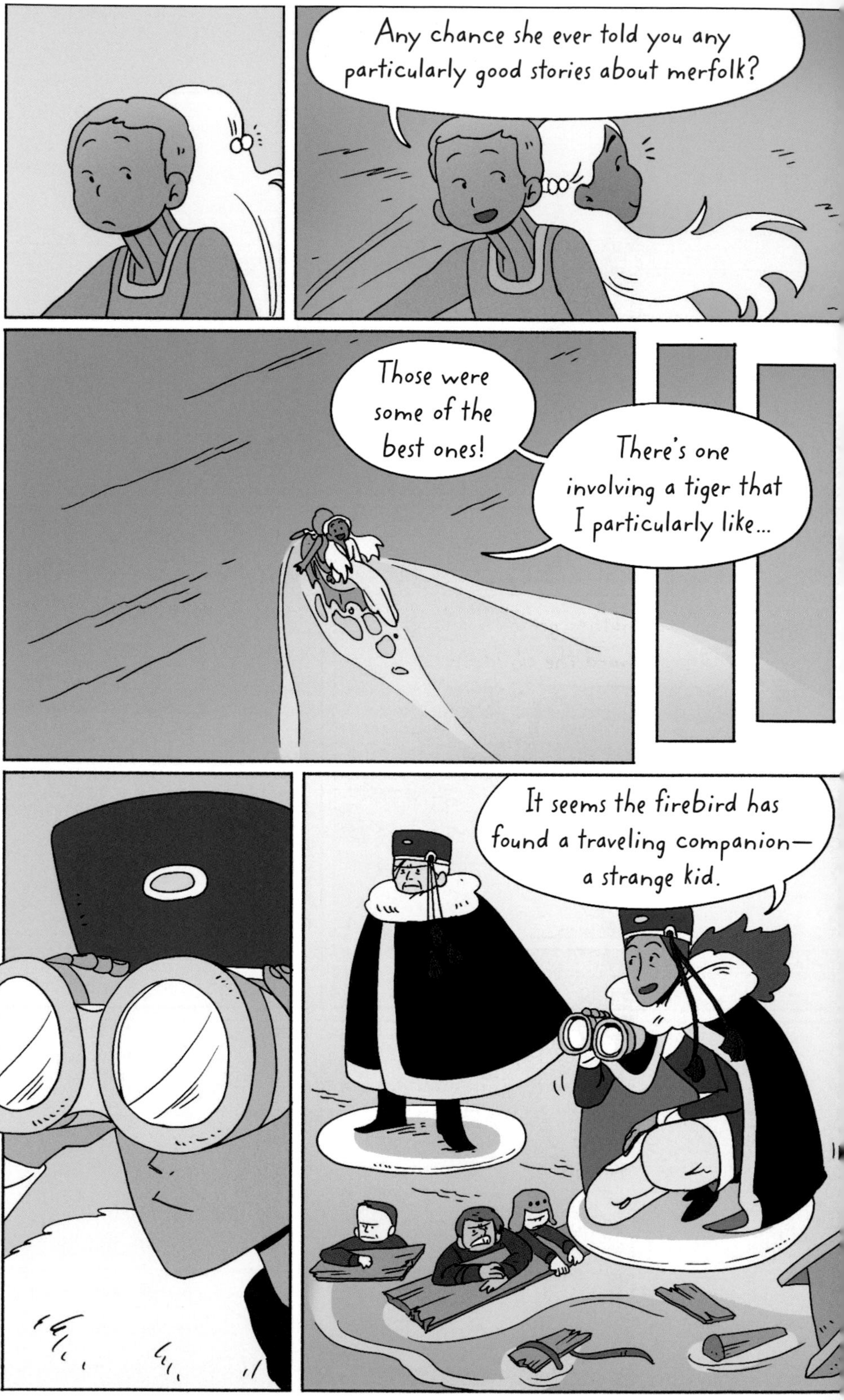
Any chance she ever told you any particularly good stories about merfolk?
Those were some of the best ones!
There's one involving a tiger that I particularly like...
It seems the firebird has found a traveling companion— a strange kid.

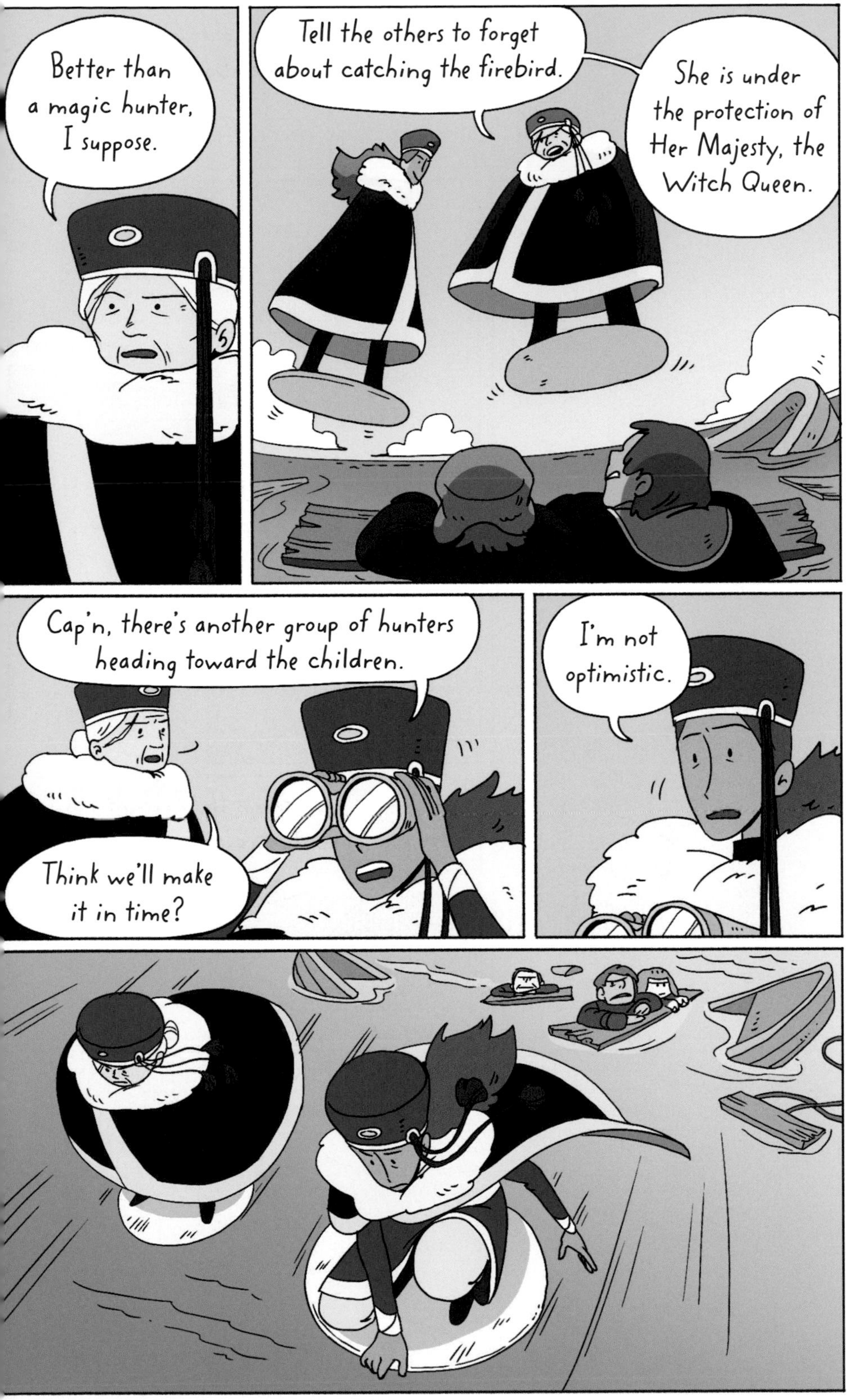

Better than a magic hunter, I suppose.
Tell the others to forget about catching the firebird.
She is under the protection of Her Majesty, the Witch Queen.
Cap'n, there's another group of hunters heading toward the children.
Think we'll make it in time?
I'm not optimistic.

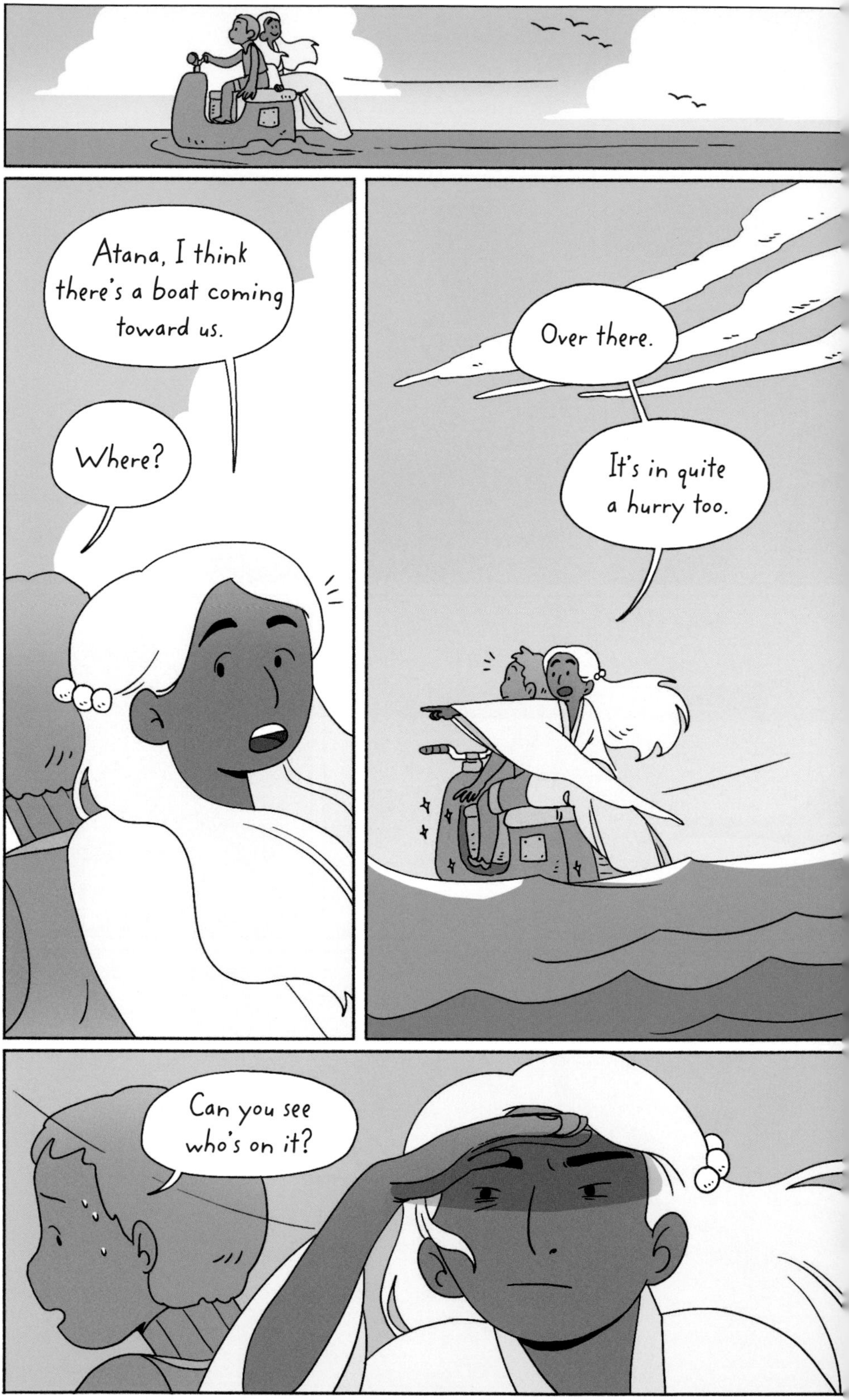
Atana, I think there's a boat coming toward us.
Where?
Over there.
It's in quite a hurry too.
Can you see who's on it?

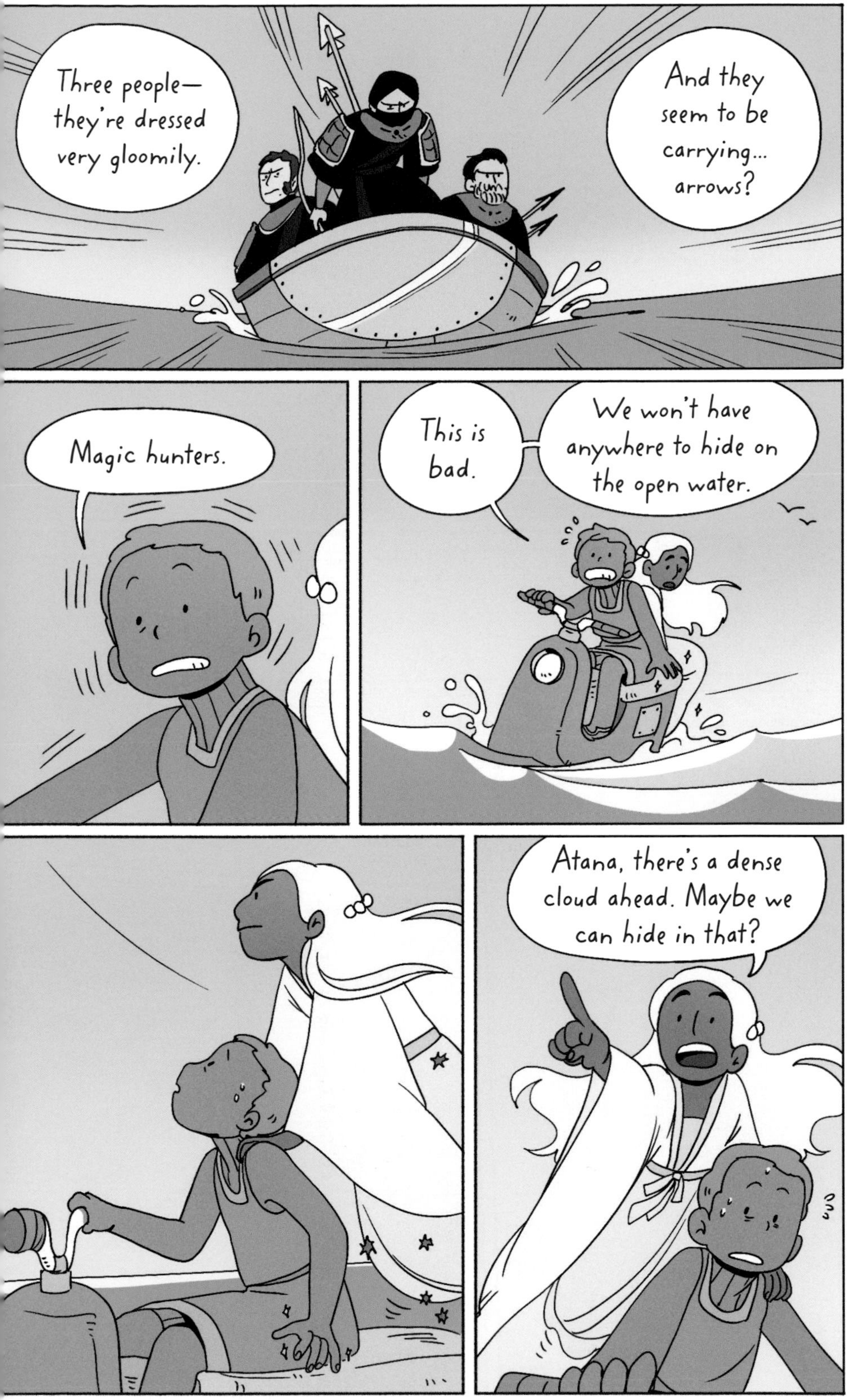
Three people—they're dressed very gloomily.
And they seem to be carrying... arrows?
Magic hunters.
This is bad.
We won't have anywhere to hide on the open water.
Atana, there's a dense cloud ahead. Maybe we can hide in that?

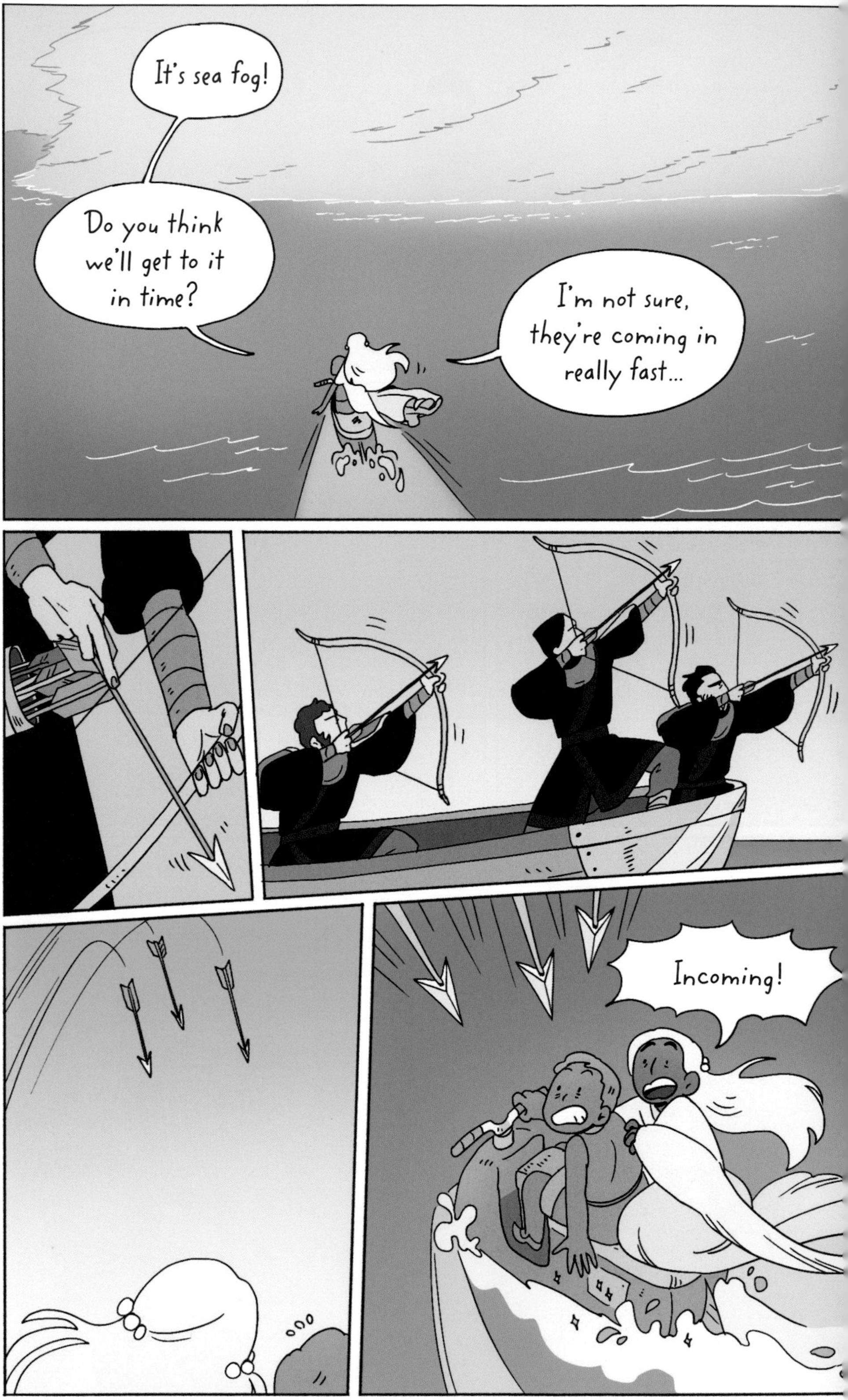
It's sea fog!
Do you think we'll get to it in time?
I'm not sure, they're coming in really fast...
Incoming!

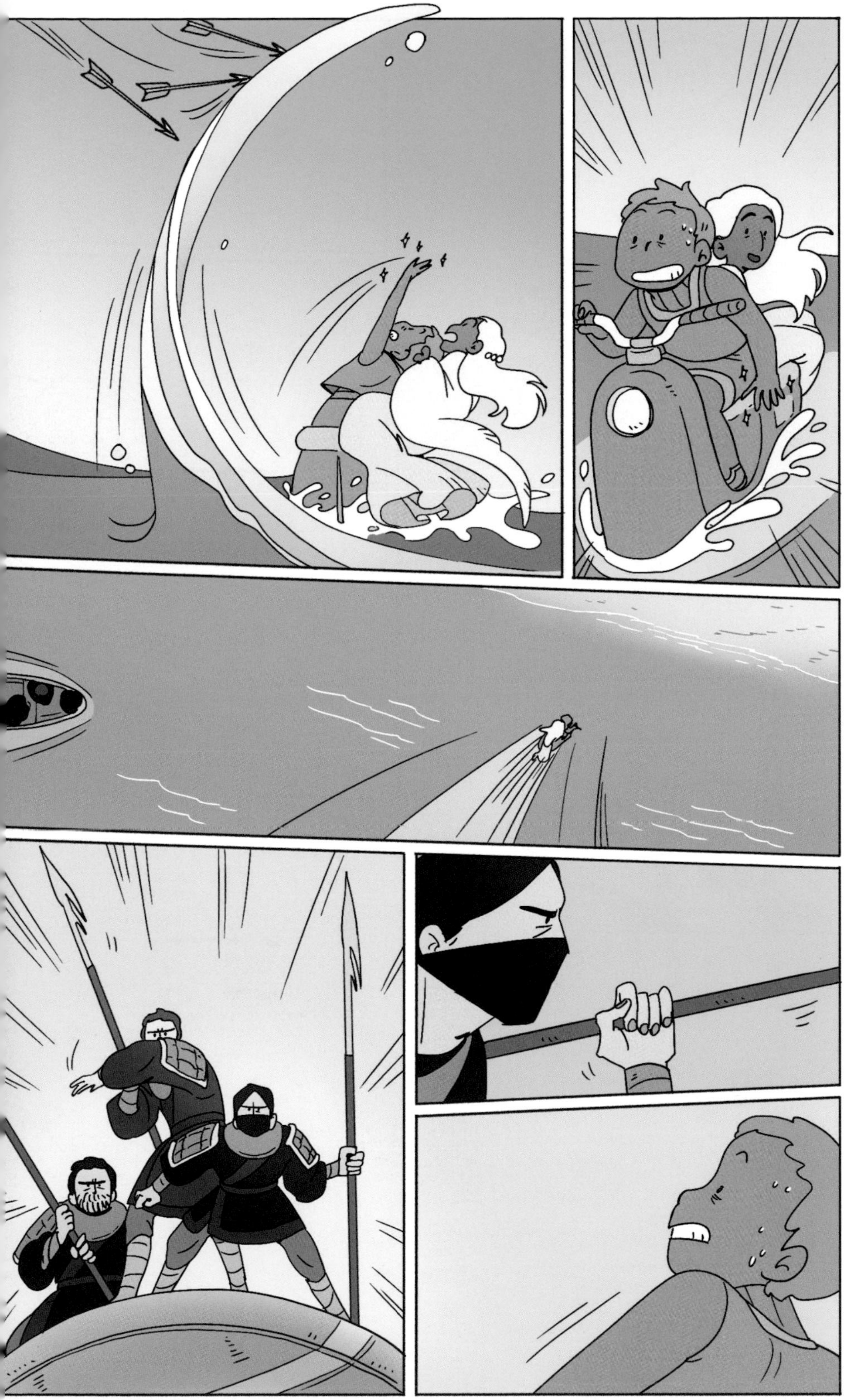

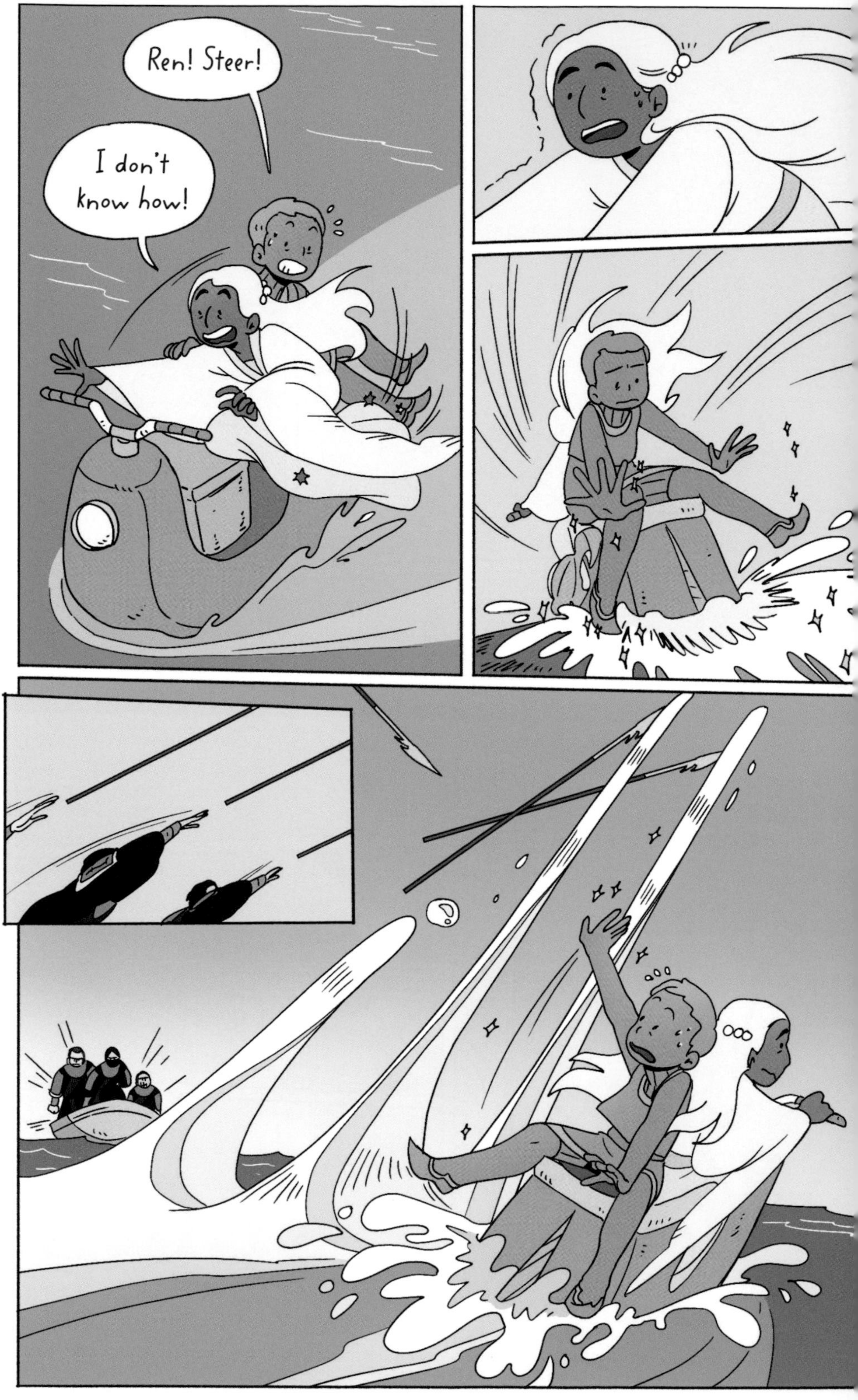
Ren! Steer!
I don't know how!

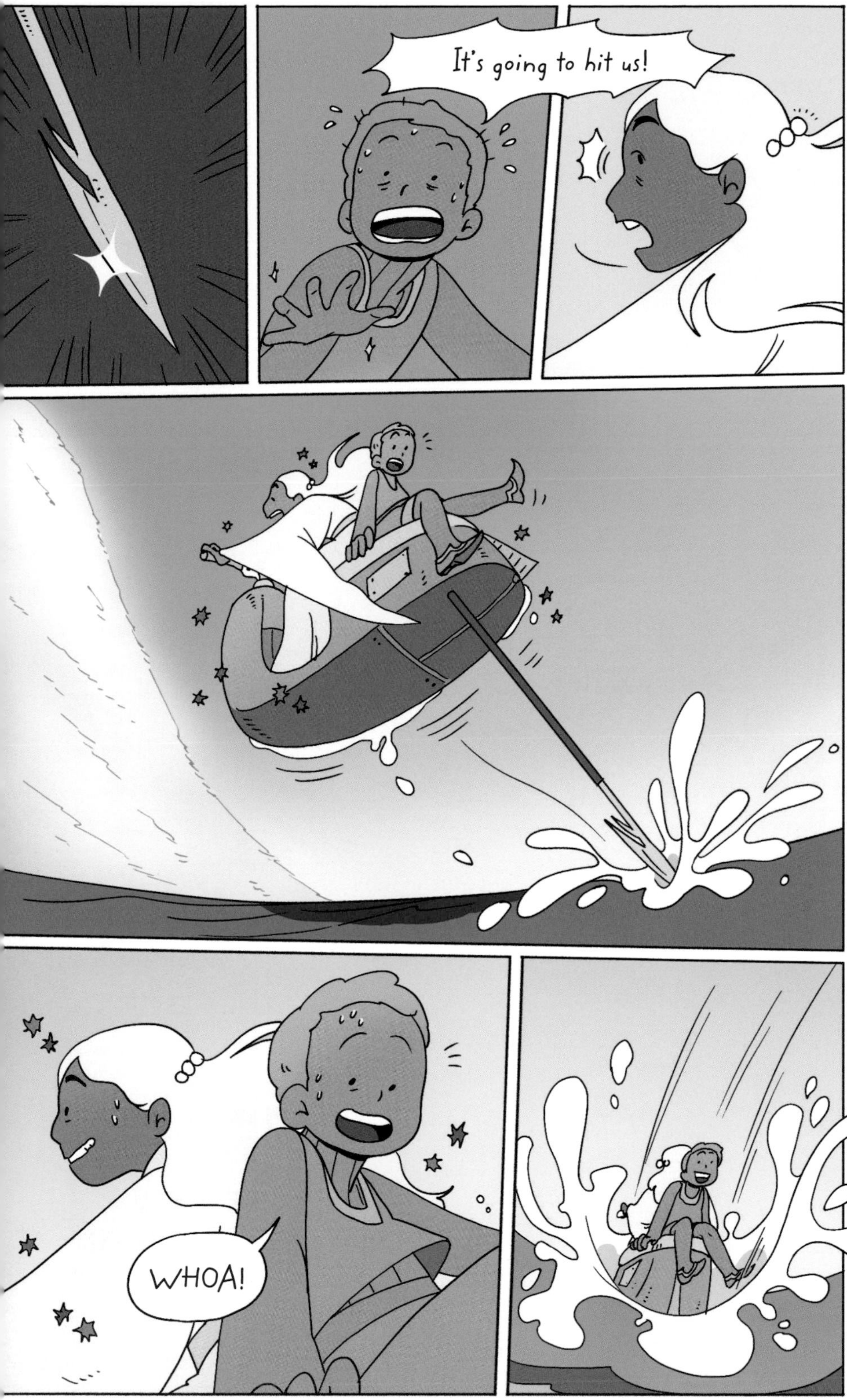
It's going to hit us!
WHOA!

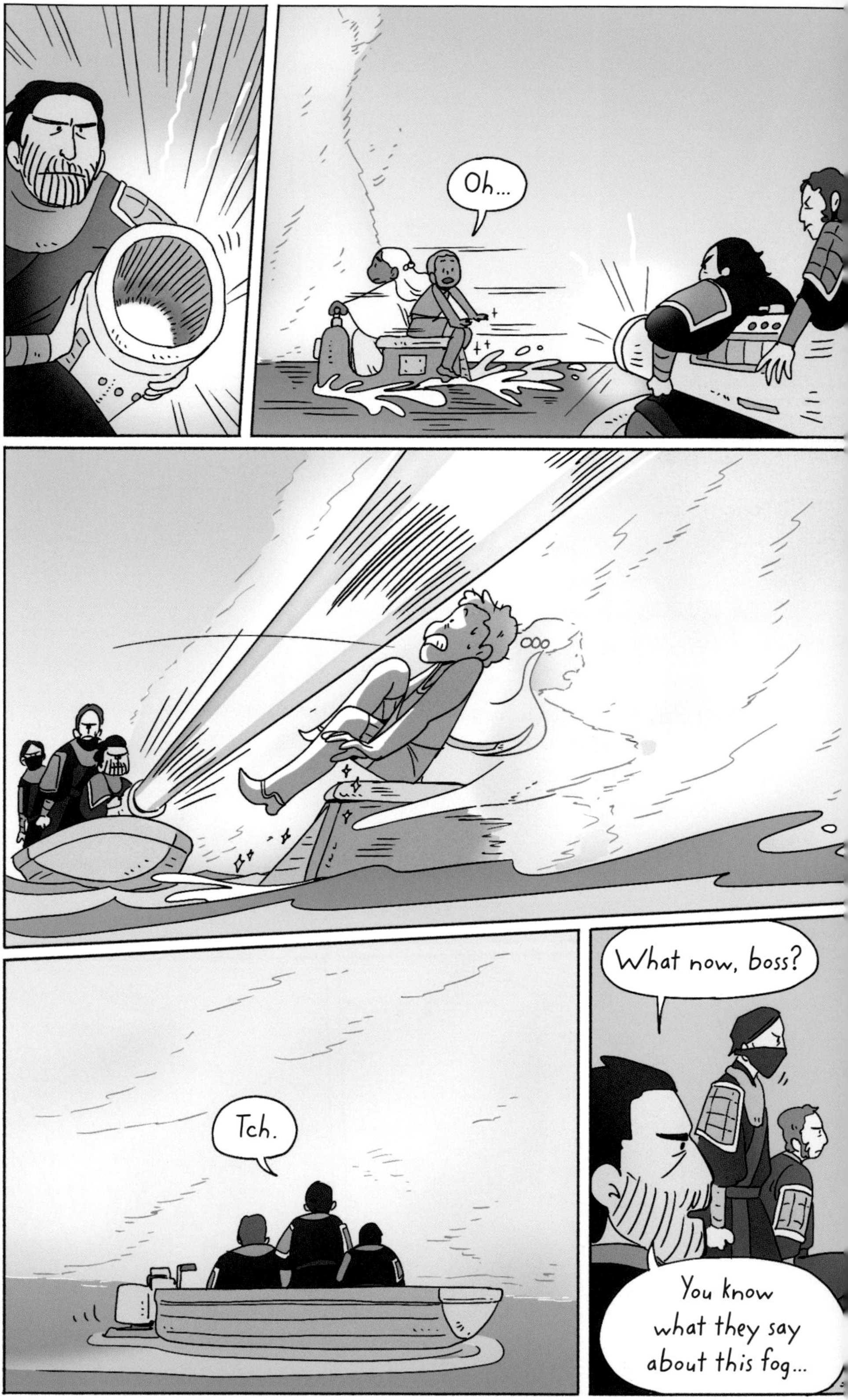
Oh...
Tch.
What now, boss?
You know what they say about this fog...

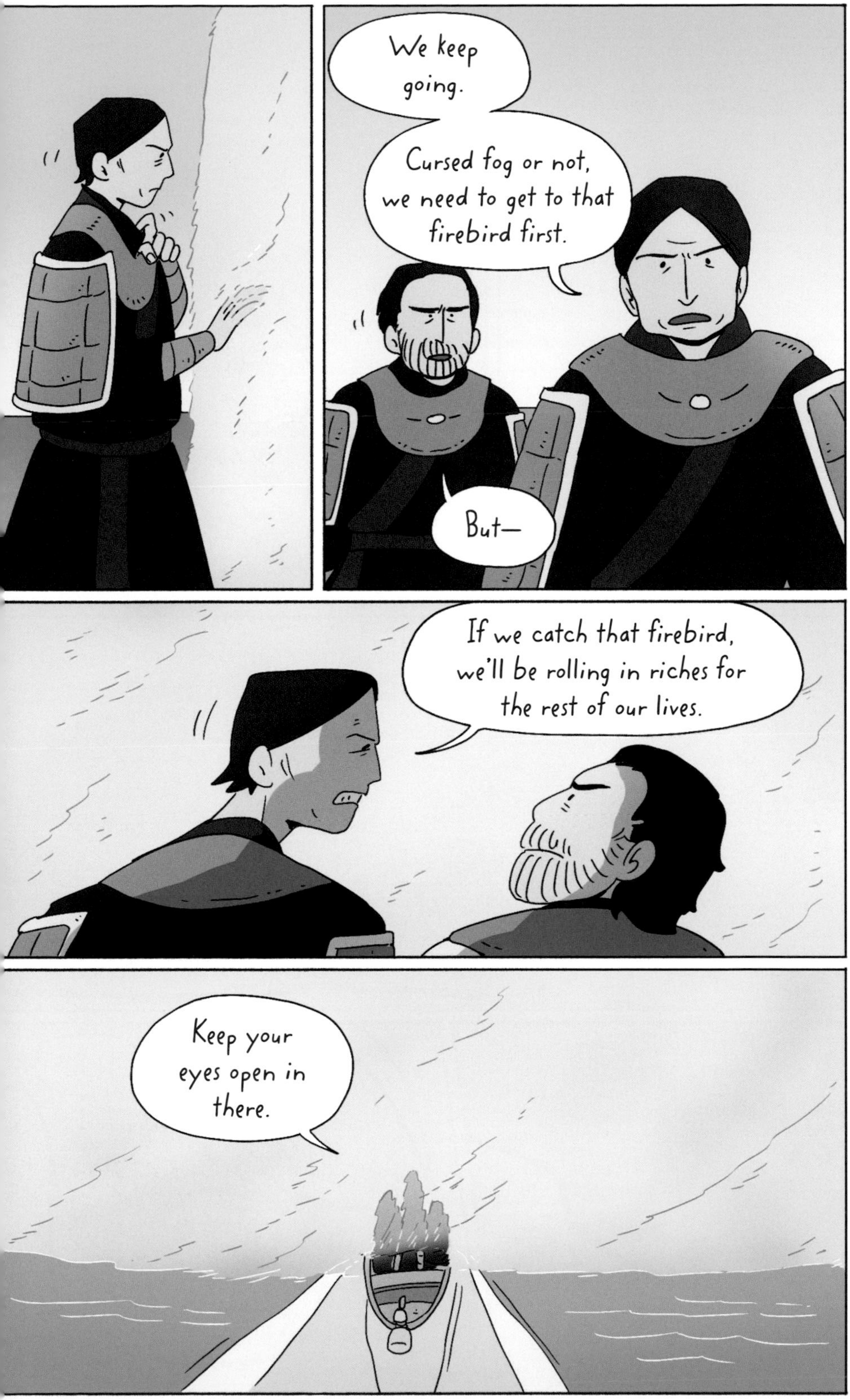
We keep going.
Cursed fog or not, we need to get to that firebird first.
But—
If we catch that firebird, we'll be rolling in riches for the rest of our lives.
Keep your eyes open in there.

CHAPTER 5

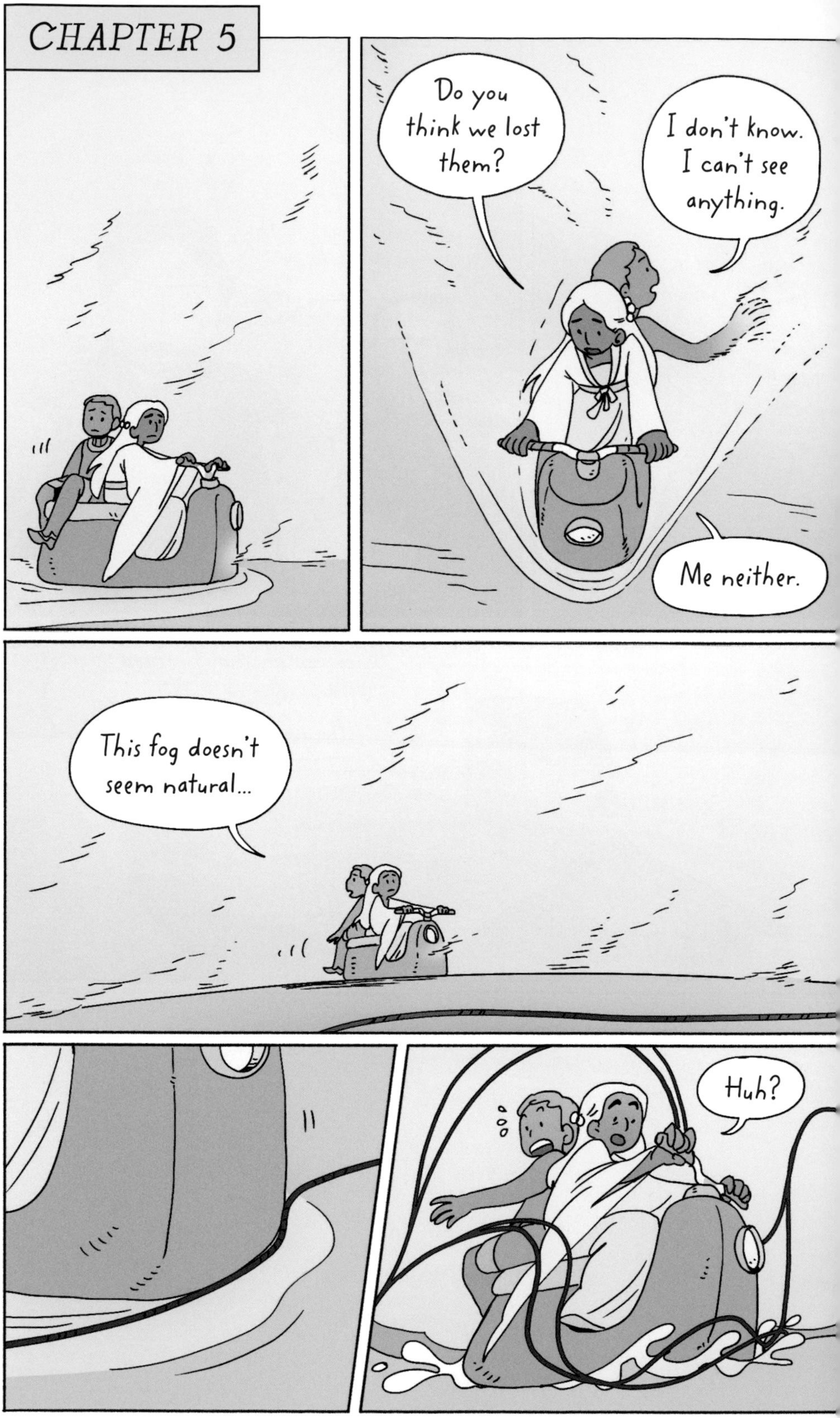
Do you think we lost them?
I don't know. I can't see anything.
Me neither.
This fog doesn't seem natural...
Huh?

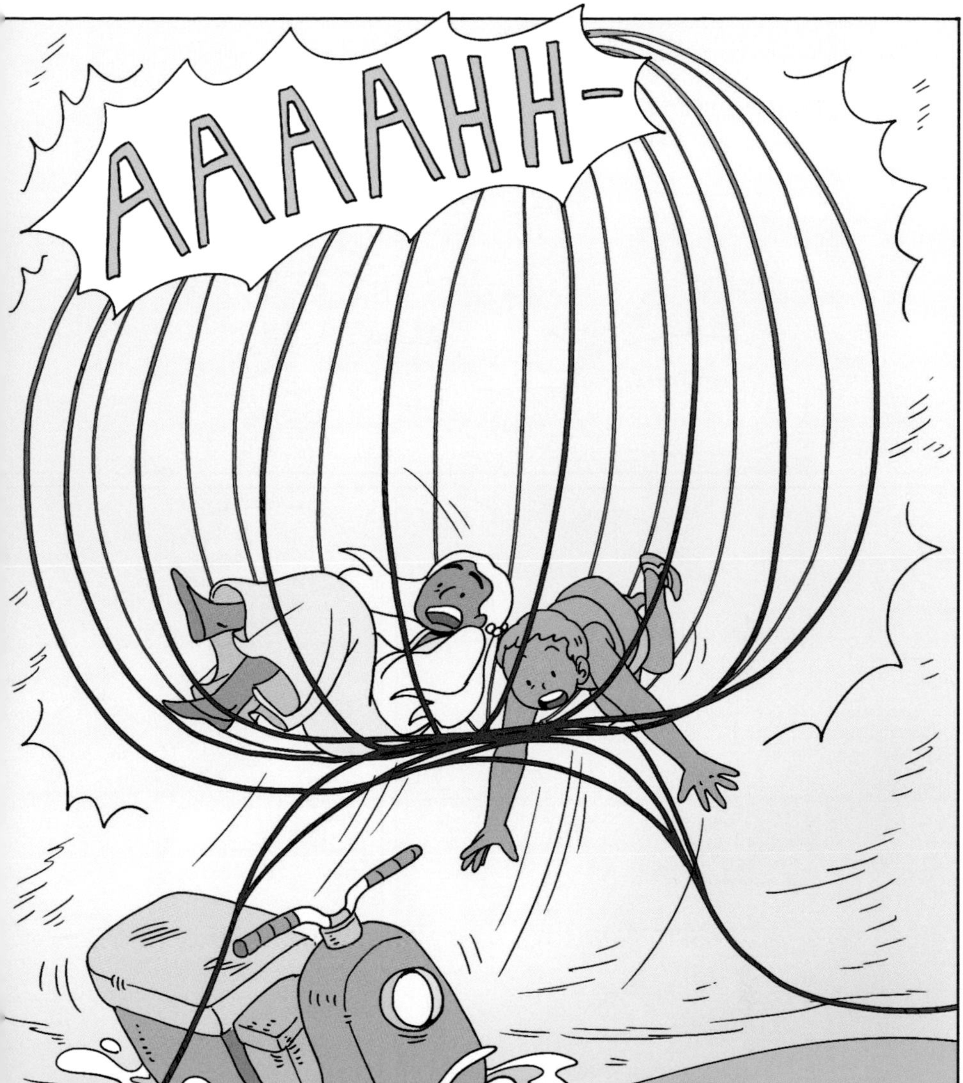
AAAAHH-

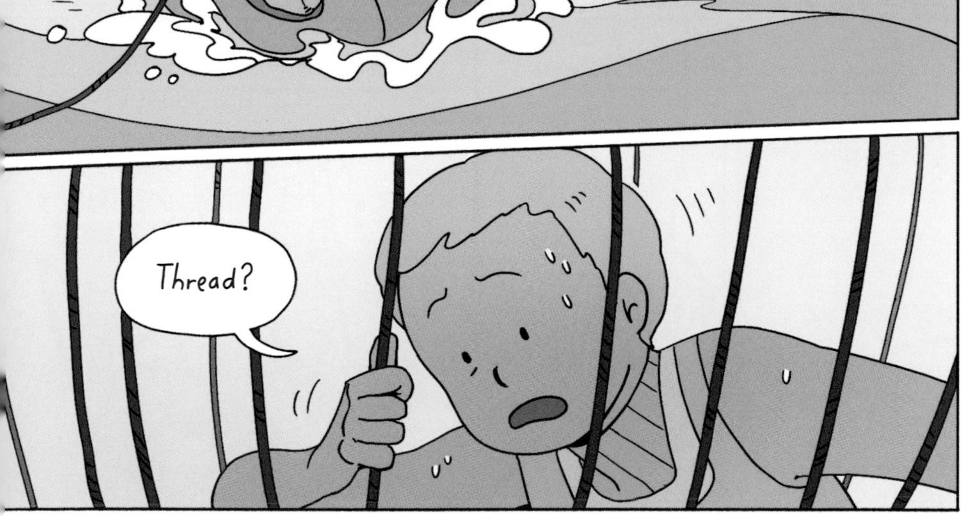
Thread?

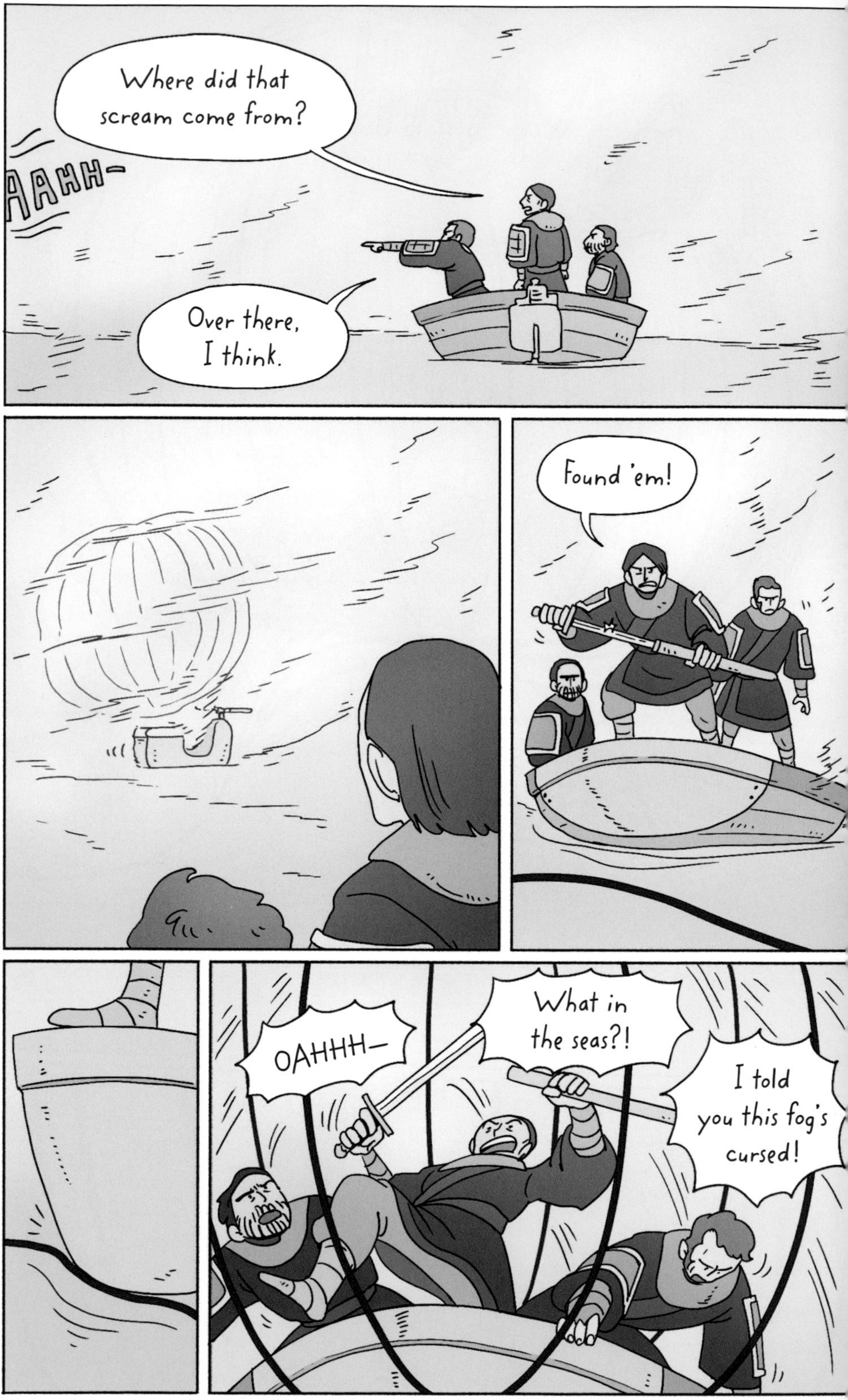

Where did that scream come from?
AAHH-
Over there, I think.
Found 'em!
OAHHH-
What in the seas?!
I told you this fog's cursed!

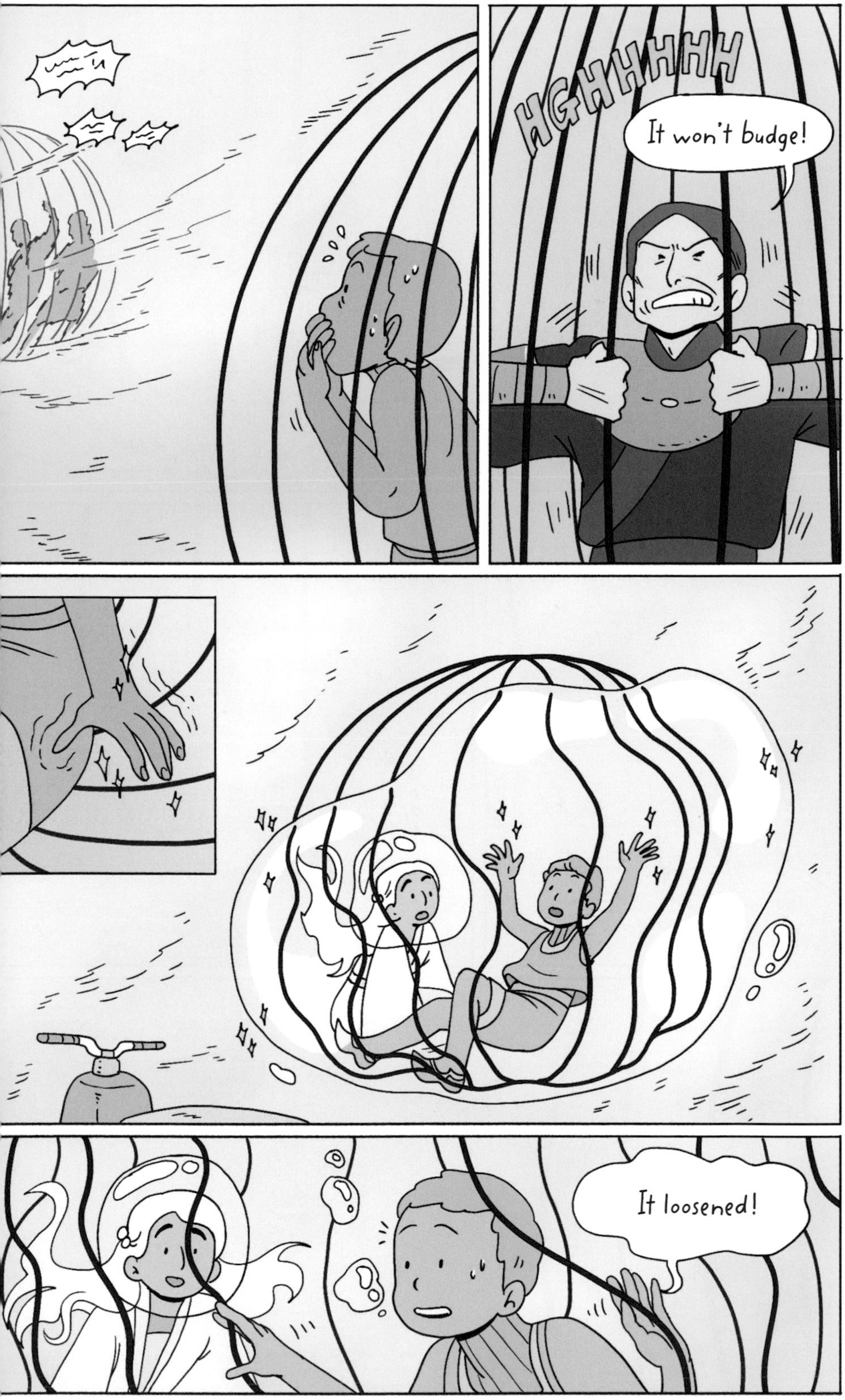
HGHHHHH
It won't budge!
It loosened!

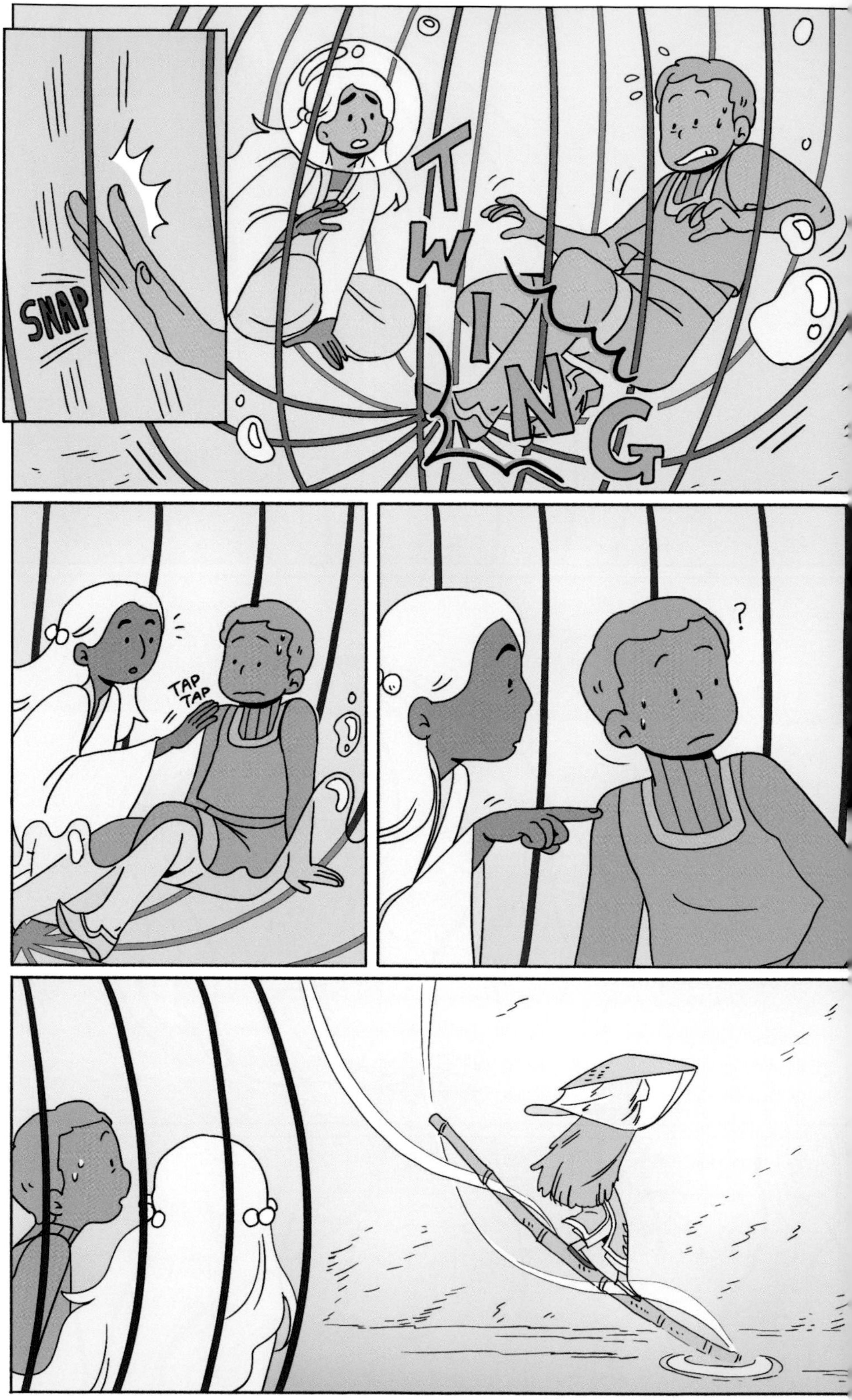
SNAP
TWING
TAP TAP
?

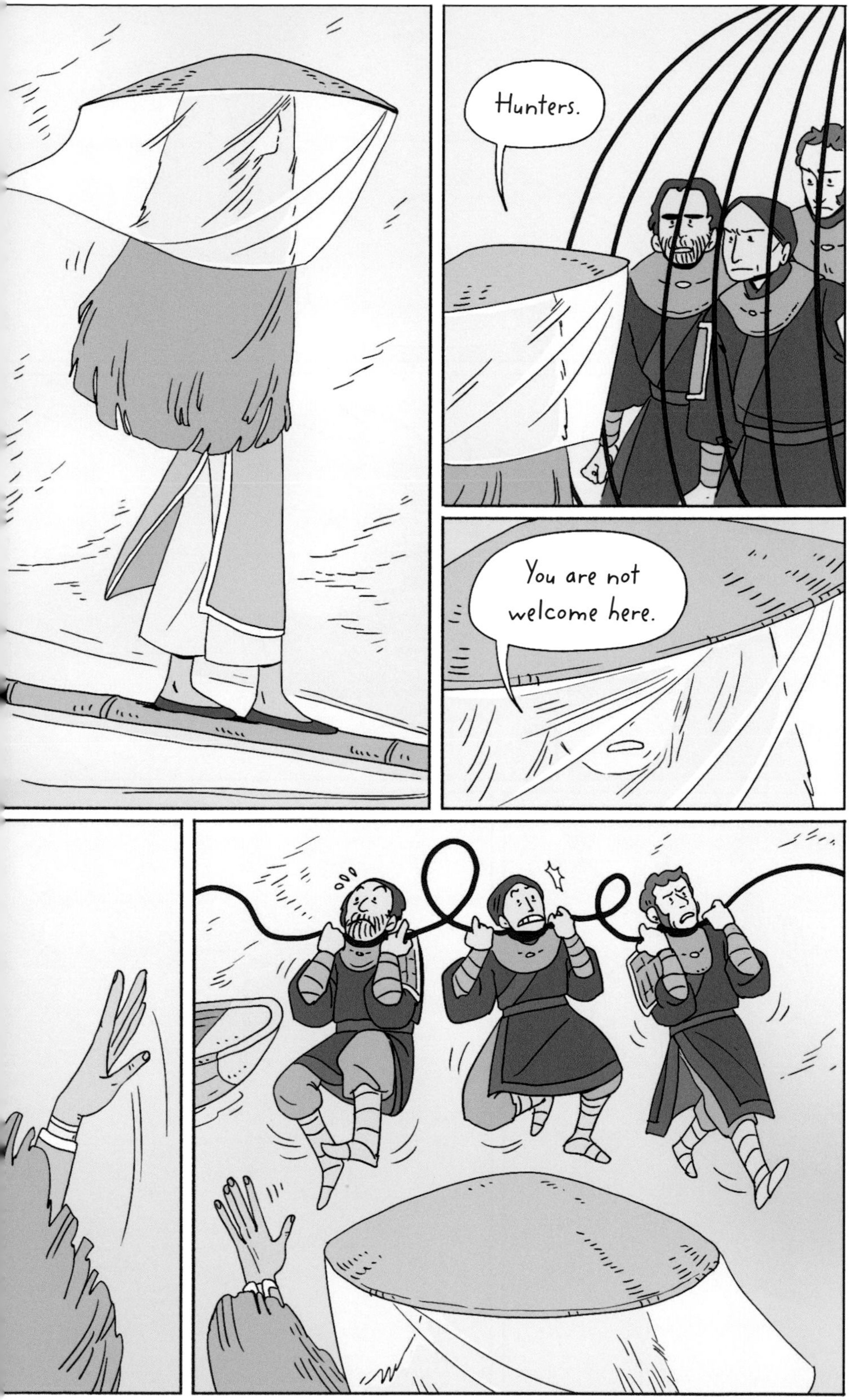
Hunters.
You are not welcome here.

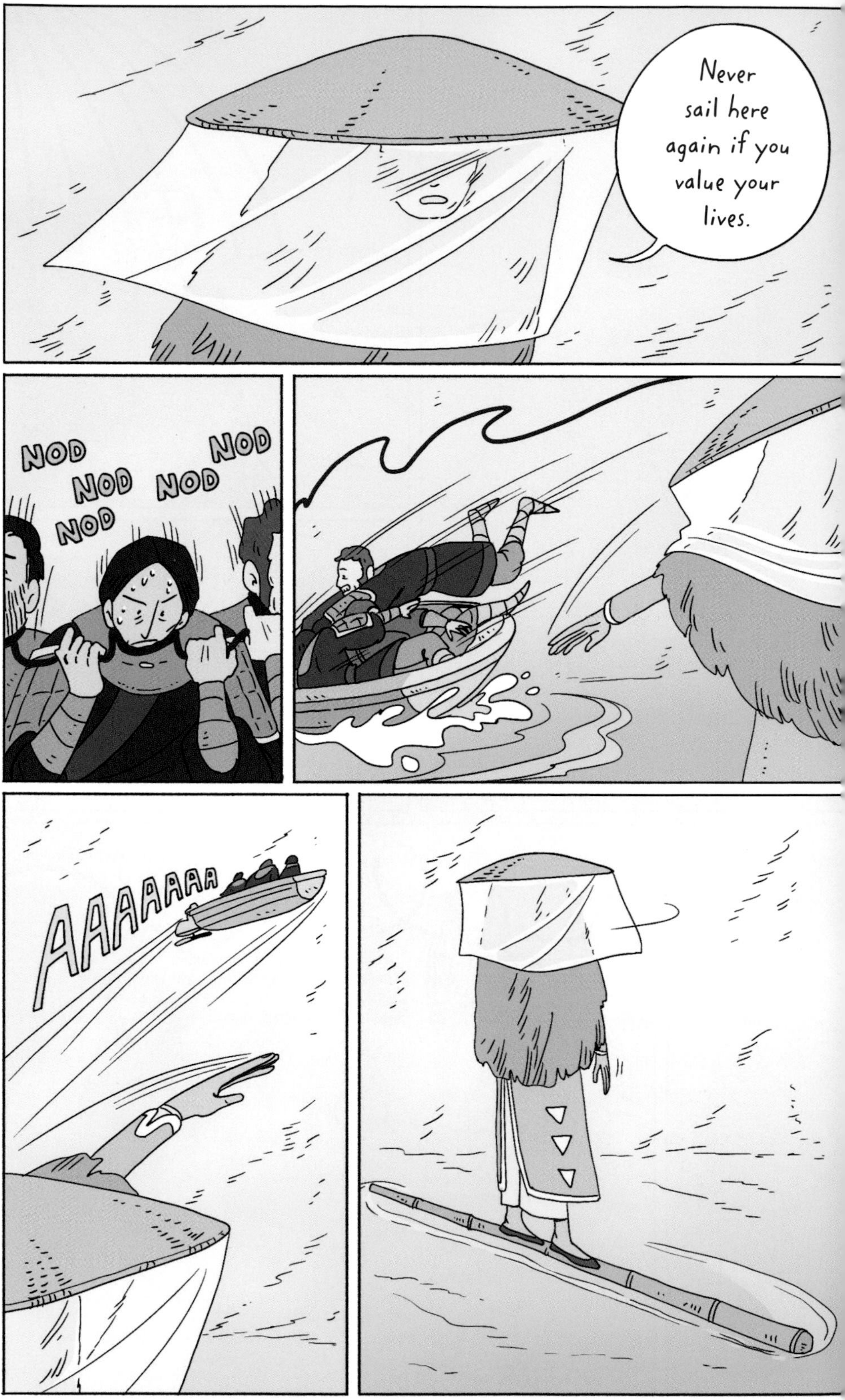
Never sail here again if you value your lives.
NOD
NOD
NOD
NOD
NOD
AAAAAAA

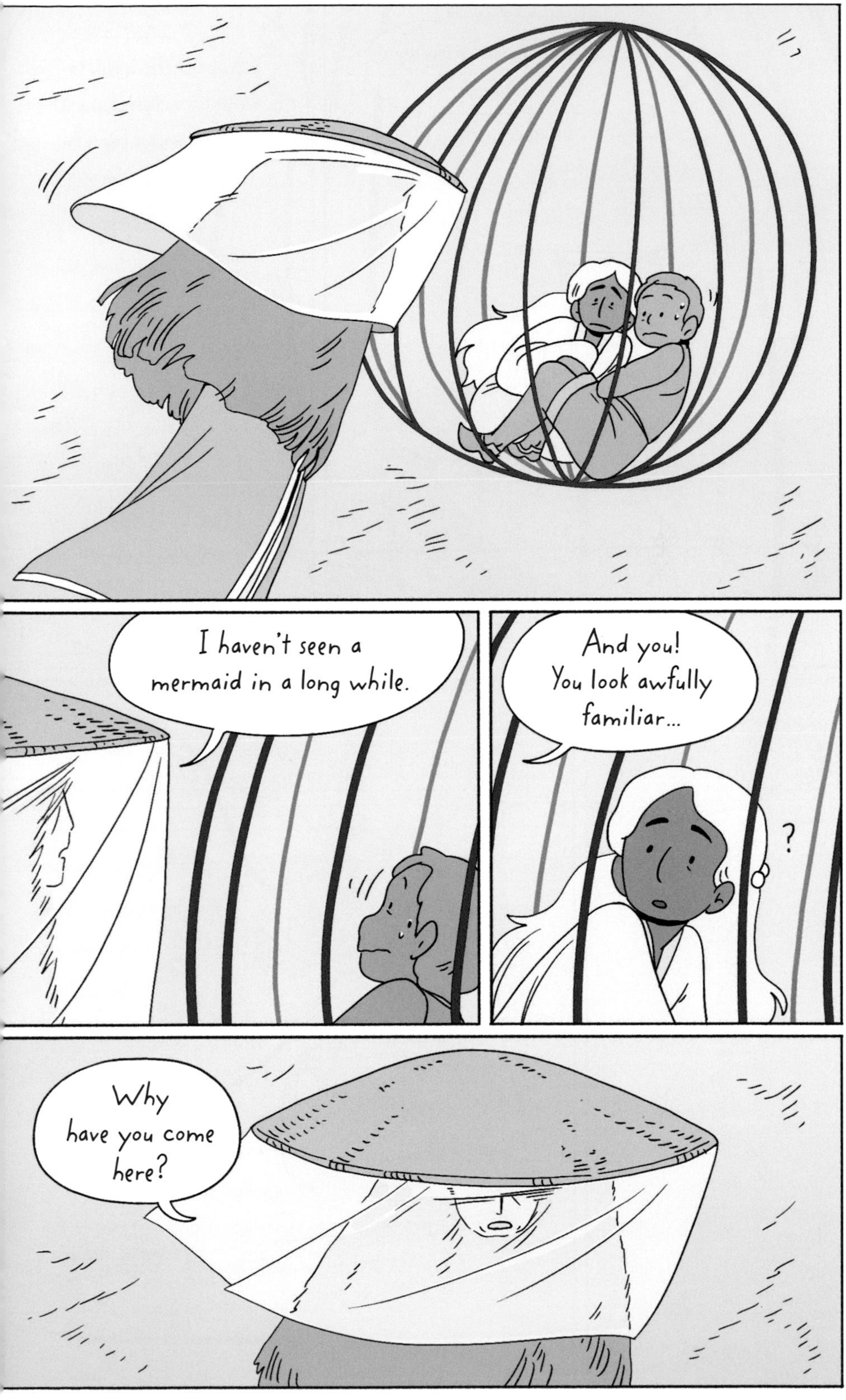
I haven't seen a mermaid in a long while.
And you! You look awfully familiar...
?
Why have you come here?

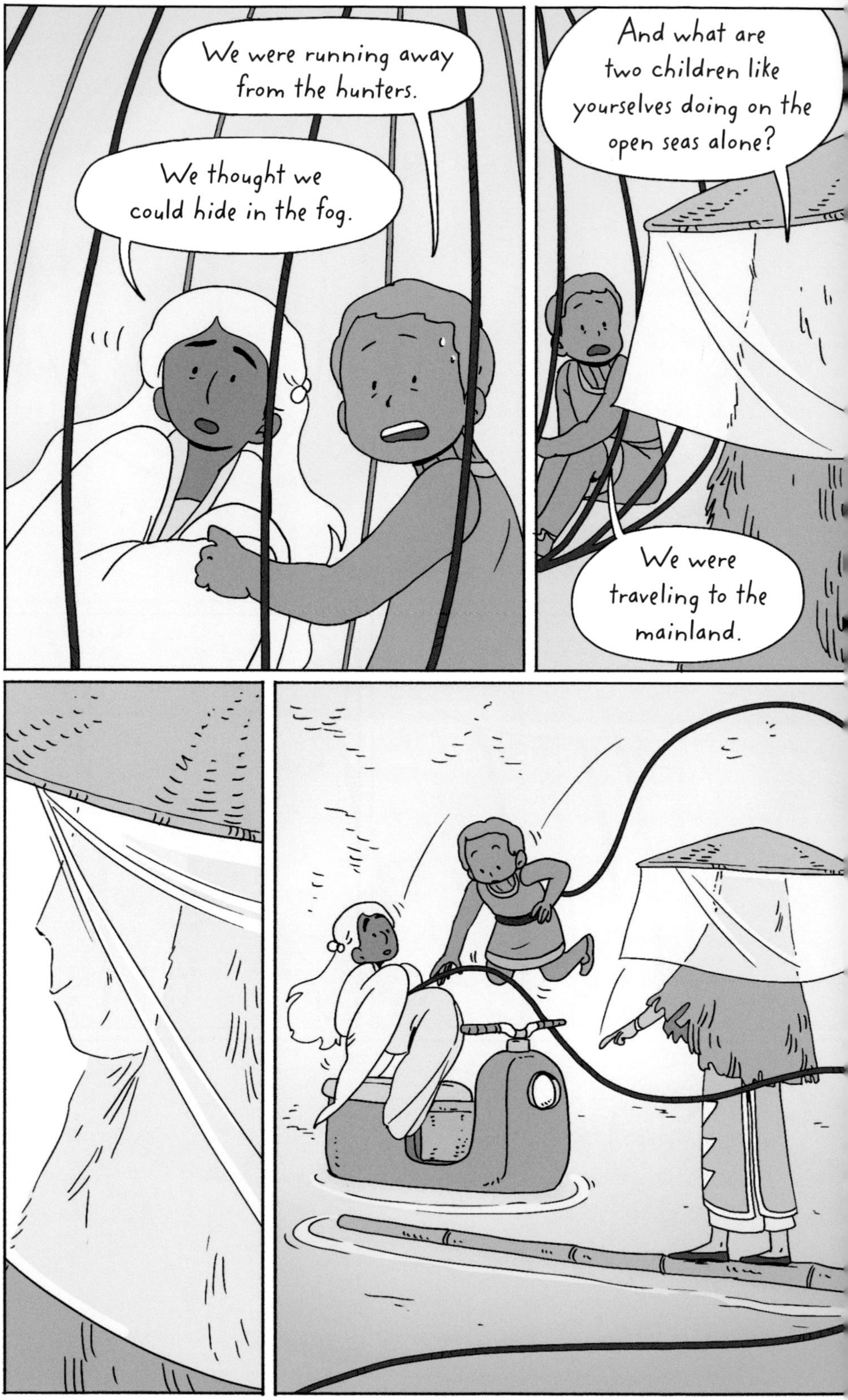
We were running away from the hunters.
We thought we could hide in the fog.
And what are two children like yourselves doing on the open seas alone?
We were traveling to the mainland.

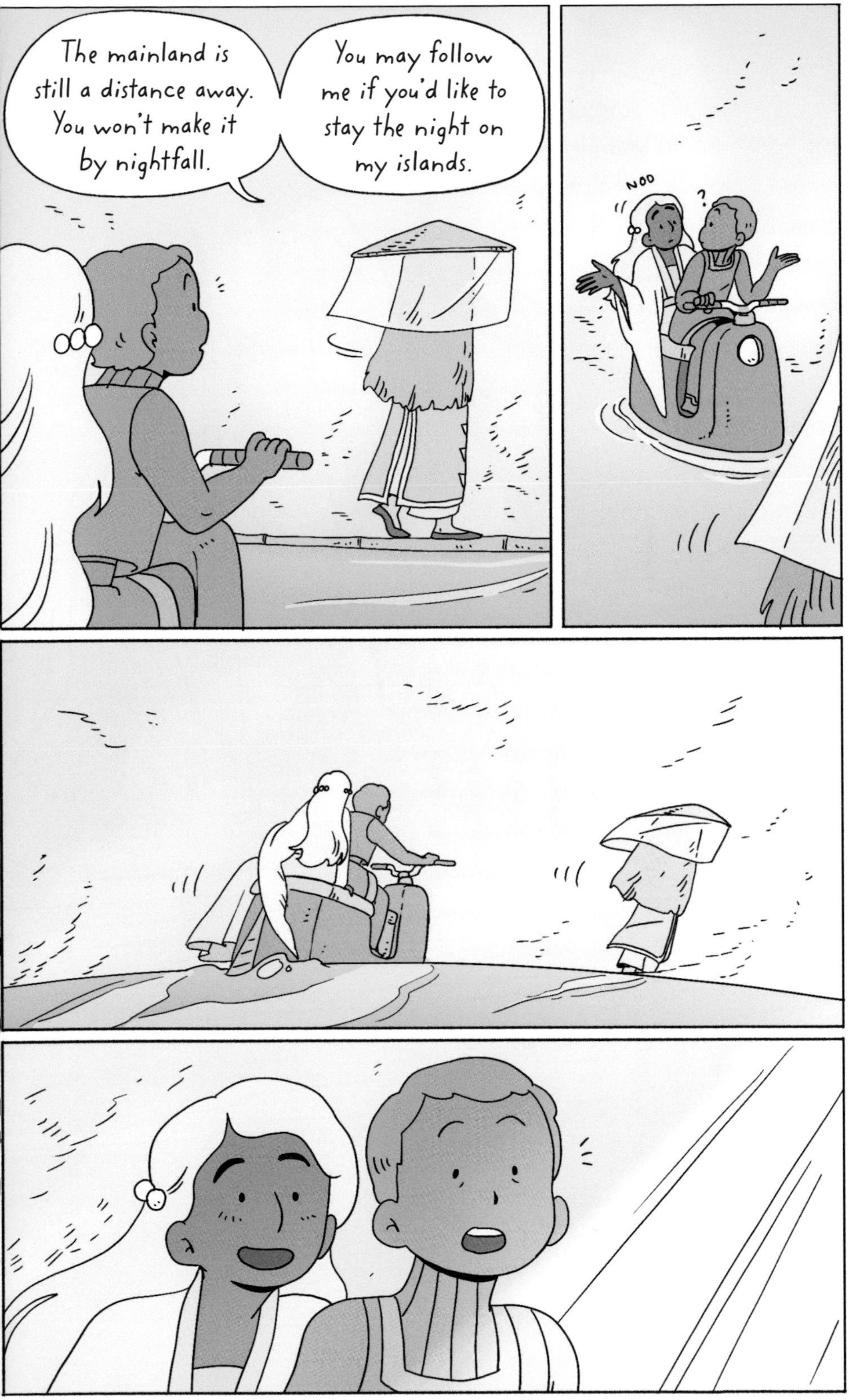
The mainland is still a distance away. You won't make it by nightfall.
You may follow me if you'd like to stay the night on my islands.
NOD
?

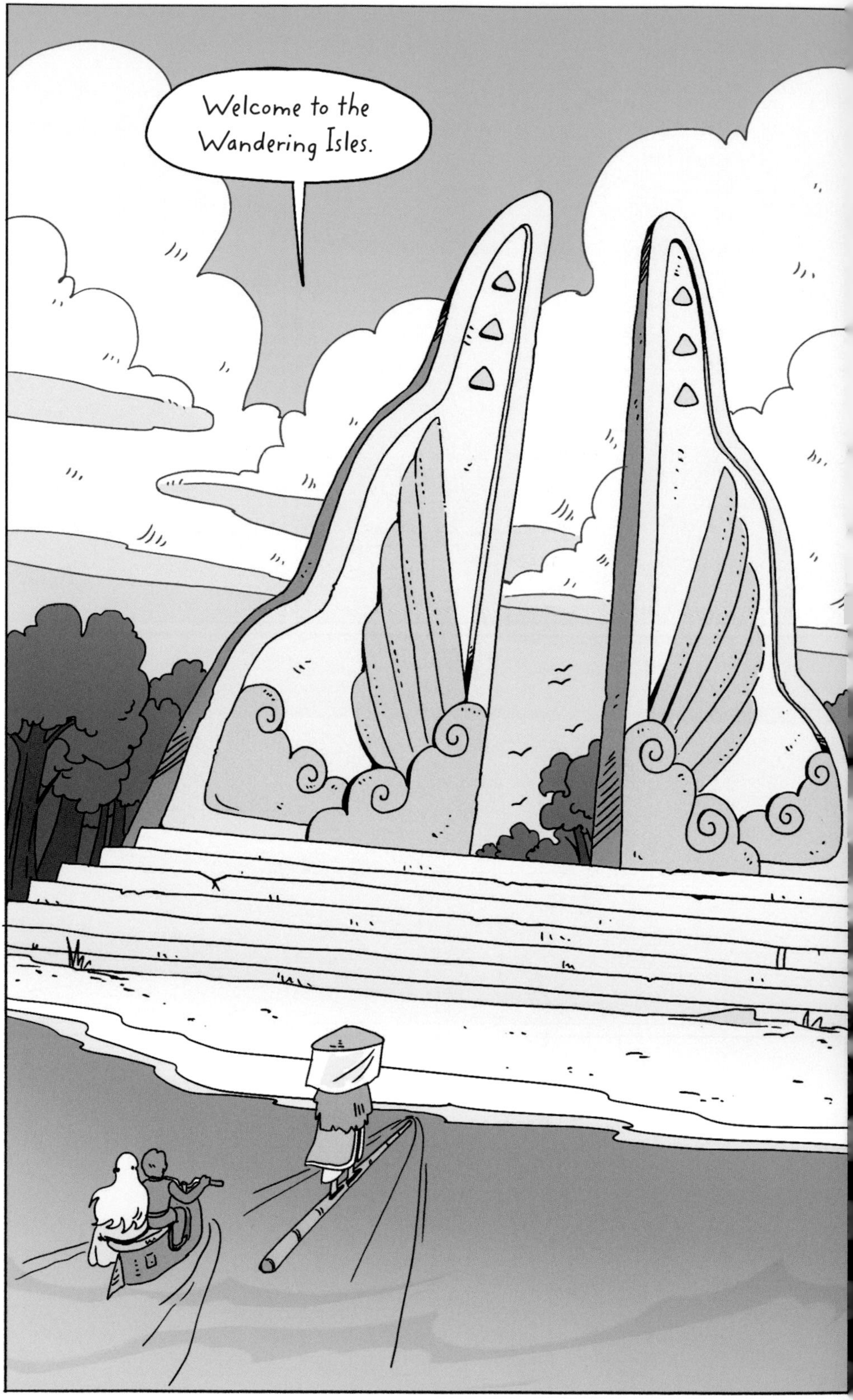
Welcome to the Wandering Isles.

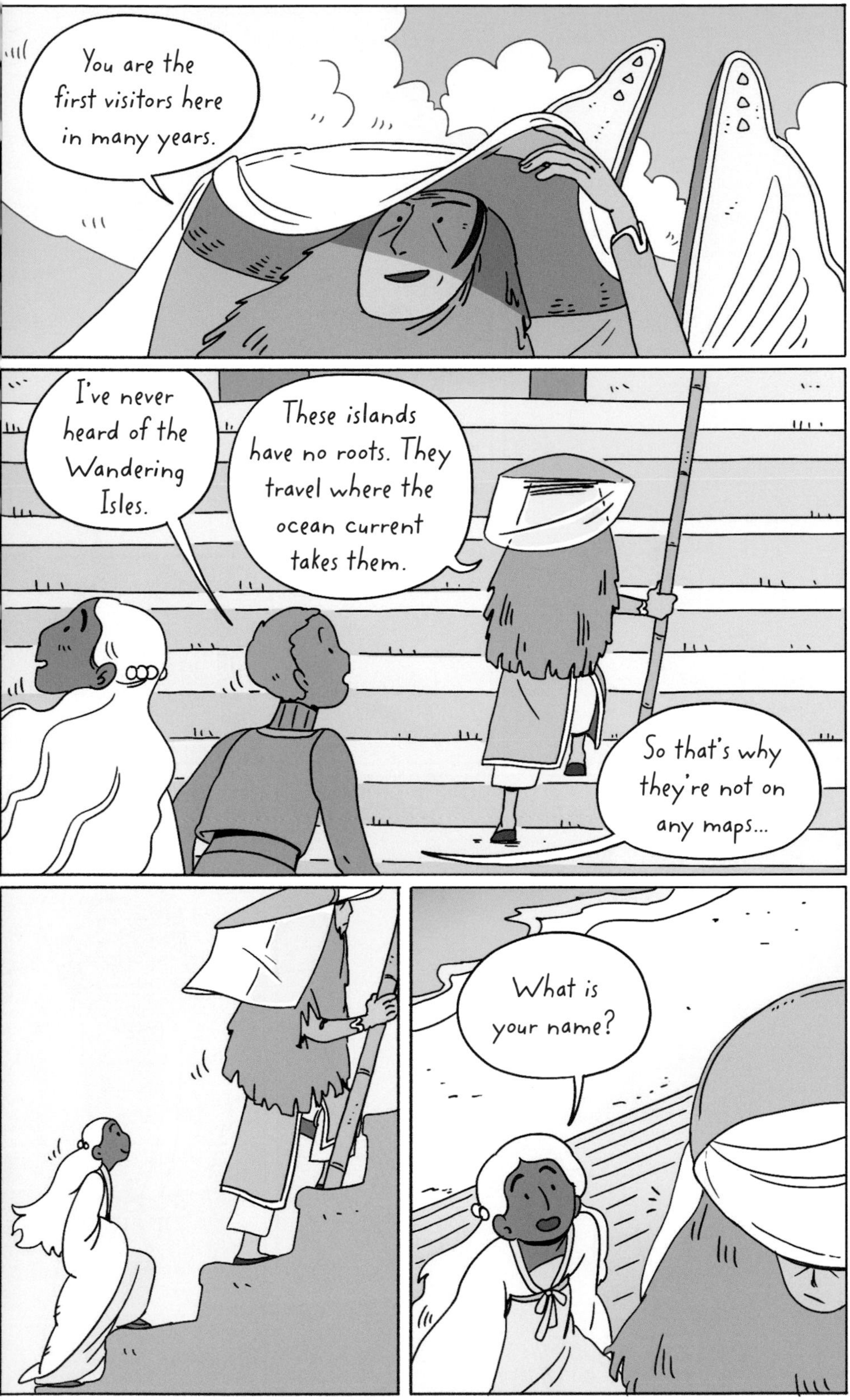
You are the first visitors here in many years.
I've never heard of the Wandering Isles.
These islands have no roots. They travel where the ocean current takes them.
So that's why they're not on any maps...
What is your name?

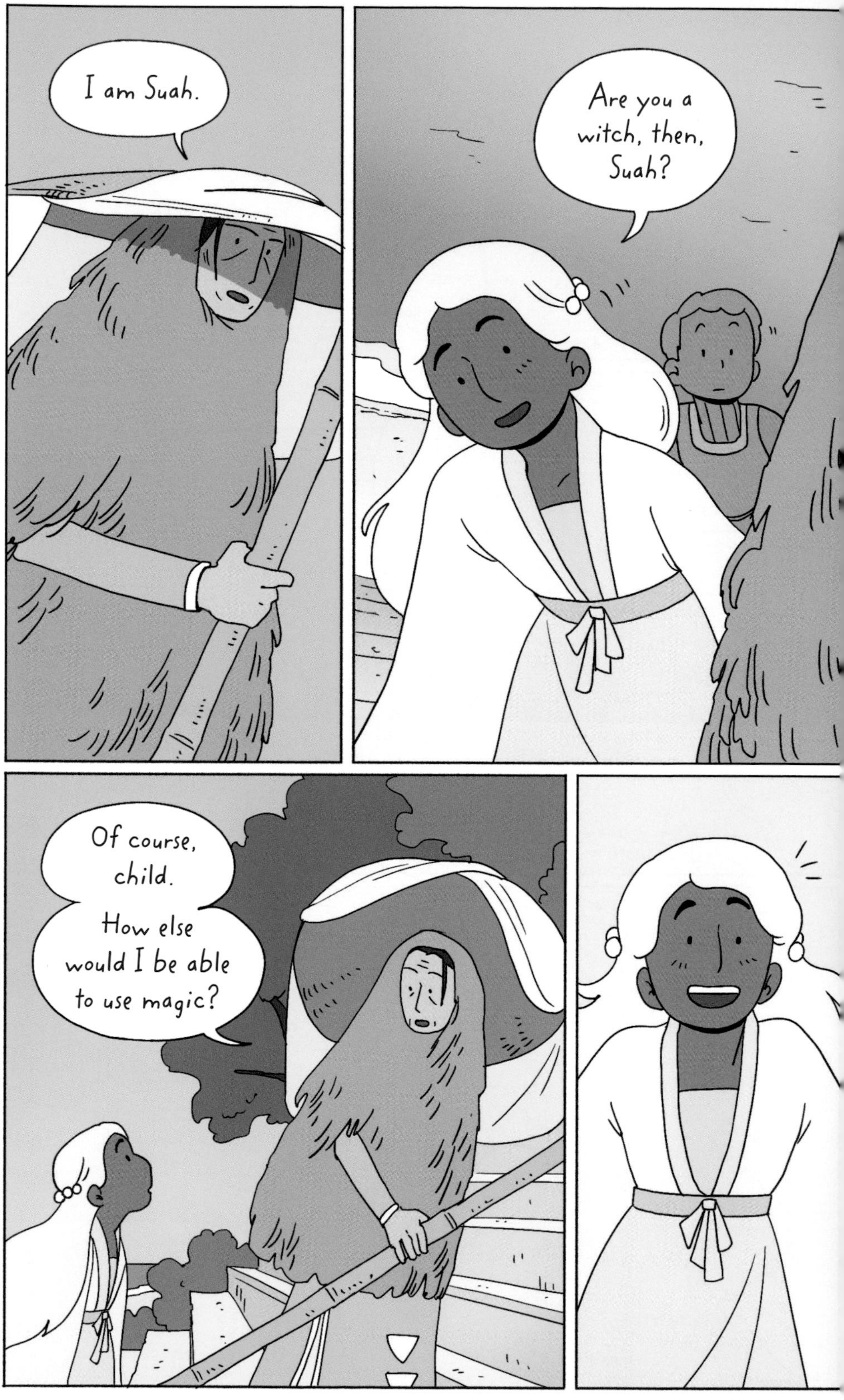
I am Suah.
Are you a witch, then, Suah?
Of course, child.
How else would I be able to use magic?

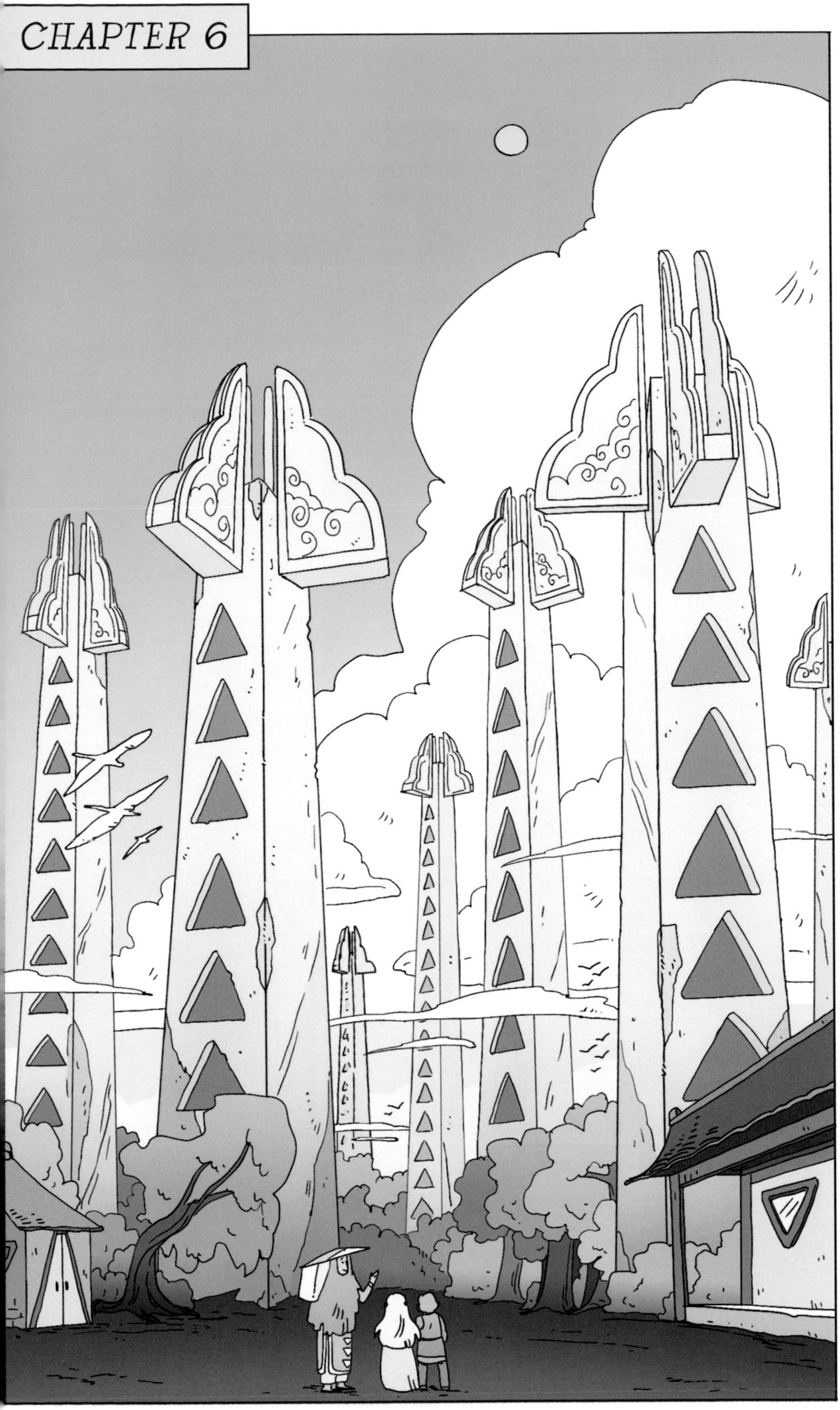
CHAPTER 6

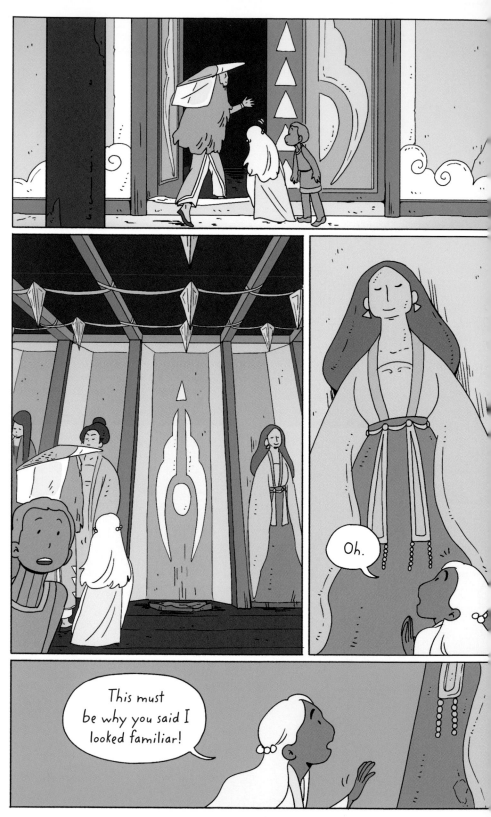

Oh.

This must be why you said I looked familiar!

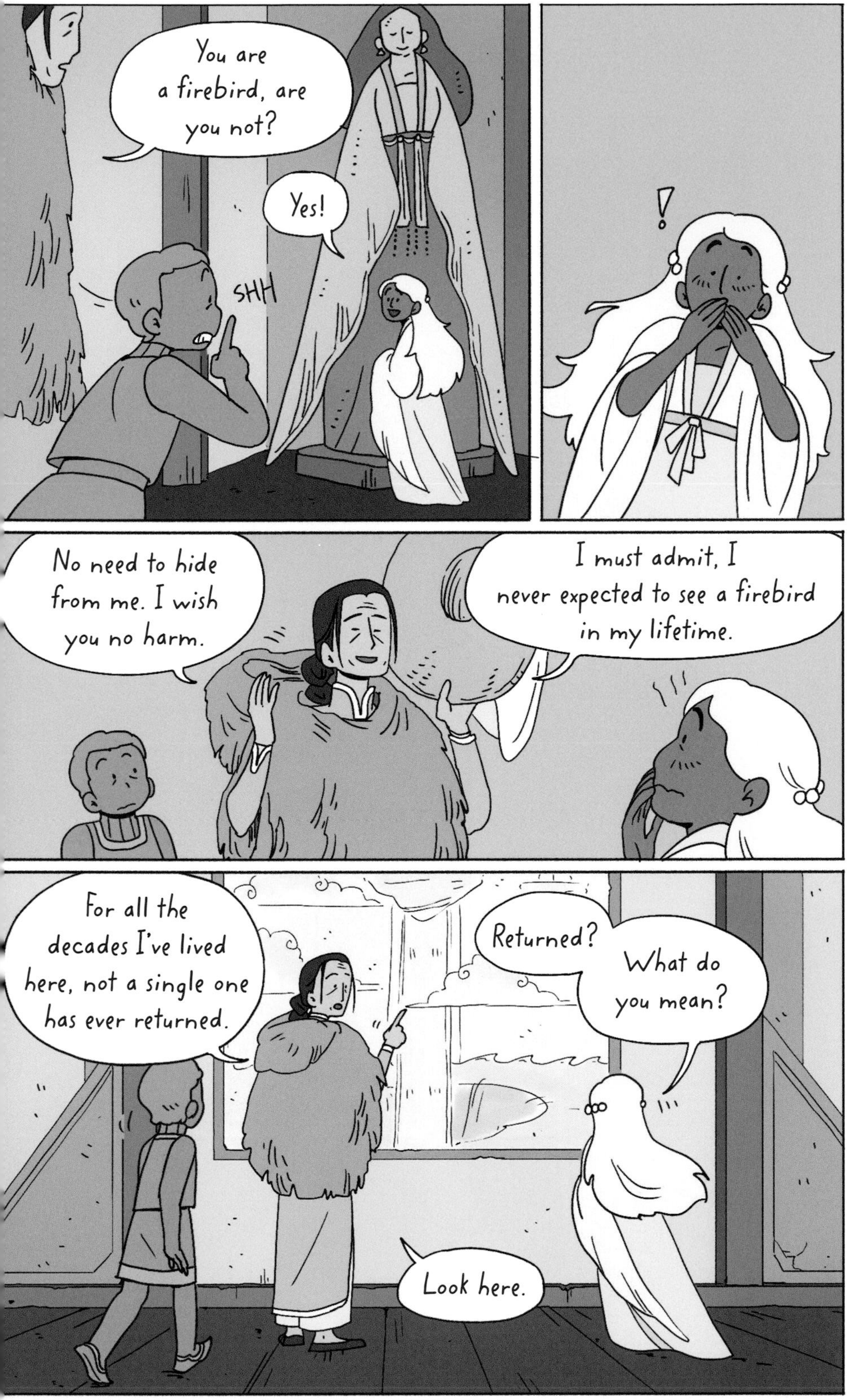
You are a firebird, are you not?
Yes!
SHH
!
No need to hide from me. I wish you no harm.
I must admit, I never expected to see a firebird in my lifetime.
For all the decades I've lived here, not a single one has ever returned.
Returned?
What do you mean?
Look here.

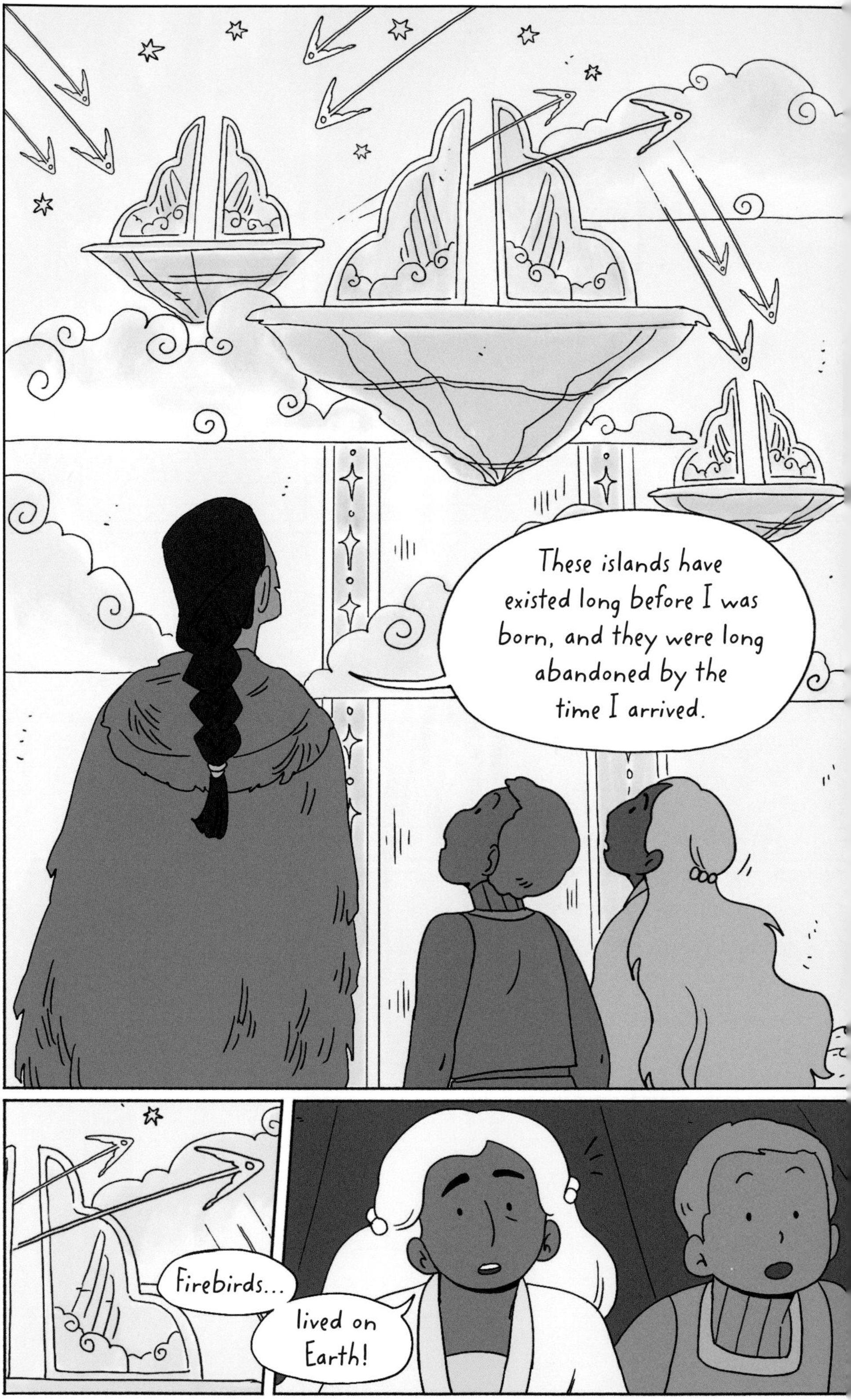
These islands have existed long before I was born, and they were long abandoned by the time I arrived.
Firebirds...
lived on Earth!

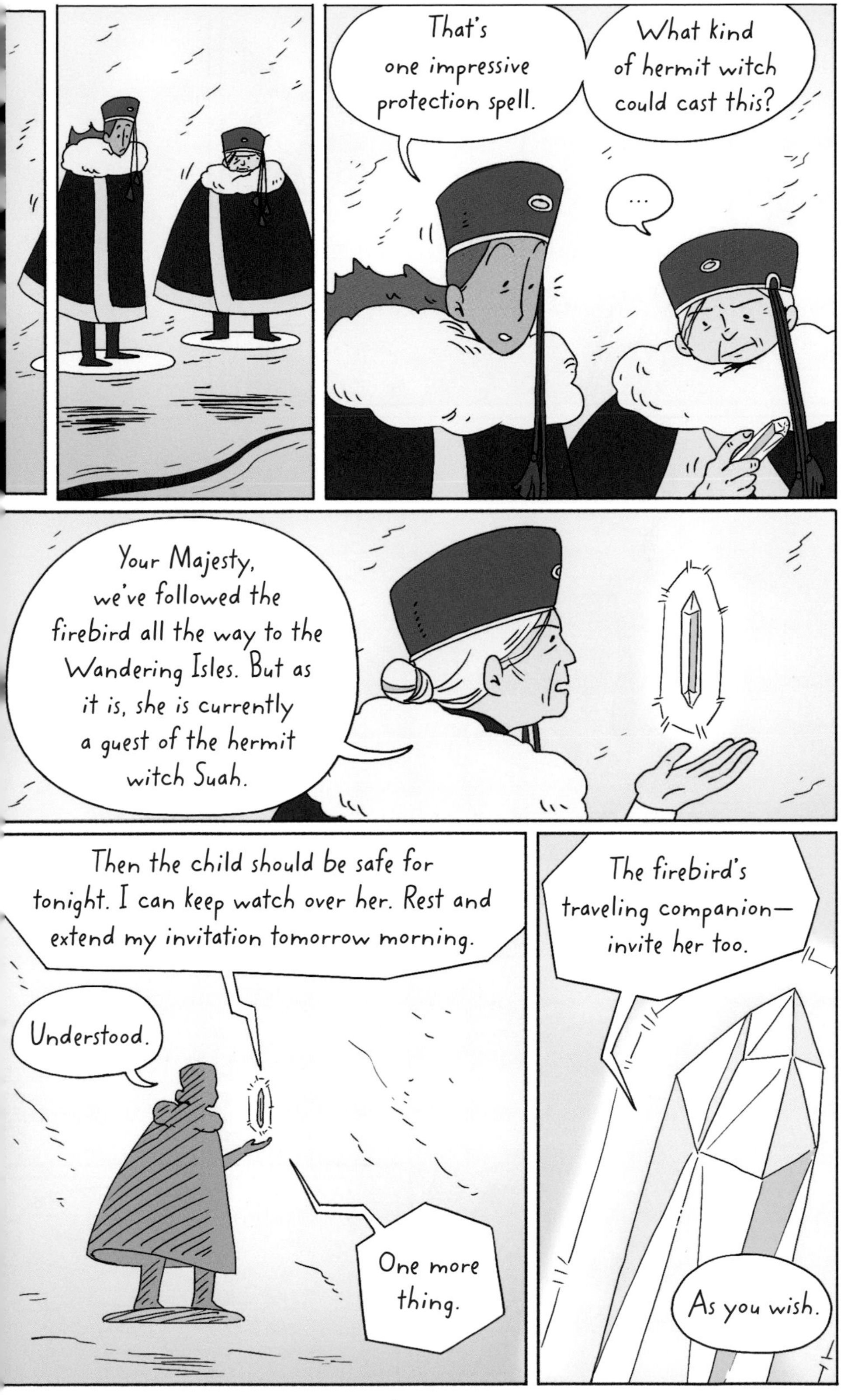
That's one impressive protection spell.
What kind of hermit witch could cast this?
...
Your Majesty, we've followed the firebird all the way to the Wandering Isles. But as it is, she is currently a guest of the hermit witch Suah.
Then the child should be safe for tonight. I can keep watch over her. Rest and extend my invitation tomorrow morning.
Understood.
One more thing.
The firebird's traveling companion—invite her too.
As you wish.

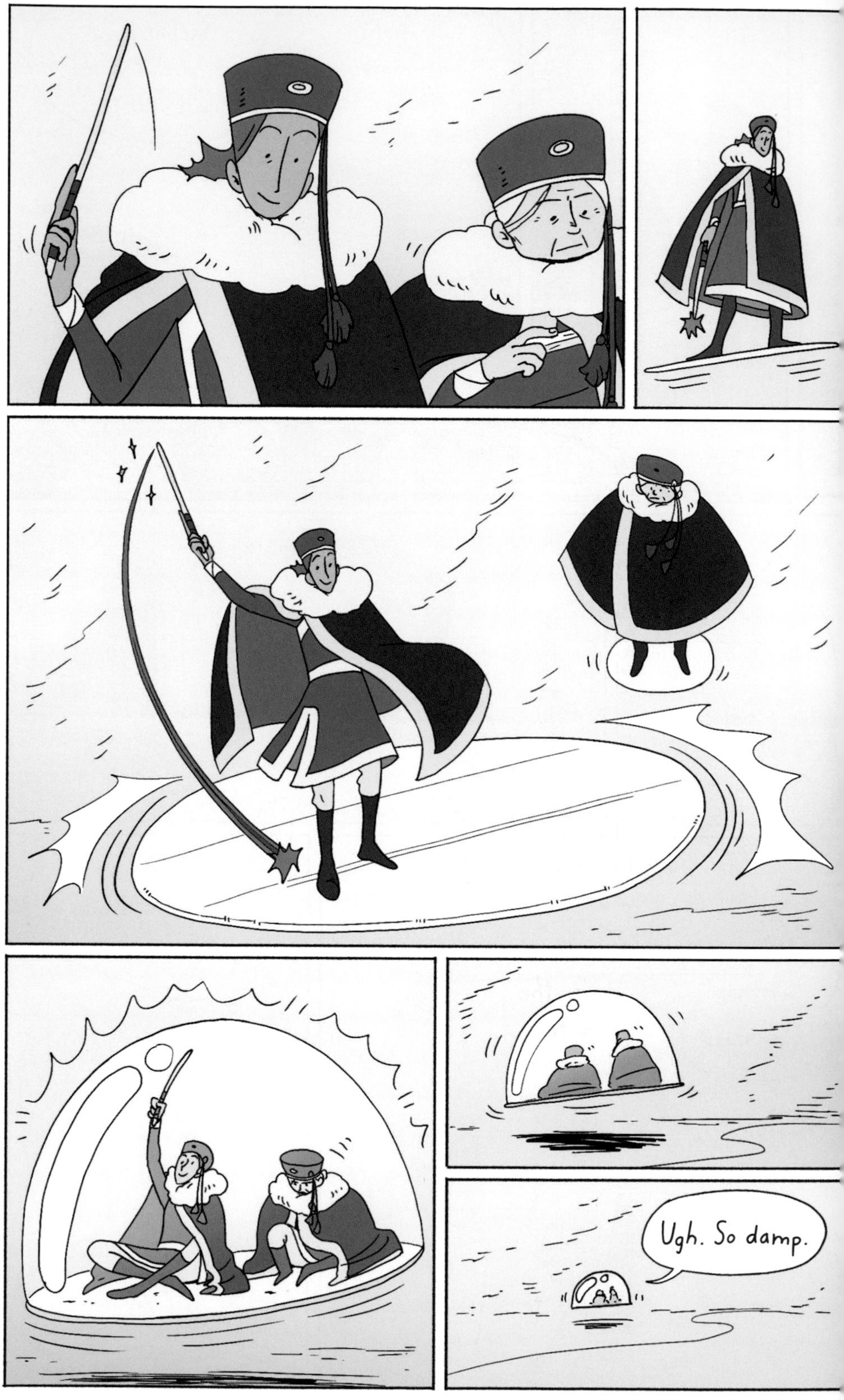
Ugh. So damp.

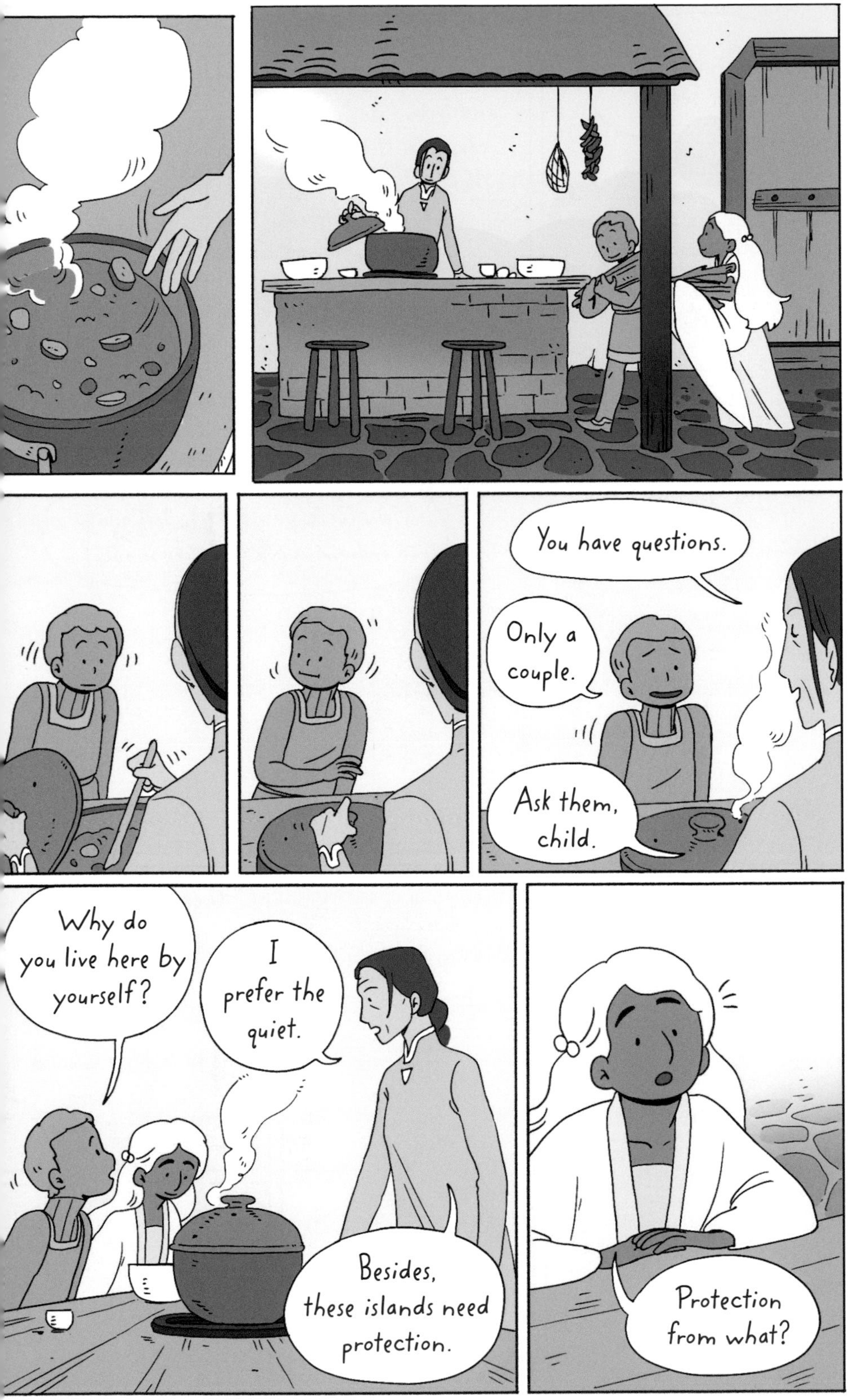
You have questions.
Only a couple.
Ask them, child.
Why do you live here by yourself?
I prefer the quiet.
Besides, these islands need protection.
Protection from what?

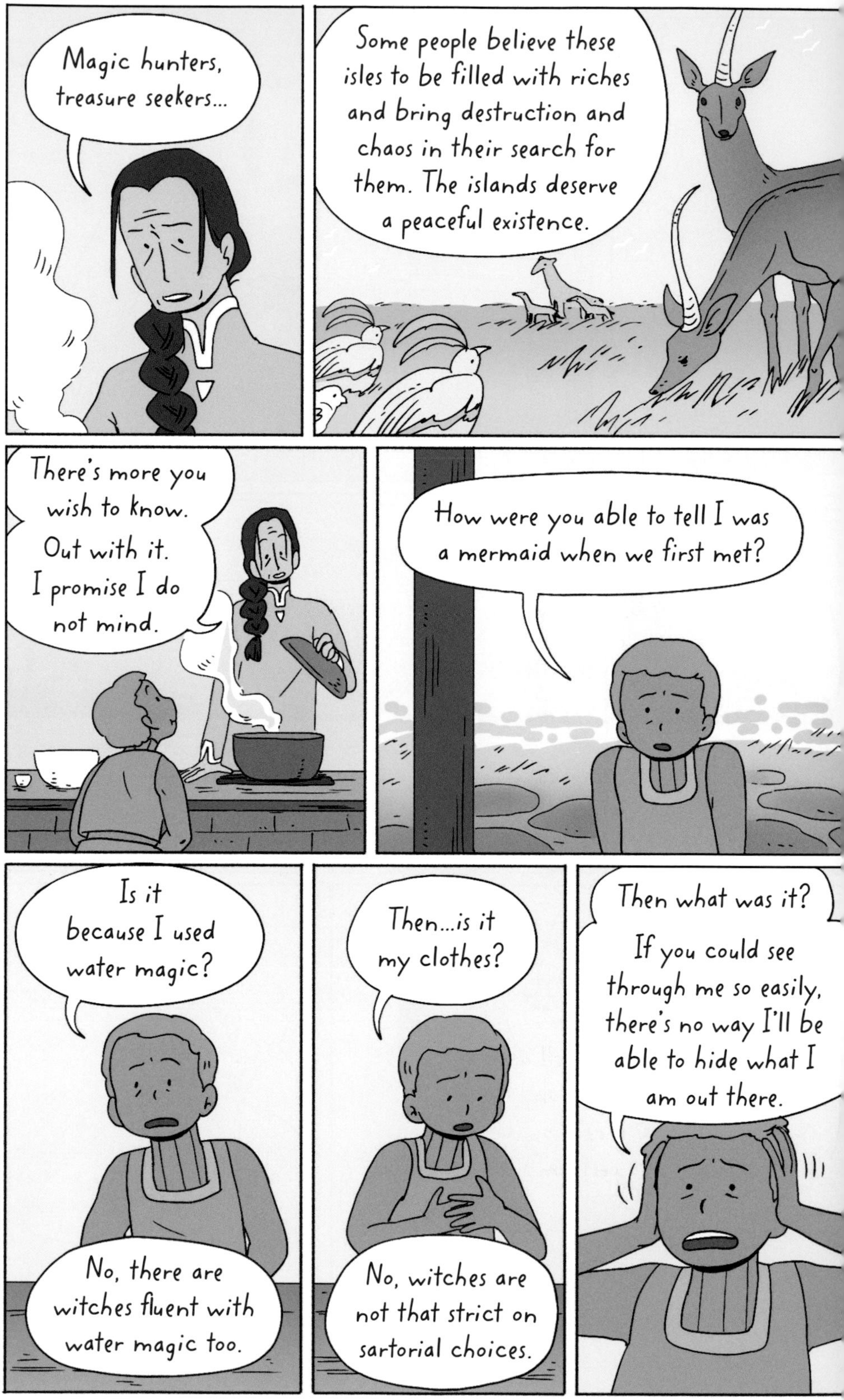
Magic hunters, treasure seekers...
Some people believe these isles to be filled with riches and bring destruction and chaos in their search for them. The islands deserve a peaceful existence.
There's more you wish to know. Out with it. I promise I do not mind.
How were you able to tell I was a mermaid when we first met?
Is it because I used water magic?
No, there are witches fluent with water magic too.
Then...is it my clothes?
No, witches are not that strict on sartorial choices.
Then what was it?
If you could see through me so easily, there's no way I'll be able to hide what I am out there.

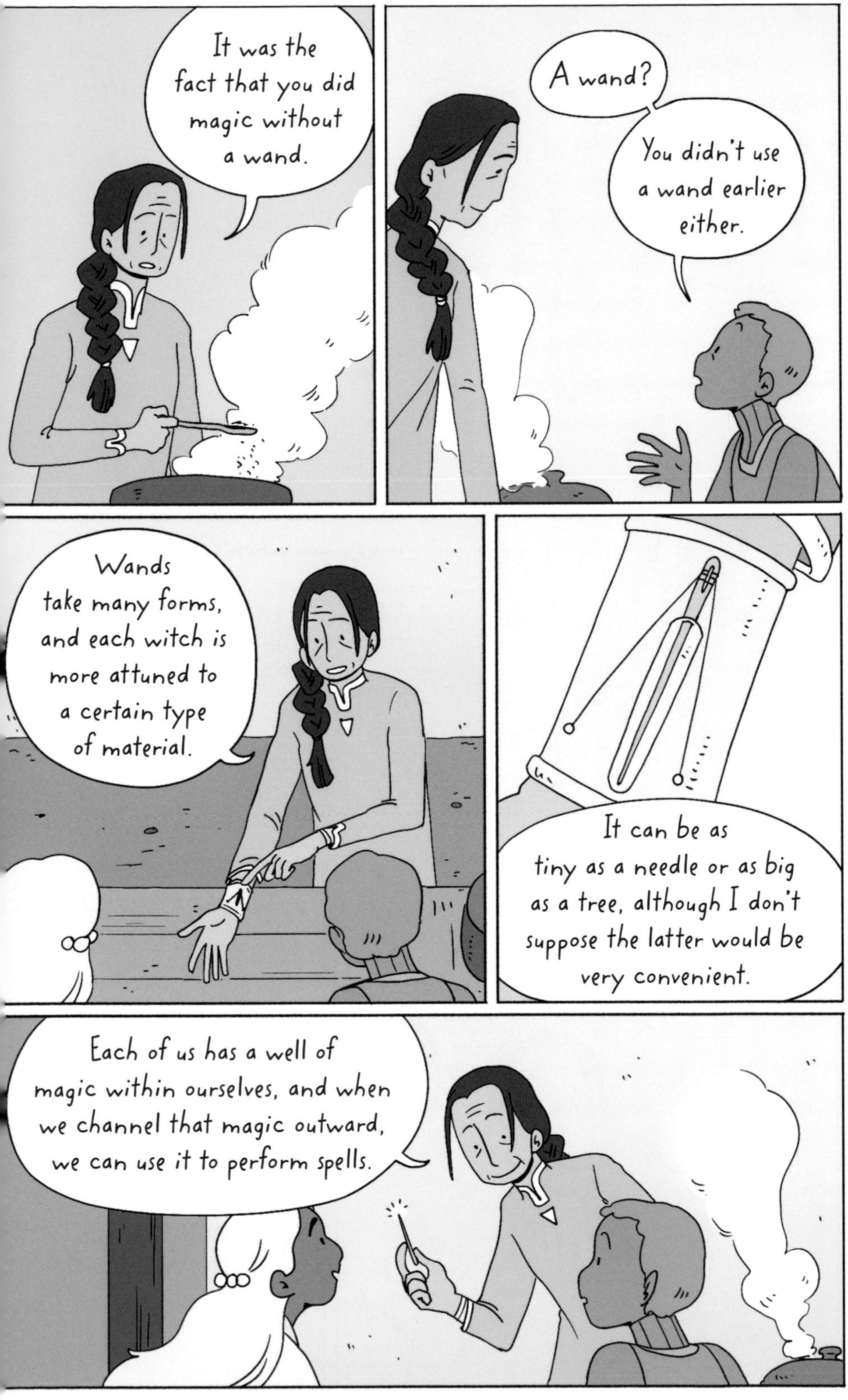
It was the fact that you did magic without a wand.
A wand?
You didn't use a wand earlier either.
Wands take many forms, and each witch is more attuned to a certain type of material.
It can be as tiny as a needle or as big as a tree, although I don't suppose the latter would be very convenient.
Each of us has a well of magic within ourselves, and when we channel that magic outward, we can use it to perform spells.

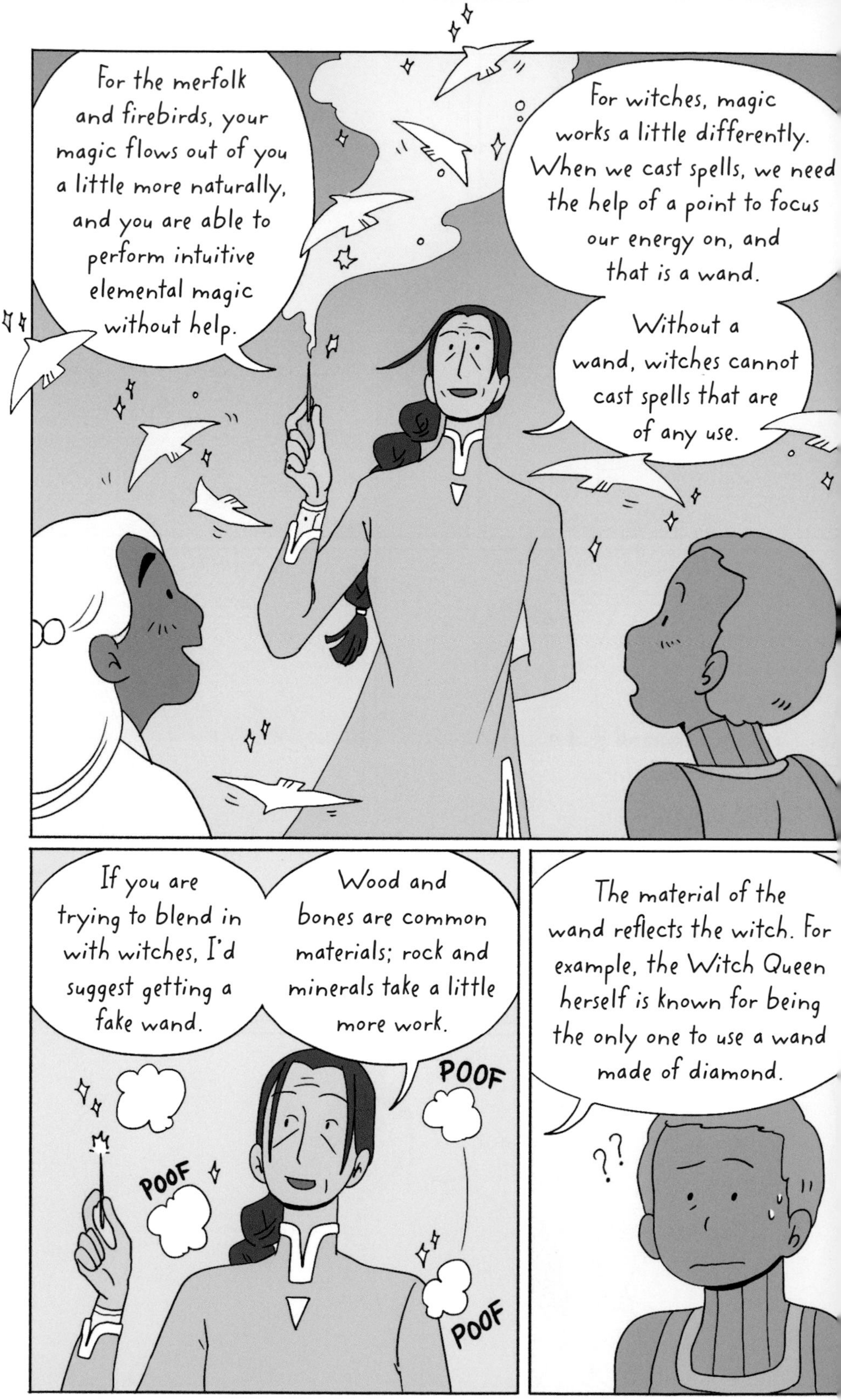
For the merfolk and firebirds, your magic flows out of you a little more naturally, and you are able to perform intuitive elemental magic without help.
For witches, magic works a little differently. When we cast spells, we need the help of a point to focus our energy on, and that is a wand.
Without a wand, witches cannot cast spells that are of any use.
If you are trying to blend in with witches, I'd suggest getting a fake wand.
Wood and bones are common materials; rock and minerals take a little more work.
POOF
POOF
POOF
The material of the wand reflects the witch. For example, the Witch Queen herself is known for being the only one to use a wand made of diamond.
??

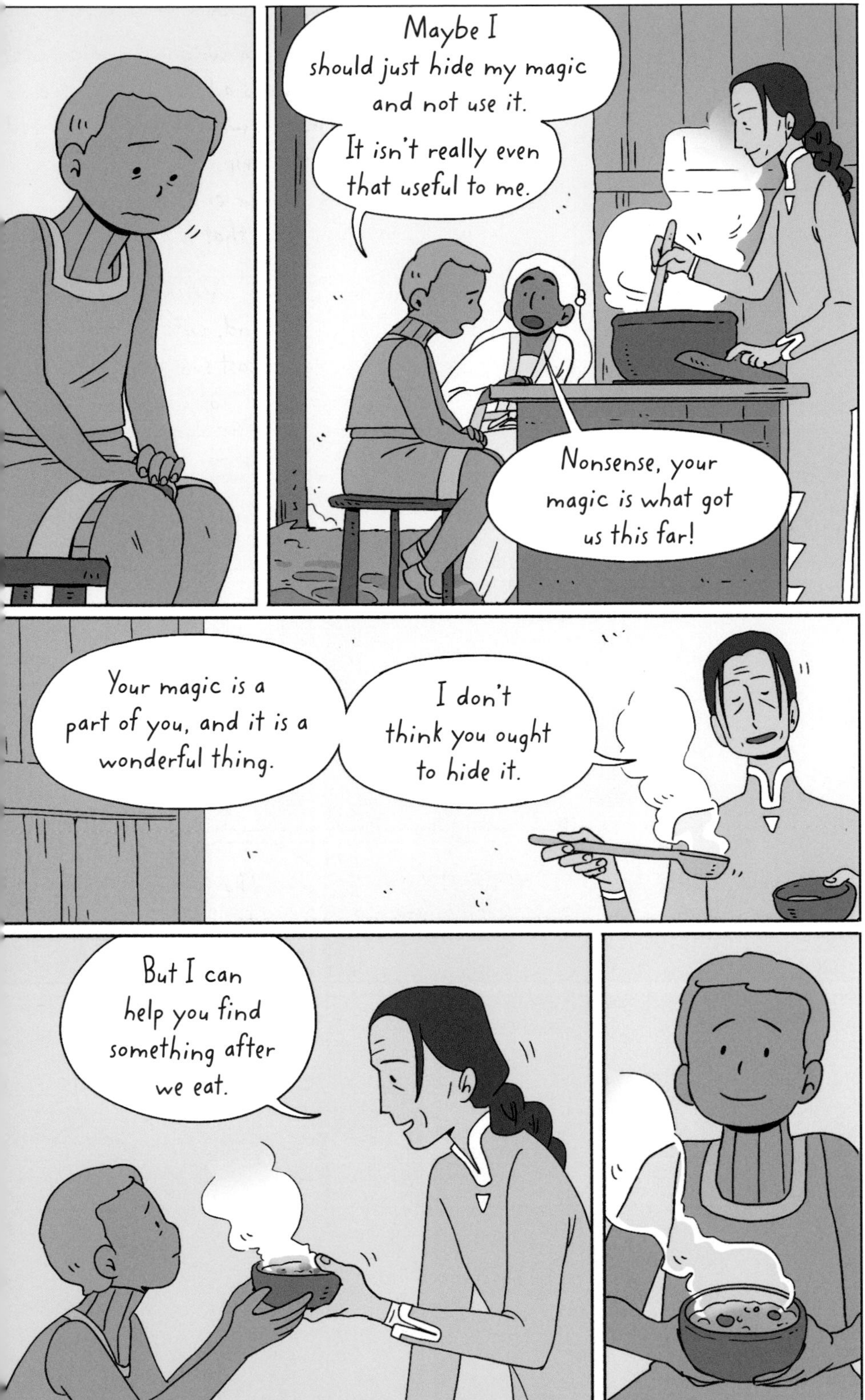
Maybe I should just hide my magic and not use it.
It isn't really even that useful to me.
Nonsense, your magic is what got us this far!
Your magic is a part of you, and it is a wonderful thing.
I don't think you ought to hide it.
But I can help you find something after we eat.

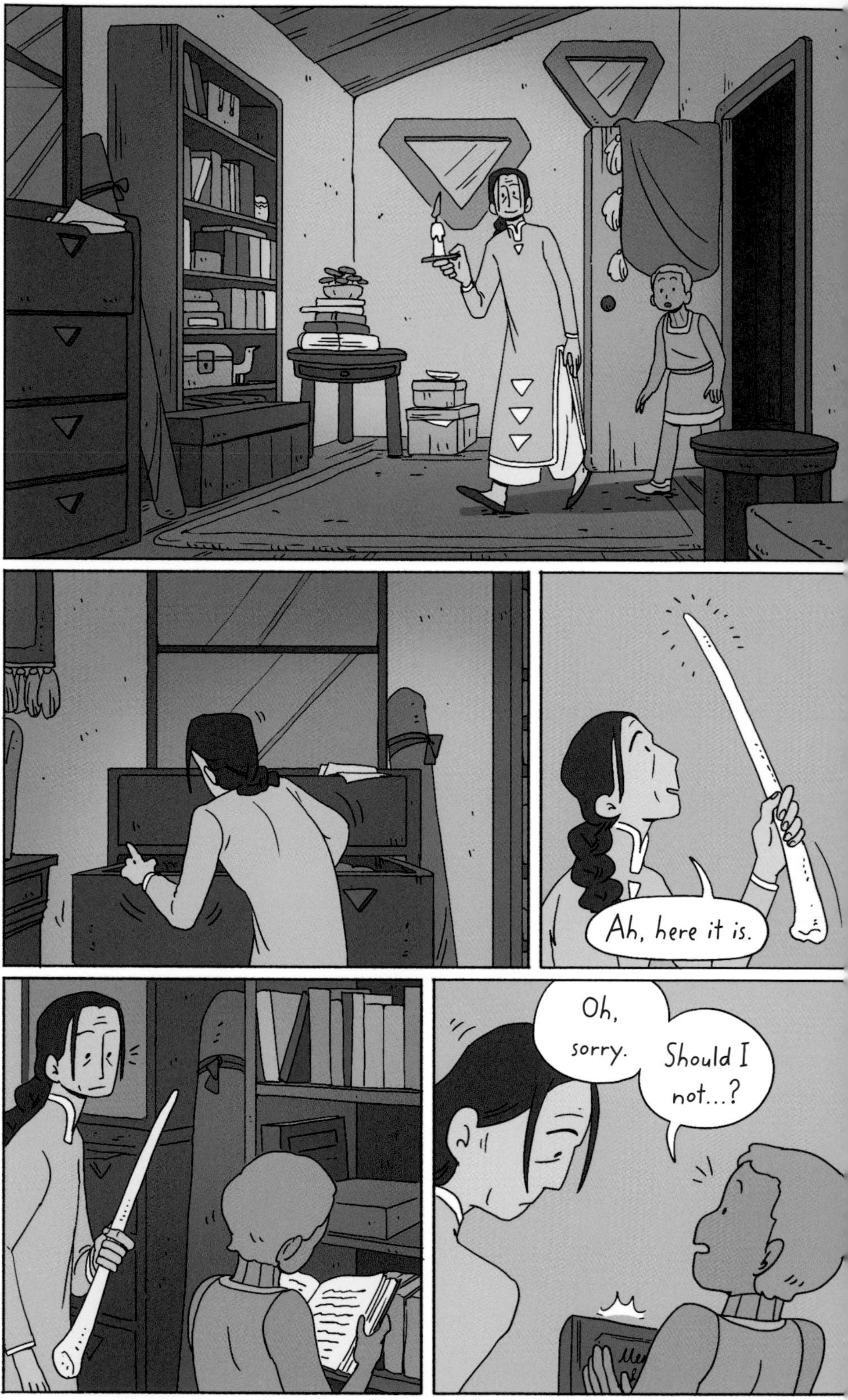
Ah, here it is.
Oh, sorry.
Should I not...?

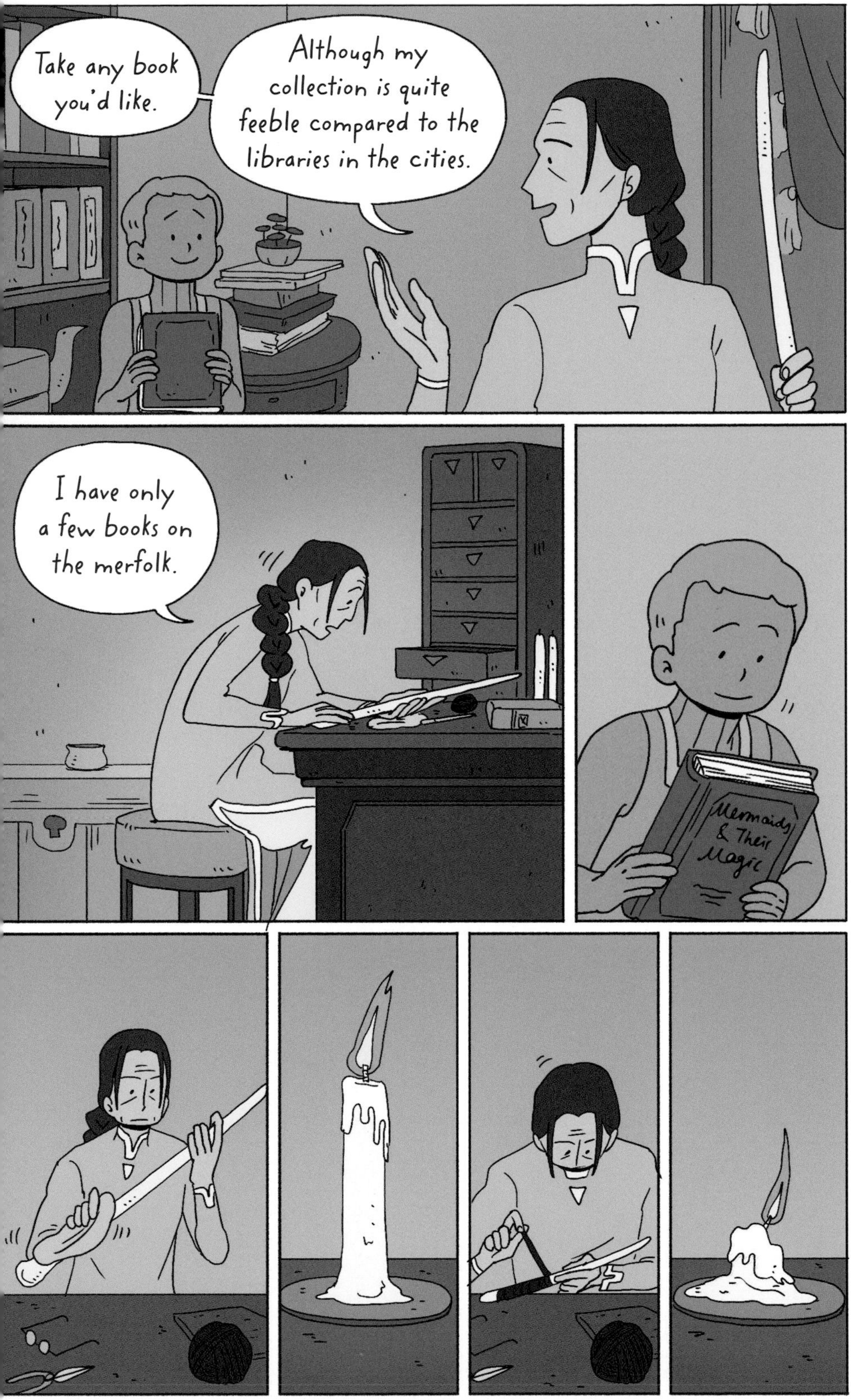
Take any book you'd like.
Although my collection is quite feeble compared to the libraries in the cities.
I have only a few books on the merfolk.
Mermaids & Their Magic

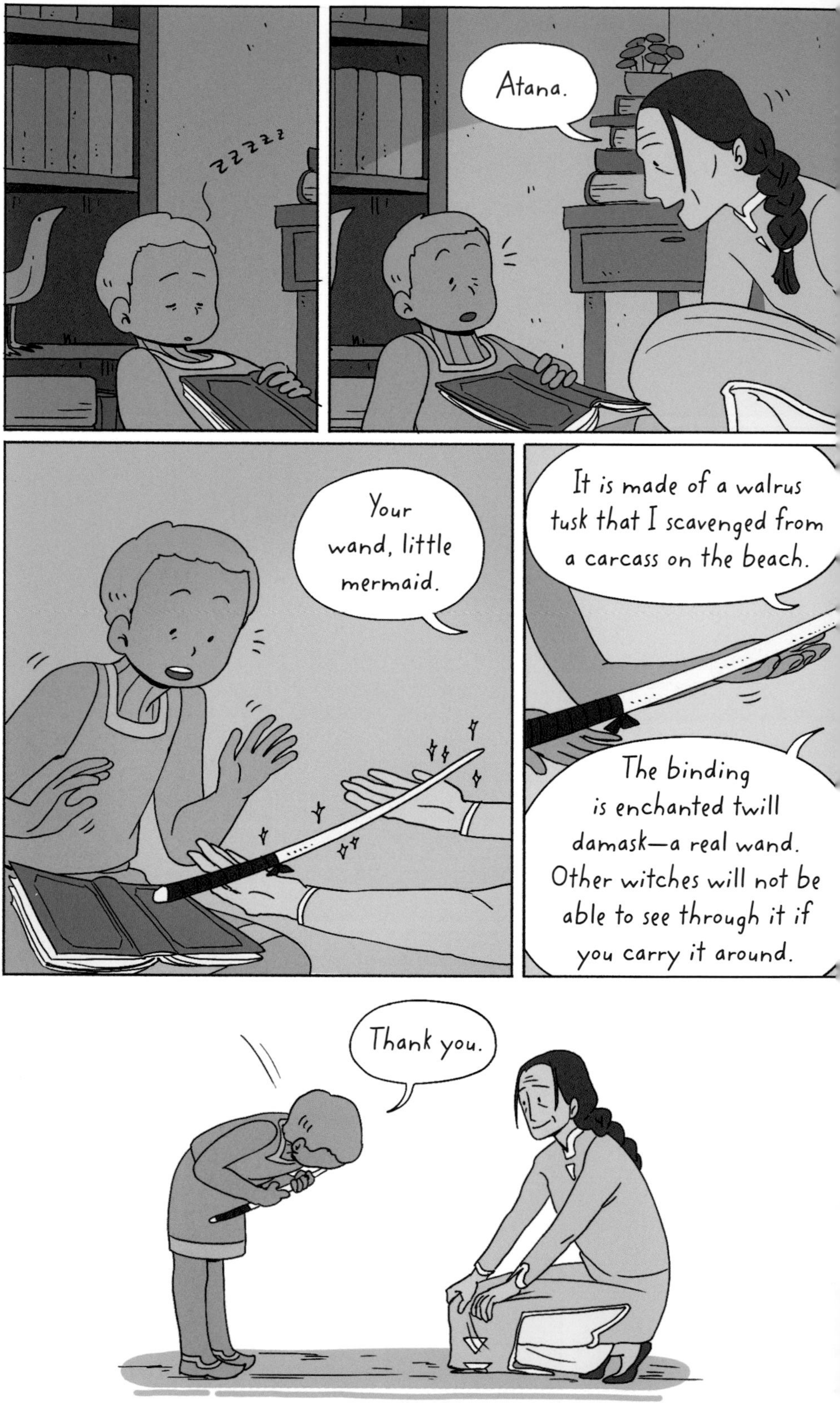
zzzzz
Atana.
Your wand, little mermaid.
It is made of a walrus tusk that I scavenged from a carcass on the beach.
The binding is enchanted twill damask—a real wand. Other witches will not be able to see through it if you carry it around.
Thank you.

CHAPTER 7

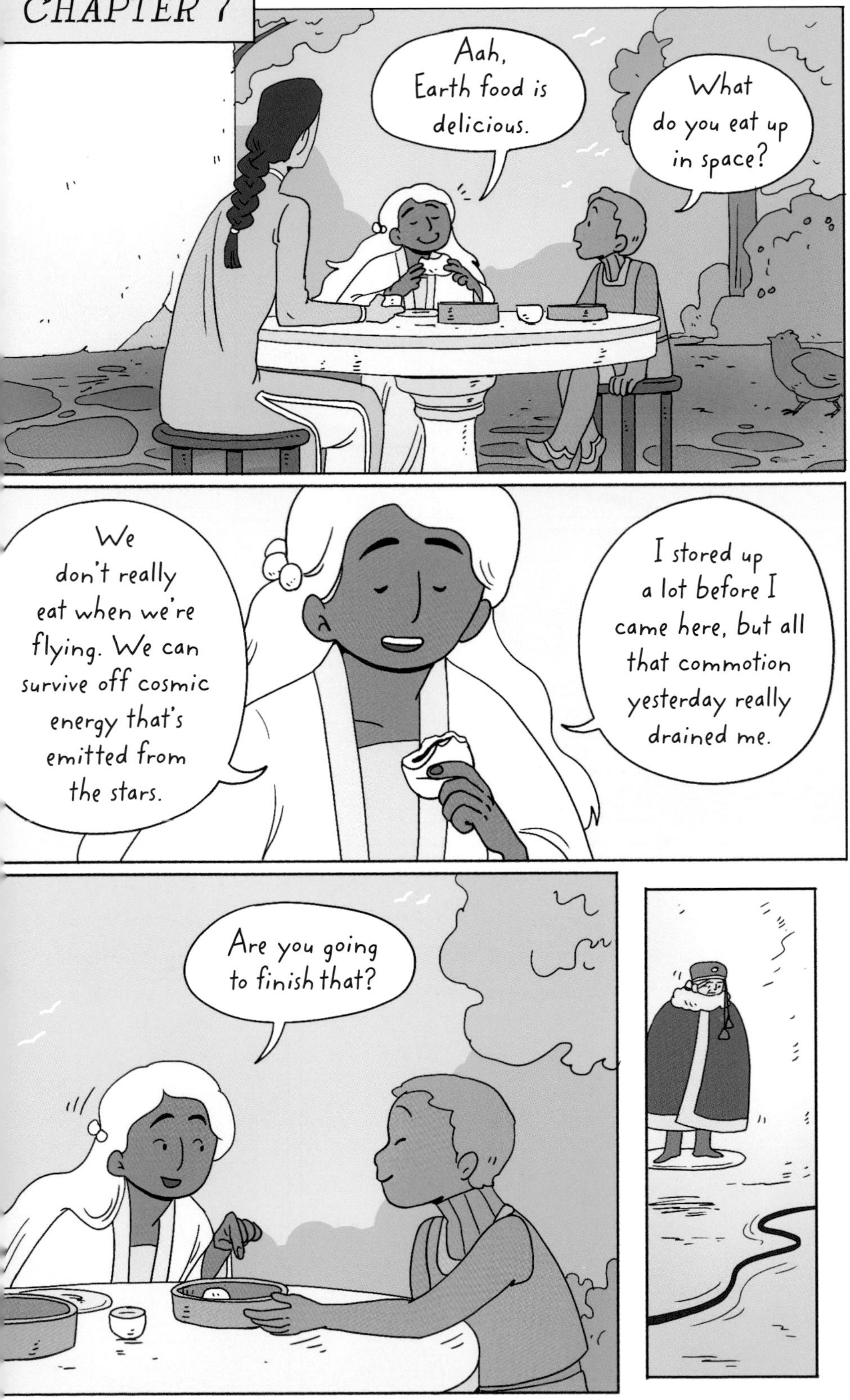

Aah, Earth food is delicious.
What do you eat up in space?
We don't really eat when we're flying. We can survive off cosmic energy that's emitted from the stars.
I stored up a lot before I came here, but all that commotion yesterday really drained me.
Are you going to finish that?

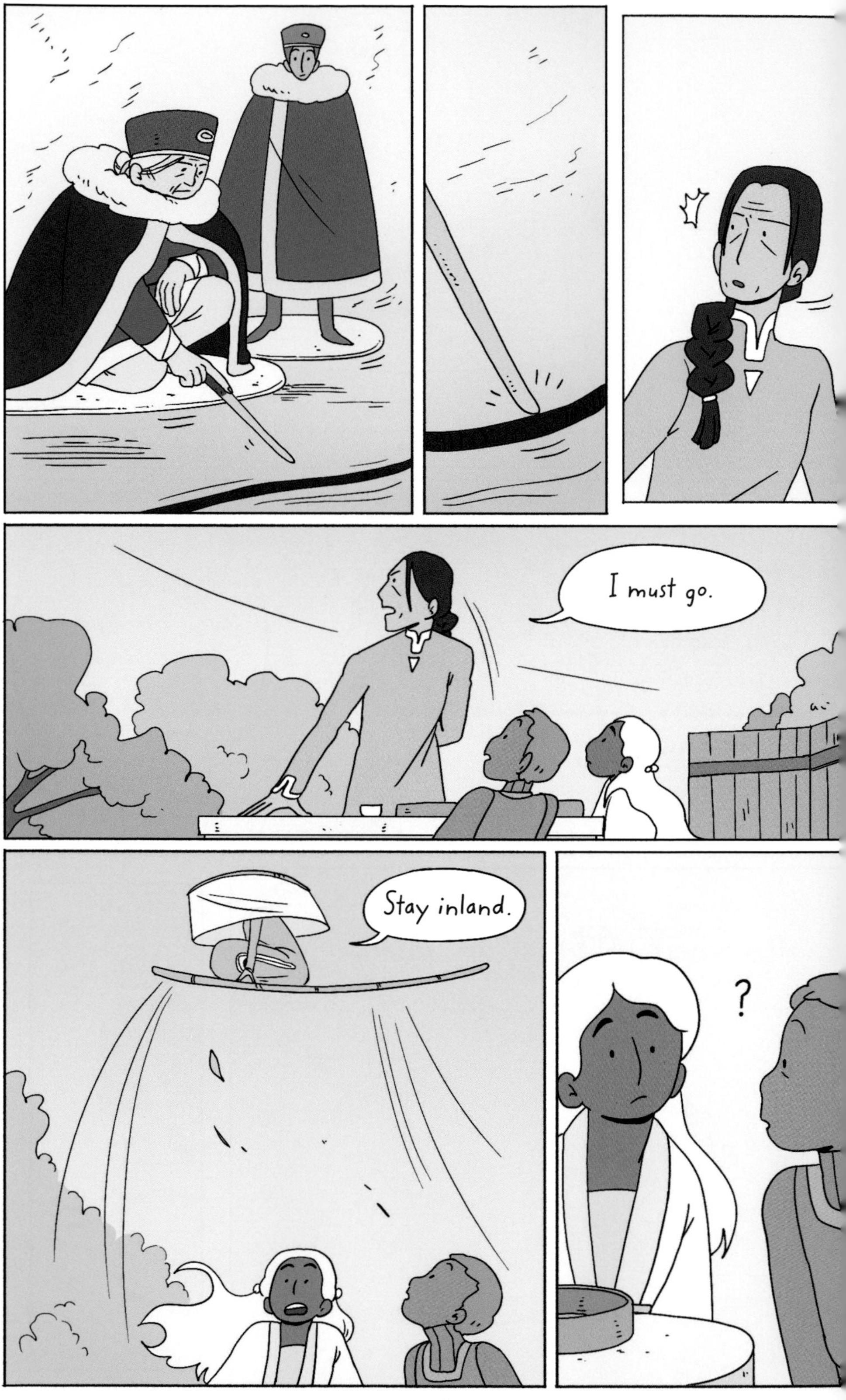
I must go.
Stay inland.
?

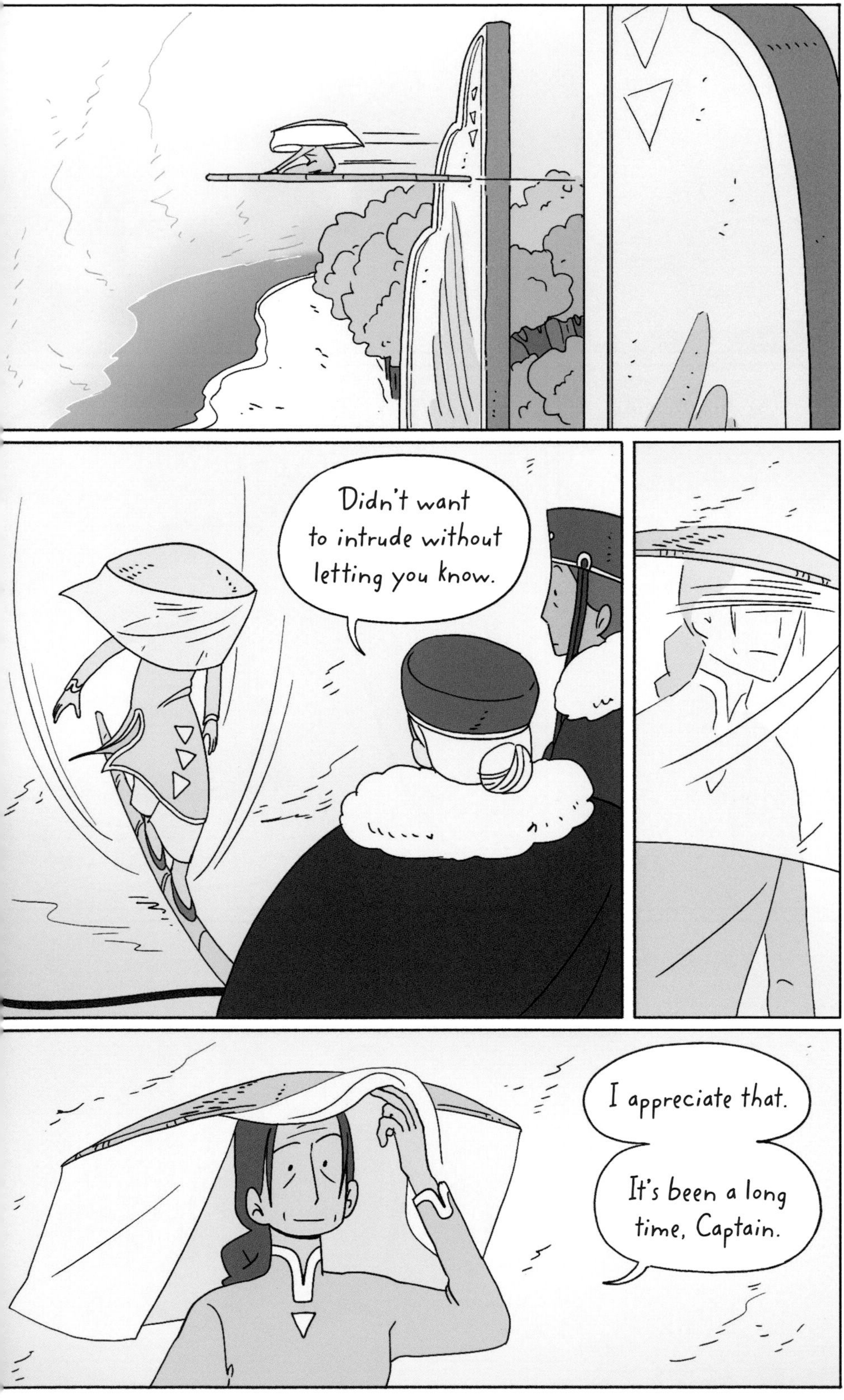

Didn't want to intrude without letting you know.
I appreciate that.
It's been a long time, Captain.

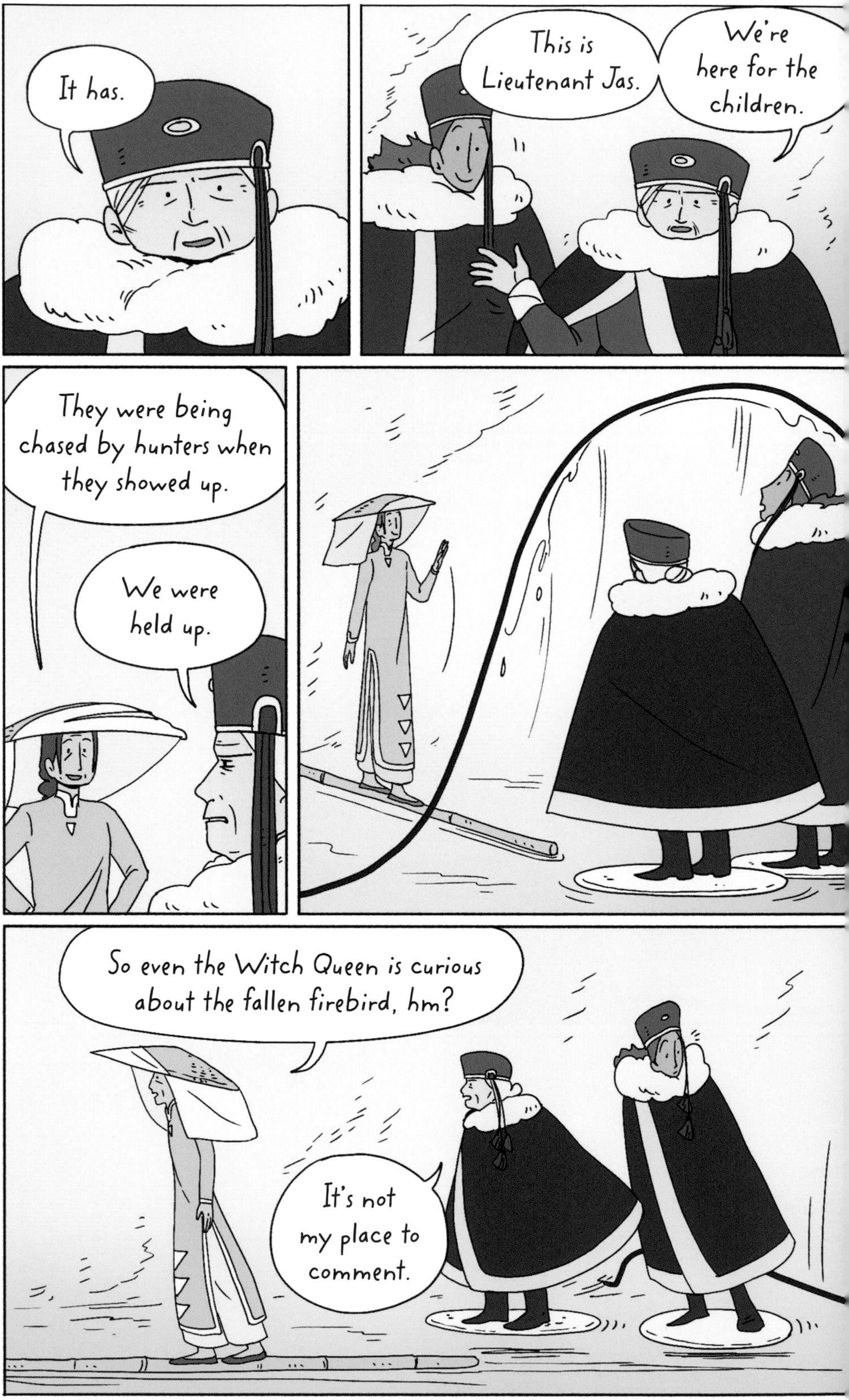
It has.
This is Lieutenant Jas.
We're here for the children.
They were being chased by hunters when they showed up.
We were held up.
So even the Witch Queen is curious about the fallen firebird, hm?
It's not my place to comment.

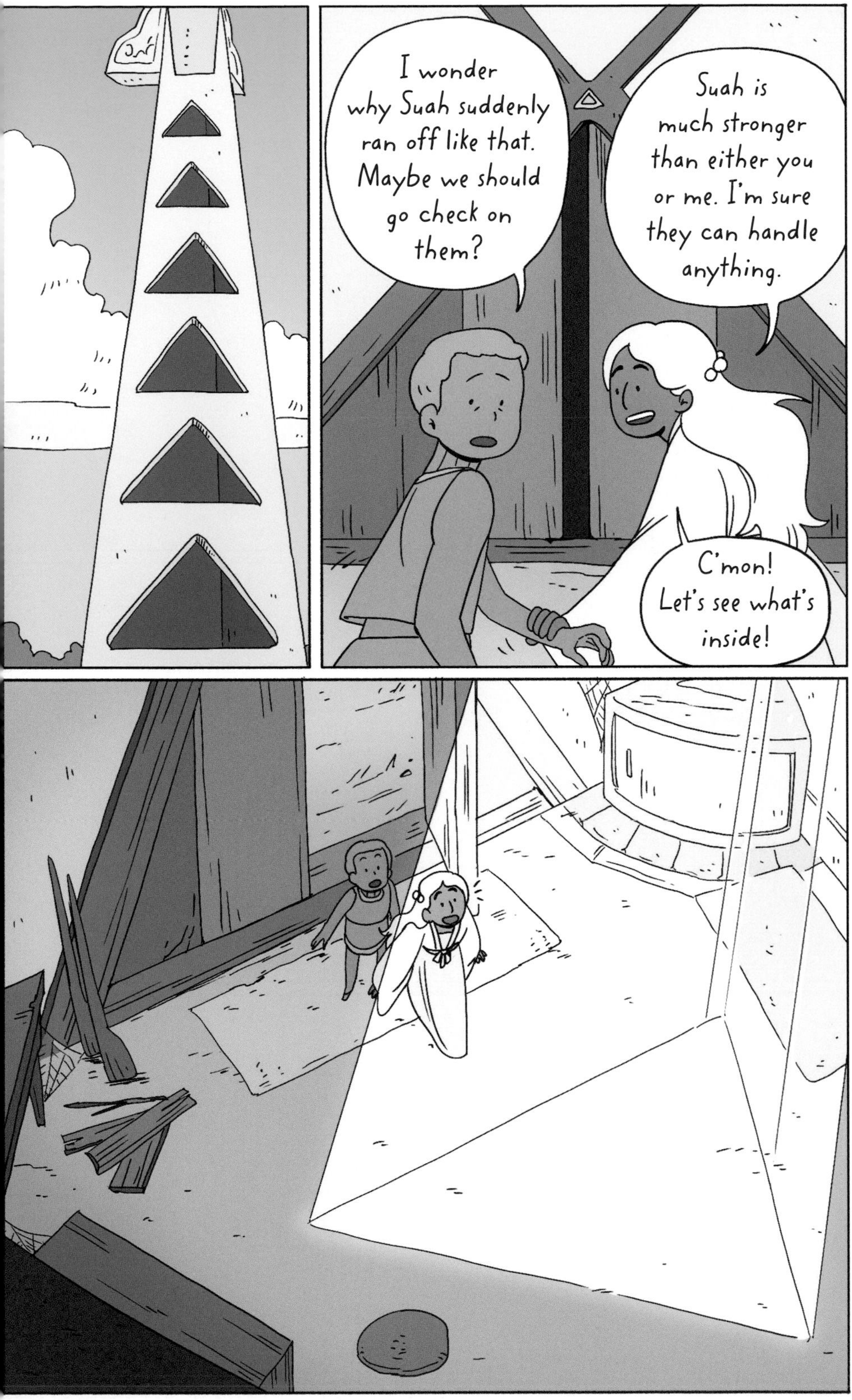

I wonder why Suah suddenly ran off like that. Maybe we should go check on them?
Suah is much stronger than either you or me. I'm sure they can handle anything.
C'mon! Let's see what's inside!

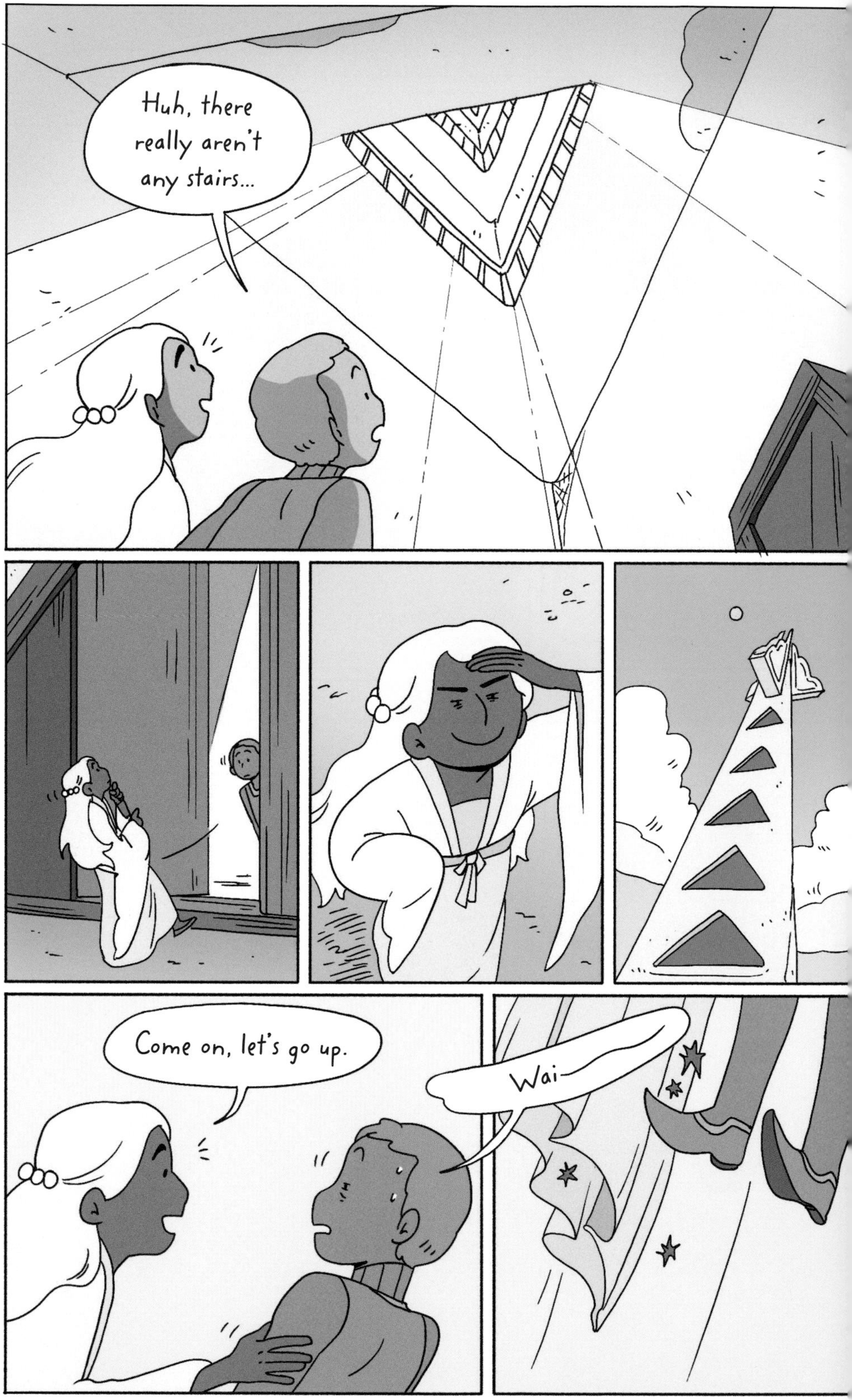
Huh, there really aren't any stairs...
Come on, let's go up.
Wai—

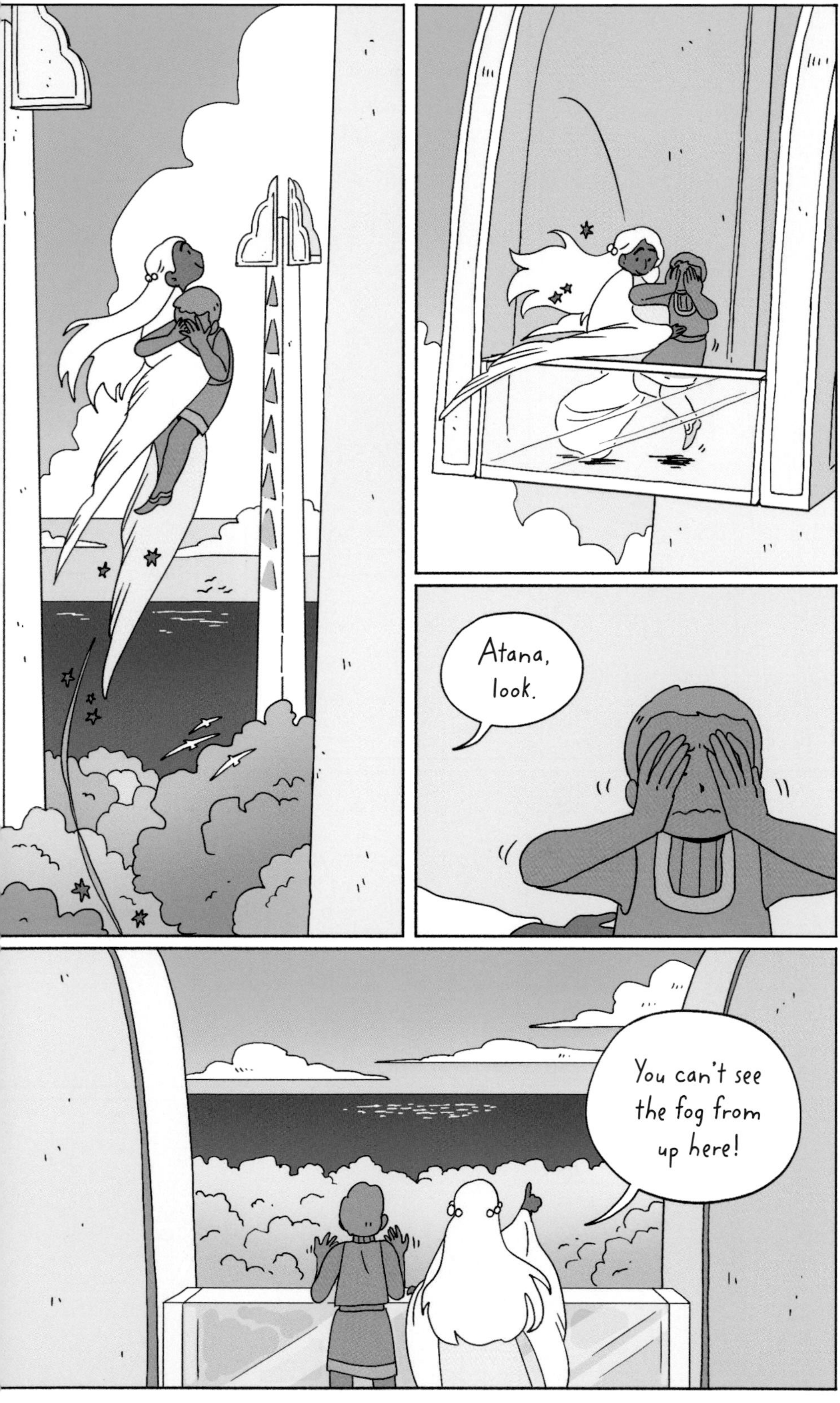
Atana, look.
You can't see the fog from up here!

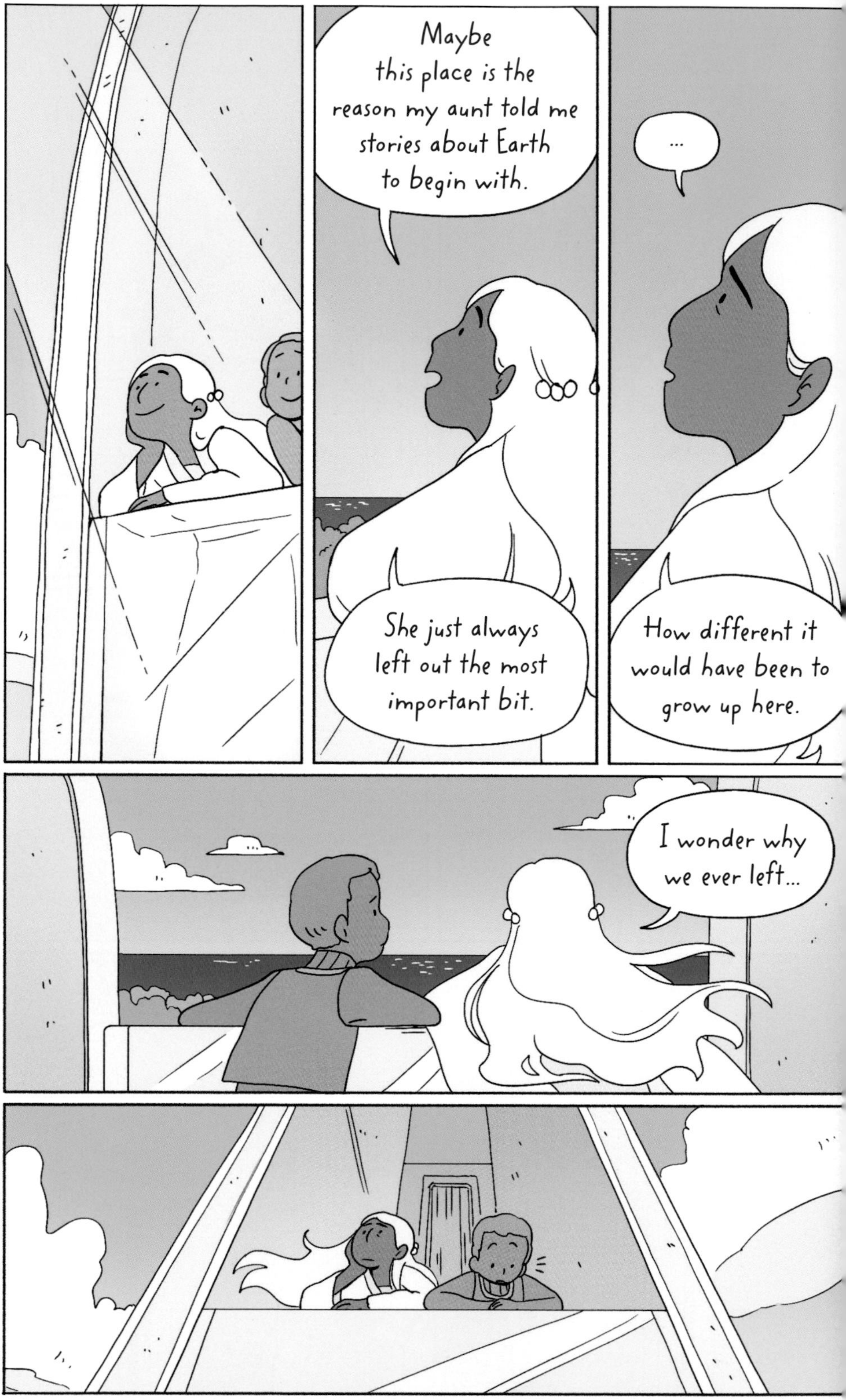

Maybe this place is the reason my aunt told me stories about Earth to begin with.
...
She just always left out the most important bit.
How different it would have been to grow up here.
I wonder why we ever left...

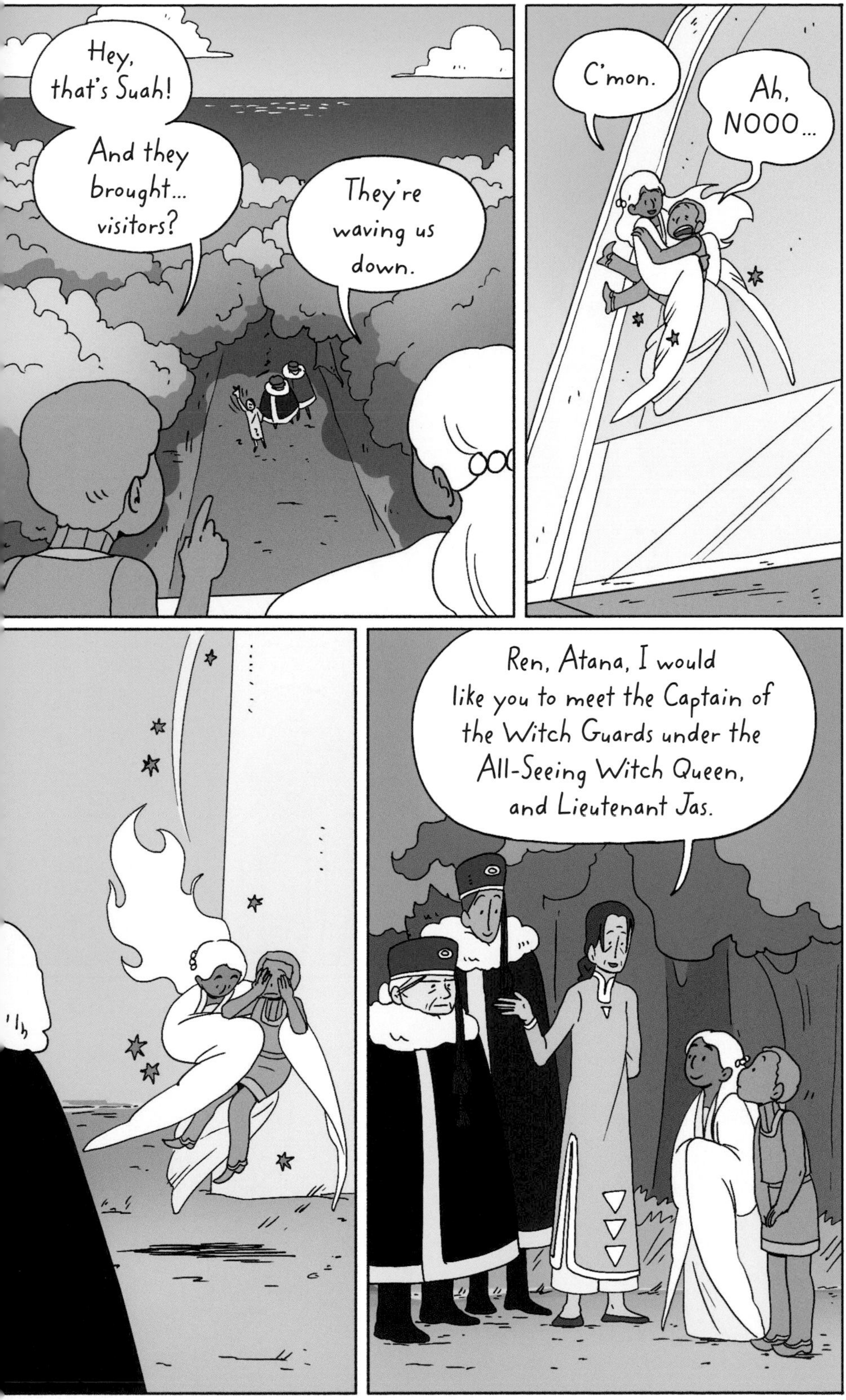
Hey, that's Suah!
And they brought... visitors?
They're waving us down.
C'mon.
Ah, NOOO...
Ren, Atana, I would like you to meet the Captain of the Witch Guards under the All-Seeing Witch Queen, and Lieutenant Jas.

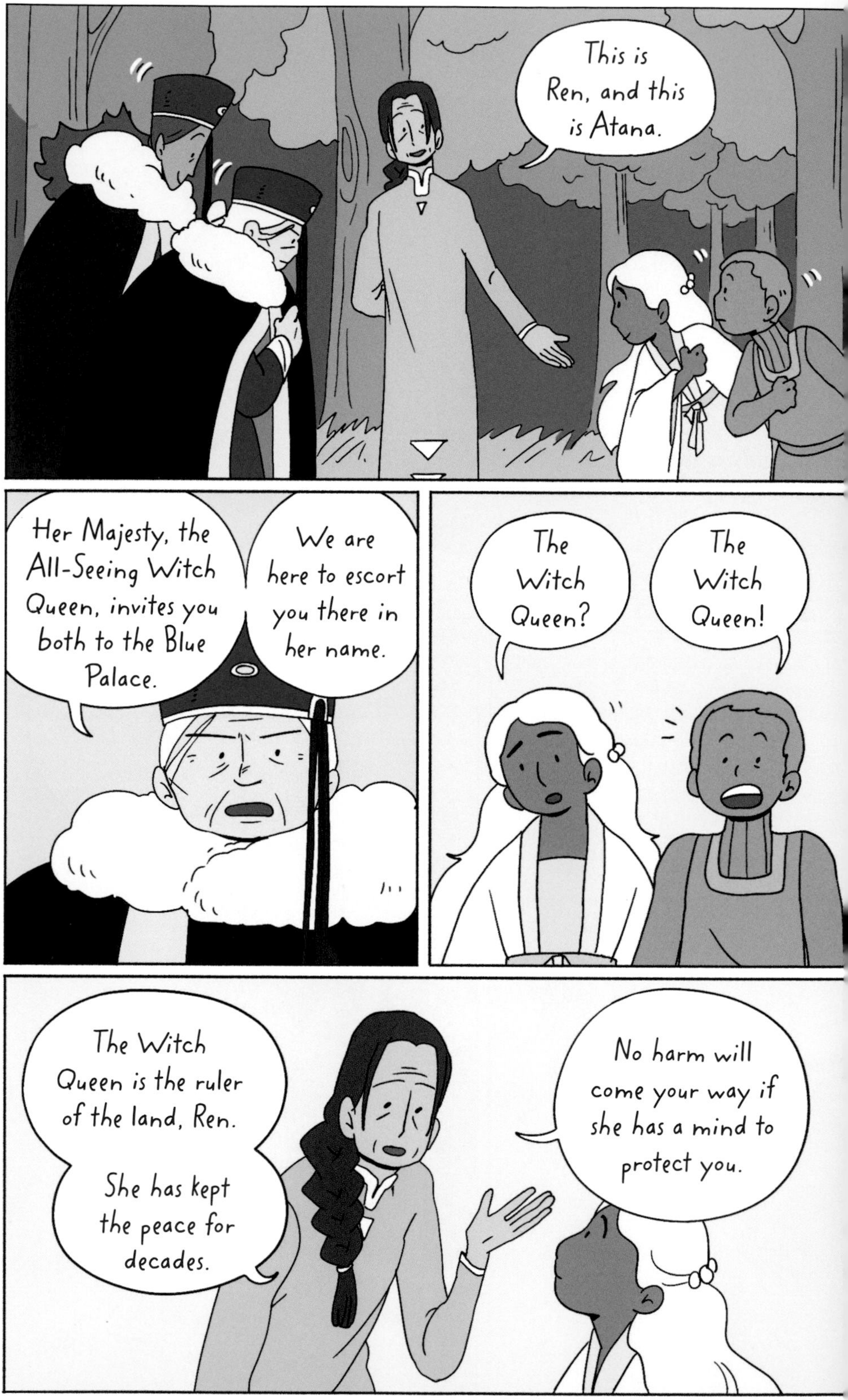
This is Ren, and this is Atana.
Her Majesty, the All-Seeing Witch Queen, invites you both to the Blue Palace.
We are here to escort you there in her name.
The Witch Queen?
The Witch Queen!
The Witch Queen is the ruler of the land, Ren.
She has kept the peace for decades.
No harm will come your way if she has a mind to protect you.

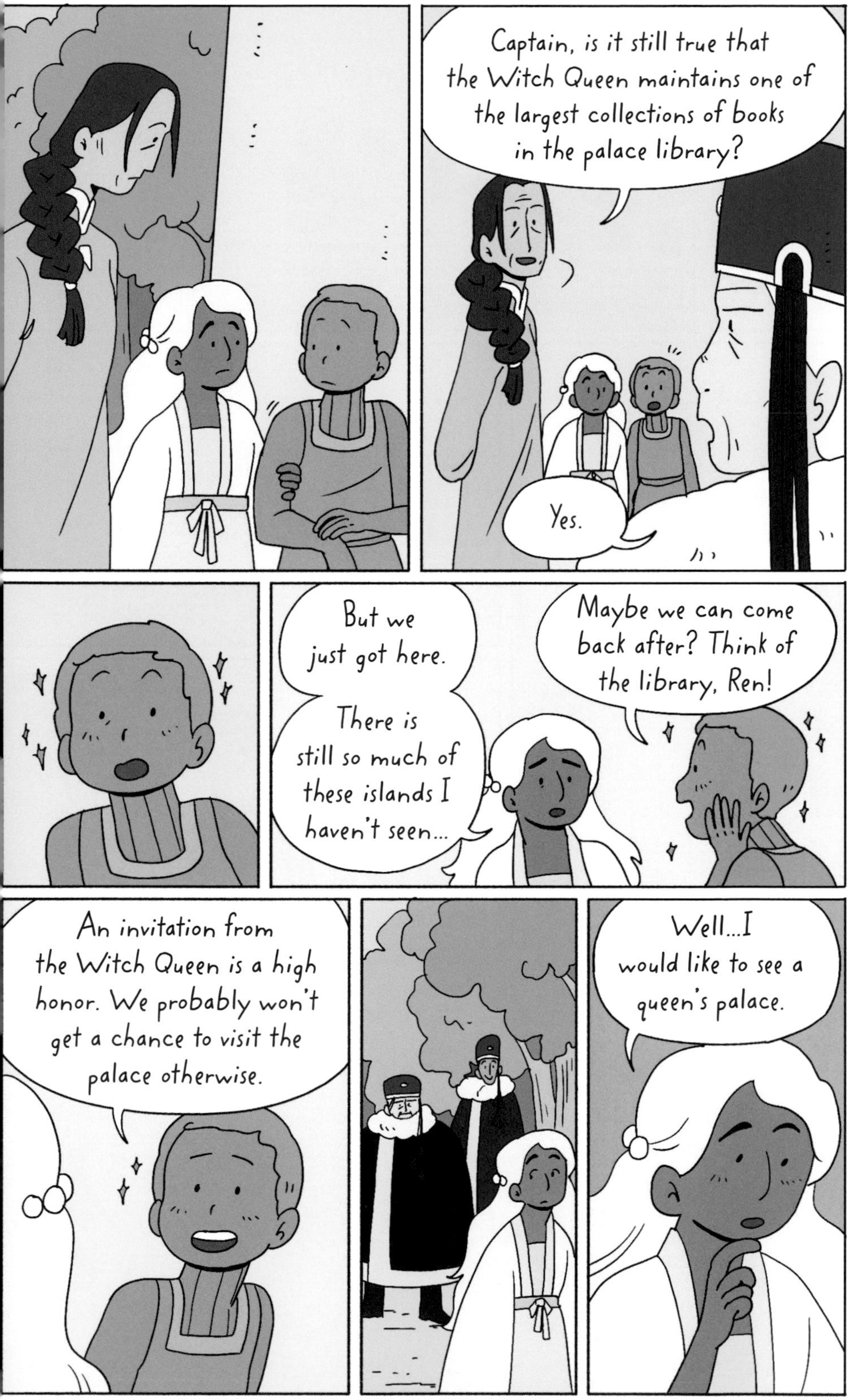
Captain, is it still true that the Witch Queen maintains one of the largest collections of books in the palace library?
Yes.
But we just got here.
There is still so much of these islands I haven't seen...
Maybe we can come back after? Think of the library, Ren!
An invitation from the Witch Queen is a high honor. We probably won't get a chance to visit the palace otherwise.
Well...I would like to see a queen's palace.

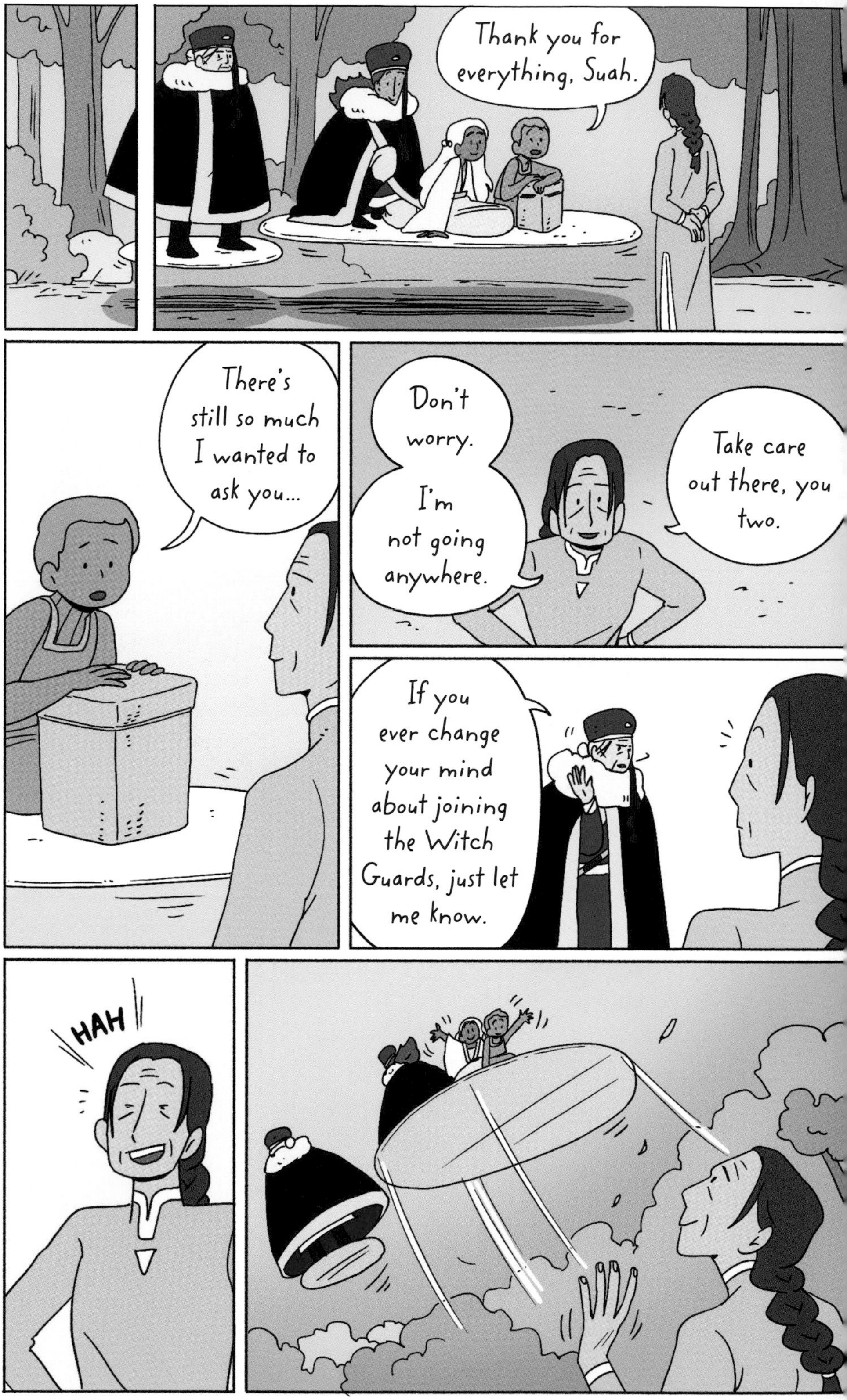
Thank you for everything, Suah.
There's still so much I wanted to ask you...
Don't worry.
I'm not going anywhere.
Take care out there, you two.
If you ever change your mind about joining the Witch Guards, just let me know.
HAH

CHAPTER 8

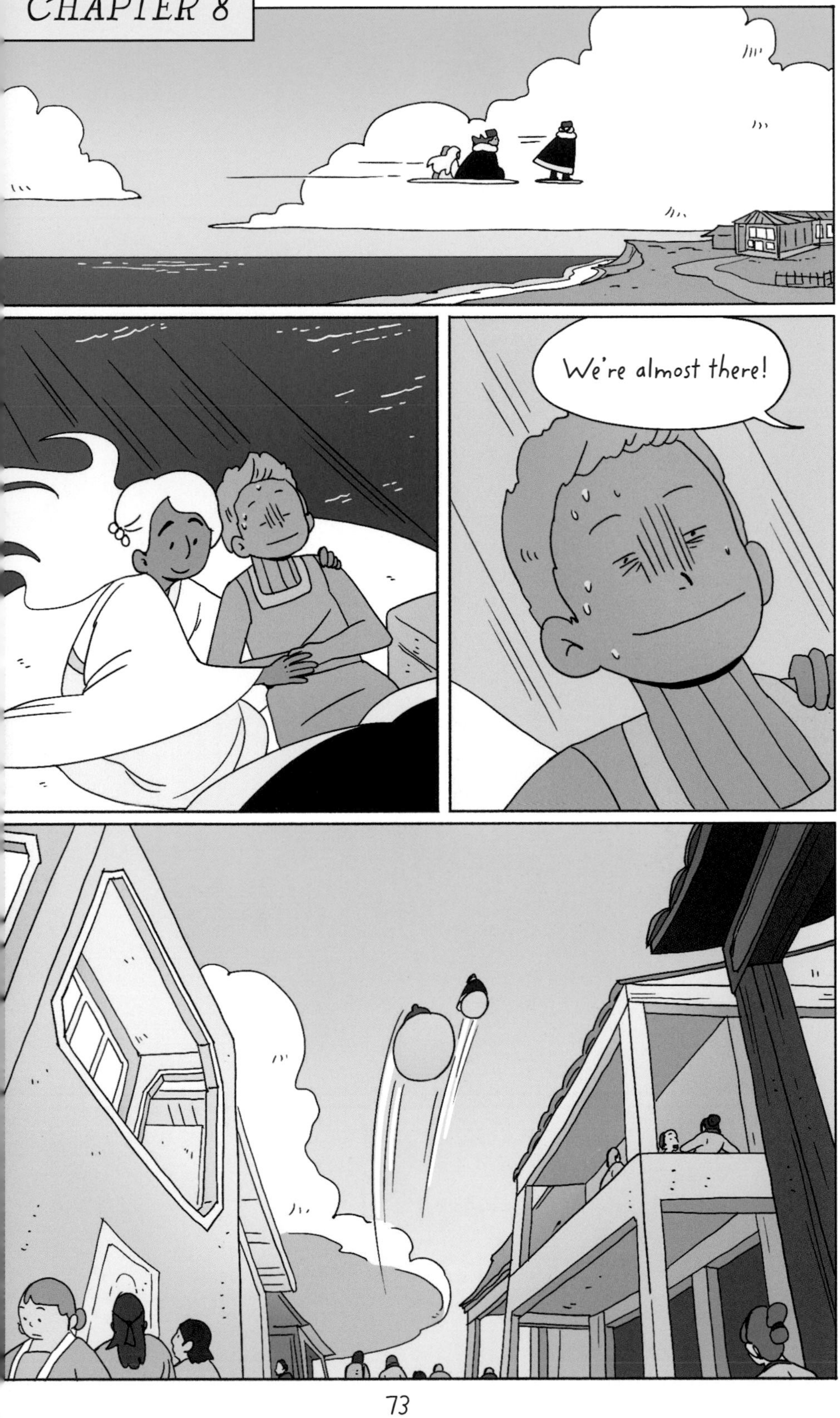
We're almost there!

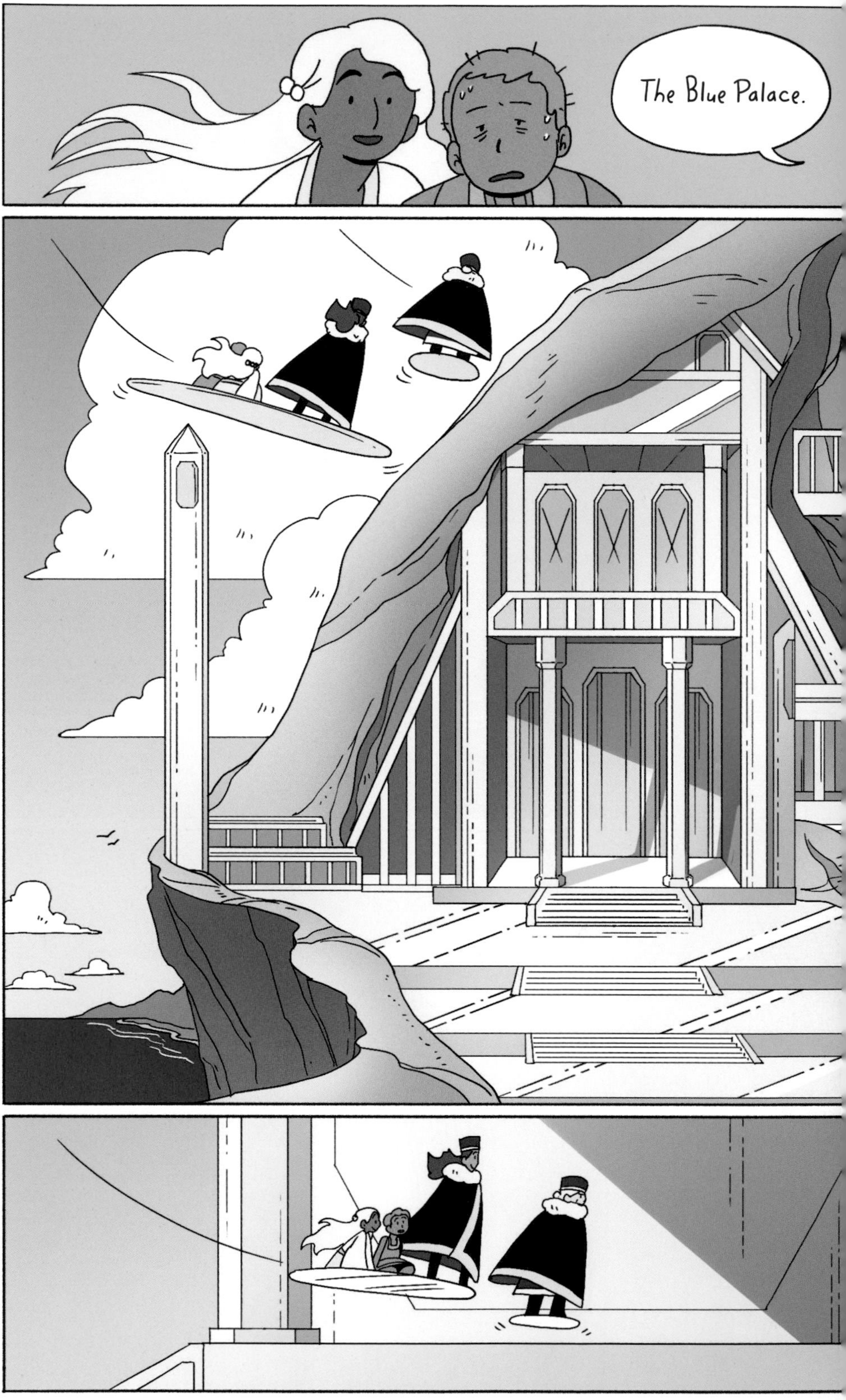
The Blue Palace.

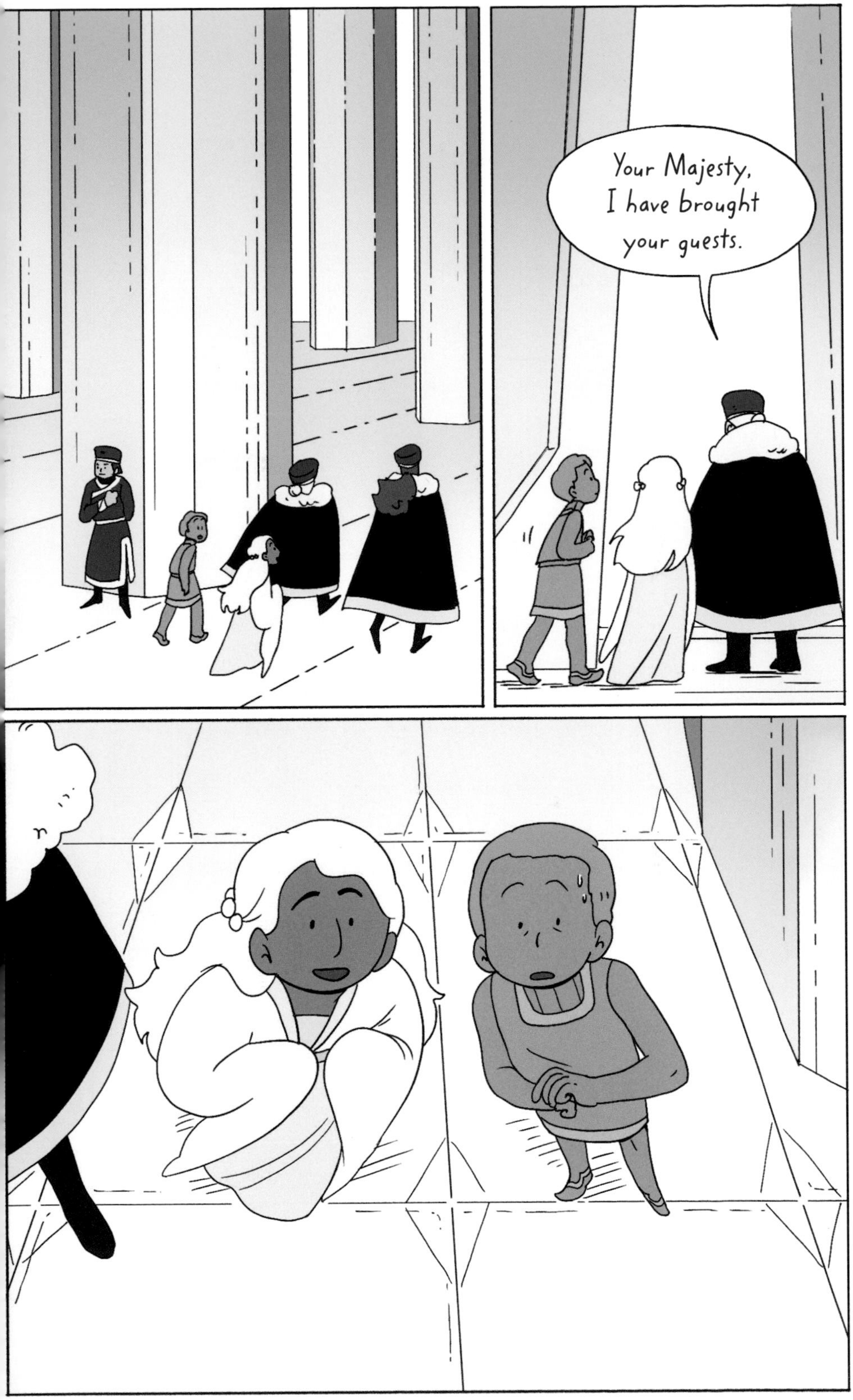
Your Majesty, I have brought your guests.

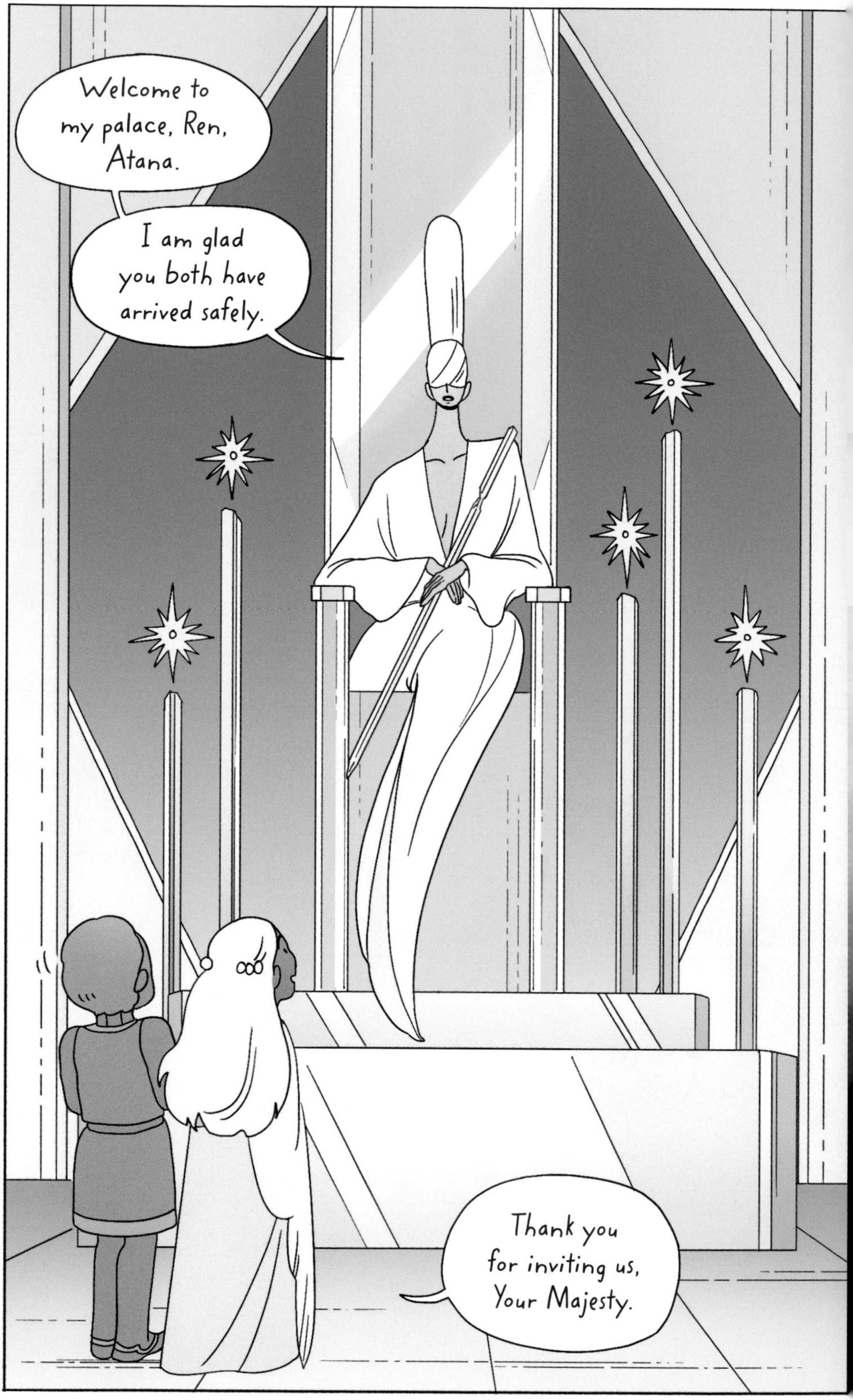
Welcome to my palace, Ren, Atana.
I am glad you both have arrived safely.
Thank you for inviting us, Your Majesty.

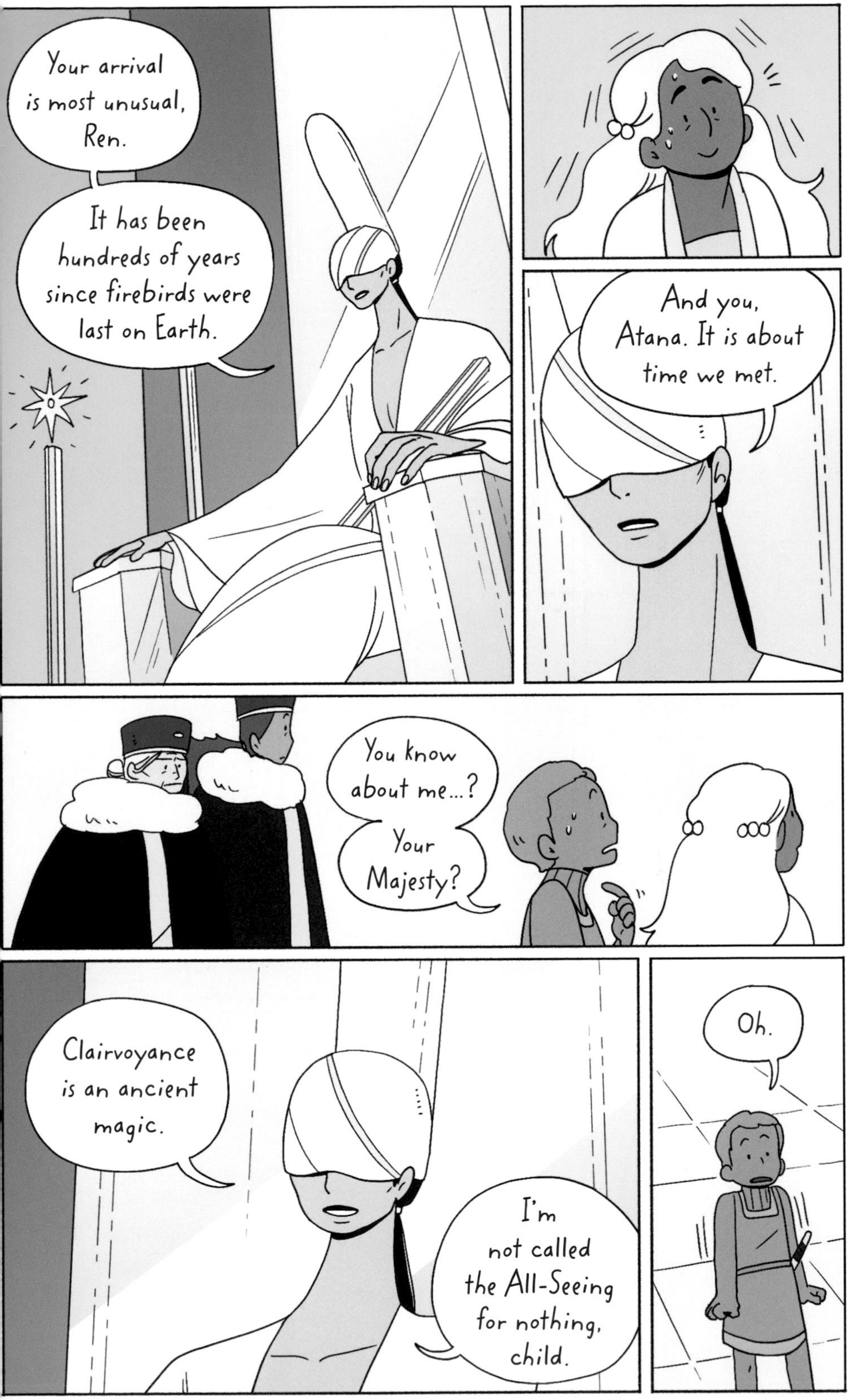
Your arrival is most unusual, Ren.
It has been hundreds of years since firebirds were last on Earth.
And you, Atana. It is about time we met.
You know about me...?
Your Majesty?
Clairvoyance is an ancient magic.
I'm not called the All-Seeing for nothing, child.
Oh.

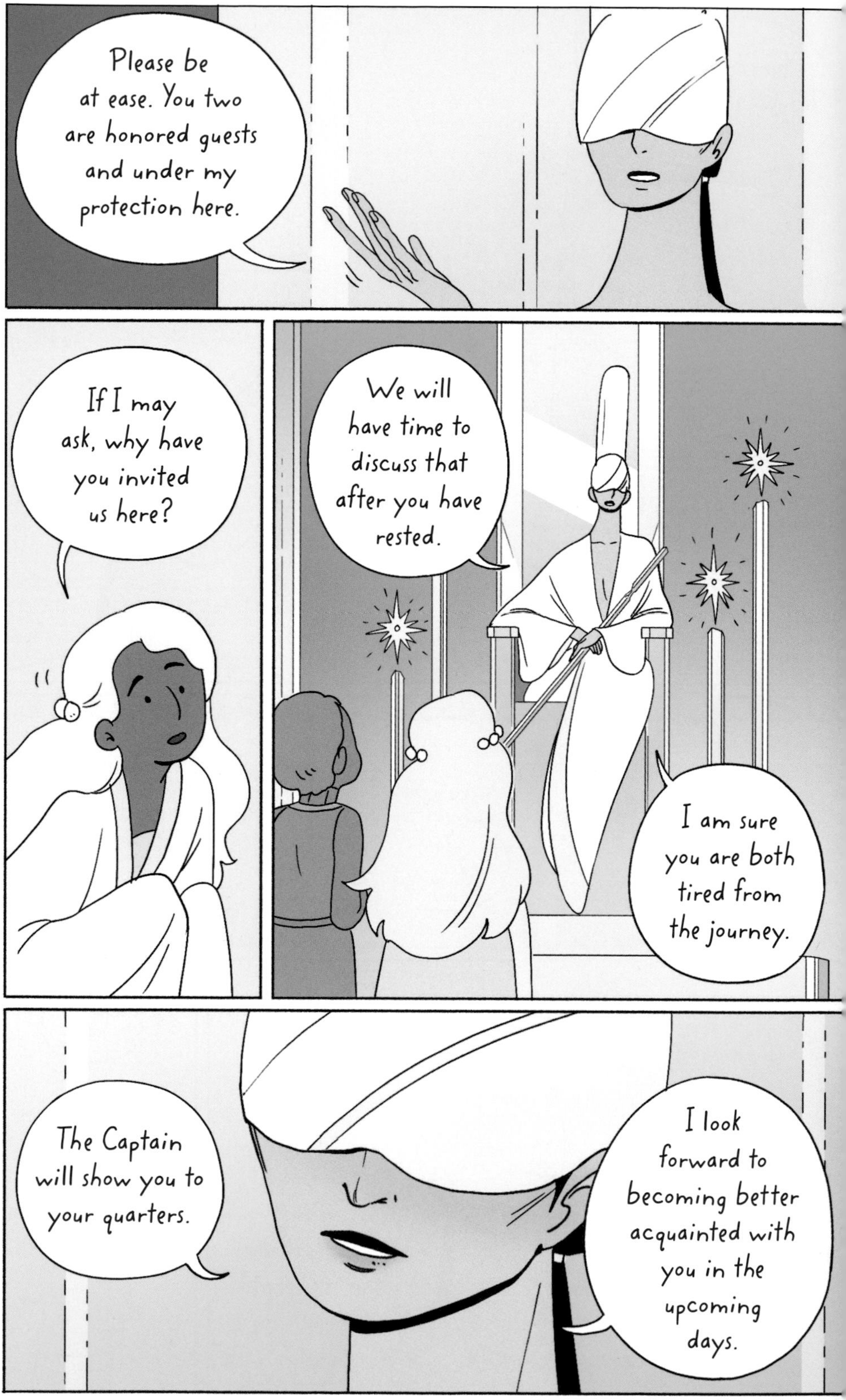
Please be at ease. You two are honored guests and under my protection here.
If I may ask, why have you invited us here?
We will have time to discuss that after you have rested.
I am sure you are both tired from the journey.
The Captain will show you to your quarters.
I look forward to becoming better acquainted with you in the upcoming days.

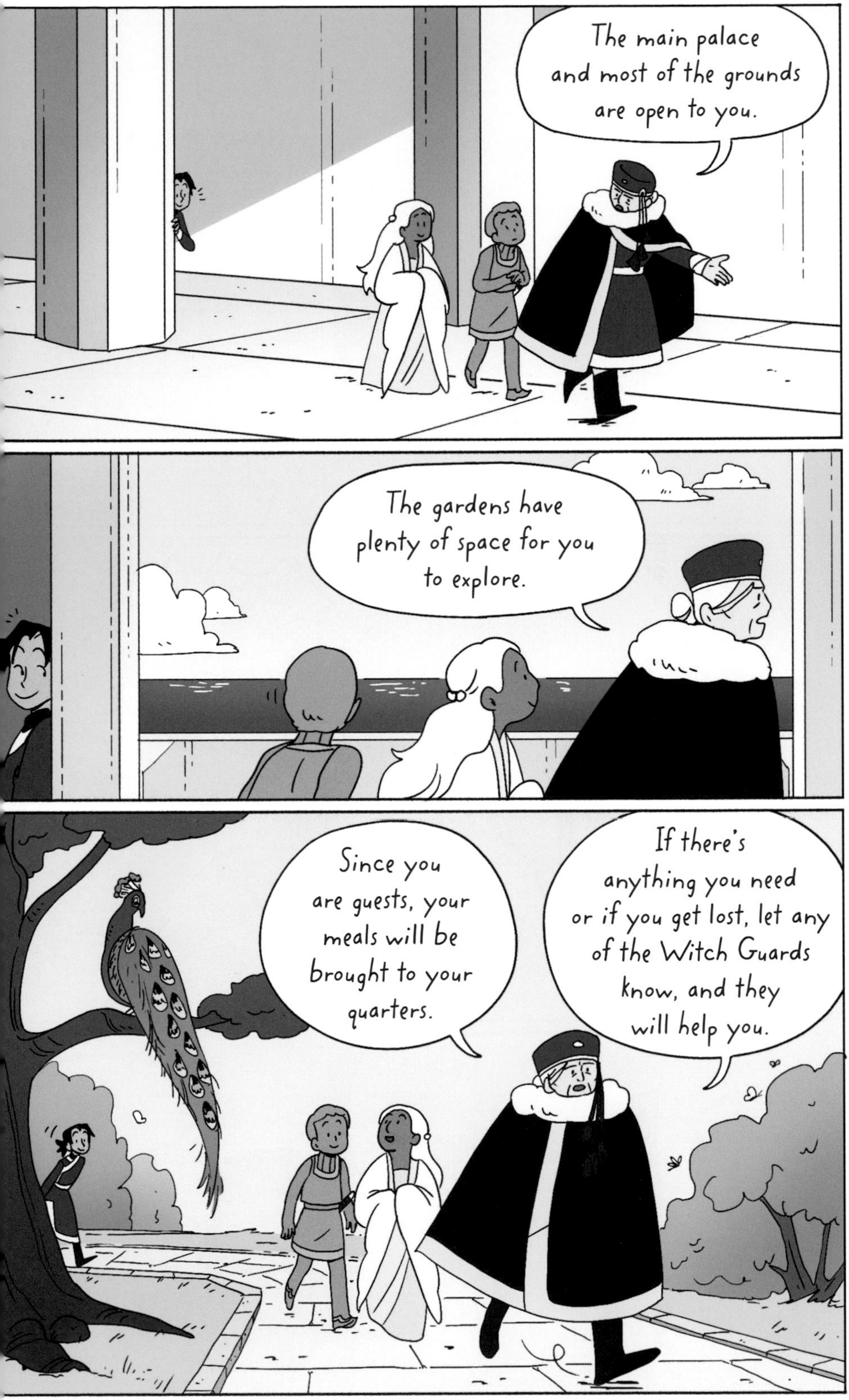
The main palace and most of the grounds are open to you.
The gardens have plenty of space for you to explore.
Since you are guests, your meals will be brought to your quarters.
If there's anything you need or if you get lost, let any of the Witch Guards know, and they will help you.

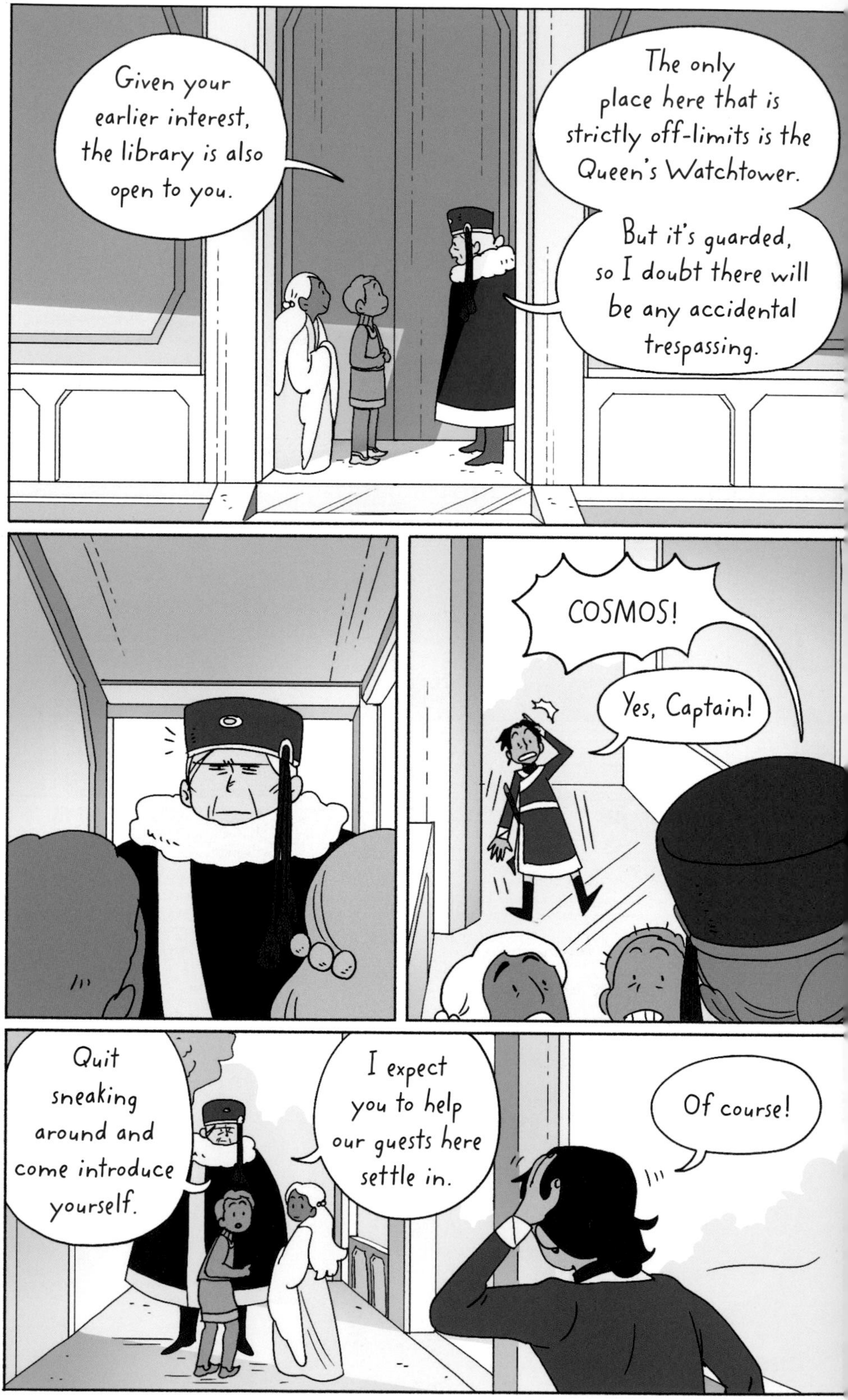
Given your earlier interest, the library is also open to you.
The only place here that is strictly off-limits is the Queen's Watchtower.
But it's guarded, so I doubt there will be any accidental trespassing.
COSMOS!
Yes, Captain!
Quit sneaking around and come introduce yourself.
I expect you to help our guests here settle in.
Of course!

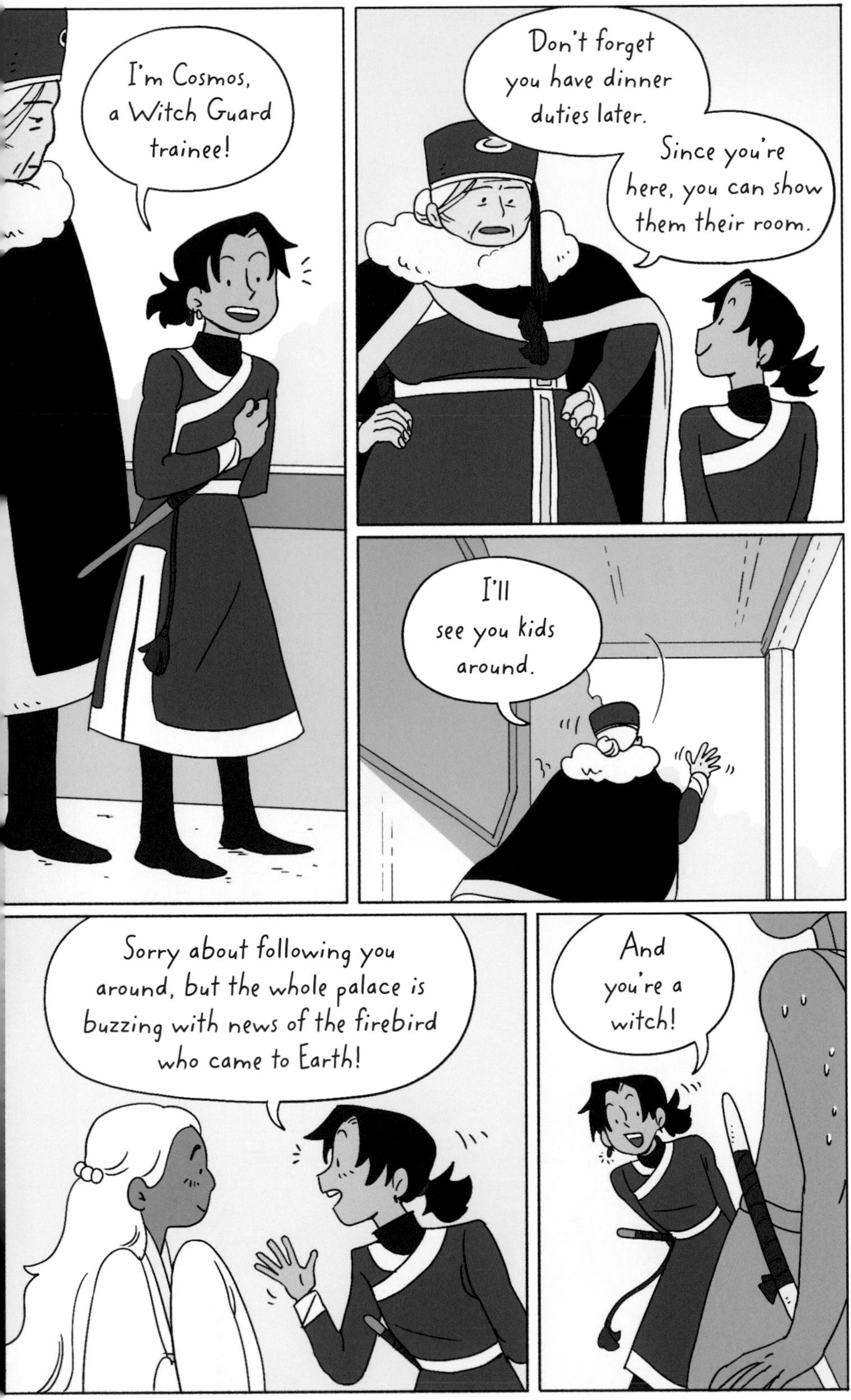
I'm Cosmos, a Witch Guard trainee!
Don't forget you have dinner duties later.
Since you're here, you can show them their room.
I'll see you kids around.
Sorry about following you around, but the whole palace is buzzing with news of the firebird who came to Earth!
And you're a witch!

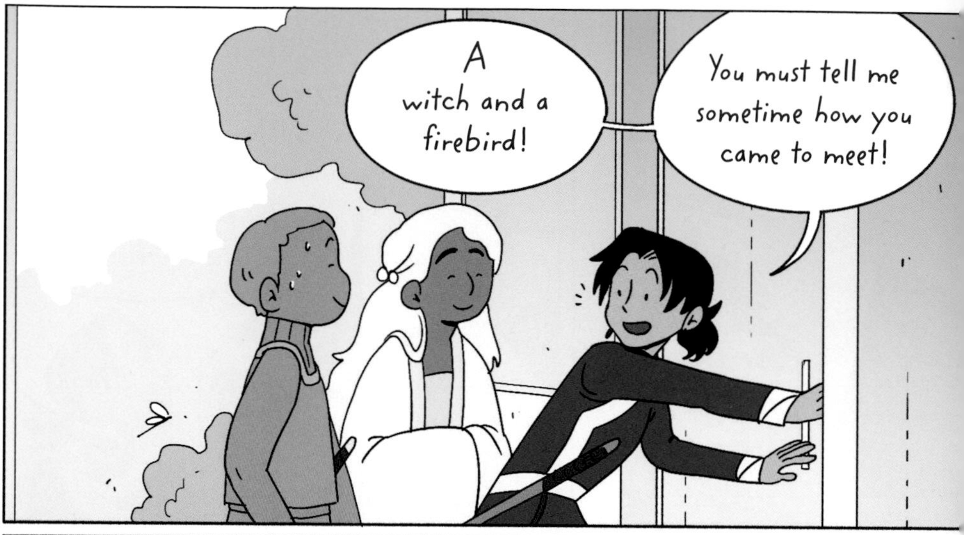
A witch and a firebird!
You must tell me sometime how you came to meet!

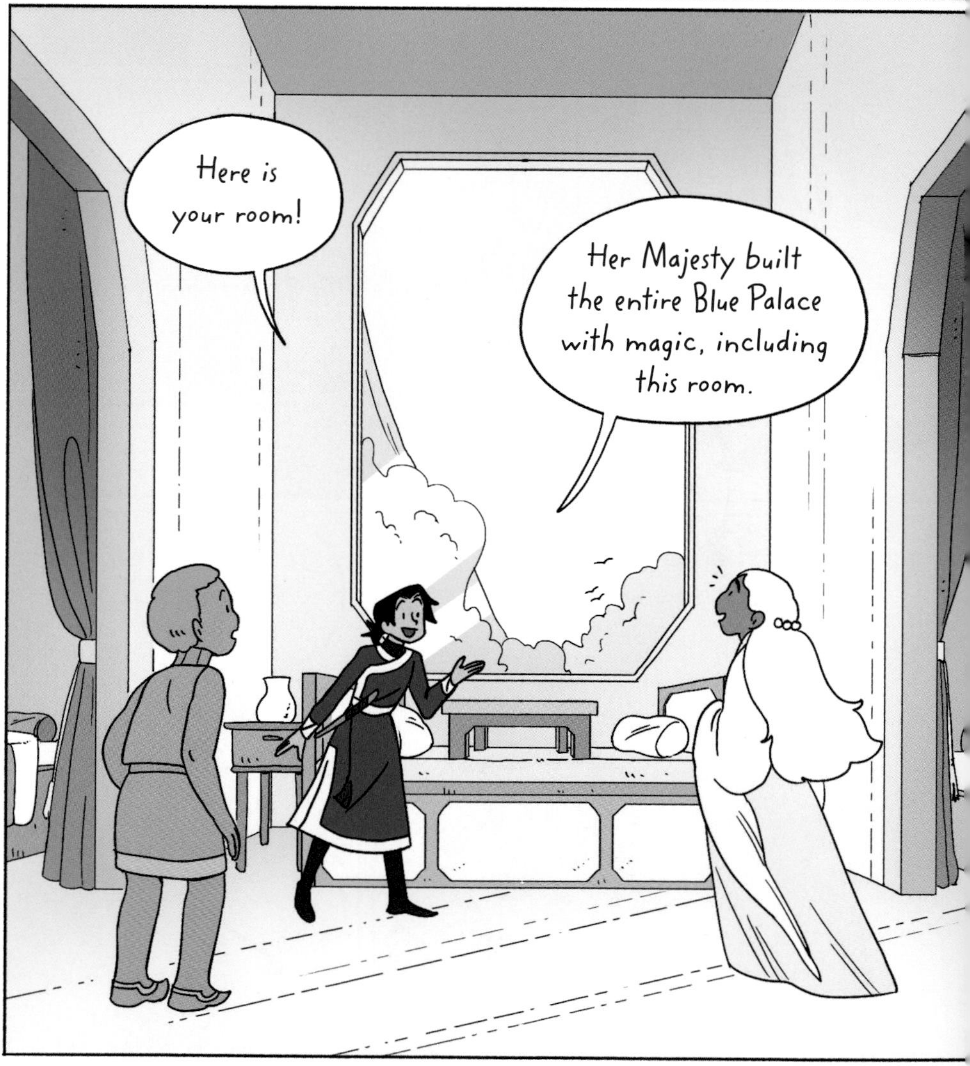
Here is your room!
Her Majesty built the entire Blue Palace with magic, including this room.

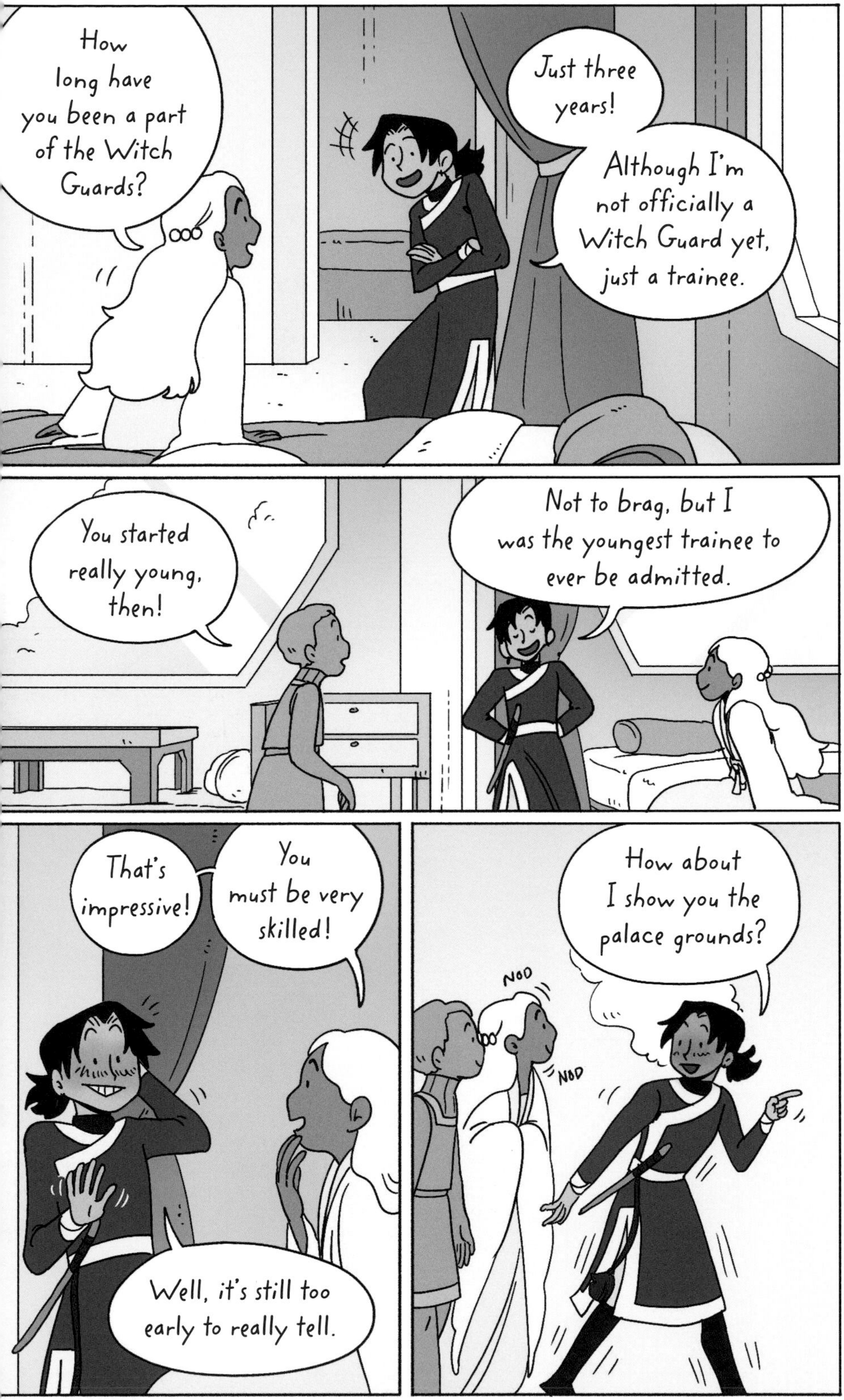
How long have you been a part of the Witch Guards?
Just three years!
Although I'm not officially a Witch Guard yet, just a trainee.
You started really young, then!
Not to brag, but I was the youngest trainee to ever be admitted.
That's impressive!
You must be very skilled!
Well, it's still too early to really tell.
How about I show you the palace grounds?
NOD
NOD

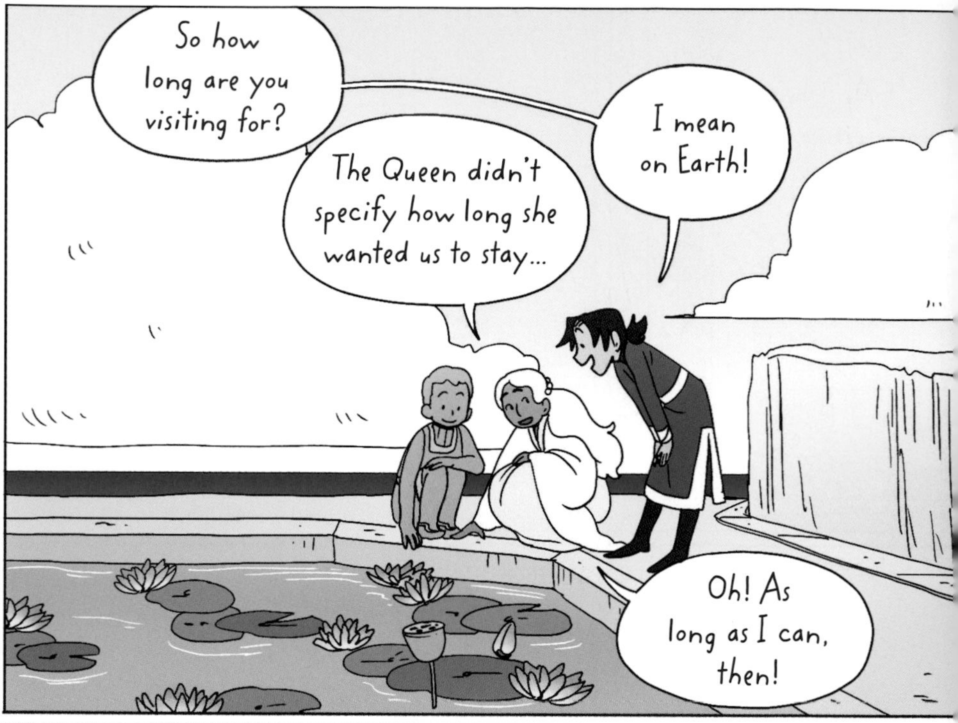
So how long are you visiting for?
I mean on Earth!
The Queen didn't specify how long she wanted us to stay...
Oh! As long as I can, then!

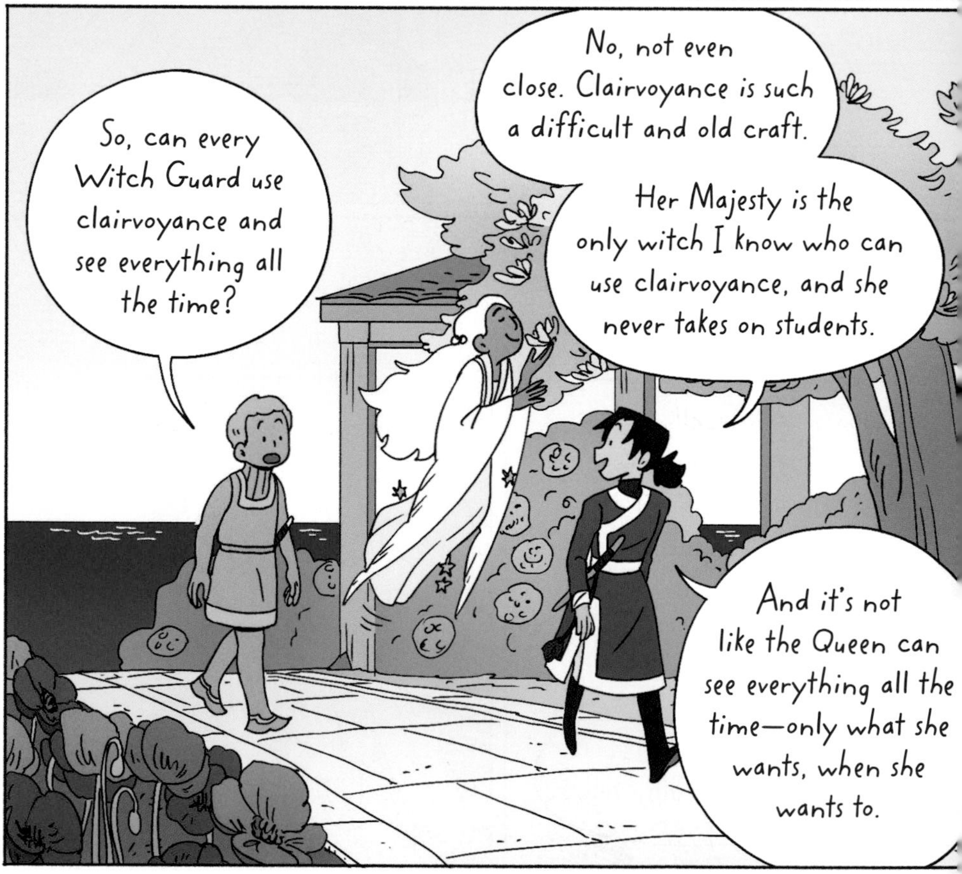
So, can every Witch Guard use clairvoyance and see everything all the time?
No, not even close. Clairvoyance is such a difficult and old craft.
Her Majesty is the only witch I know who can use clairvoyance, and she never takes on students.
And it's not like the Queen can see everything all the time—only what she wants, when she wants to.

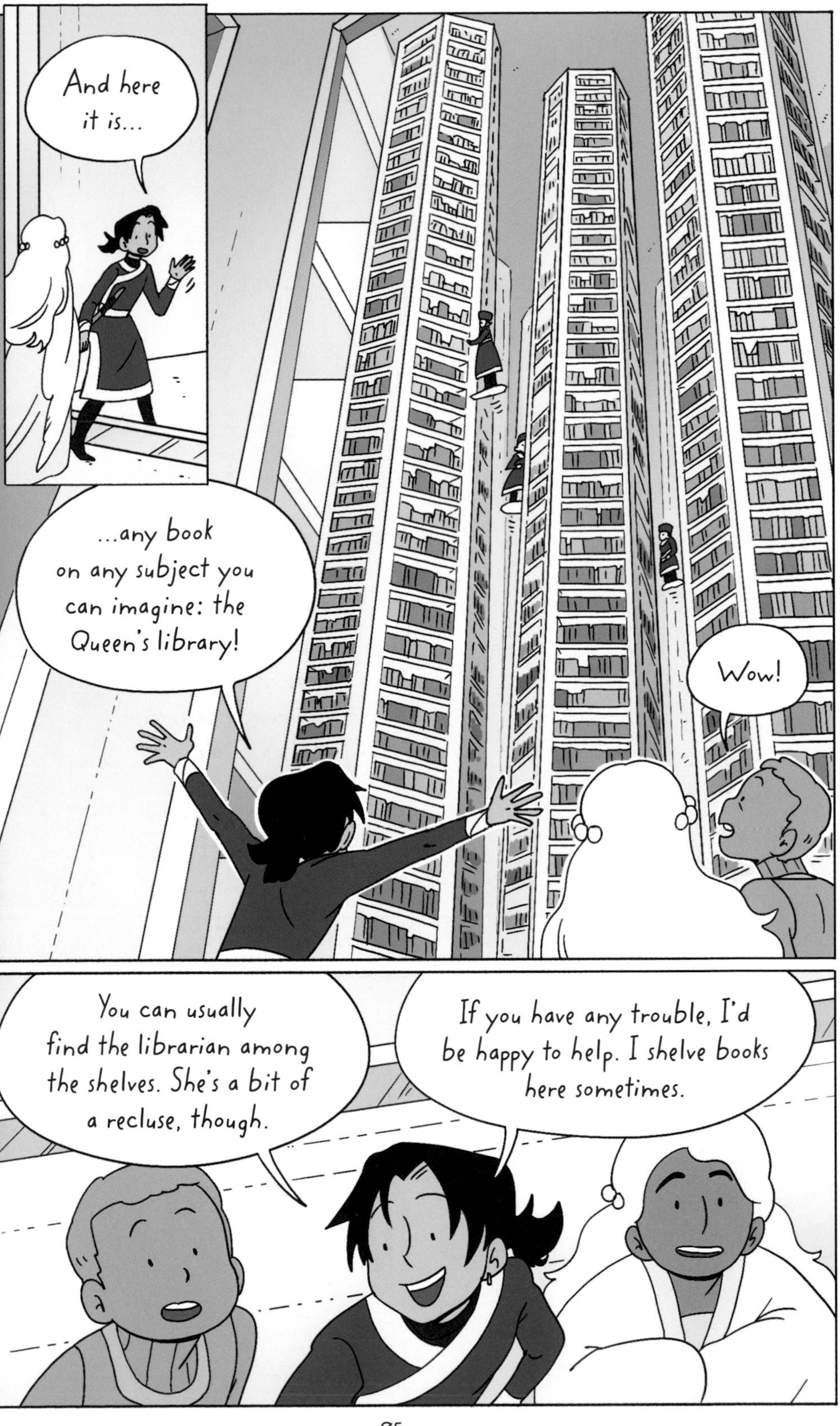
And here it is...
...any book on any subject you can imagine: the Queen's library!
Wow!
You can usually find the librarian among the shelves. She's a bit of a recluse, though.
If you have any trouble, I'd be happy to help. I shelve books here sometimes.

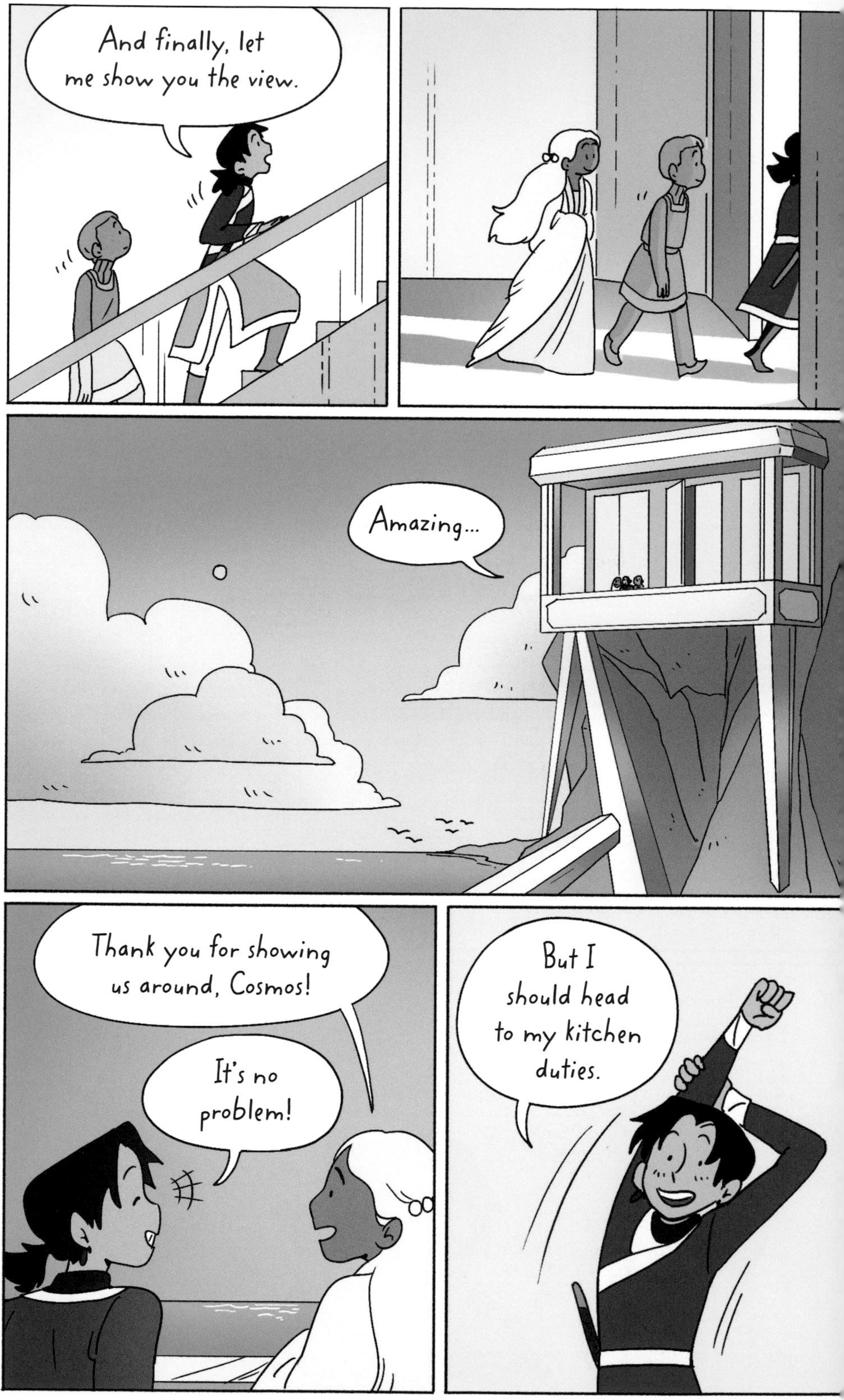
And finally, let me show you the view.
Amazing...
Thank you for showing us around, Cosmos!
It's no problem!
But I should head to my kitchen duties.

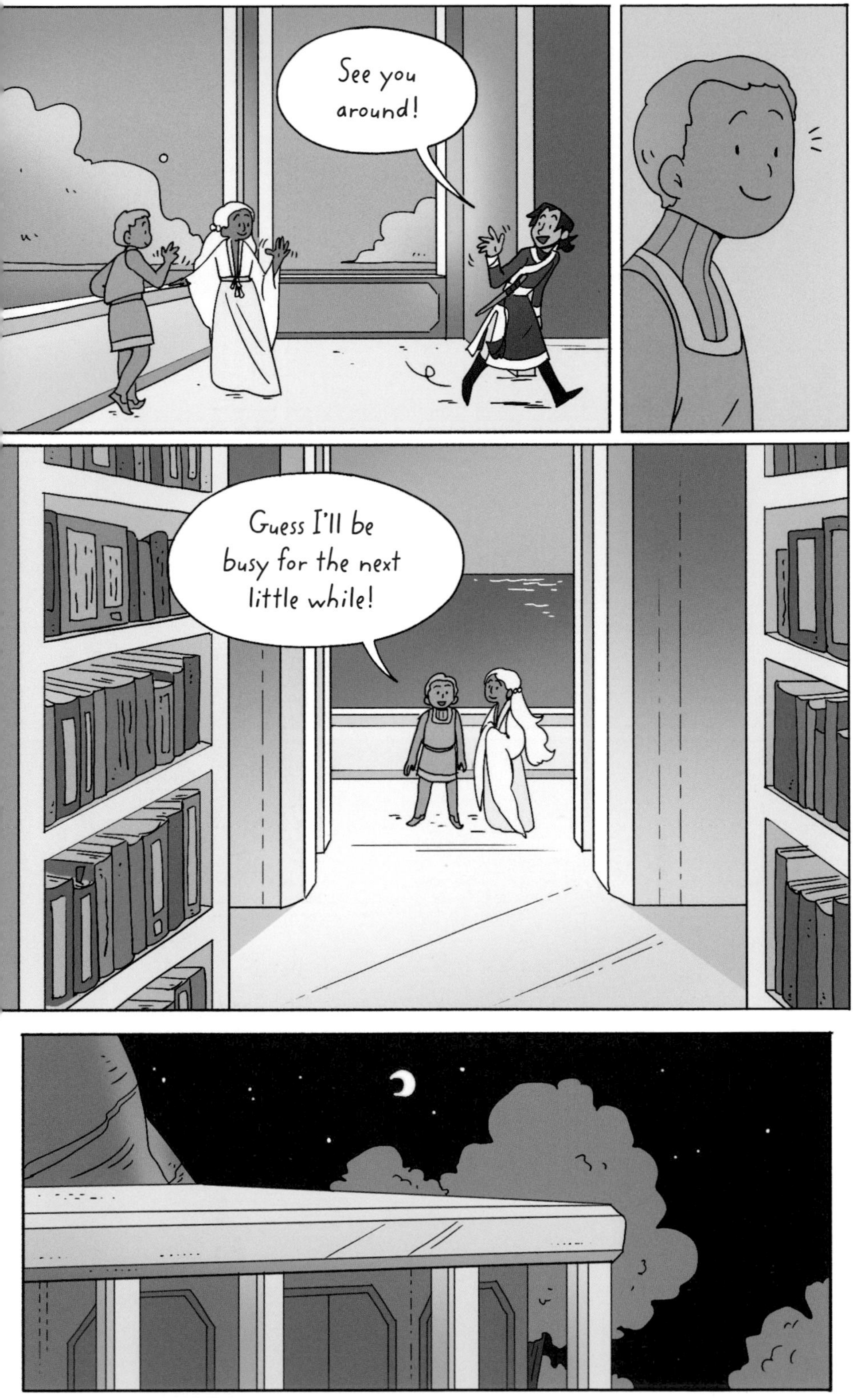
See you around!
Guess I'll be busy for the next little while!

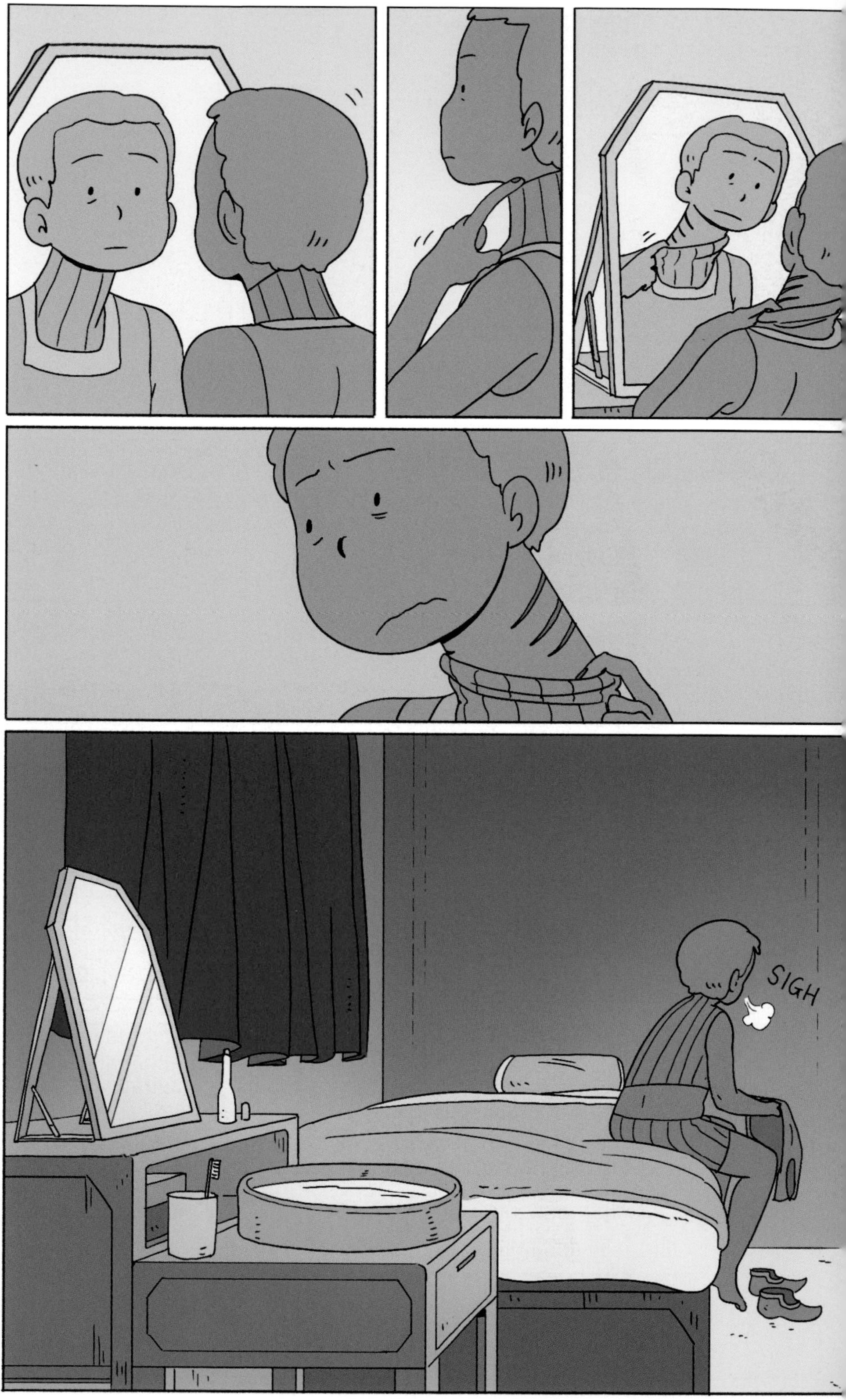
SIGH

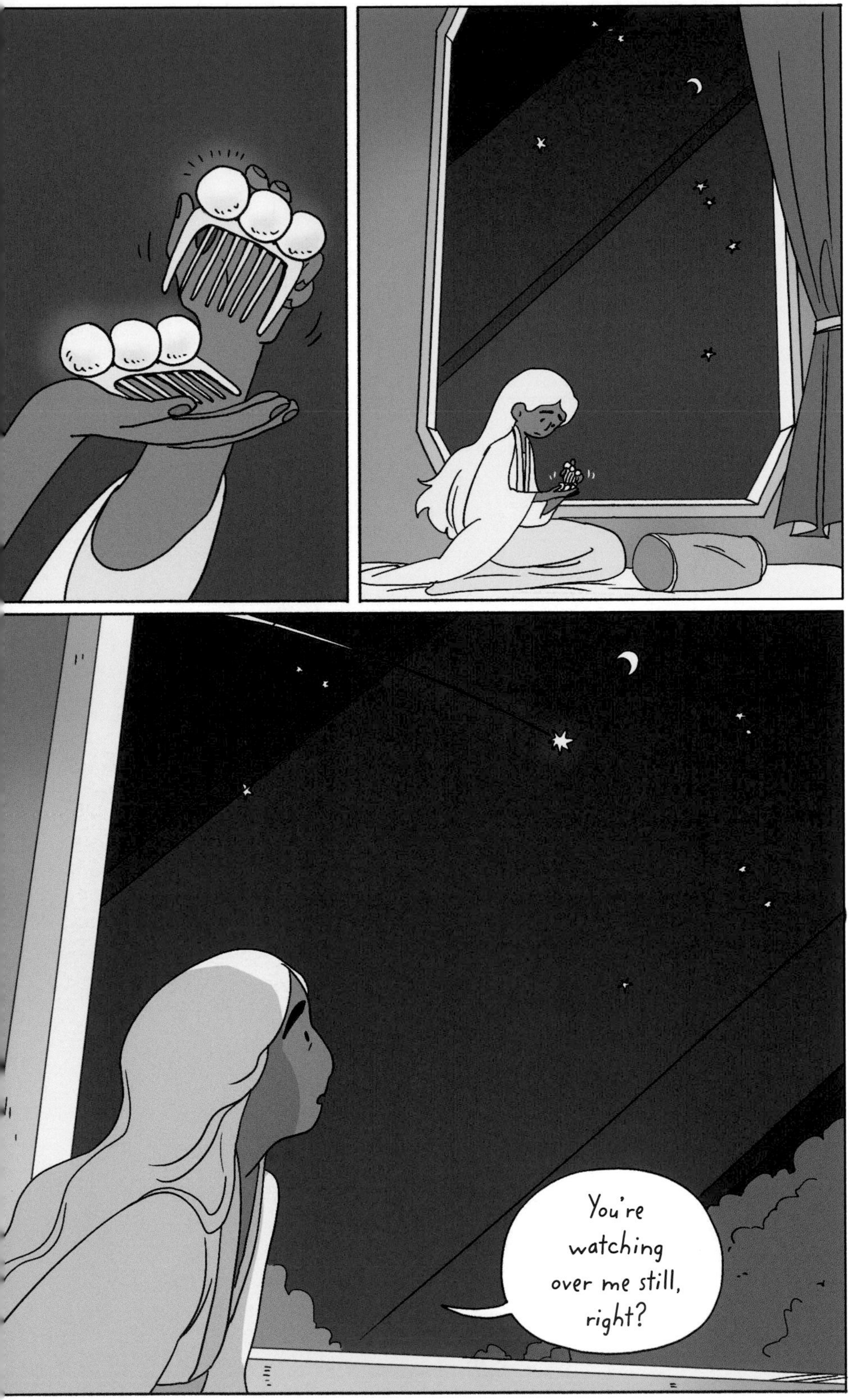
You're watching over me still, right?

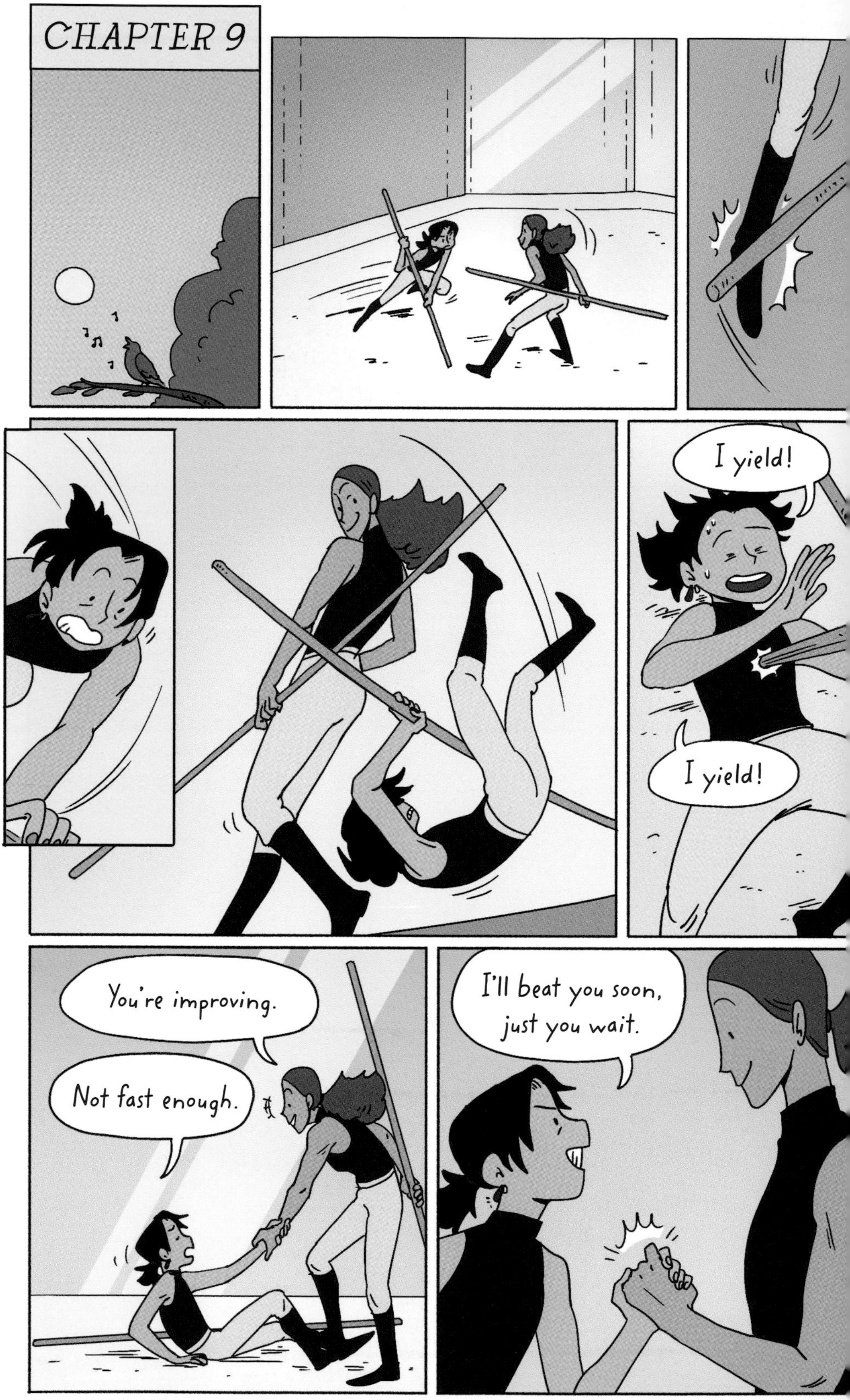
CHAPTER 9
I yield!
I yield!
You're improving.
Not fast enough.
I'll beat you soon, just you wait.

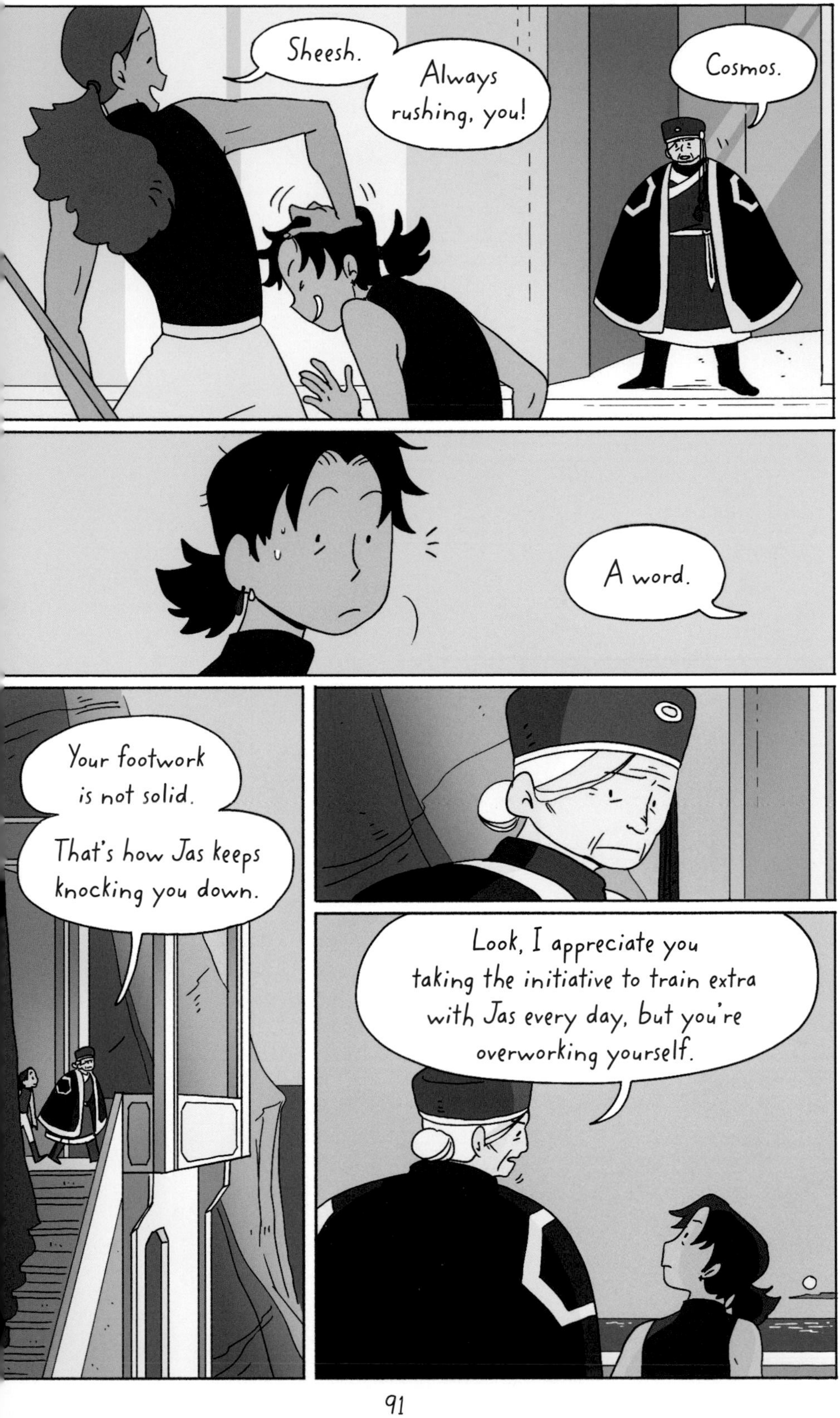
Sheesh.
Always rushing, you!
Cosmos.
A word.
Your footwork is not solid.
That's how Jas keeps knocking you down.
Look, I appreciate you taking the initiative to train extra with Jas every day, but you're overworking yourself.

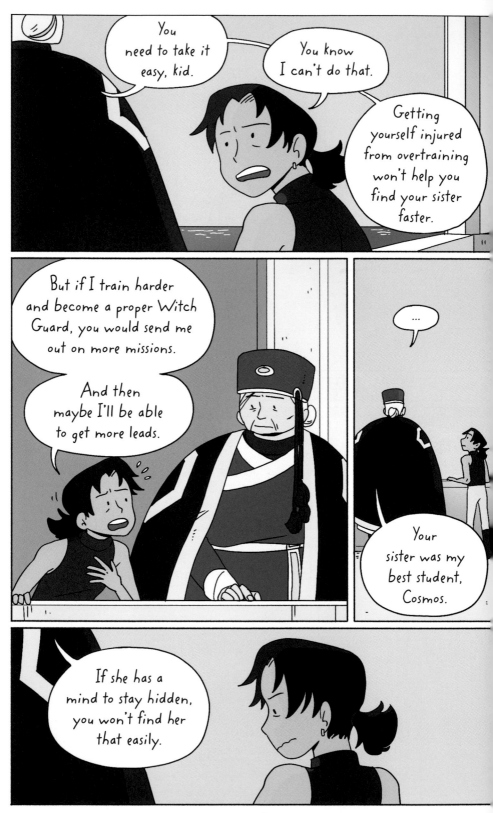

You need to take it easy, kid.

You know I can't do that.

Getting yourself injured from overtraining won't help you find your sister faster.

But if I train harder and become a proper Witch Guard, you would send me out on more missions.

And then maybe I'll be able to get more leads.

...

Your sister was my best student, Cosmos.

If she has a mind to stay hidden, you won't find her that easily.

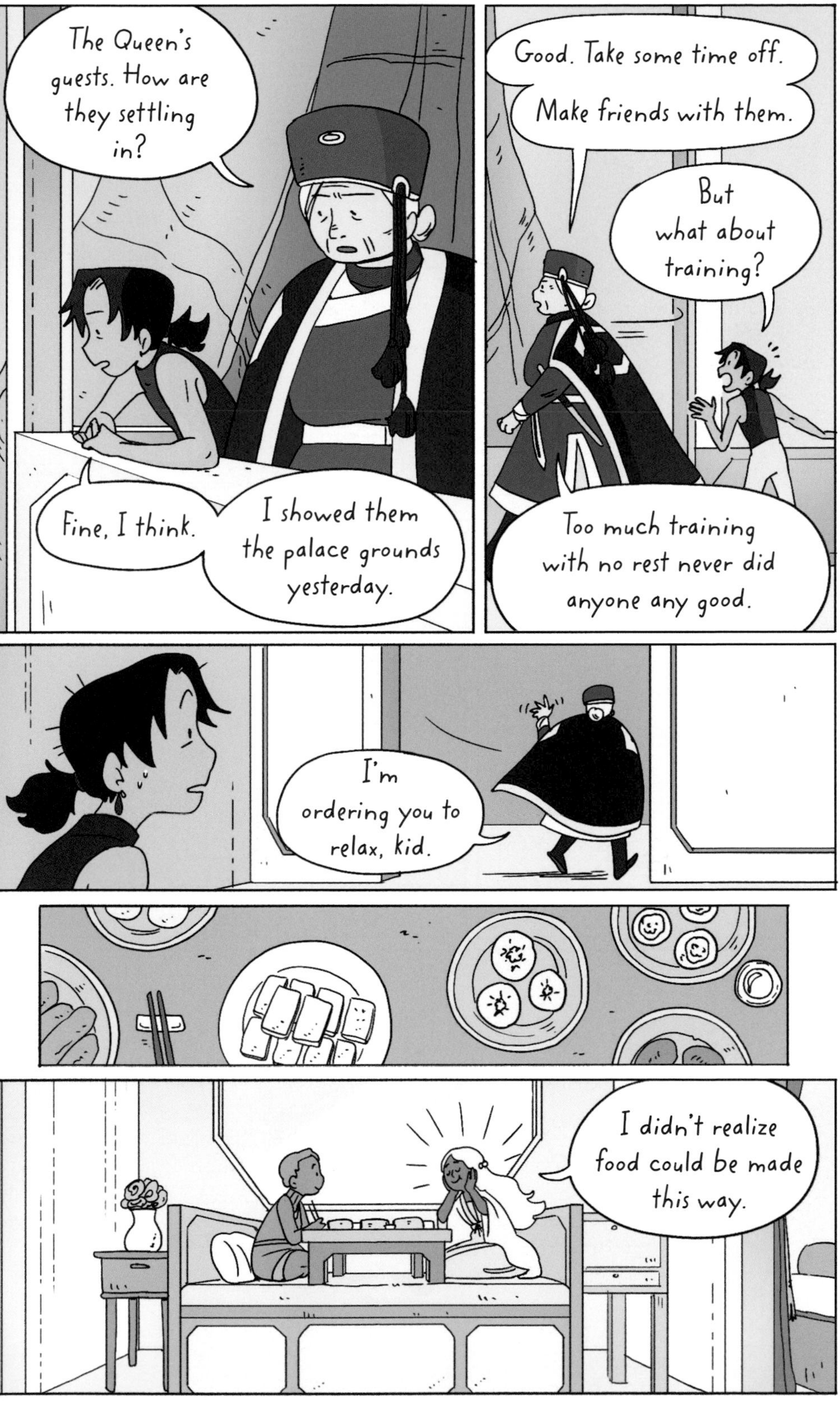
The Queen's guests. How are they settling in?
Fine, I think.
I showed them the palace grounds yesterday.
Good. Take some time off.
Make friends with them.
But what about training?
Too much training with no rest never did anyone any good.
I'm ordering you to relax, kid.
I didn't realize food could be made this way.

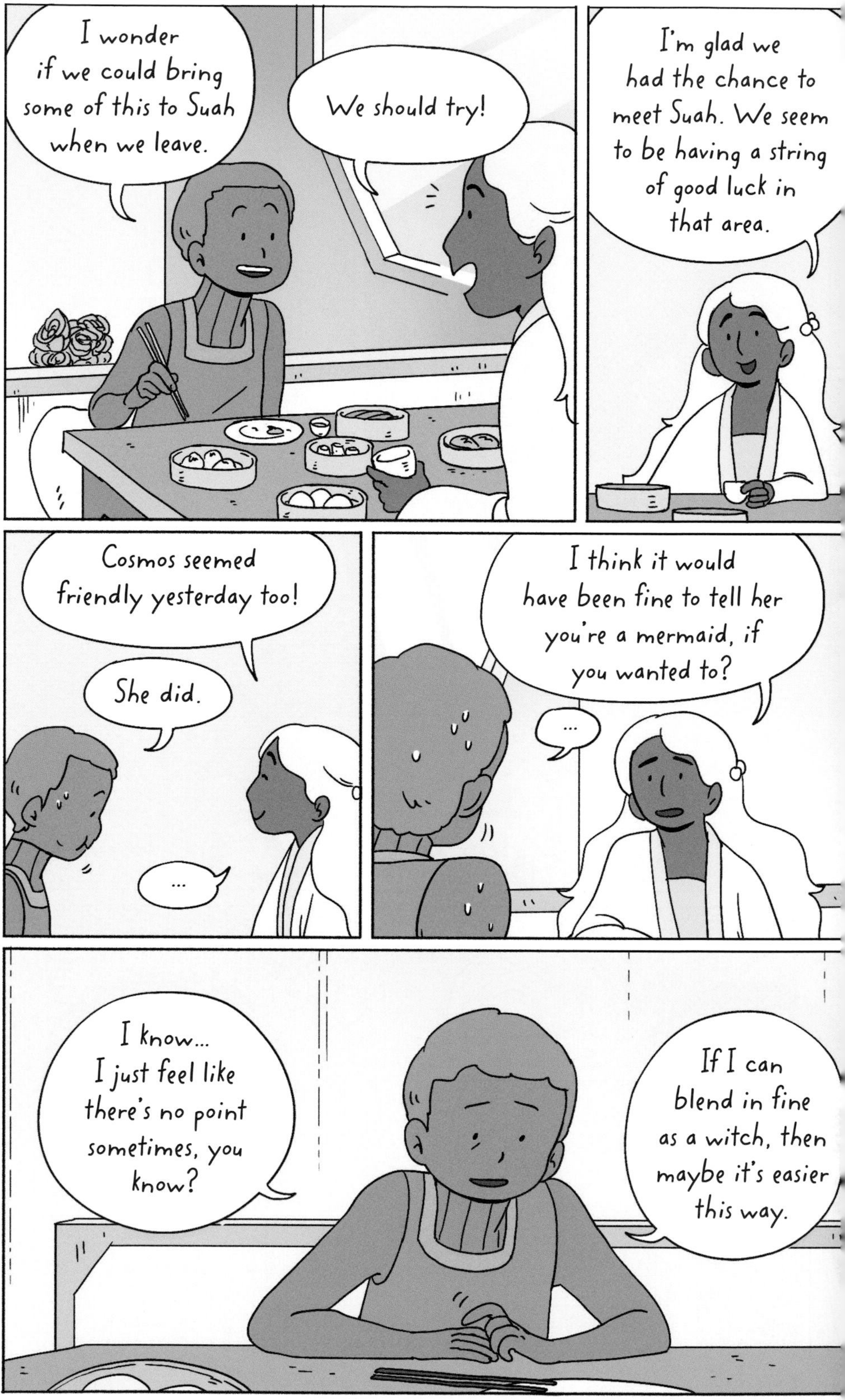

I wonder if we could bring some of this to Suah when we leave.
We should try!
I'm glad we had the chance to meet Suah. We seem to be having a string of good luck in that area.
Cosmos seemed friendly yesterday too!
She did.
...
I think it would have been fine to tell her you're a mermaid, if you wanted to?
...
I know... I just feel like there's no point sometimes, you know?
If I can blend in fine as a witch, then maybe it's easier this way.

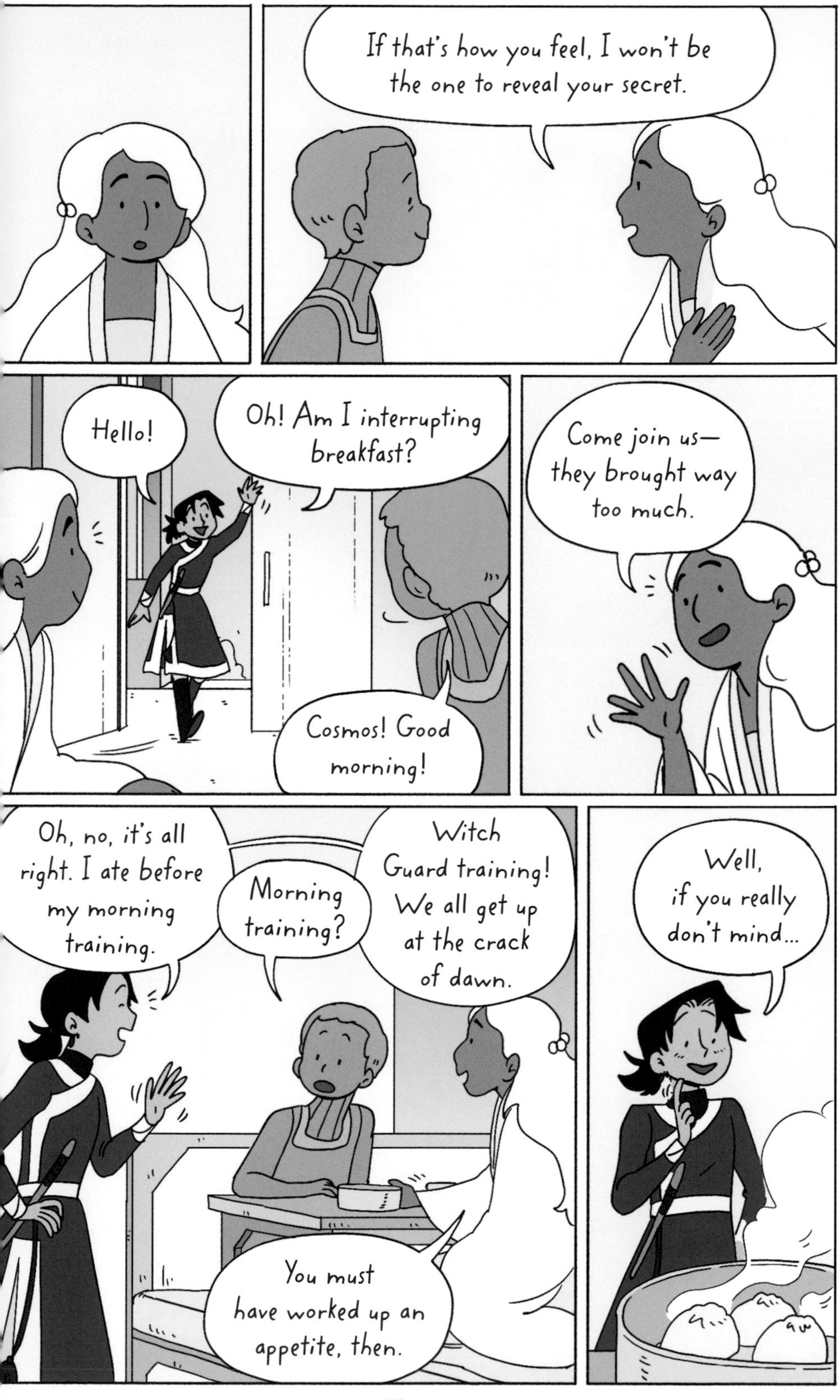
If that's how you feel, I won't be the one to reveal your secret.
Hello!
Oh! Am I interrupting breakfast?
Cosmos! Good morning!
Come join us—they brought way too much.
Oh, no, it's all right. I ate before my morning training.
Morning training?
Witch Guard training! We all get up at the crack of dawn.
You must have worked up an appetite, then.
Well, if you really don't mind...

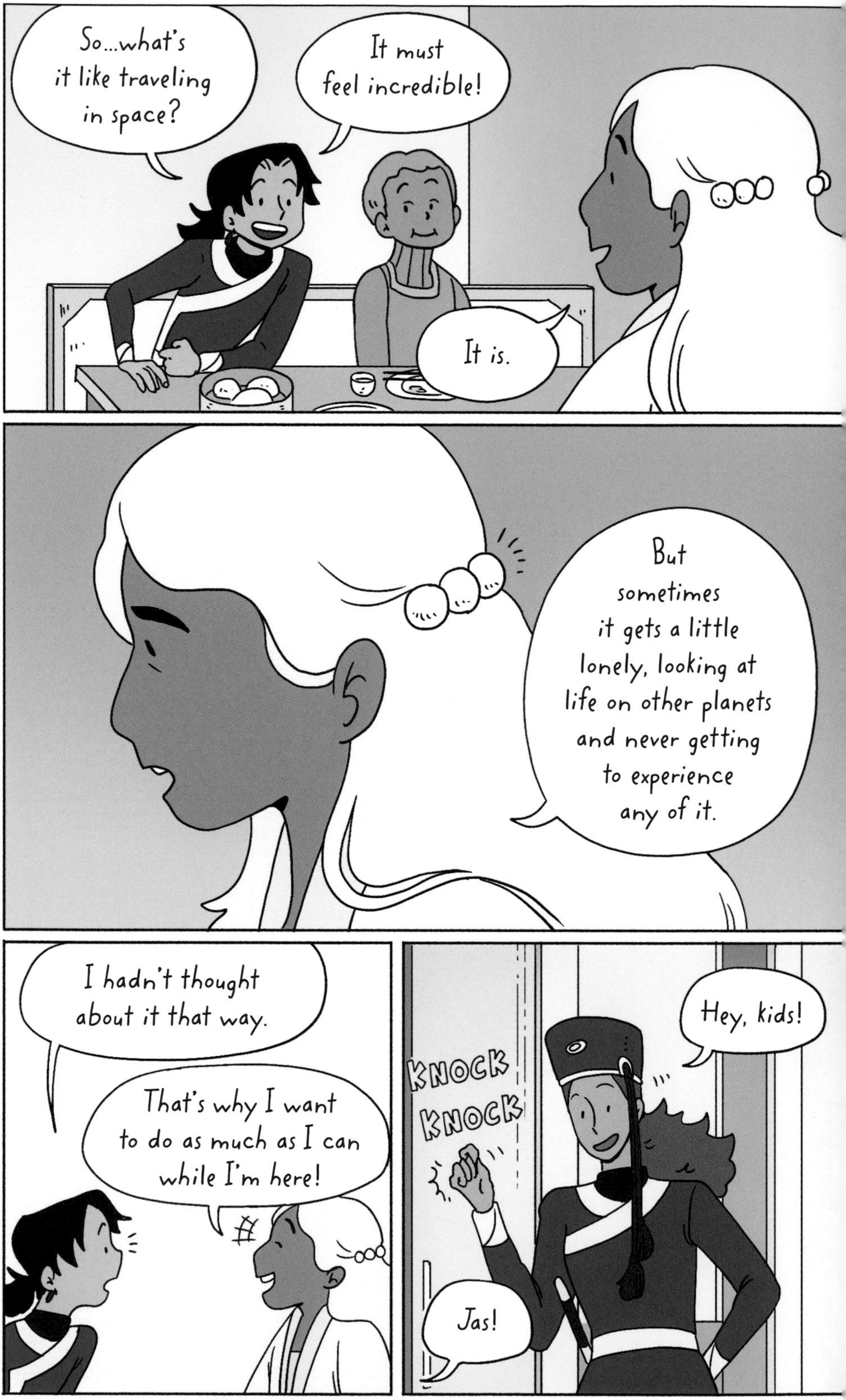
So...what's it like traveling in space?
It must feel incredible!
It is.
But sometimes it gets a little lonely, looking at life on other planets and never getting to experience any of it.
I hadn't thought about it that way.
That's why I want to do as much as I can while I'm here!
KNOCK KNOCK
Hey, kids!
Jas!

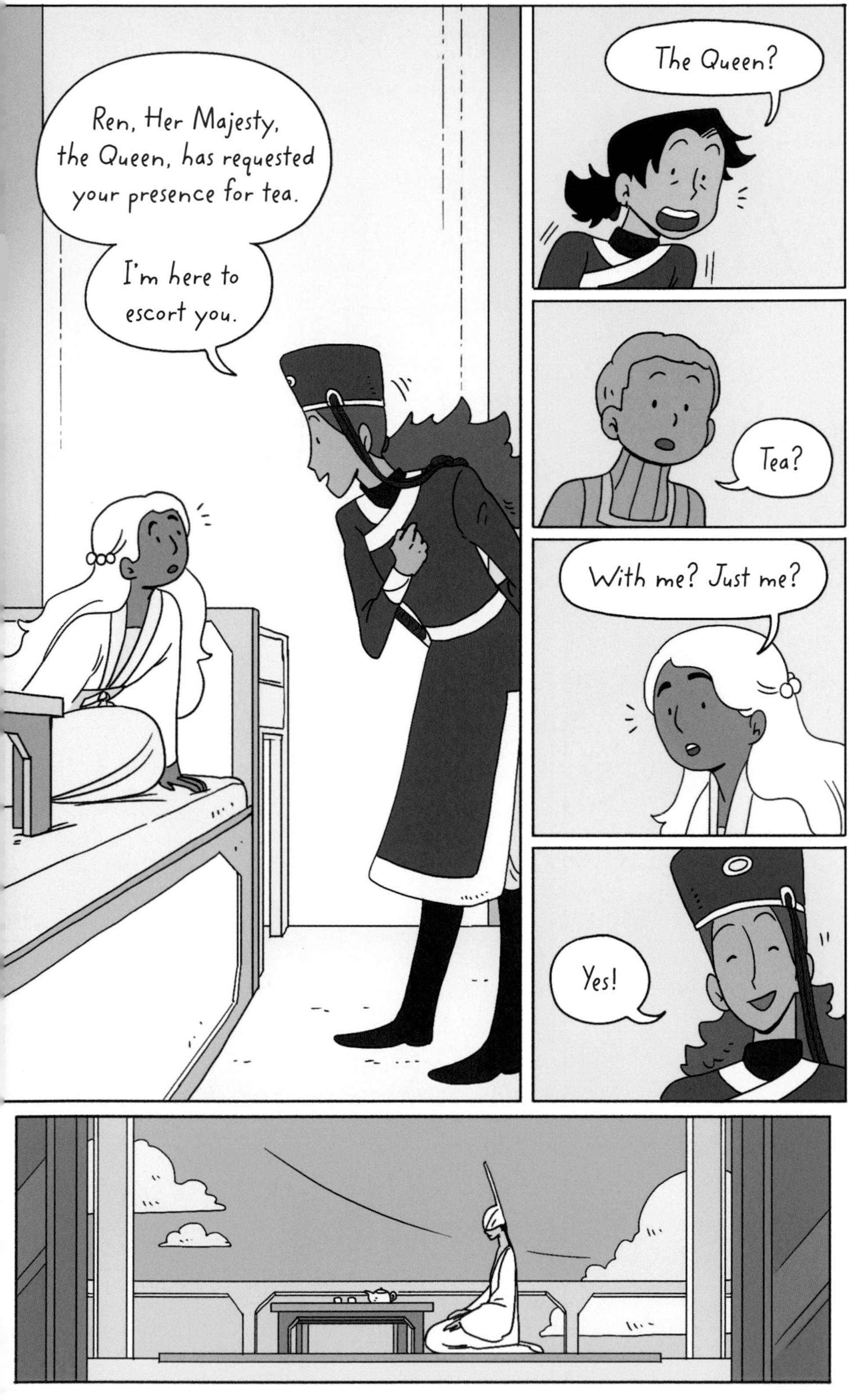

Ren, Her Majesty, the Queen, has requested your presence for tea.
I'm here to escort you.
The Queen?
Tea?
With me? Just me?
Yes!

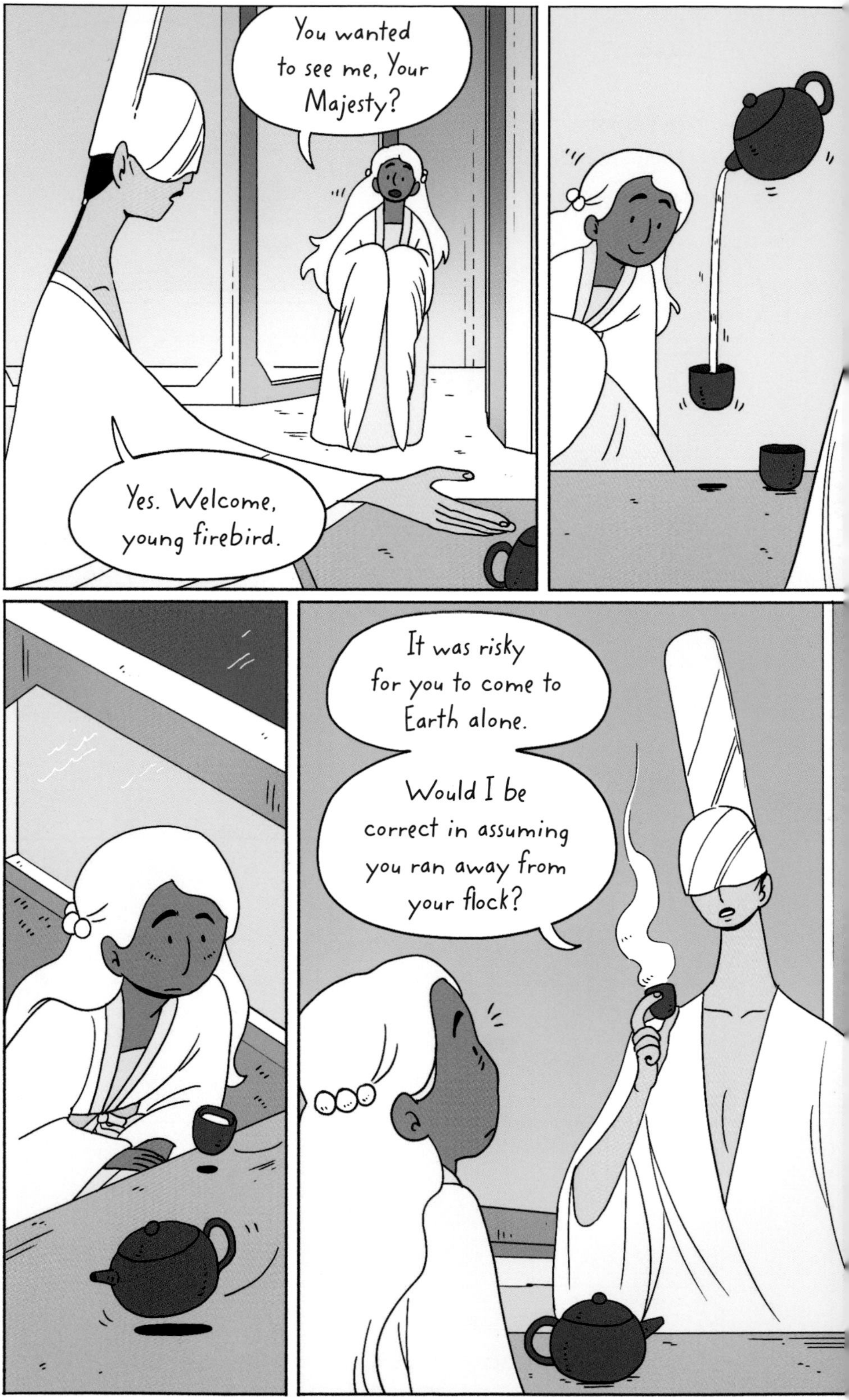
You wanted to see me, Your Majesty?
Yes. Welcome, young firebird.
It was risky for you to come to Earth alone.
Would I be correct in assuming you ran away from your flock?

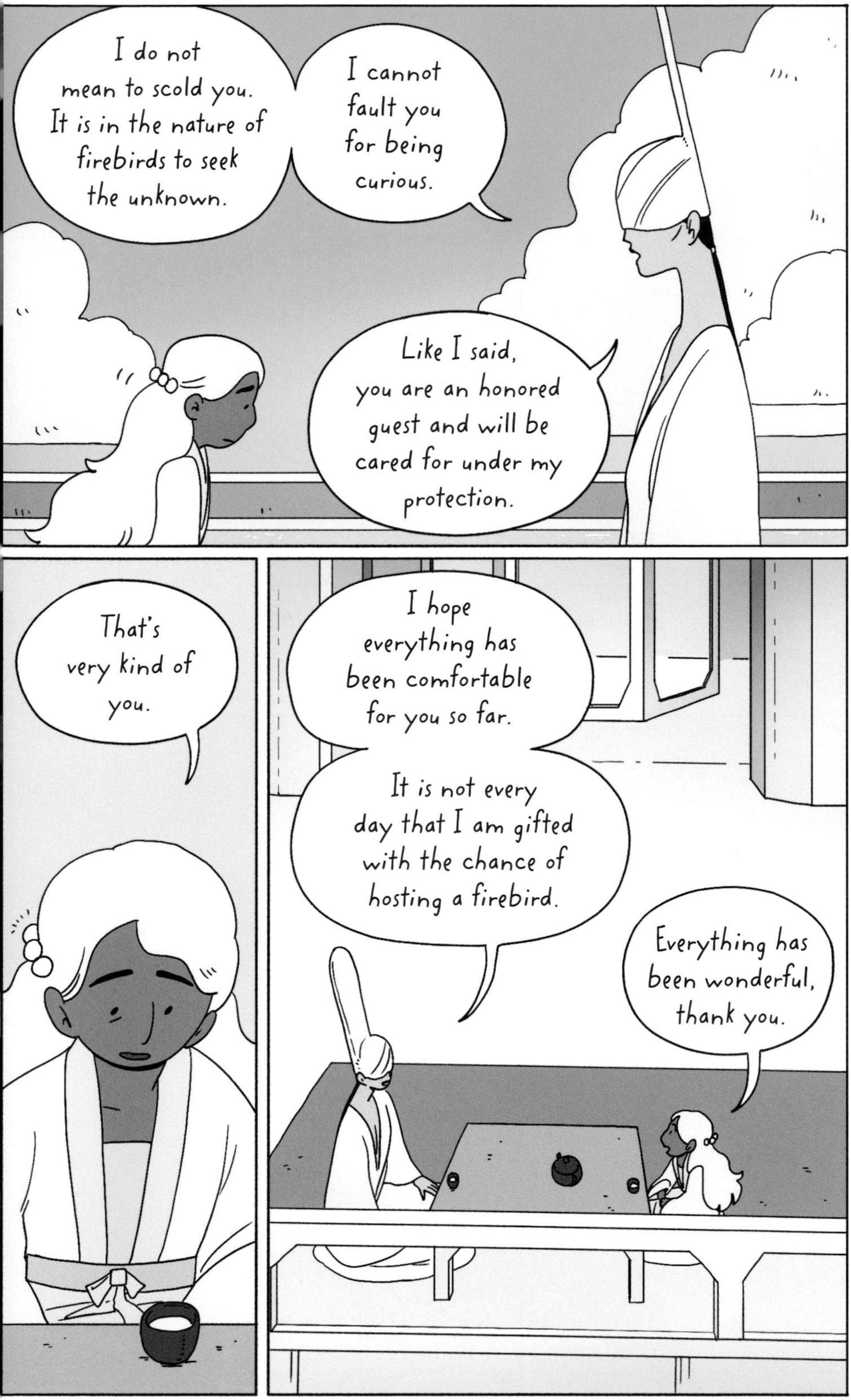
I do not mean to scold you. It is in the nature of firebirds to seek the unknown.
I cannot fault you for being curious.
Like I said, you are an honored guest and will be cared for under my protection.
That's very kind of you.
I hope everything has been comfortable for you so far.
It is not every day that I am gifted with the chance of hosting a firebird.
Everything has been wonderful, thank you.

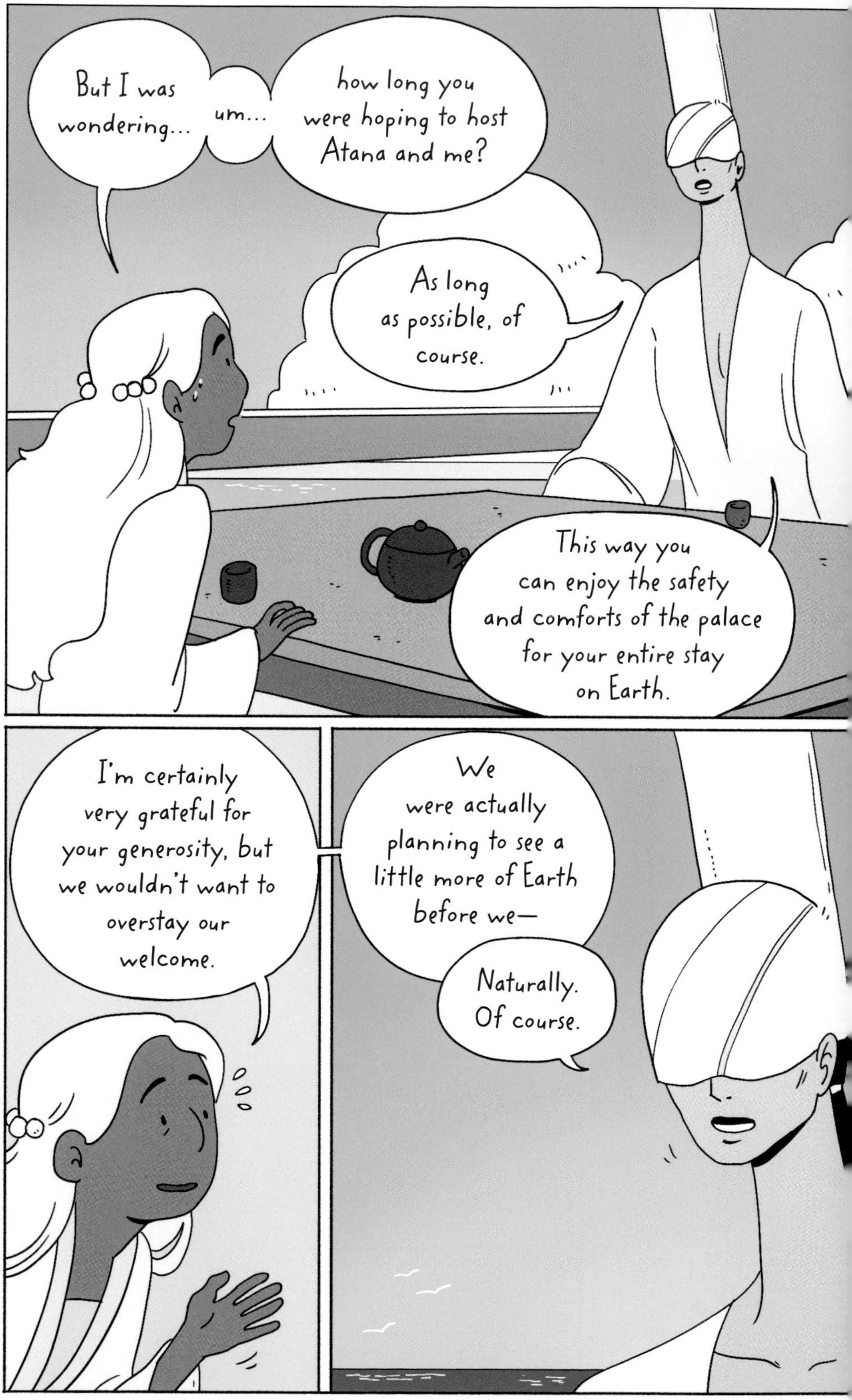
But I was wondering...
um...
how long you were hoping to host Atana and me?
As long as possible, of course.
This way you can enjoy the safety and comforts of the palace for your entire stay on Earth.
I'm certainly very grateful for your generosity, but we wouldn't want to overstay our welcome.
We were actually planning to see a little more of Earth before we—
Naturally. Of course.

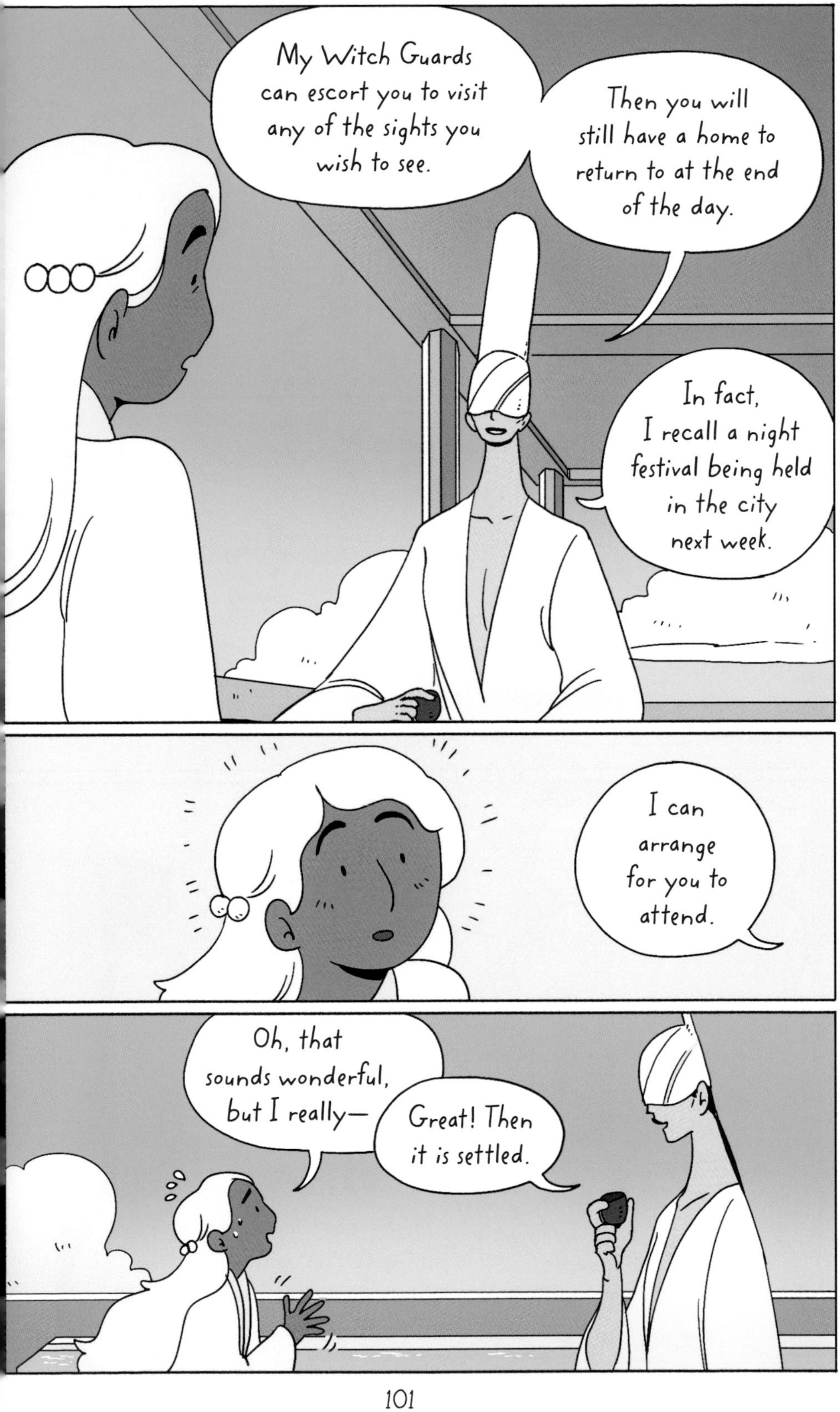
My Witch Guards can escort you to visit any of the sights you wish to see.
Then you will still have a home to return to at the end of the day.
In fact, I recall a night festival being held in the city next week.
I can arrange for you to attend.
Oh, that sounds wonderful, but I really—
Great! Then it is settled.

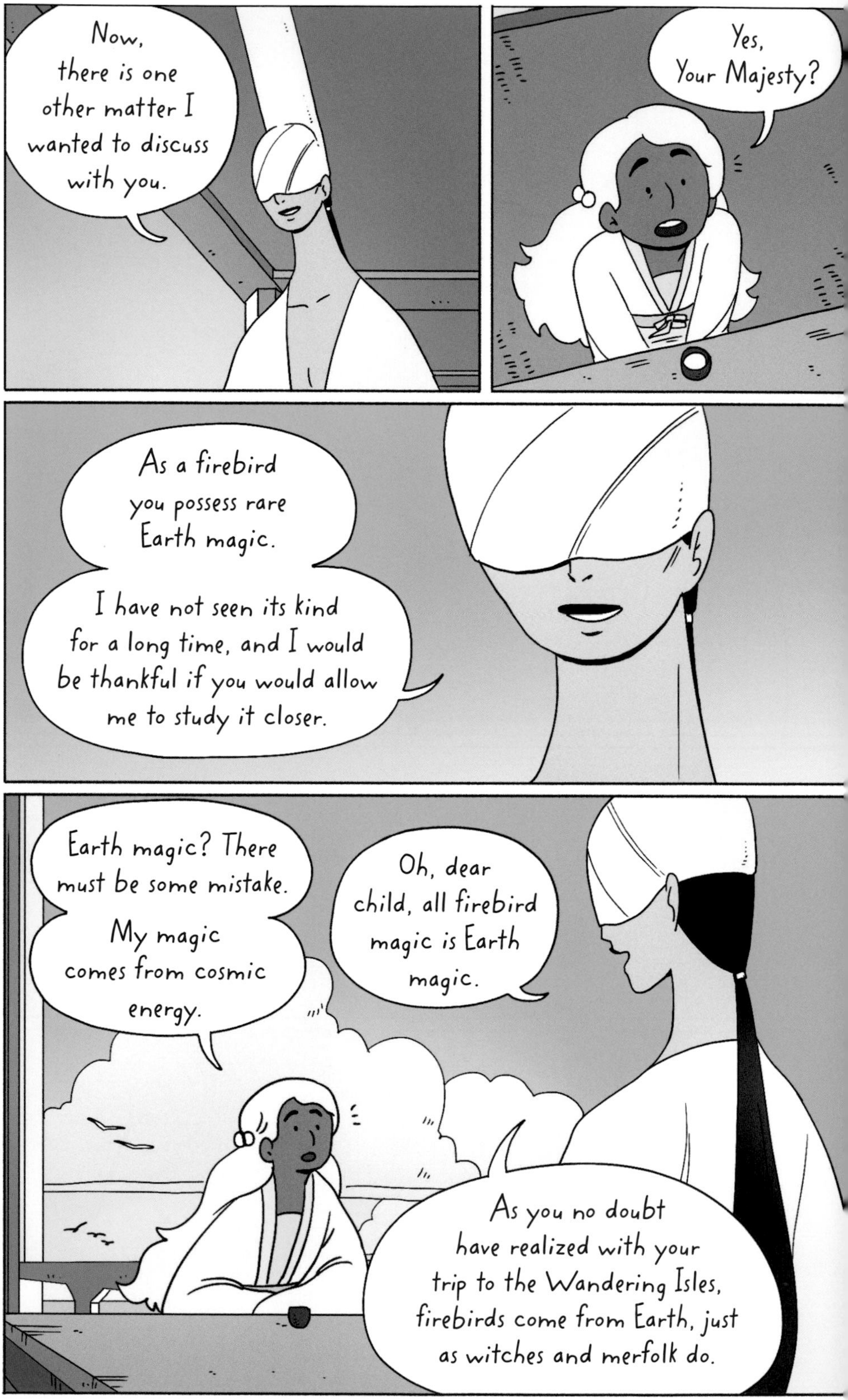
Now, there is one other matter I wanted to discuss with you.
Yes, Your Majesty?
As a firebird you possess rare Earth magic.
I have not seen its kind for a long time, and I would be thankful if you would allow me to study it closer.
Earth magic? There must be some mistake.
My magic comes from cosmic energy.
Oh, dear child, all firebird magic is Earth magic.
As you no doubt have realized with your trip to the Wandering Isles, firebirds come from Earth, just as witches and merfolk do.

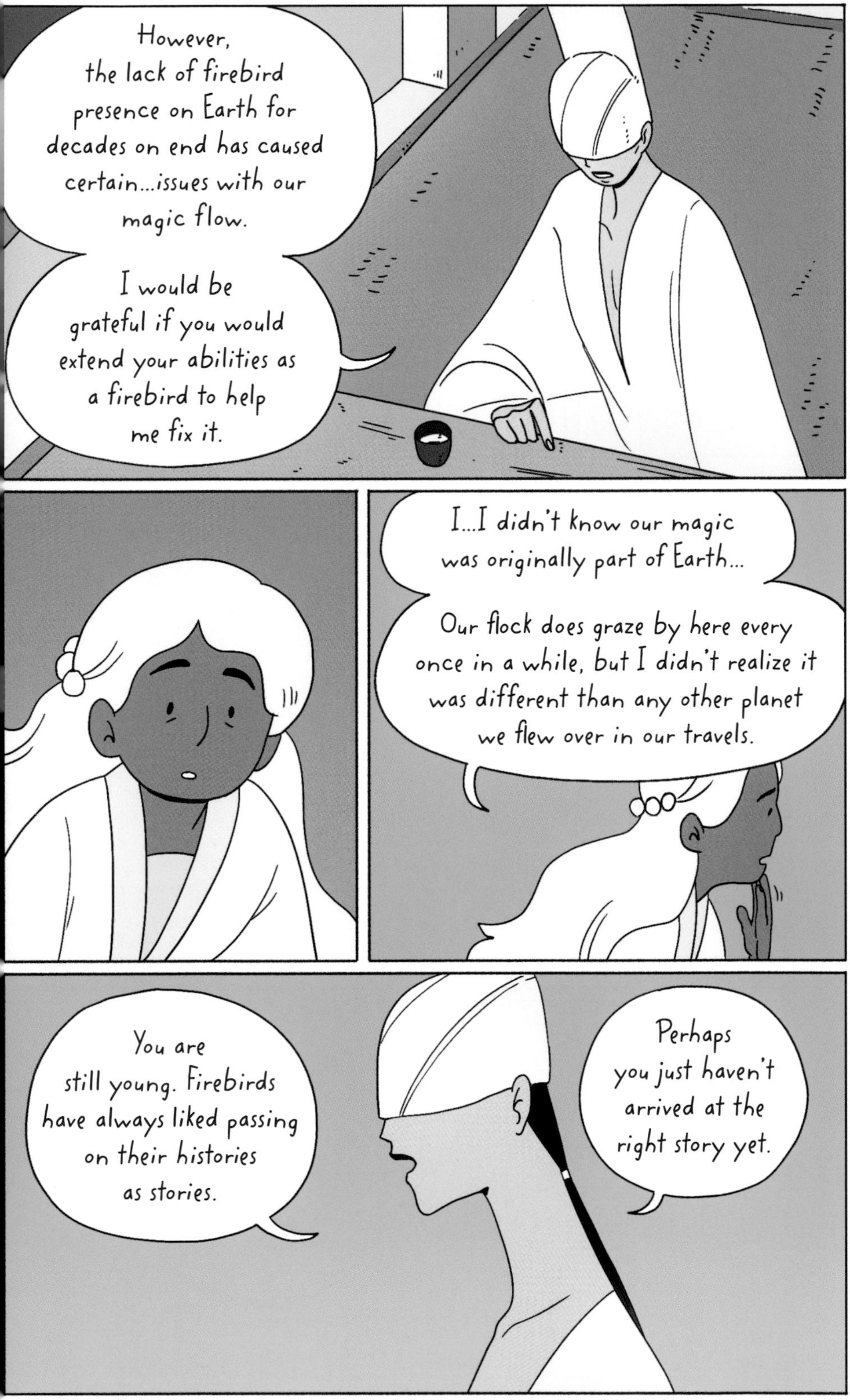
However, the lack of firebird presence on Earth for decades on end has caused certain...issues with our magic flow.
I would be grateful if you would extend your abilities as a firebird to help me fix it.
I...I didn't know our magic was originally part of Earth...
Our flock does graze by here every once in a while, but I didn't realize it was different than any other planet we flew over in our travels.
You are still young. Firebirds have always liked passing on their histories as stories.
Perhaps you just haven't arrived at the right story yet.

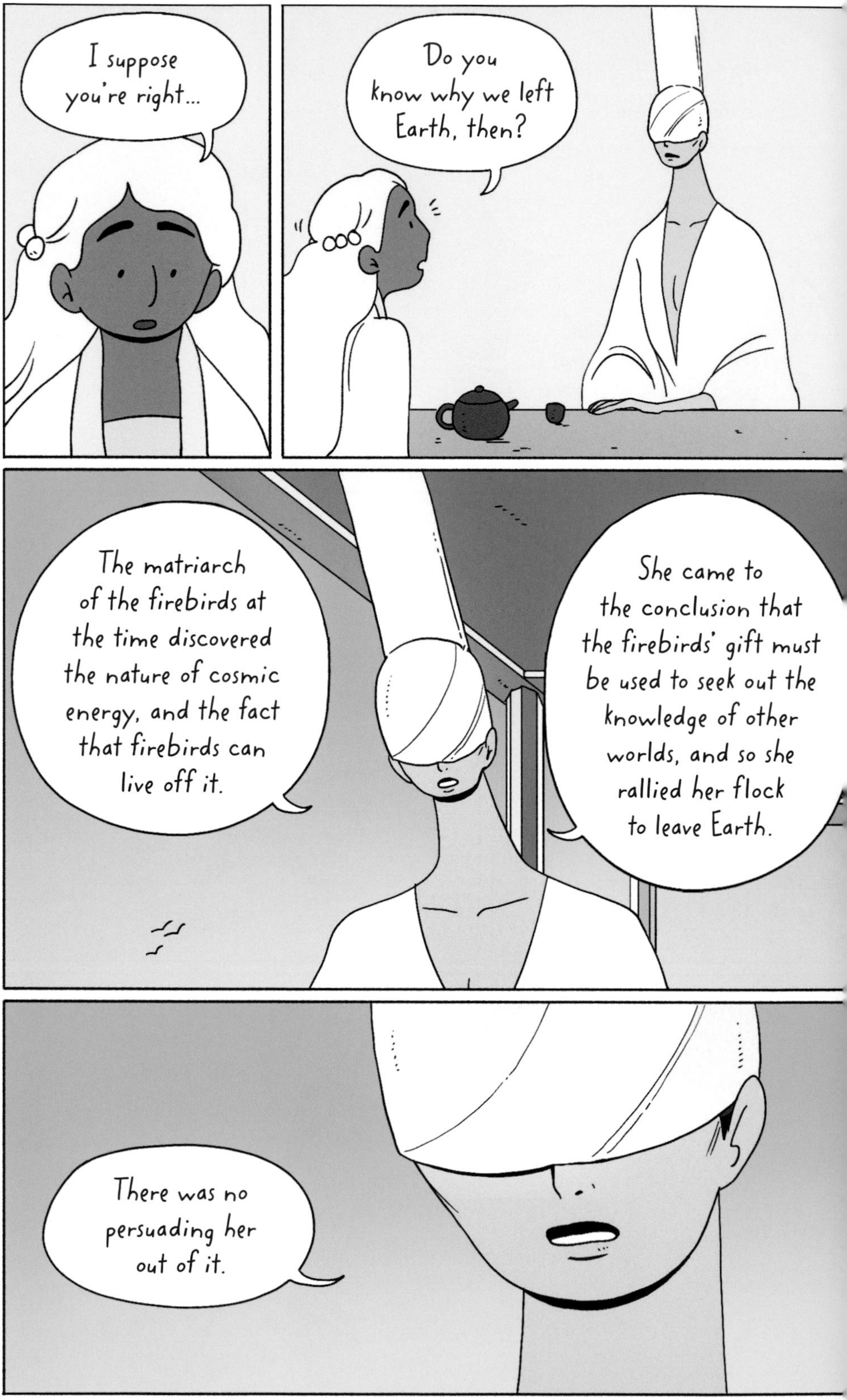
I suppose you're right...
Do you know why we left Earth, then?
The matriarch of the firebirds at the time discovered the nature of cosmic energy, and the fact that firebirds can live off it.
She came to the conclusion that the firebirds' gift must be used to seek out the knowledge of other worlds, and so she rallied her flock to leave Earth.
There was no persuading her out of it.

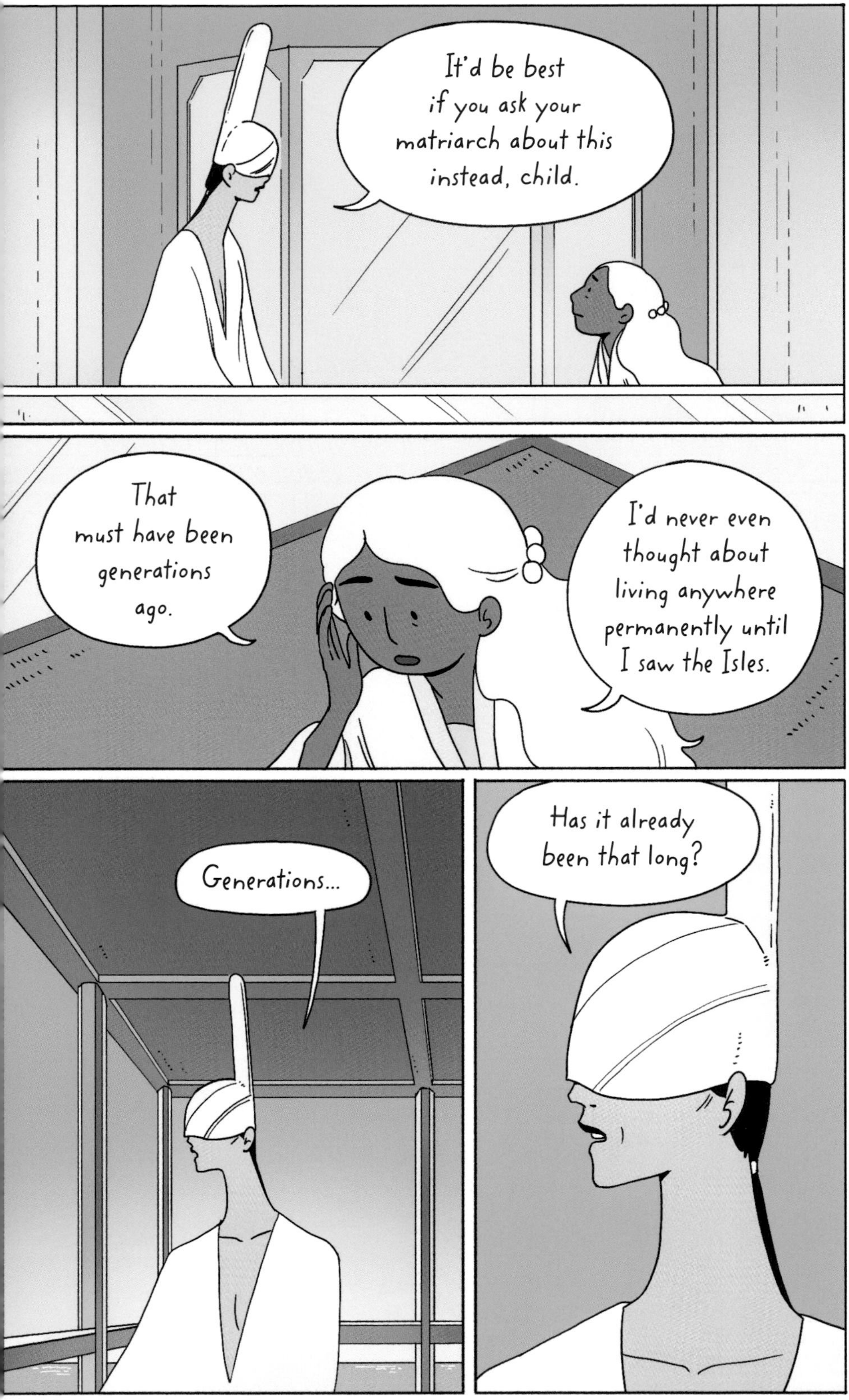
It'd be best if you ask your matriarch about this instead, child.
That must have been generations ago.
I'd never even thought about living anywhere permanently until I saw the Isles.
Generations...
Has it already been that long?

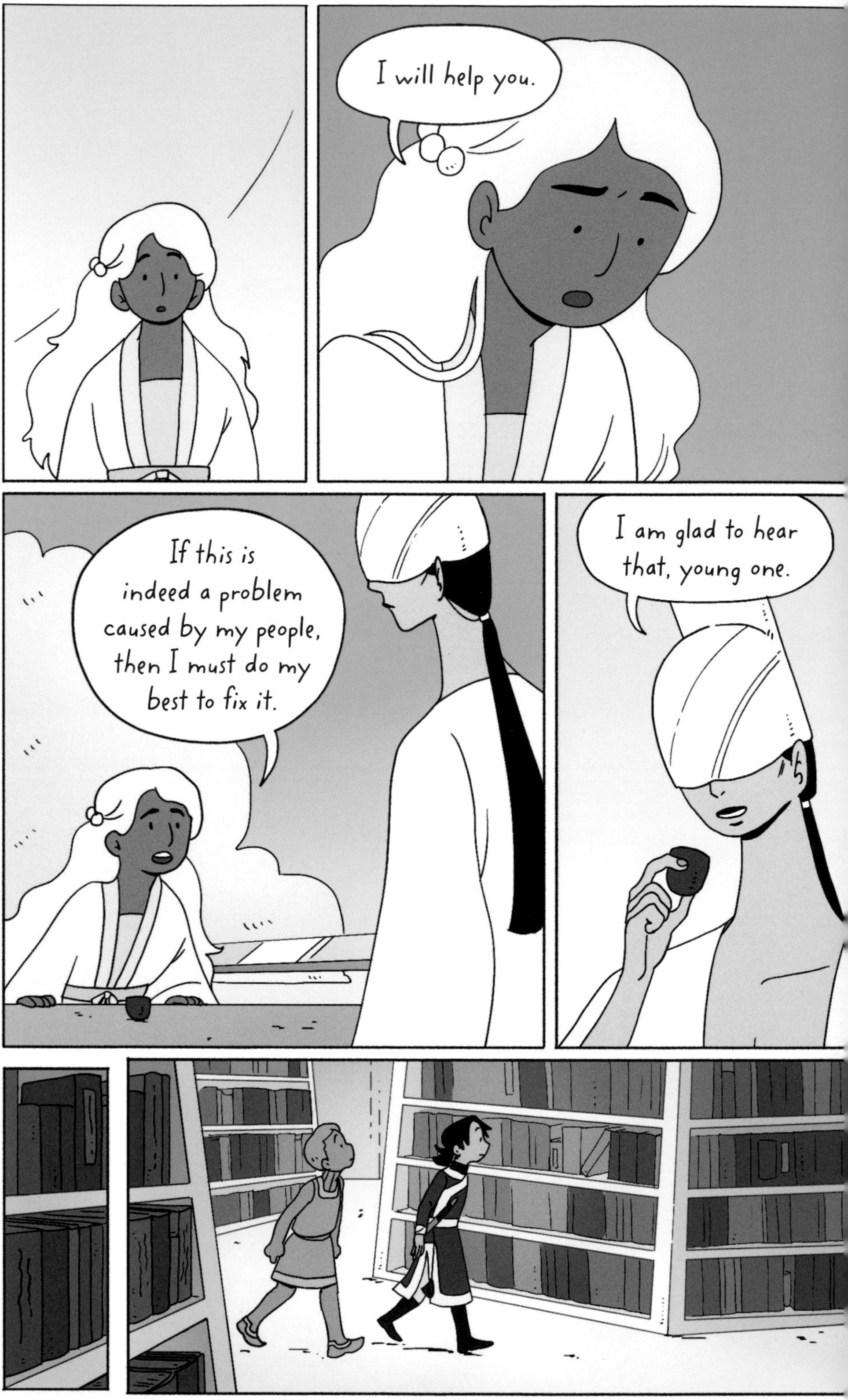
I will help you.
If this is indeed a problem caused by my people, then I must do my best to fix it.
I am glad to hear that, young one.

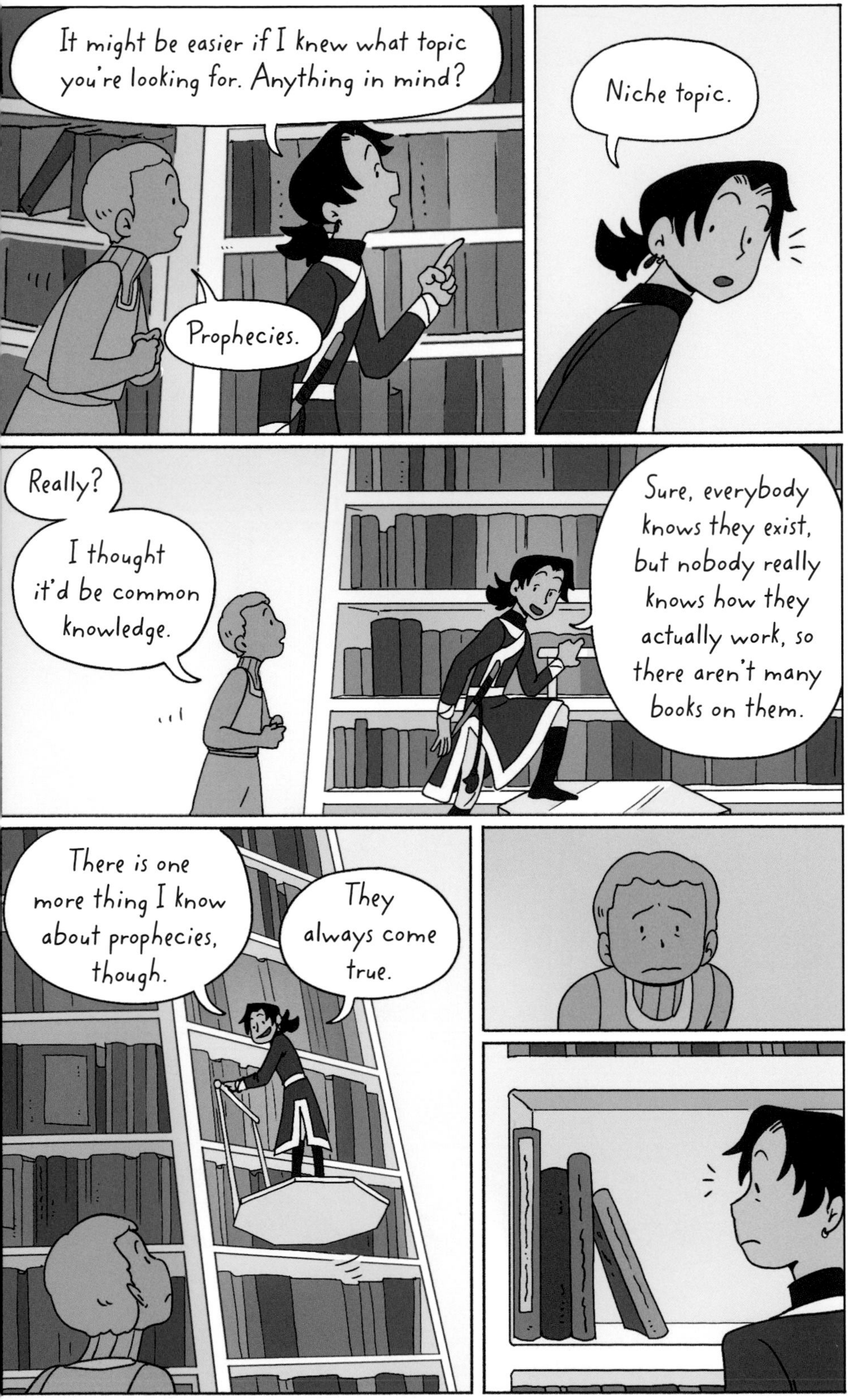
It might be easier if I knew what topic you're looking for. Anything in mind?
...
Prophecies.
Niche topic.
Really?
I thought it'd be common knowledge.
...
Sure, everybody knows they exist, but nobody really knows how they actually work, so there aren't many books on them.
There is one more thing I know about prophecies, though.
They always come true.

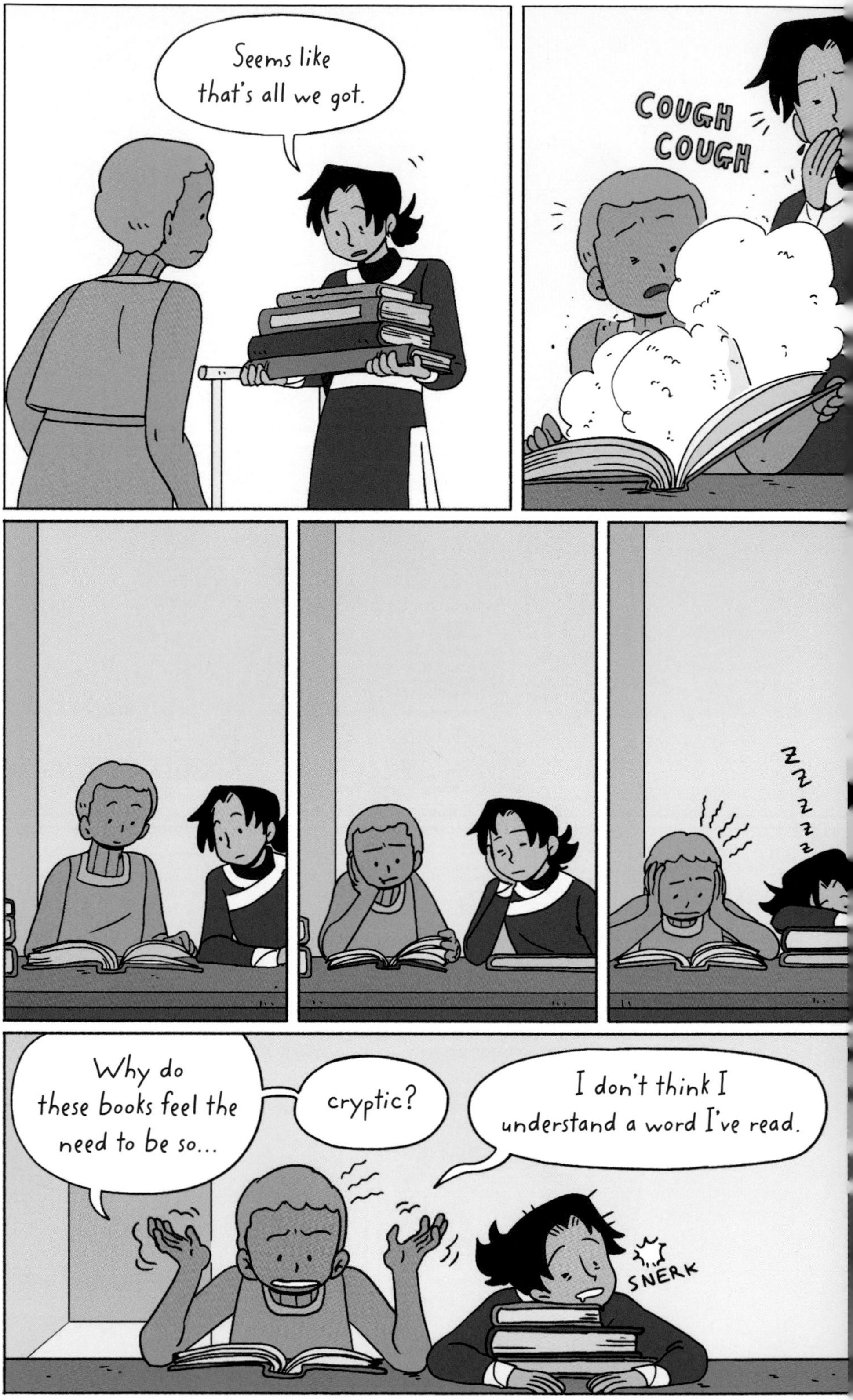
Seems like that's all we got.
COUGH COUGH
Z Z Z Z Z
Why do these books feel the need to be so...
cryptic?
I don't think I understand a word I've read.
SNERK

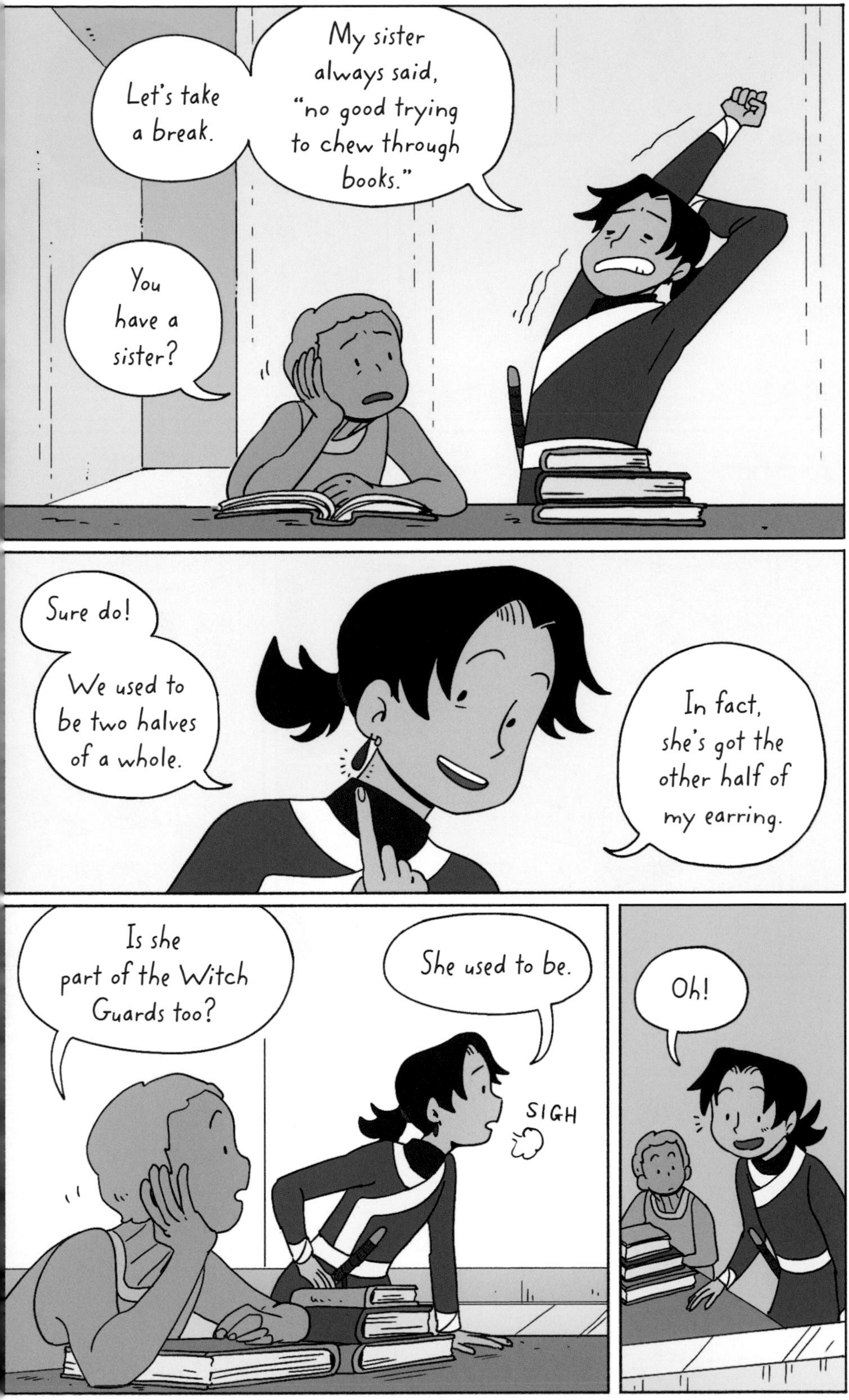
Let's take a break.
My sister always said, "no good trying to chew through books."
You have a sister?
Sure do!
We used to be two halves of a whole.
In fact, she's got the other half of my earring.
Is she part of the Witch Guards too?
She used to be.
SIGH
Oh!

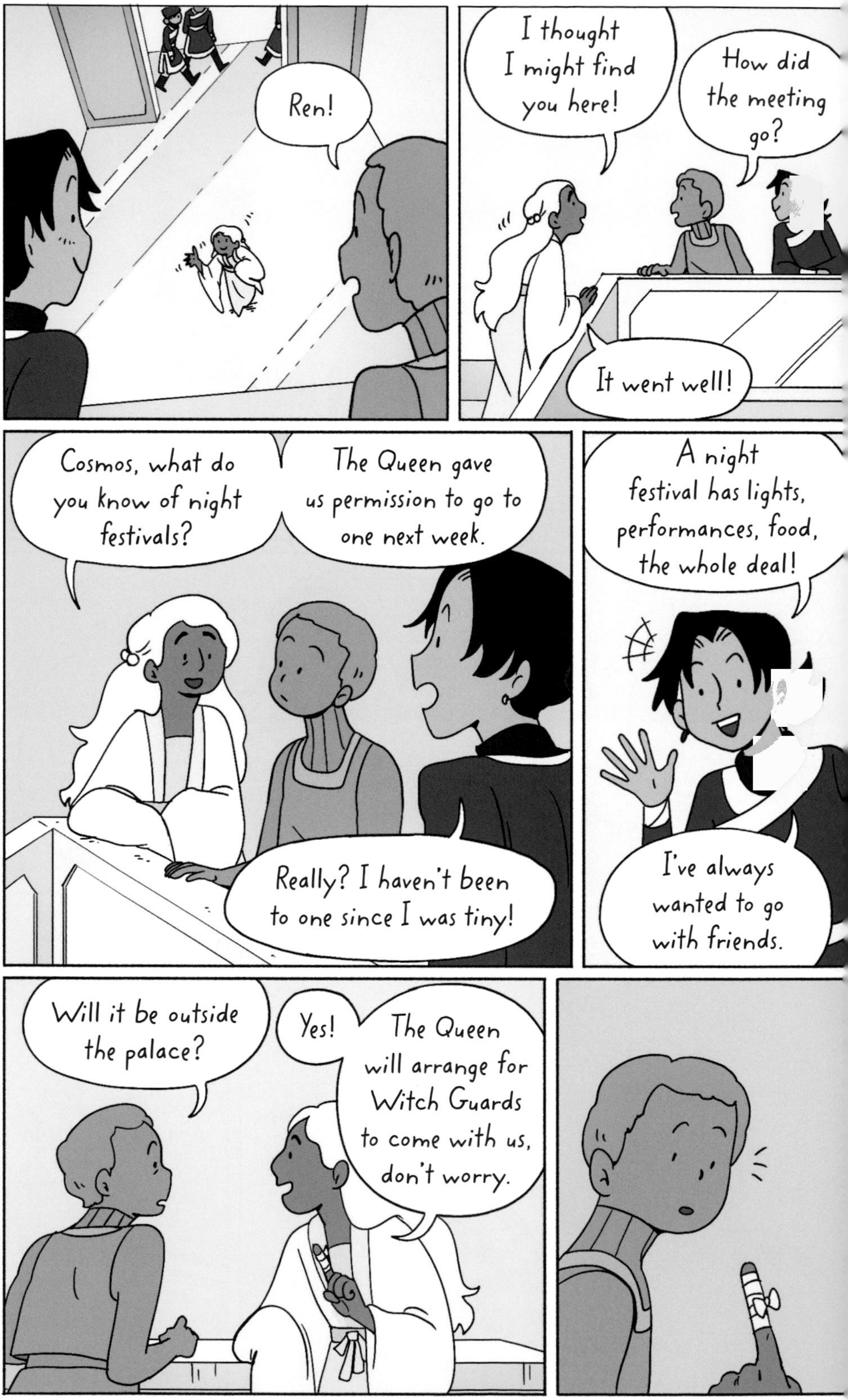
Ren!
I thought I might find you here!
How did the meeting go?
It went well!
Cosmos, what do you know of night festivals?
The Queen gave us permission to go to one next week.
Really? I haven't been to one since I was tiny!
A night festival has lights, performances, food, the whole deal!
I've always wanted to go with friends.
Will it be outside the palace?
Yes!
The Queen will arrange for Witch Guards to come with us, don't worry.

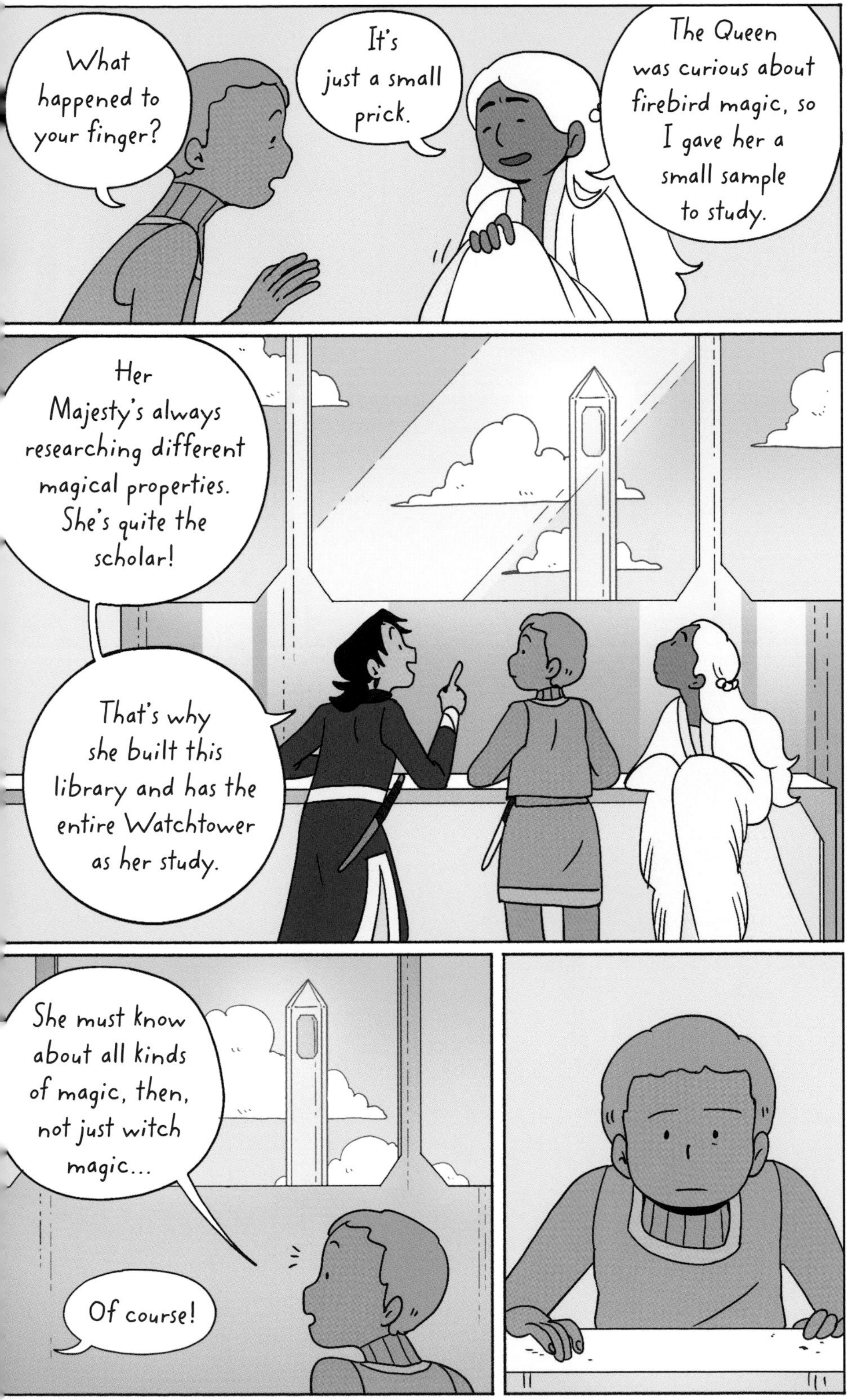
What happened to your finger?
It's just a small prick.
The Queen was curious about firebird magic, so I gave her a small sample to study.
Her Majesty's always researching different magical properties. She's quite the scholar!
That's why she built this library and has the entire Watchtower as her study.
She must know about all kinds of magic, then, not just witch magic...
Of course!

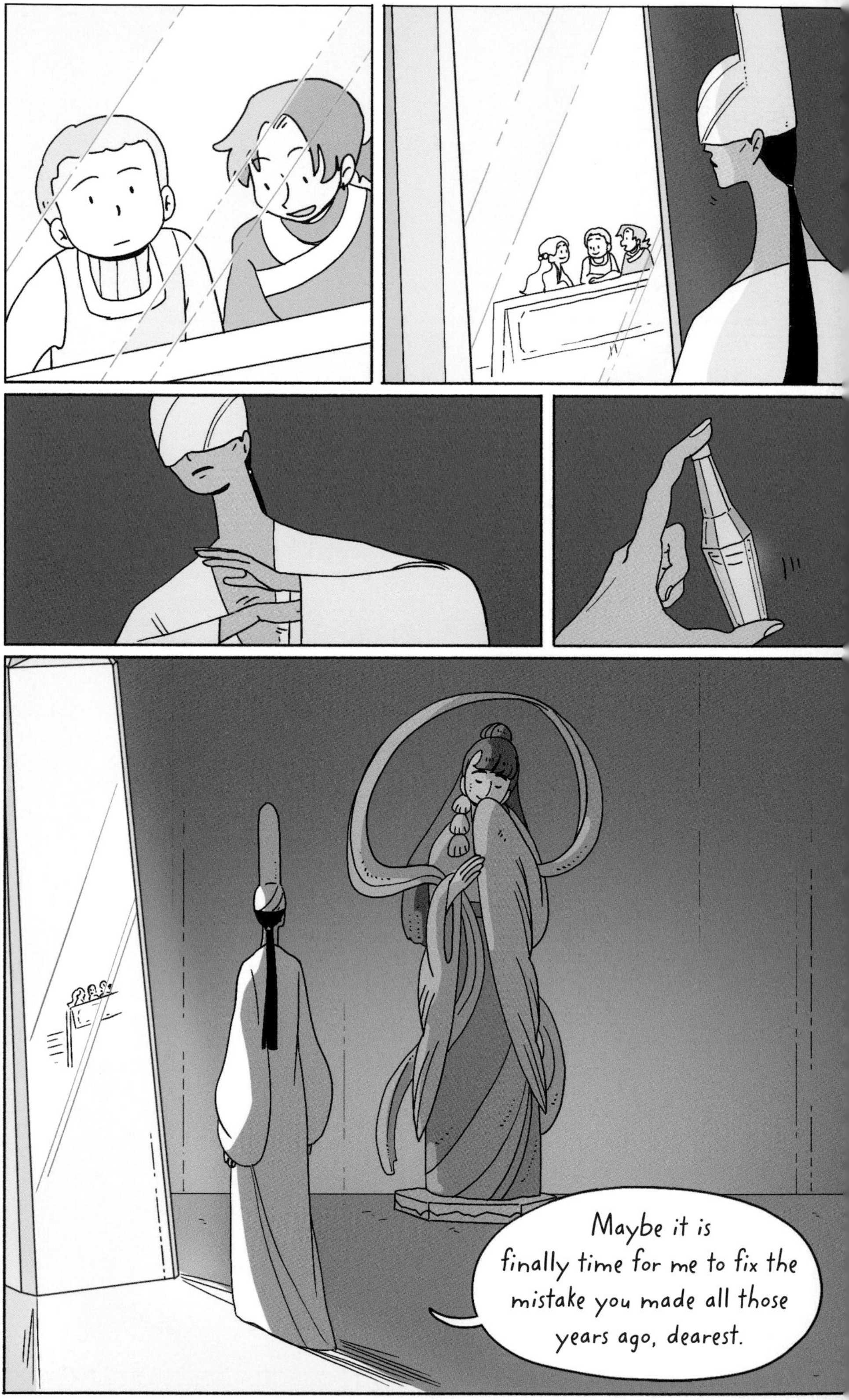
Maybe it is finally time for me to fix the mistake you made all those years ago, dearest.

CHAPTER 10

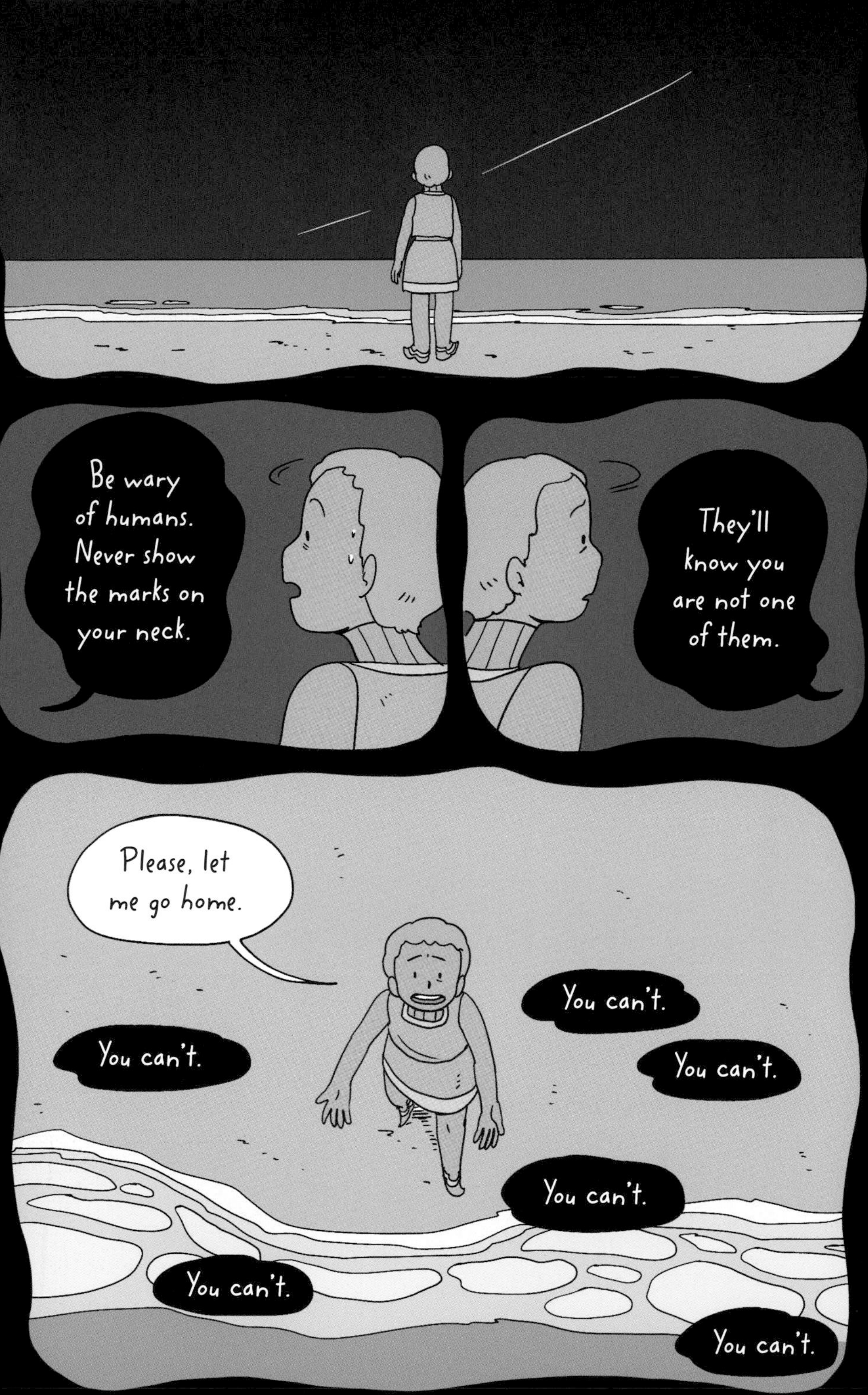

Be wary of humans. Never show the marks on your neck.
They'll know you are not one of them.
Please, let me go home.
You can't.
You can't.
You can't.
You can't.
You can't.
You can't.

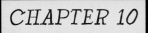

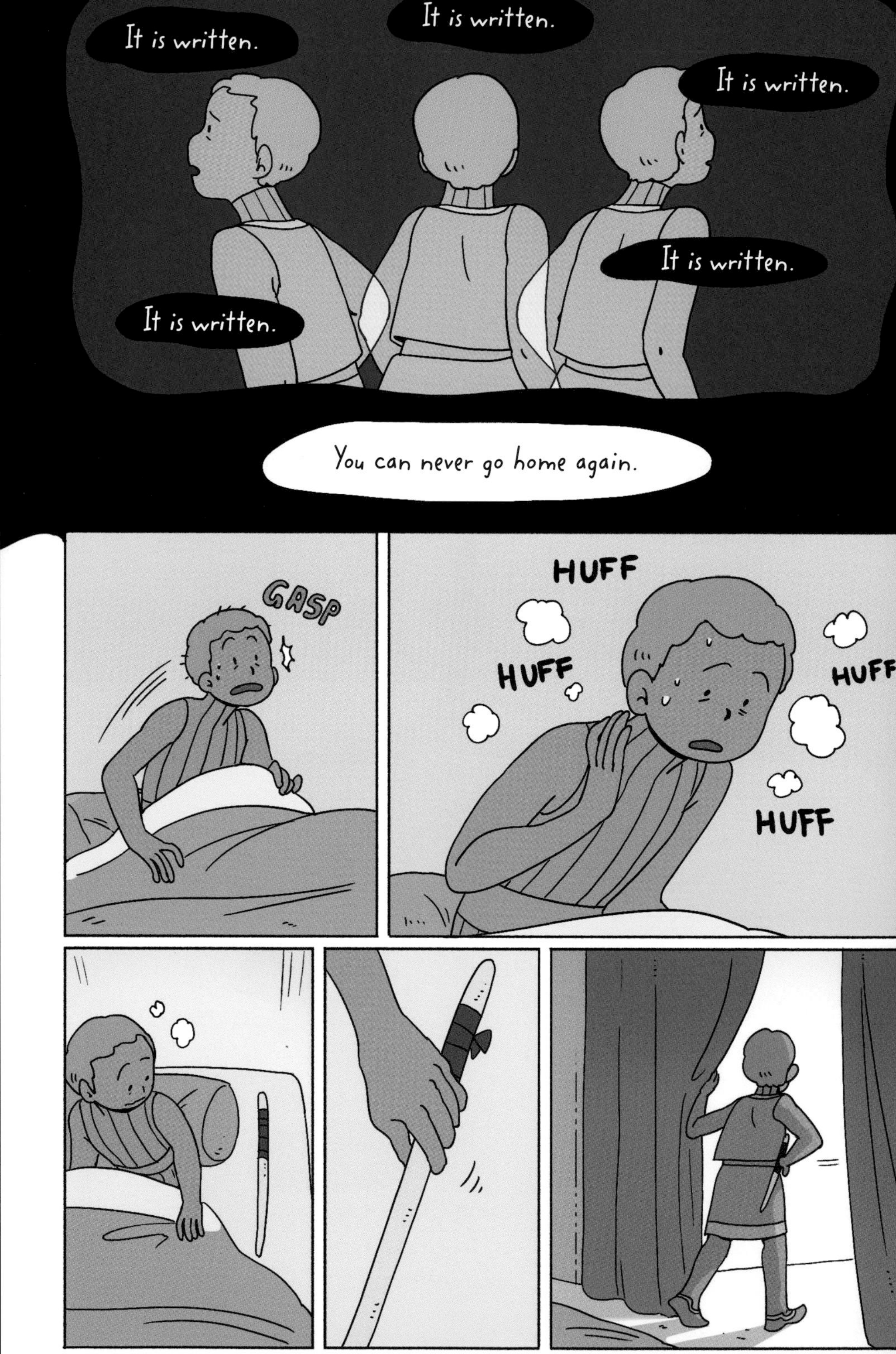
It is written.
It is written.
It is written.
It is written.
It is written.
You can never go home again.
GASP
HUFF
HUFF
HUFF
HUFF

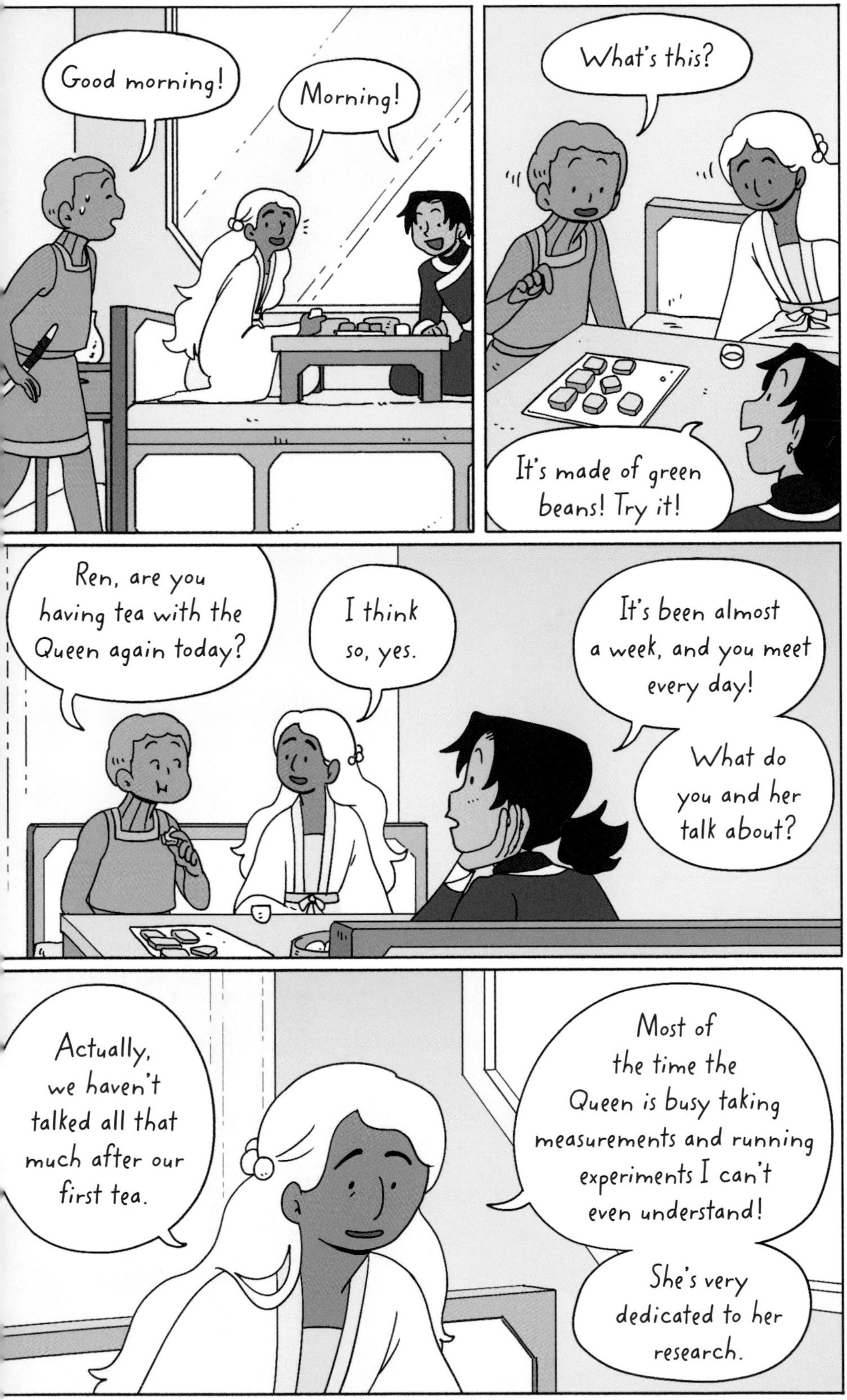
Good morning!
Morning!
What's this?
It's made of green beans! Try it!
Ren, are you having tea with the Queen again today?
I think so, yes.
It's been almost a week, and you meet every day!
What do you and her talk about?
Actually, we haven't talked all that much after our first tea.
Most of the time the Queen is busy taking measurements and running experiments I can't even understand!
She's very dedicated to her research.

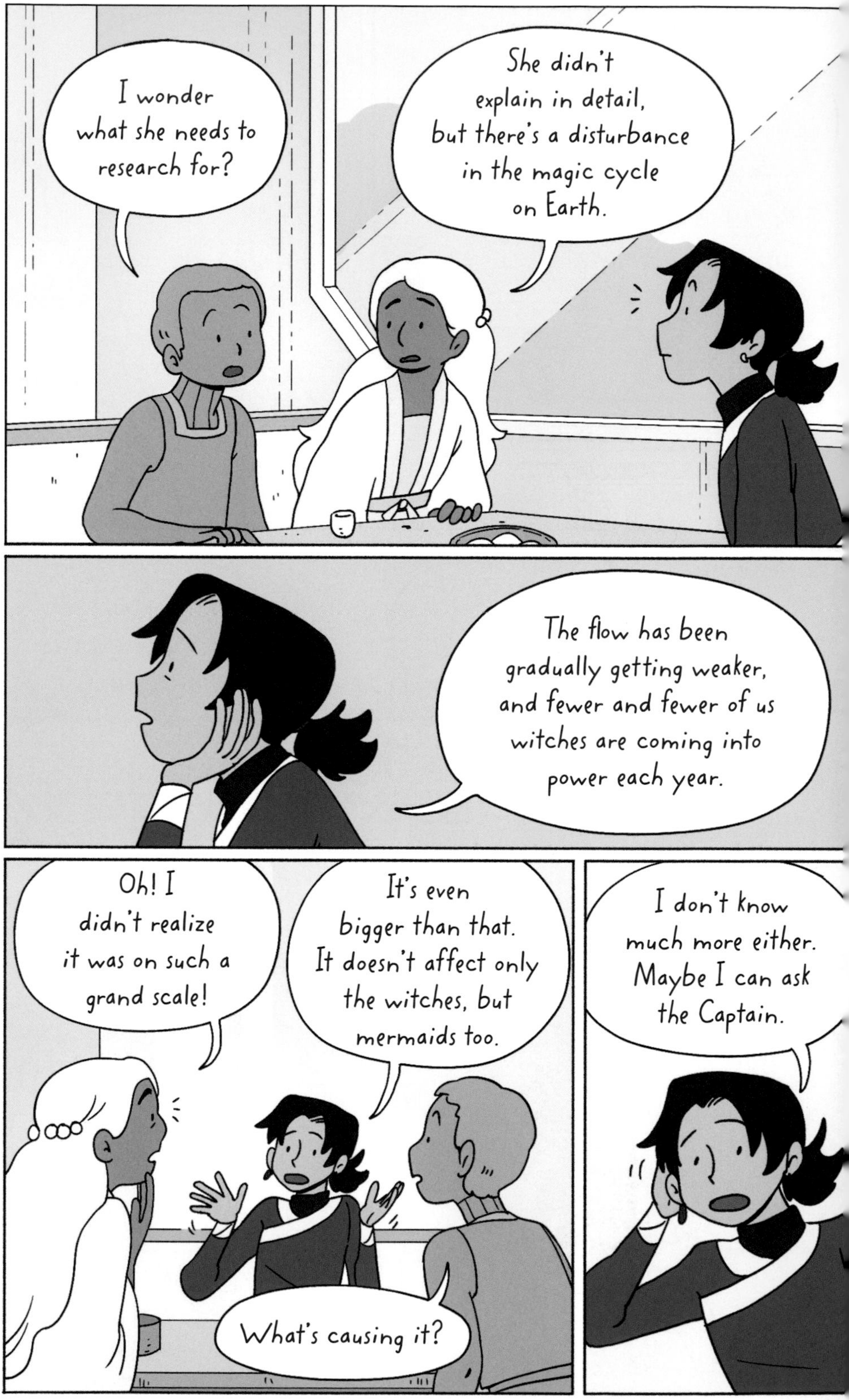
I wonder what she needs to research for?
She didn't explain in detail, but there's a disturbance in the magic cycle on Earth.
The flow has been gradually getting weaker, and fewer and fewer of us witches are coming into power each year.
Oh! I didn't realize it was on such a grand scale!
It's even bigger than that. It doesn't affect only the witches, but mermaids too.
What's causing it?
I don't know much more either. Maybe I can ask the Captain.

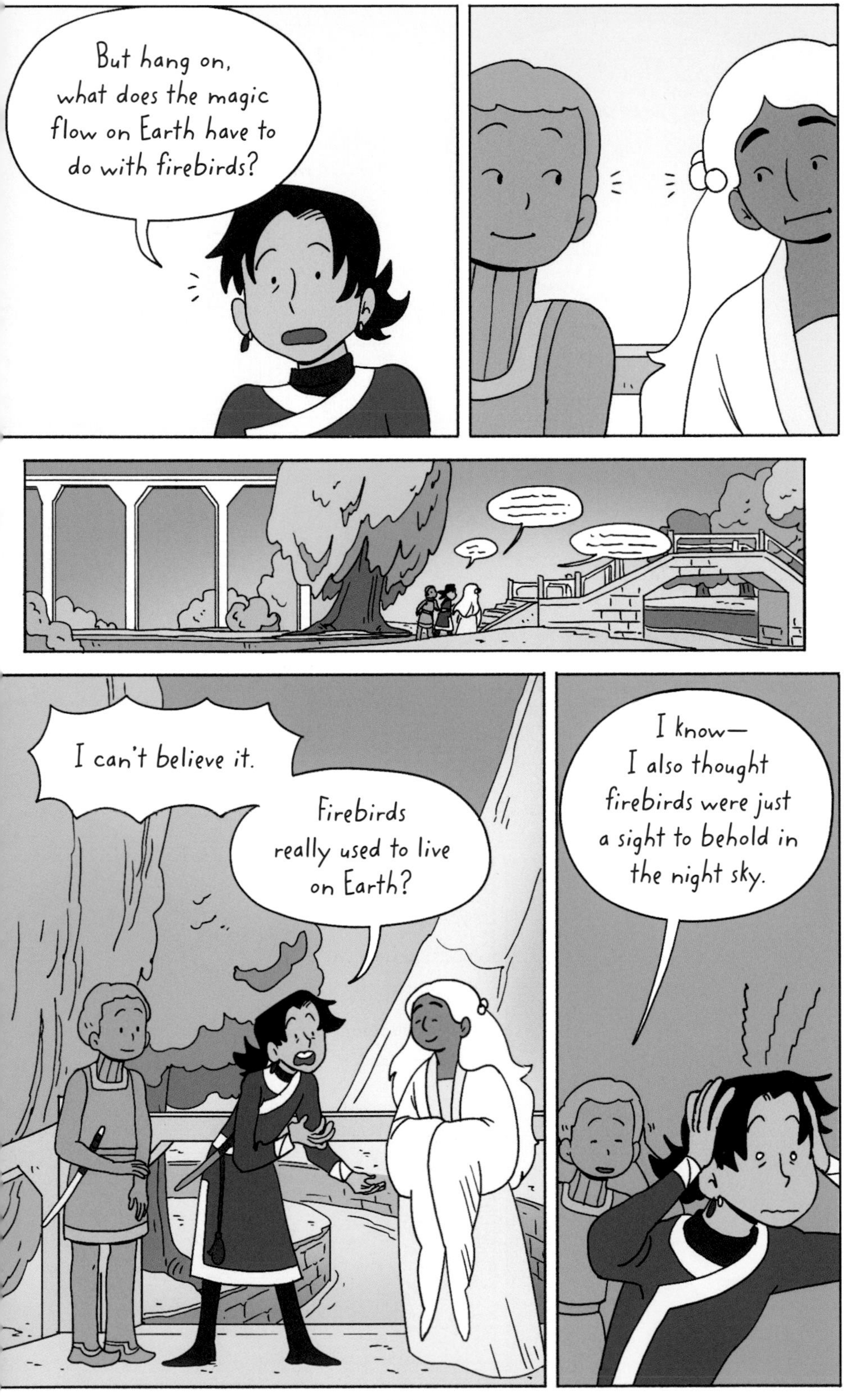
But hang on, what does the magic flow on Earth have to do with firebirds?
I can't believe it.
Firebirds really used to live on Earth?
I know— I also thought firebirds were just a sight to behold in the night sky.

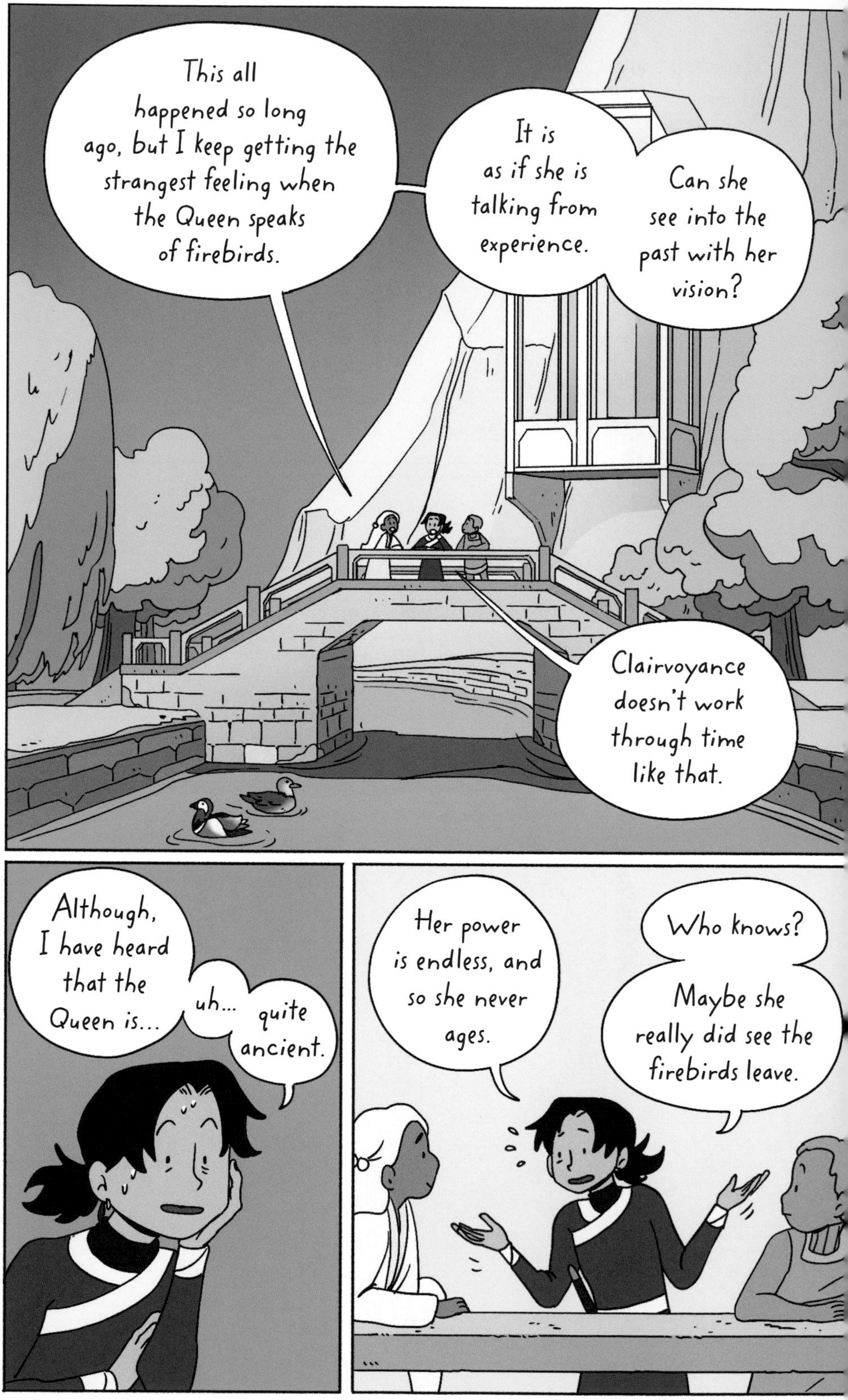
This all happened so long ago, but I keep getting the strangest feeling when the Queen speaks of firebirds.
It is as if she is talking from experience.
Can she see into the past with her vision?
Clairvoyance doesn't work through time like that.
Although, I have heard that the Queen is...
uh...
quite ancient.
Her power is endless, and so she never ages.
Who knows?
Maybe she really did see the firebirds leave.

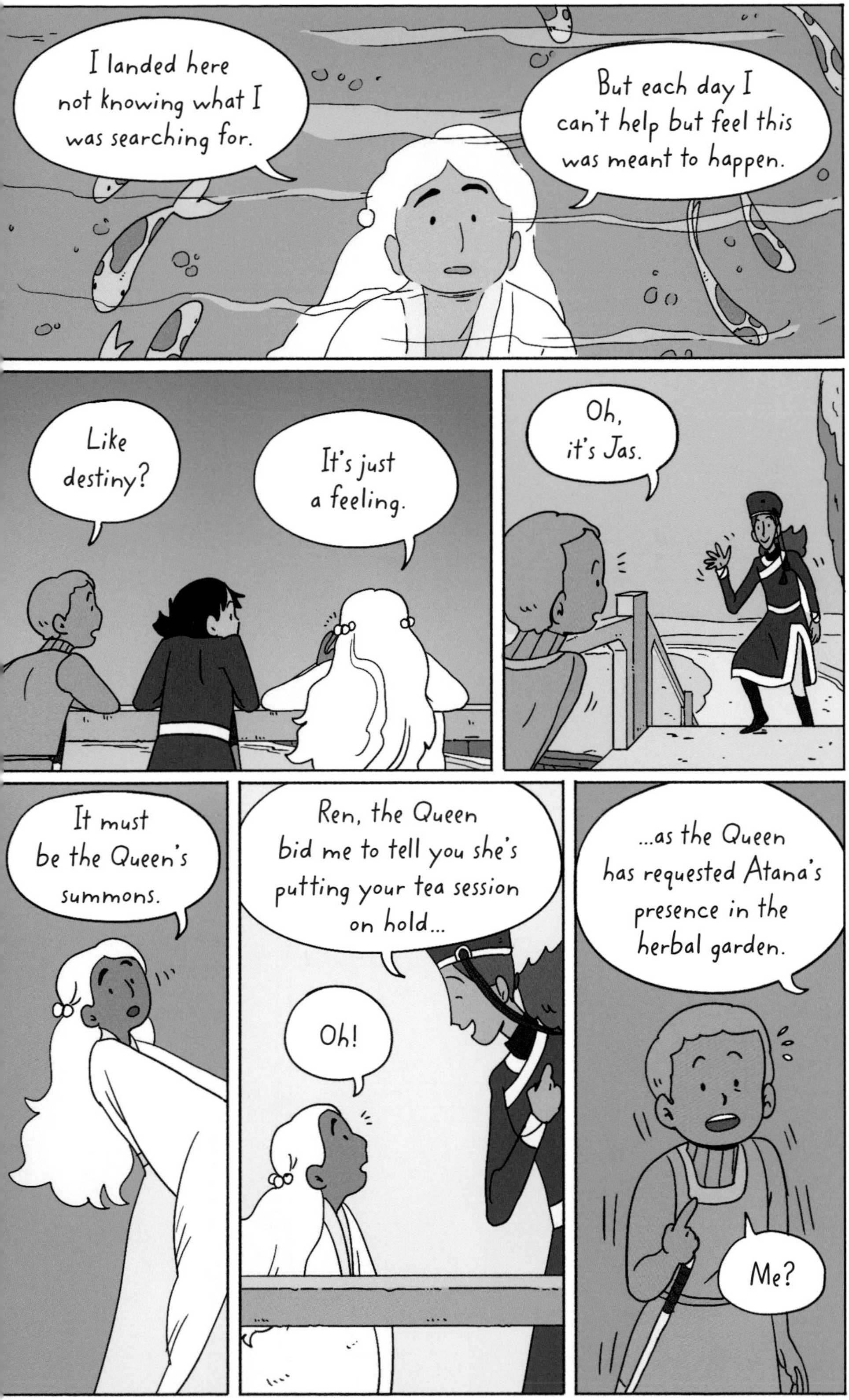

I landed here not knowing what I was searching for.
But each day I can't help but feel this was meant to happen.
Like destiny?
It's just a feeling.
Oh, it's Jas.
It must be the Queen's summons.
Ren, the Queen bid me to tell you she's putting your tea session on hold...
Oh!
...as the Queen has requested Atana's presence in the herbal garden.
Me?

CHAPTER 11

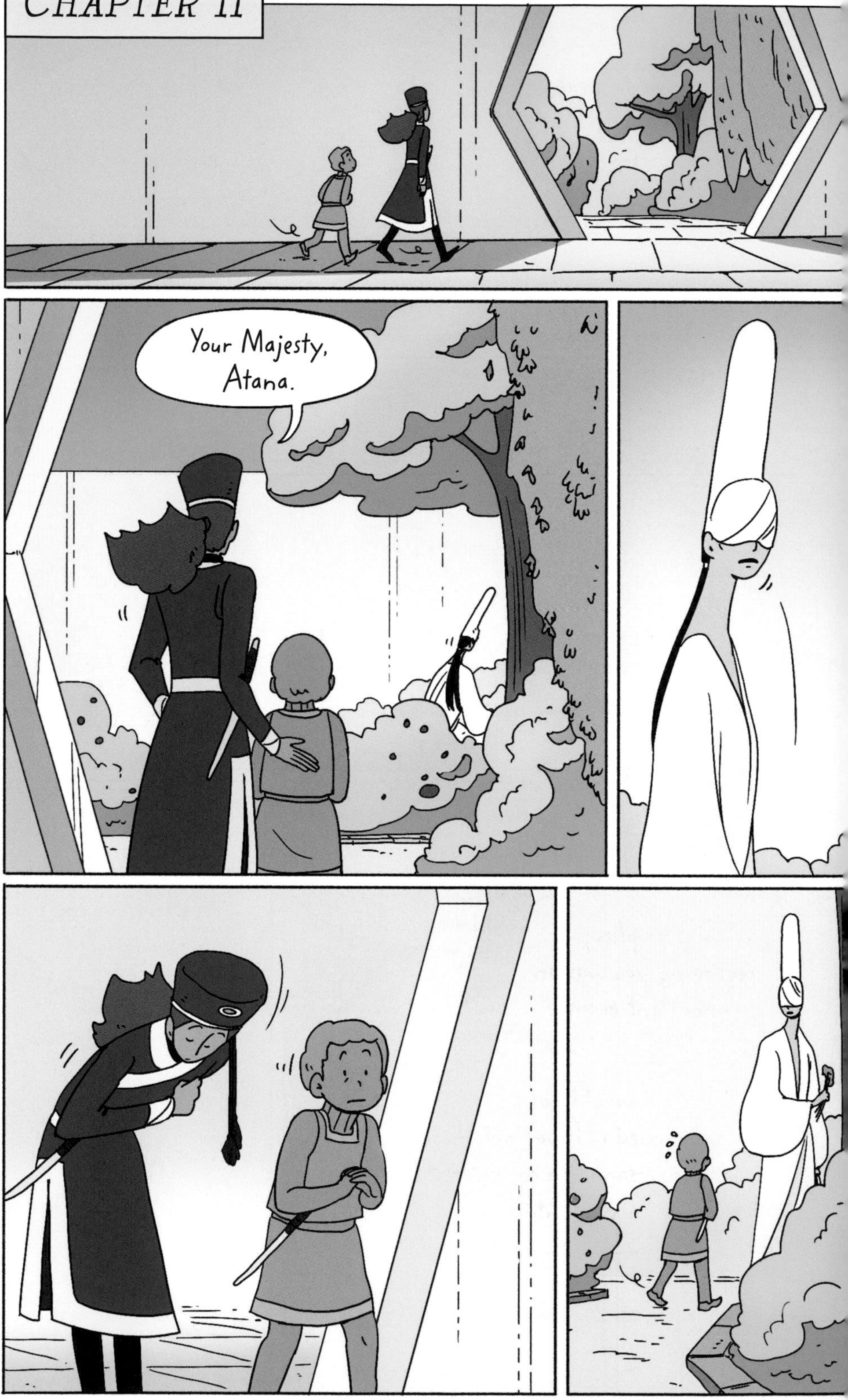
Your Majesty, Atana.

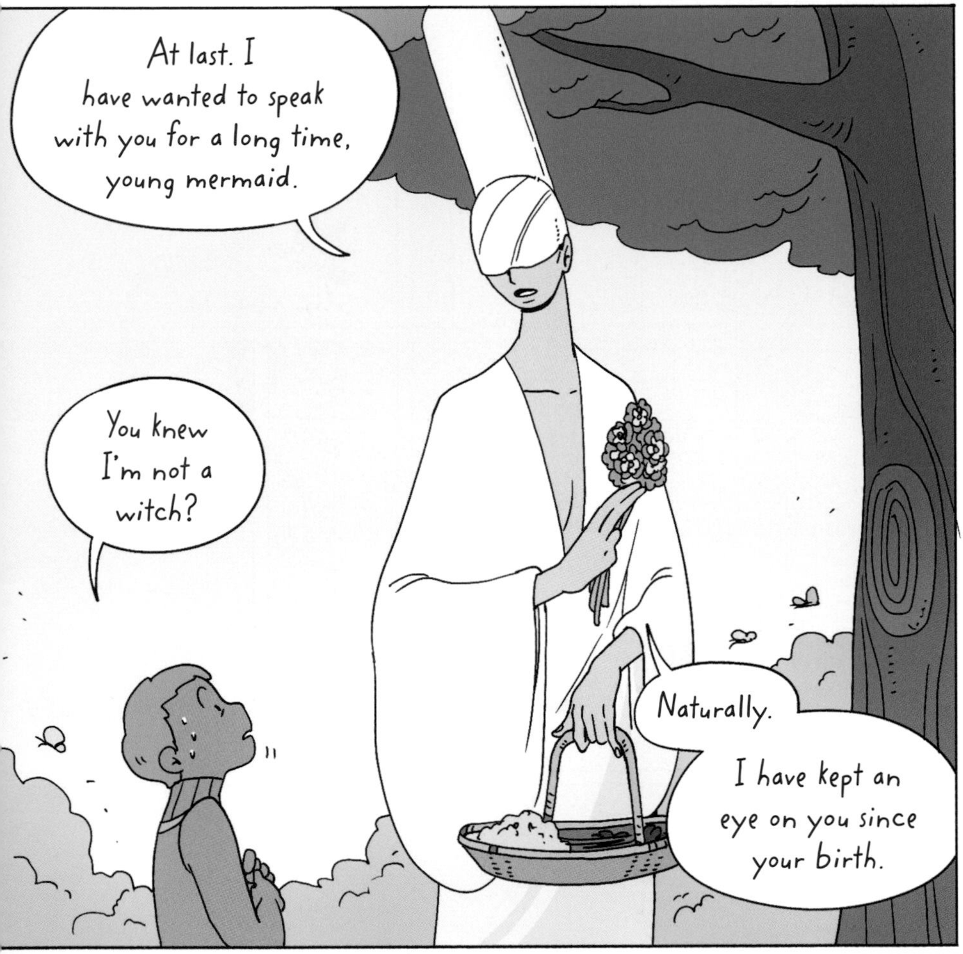
At last. I have wanted to speak with you for a long time, young mermaid.
You knew I'm not a witch?
Naturally.
I have kept an eye on you since your birth.

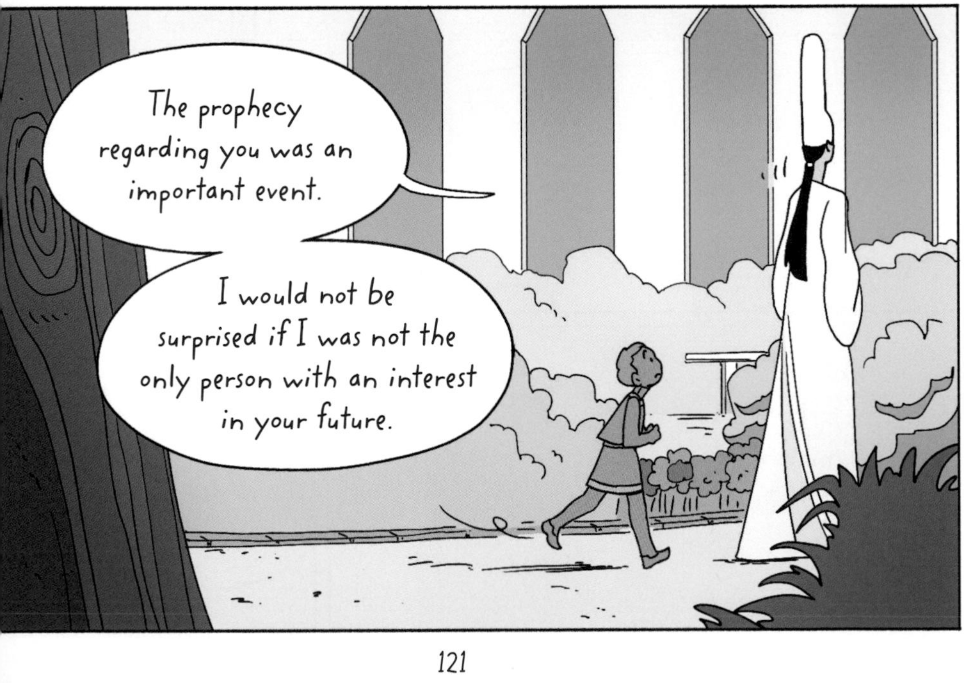
The prophecy regarding you was an important event.
I would not be surprised if I was not the only person with an interest in your future.

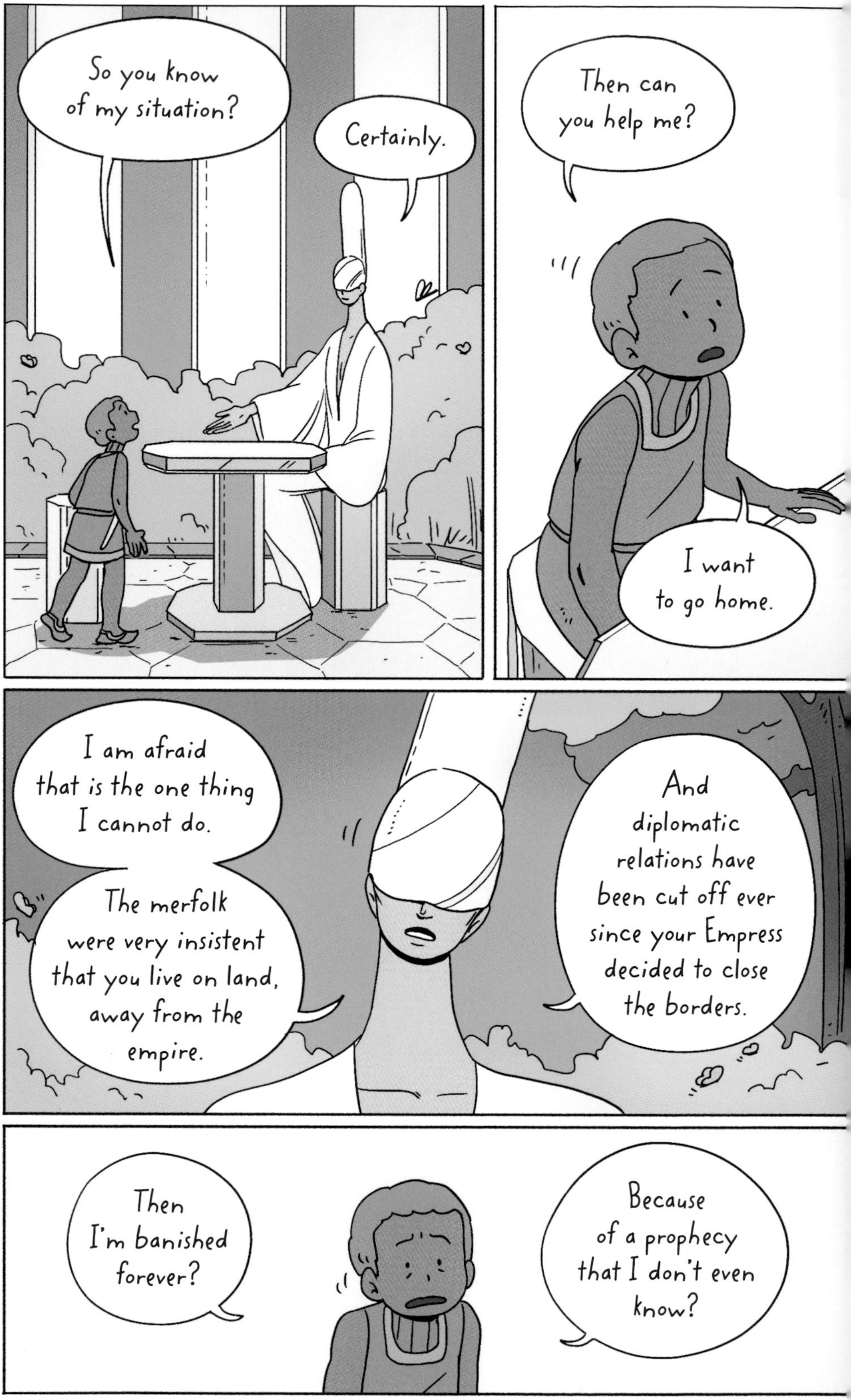
So you know of my situation?
Certainly.
Then can you help me?
I want to go home.
I am afraid that is the one thing I cannot do.
The merfolk were very insistent that you live on land, away from the empire.
And diplomatic relations have been cut off ever since your Empress decided to close the borders.
Then I'm banished forever?
Because of a prophecy that I don't even know?

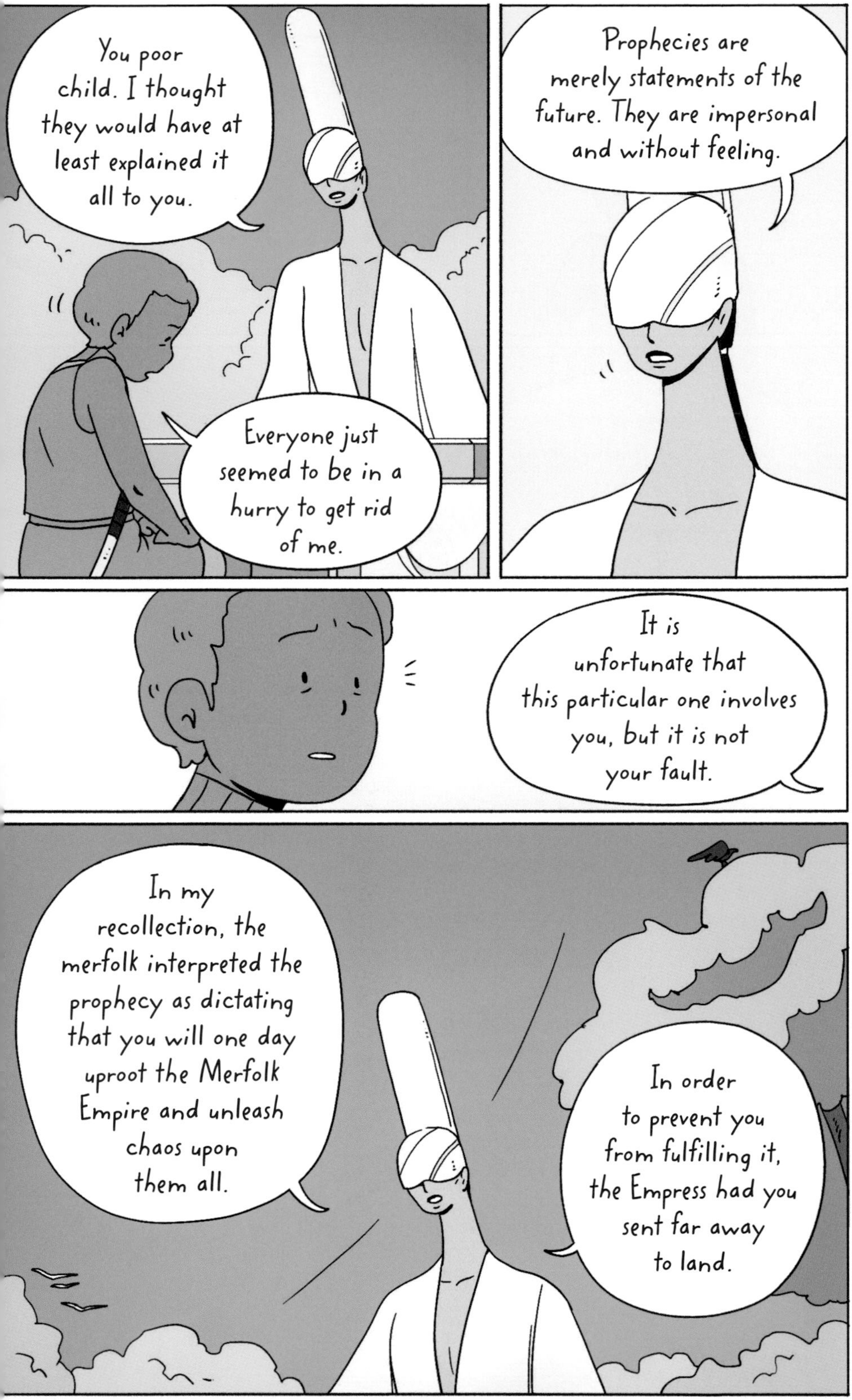
You poor child. I thought they would have at least explained it all to you.
Everyone just seemed to be in a hurry to get rid of me.
Prophecies are merely statements of the future. They are impersonal and without feeling.
It is unfortunate that this particular one involves you, but it is not your fault.
In my recollection, the merfolk interpreted the prophecy as dictating that you will one day uproot the Merfolk Empire and unleash chaos upon them all.
In order to prevent you from fulfilling it, the Empress had you sent far away to land.

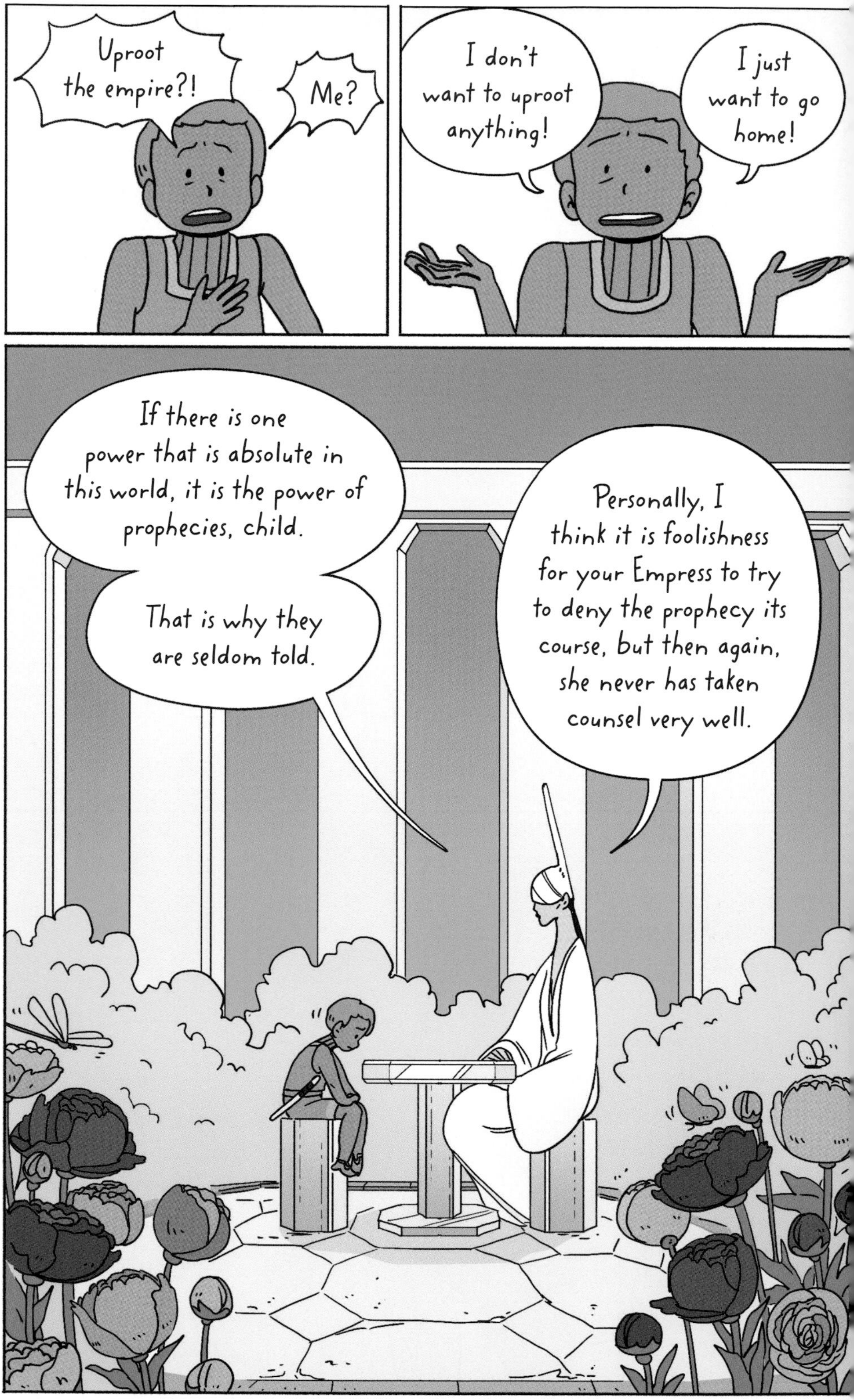
Uproot the empire?!
Me?
I don't want to uproot anything!
I just want to go home!
If there is one power that is absolute in this world, it is the power of prophecies, child.
That is why they are seldom told.
Personally, I think it is foolishness for your Empress to try to deny the prophecy its course, but then again, she never has taken counsel very well.

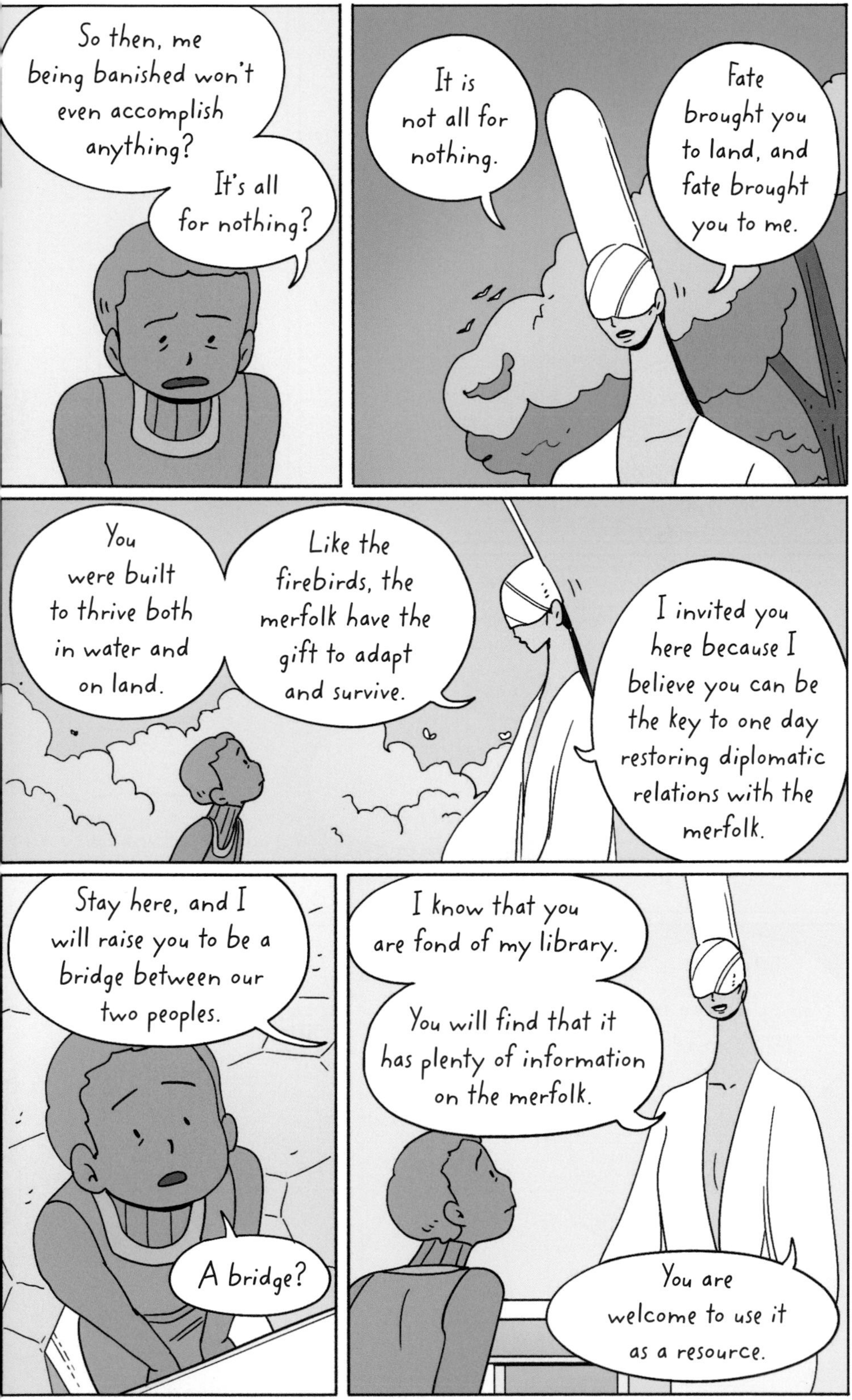
So then, me being banished won't even accomplish anything?
It's all for nothing?
It is not all for nothing.
Fate brought you to land, and fate brought you to me.
You were built to thrive both in water and on land.
Like the firebirds, the merfolk have the gift to adapt and survive.
I invited you here because I believe you can be the key to one day restoring diplomatic relations with the merfolk.
Stay here, and I will raise you to be a bridge between our two peoples.
A bridge?
I know that you are fond of my library.
You will find that it has plenty of information on the merfolk.
You are welcome to use it as a resource.

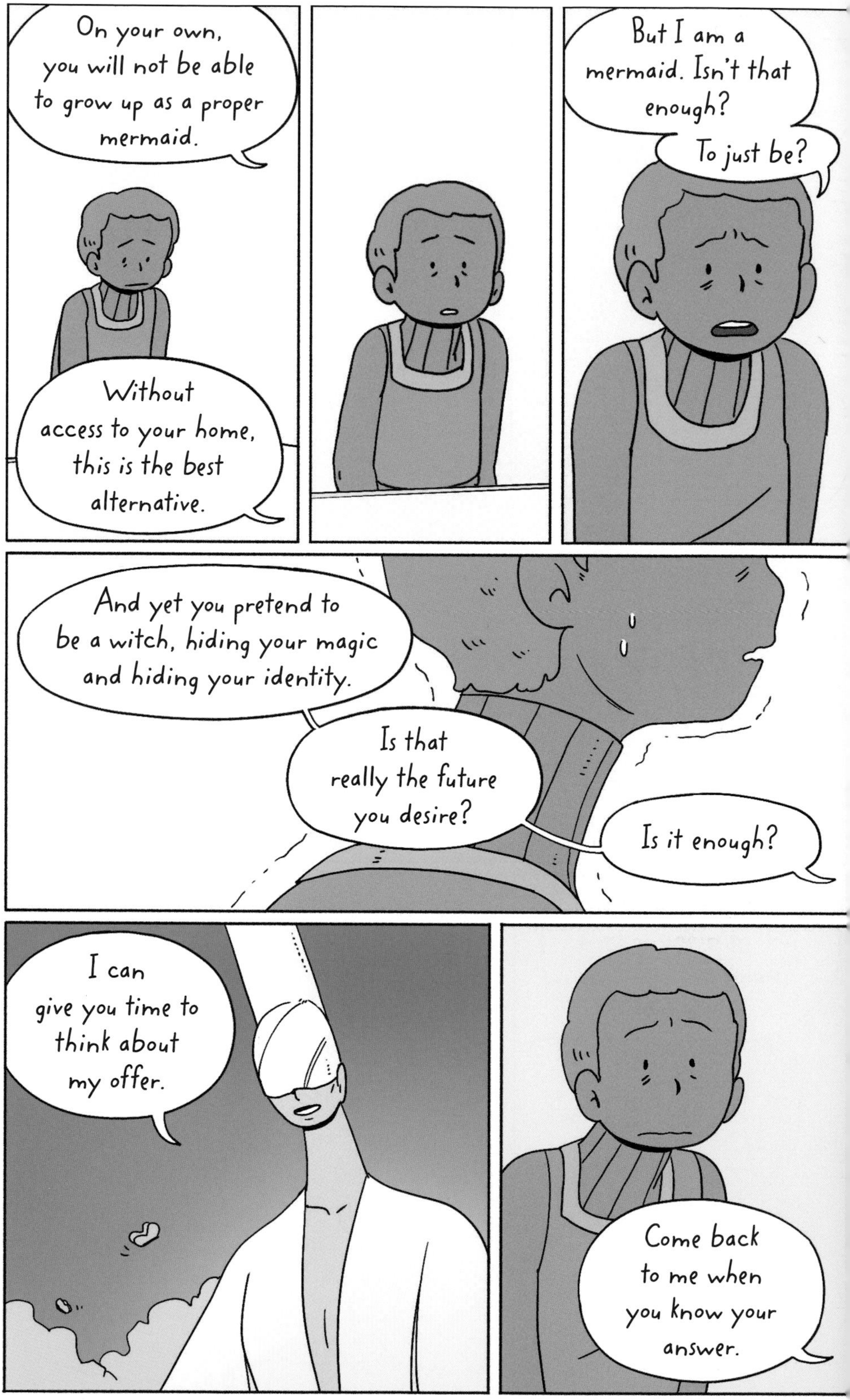
On your own, you will not be able to grow up as a proper mermaid.
Without access to your home, this is the best alternative.
But I am a mermaid. Isn't that enough?
To just be?
And yet you pretend to be a witch, hiding your magic and hiding your identity.
Is that really the future you desire?
Is it enough?
I can give you time to think about my offer.
Come back to me when you know your answer.

CHAPTER 12

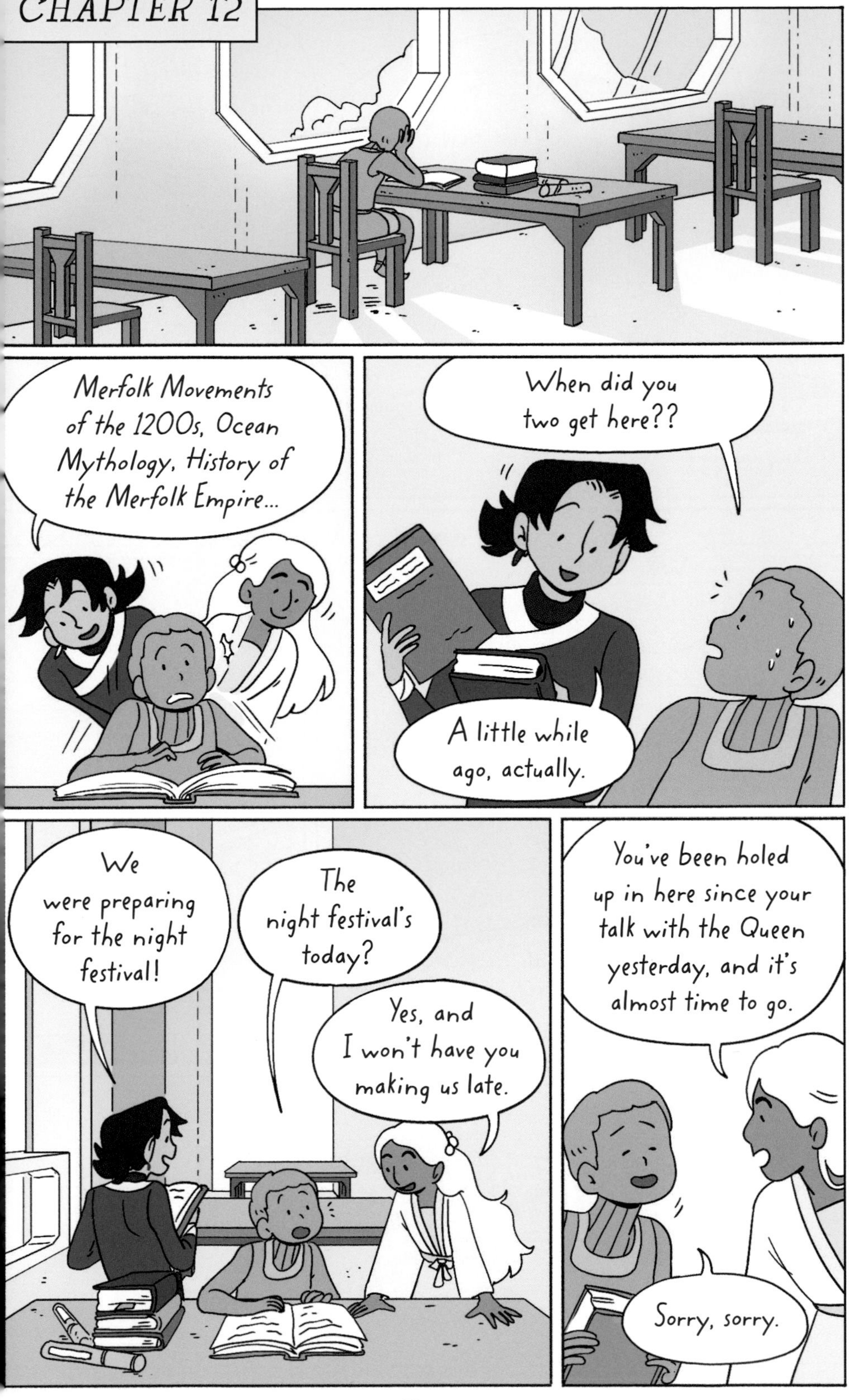

Merfolk Movements of the 1200s, Ocean Mythology, History of the Merfolk Empire...
When did you two get here??
A little while ago, actually.
We were preparing for the night festival!
The night festival's today?
Yes, and I won't have you making us late.
You've been holed up in here since your talk with the Queen yesterday, and it's almost time to go.
Sorry, sorry.

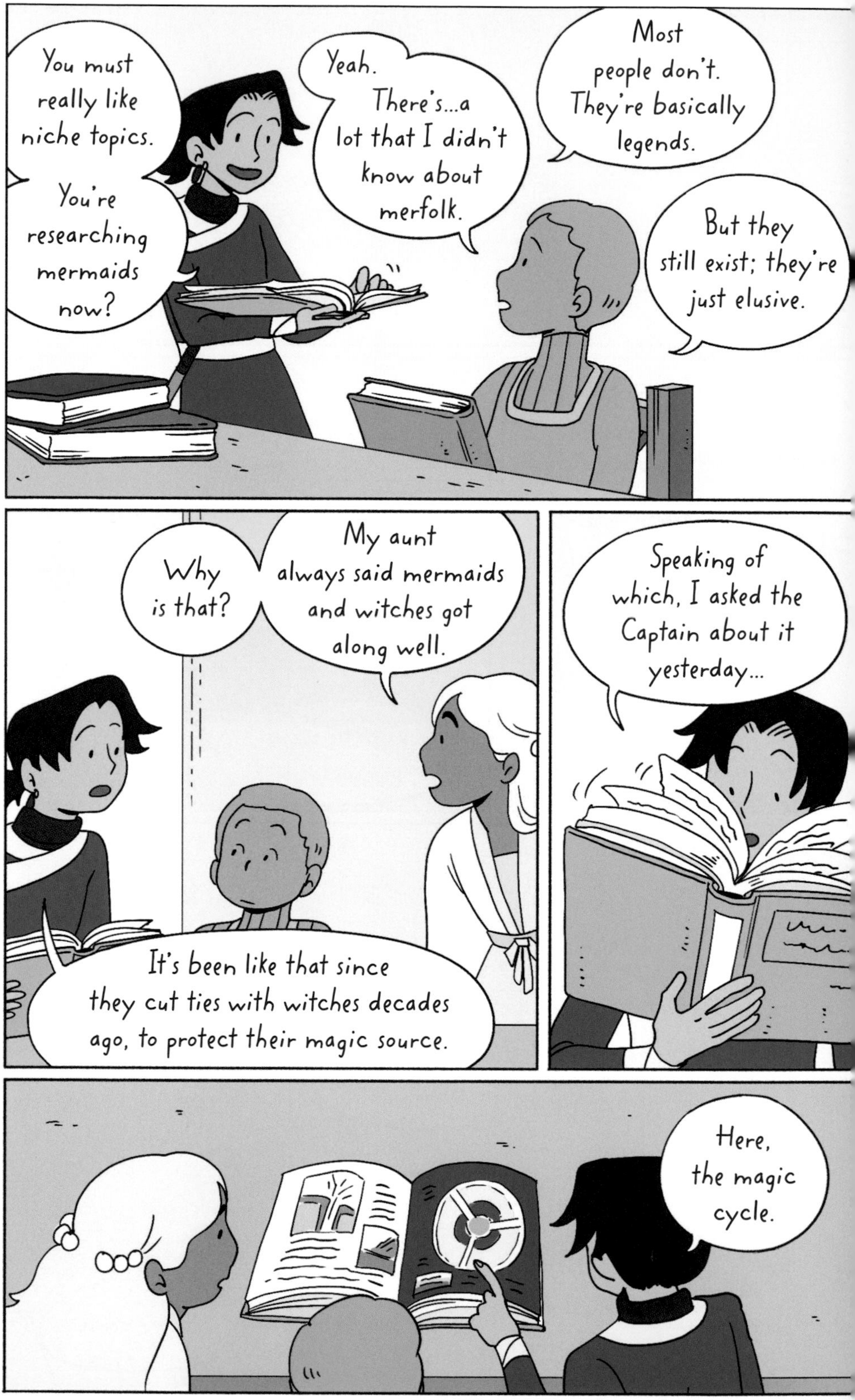
You must really like niche topics.
You're researching mermaids now?
Yeah. There's...a lot that I didn't know about merfolk.
Most people don't. They're basically legends.
But they still exist; they're just elusive.
Why is that?
My aunt always said mermaids and witches got along well.
It's been like that since they cut ties with witches decades ago, to protect their magic source.
Speaking of which, I asked the Captain about it yesterday...
Here, the magic cycle.

There are three magic sources on Earth, one for the witches, one for the merfolk, and one for the firebirds.

Magic is generated in Earth's core, and then it floats up to the surface in the spots we call magic sources.

There, it gets released into the atmosphere and is absorbed by living creatures.

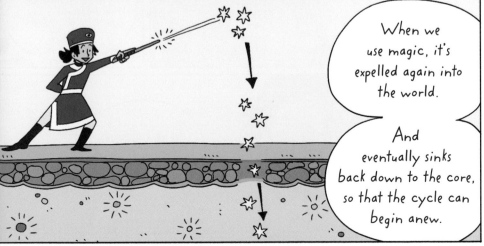

When we use magic, it's expelled again into the world.

And eventually sinks back down to the core, so that the cycle can begin anew.

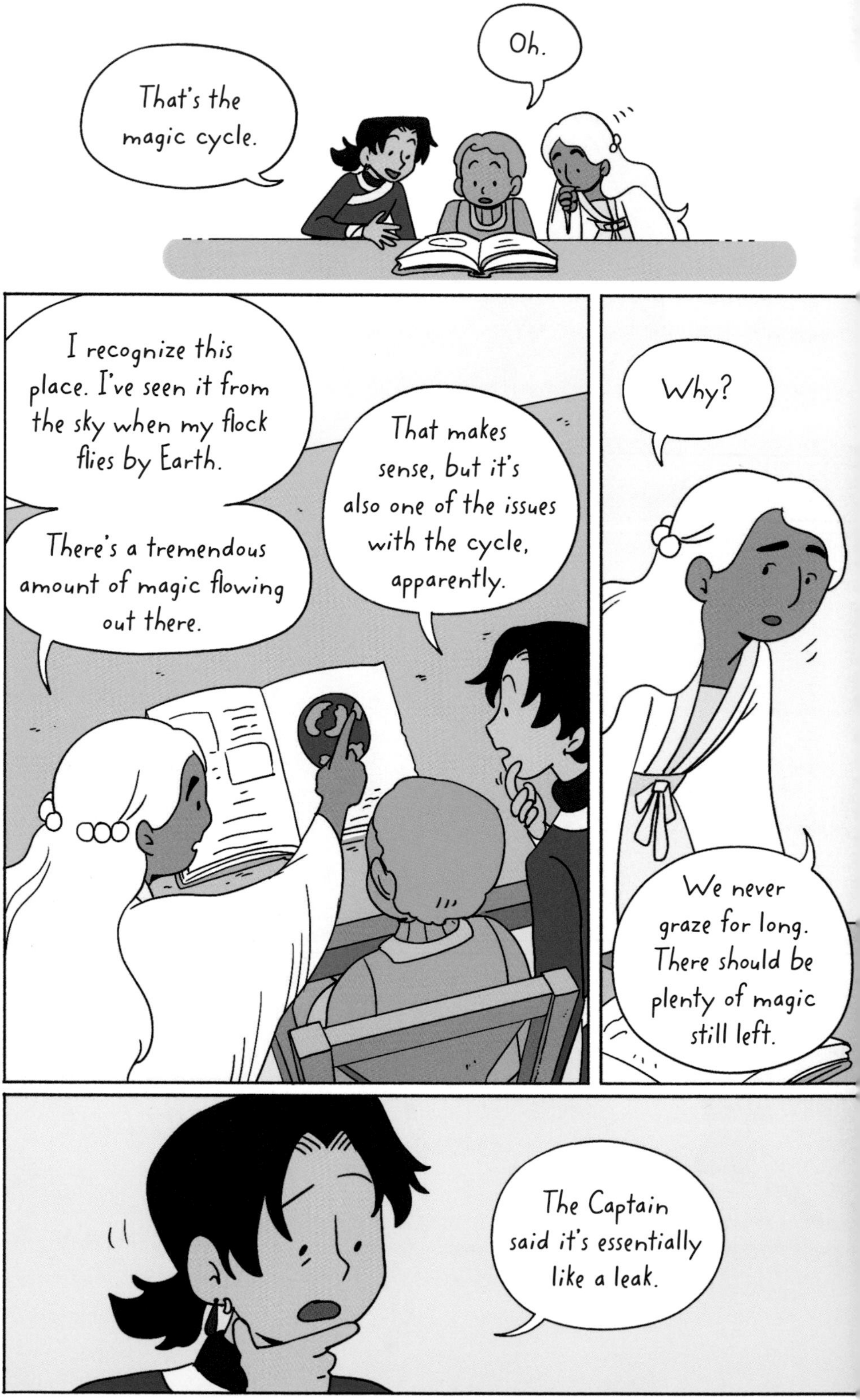
That's the magic cycle.
Oh.
I recognize this place. I've seen it from the sky when my flock flies by Earth.
There's a tremendous amount of magic flowing out there.
That makes sense, but it's also one of the issues with the cycle, apparently.
Why?
We never graze for long. There should be plenty of magic still left.
The Captain said it's essentially like a leak.

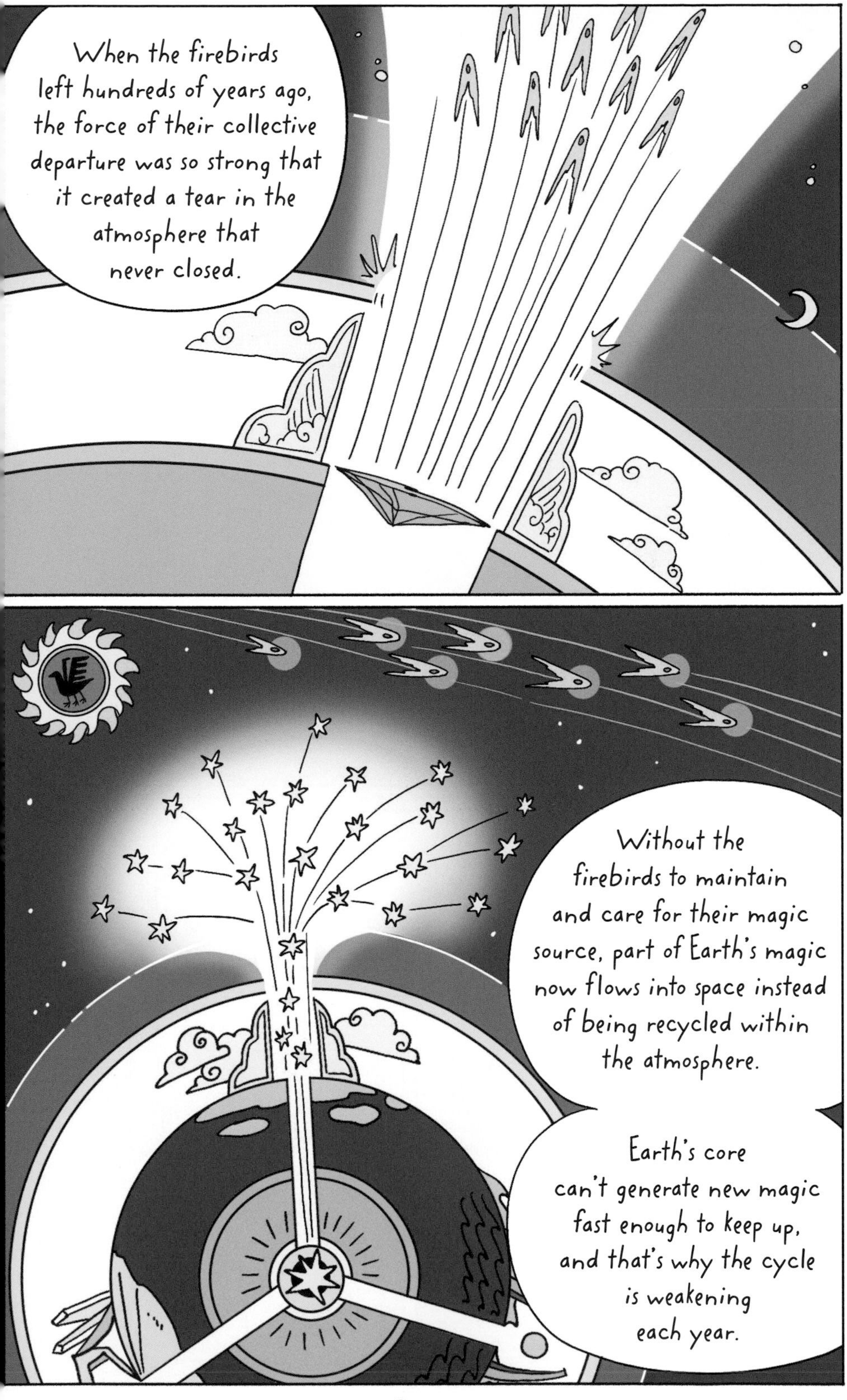
When the firebirds left hundreds of years ago, the force of their collective departure was so strong that it created a tear in the atmosphere that never closed.
Without the firebirds to maintain and care for their magic source, part of Earth's magic now flows into space instead of being recycled within the atmosphere.
Earth's core can't generate new magic fast enough to keep up, and that's why the cycle is weakening each year.

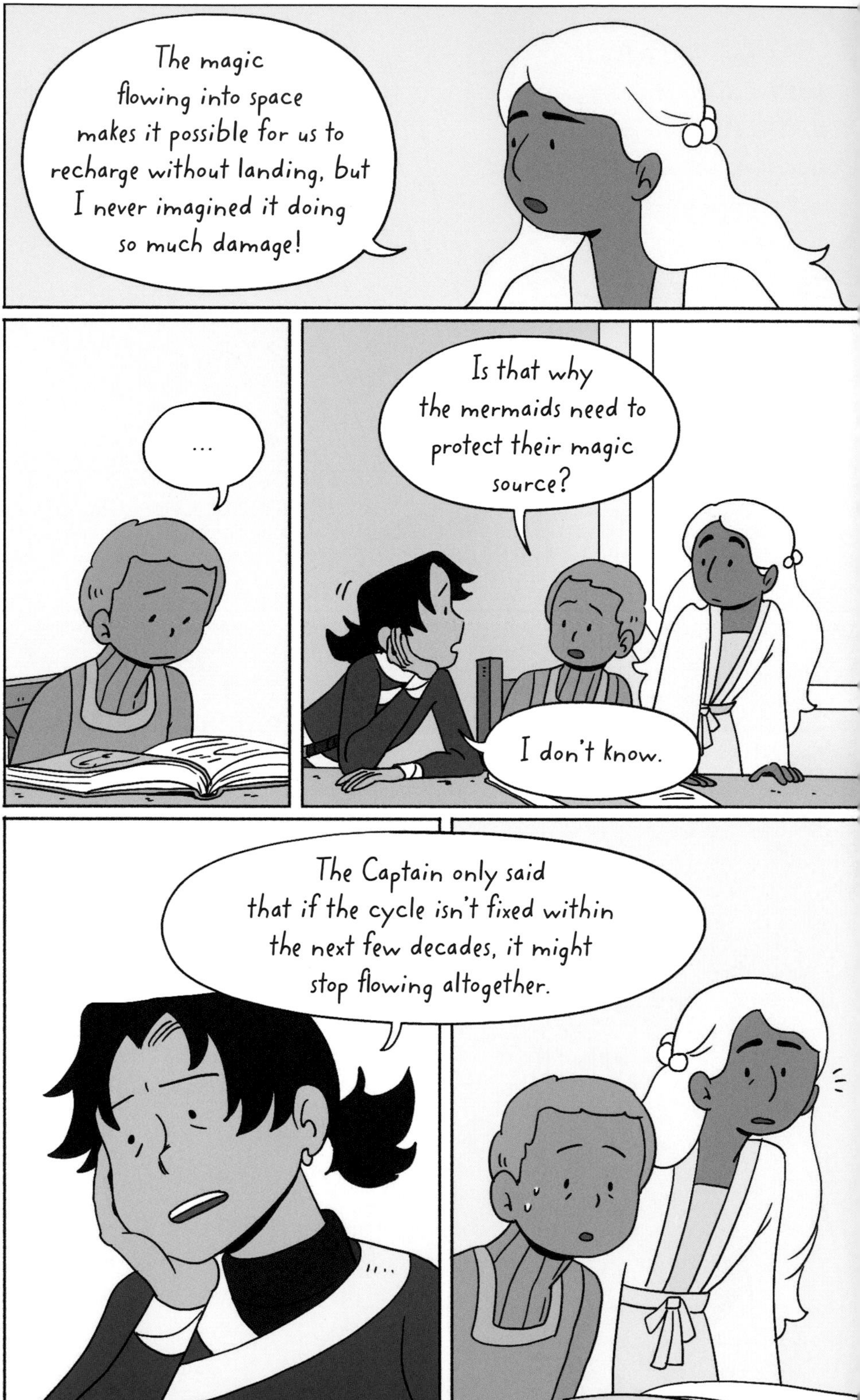
The magic flowing into space makes it possible for us to recharge without landing, but I never imagined it doing so much damage!
...
Is that why the mermaids need to protect their magic source?
I don't know.
The Captain only said that if the cycle isn't fixed within the next few decades, it might stop flowing altogether.

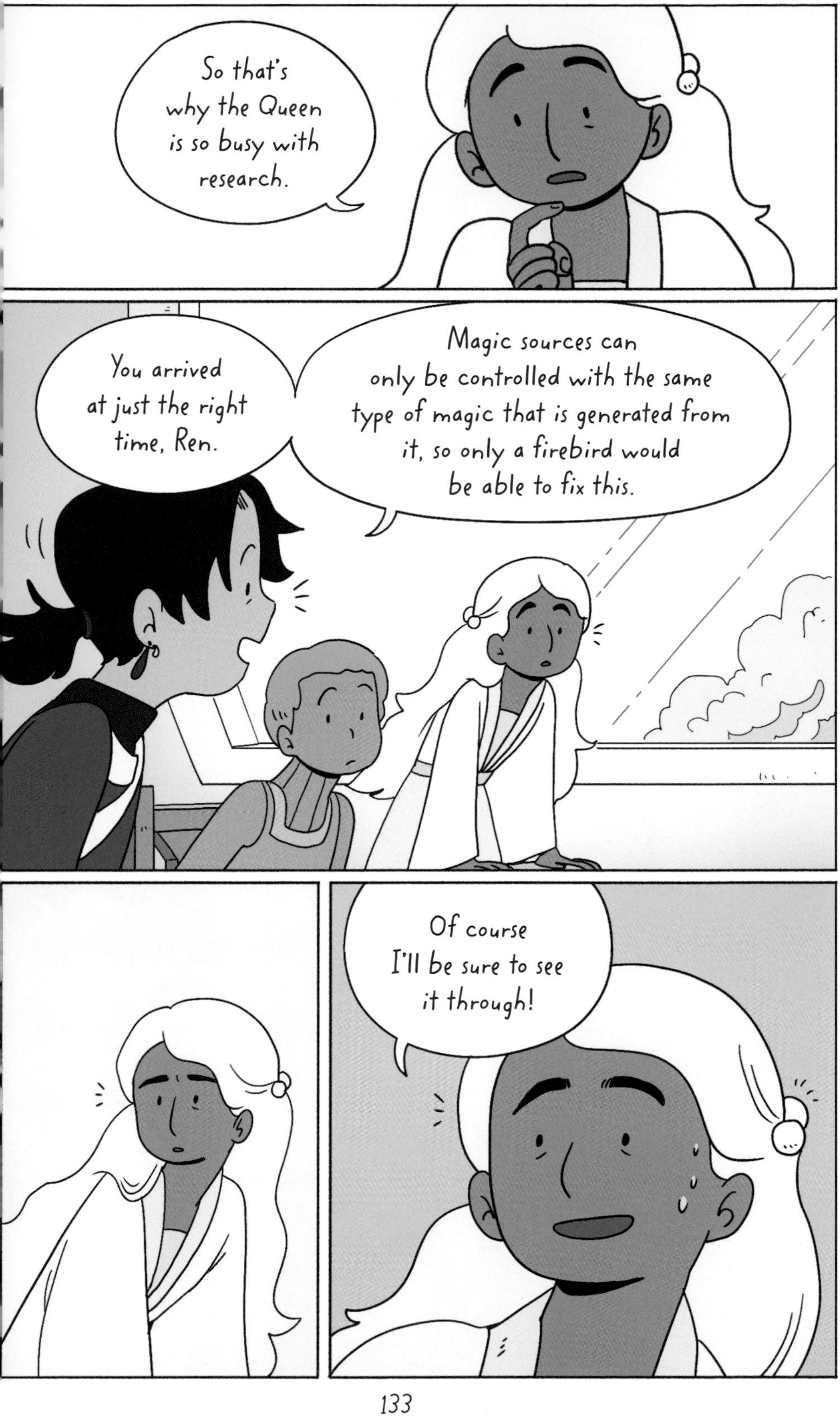
So that's why the Queen is so busy with research.
You arrived at just the right time, Ren.
Magic sources can only be controlled with the same type of magic that is generated from it, so only a firebird would be able to fix this.
Of course I'll be sure to see it through!

CHAPTER 13

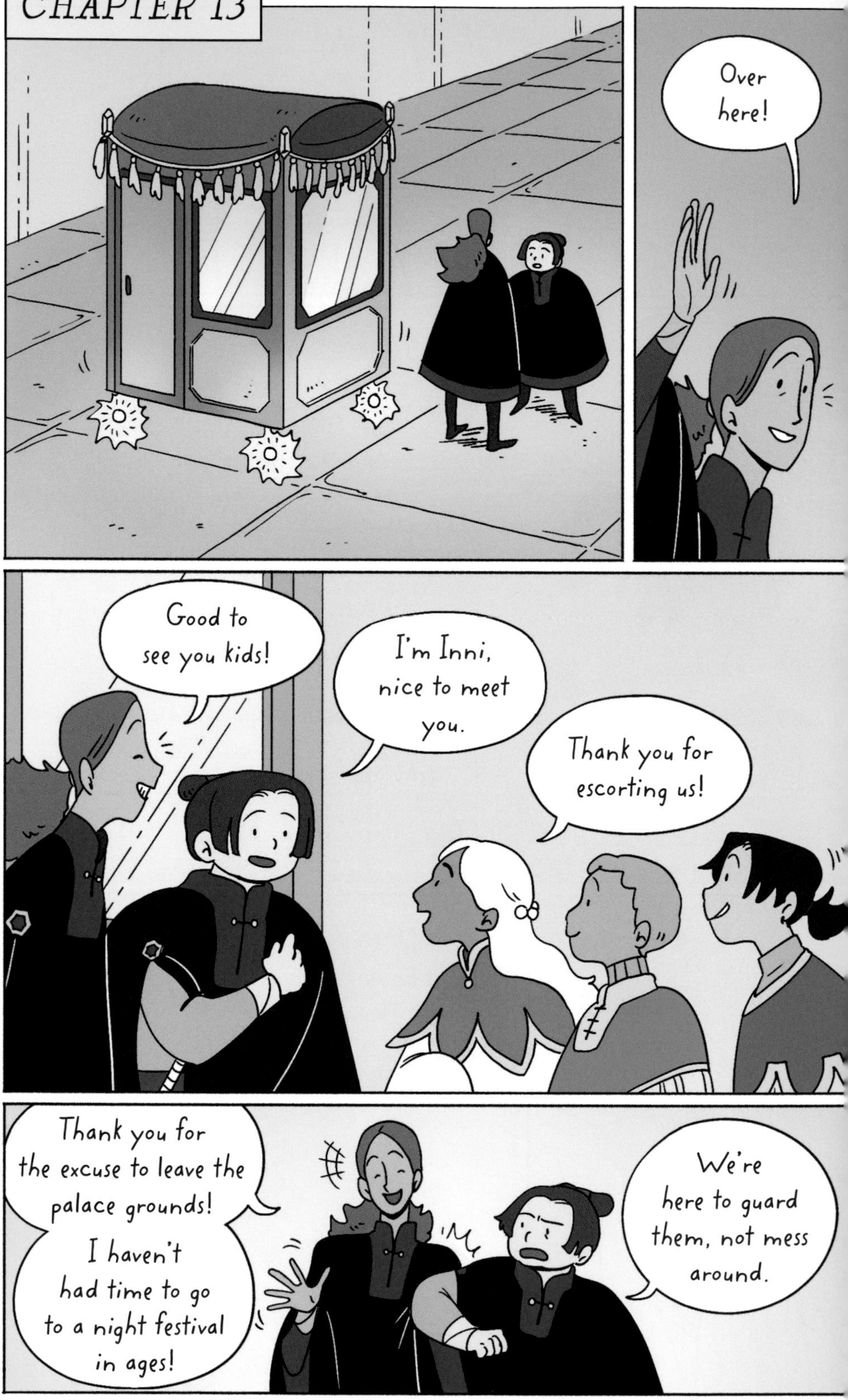
Over here!
Good to see you kids!
I'm Inni, nice to meet you.
Thank you for escorting us!
Thank you for the excuse to leave the palace grounds!
I haven't had time to go to a night festival in ages!
We're here to guard them, not mess around.

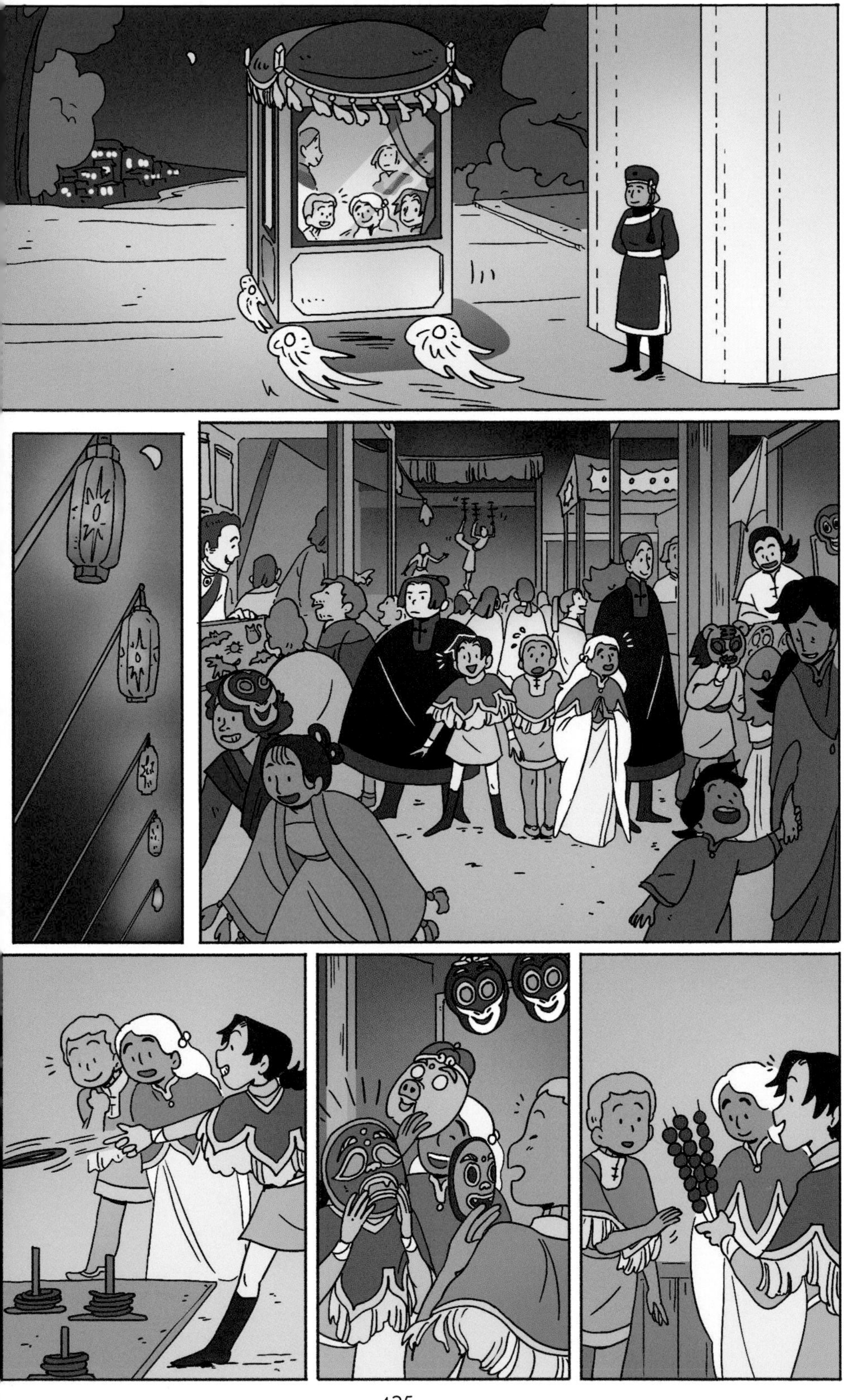

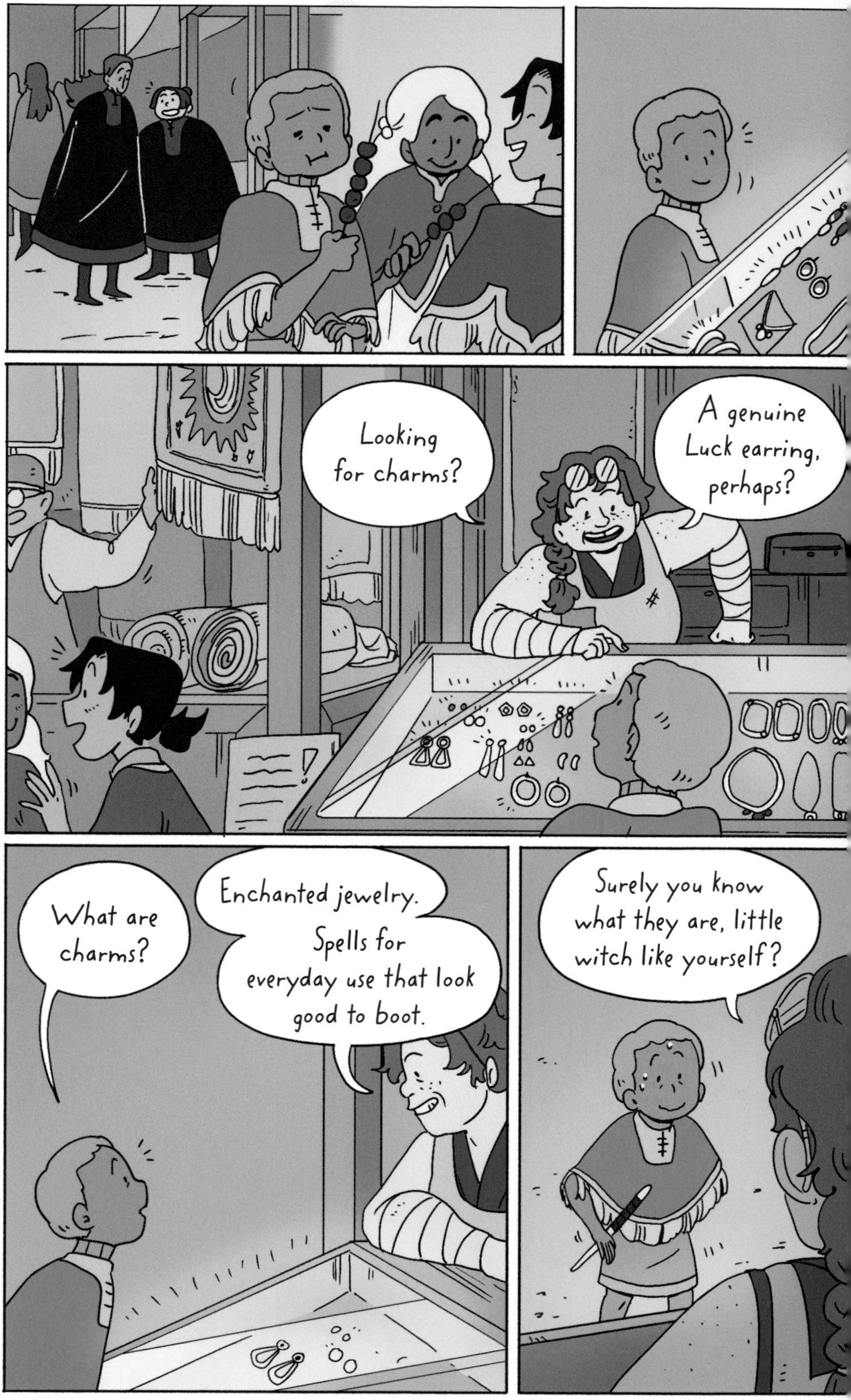
Looking for charms?
A genuine Luck earring, perhaps?
What are charms?
Enchanted jewelry.
Spells for everyday use that look good to boot.
Surely you know what they are, little witch like yourself?

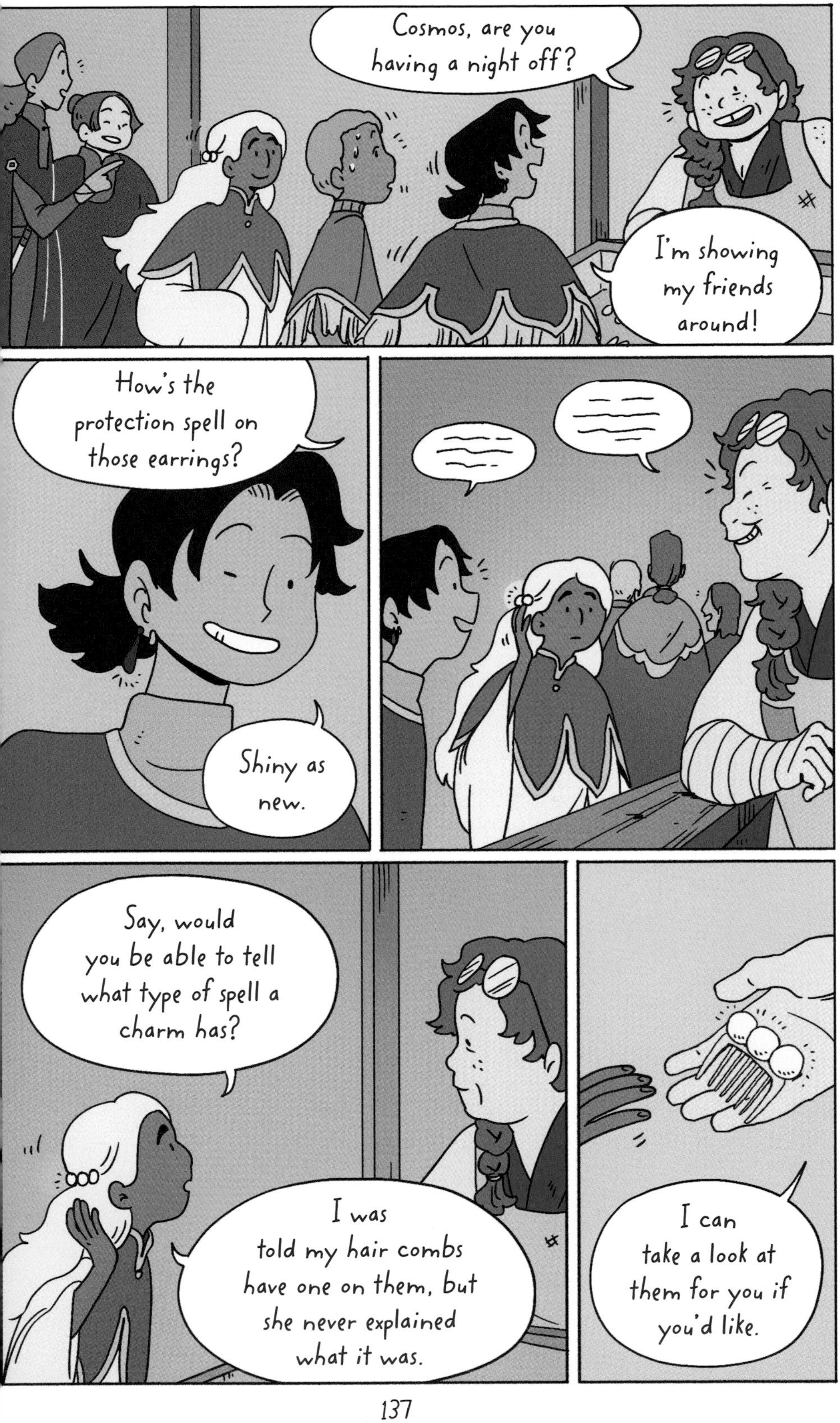
Cosmos, are you having a night off?
I'm showing my friends around!
How's the protection spell on those earrings?
Shiny as new.
Say, would you be able to tell what type of spell a charm has?
I was told my hair combs have one on them, but she never explained what it was.
I can take a look at them for you if you'd like.

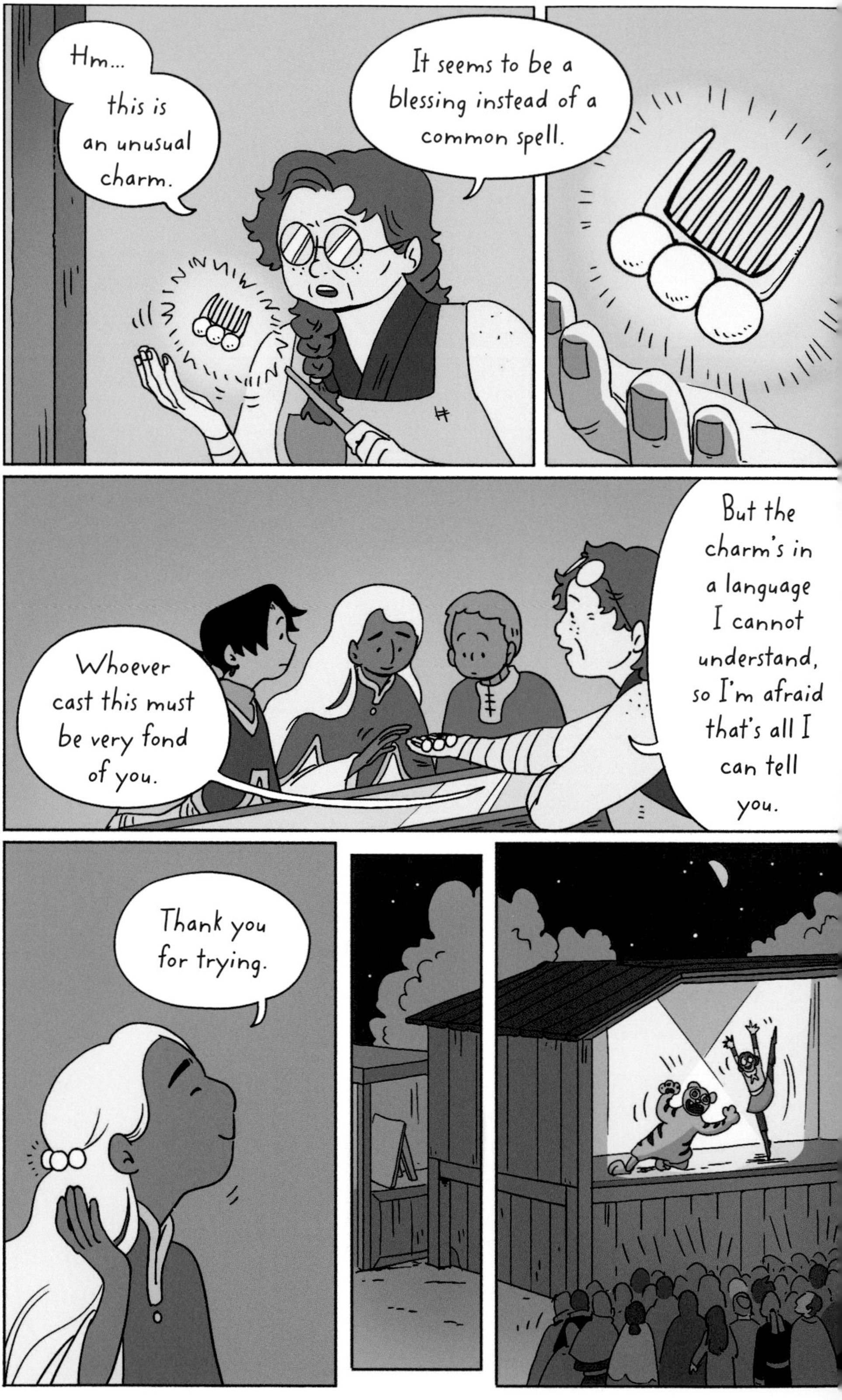
Hm... this is an unusual charm.
It seems to be a blessing instead of a common spell.
But the charm's in a language I cannot understand, so I'm afraid that's all I can tell you.
Whoever cast this must be very fond of you.
Thank you for trying.

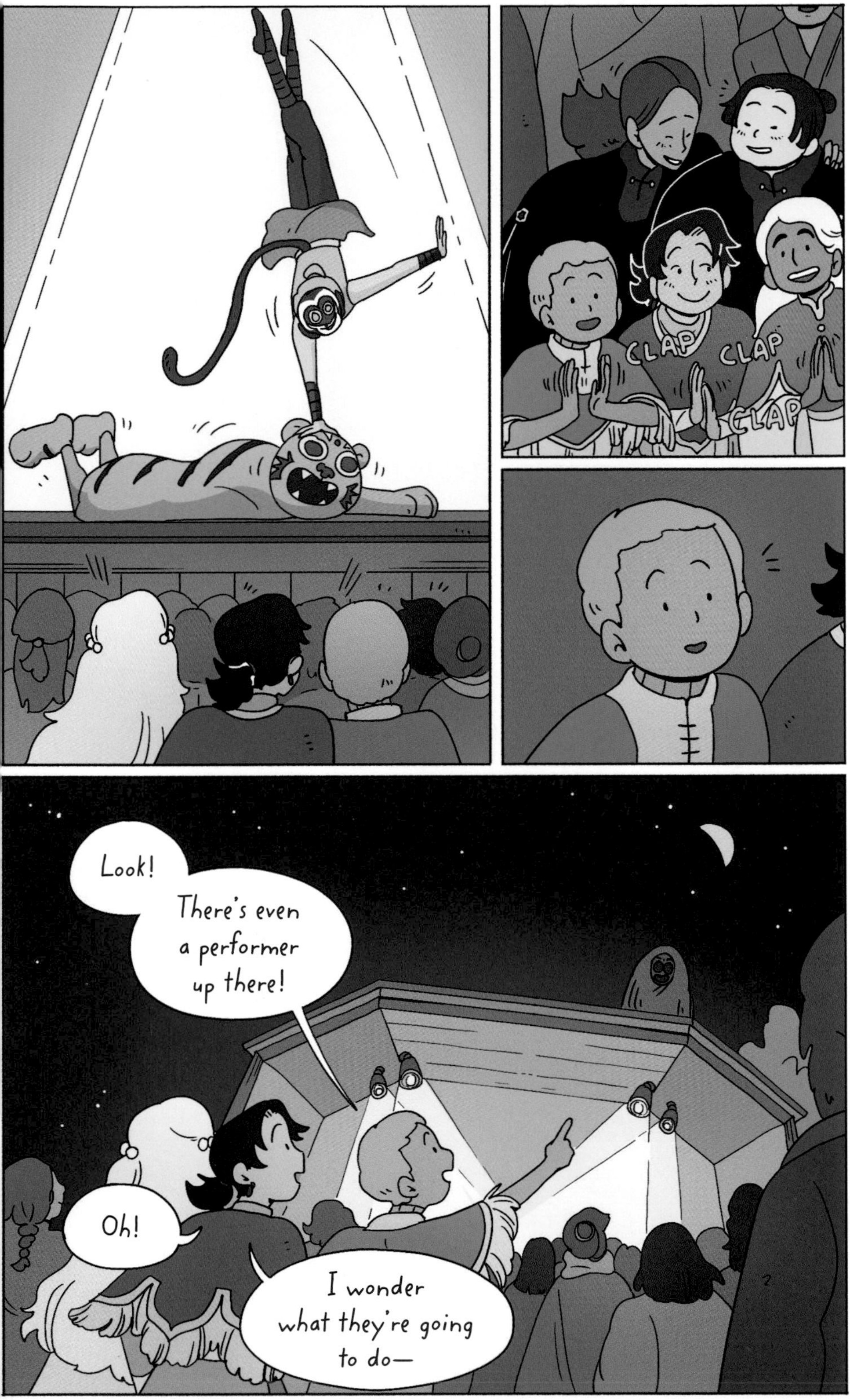
CLAP
CLAP
CLAP
Look!
There's even a performer up there!
Oh!
I wonder what they're going to do—

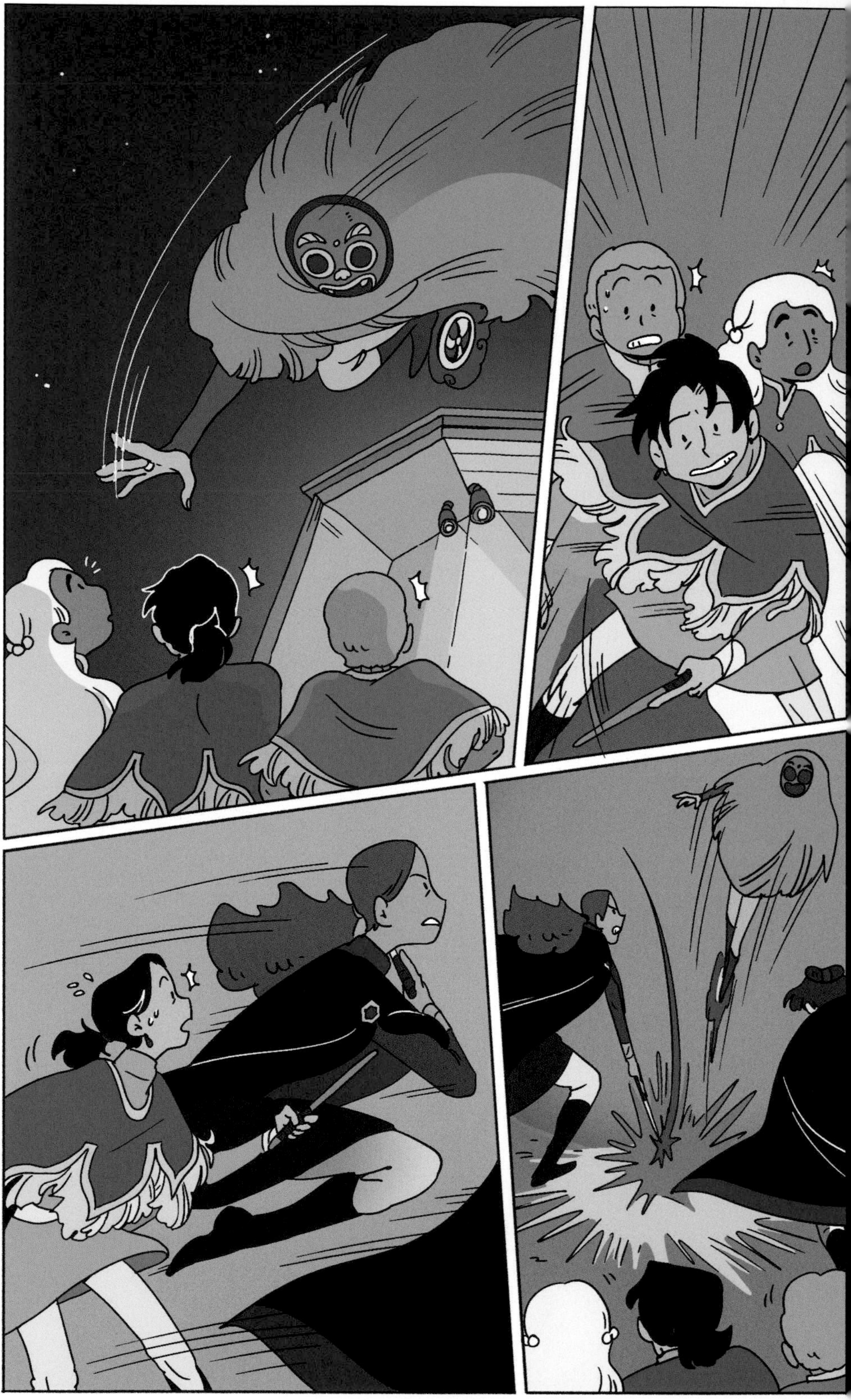

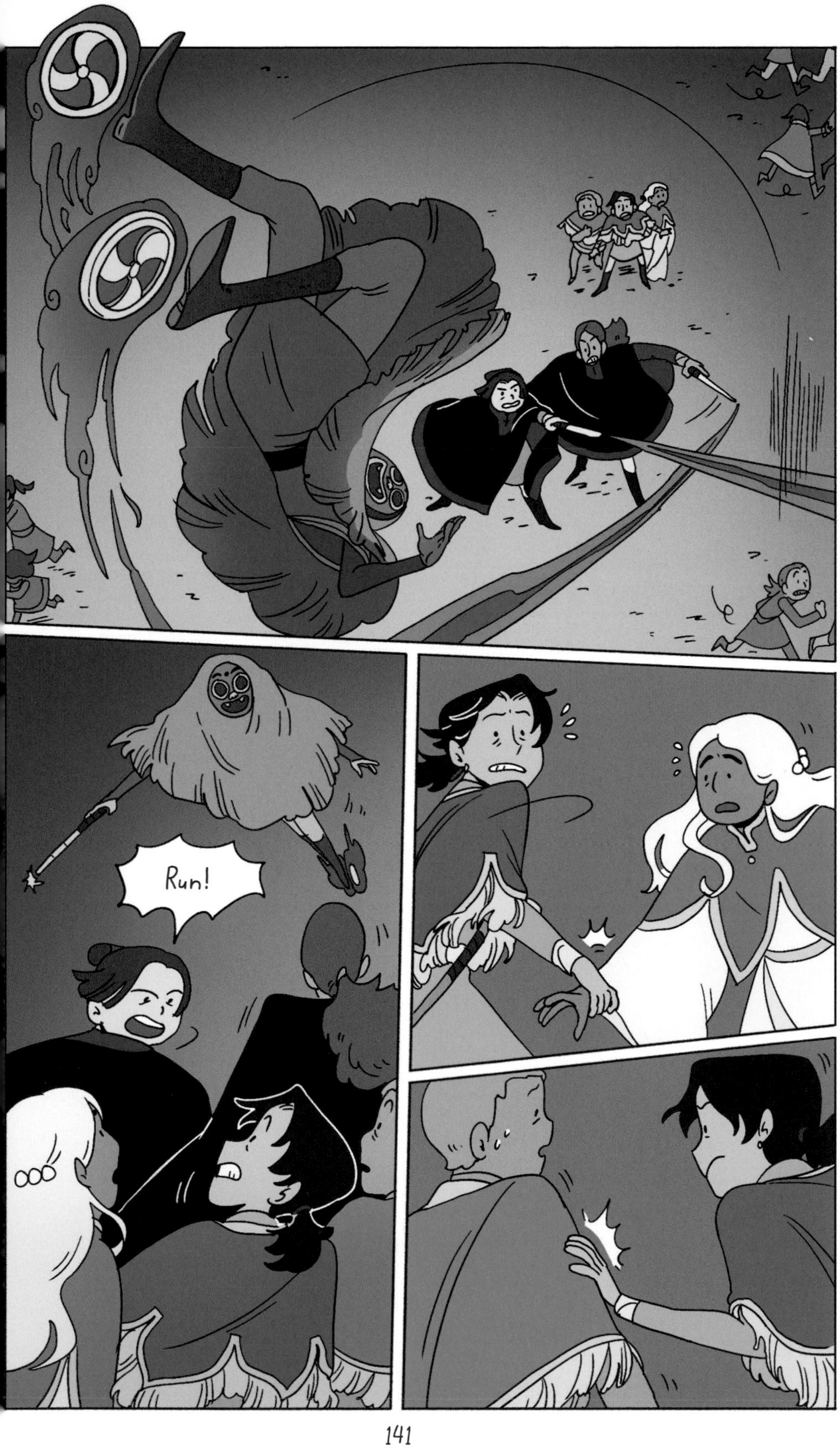
Run!

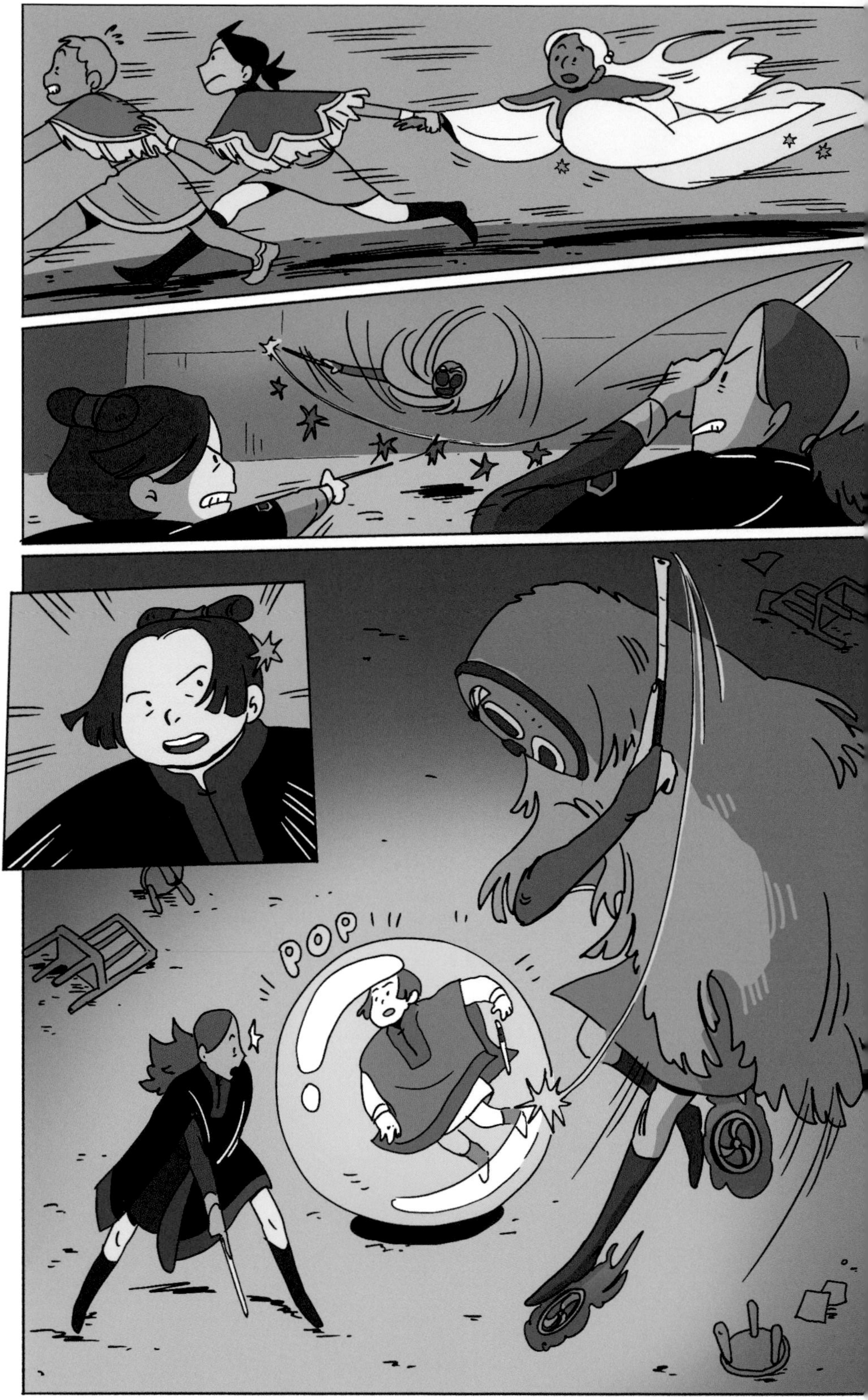
POP

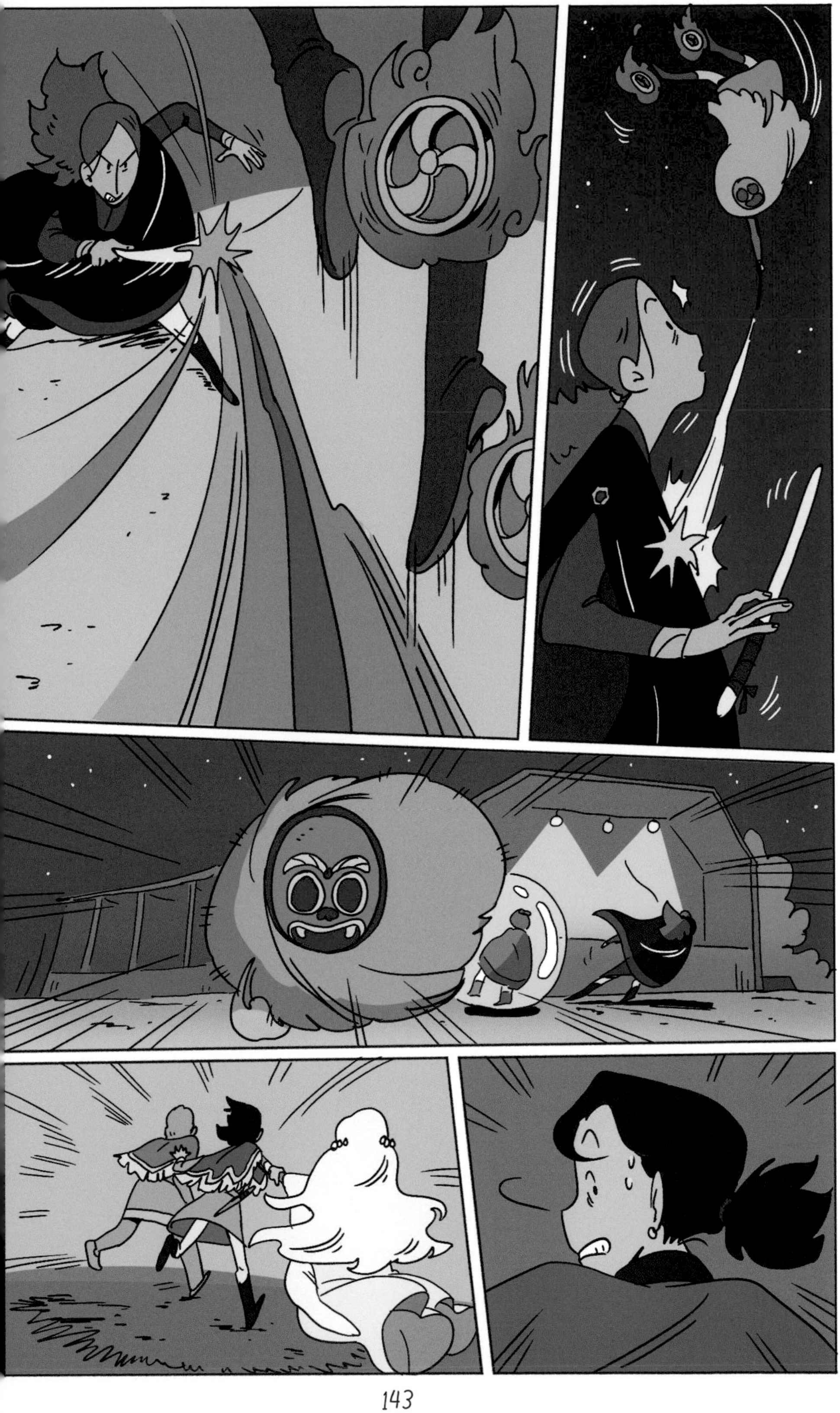

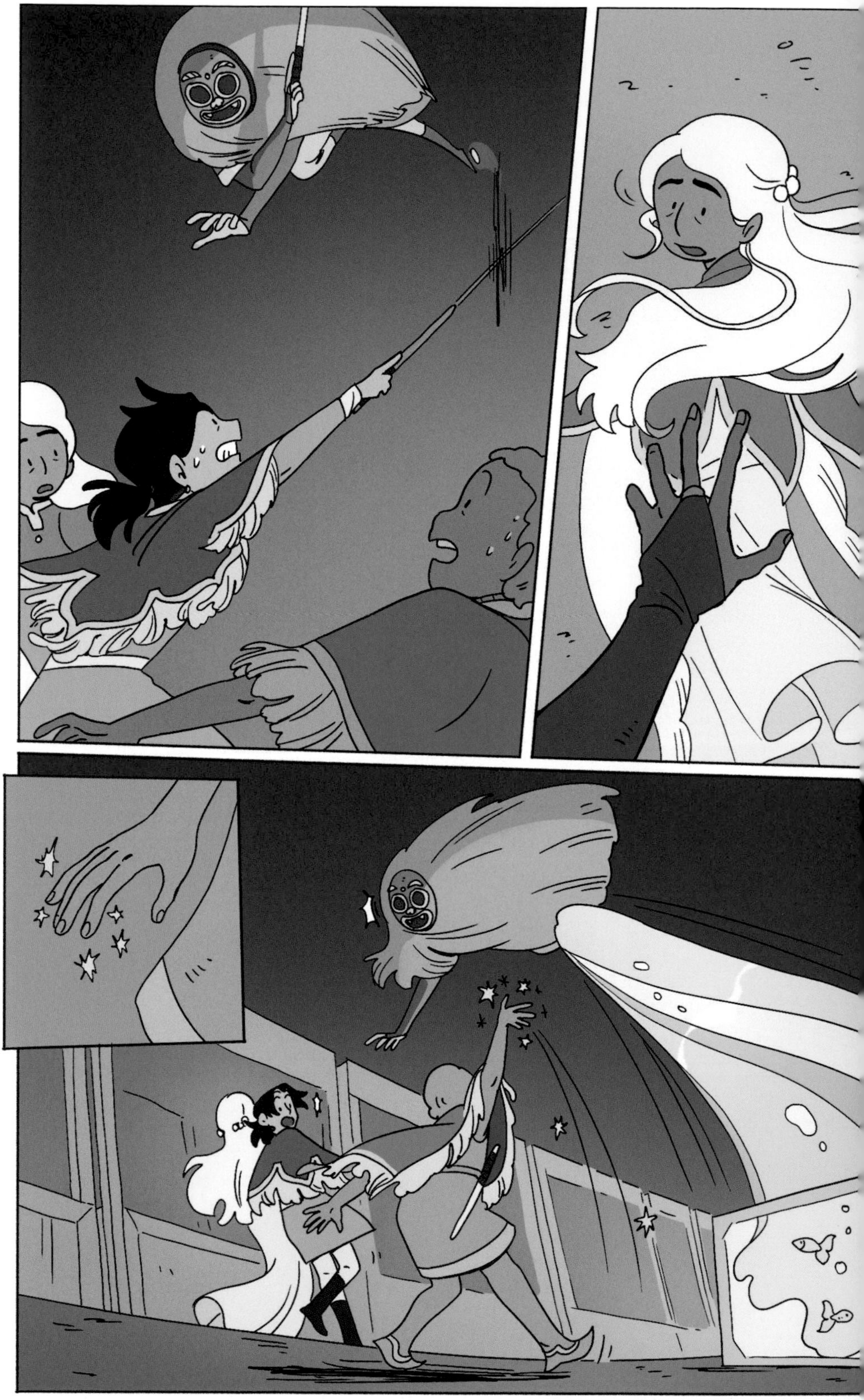

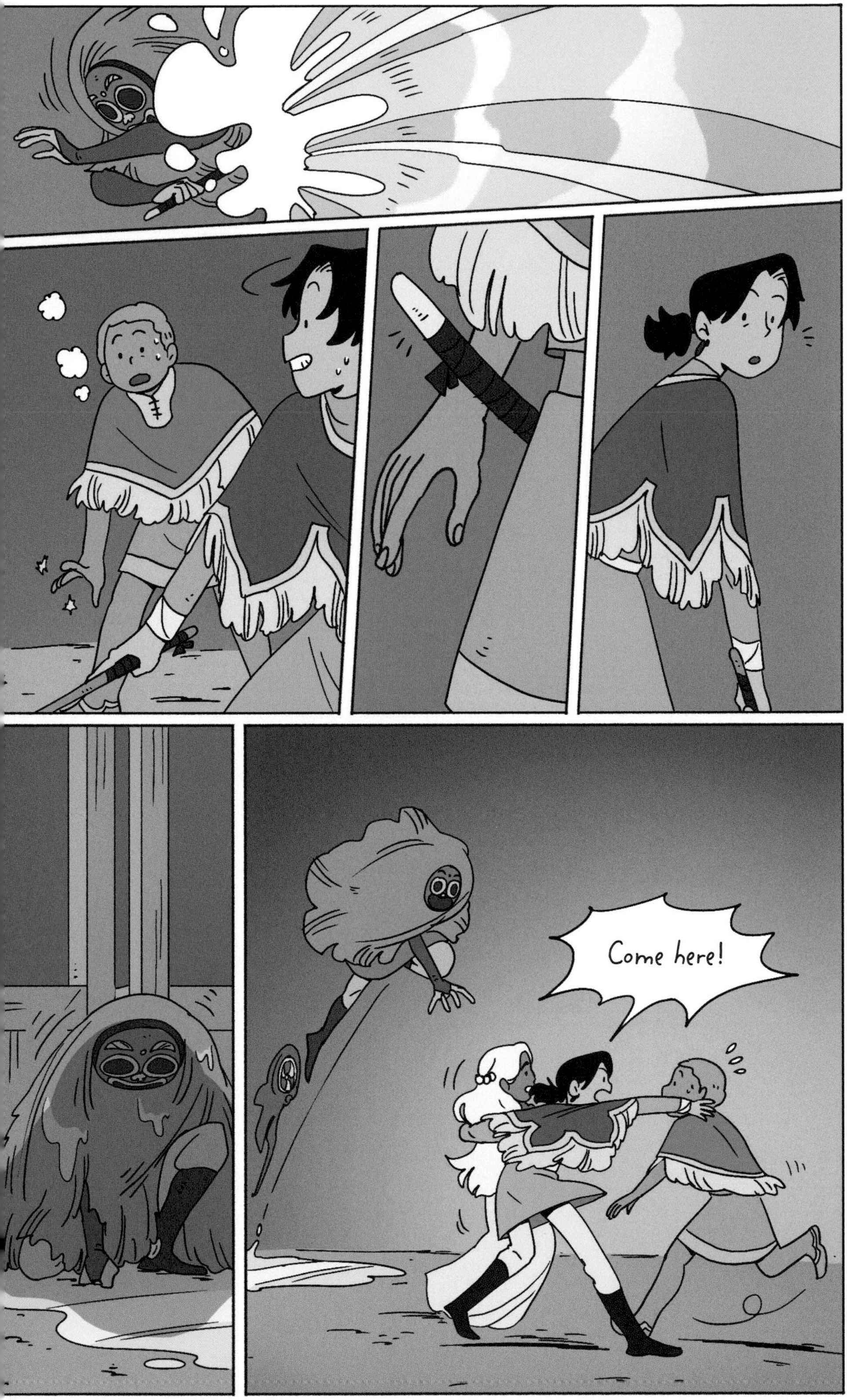
Come here!

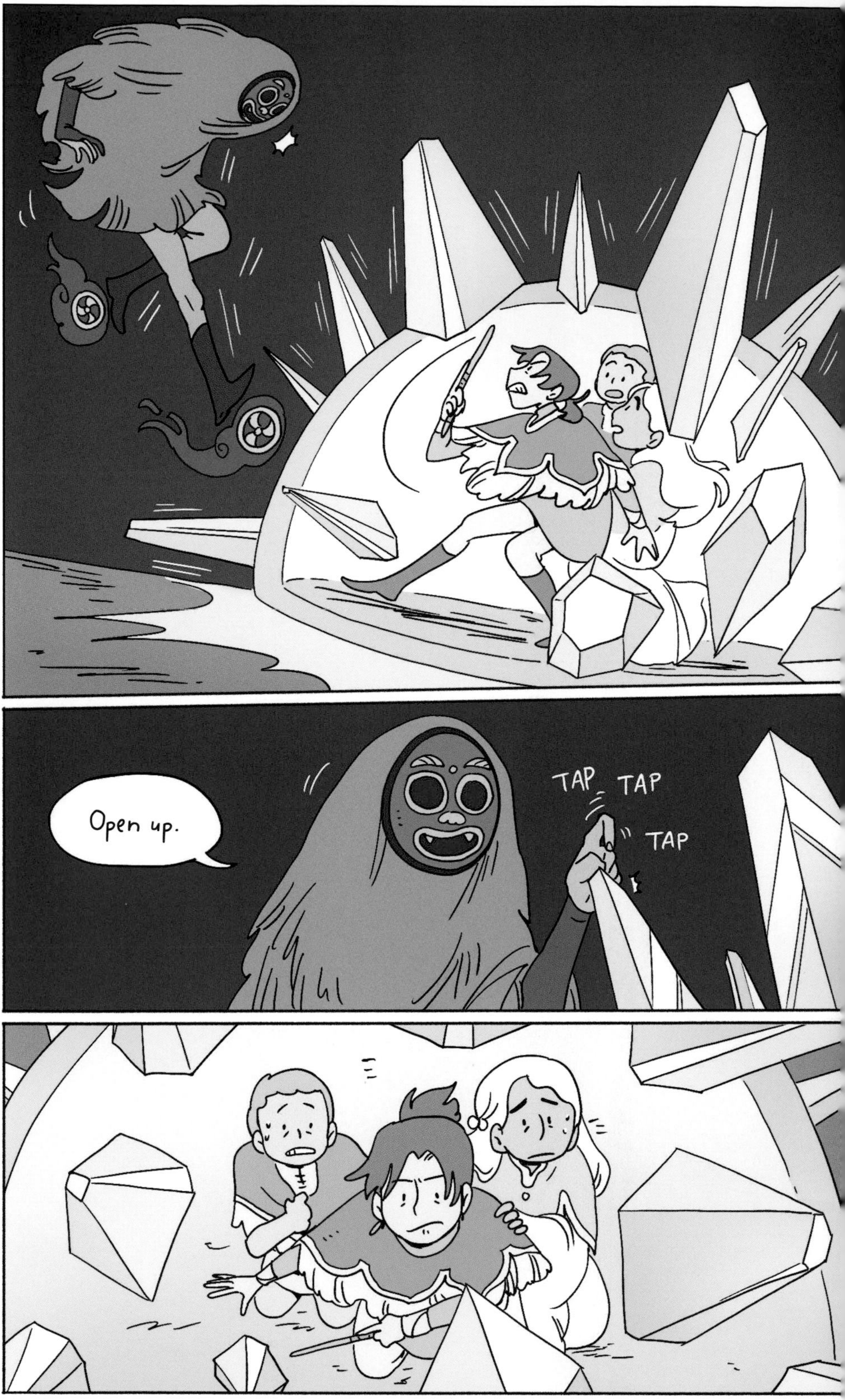
Open up.
TAP TAP
TAP

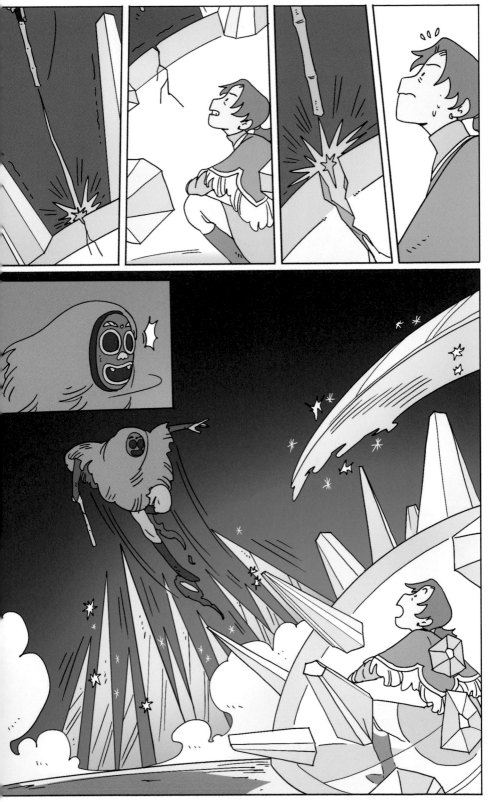

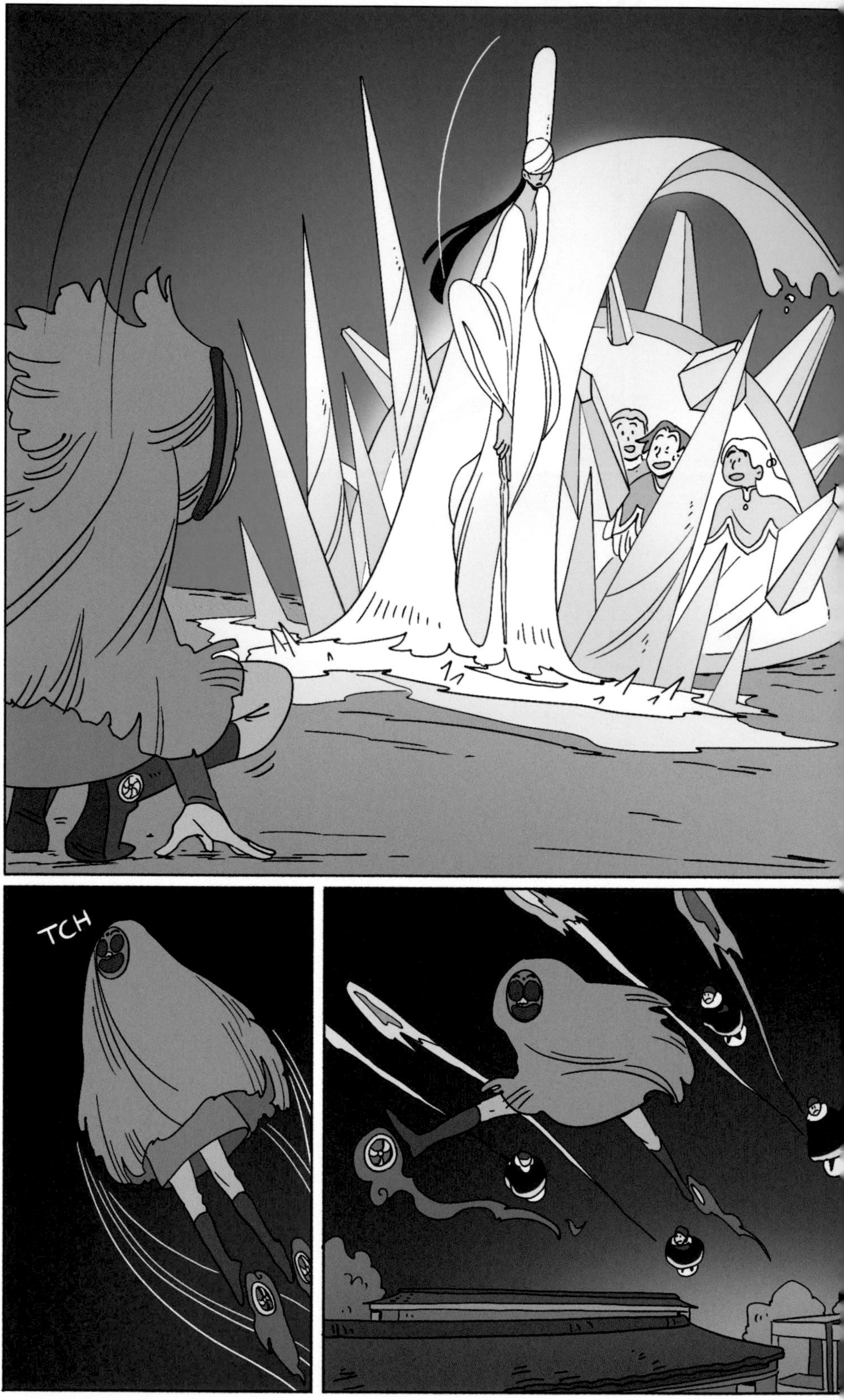
TCH

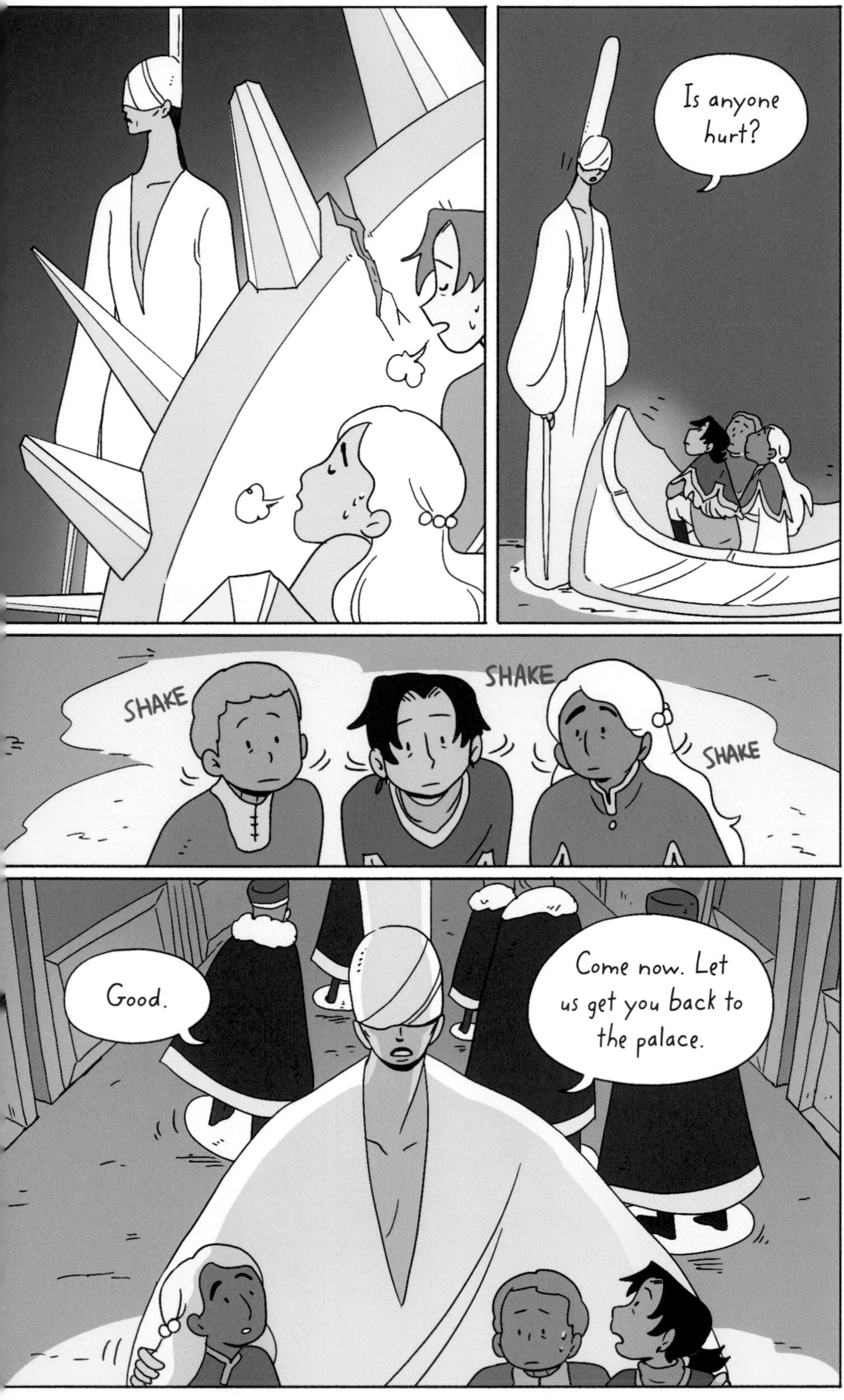
Is anyone hurt?
SHAKE
SHAKE
SHAKE
Good.
Come now. Let us get you back to the palace.

CHAPTER 14

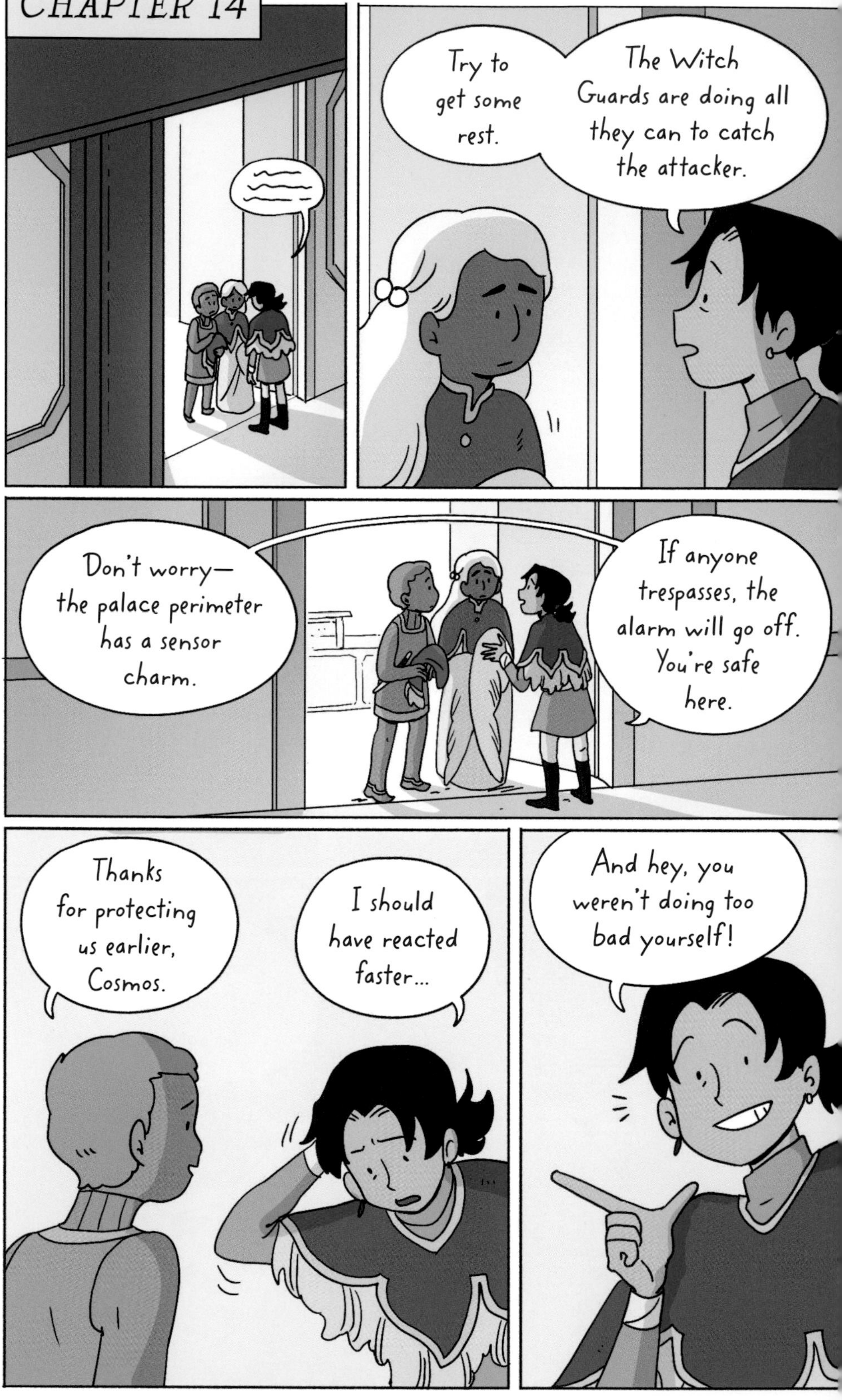
Try to get some rest.
The Witch Guards are doing all they can to catch the attacker.
Don't worry— the palace perimeter has a sensor charm.
If anyone trespasses, the alarm will go off. You're safe here.
Thanks for protecting us earlier, Cosmos.
I should have reacted faster...
And hey, you weren't doing too bad yourself!

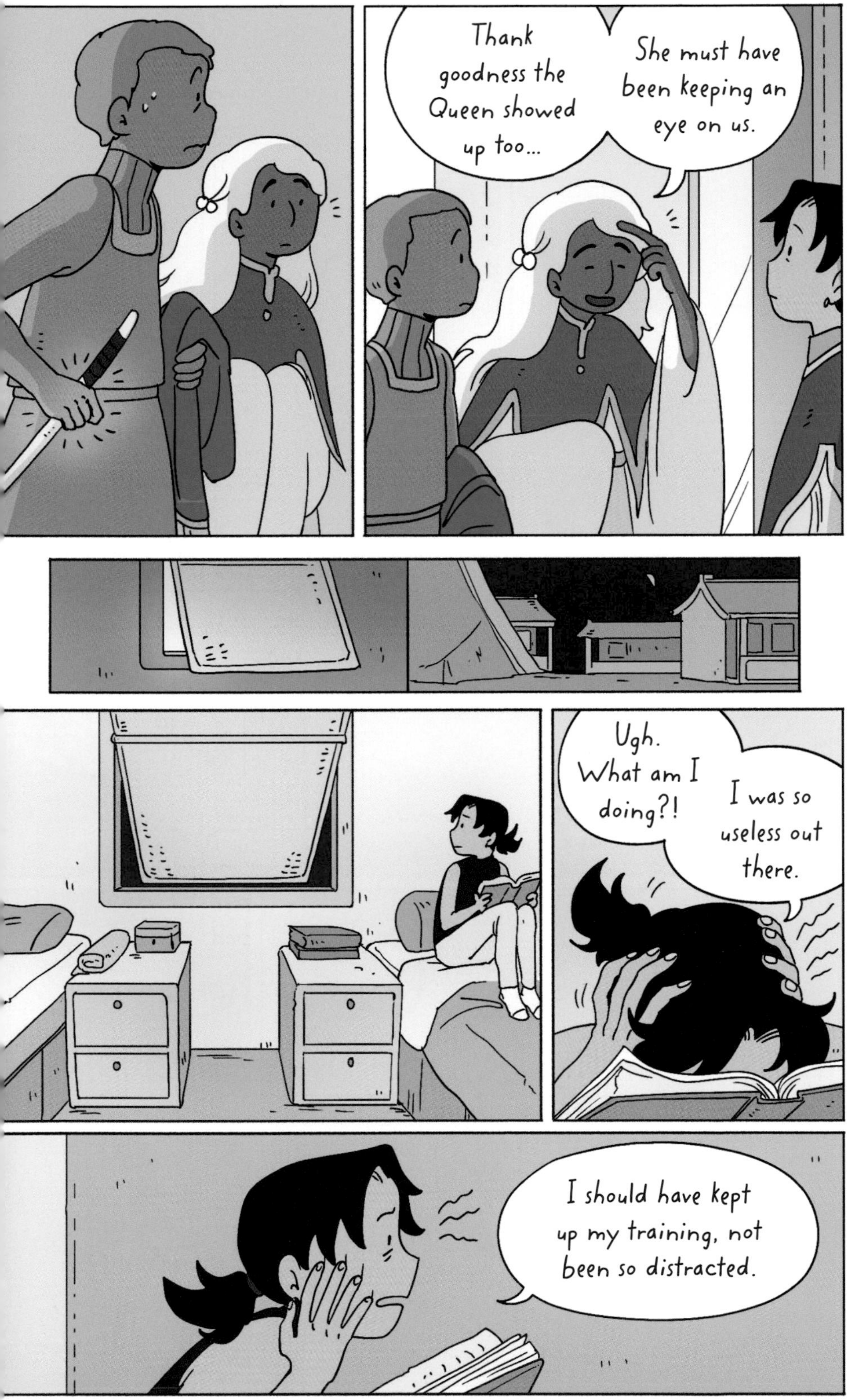
Thank goodness the Queen showed up too...
She must have been keeping an eye on us.
Ugh. What am I doing?!
I was so useless out there.
I should have kept up my training, not been so distracted.

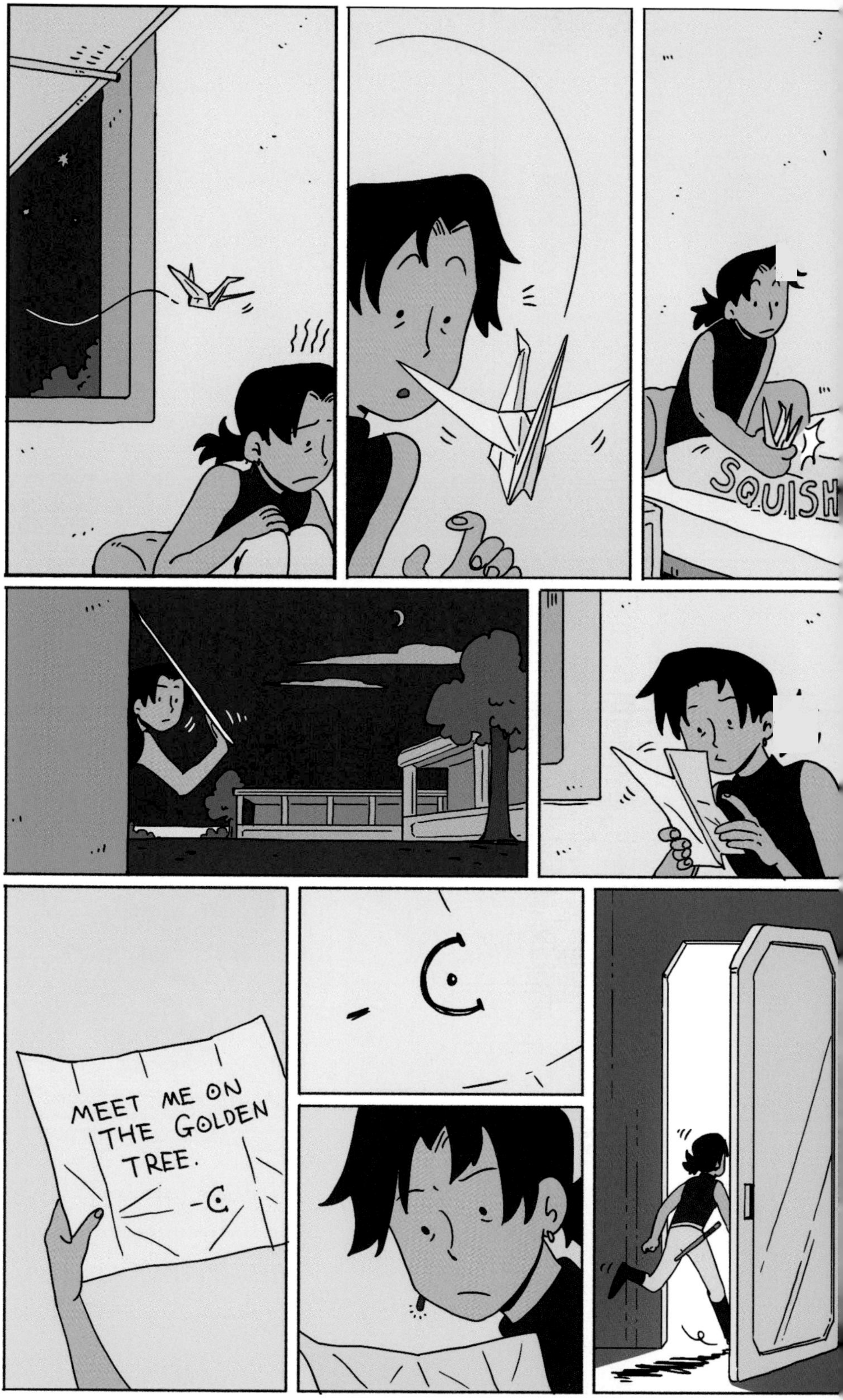
SQUISH
MEET ME ON
THE GOLDEN
TREE.
-C
-C

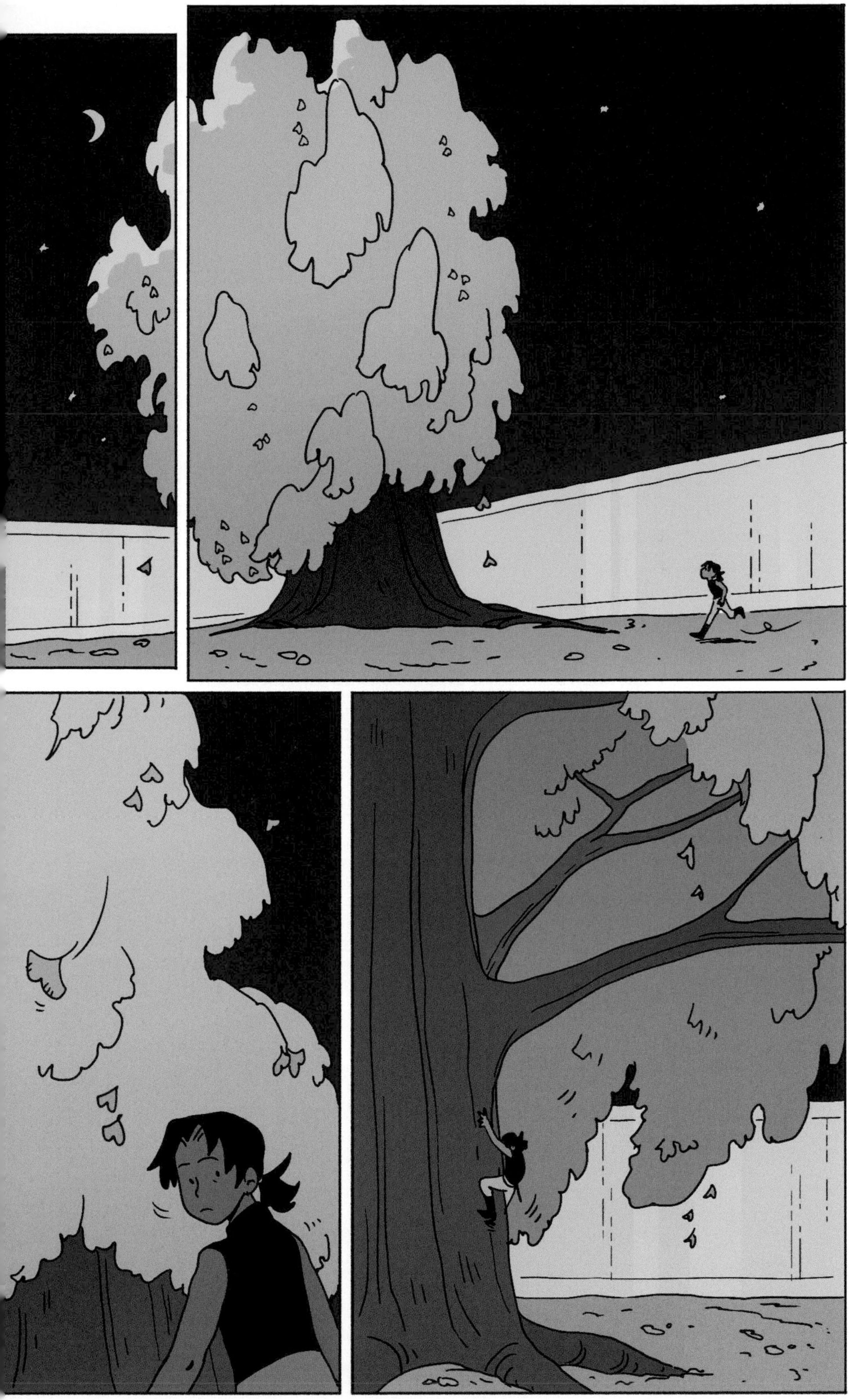

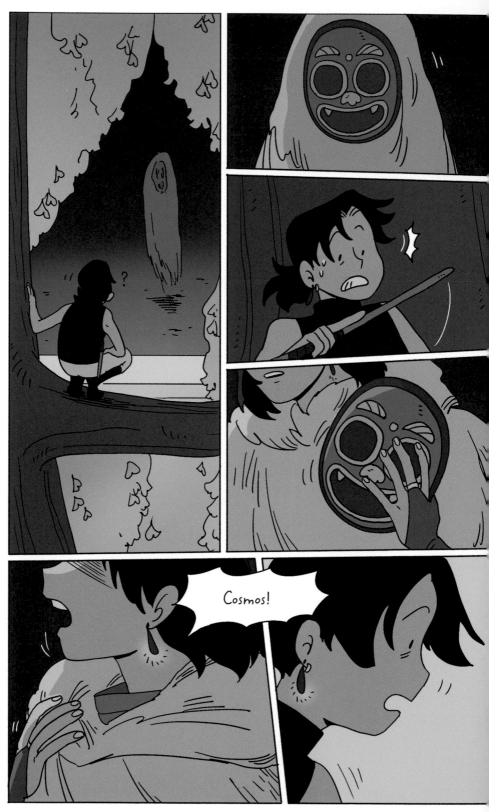

Cosmos!

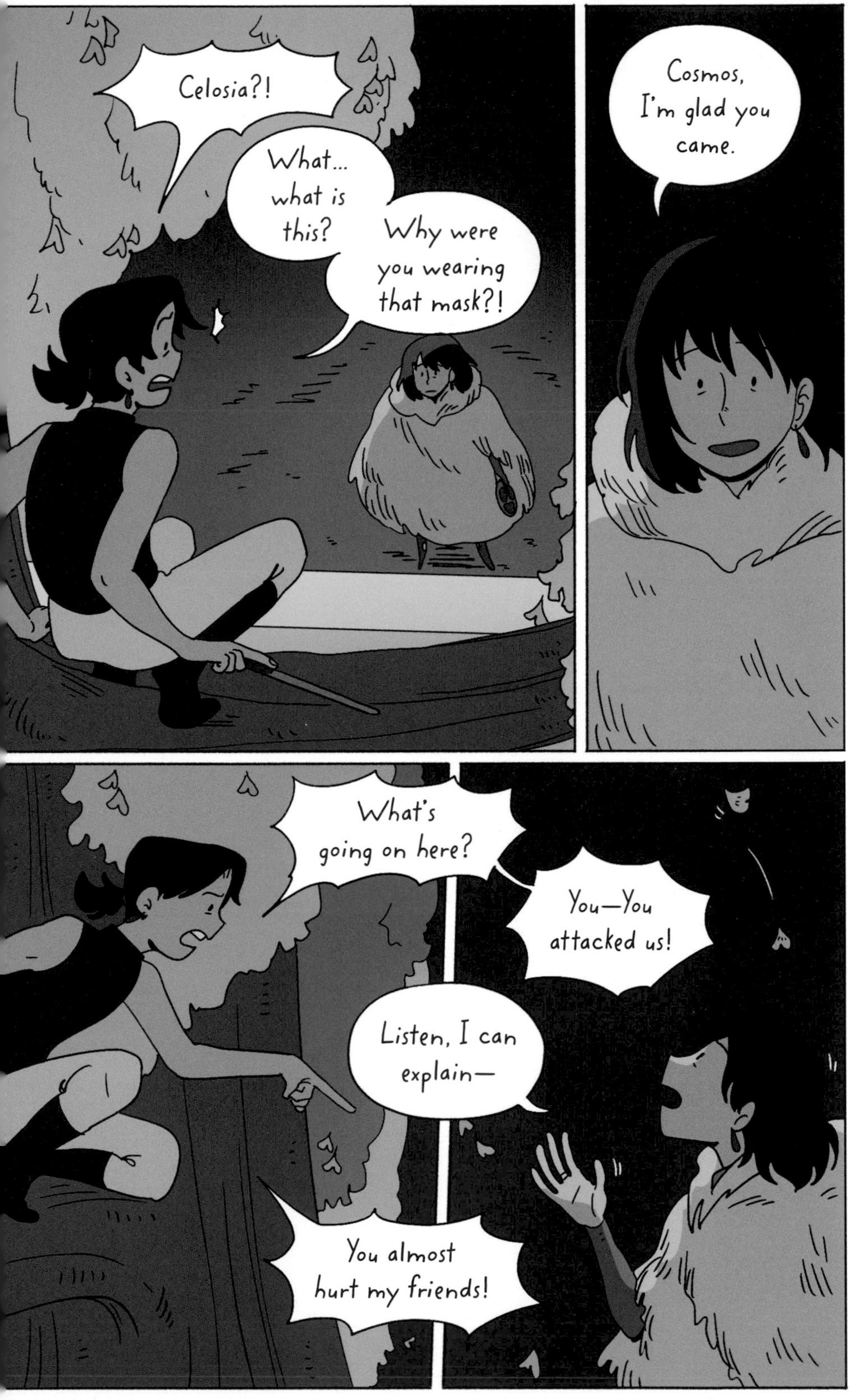
Celosia?!
What... what is this?
Why were you wearing that mask?!
Cosmos, I'm glad you came.
What's going on here?
You—You attacked us!
Listen, I can explain—
You almost hurt my friends!

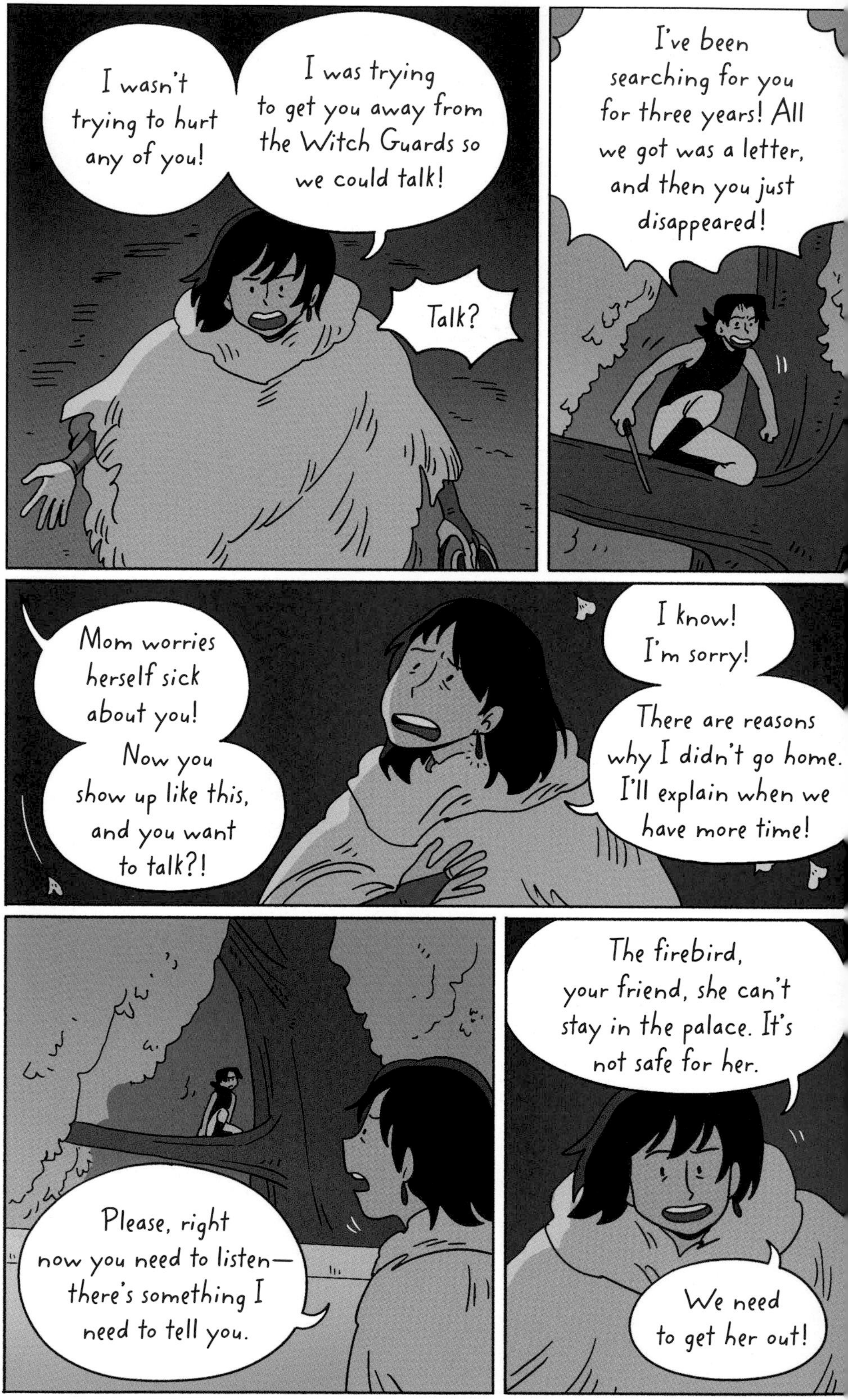
I wasn't trying to hurt any of you!
I was trying to get you away from the Witch Guards so we could talk!
Talk?
I've been searching for you for three years! All we got was a letter, and then you just disappeared!
Mom worries herself sick about you!
Now you show up like this, and you want to talk?!
I know! I'm sorry!
There are reasons why I didn't go home. I'll explain when we have more time!
Please, right now you need to listen— there's something I need to tell you.
The firebird, your friend, she can't stay in the palace. It's not safe for her.
We need to get her out!

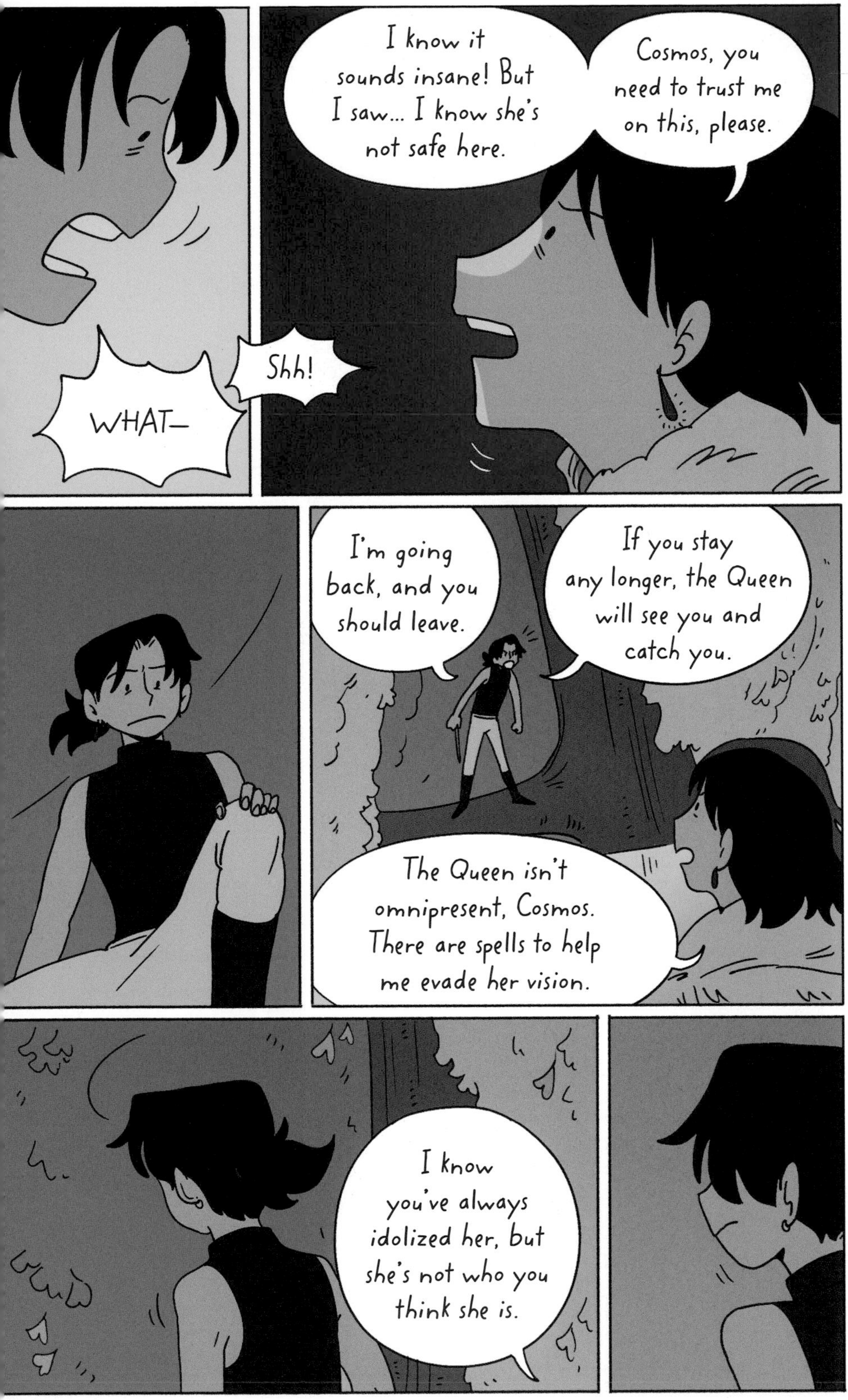
WHAT—
Shh!
I know it sounds insane! But I saw... I know she's not safe here.
Cosmos, you need to trust me on this, please.
I'm going back, and you should leave.
If you stay any longer, the Queen will see you and catch you.
The Queen isn't omnipresent, Cosmos. There are spells to help me evade her vision.
I know you've always idolized her, but she's not who you think she is.

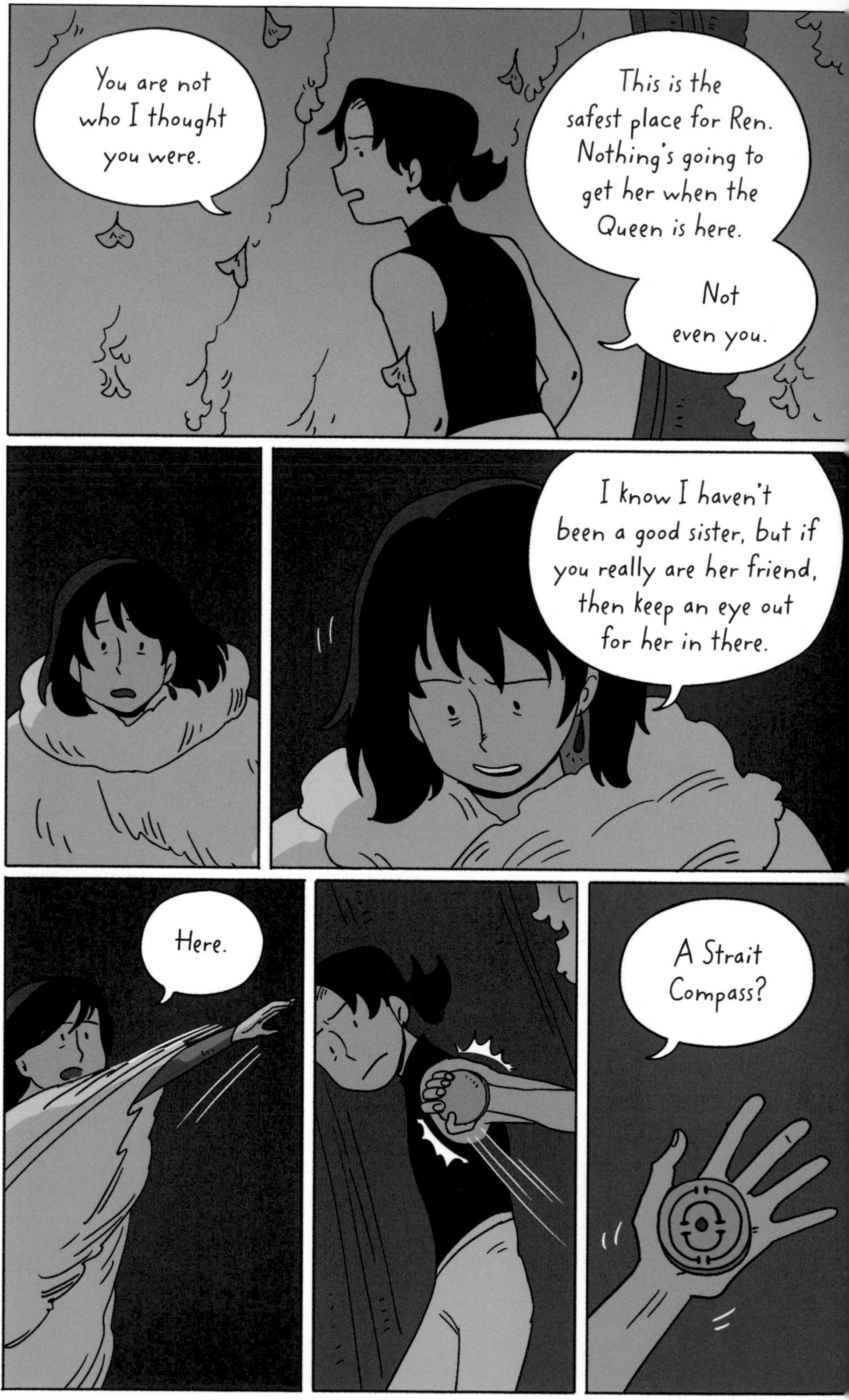
You are not who I thought you were.
This is the safest place for Ren. Nothing's going to get her when the Queen is here.
Not even you.
I know I haven't been a good sister, but if you really are her friend, then keep an eye out for her in there.
Here.
A Strait Compass?

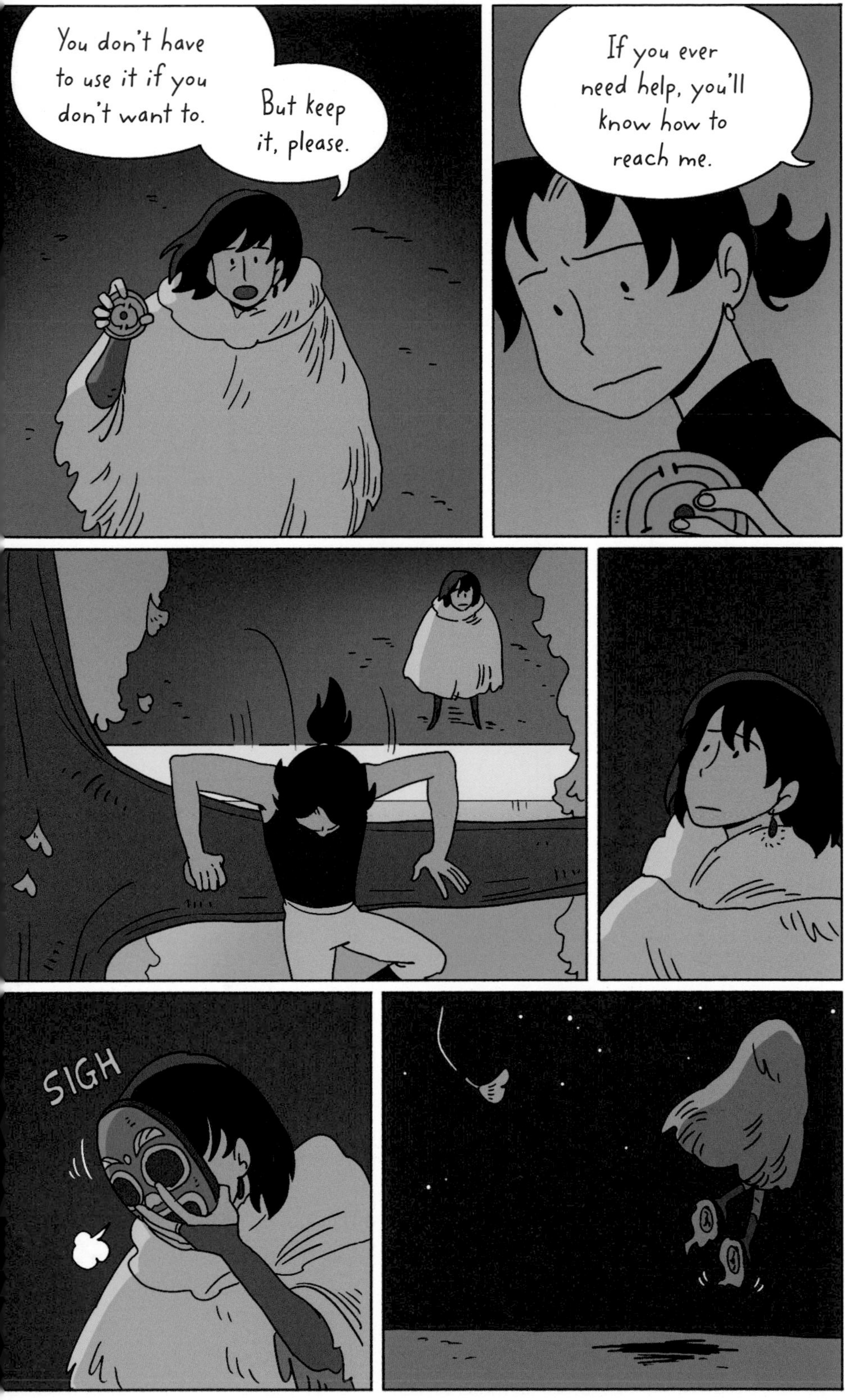
You don't have to use it if you don't want to.
But keep it, please.
If you ever need help, you'll know how to reach me.
SIGH

CHAPTER 15

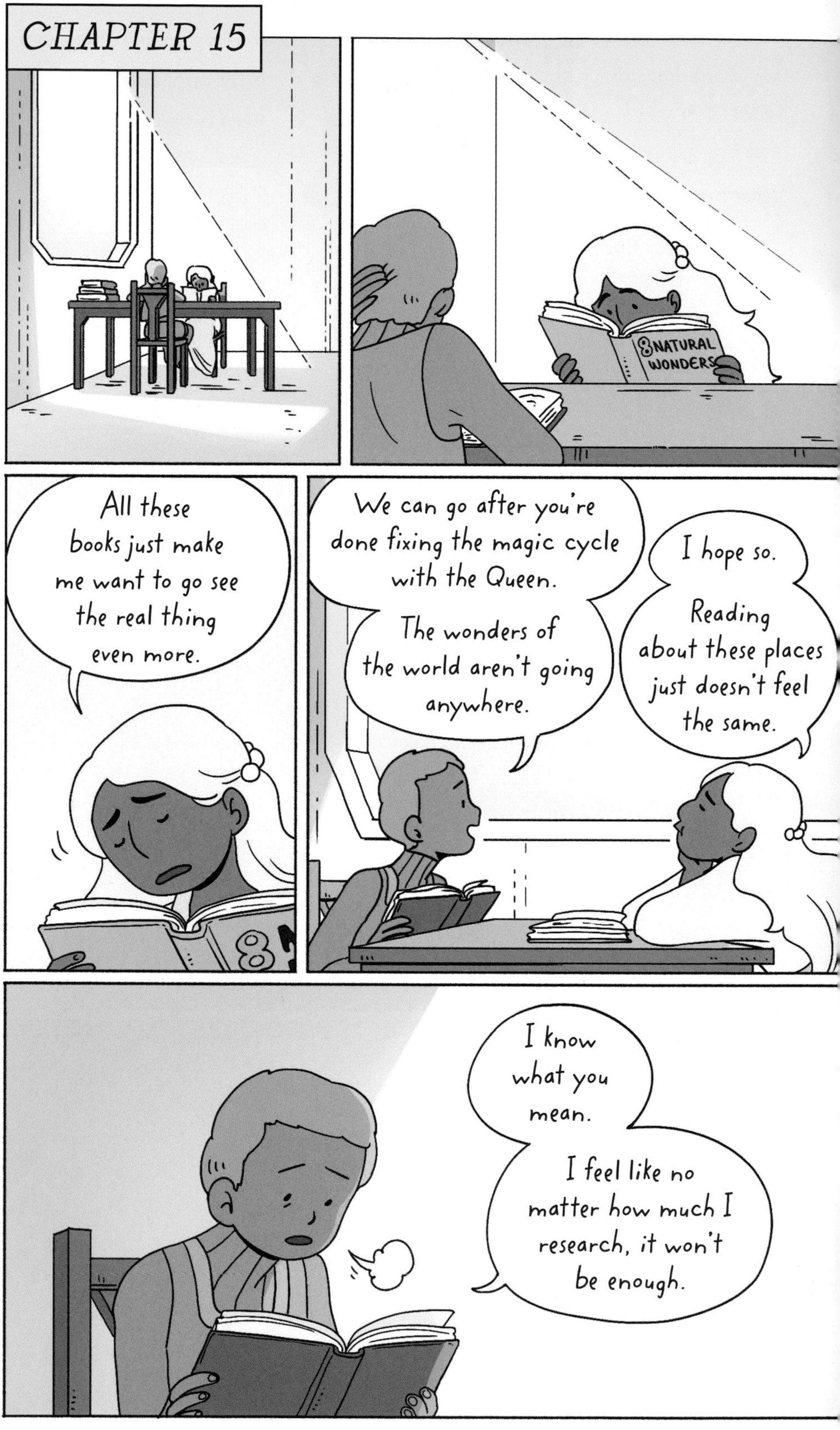
8 NATURAL WONDERS
All these books just make me want to go see the real thing even more.
We can go after you're done fixing the magic cycle with the Queen.
The wonders of the world aren't going anywhere.
I hope so.
Reading about these places just doesn't feel the same.
I know what you mean.
I feel like no matter how much I research, it won't be enough.

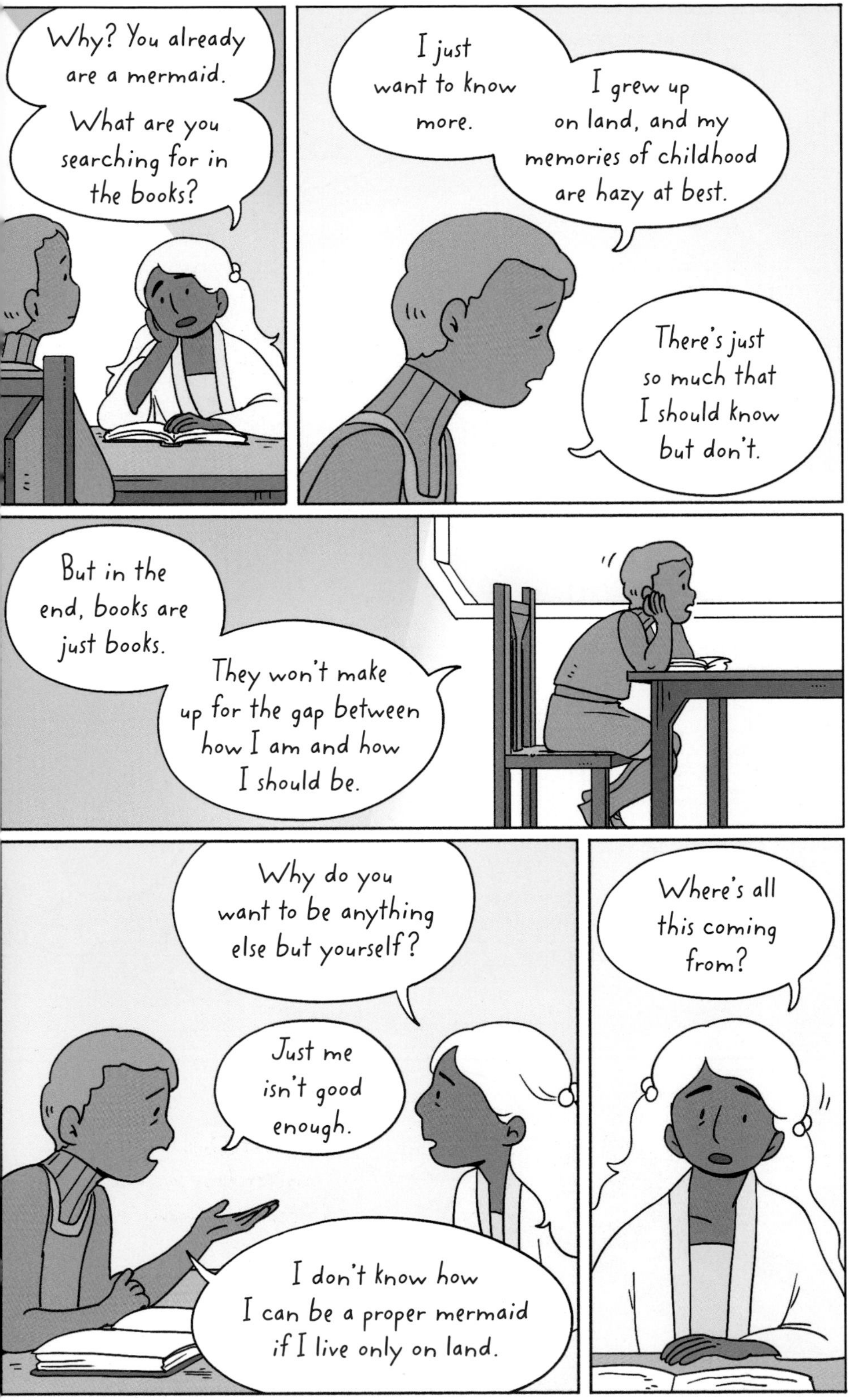
Why? You already are a mermaid.
What are you searching for in the books?
I just want to know more.
I grew up on land, and my memories of childhood are hazy at best.
There's just so much that I should know but don't.
But in the end, books are just books.
They won't make up for the gap between how I am and how I should be.
Why do you want to be anything else but yourself?
Just me isn't good enough.
I don't know how I can be a proper mermaid if I live only on land.
Where's all this coming from?

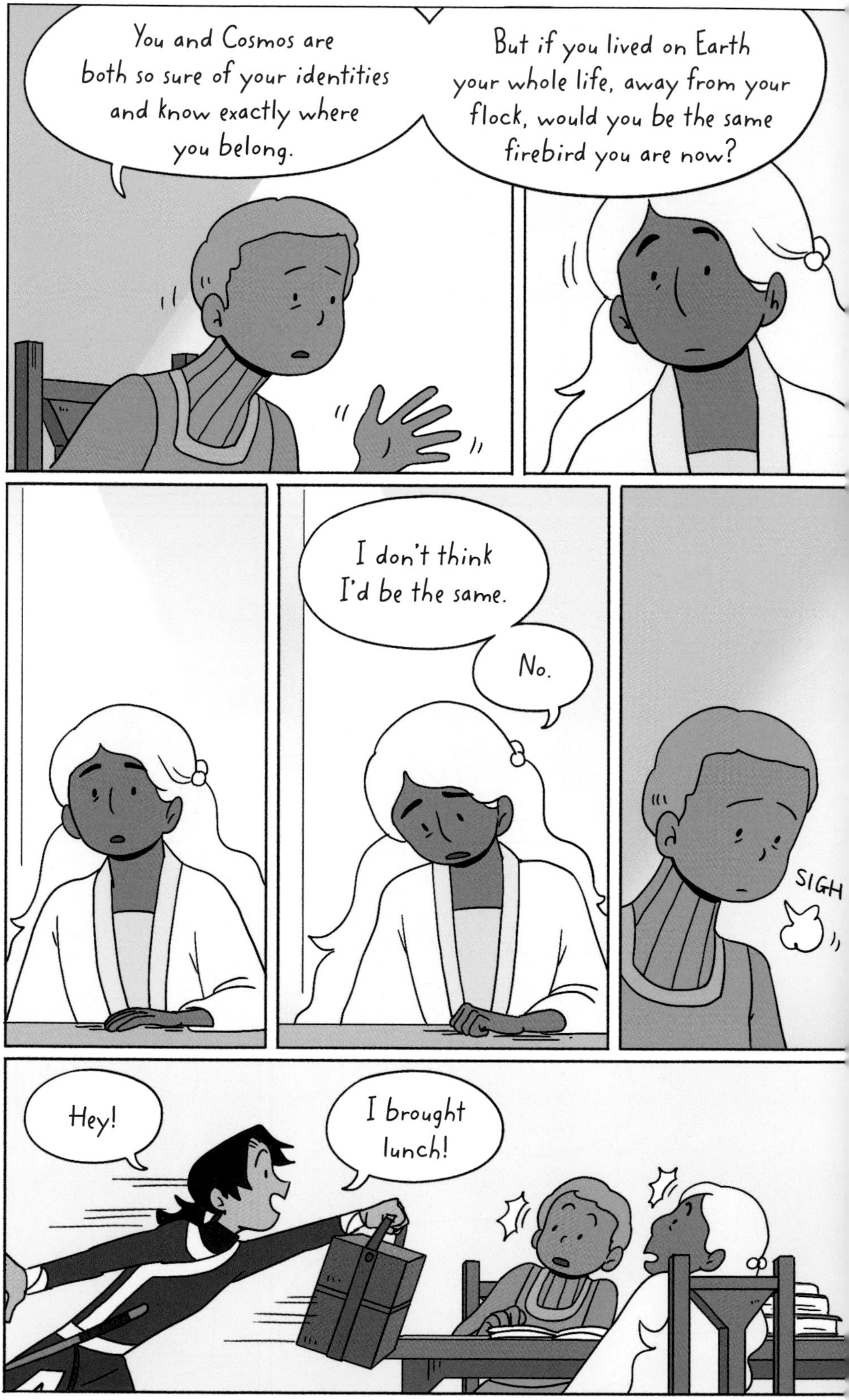
You and Cosmos are both so sure of your identities and know exactly where you belong.
But if you lived on Earth your whole life, away from your flock, would you be the same firebird you are now?
I don't think I'd be the same.
No.
SIGH
Hey!
I brought lunch!

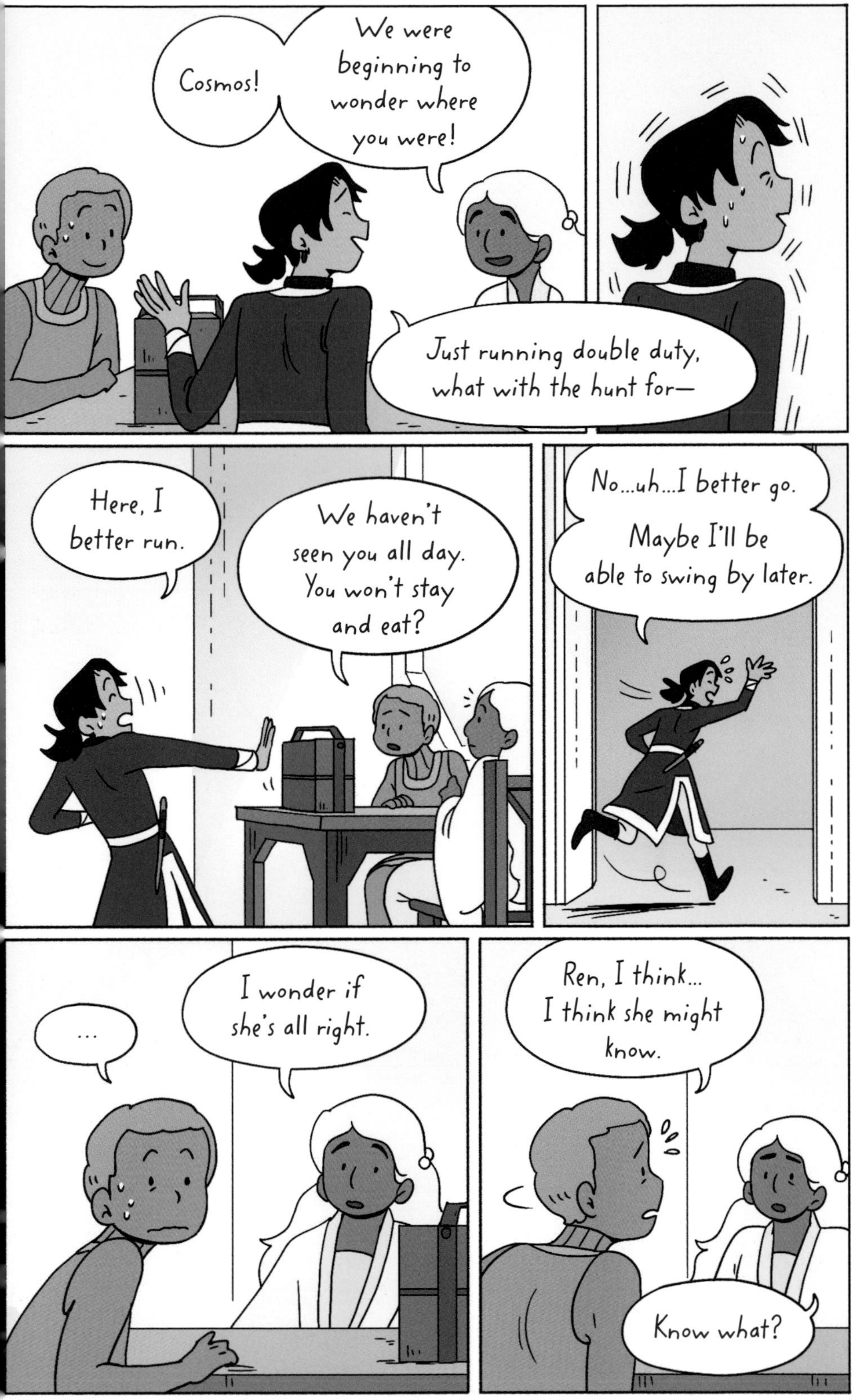
Cosmos!
We were beginning to wonder where you were!
Just running double duty, what with the hunt for—
Here, I better run.
We haven't seen you all day. You won't stay and eat?
No...uh...I better go.
Maybe I'll be able to swing by later.
...
I wonder if she's all right.
Ren, I think... I think she might know.
Know what?

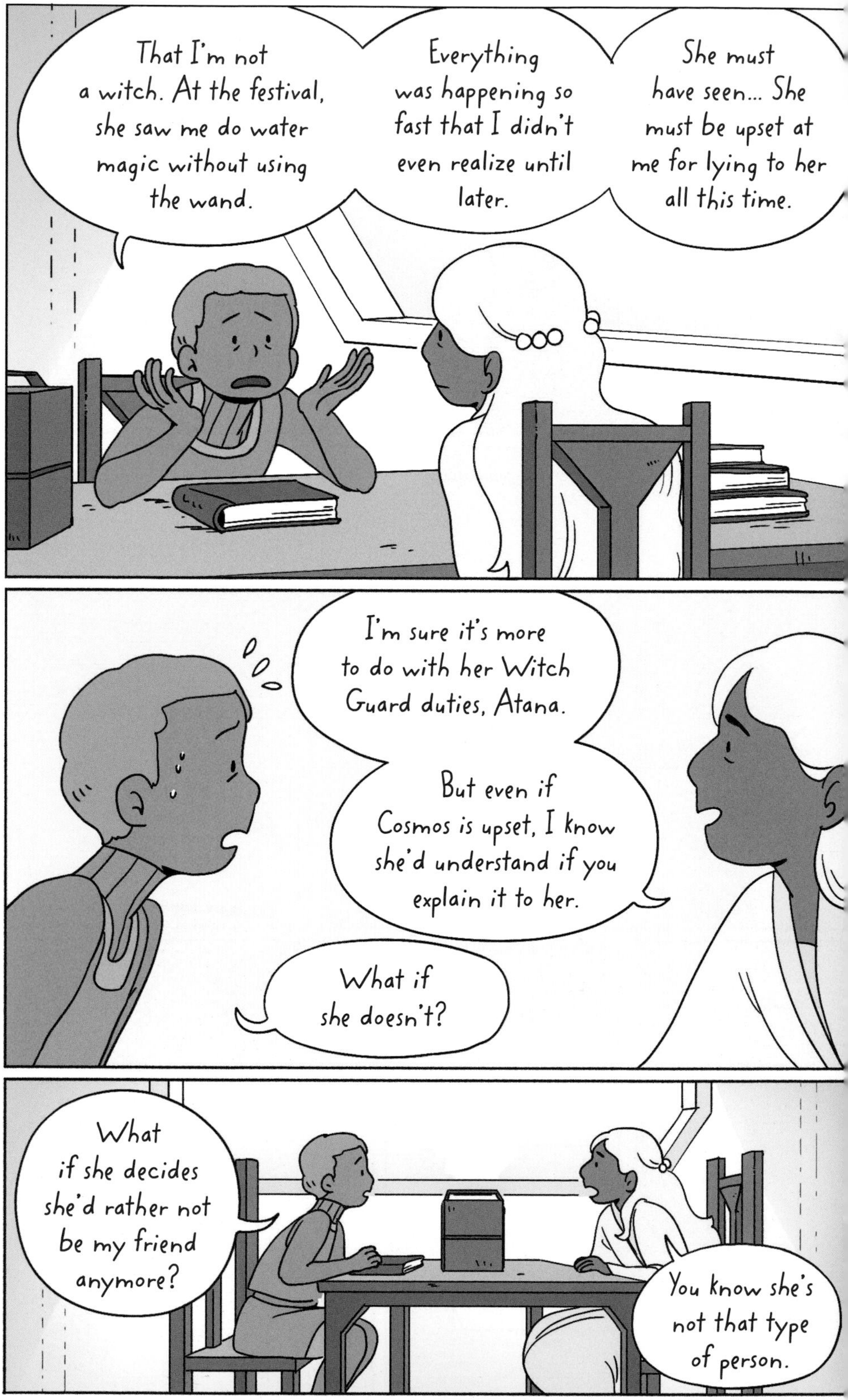
That I'm not a witch. At the festival, she saw me do water magic without using the wand.
Everything was happening so fast that I didn't even realize until later.
She must have seen... She must be upset at me for lying to her all this time.
I'm sure it's more to do with her Witch Guard duties, Atana.
But even if Cosmos is upset, I know she'd understand if you explain it to her.
What if she doesn't?
What if she decides she'd rather not be my friend anymore?
You know she's not that type of person.

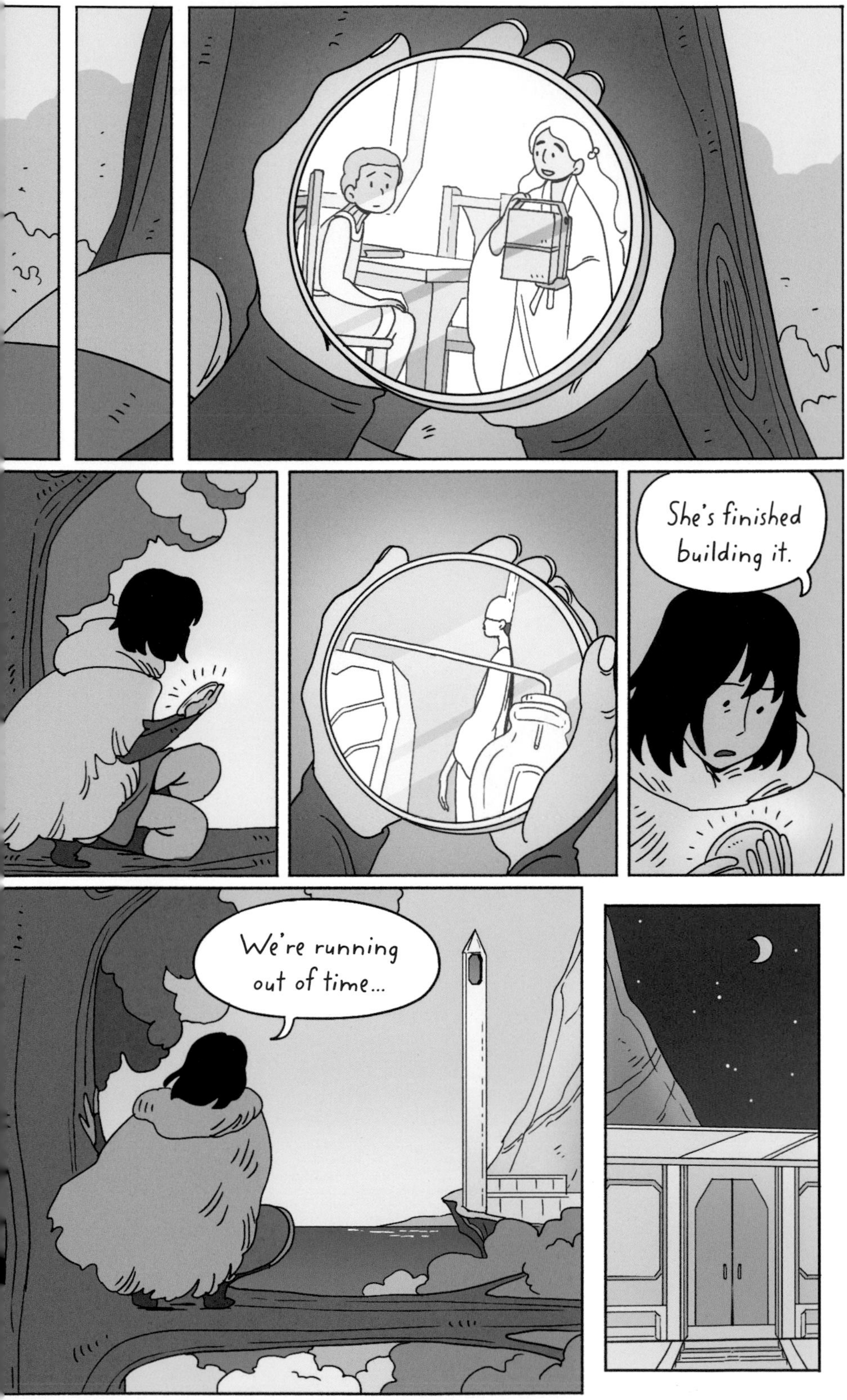

She's finished building it.
We're running out of time...

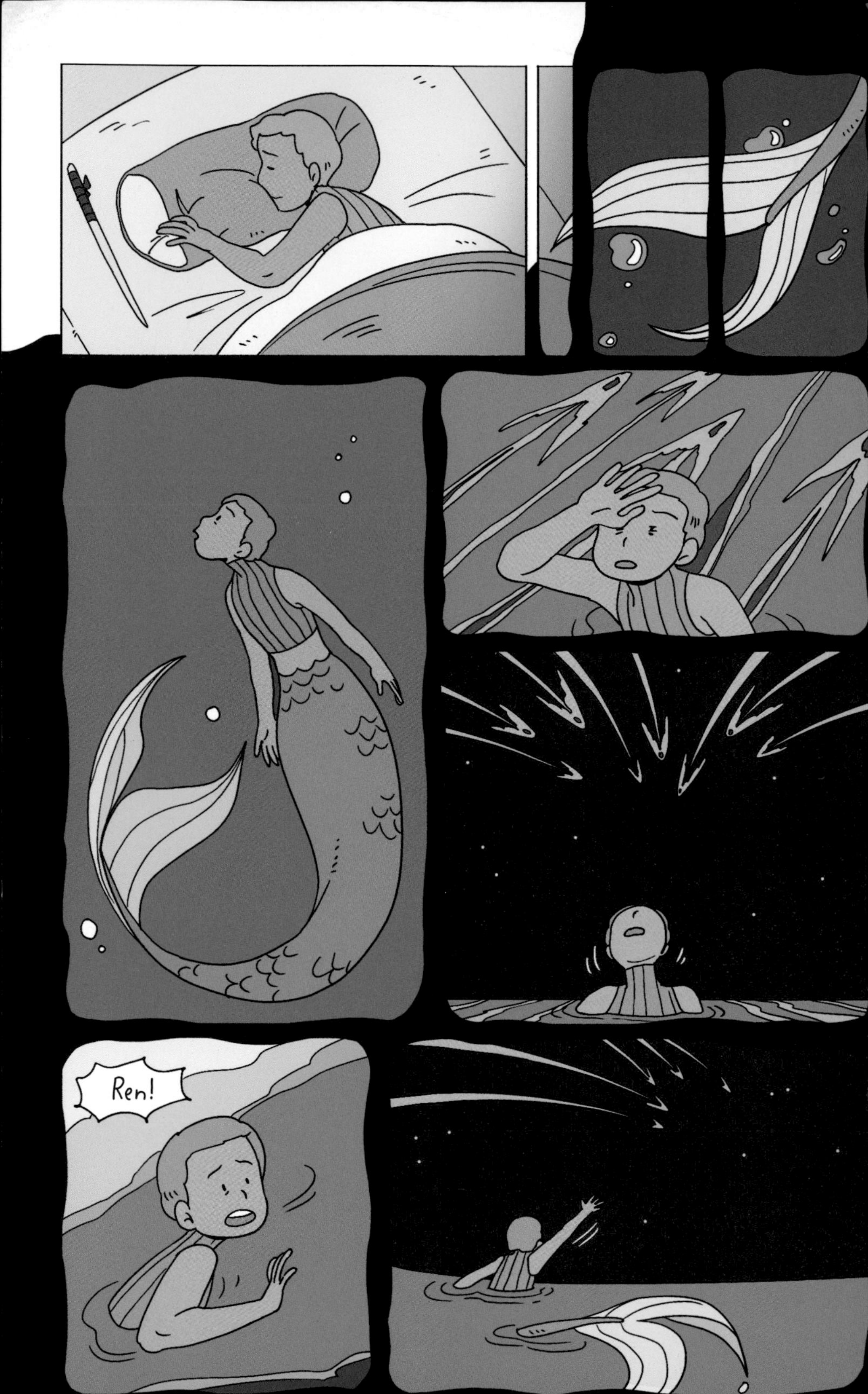
Ren!

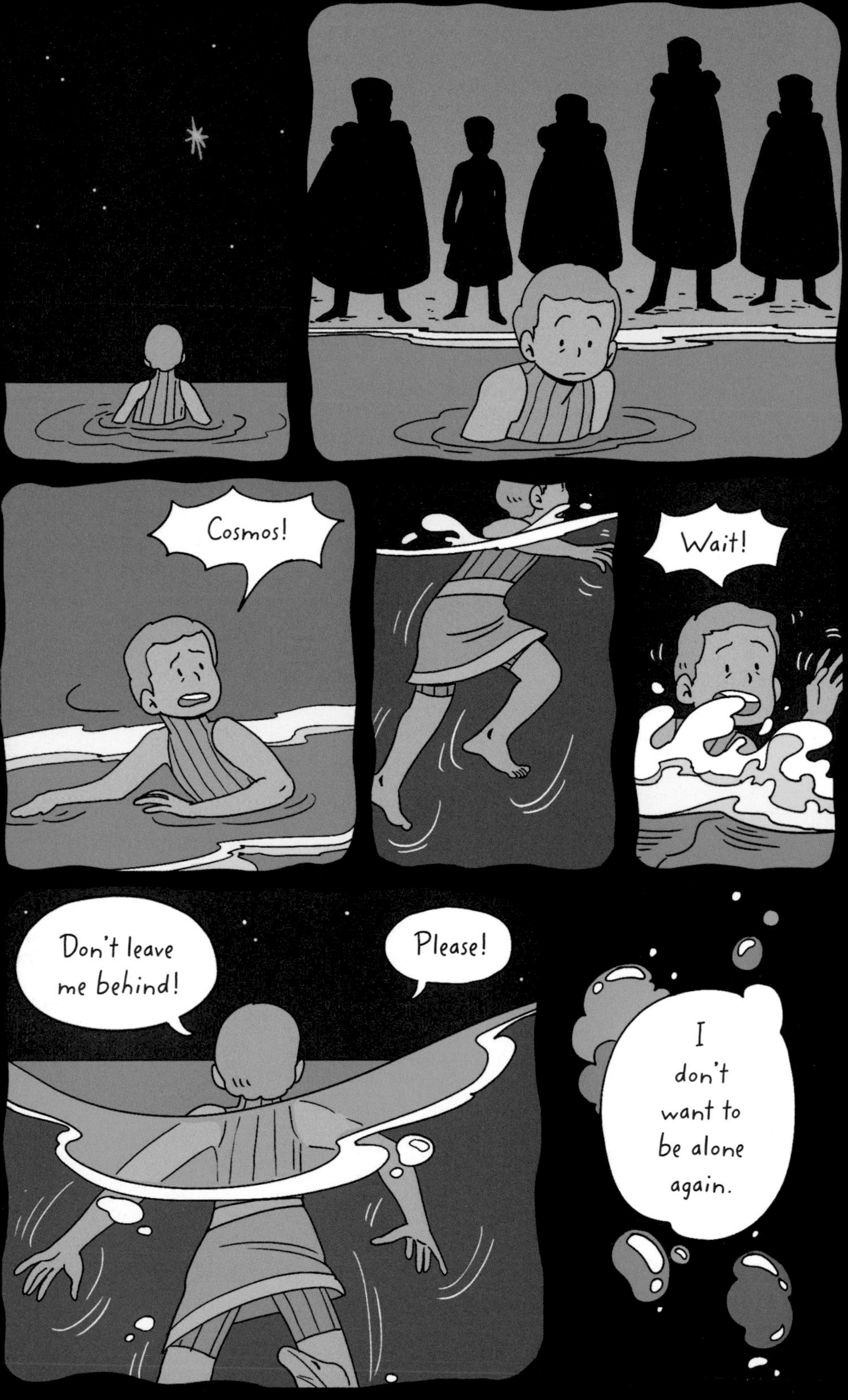
Cosmos!
Wait!
Don't leave me behind!
Please!
I don't want to be alone again.

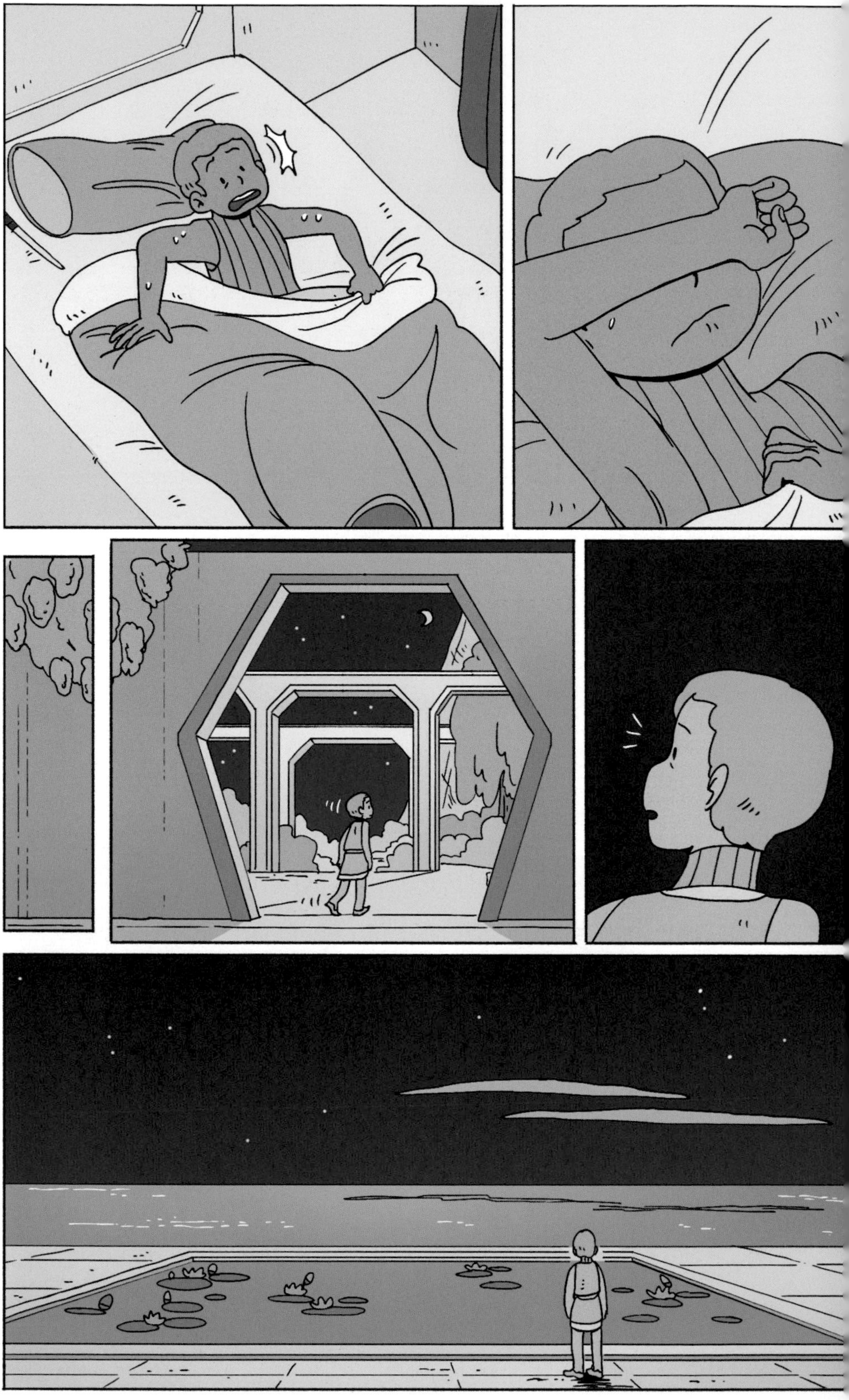

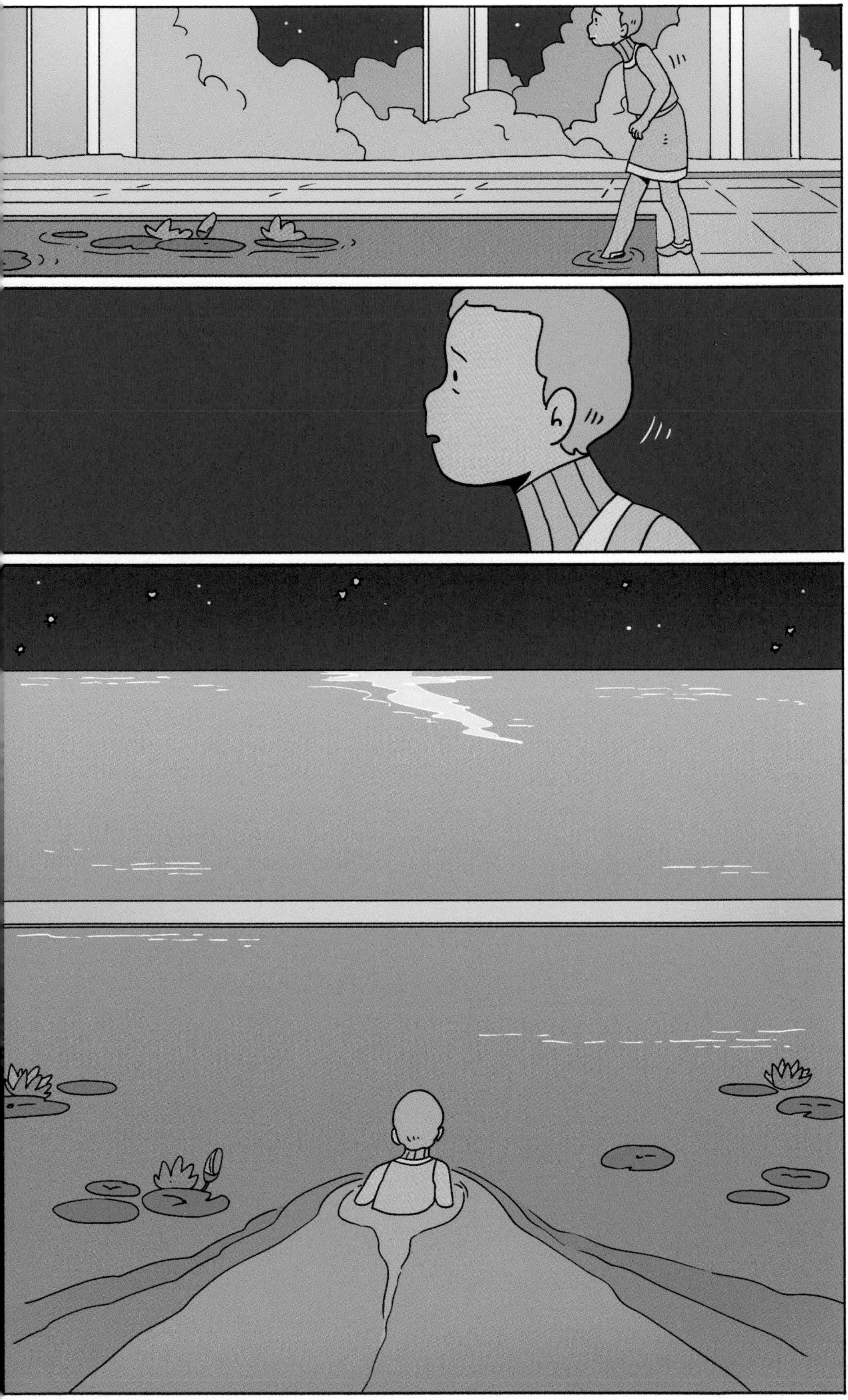

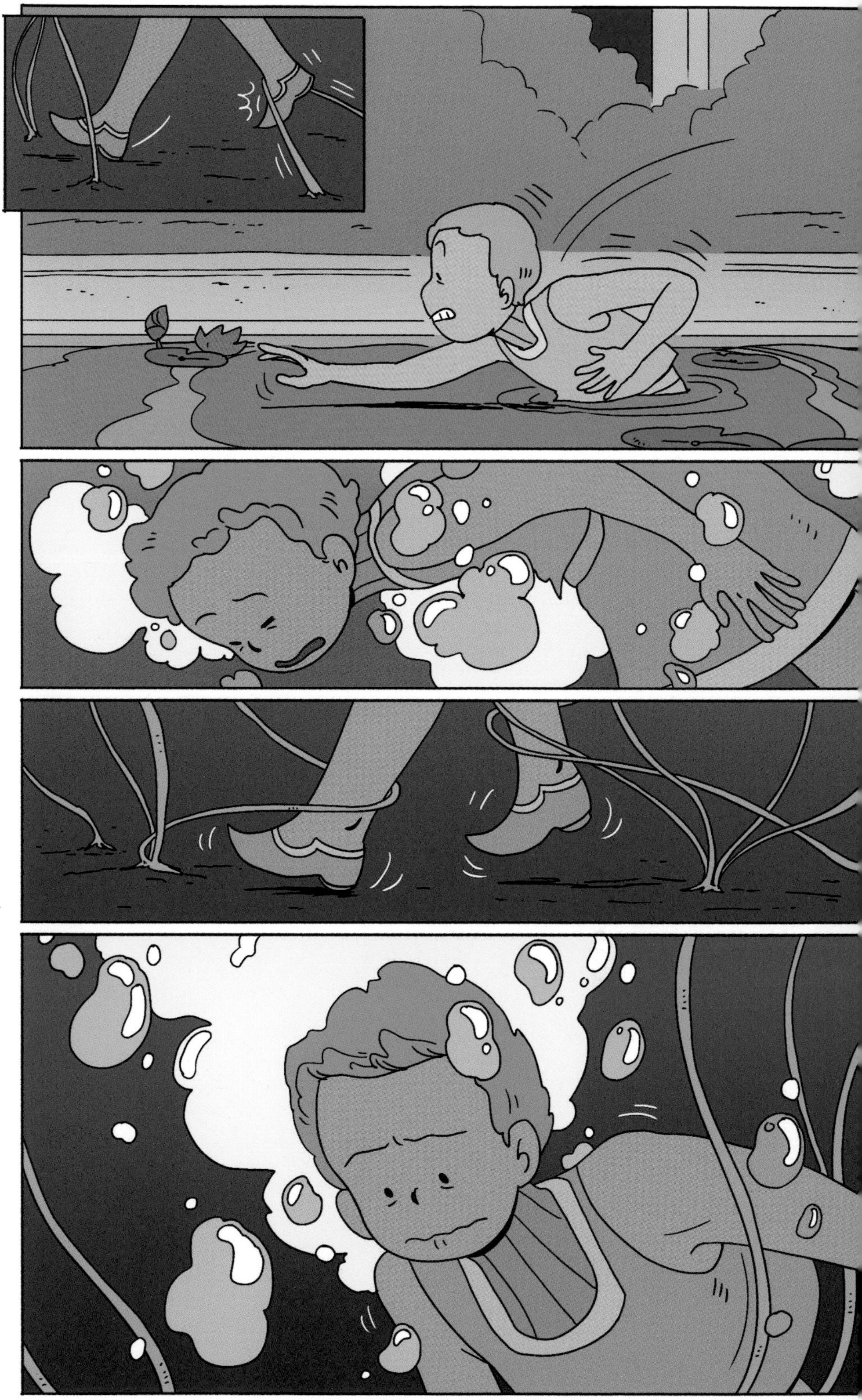

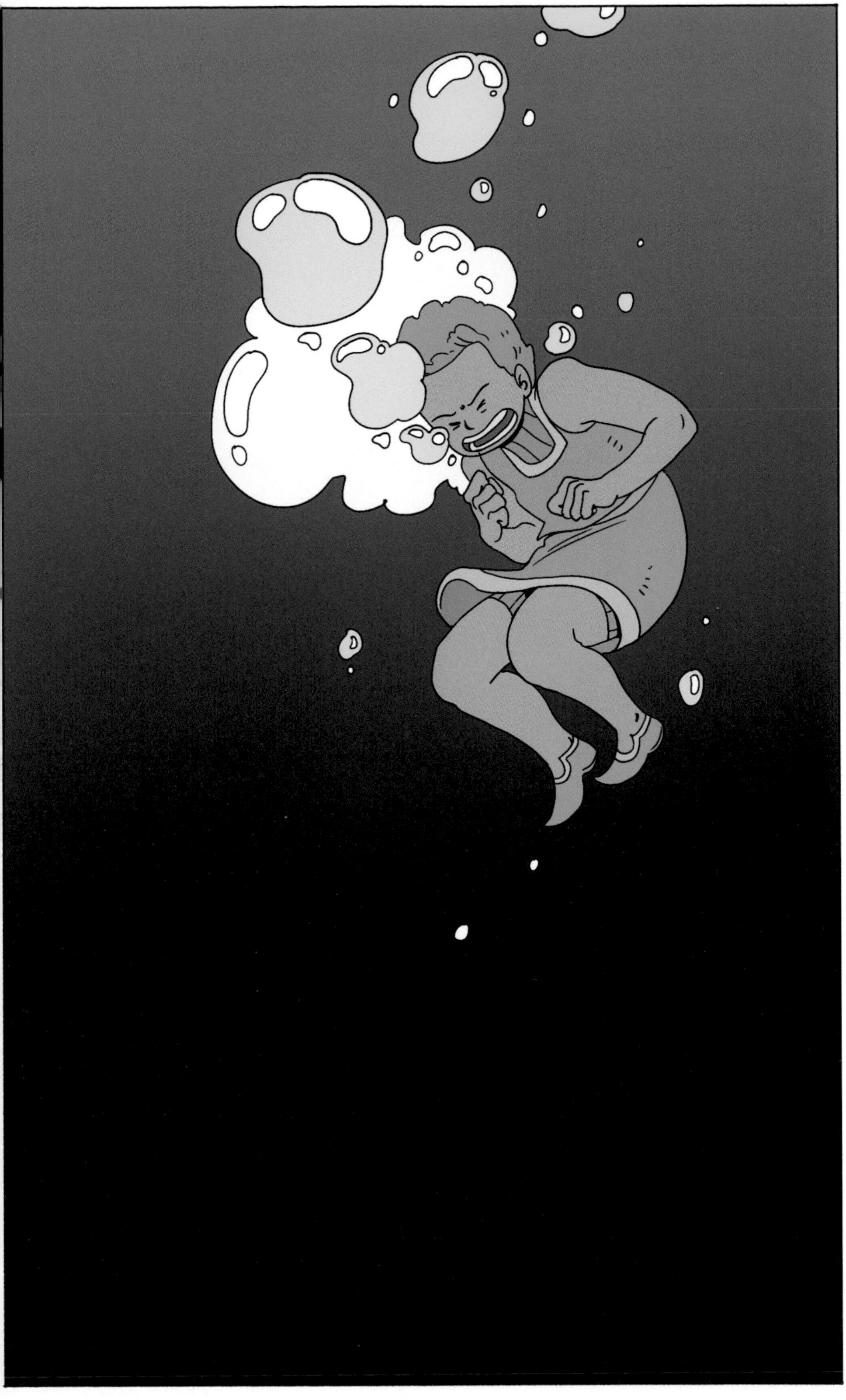

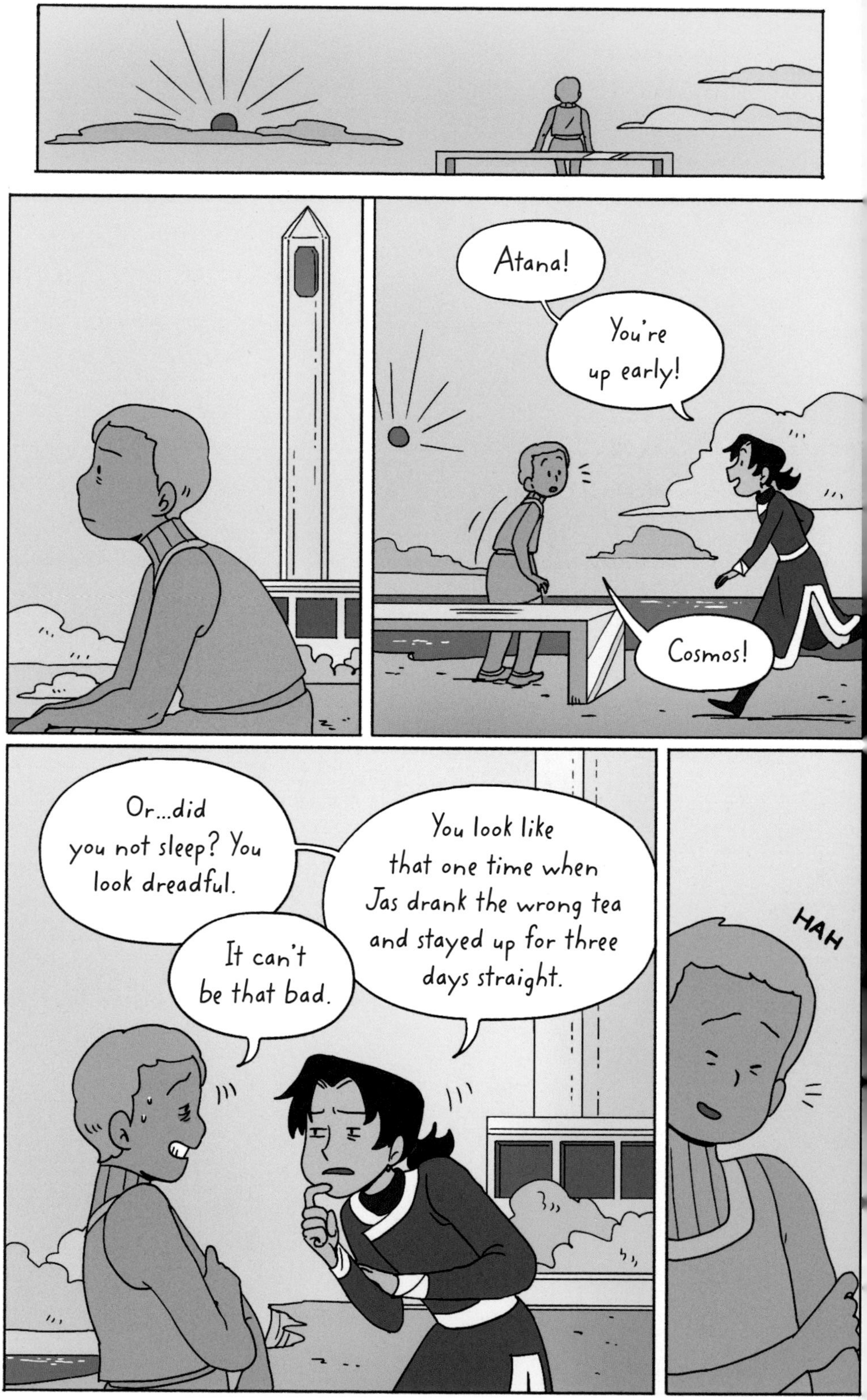

Atana!
You're up early!
Cosmos!
Or...did you not sleep? You look dreadful.
You look like that one time when Jas drank the wrong tea and stayed up for three days straight.
It can't be that bad.
HAH

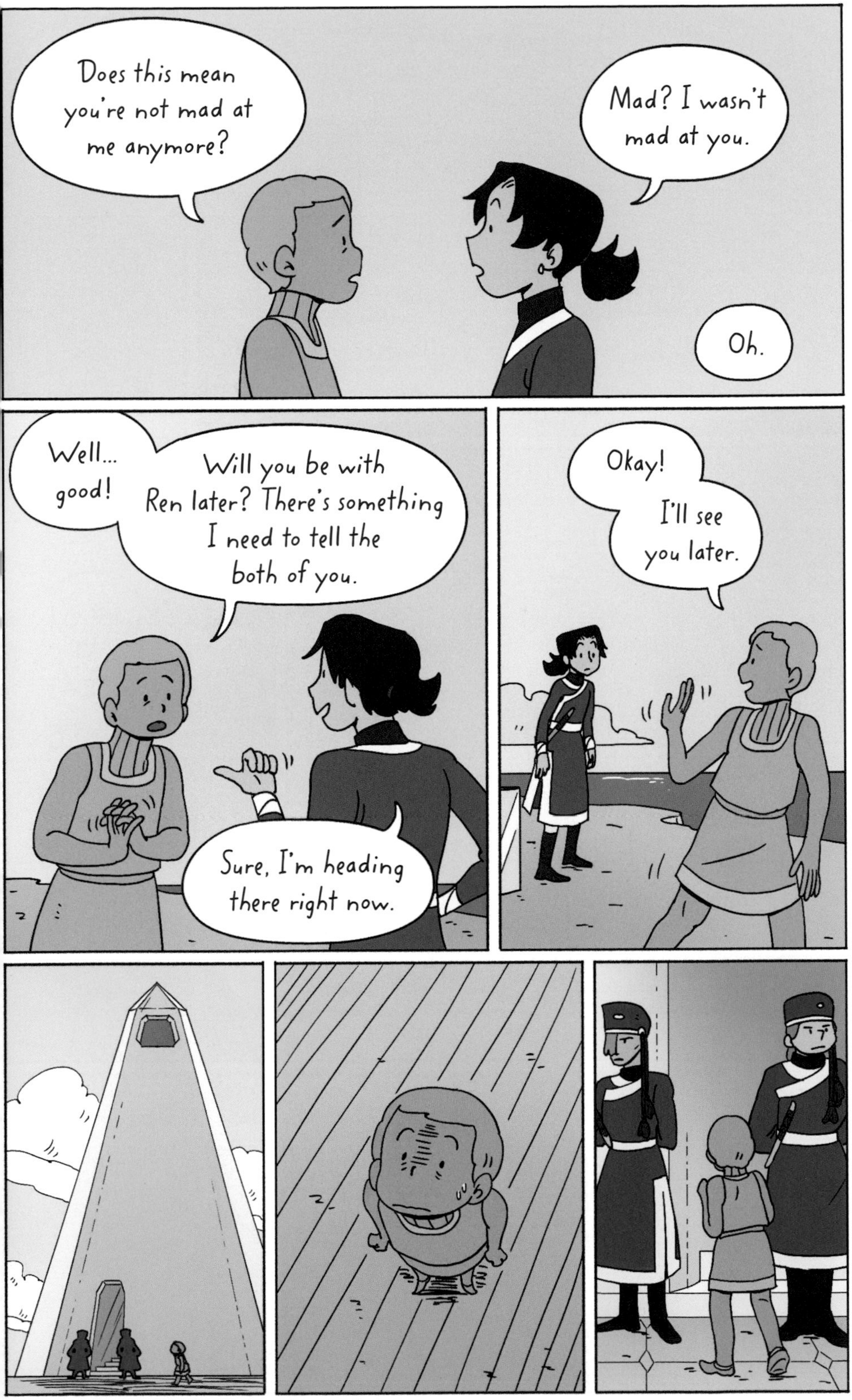
Does this mean you're not mad at me anymore?
Mad? I wasn't mad at you.
Oh.
Well... good!
Will you be with Ren later? There's something I need to tell the both of you.
Sure, I'm heading there right now.
Okay!
I'll see you later.

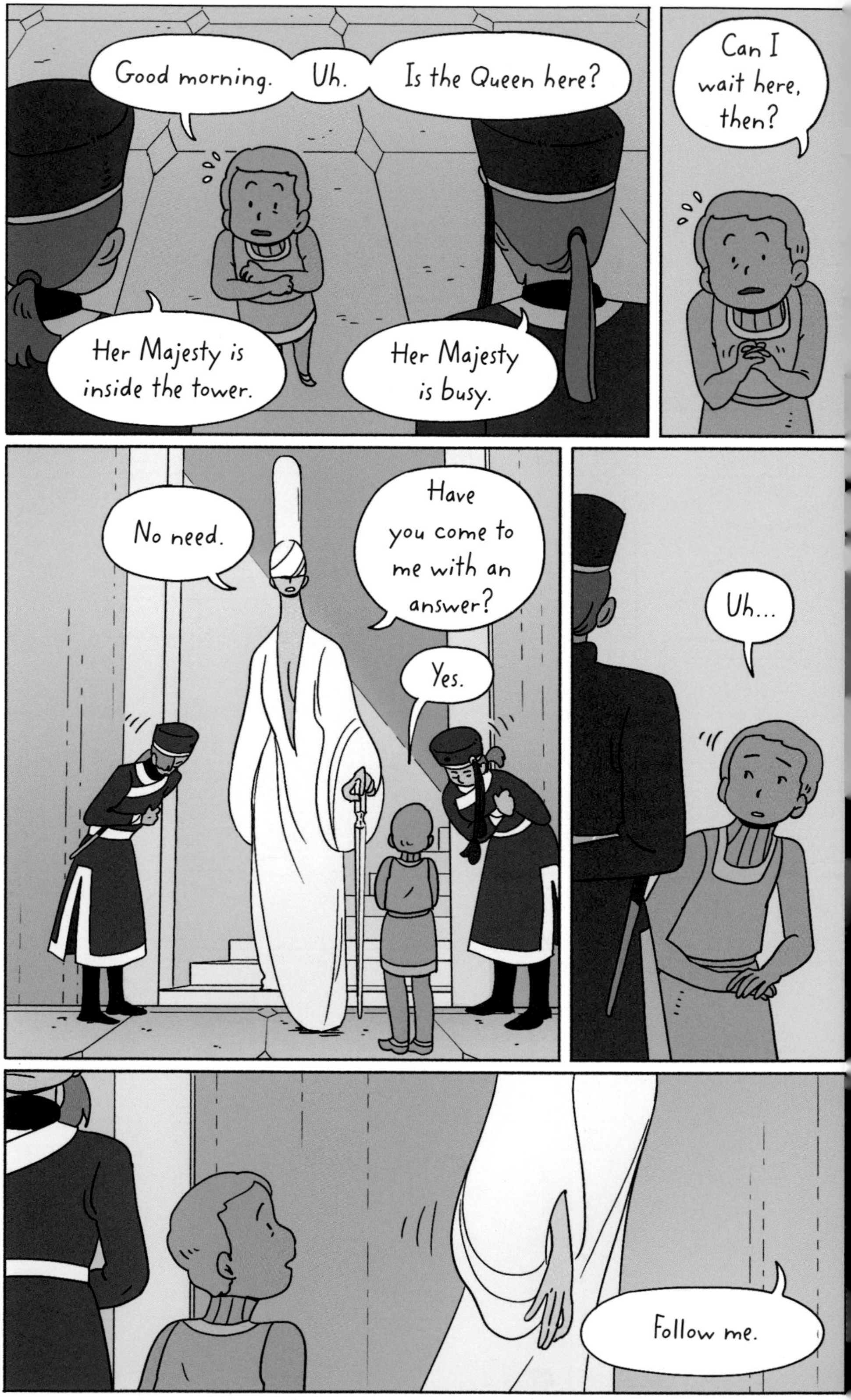
Good morning.
Uh.
Is the Queen here?
Her Majesty is inside the tower.
Her Majesty is busy.
Can I wait here, then?
No need.
Have you come to me with an answer?
Yes.
Uh...
Follow me.

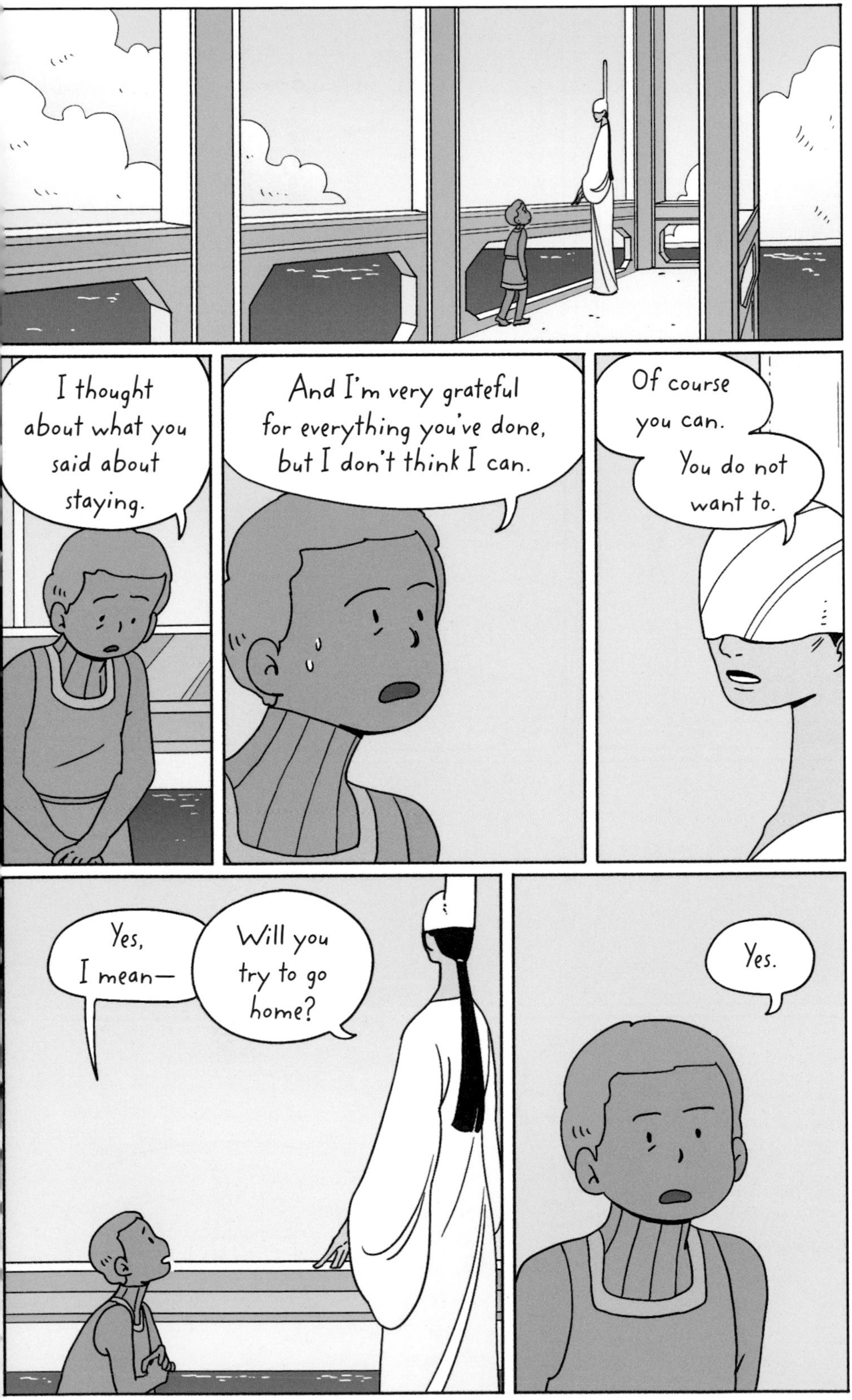
I thought about what you said about staying.
And I'm very grateful for everything you've done, but I don't think I can.
Of course you can.
You do not want to.
Yes, I mean—
Will you try to go home?
Yes.

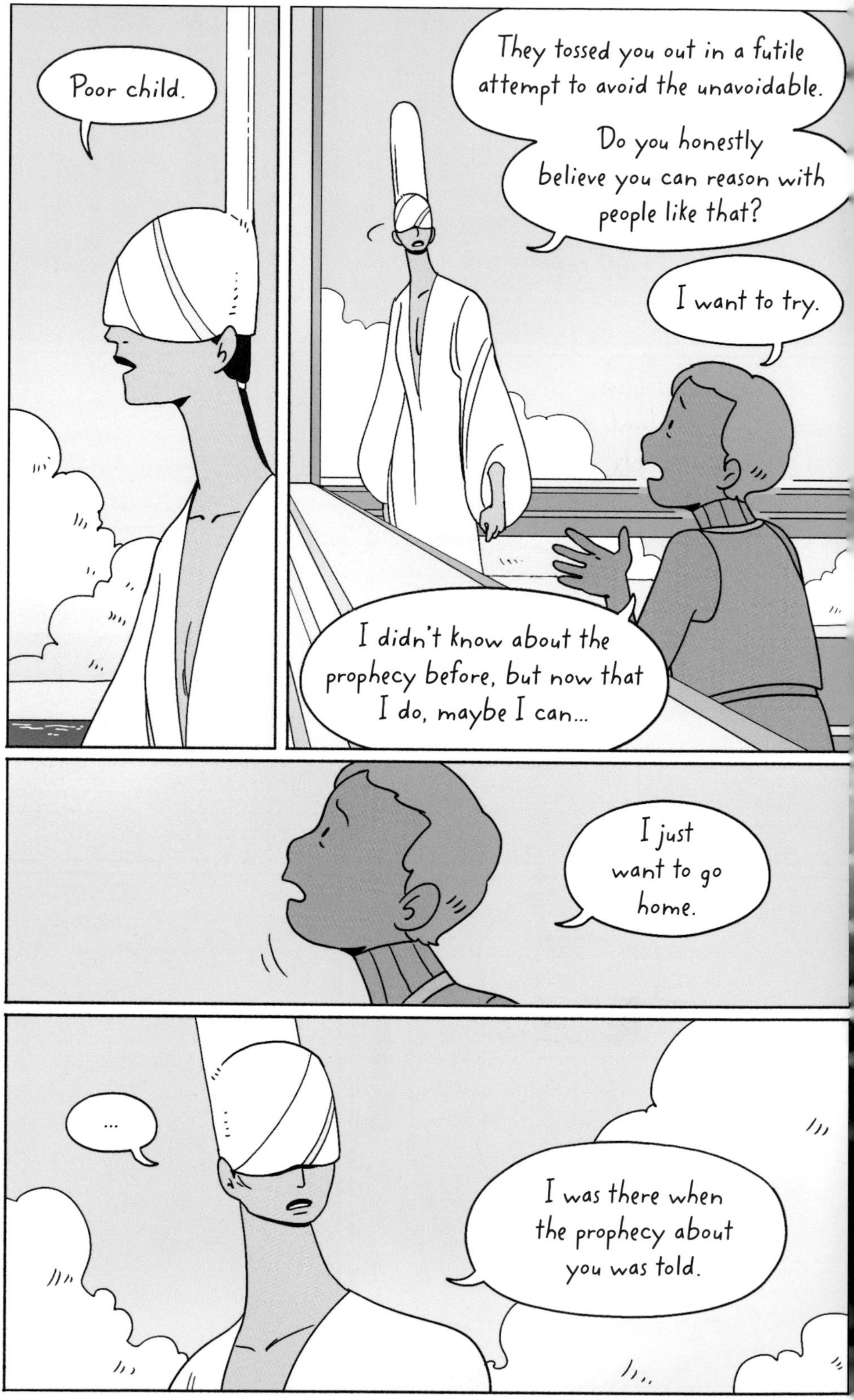
Poor child.
They tossed you out in a futile attempt to avoid the unavoidable.
Do you honestly believe you can reason with people like that?
I want to try.
I didn't know about the prophecy before, but now that I do, maybe I can...
I just want to go home.
...
I was there when the prophecy about you was told.

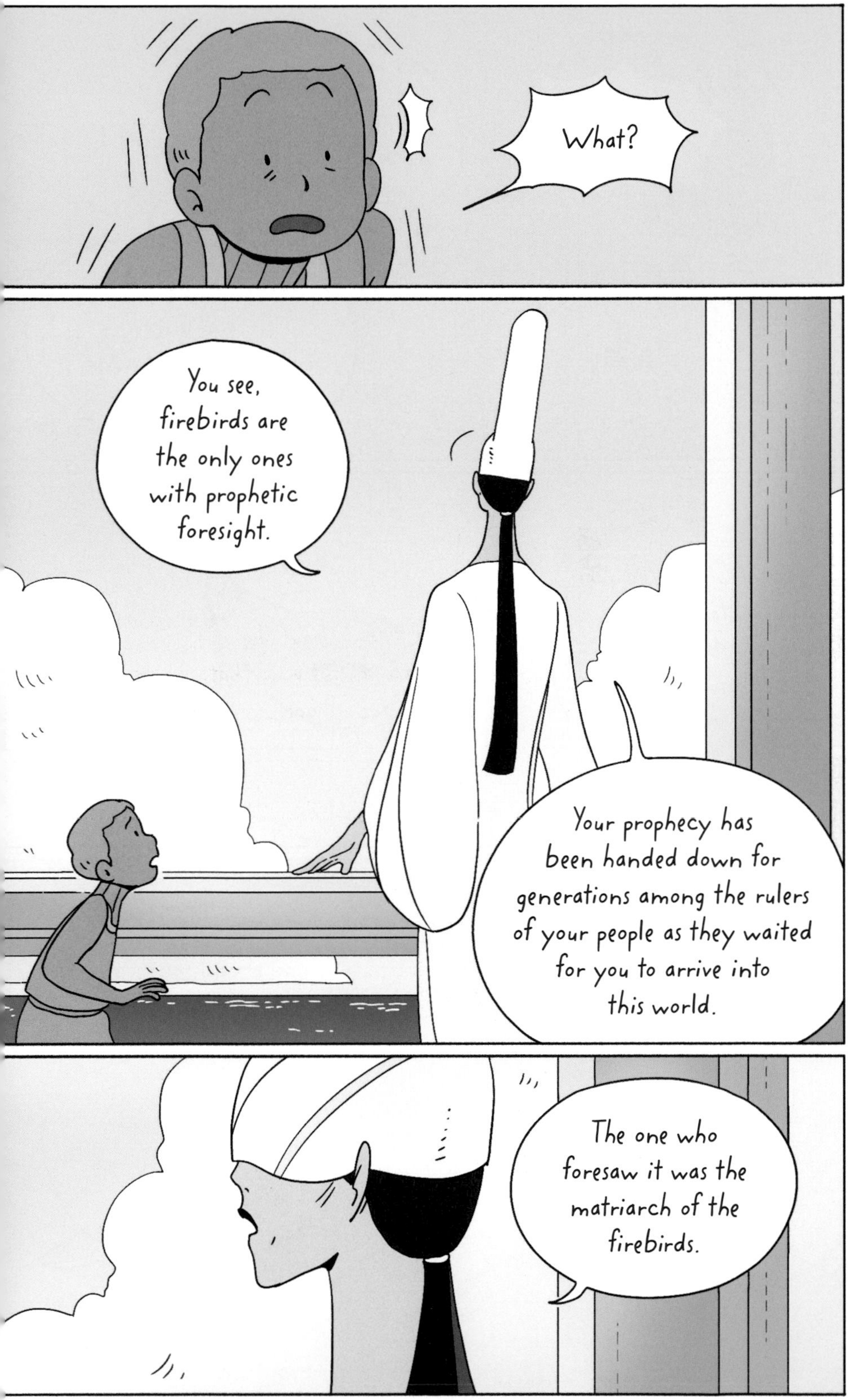
What?
You see, firebirds are the only ones with prophetic foresight.
Your prophecy has been handed down for generations among the rulers of your people as they waited for you to arrive into this world.
The one who foresaw it was the matriarch of the firebirds.

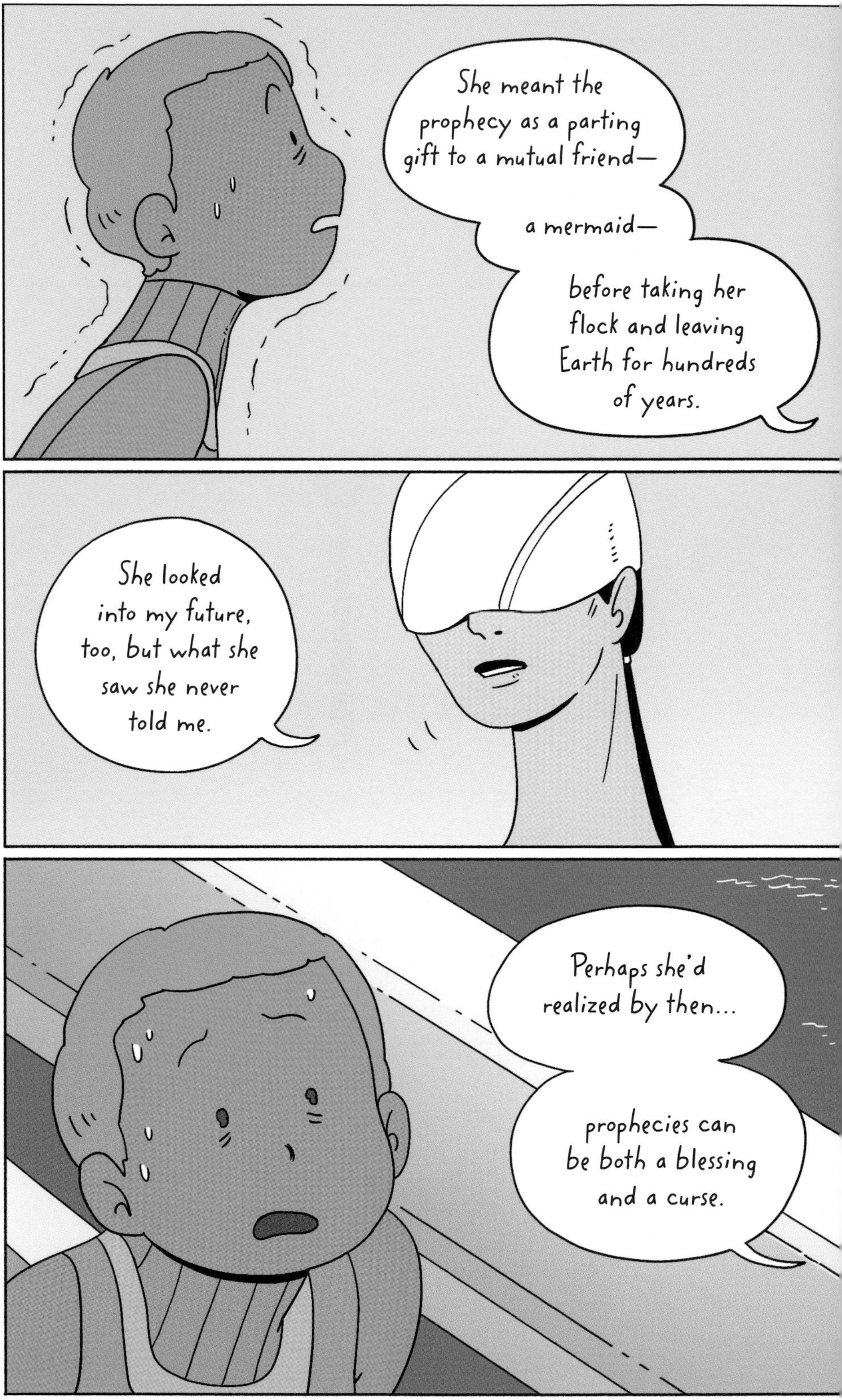
She meant the prophecy as a parting gift to a mutual friend—
a mermaid—
before taking her flock and leaving Earth for hundreds of years.
She looked into my future, too, but what she saw she never told me.
Perhaps she'd realized by then...
prophecies can be both a blessing and a curse.

CHAPTER 16

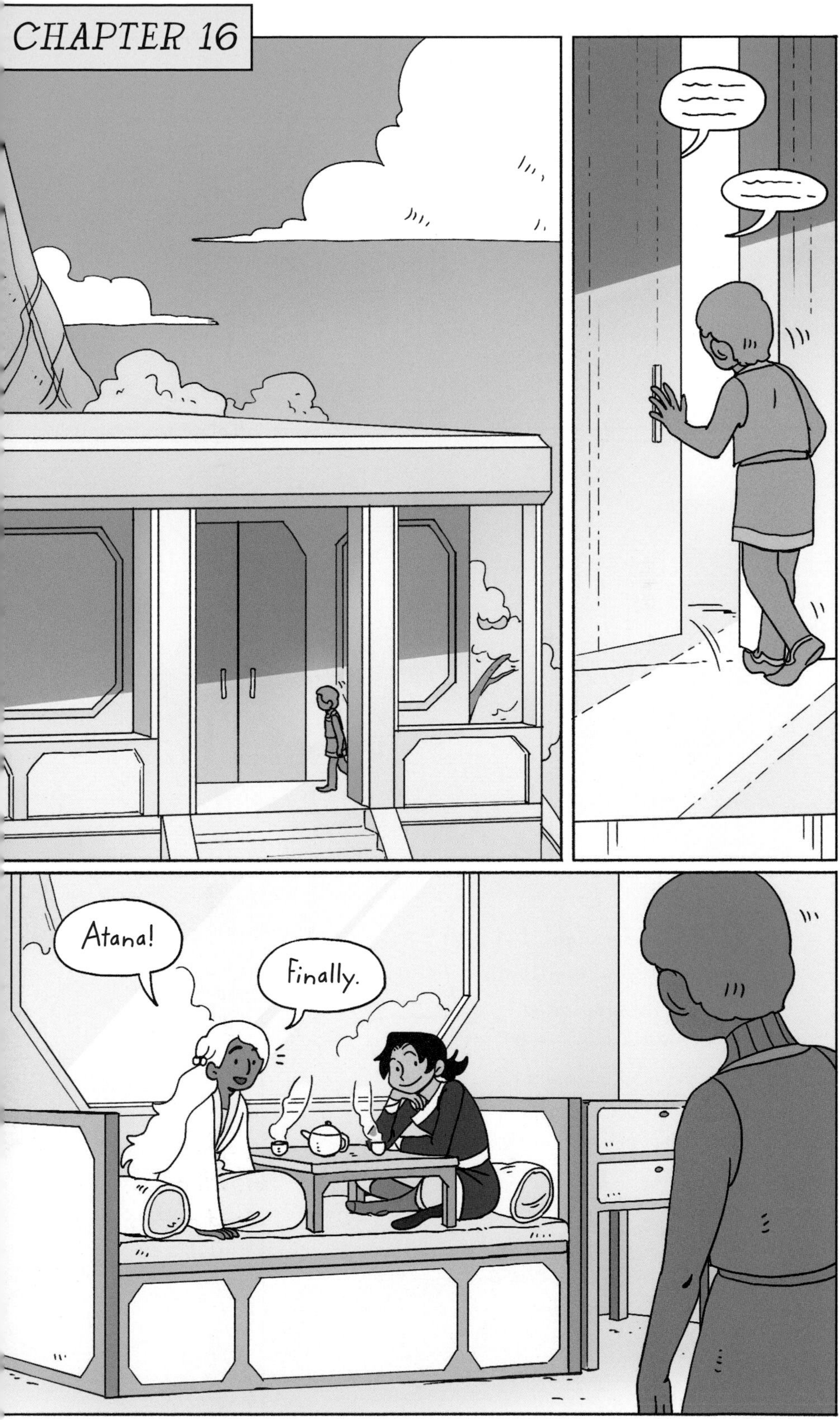
Atana!
Finally.

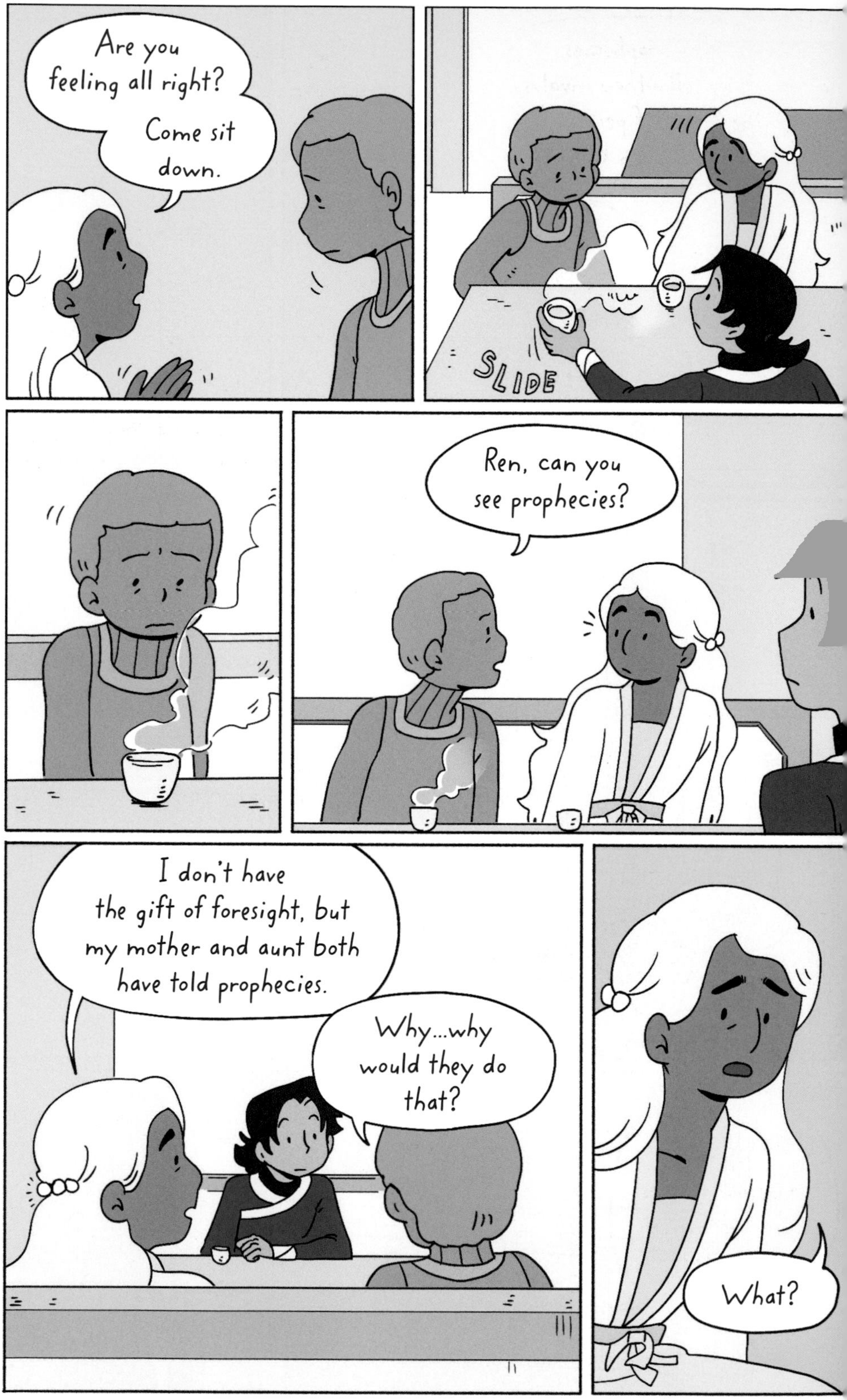
Are you feeling all right?
Come sit down.
SLIDE
Ren, can you see prophecies?
I don't have the gift of foresight, but my mother and aunt both have told prophecies.
Why...why would they do that?
What?

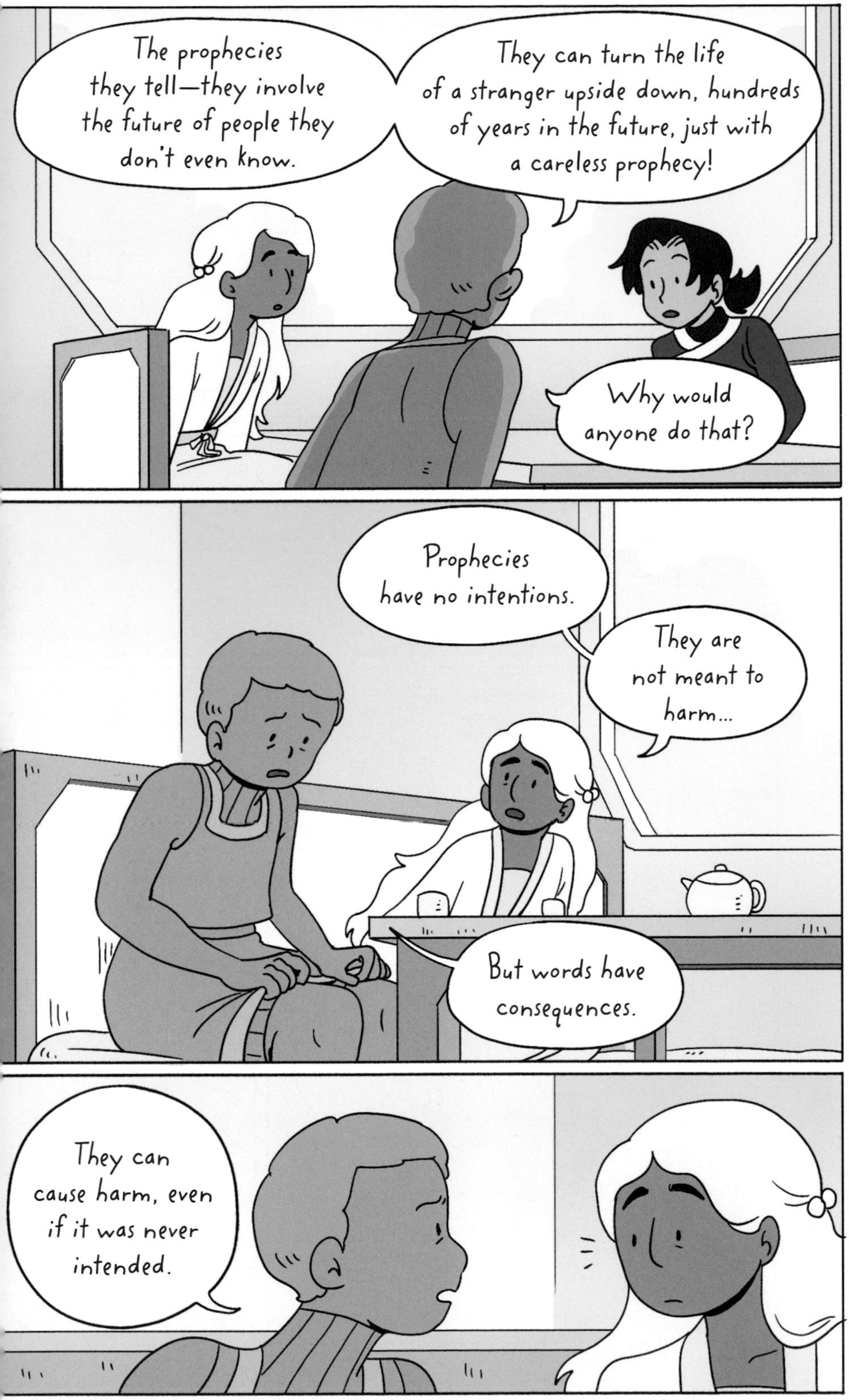
The prophecies they tell—they involve the future of people they don't even know.
They can turn the life of a stranger upside down, hundreds of years in the future, just with a careless prophecy!
Why would anyone do that?
Prophecies have no intentions.
They are not meant to harm...
But words have consequences.
They can cause harm, even if it was never intended.

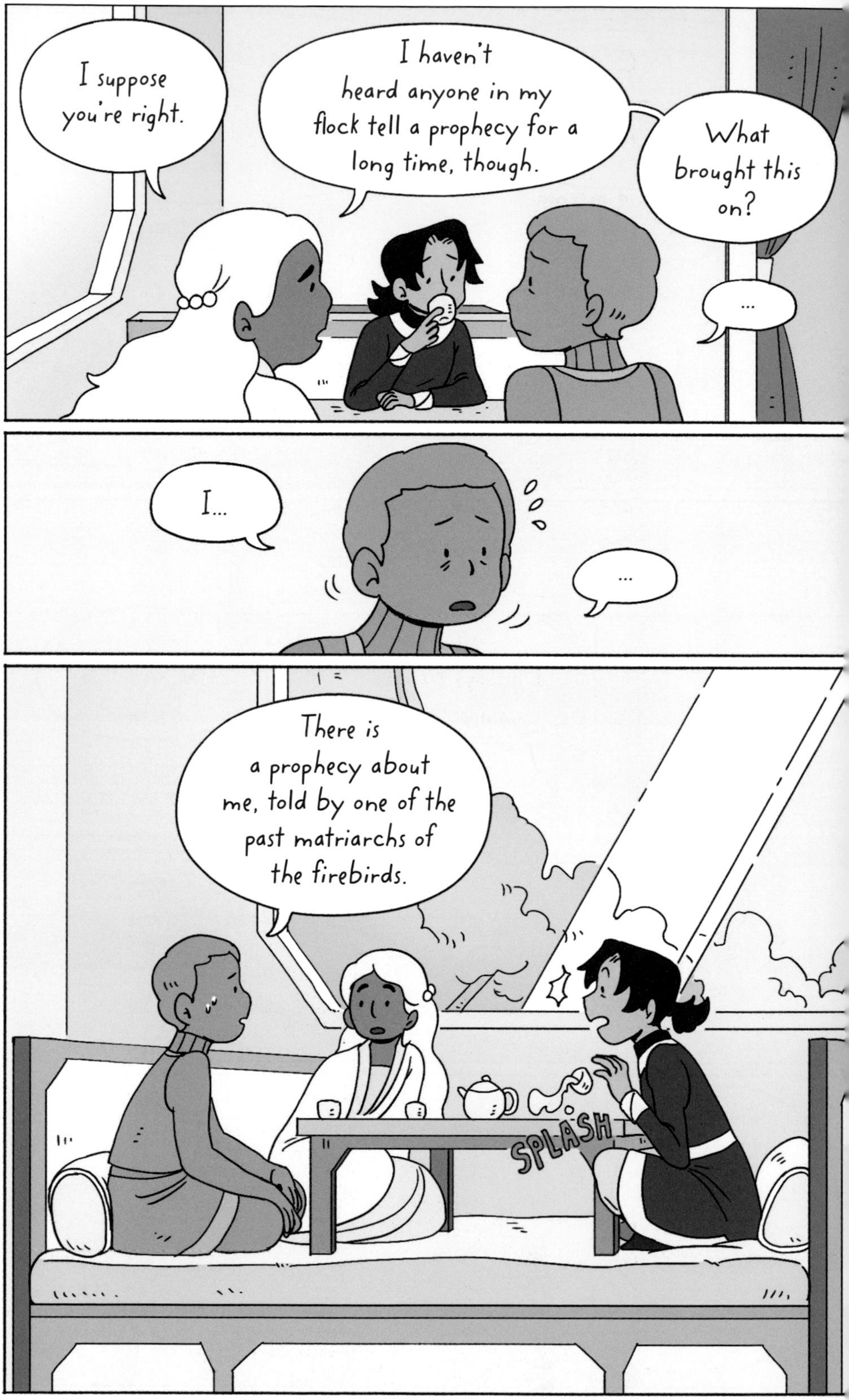
I suppose you're right.
I haven't heard anyone in my flock tell a prophecy for a long time, though.
What brought this on?
...
I...
...
There is a prophecy about me, told by one of the past matriarchs of the firebirds.
SPLASH

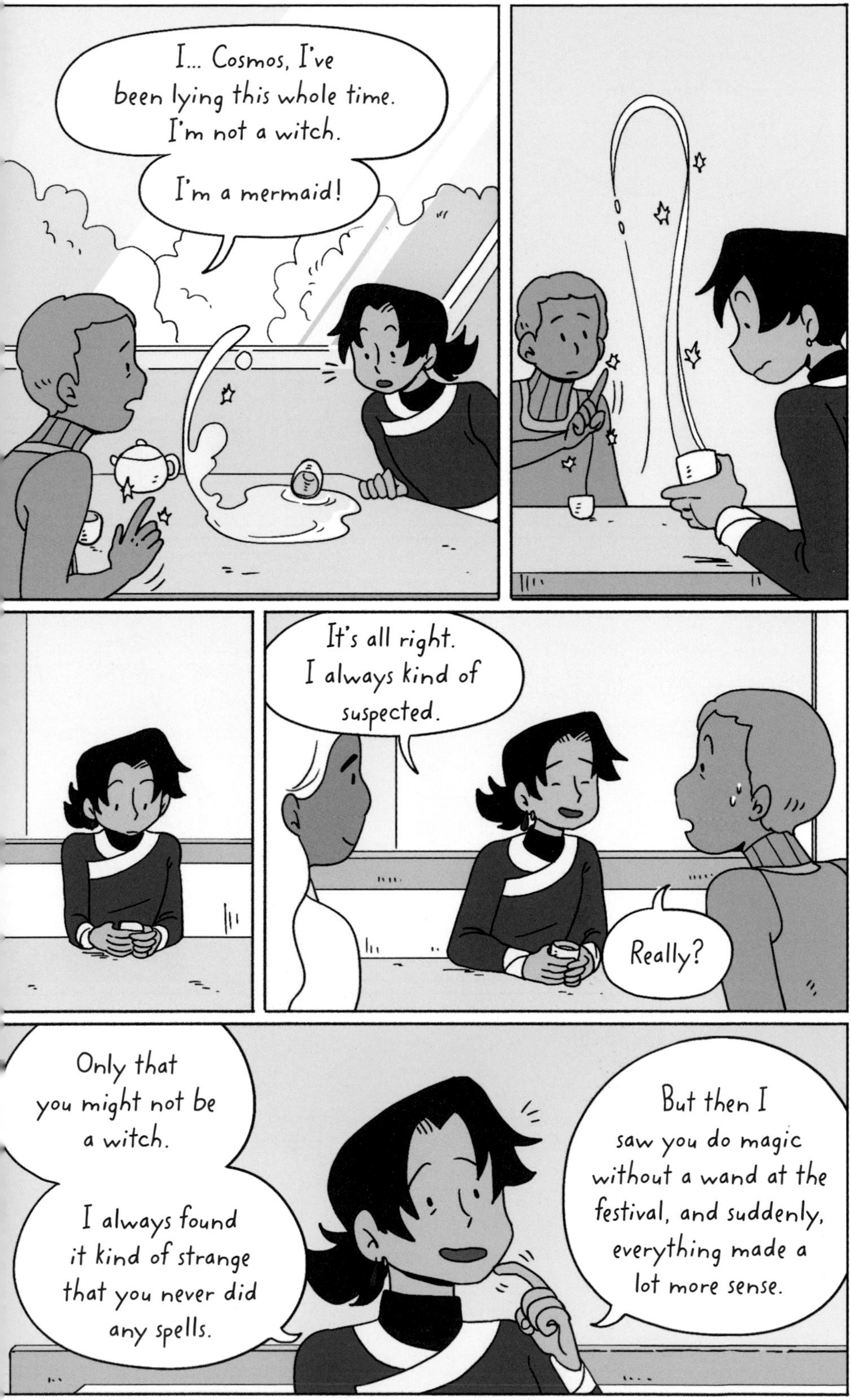
I... Cosmos, I've been lying this whole time. I'm not a witch.
I'm a mermaid!
It's all right. I always kind of suspected.
Really?
Only that you might not be a witch.
I always found it kind of strange that you never did any spells.
But then I saw you do magic without a wand at the festival, and suddenly, everything made a lot more sense.

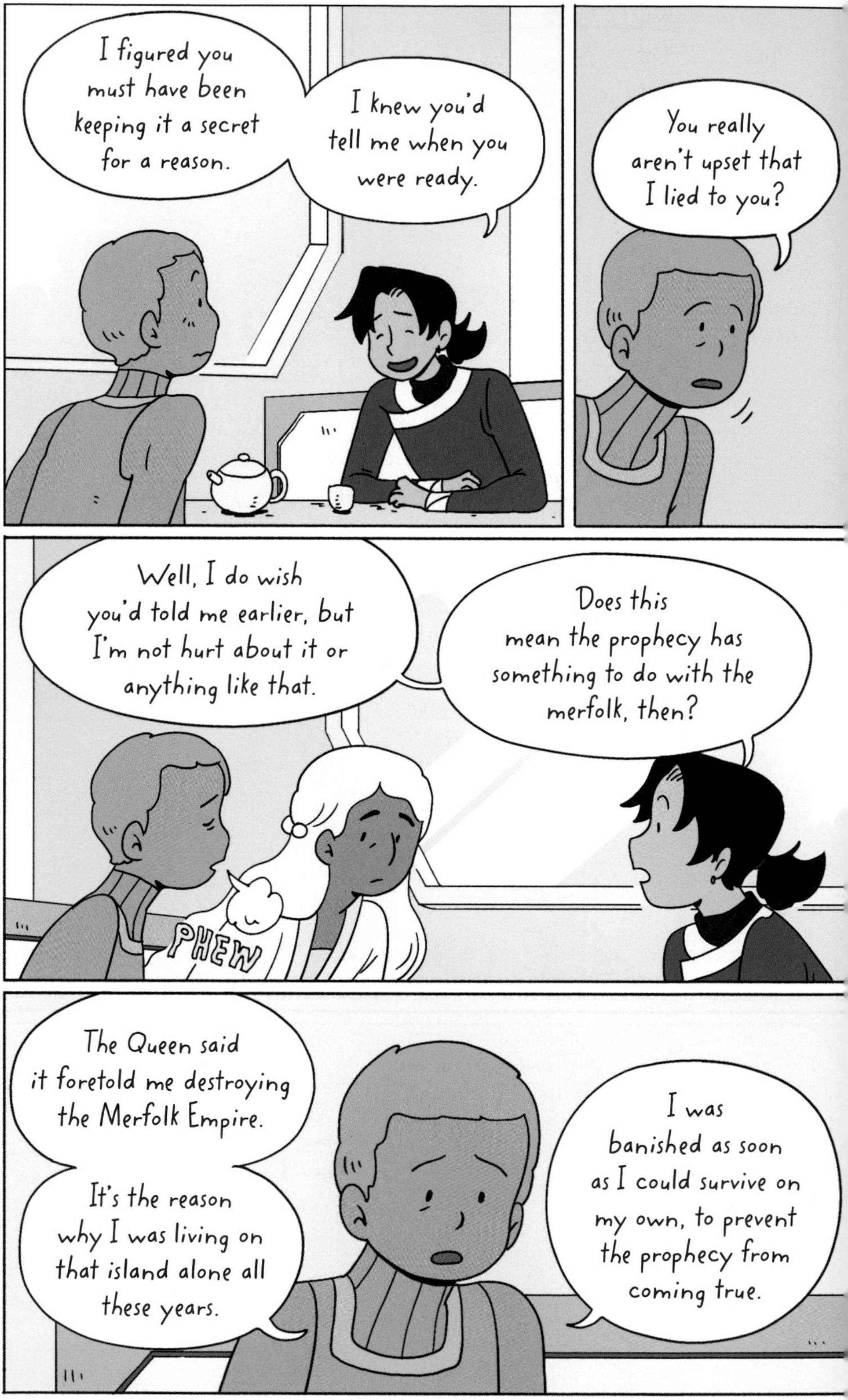
I figured you must have been keeping it a secret for a reason.
I knew you'd tell me when you were ready.
You really aren't upset that I lied to you?
Well, I do wish you'd told me earlier, but I'm not hurt about it or anything like that.
Does this mean the prophecy has something to do with the merfolk, then?
PHEW
The Queen said it foretold me destroying the Merfolk Empire.
It's the reason why I was living on that island alone all these years.
I was banished as soon as I could survive on my own, to prevent the prophecy from coming true.

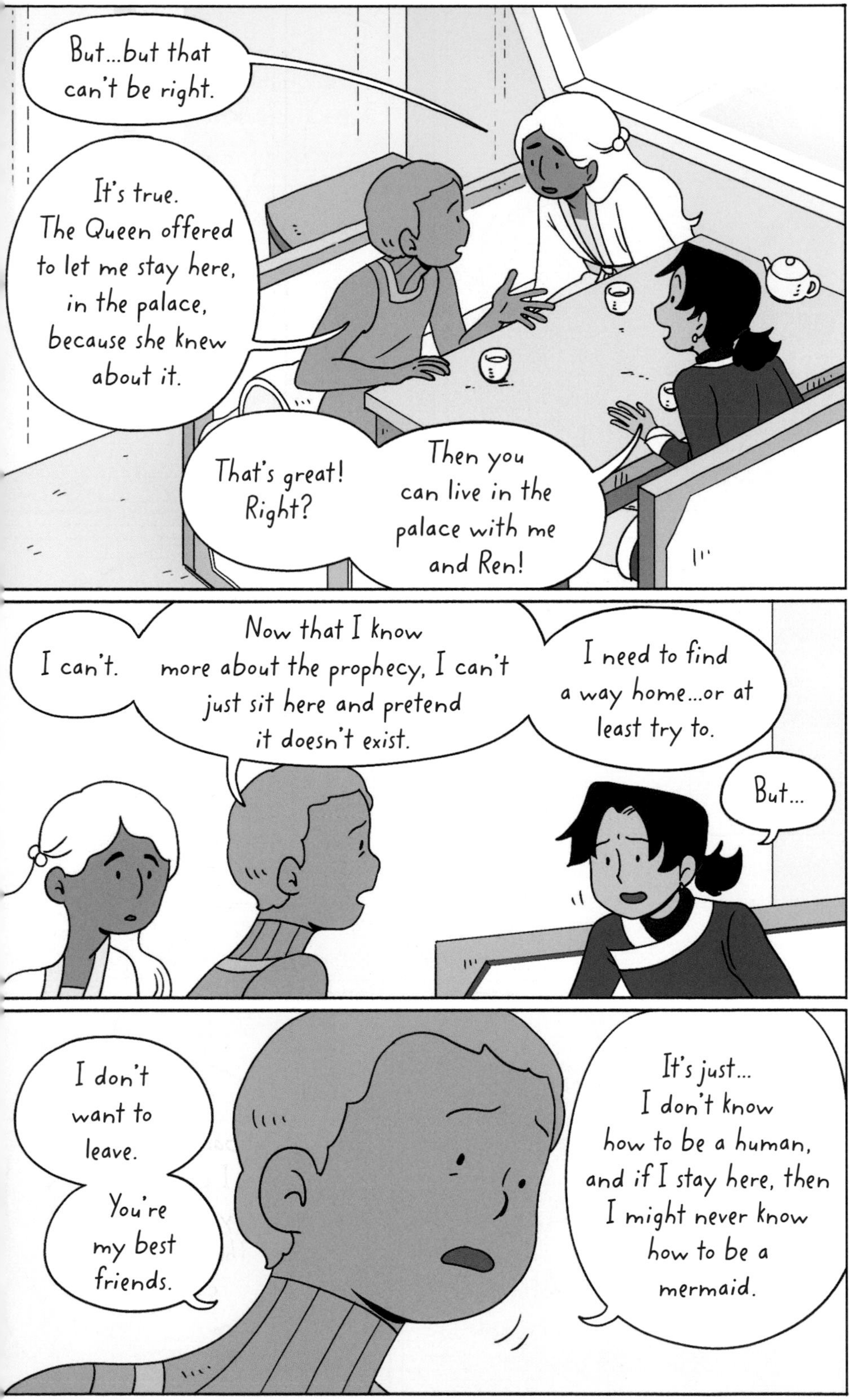
But...but that can't be right.
It's true. The Queen offered to let me stay here, in the palace, because she knew about it.
That's great! Right?
Then you can live in the palace with me and Ren!
I can't.
Now that I know more about the prophecy, I can't just sit here and pretend it doesn't exist.
I need to find a way home...or at least try to.
But...
I don't want to leave.
You're my best friends.
It's just... I don't know how to be a human, and if I stay here, then I might never know how to be a mermaid.

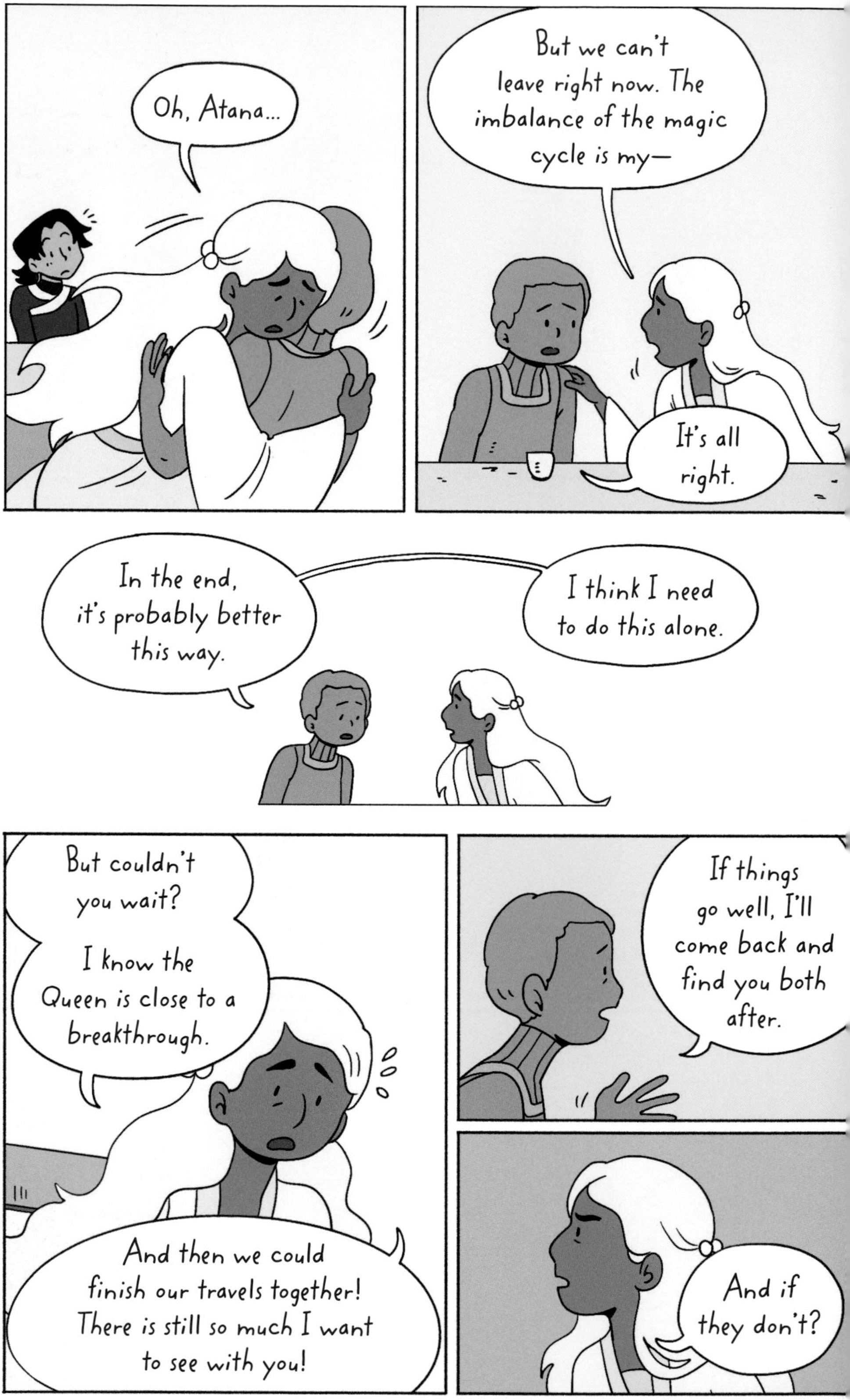
Oh, Atana...
But we can't leave right now. The imbalance of the magic cycle is my—
It's all right.
In the end, it's probably better this way.
I think I need to do this alone.
But couldn't you wait?
I know the Queen is close to a breakthrough.
And then we could finish our travels together! There is still so much I want to see with you!
If things go well, I'll come back and find you both after.
And if they don't?

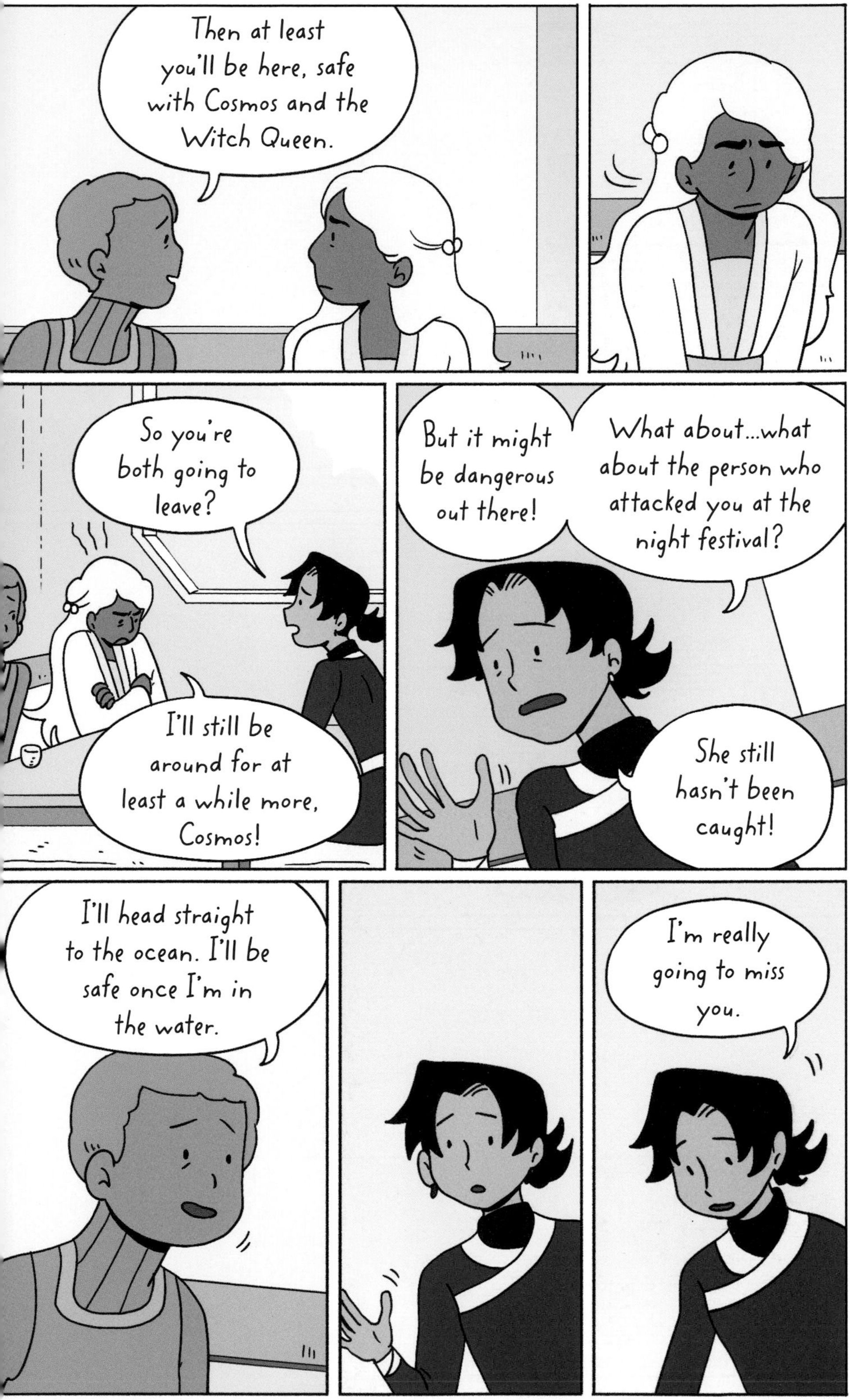
Then at least you'll be here, safe with Cosmos and the Witch Queen.
So you're both going to leave?
I'll still be around for at least a while more, Cosmos!
But it might be dangerous out there!
What about...what about the person who attacked you at the night festival?
She still hasn't been caught!
I'll head straight to the ocean. I'll be safe once I'm in the water.
I'm really going to miss you.

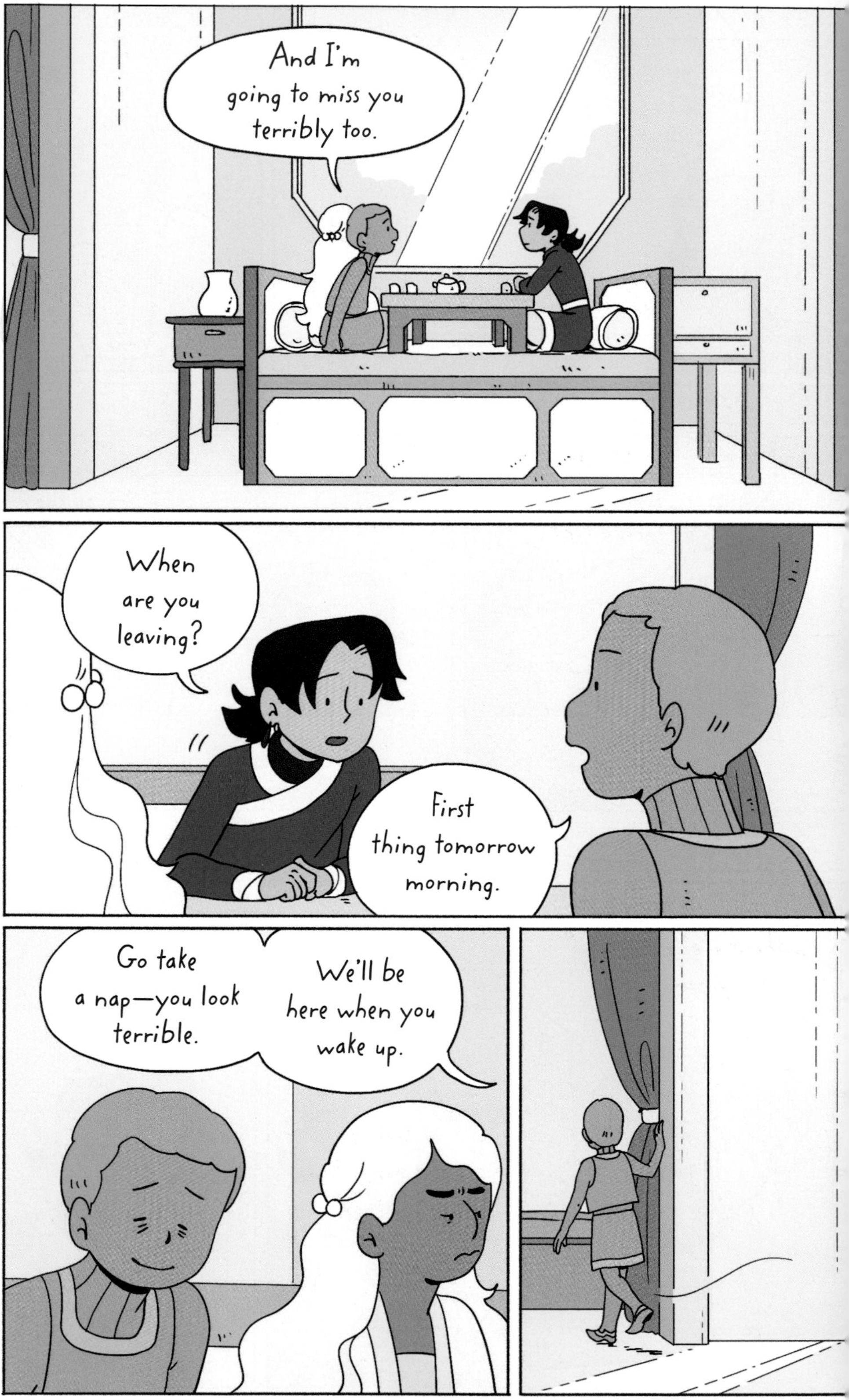
And I'm going to miss you terribly too.
When are you leaving?
First thing tomorrow morning.
Go take a nap—you look terrible.
We'll be here when you wake up.

CHAPTER 17

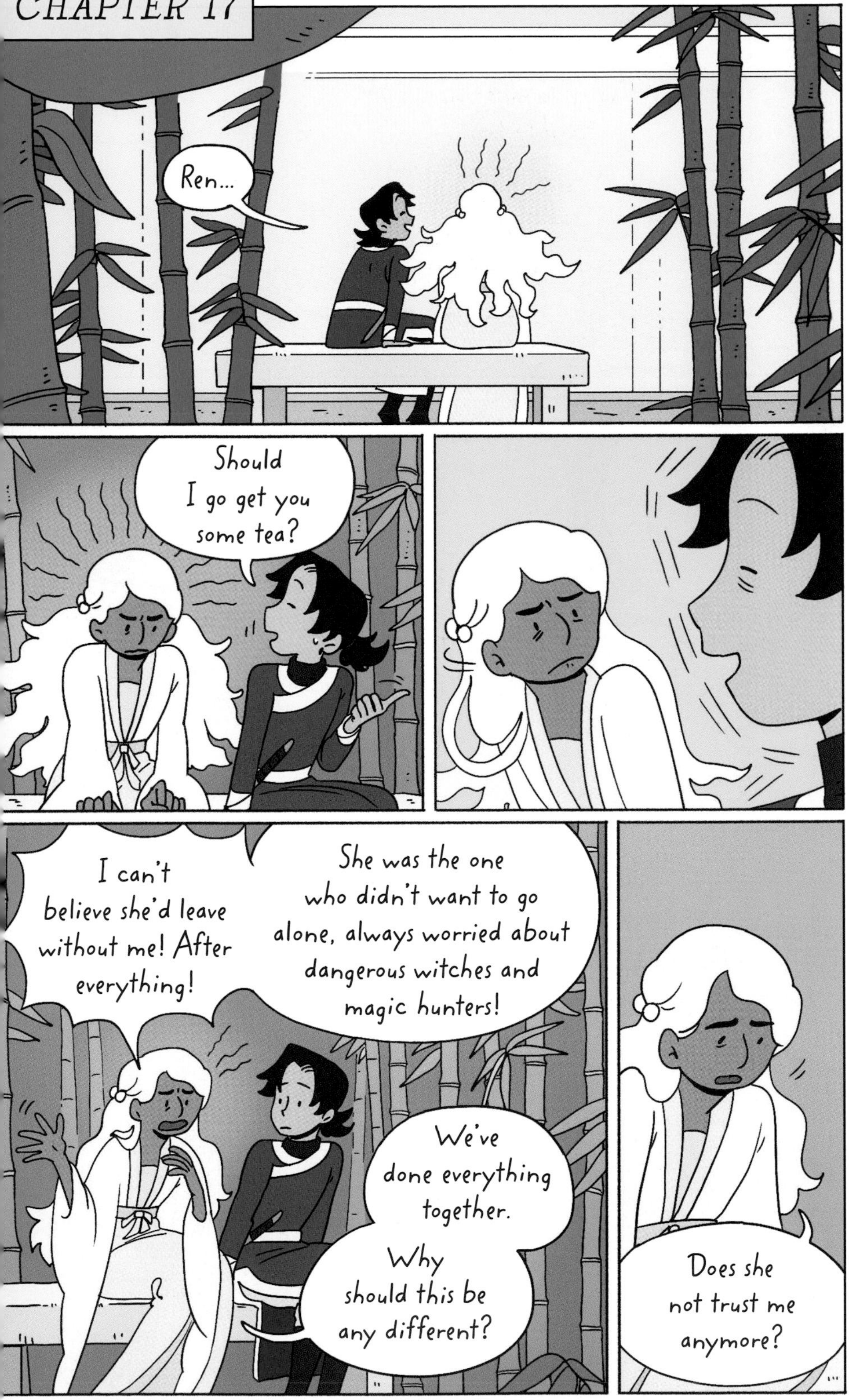

Ren...
Should I go get you some tea?
I can't believe she'd leave without me! After everything!
She was the one who didn't want to go alone, always worried about dangerous witches and magic hunters!
We've done everything together.
Why should this be any different?
Does she not trust me anymore?

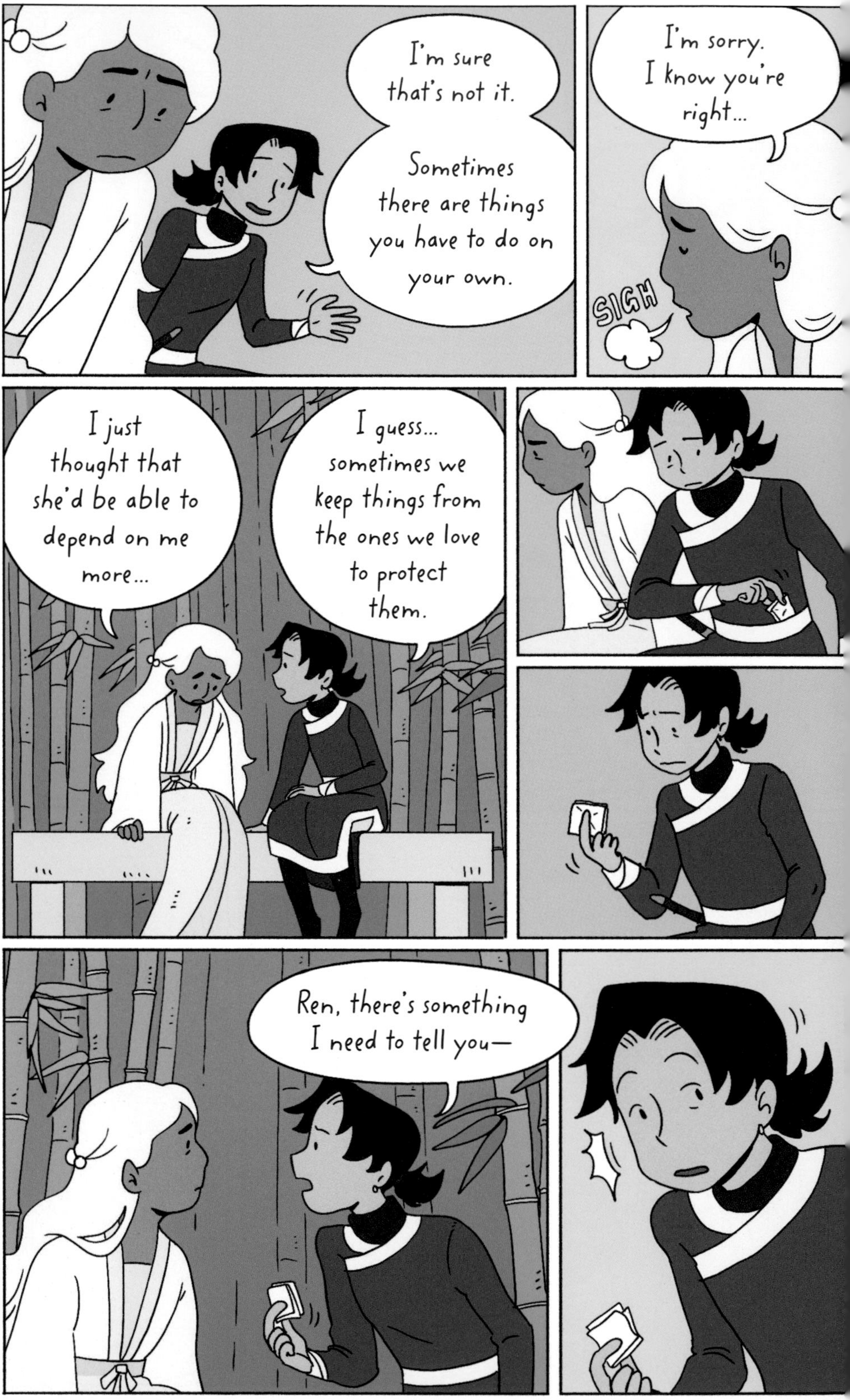
I'm sure that's not it.
Sometimes there are things you have to do on your own.
I'm sorry. I know you're right...
SIGH
I just thought that she'd be able to depend on me more...
I guess... sometimes we keep things from the ones we love to protect them.
Ren, there's something I need to tell you—

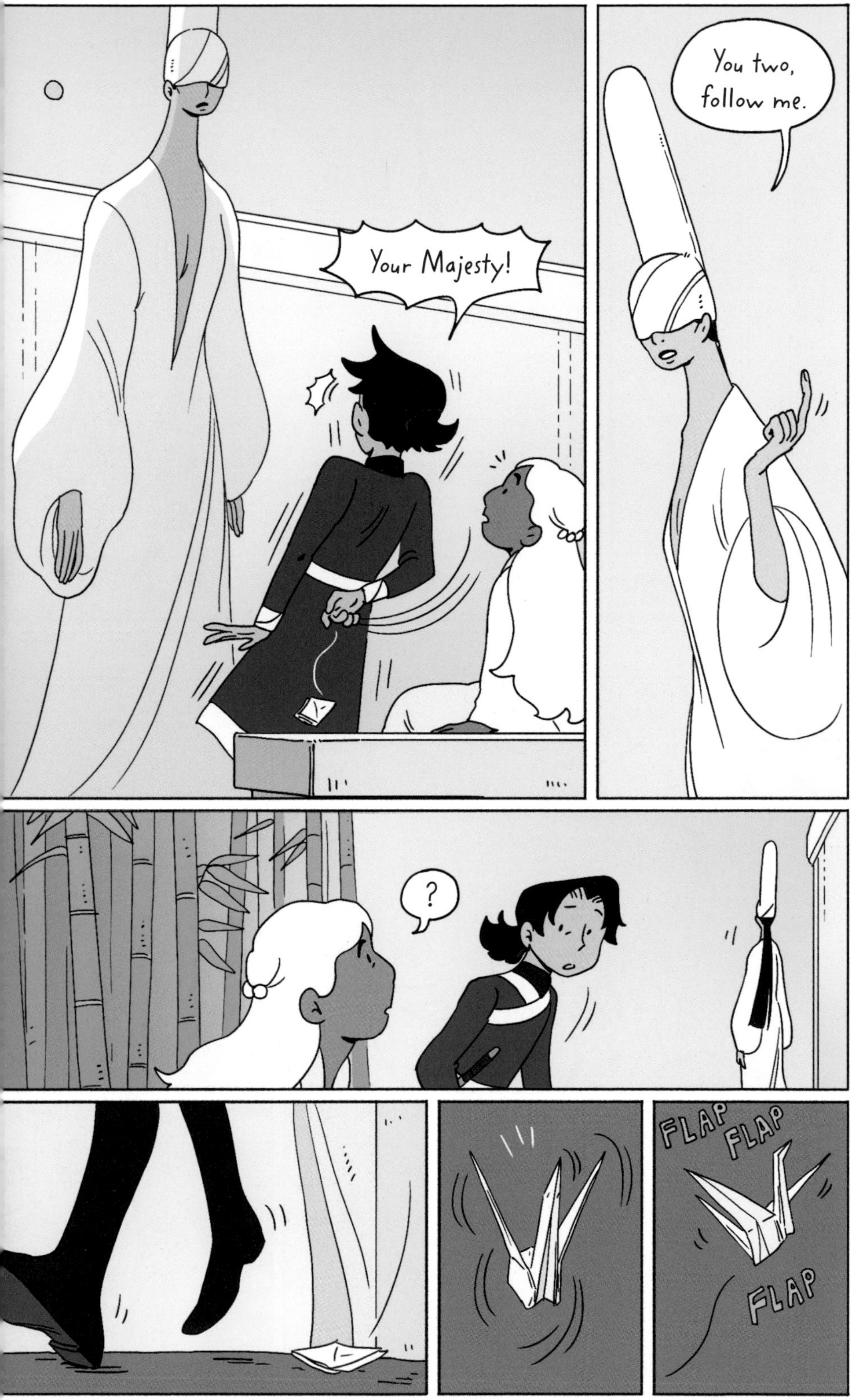
Your Majesty!
You two, follow me.
?
FLAP
FLAP
FLAP

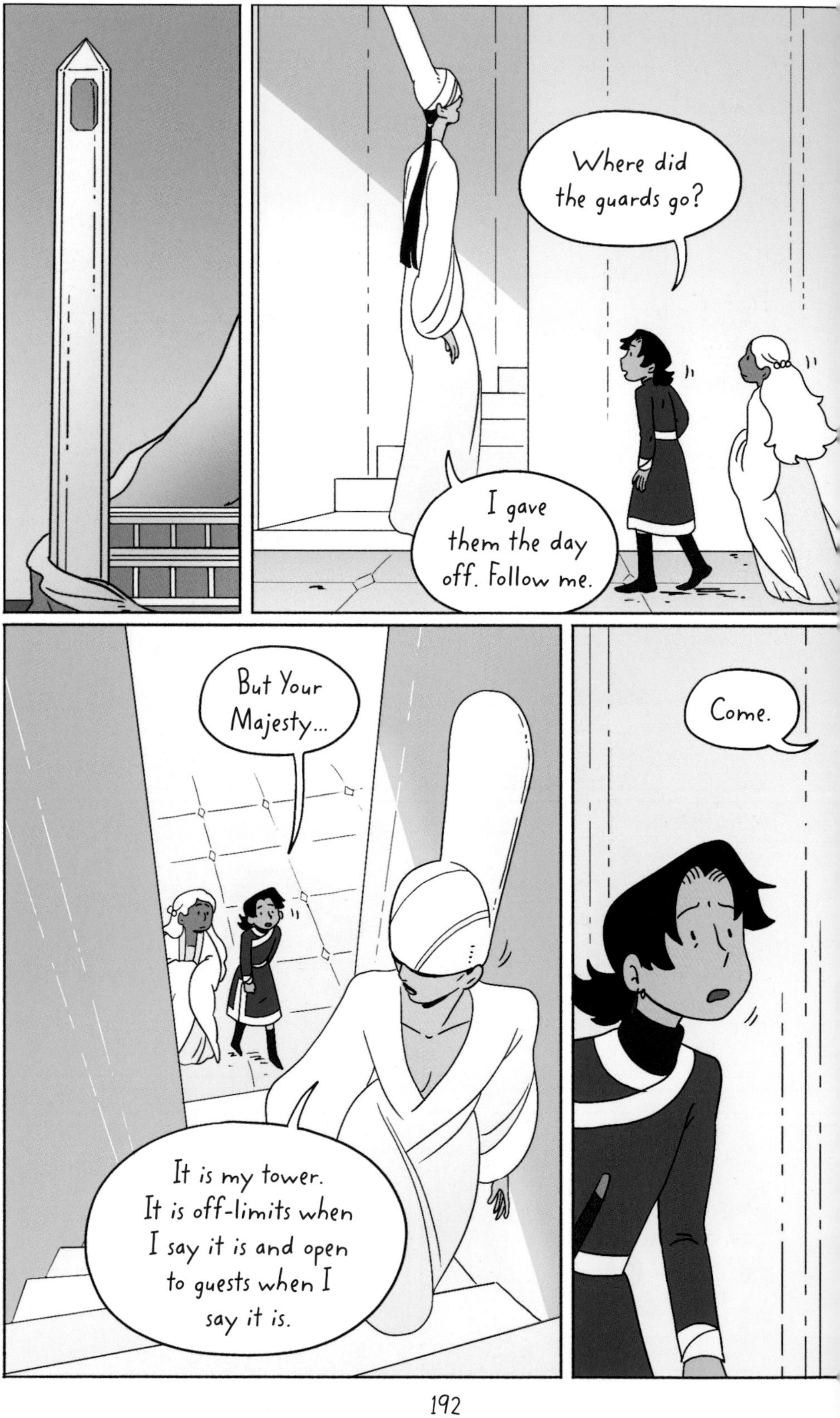
Where did the guards go?
I gave them the day off. Follow me.
But Your Majesty...
It is my tower. It is off-limits when I say it is and open to guests when I say it is.
Come.

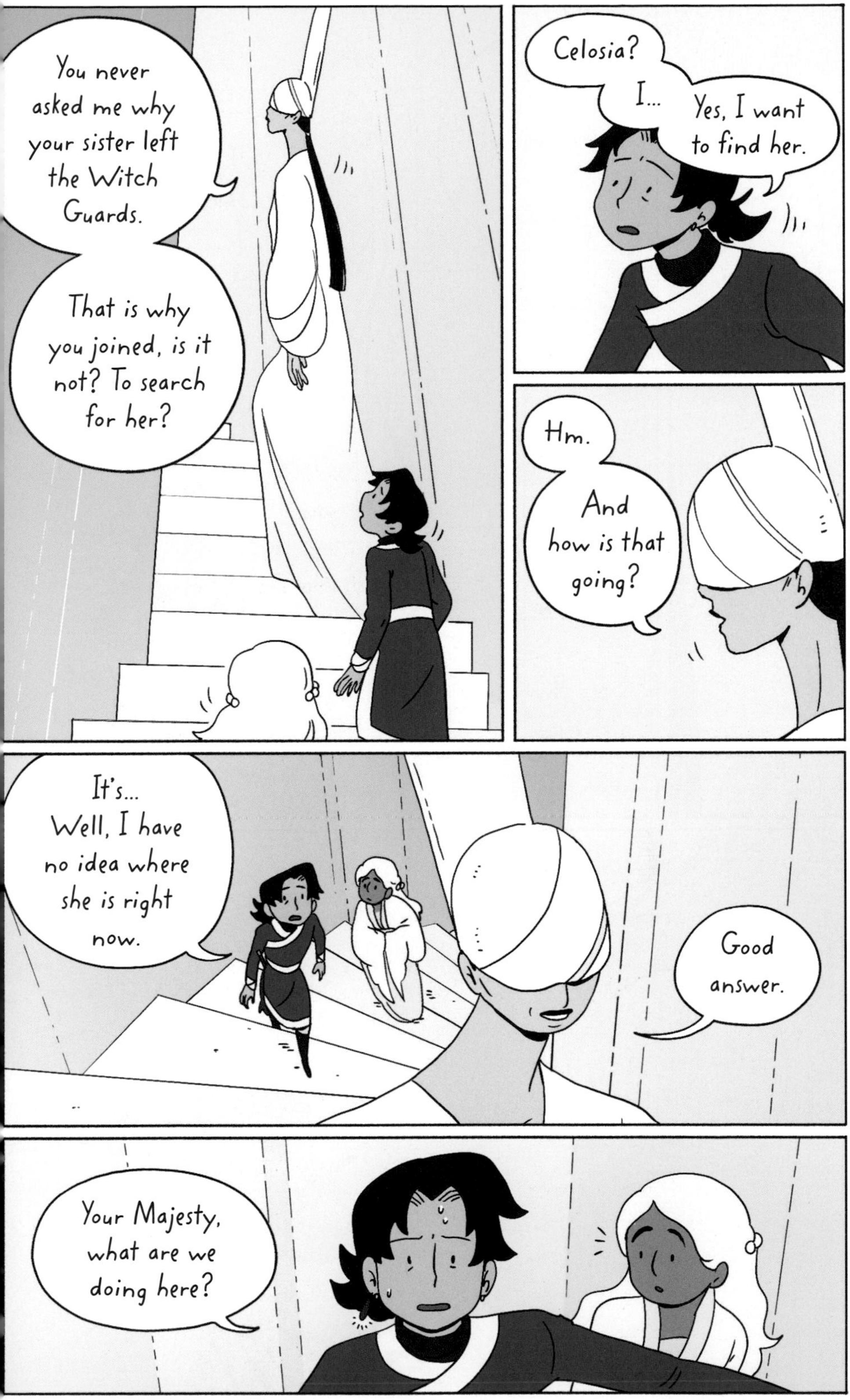
You never asked me why your sister left the Witch Guards.
That is why you joined, is it not? To search for her?
Celosia?
I...
Yes, I want to find her.
Hm.
And how is that going?
It's... Well, I have no idea where she is right now.
Good answer.
Your Majesty, what are we doing here?

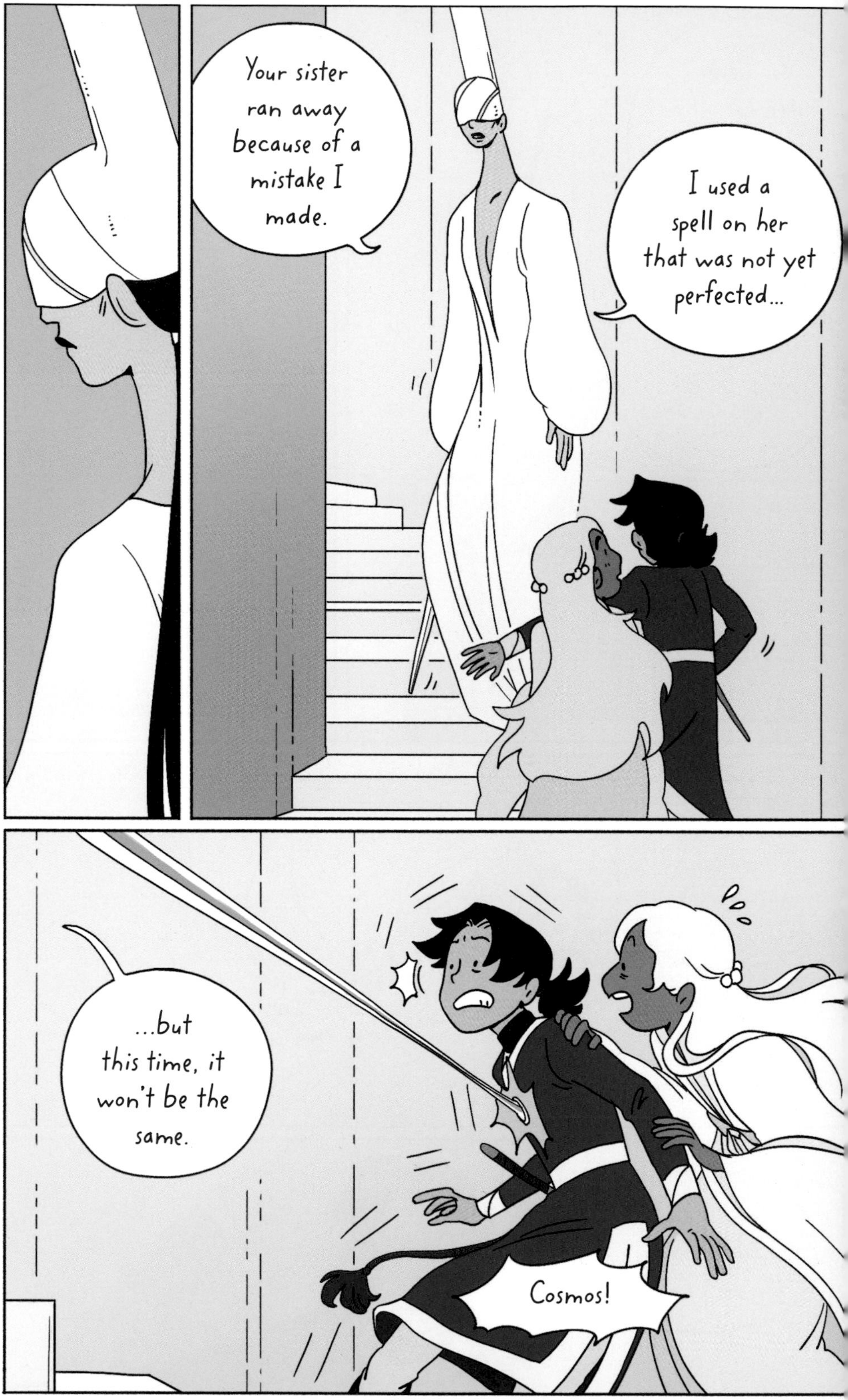
Your sister ran away because of a mistake I made.
I used a spell on her that was not yet perfected...
...but this time, it won't be the same.
Cosmos!

CHAPTER 18

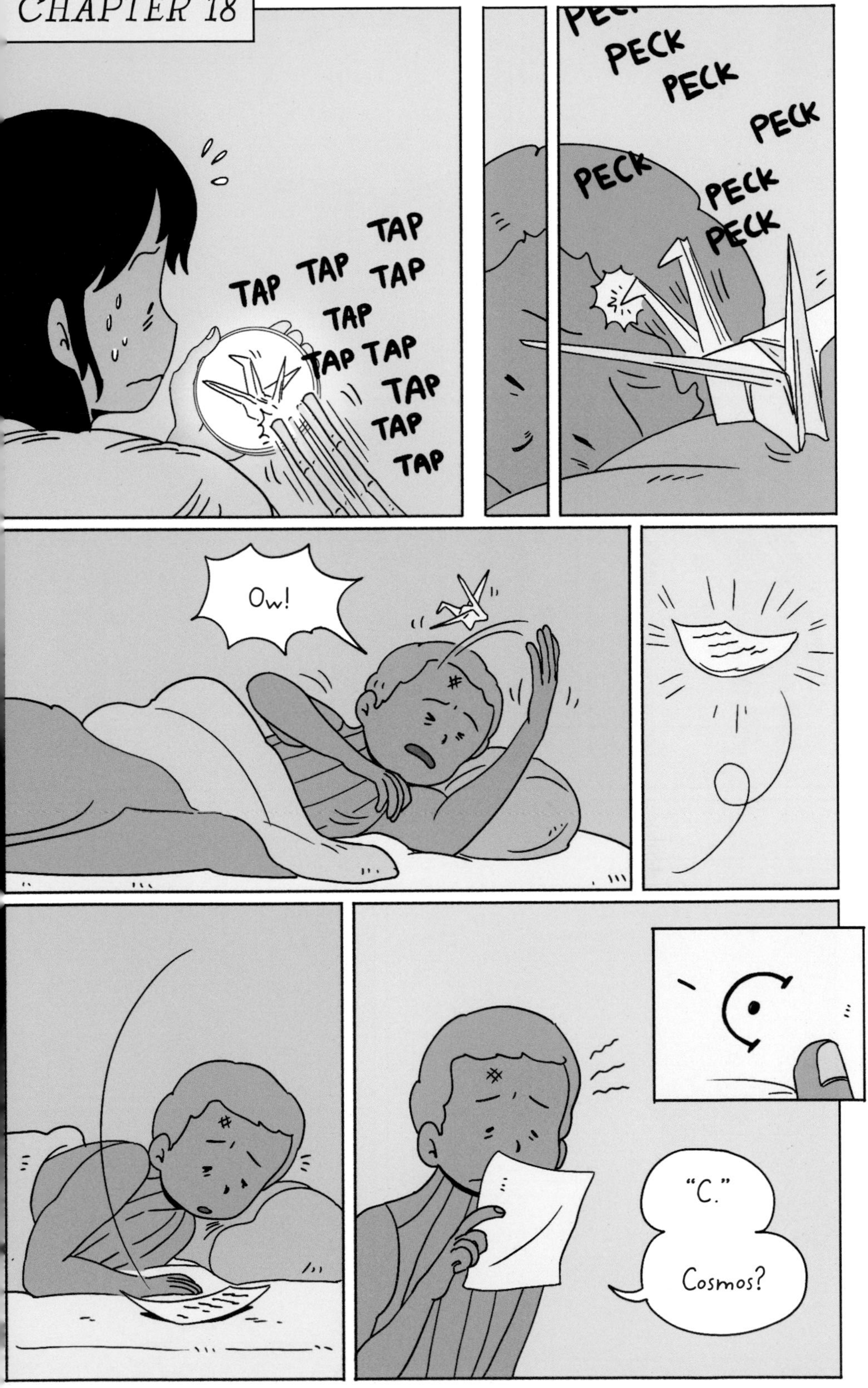
TAP TAP TAP TAP TAP TAP TAP TAP TAP TAP
PECK PECK PECK PECK PECK PECK
Ow!
"C."
Cosmos?

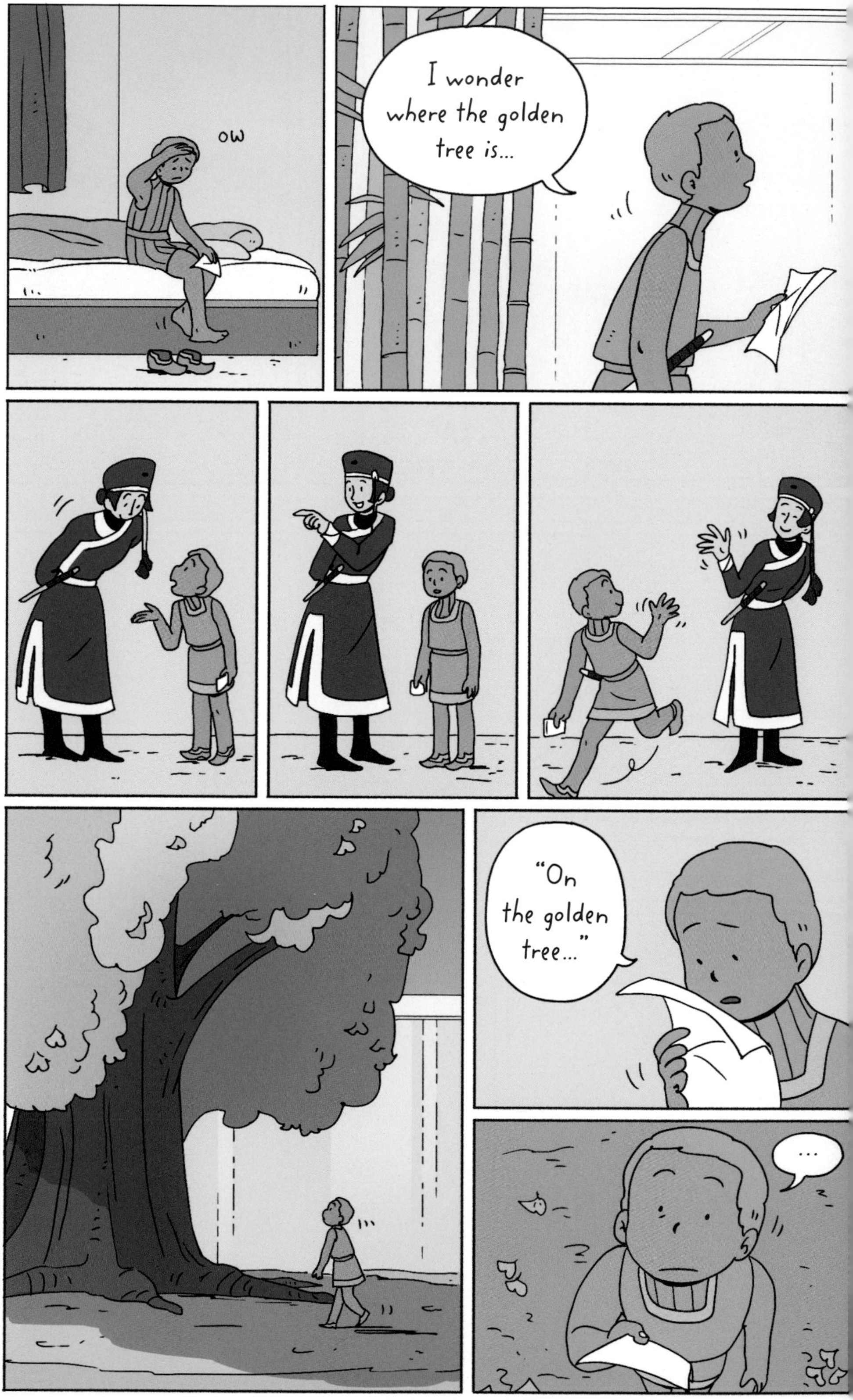
ow
I wonder where the golden tree is...
"On the golden tree..."
...

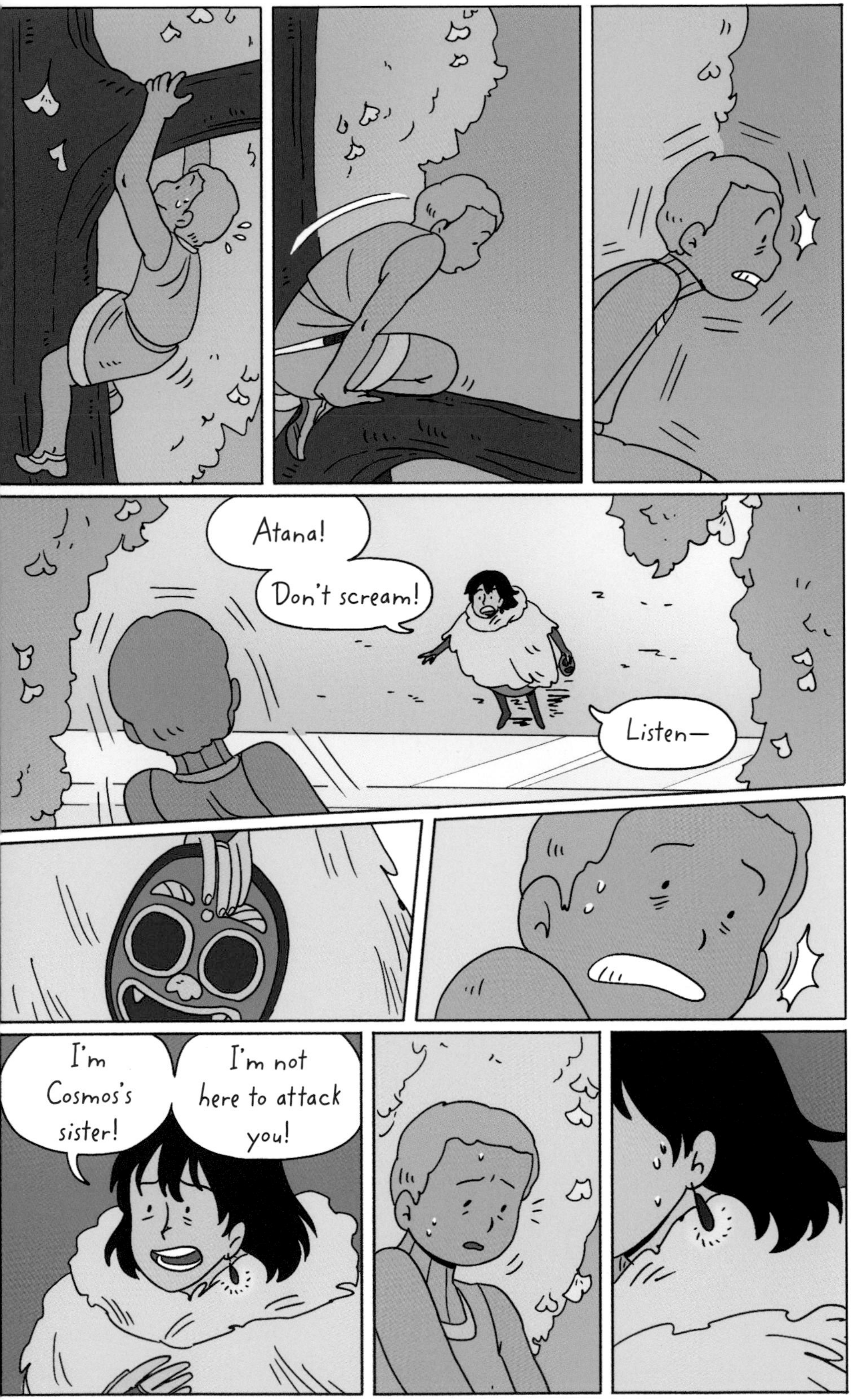
Atana!
Don't scream!
Listen—
I'm Cosmos's sister!
I'm not here to attack you!

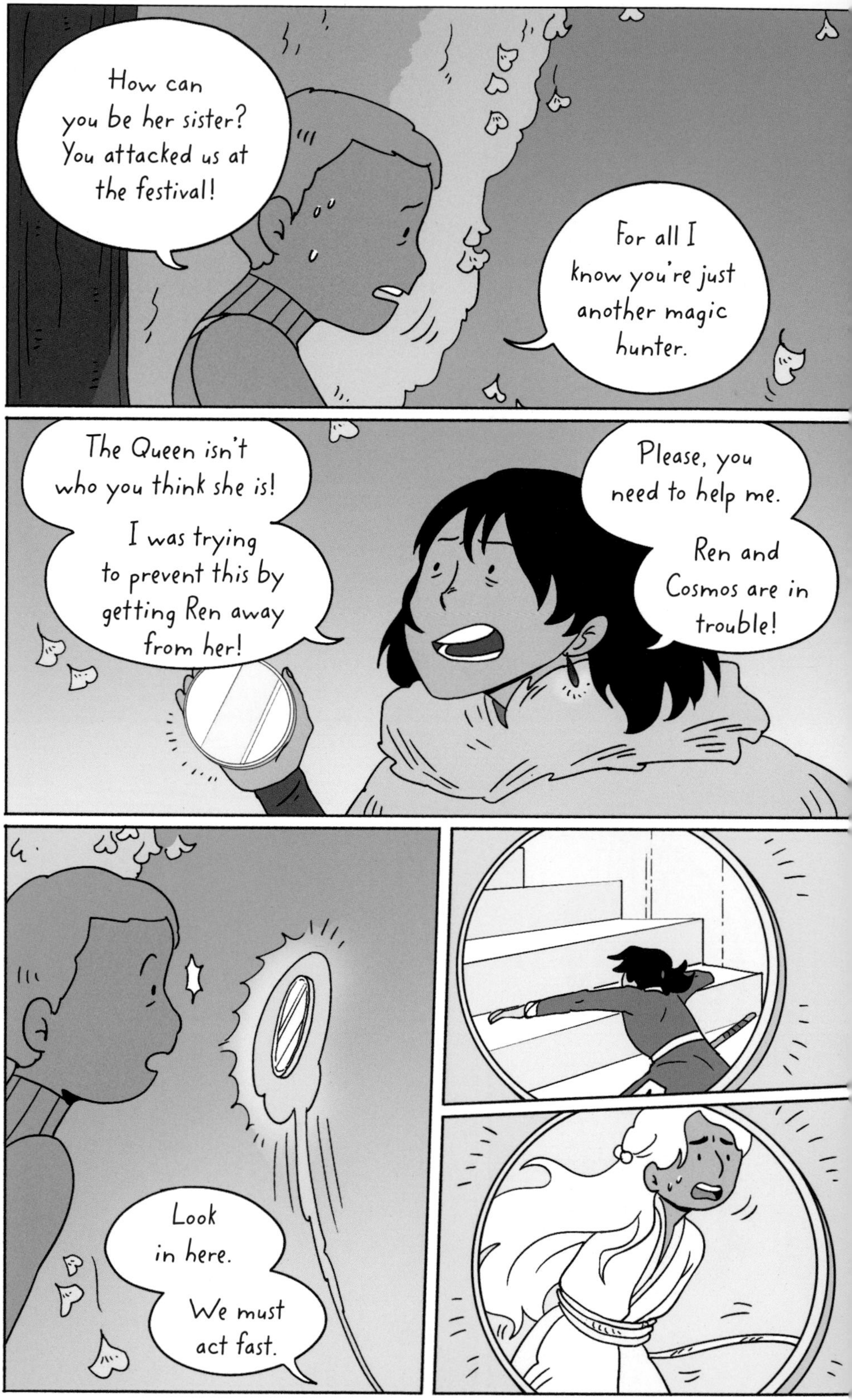
How can you be her sister? You attacked us at the festival!
For all I know you're just another magic hunter.
The Queen isn't who you think she is!
I was trying to prevent this by getting Ren away from her!
Please, you need to help me.
Ren and Cosmos are in trouble!
Look in here.
We must act fast.

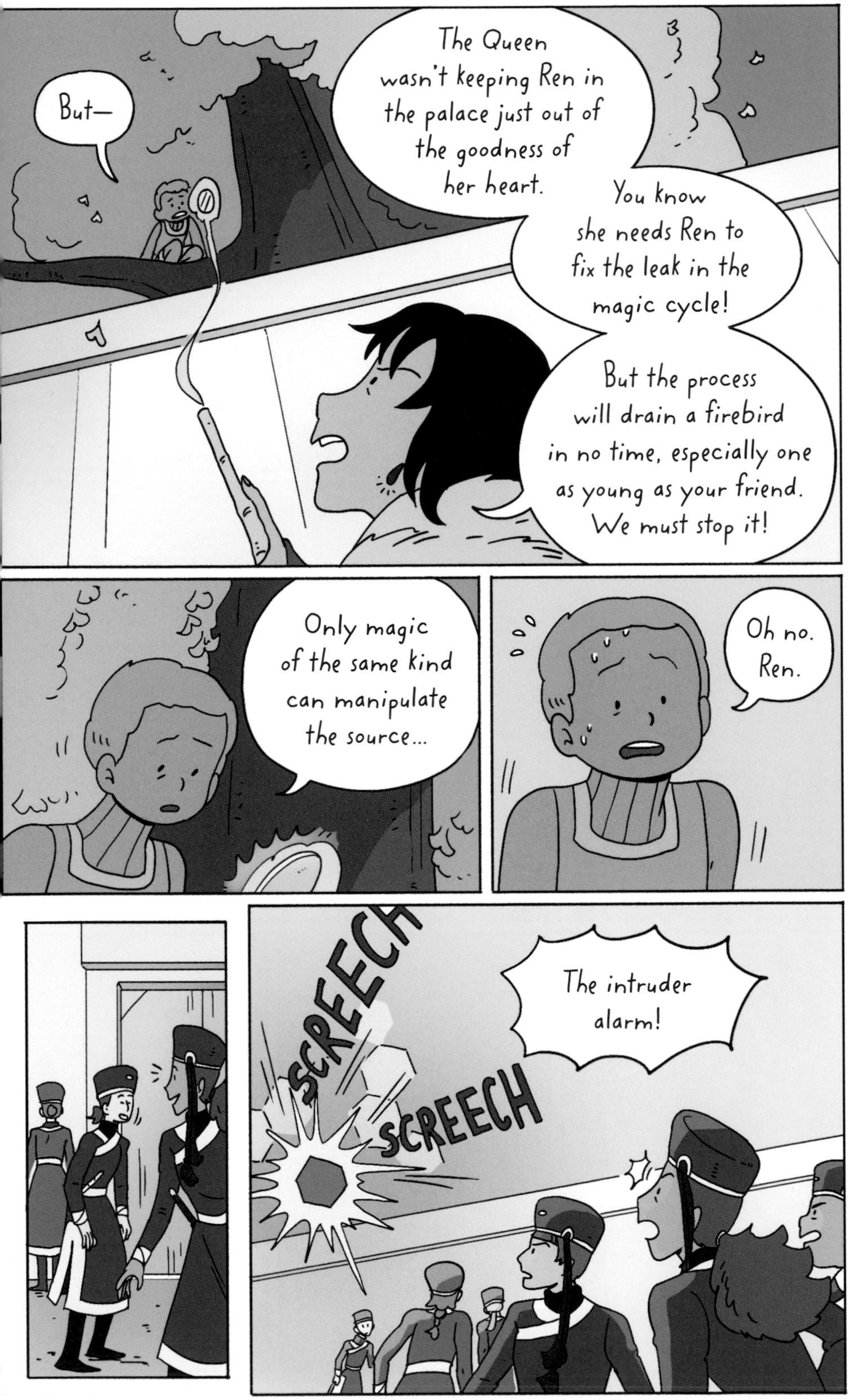
But—
The Queen wasn't keeping Ren in the palace just out of the goodness of her heart.
You know she needs Ren to fix the leak in the magic cycle!
But the process will drain a firebird in no time, especially one as young as your friend. We must stop it!
Only magic of the same kind can manipulate the source...
Oh no. Ren.
SCREECH
SCREECH
The intruder alarm!

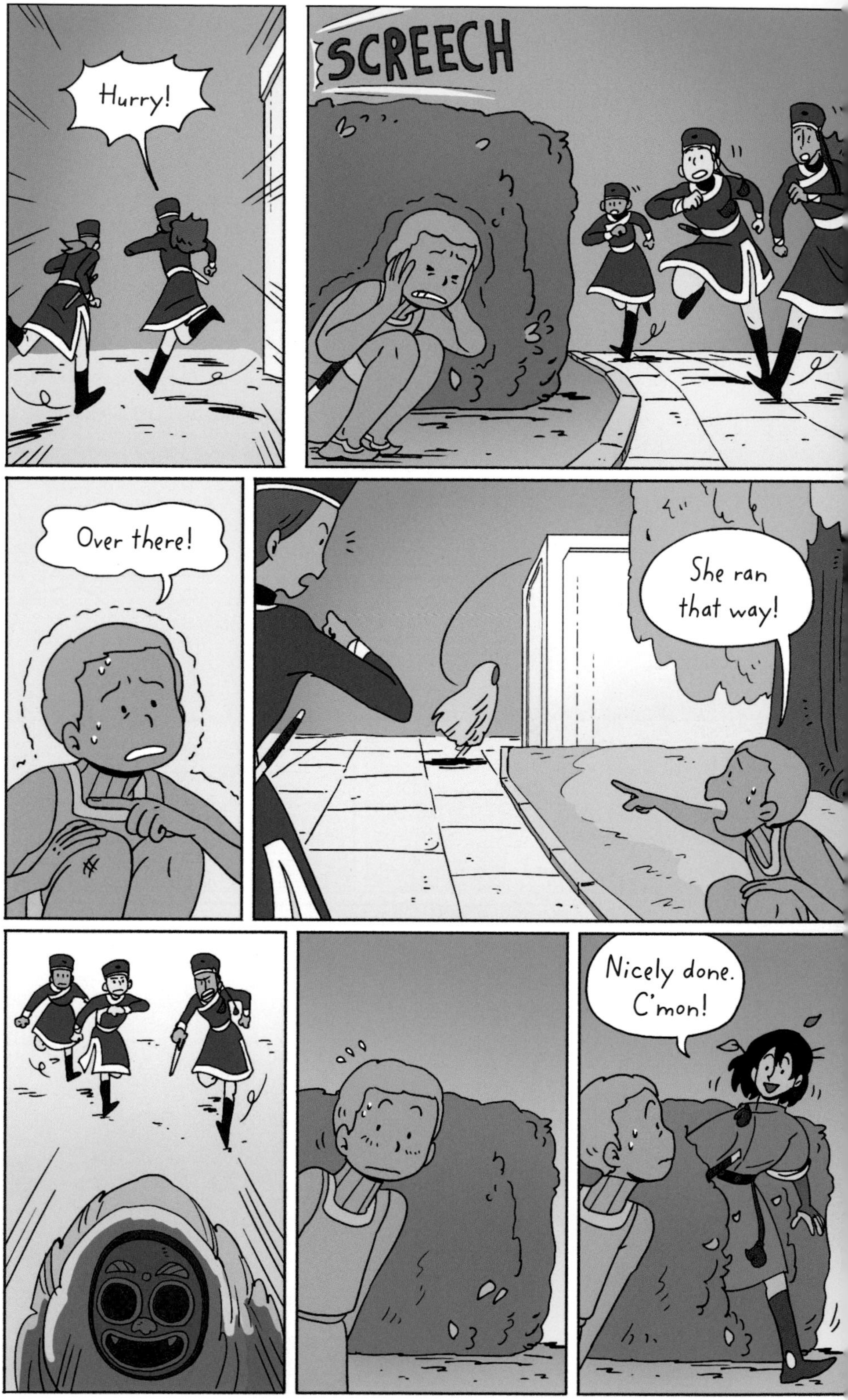
Hurry!
SCREECH
Over there!
She ran that way!
Nicely done. C'mon!

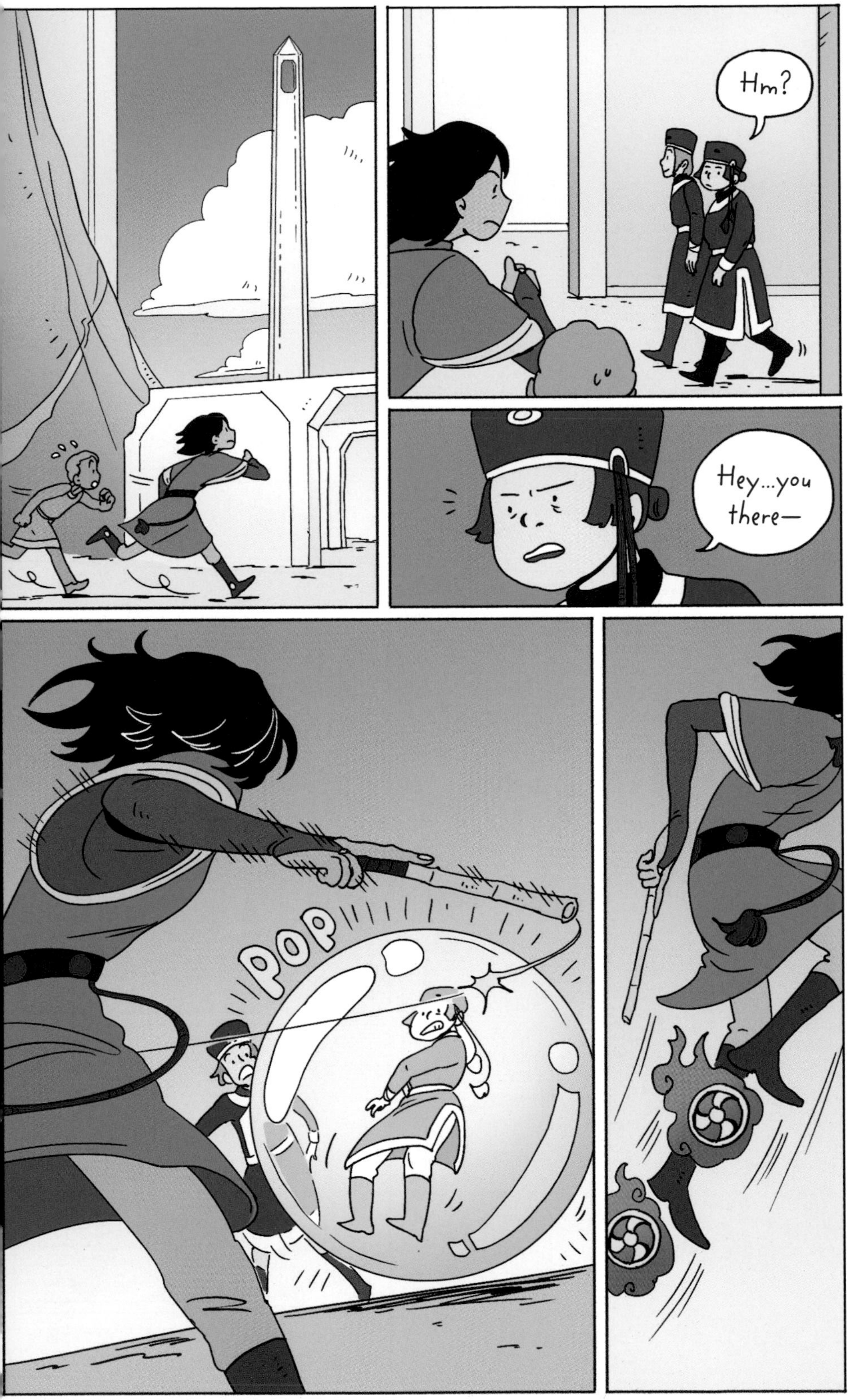
Hm?
Hey...you there—
POP

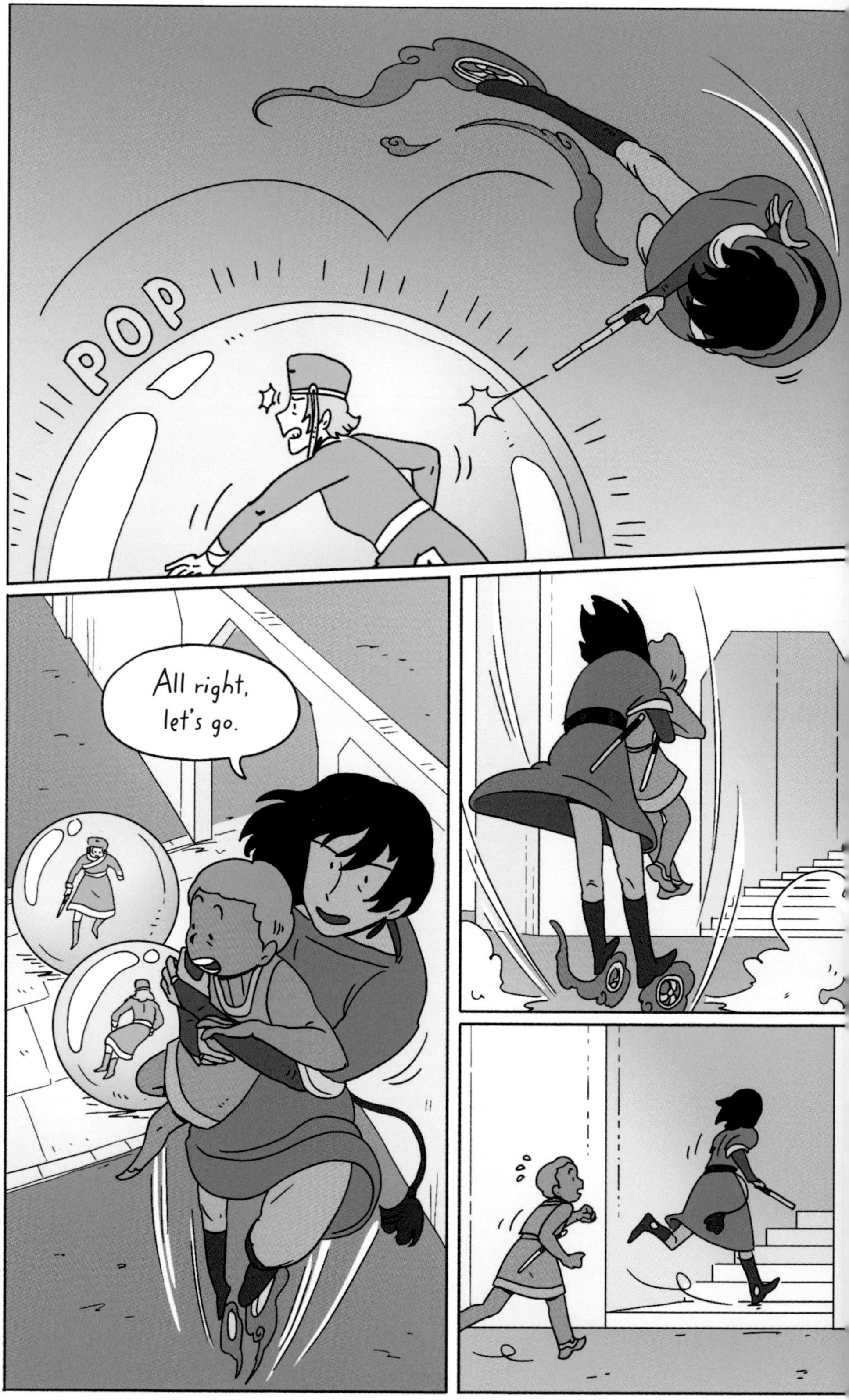
POP
All right, let's go.

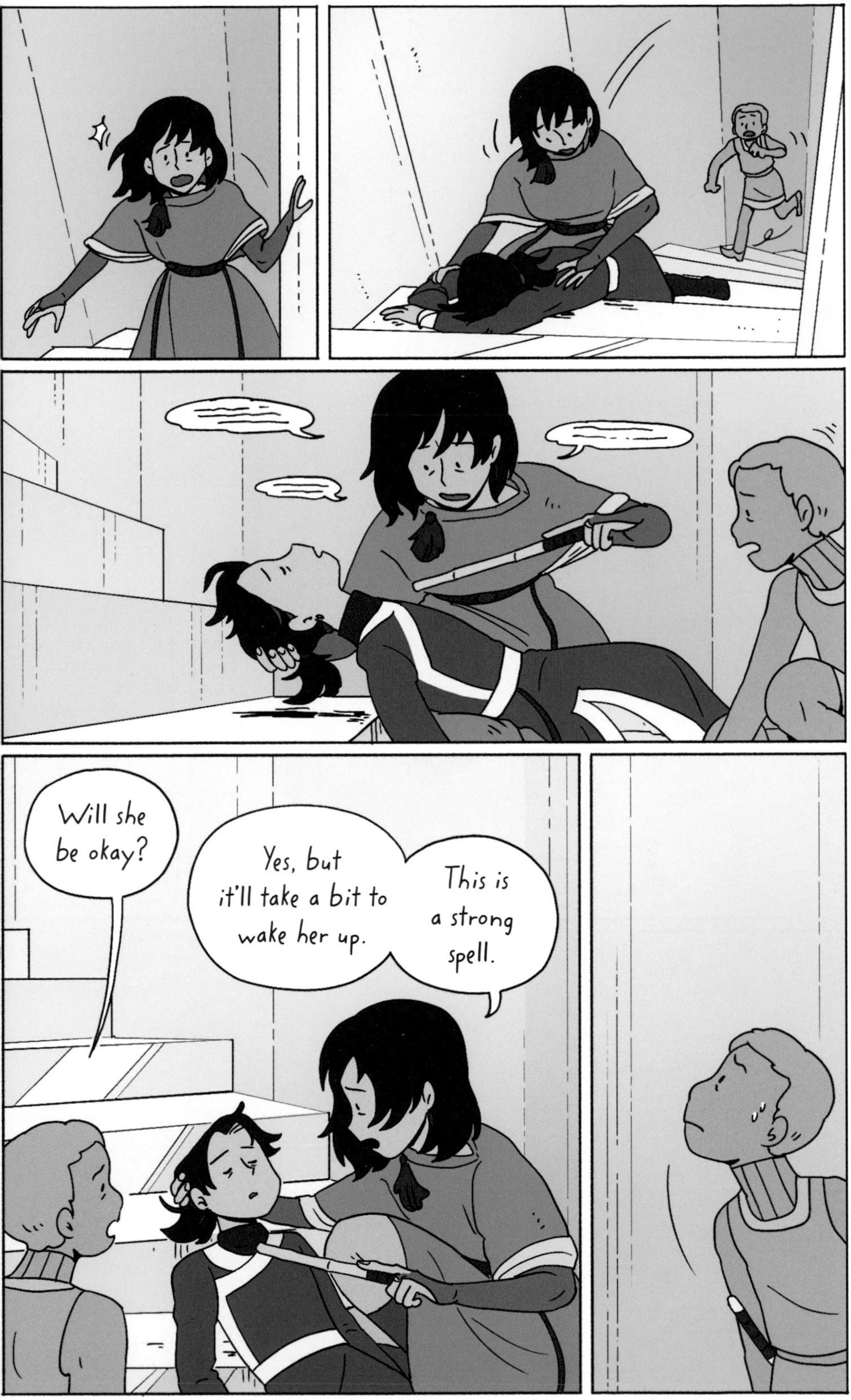
Will she be okay?
Yes, but it'll take a bit to wake her up.
This is a strong spell.

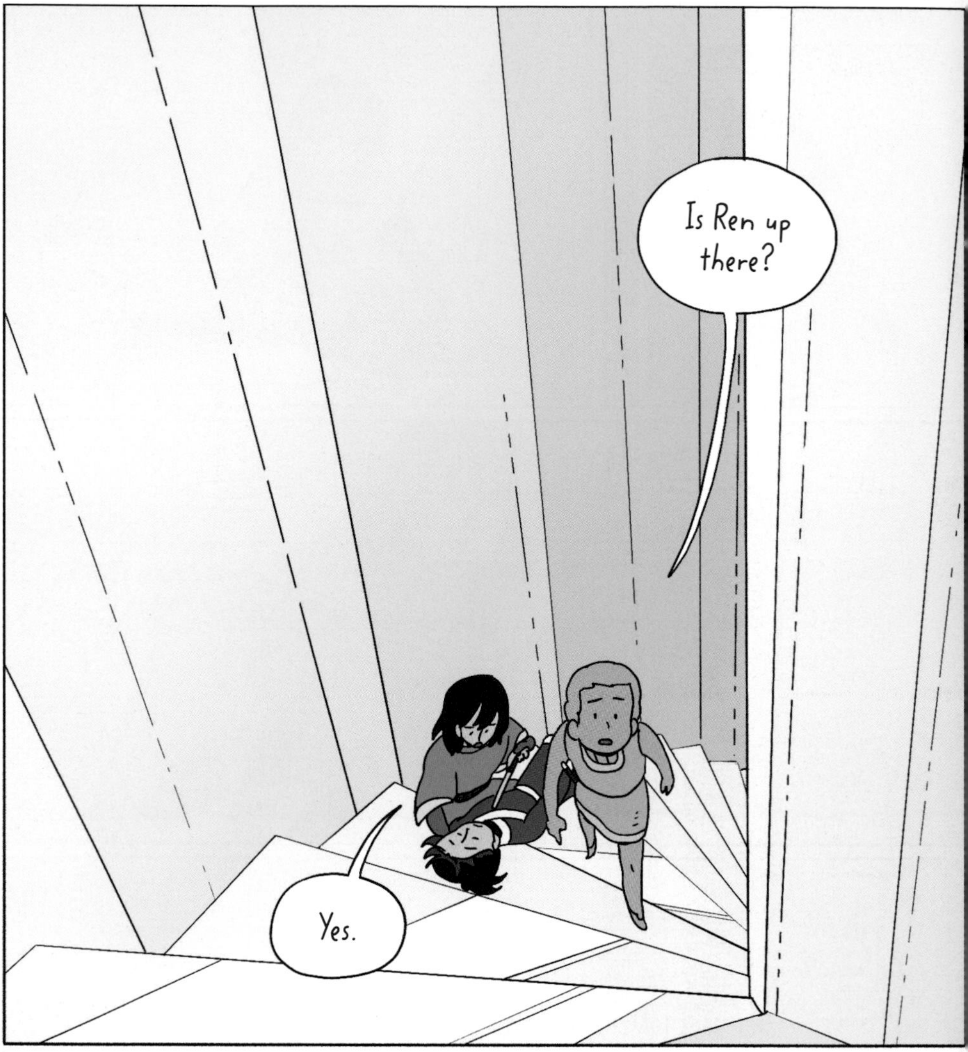
Is Ren up there?
Yes.

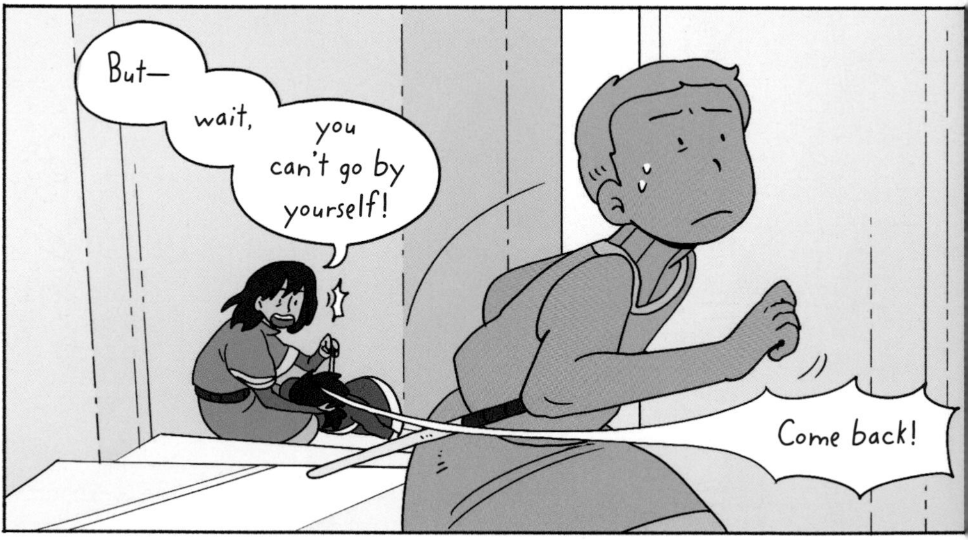
But—
wait,
you can't go by yourself!
Come back!

CHAPTER 19

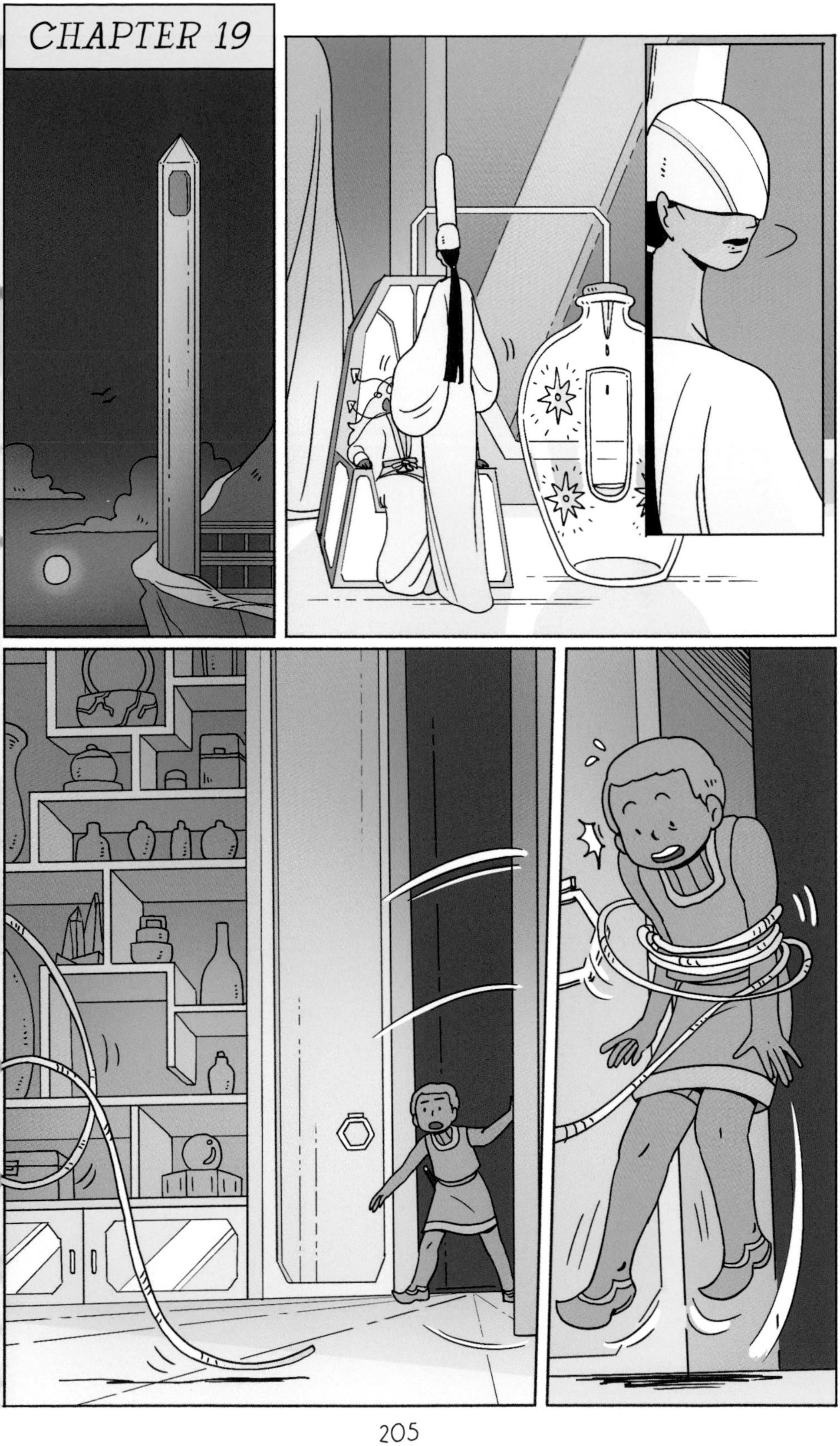

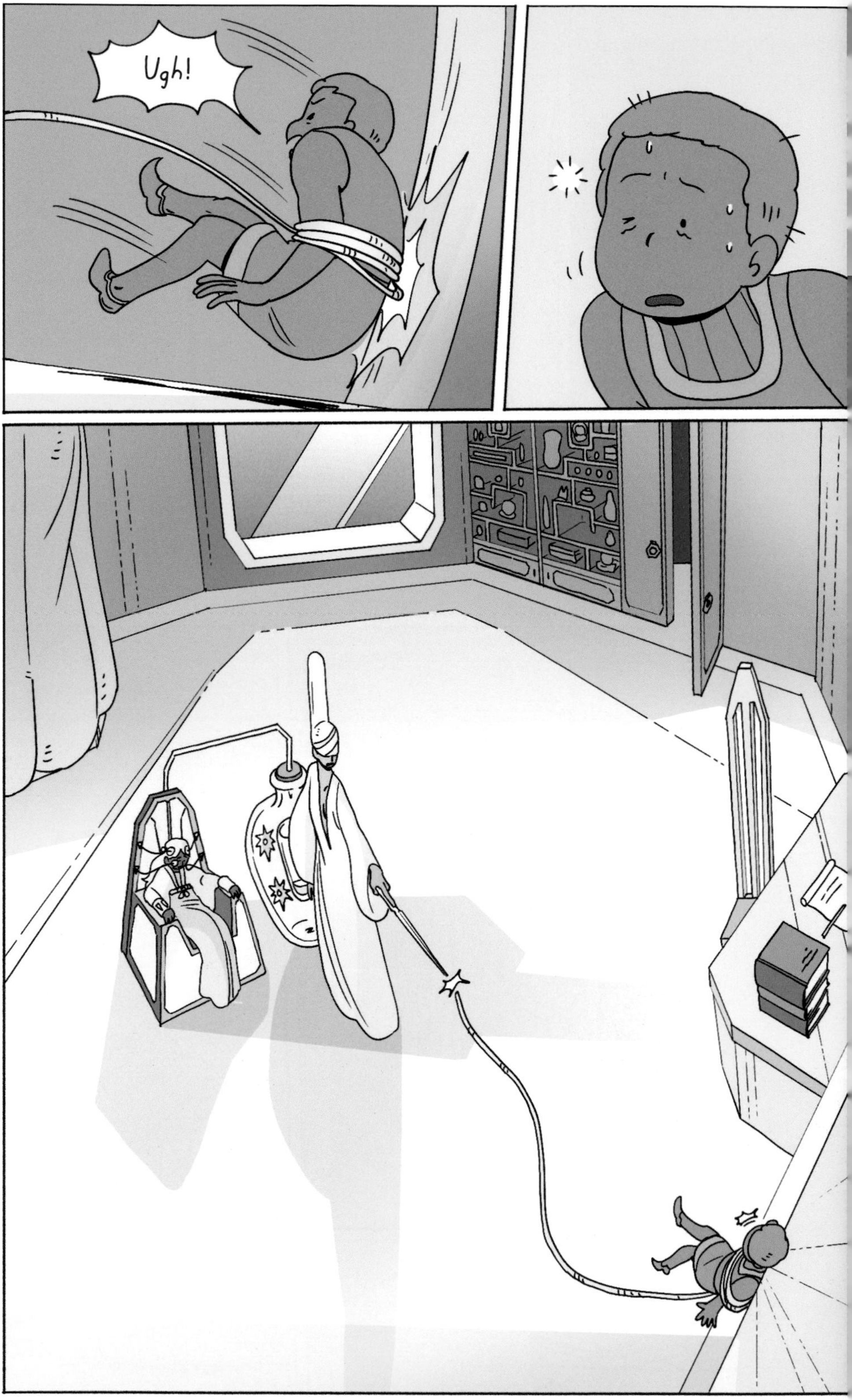
Ugh!

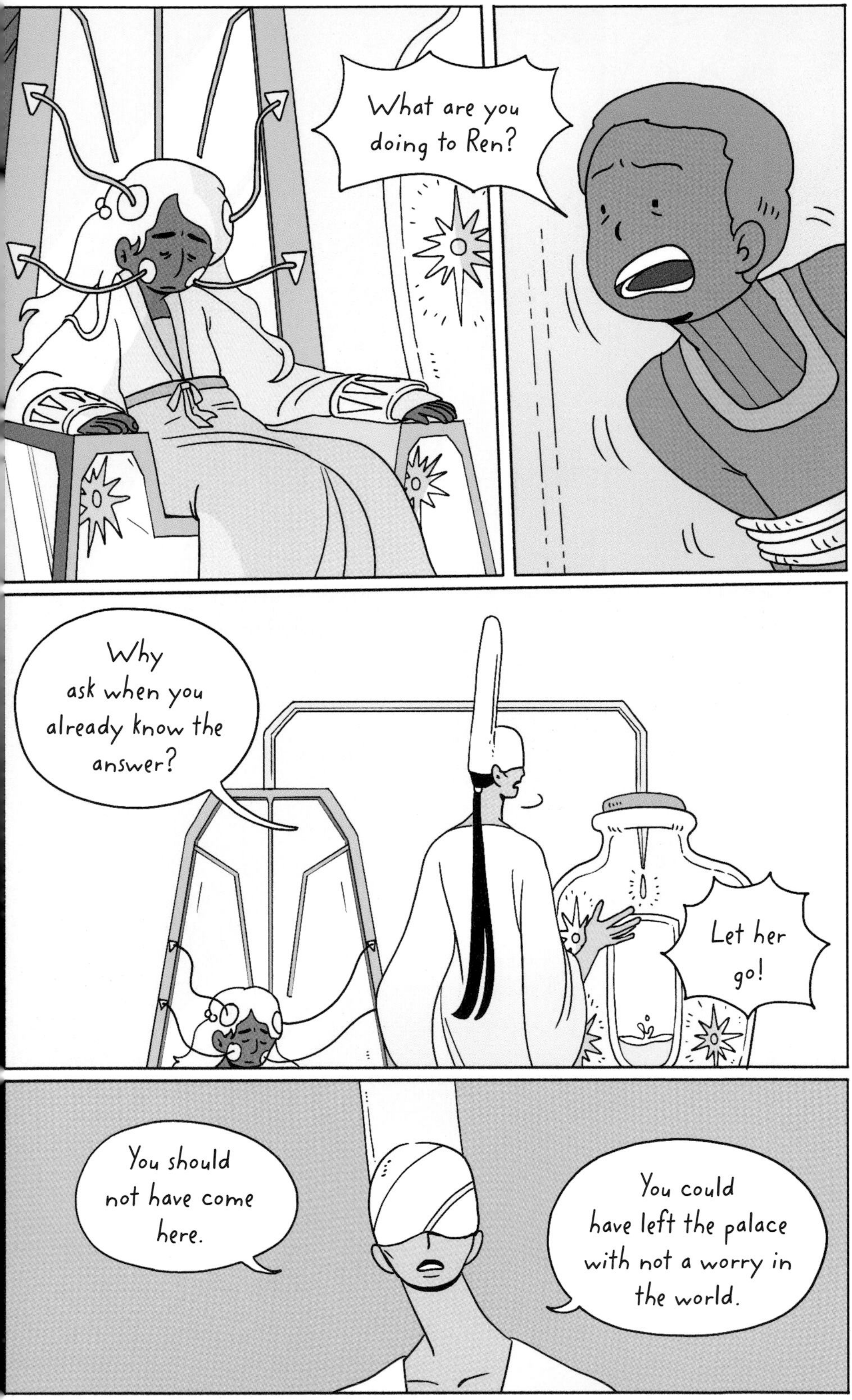
What are you doing to Ren?
Why ask when you already know the answer?
Let her go!
You should not have come here.
You could have left the palace with not a worry in the world.

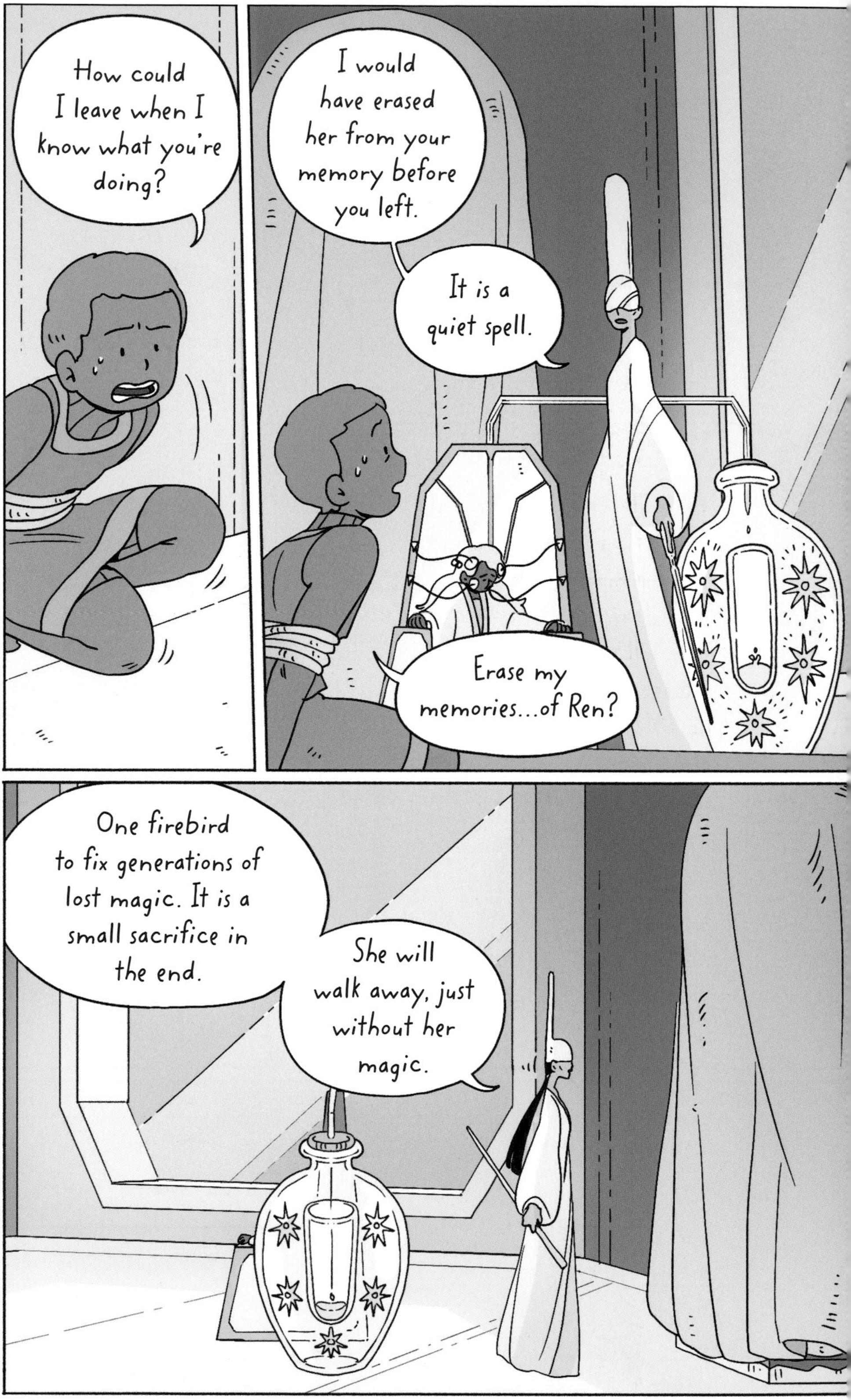
How could I leave when I know what you're doing?
I would have erased her from your memory before you left.
It is a quiet spell.
Erase my memories...of Ren?
One firebird to fix generations of lost magic. It is a small sacrifice in the end.
She will walk away, just without her magic.

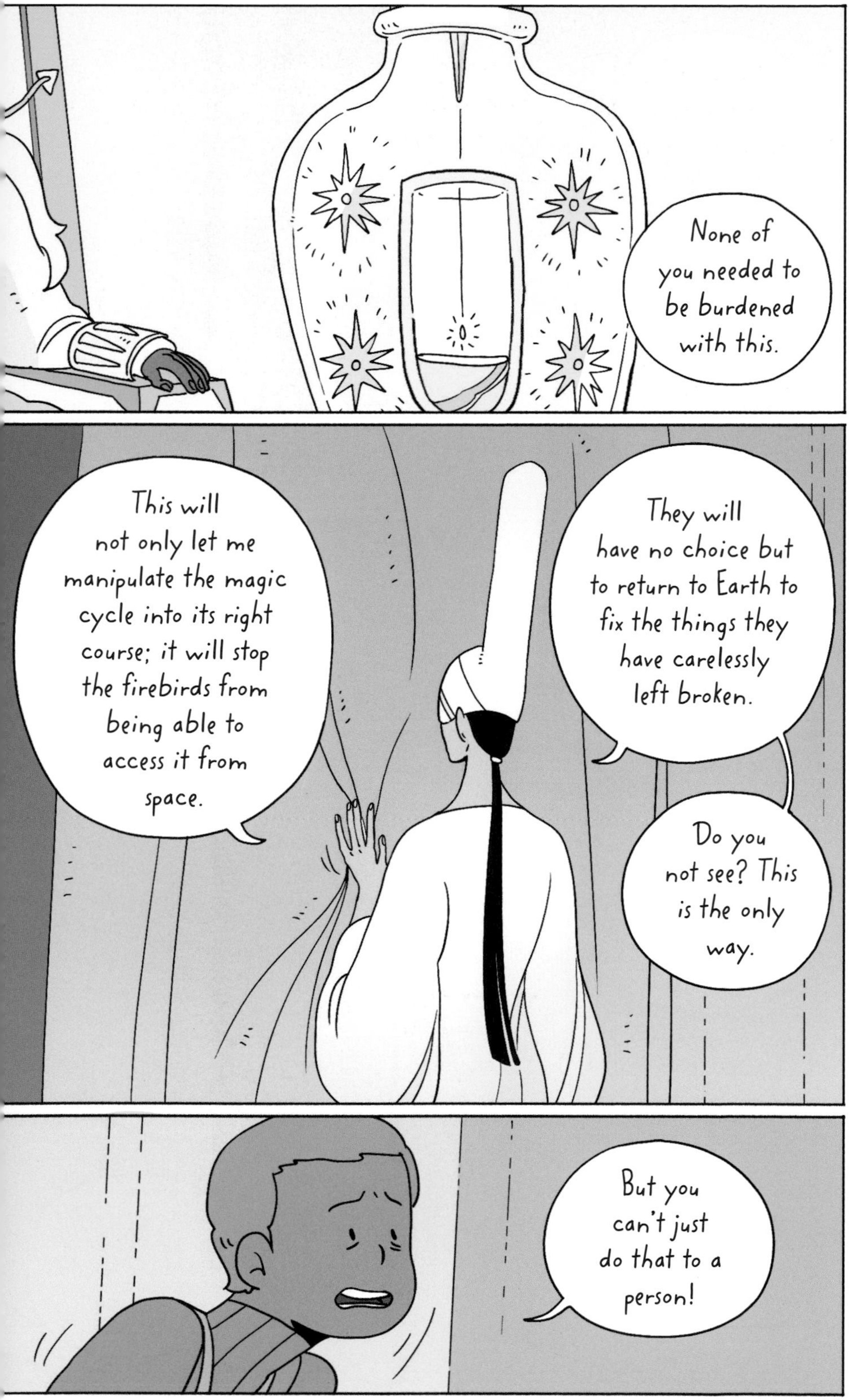
None of you needed to be burdened with this.
This will not only let me manipulate the magic cycle into its right course; it will stop the firebirds from being able to access it from space.
They will have no choice but to return to Earth to fix the things they have carelessly left broken.
Do you not see? This is the only way.
But you can't just do that to a person!

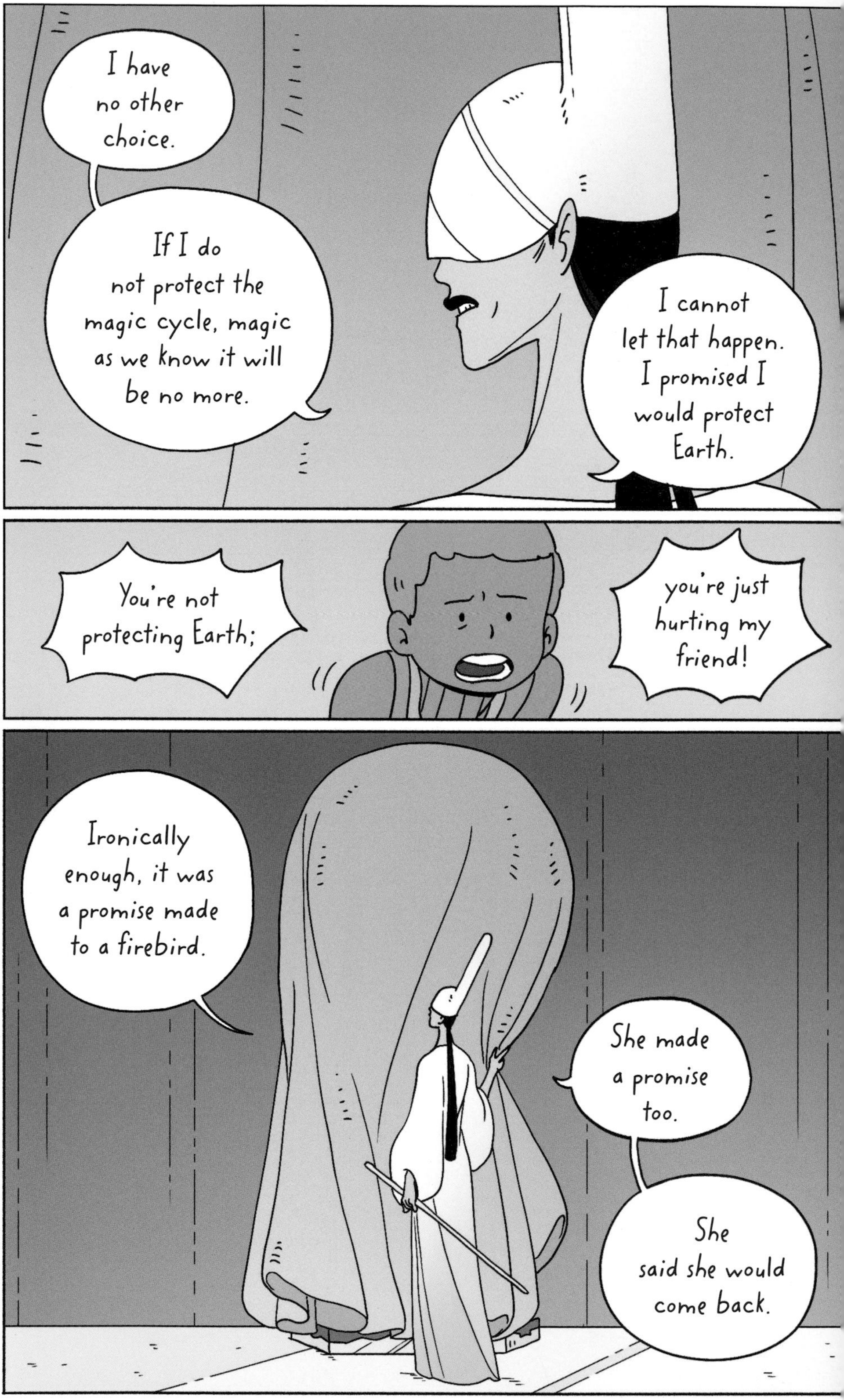
I have no other choice.
If I do not protect the magic cycle, magic as we know it will be no more.
I cannot let that happen. I promised I would protect Earth.
You're not protecting Earth;
you're just hurting my friend!
Ironically enough, it was a promise made to a firebird.
She made a promise too.
She said she would come back.

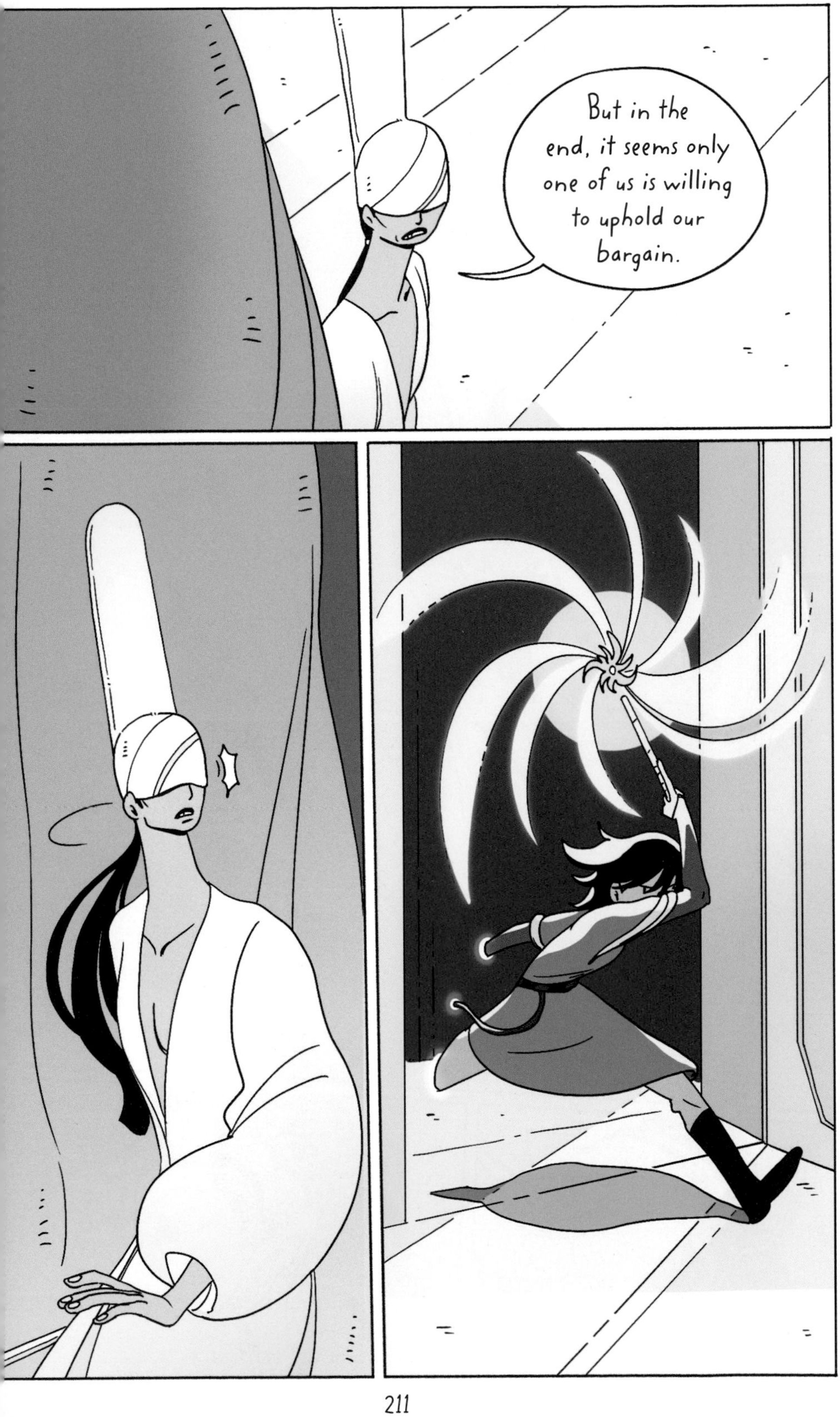
But in the end, it seems only one of us is willing to uphold our bargain.

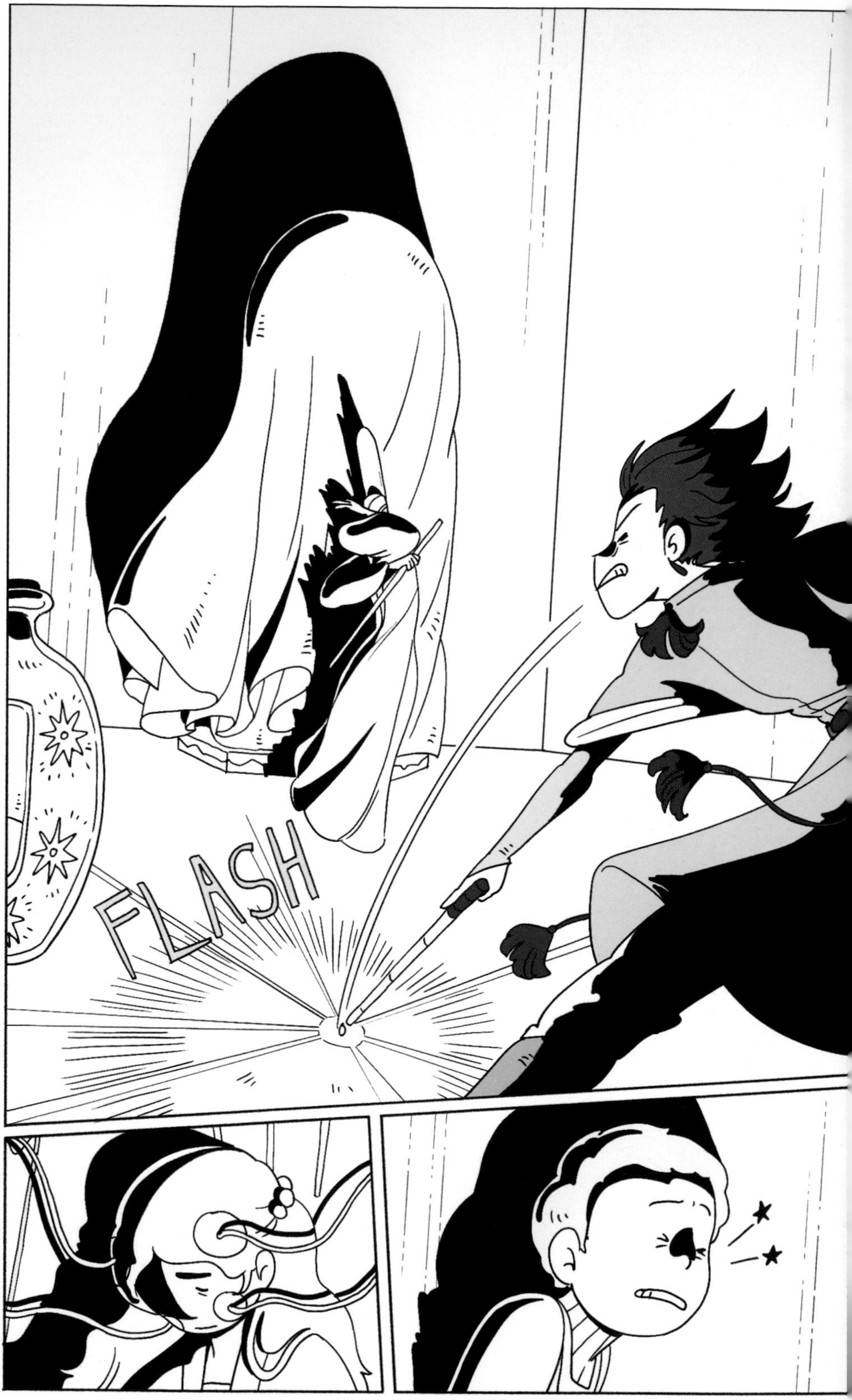
FLASH

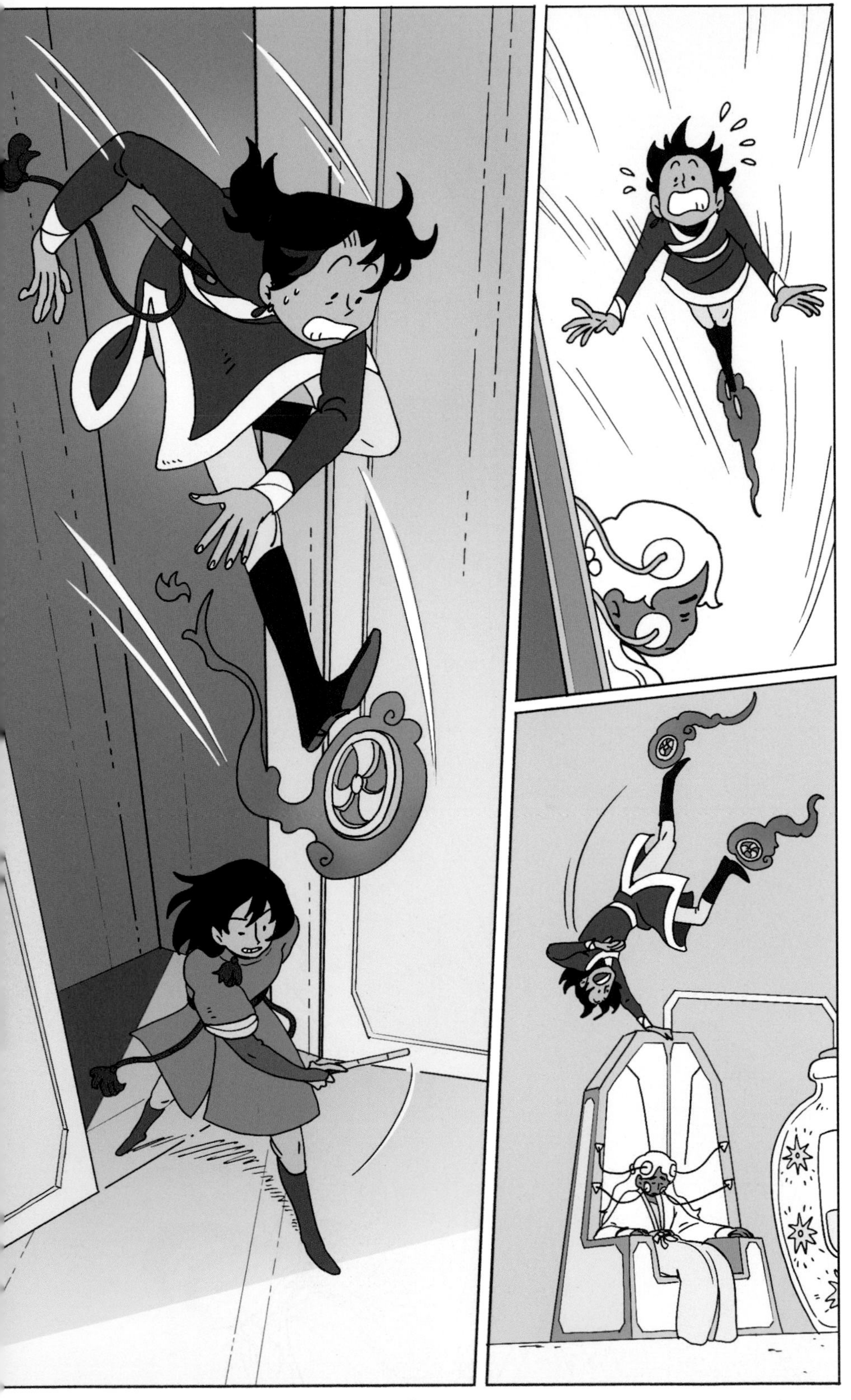

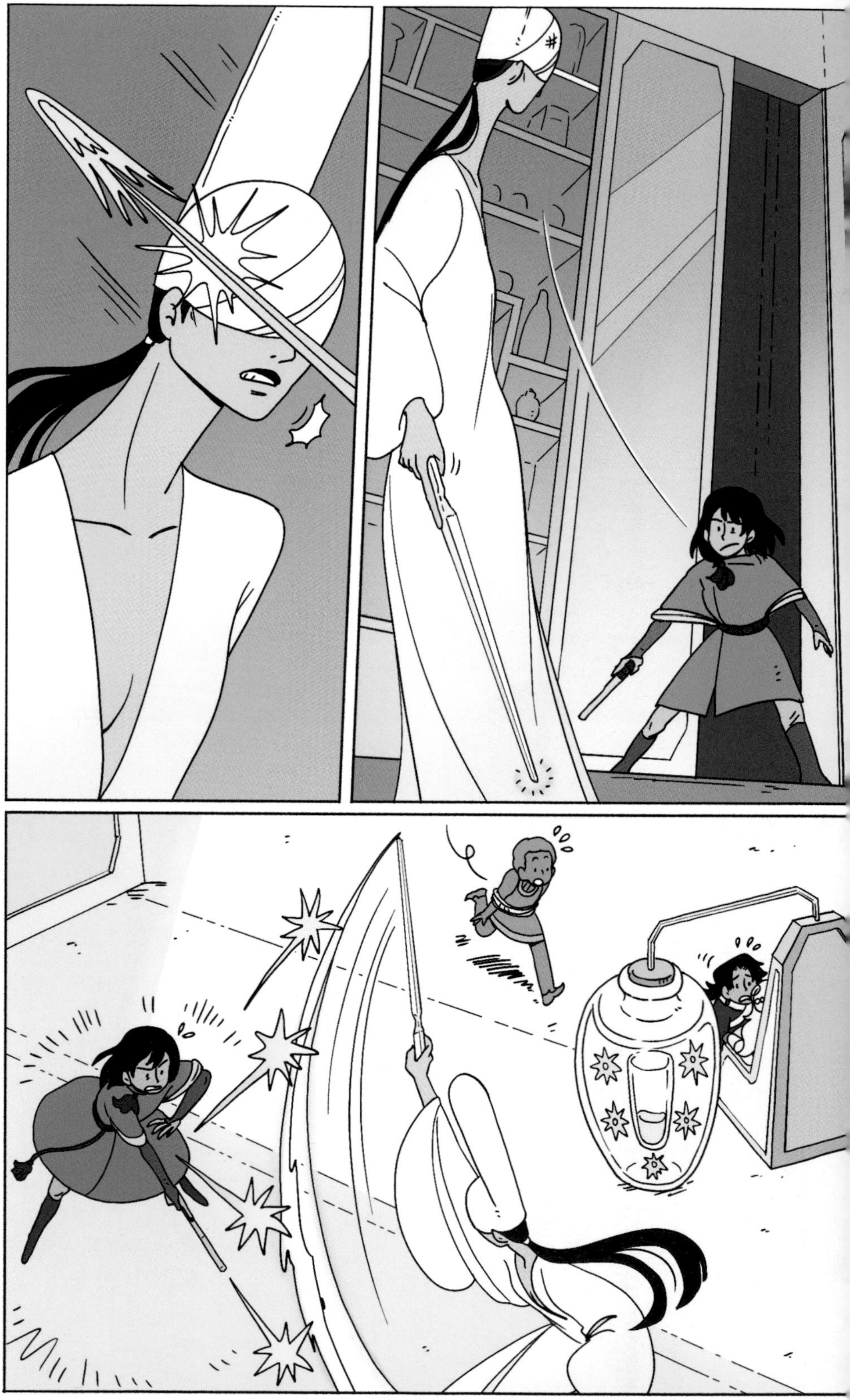

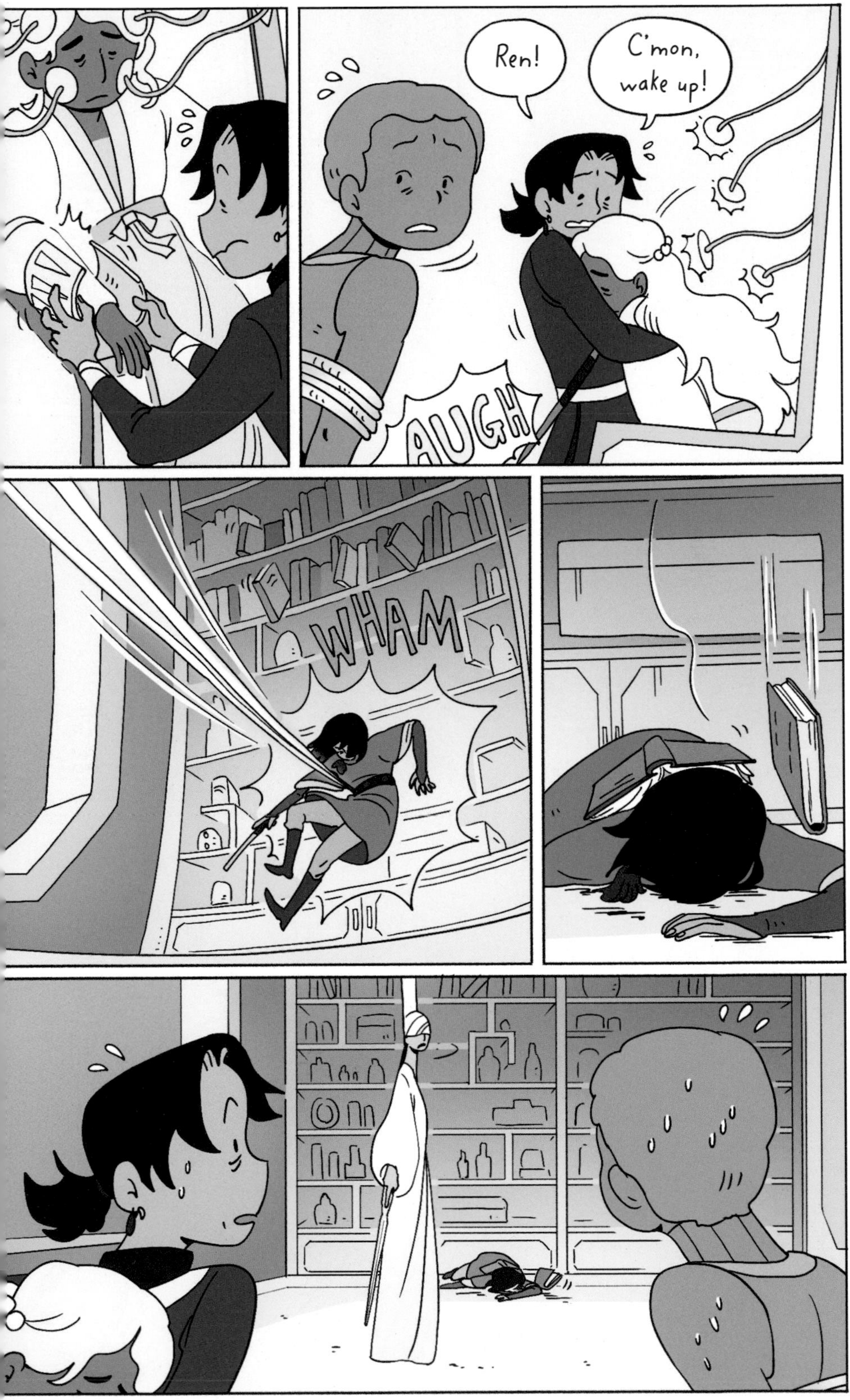
Ren!
C'mon, wake up!
AUGH
WHAM

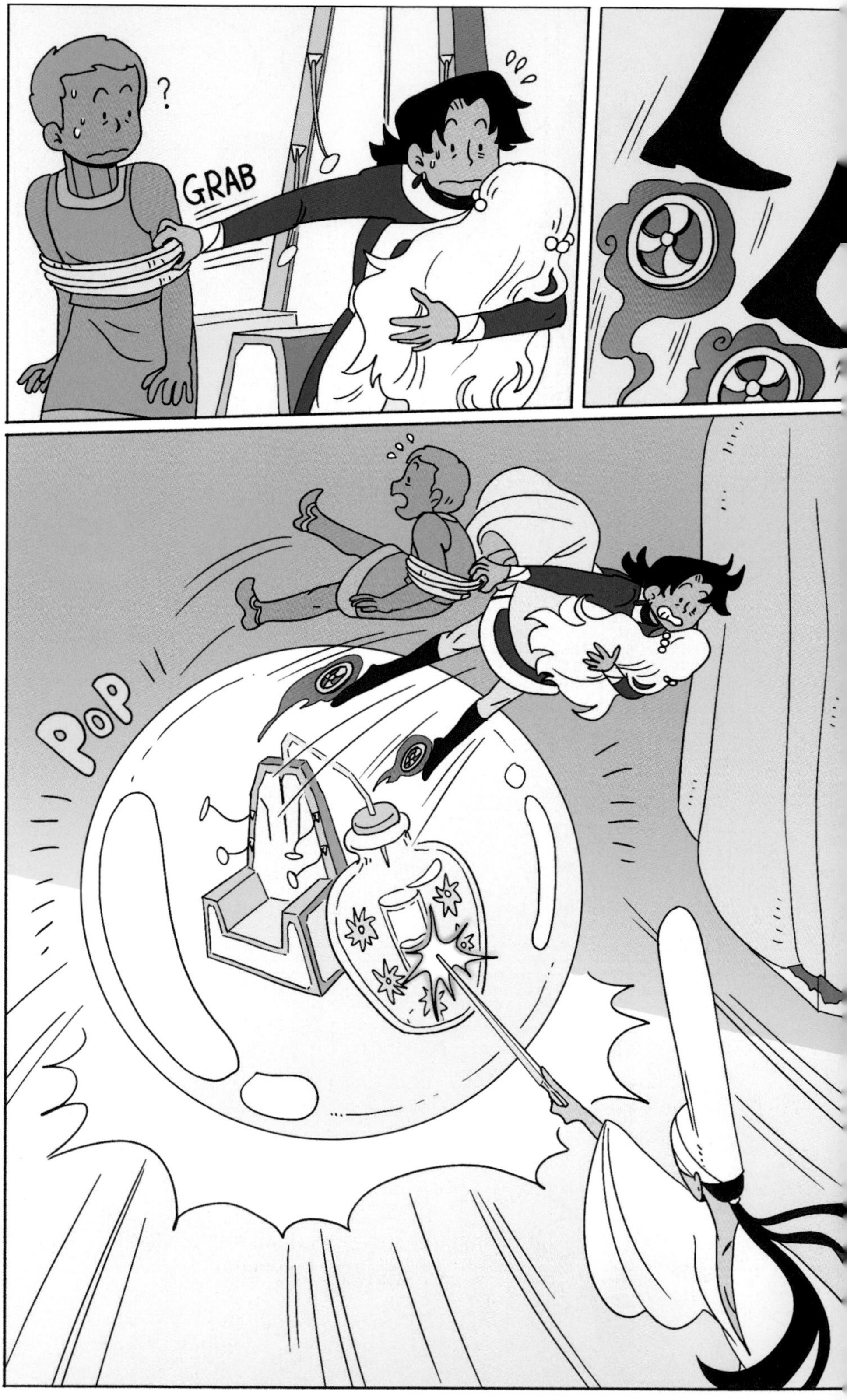
?
GRAB
POP

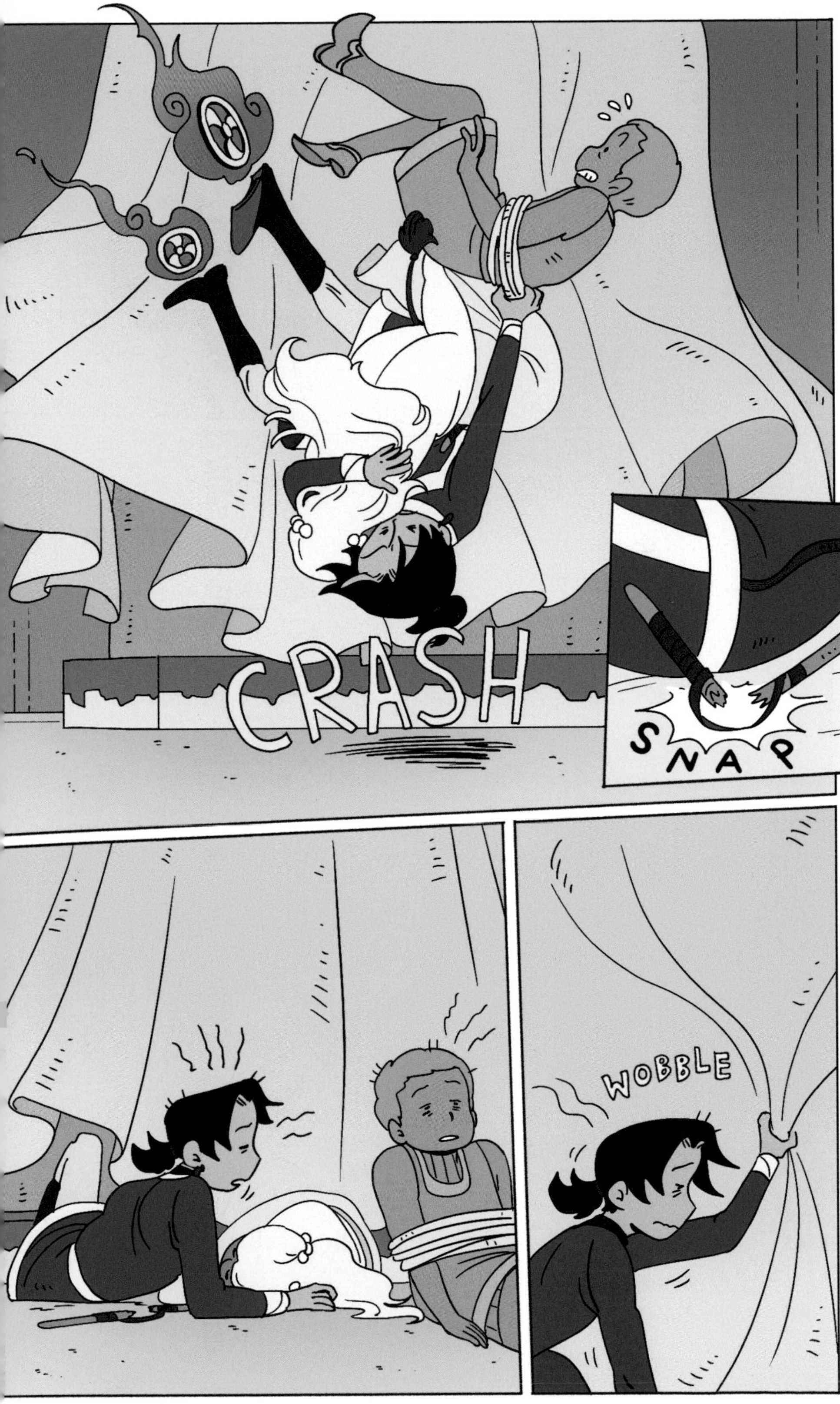
CRASH
SNAP
WOBBLE

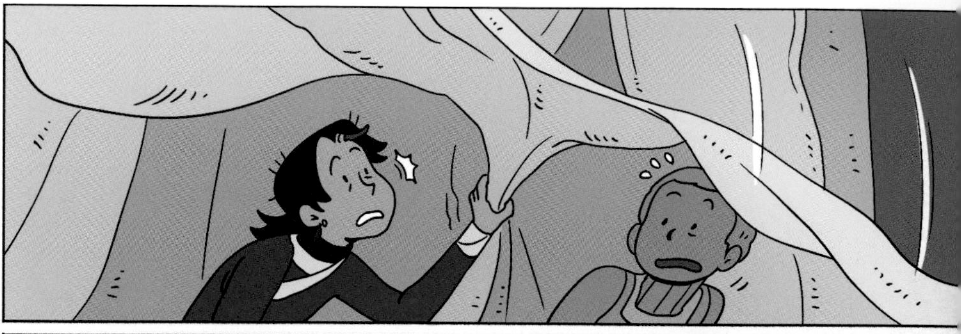
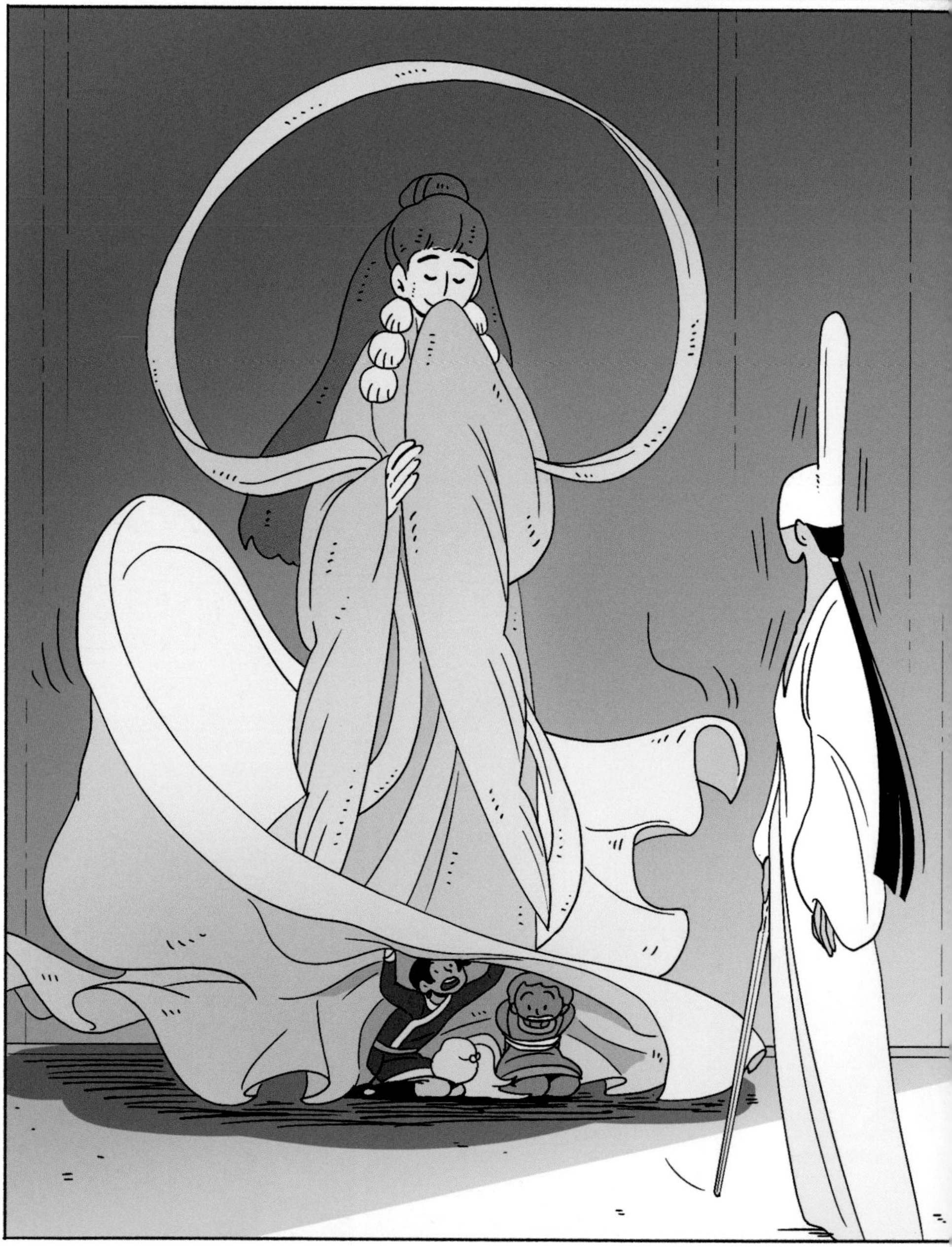

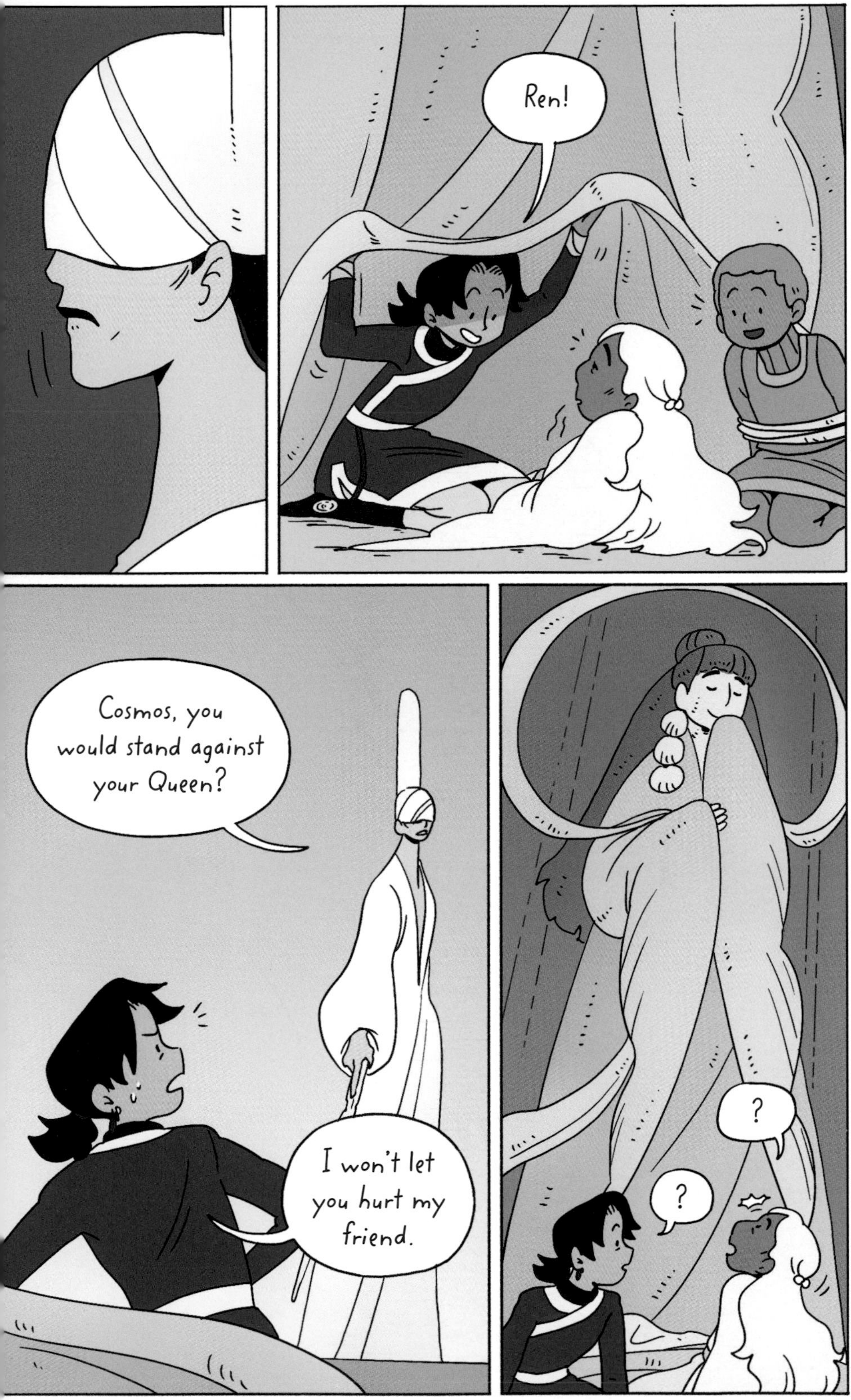
Ren!
Cosmos, you would stand against your Queen?
I won't let you hurt my friend.
?
?

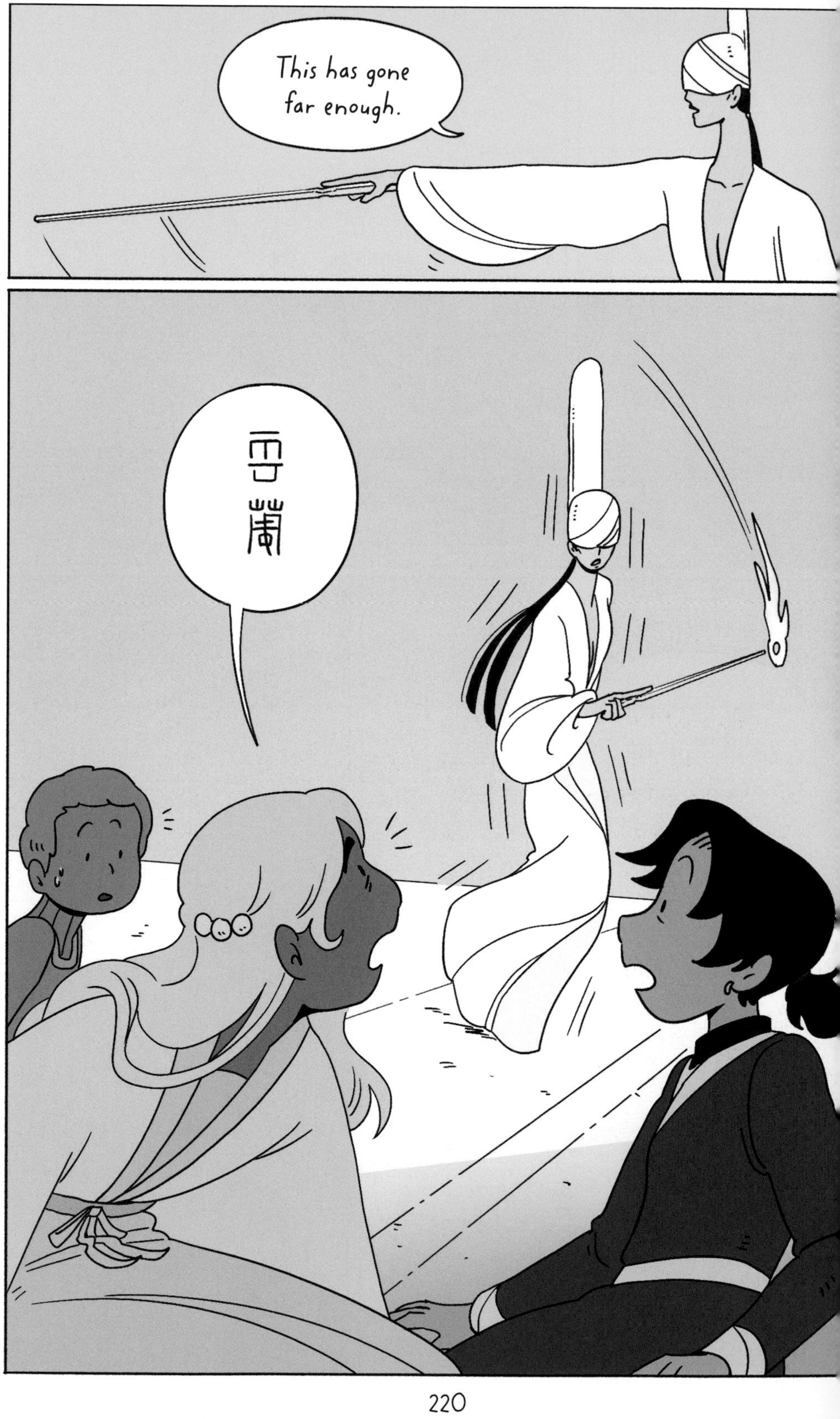
This has gone far enough.

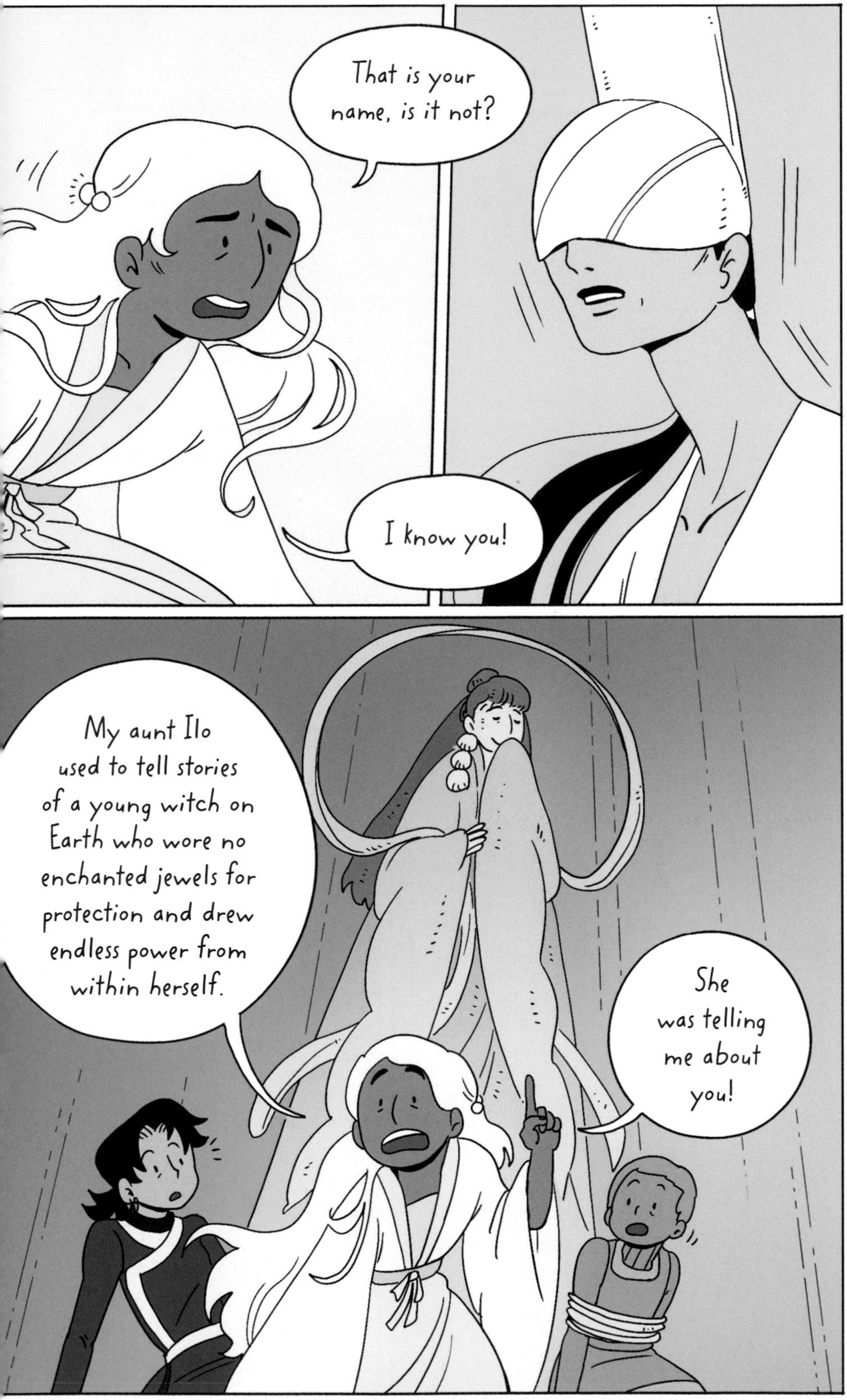
That is your name, is it not?
I know you!
My aunt Ilo used to tell stories of a young witch on Earth who wore no enchanted jewels for protection and drew endless power from within herself.
She was telling me about you!

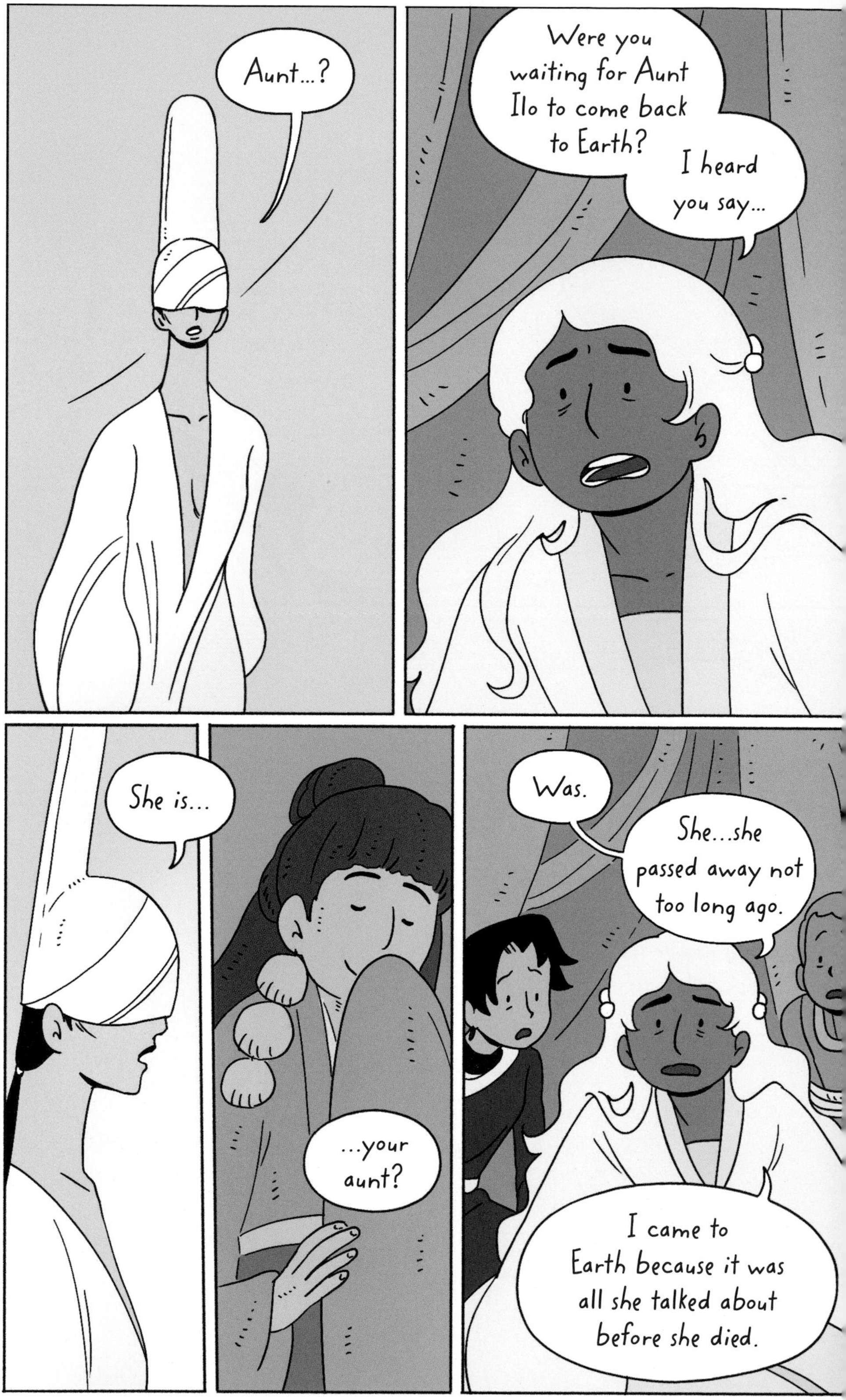
Aunt...?
Were you waiting for Aunt Ilo to come back to Earth?
I heard you say...
She is...
...your aunt?
Was.
She...she passed away not too long ago.
I came to Earth because it was all she talked about before she died.

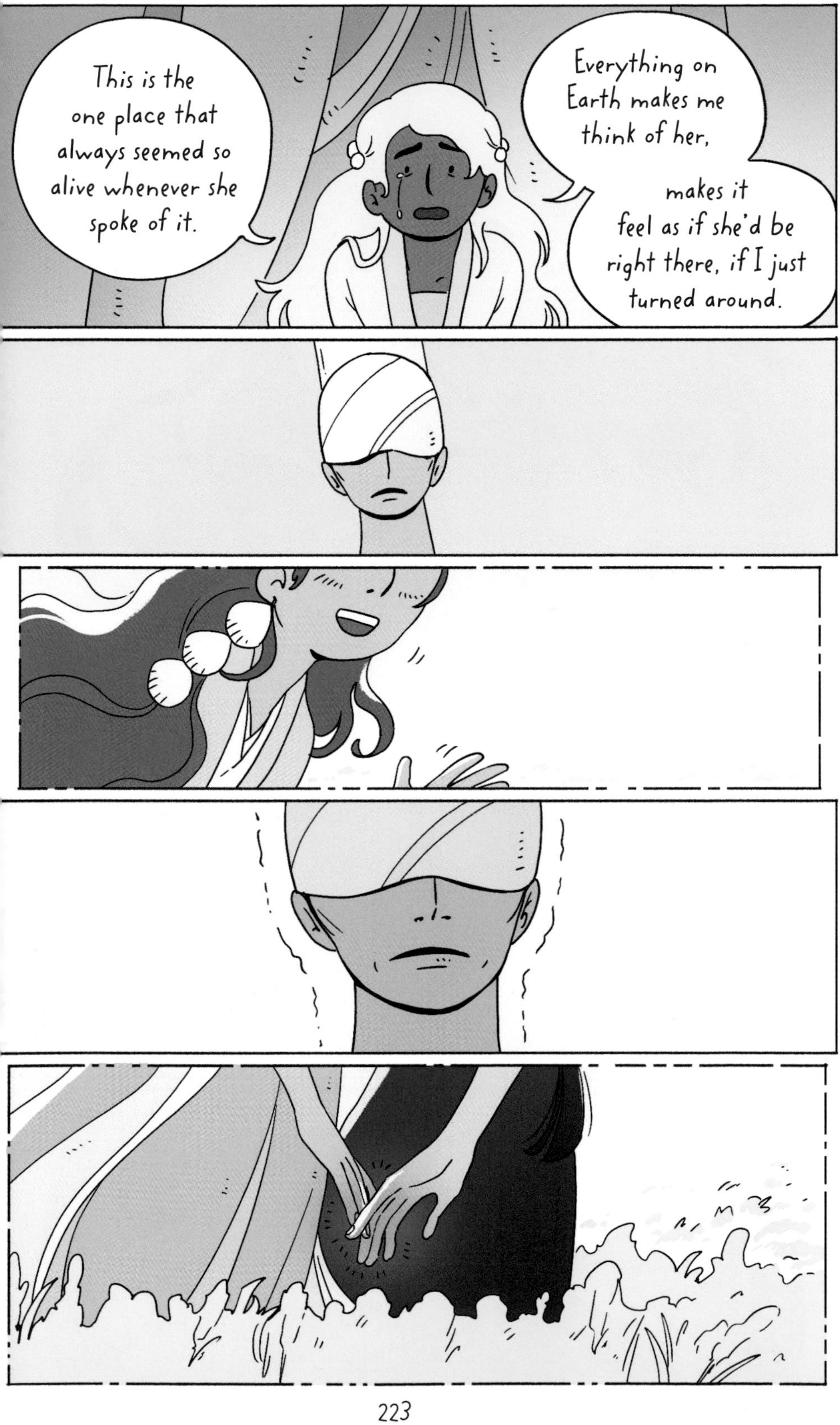
This is the one place that always seemed so alive whenever she spoke of it.
Everything on Earth makes me think of her,
makes it feel as if she'd be right there, if I just turned around.

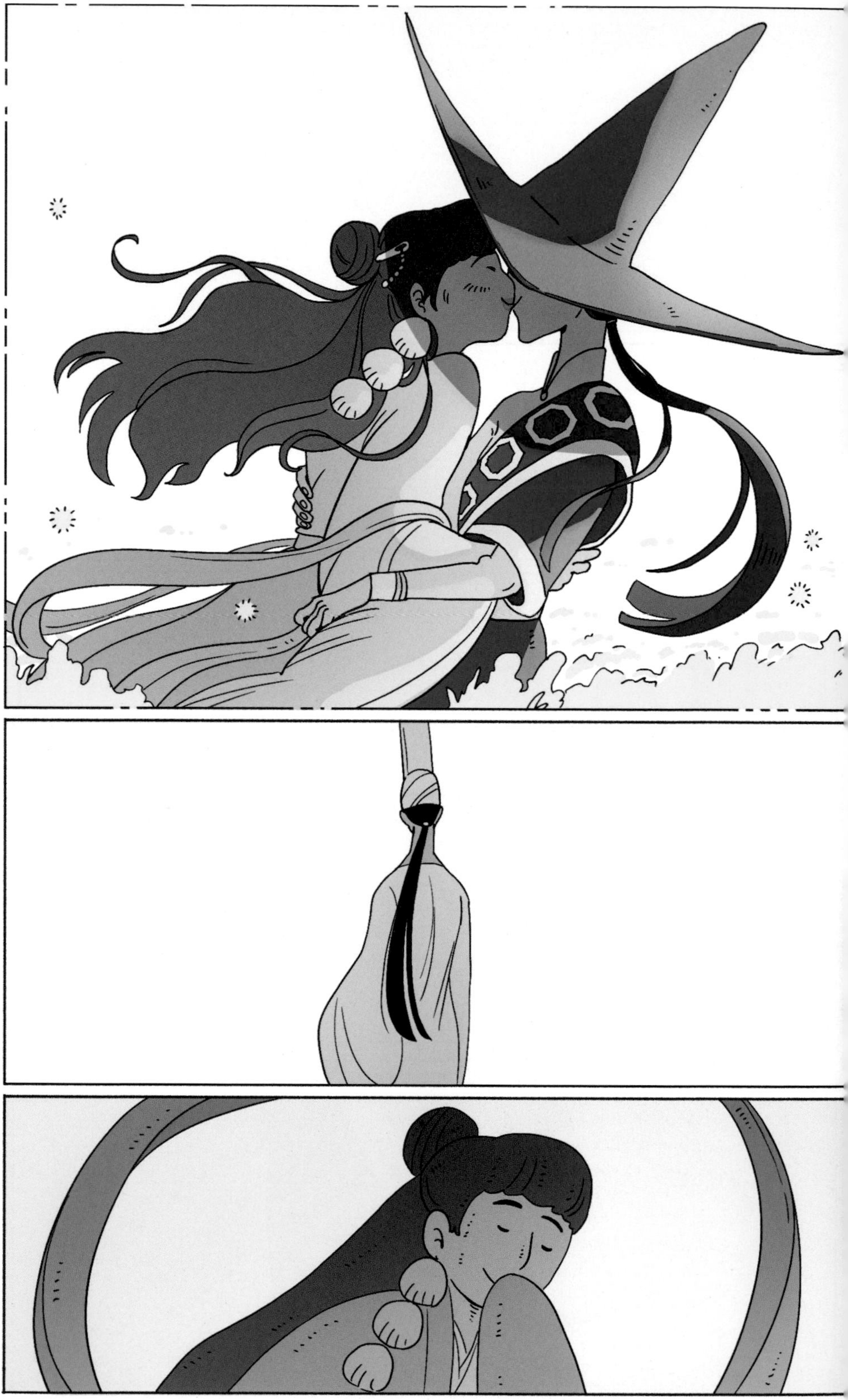

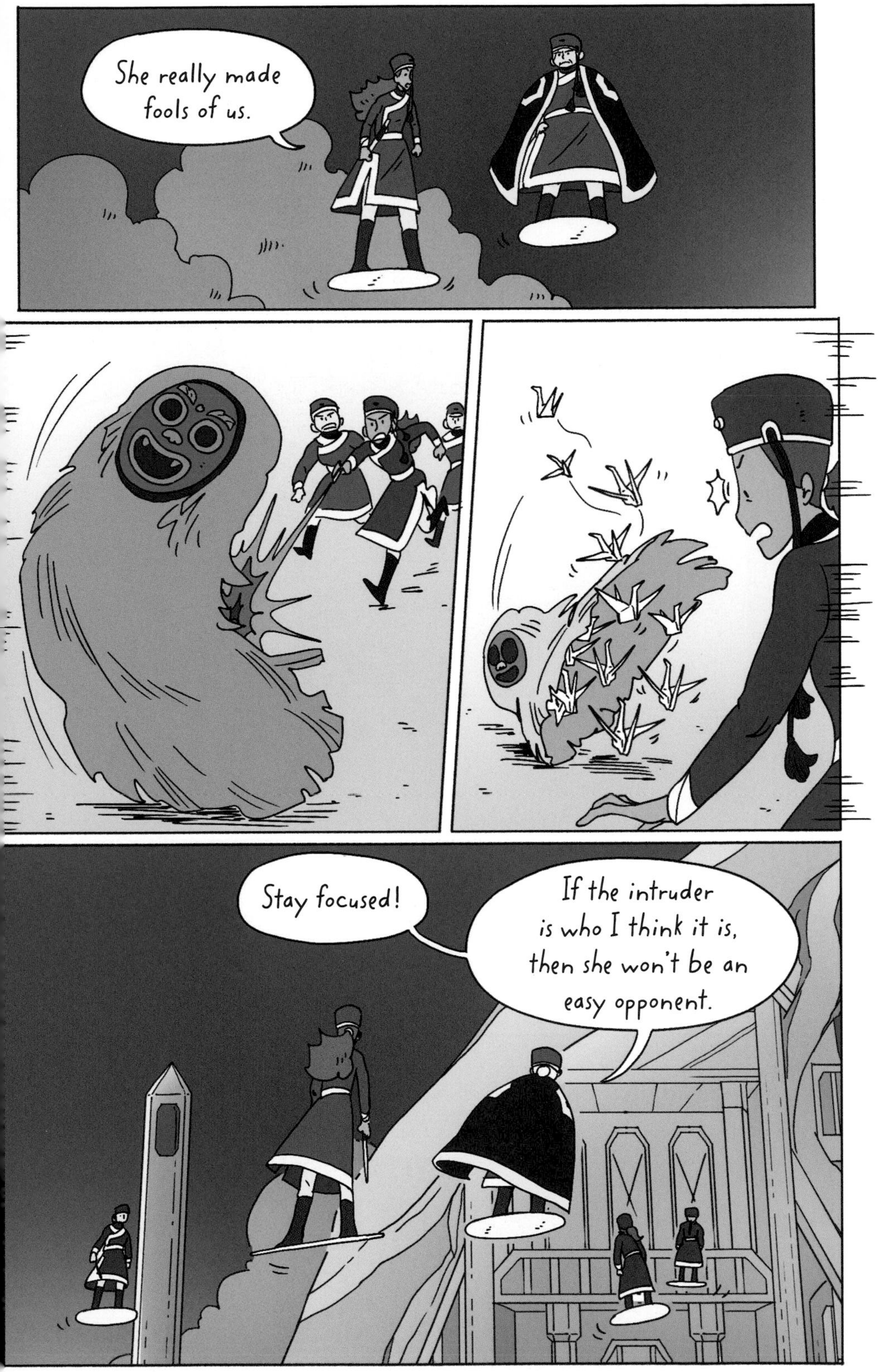
She really made fools of us.
Stay focused!
If the intruder is who I think it is, then she won't be an easy opponent.

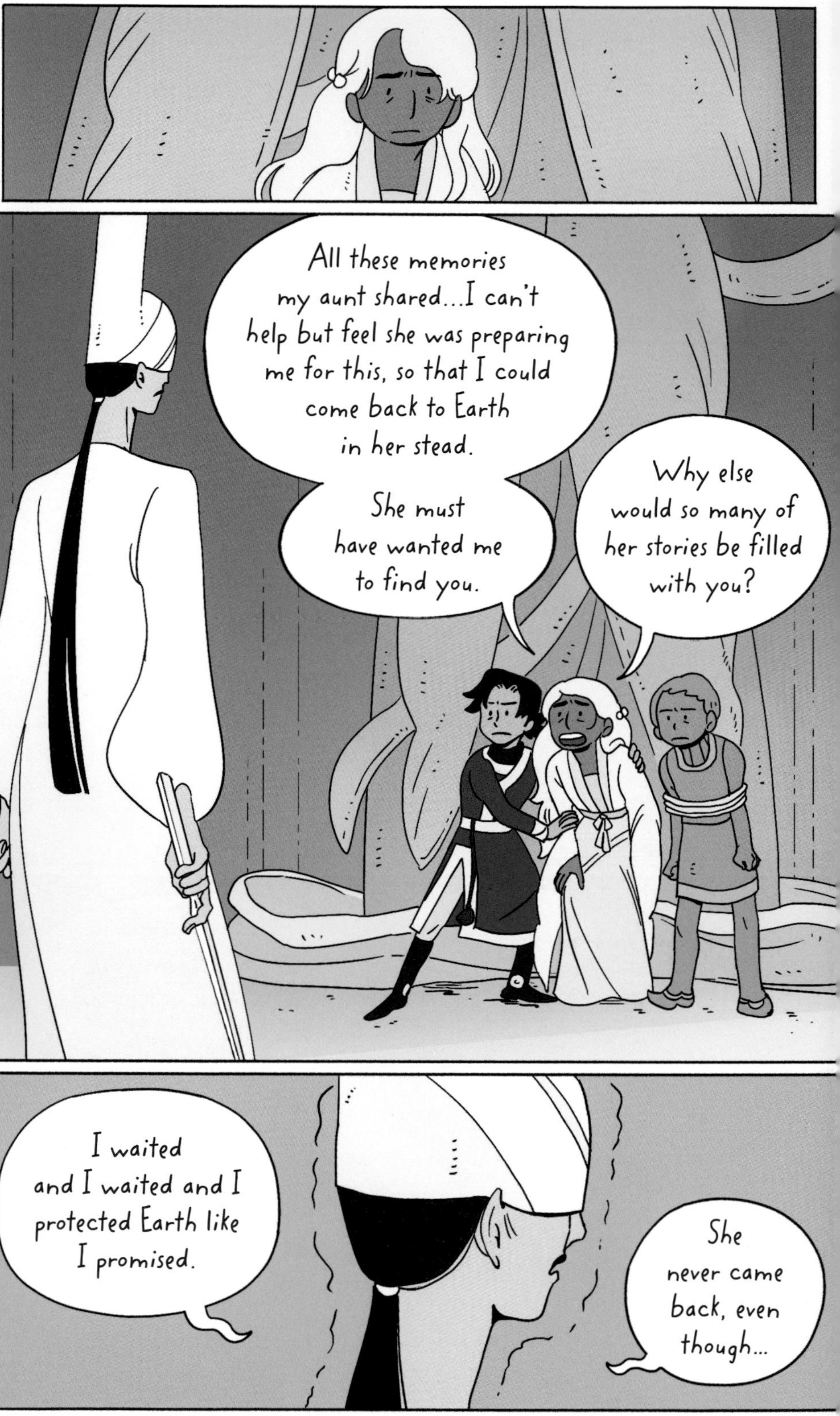
All these memories my aunt shared...I can't help but feel she was preparing me for this, so that I could come back to Earth in her stead.
She must have wanted me to find you.
Why else would so many of her stories be filled with you?
I waited and I waited and I protected Earth like I promised.
She never came back, even though...

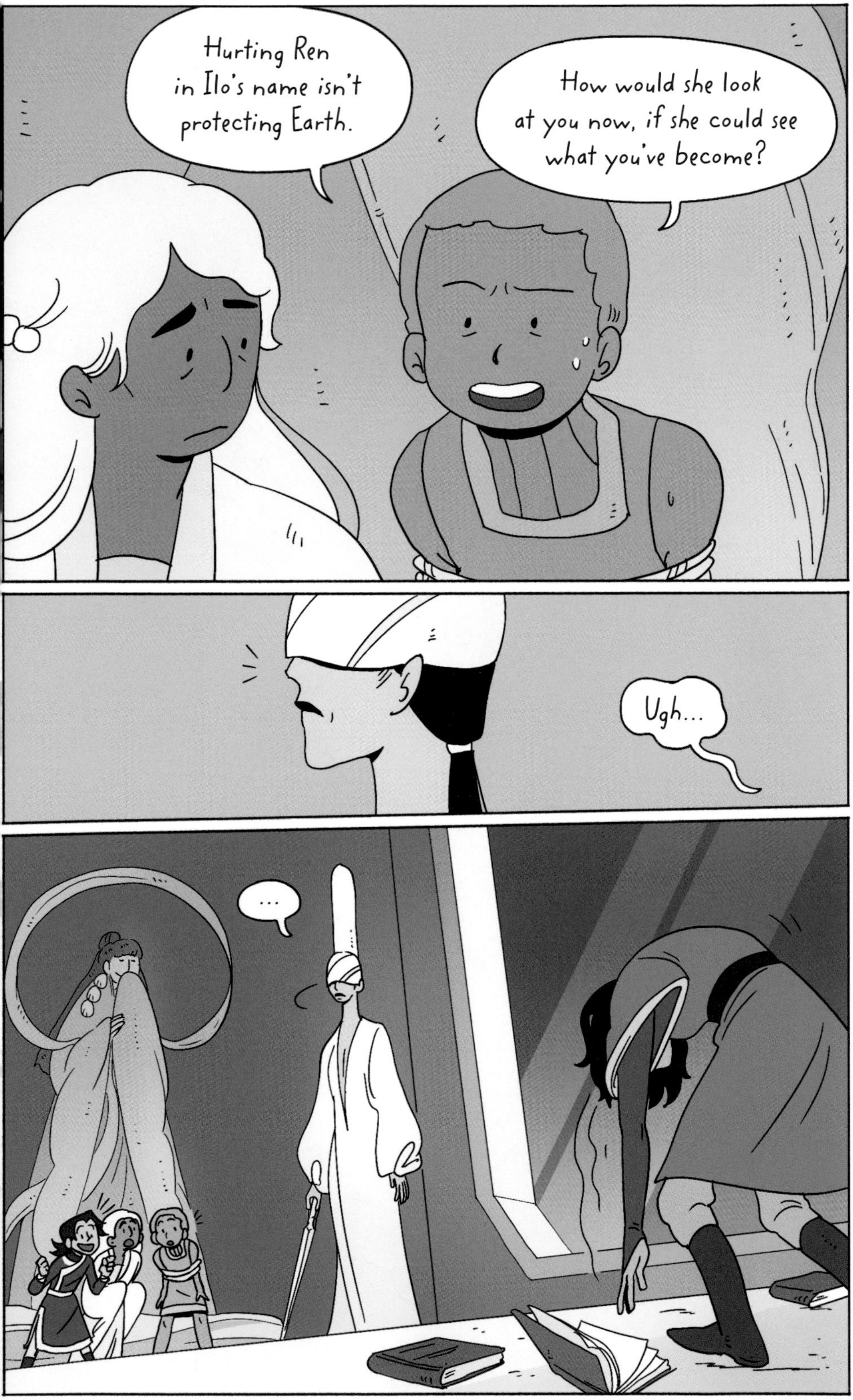
Hurting Ren in Ilo's name isn't protecting Earth.
How would she look at you now, if she could see what you've become?
Ugh...
...

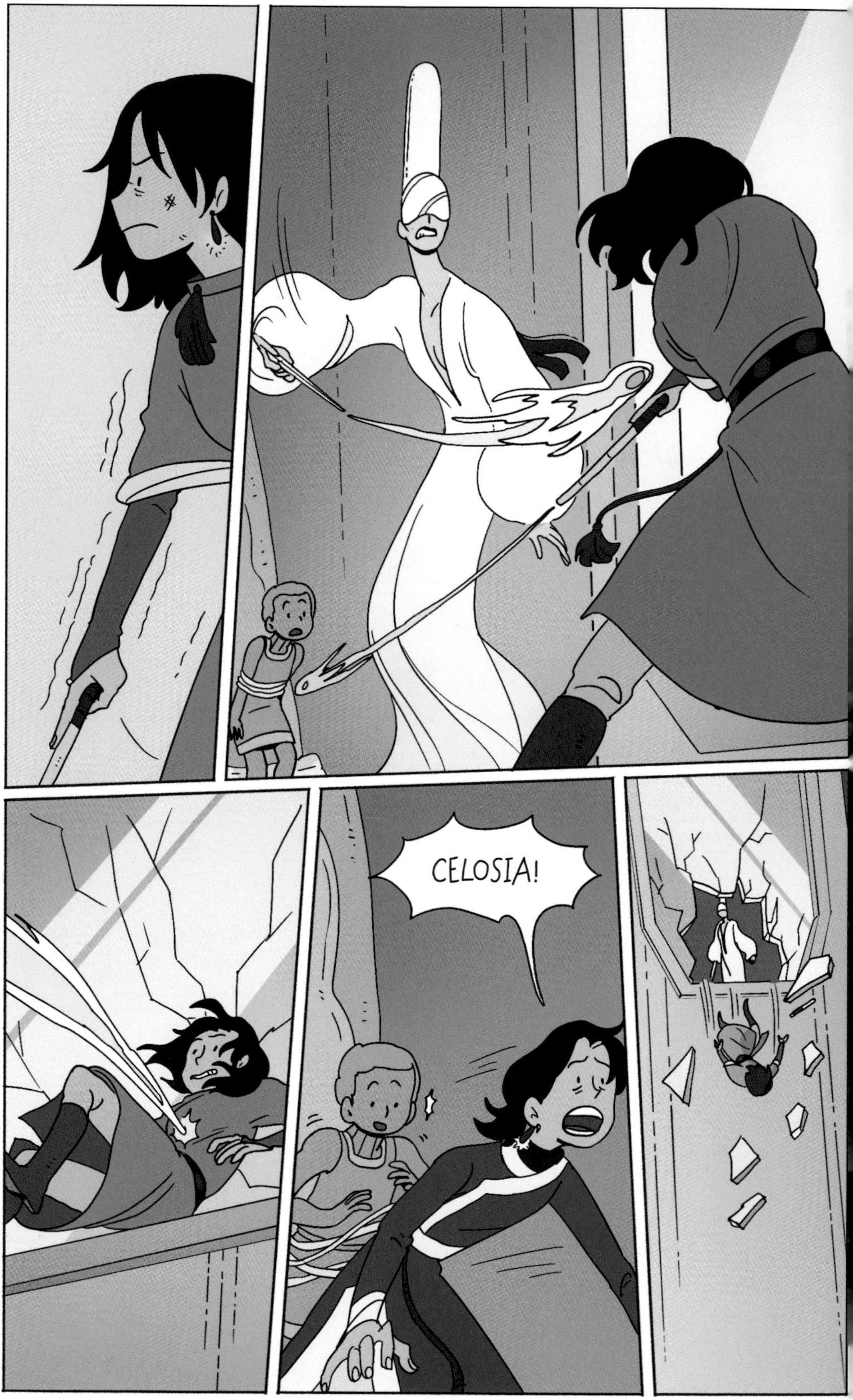
CELOSIA!

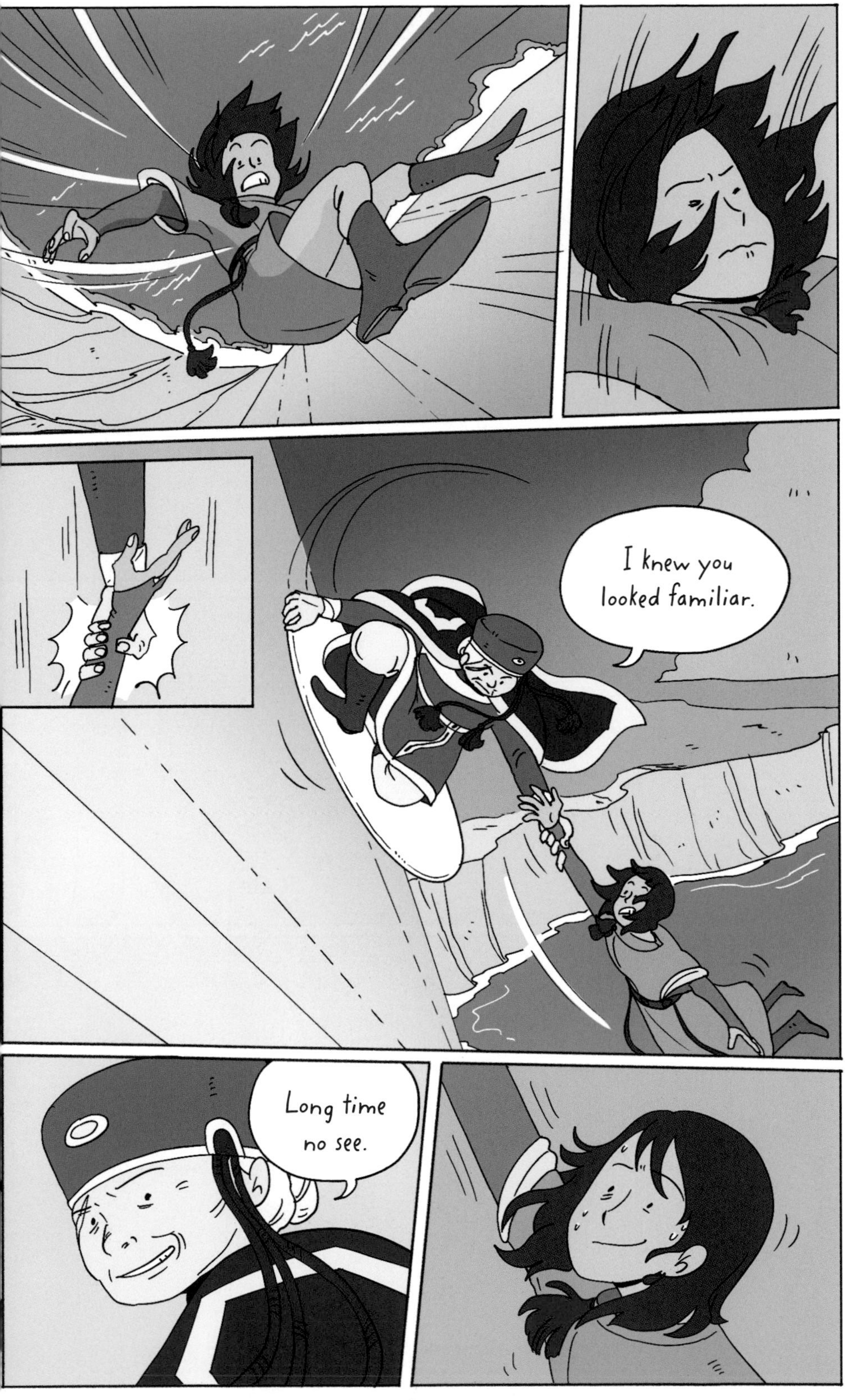
I knew you looked familiar.
Long time no see.

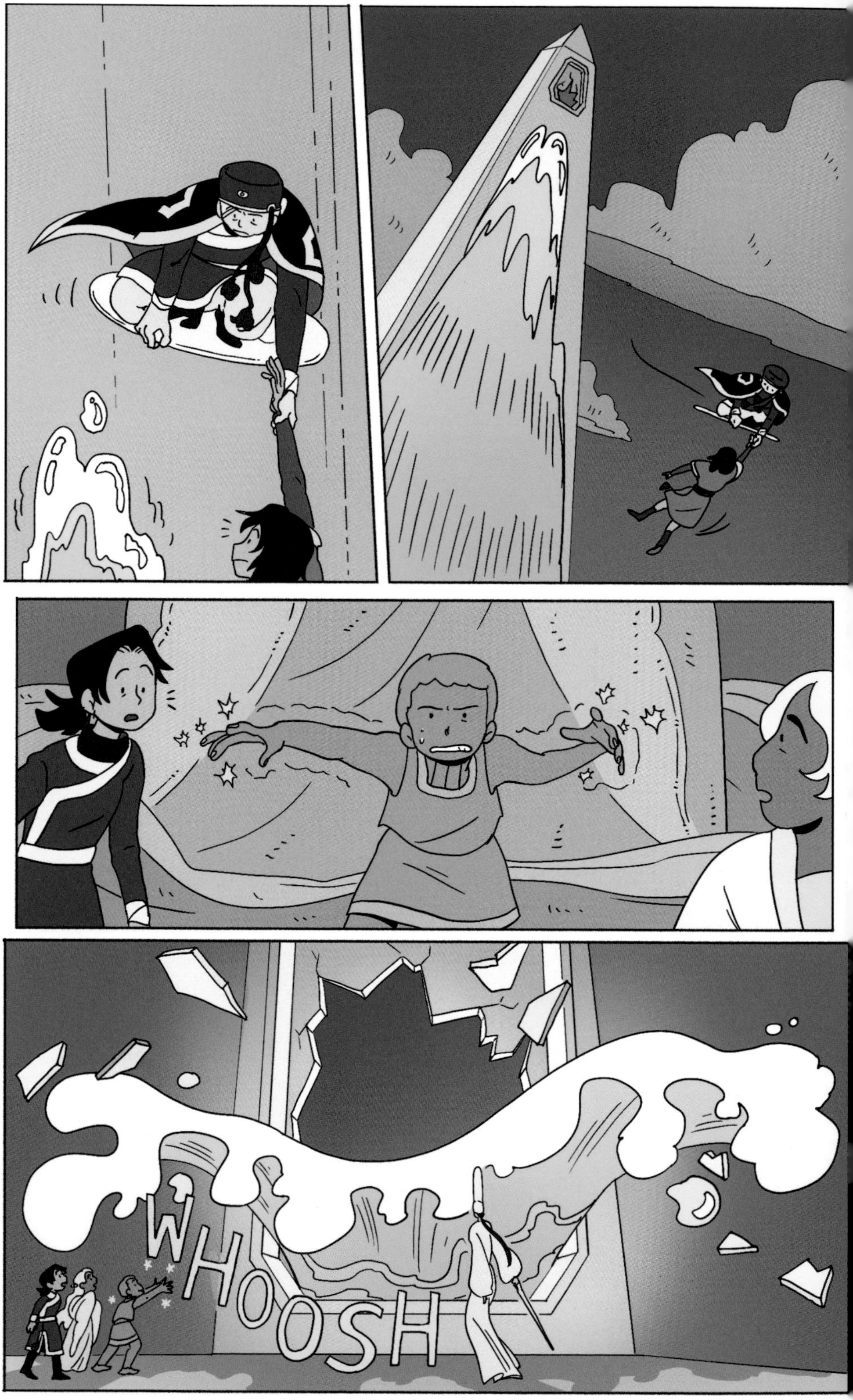
WHOOSH

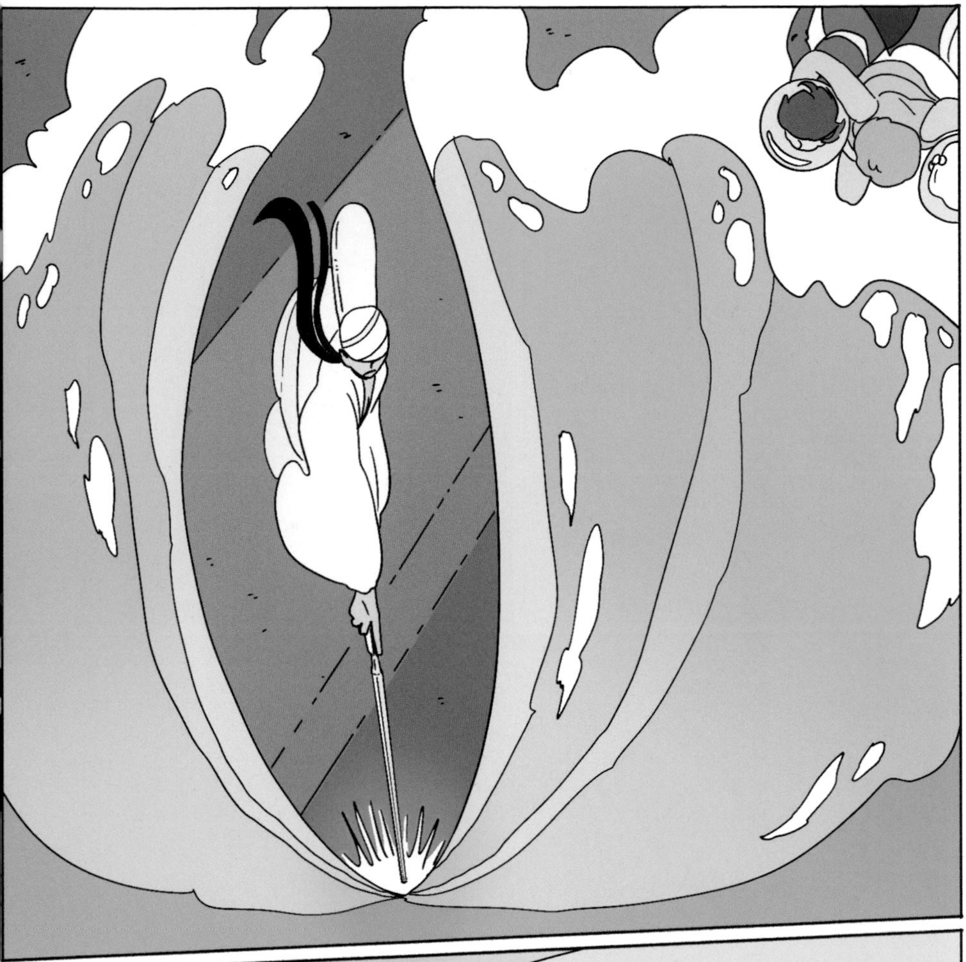

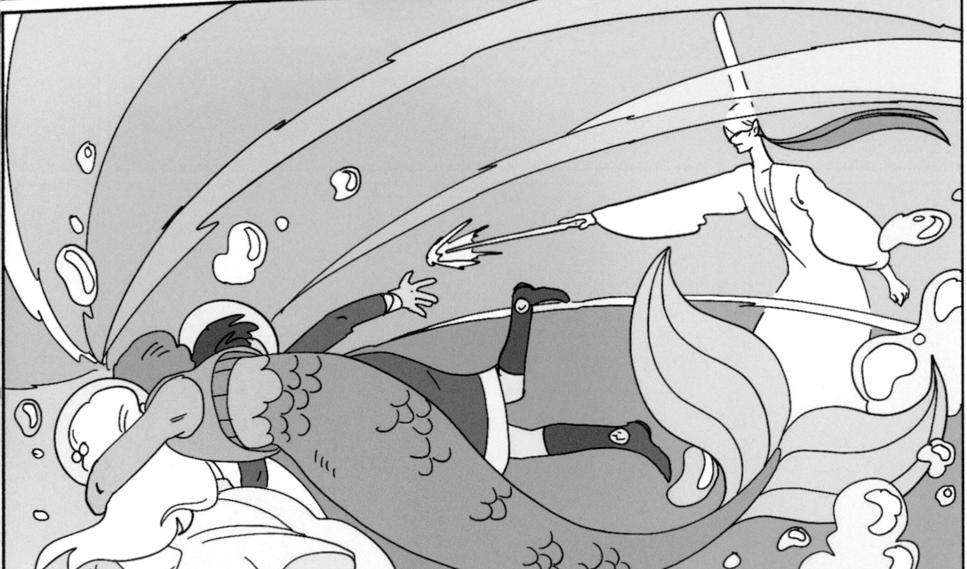

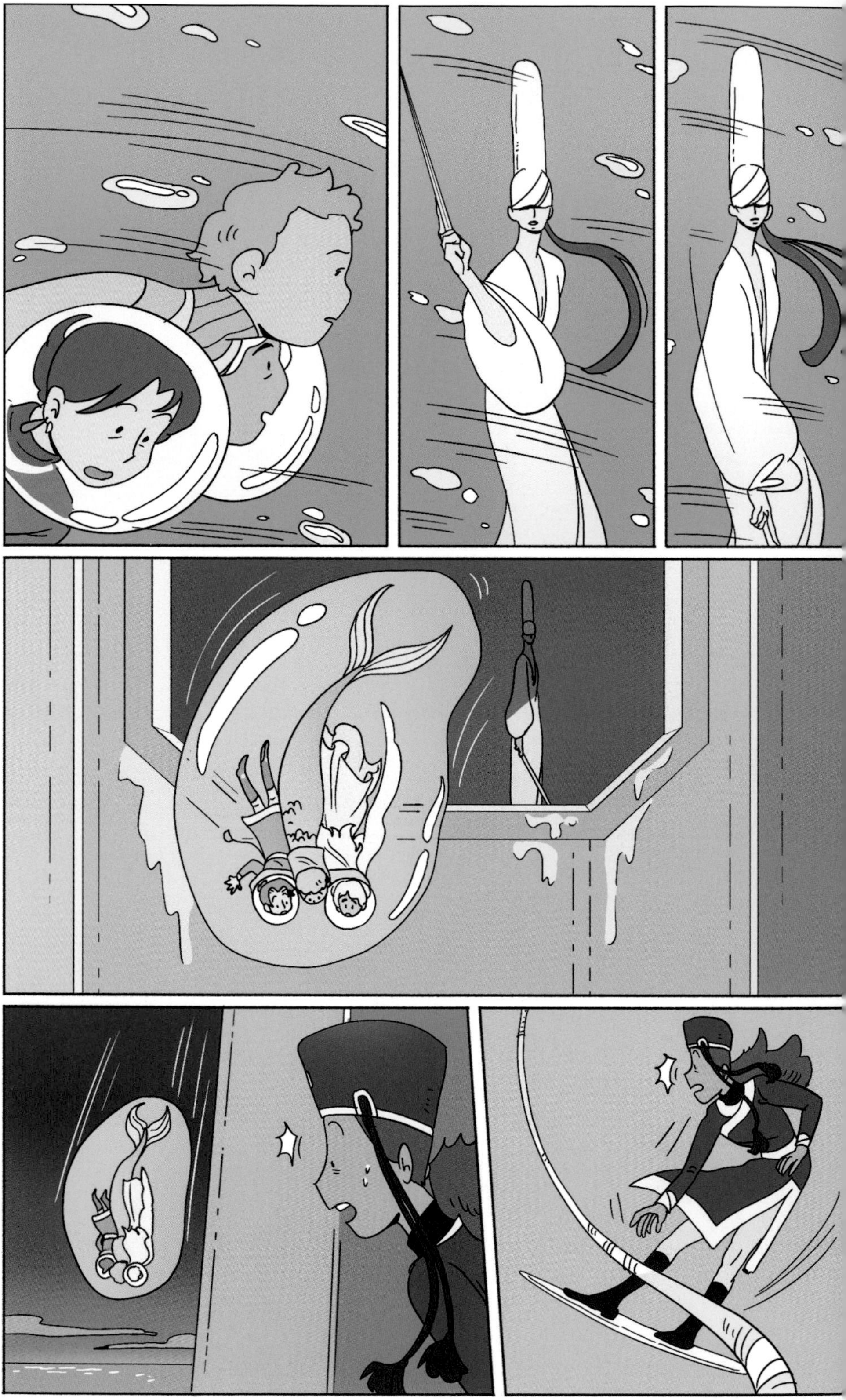

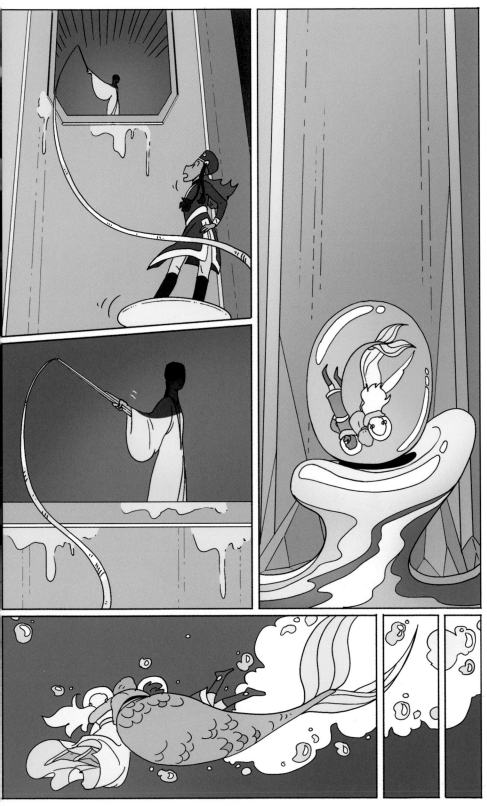

233

CHAPTER 20

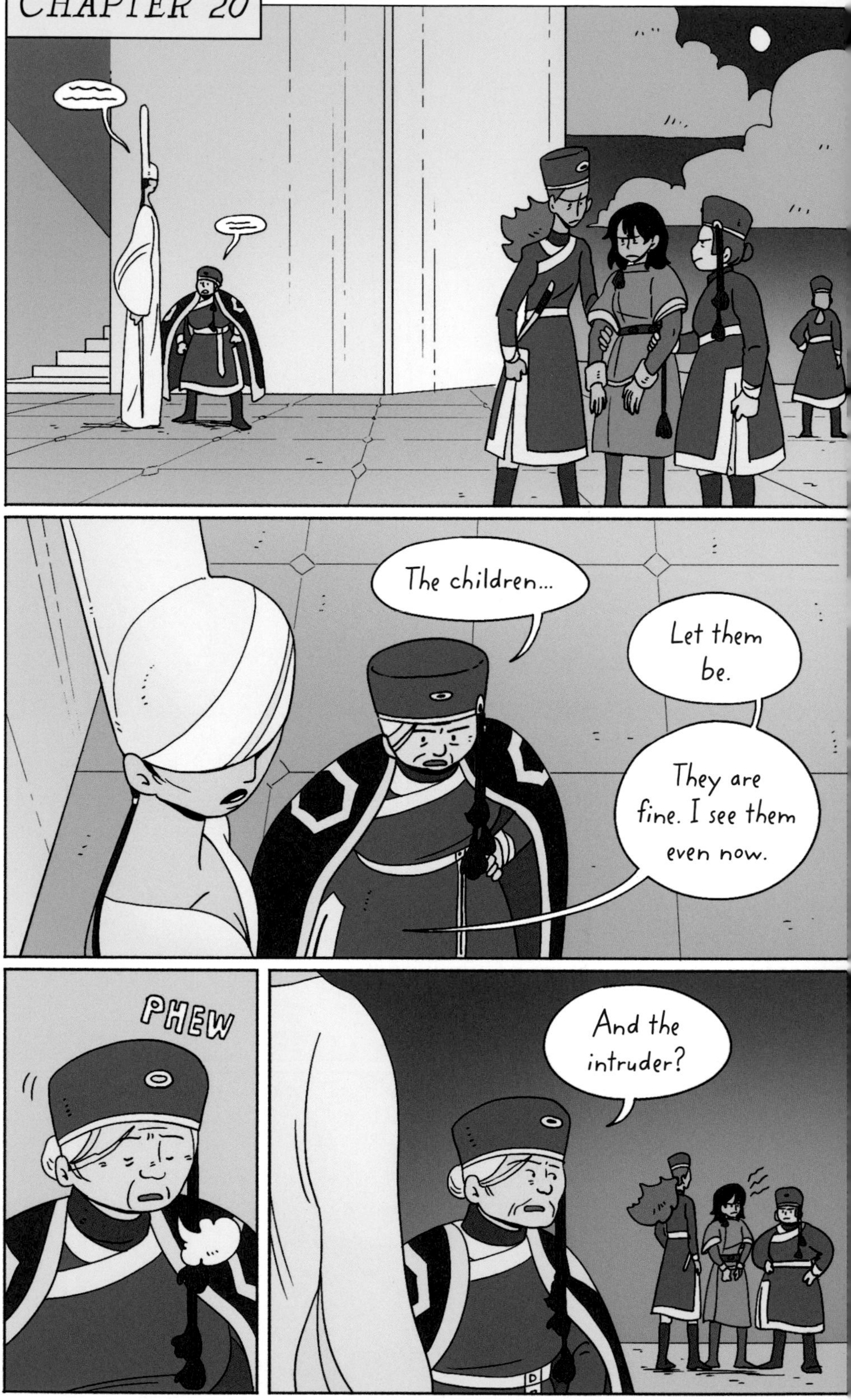
The children...
Let them be.
They are fine. I see them even now.
PHEW
And the intruder?

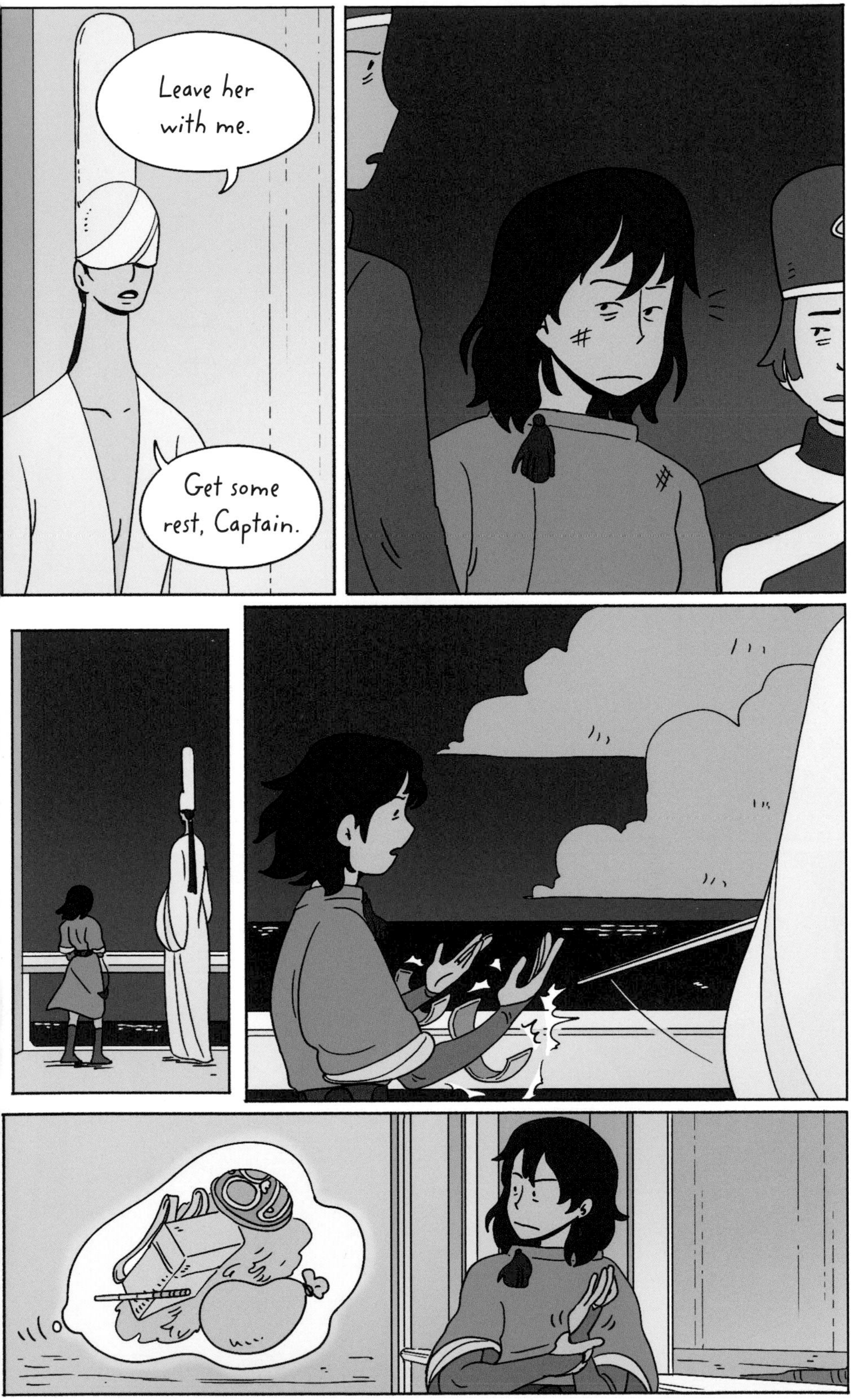
Leave her with me.
Get some rest, Captain.

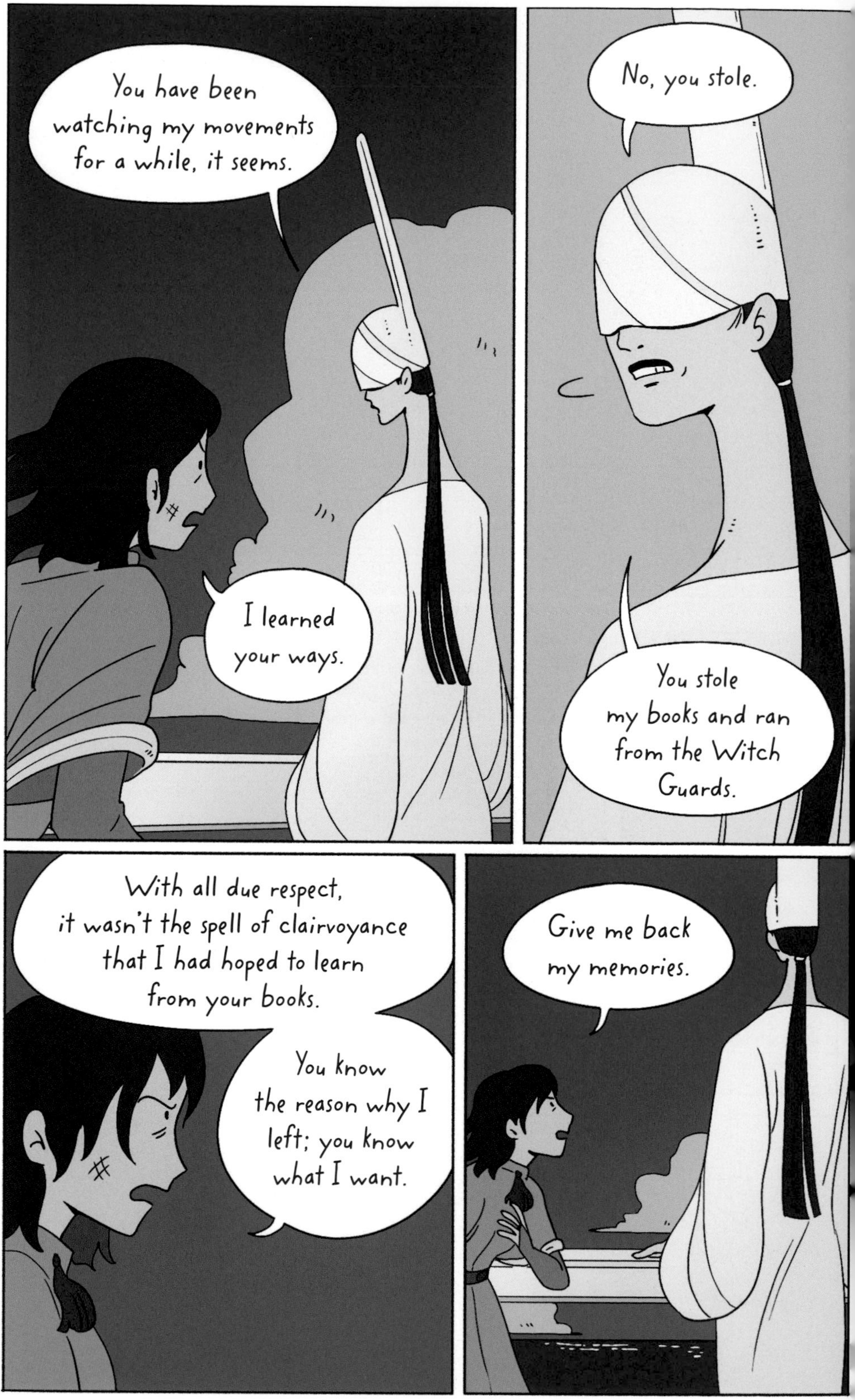
You have been watching my movements for a while, it seems.
I learned your ways.
No, you stole.
You stole my books and ran from the Witch Guards.
With all due respect, it wasn't the spell of clairvoyance that I had hoped to learn from your books.
You know the reason why I left; you know what I want.
Give me back my memories.

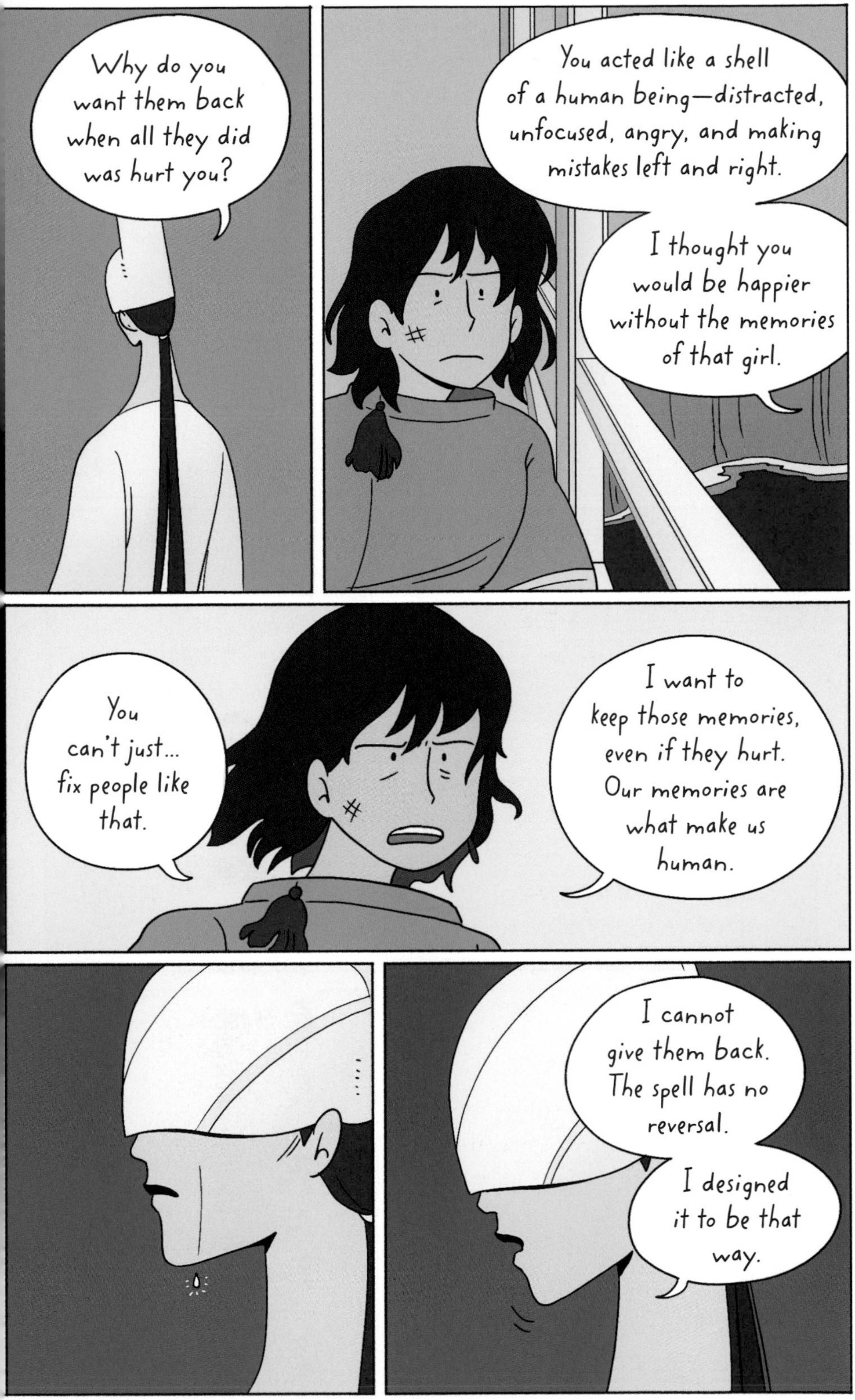
Why do you want them back when all they did was hurt you?
You acted like a shell of a human being—distracted, unfocused, angry, and making mistakes left and right.
I thought you would be happier without the memories of that girl.
You can't just... fix people like that.
I want to keep those memories, even if they hurt. Our memories are what make us human.
I cannot give them back. The spell has no reversal.
I designed it to be that way.

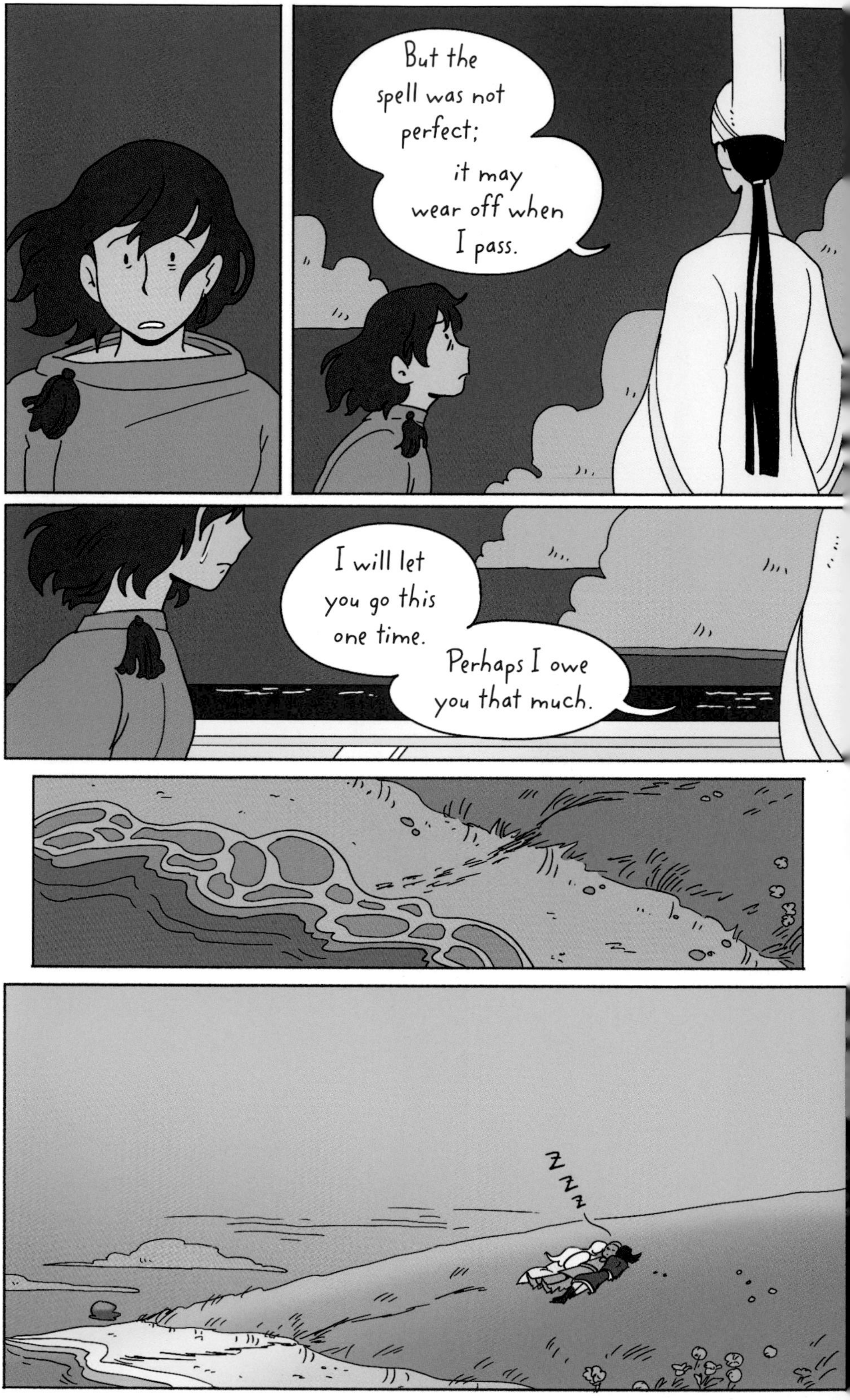
But the spell was not perfect;
it may wear off when I pass.
I will let you go this one time.
Perhaps I owe you that much.
Z Z Z

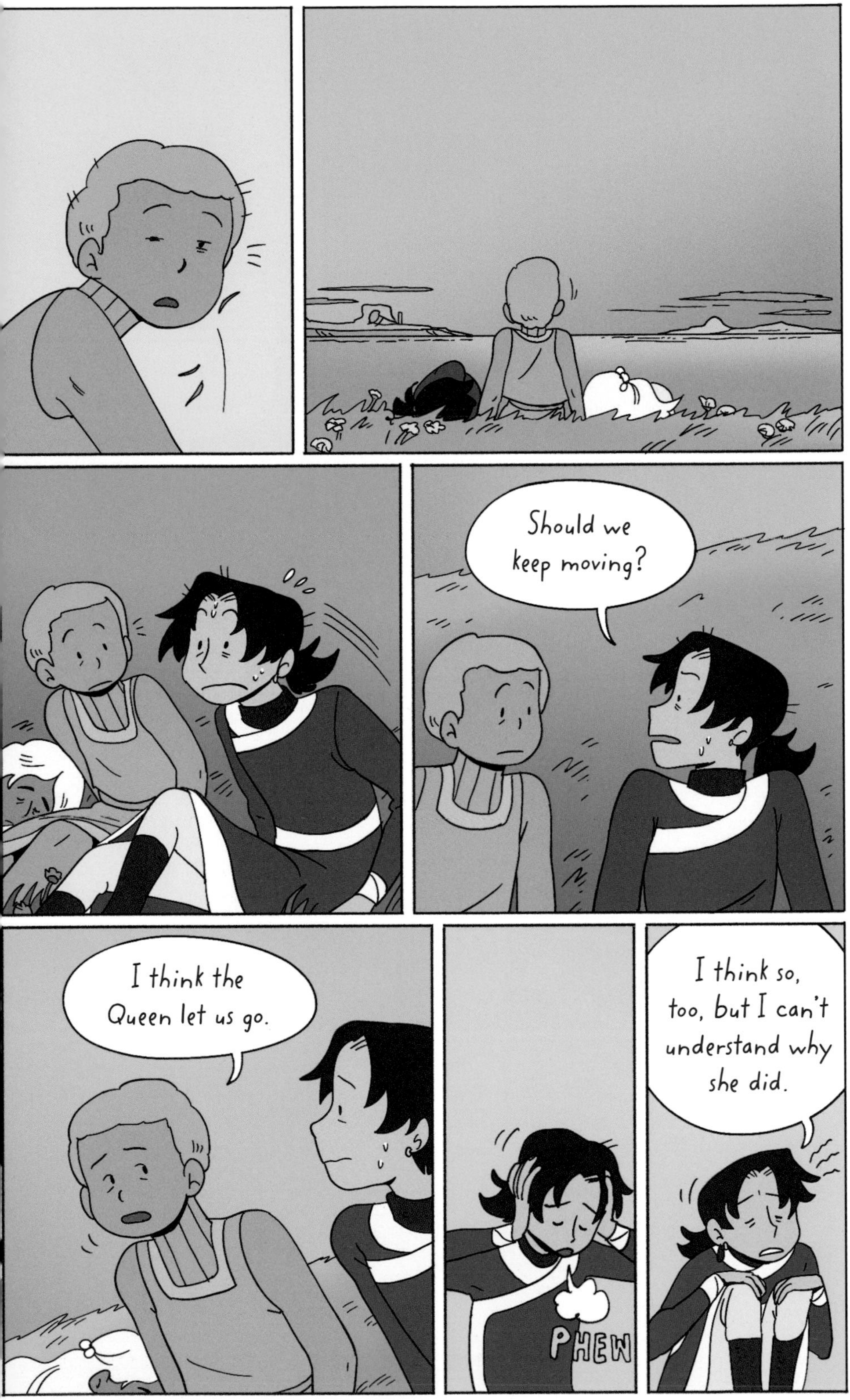
Should we keep moving?
I think the Queen let us go.
PHEW
I think so, too, but I can't understand why she did.

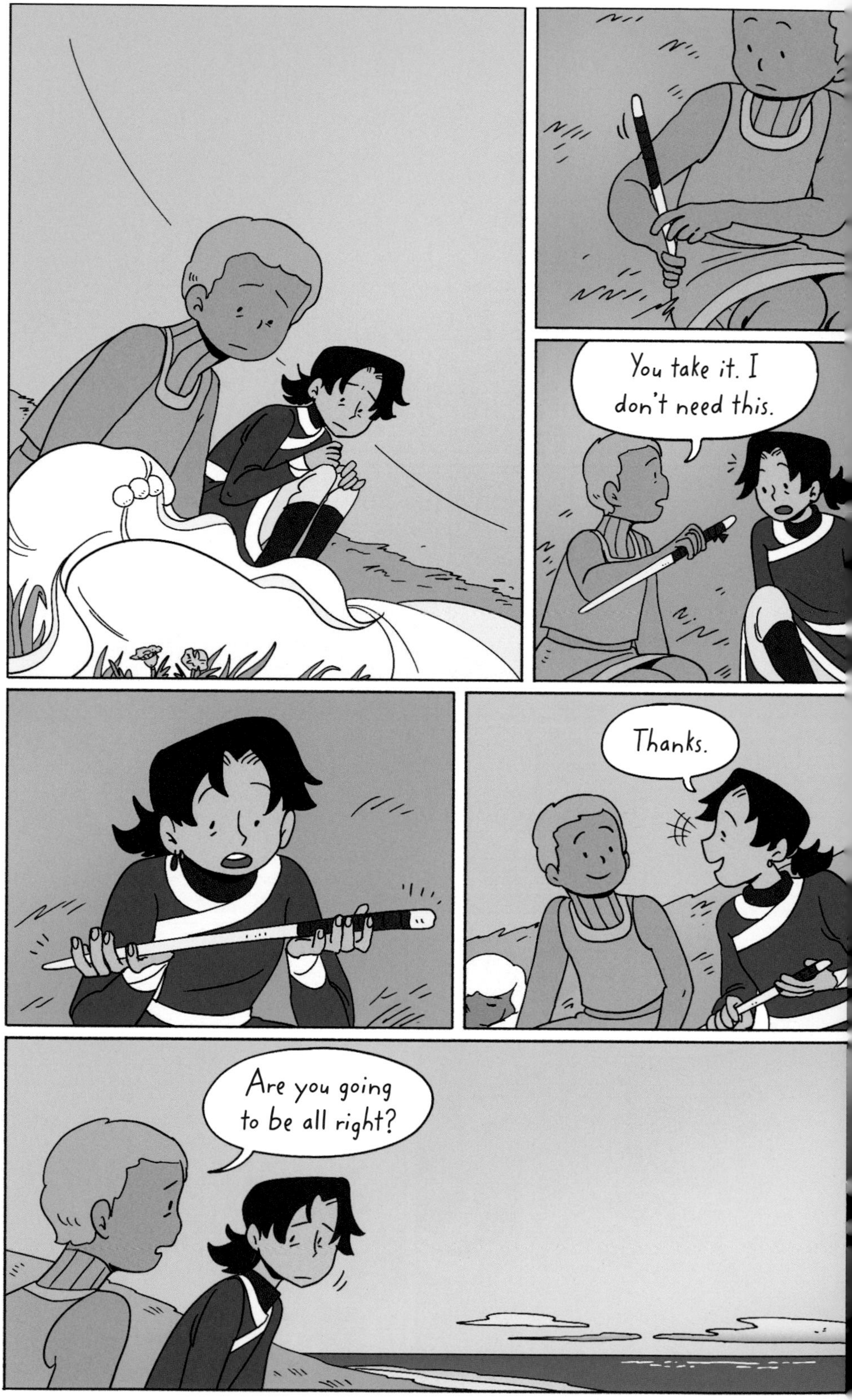
You take it. I don't need this.
Thanks.
Are you going to be all right?

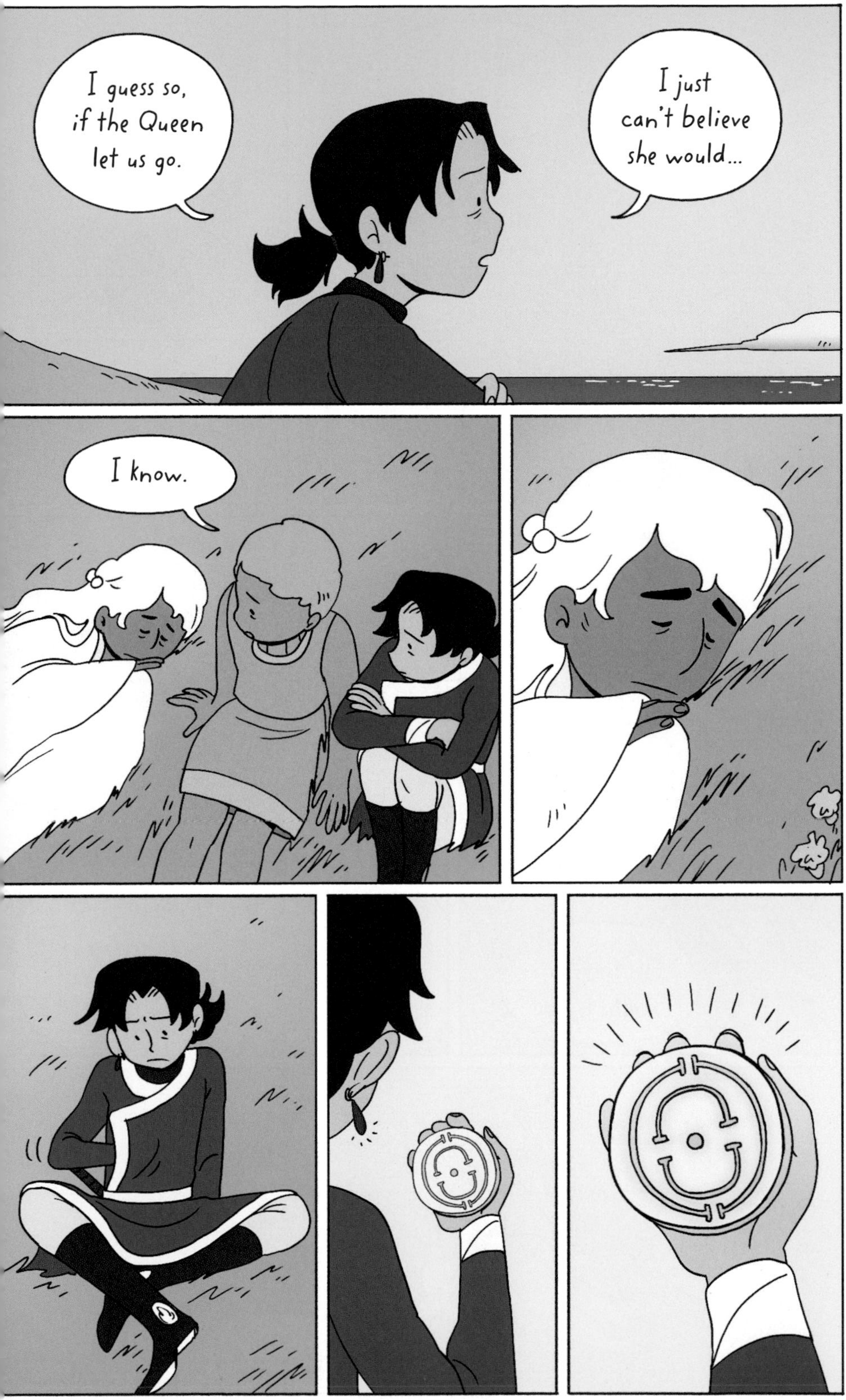
I guess so, if the Queen let us go.
I just can't believe she would...
I know.

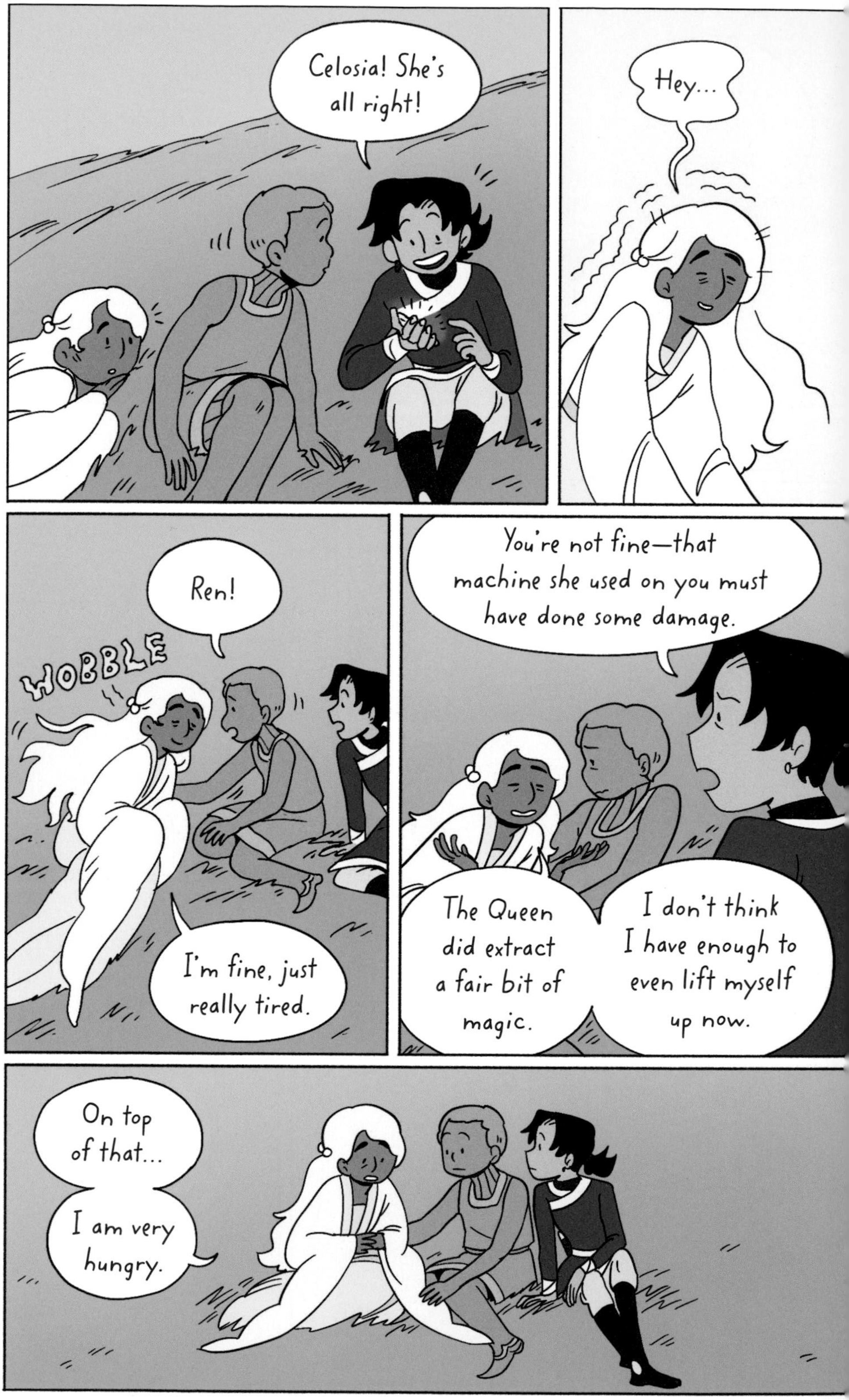
Celosia! She's all right!
Hey...
Ren!
WOBBLE
I'm fine, just really tired.
You're not fine—that machine she used on you must have done some damage.
The Queen did extract a fair bit of magic.
I don't think I have enough to even lift myself up now.
On top of that...
I am very hungry.

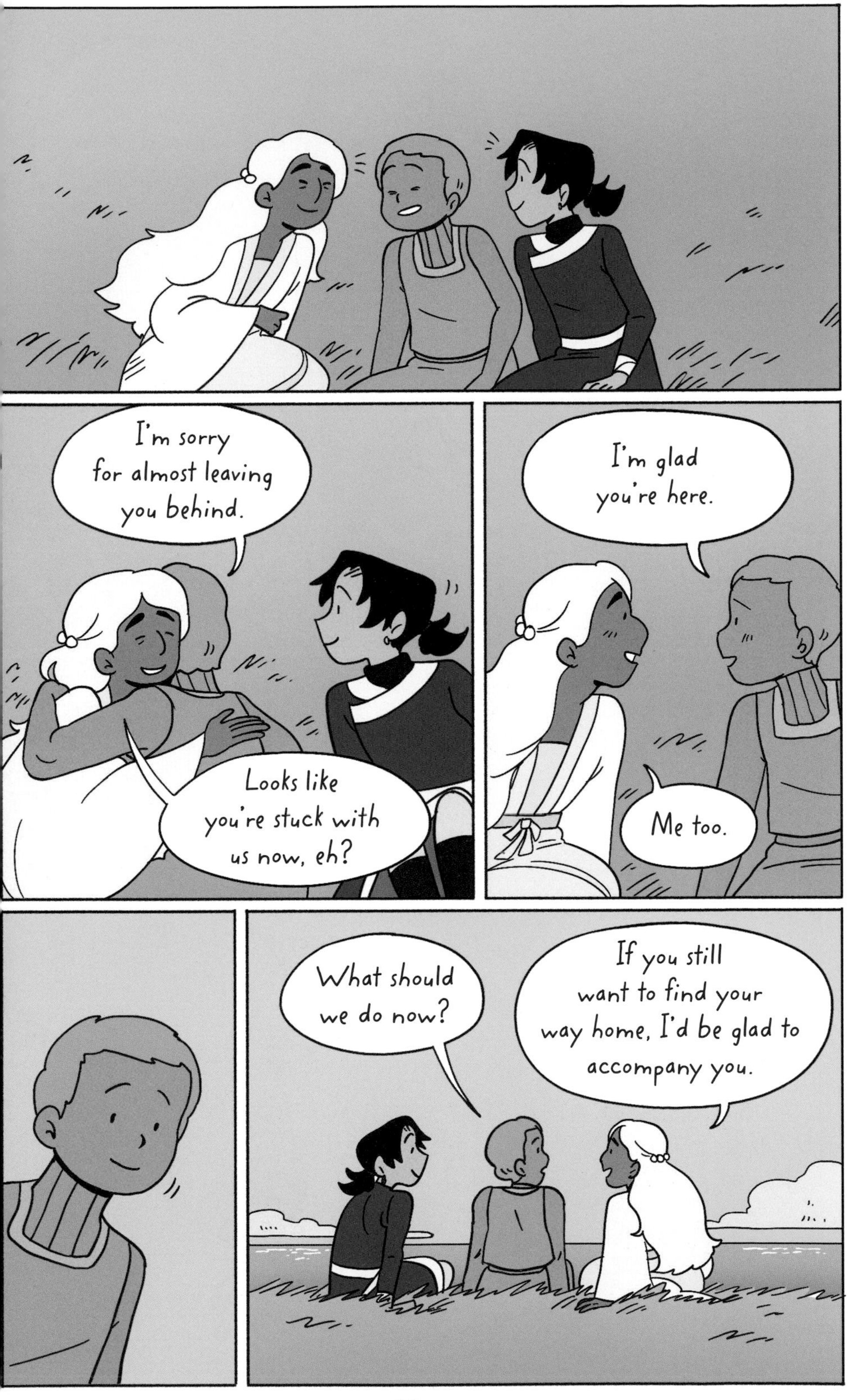

I'm sorry for almost leaving you behind.
Looks like you're stuck with us now, eh?
I'm glad you're here.
Me too.
What should we do now?
If you still want to find your way home, I'd be glad to accompany you.

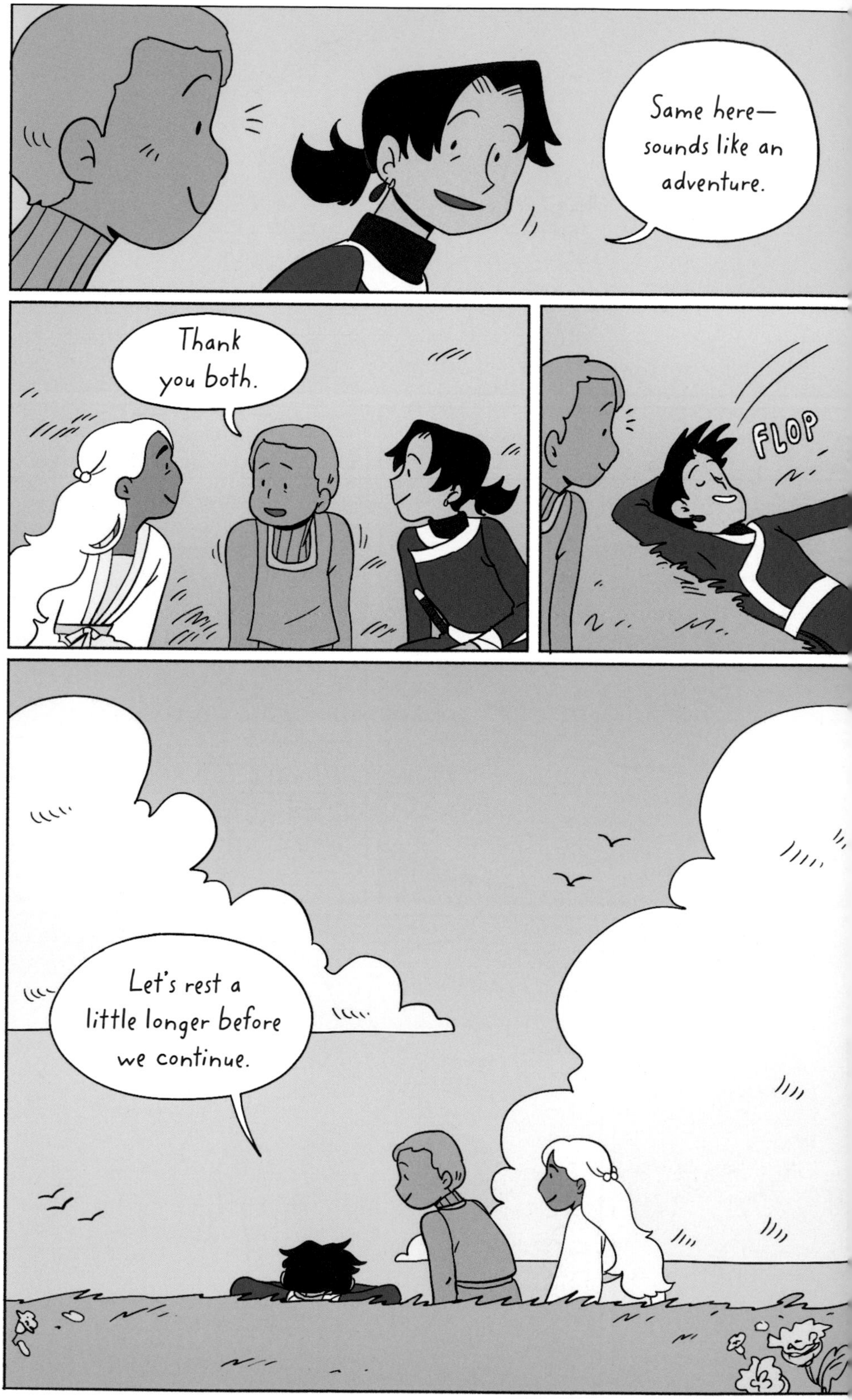
Same here—sounds like an adventure.
Thank you both.
FLOP
Let's rest a little longer before we continue.

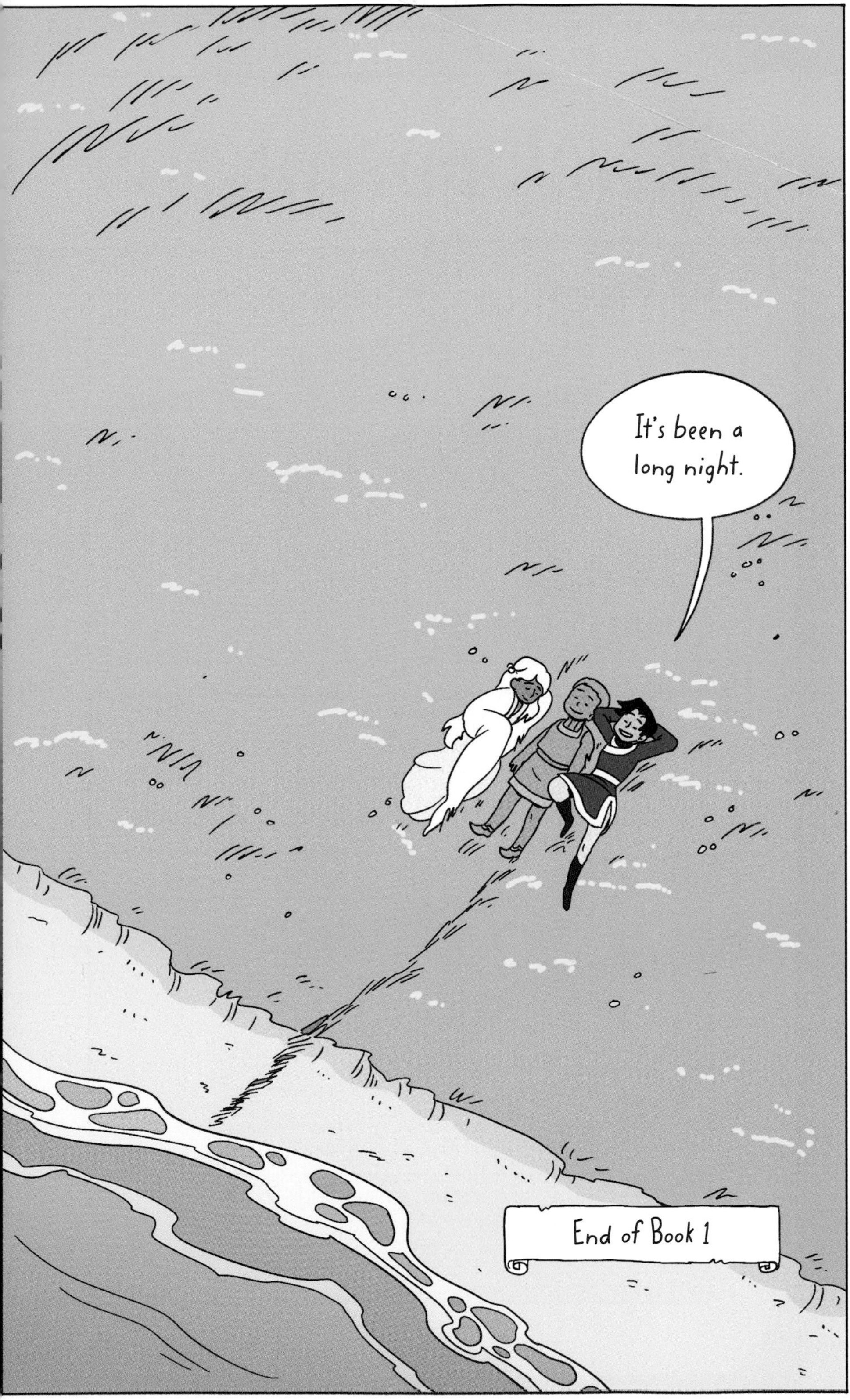
It's been a long night.
End of Book 1

Development Art

The first pieces of finished Atana art I ever made. These were drawn together in the same afternoon, so I've always considered them a set.

The second piece of Atana art I ever made.

This scene with Atana and Ren is the only thing that never changed through all the iterations of the story, from start to end.

Atana's and Ren's designs haven't changed much since I first came up with them, so I have lots of early paintings of the two of them, but not of Cosmos. (Sorry, Cosmos!)

Acknowledgments

Thank you first and foremost to my parents, for always encouraging me to pursue my interests and dreams, and for tirelessly supporting me and believing in me. To my agent, Thao Le, for taking Atana under your wing and finding her a wonderful home. To my editor, Carolina Ortiz, for patiently tailoring this story with me, and everything that you've taught me in the process. To Marisa Rother, Elaine Lopez-Levine, and everyone at HarperAlley who had a hand in making this book a reality. Thank you also to Atla Hrafney, for your thoughtful feedback and encouragement.

Thank you to Darcy, for always having spared the time to listen to me ramble on about this story, even when it was only a vague jumble of ideas. To Youjia and Aimee, for being the best moral support anyone could ever ask for. To Mac, for all the reference photos that made the world of Atana a richer place. Thank you to Fruit Salad Comics, for being lovely and energetic and constantly making me excited about comics.

Last but not least, thank you to the Canada Council for the Arts, for the grant that allowed me to start working on this story full-time.

I am truly grateful for you all.

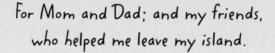

For Mom and Dad; and my friends,
who helped me leave my island.

The author acknowledges the support
of the Canada Council for the Arts.

HarperAlley is an imprint of HarperCollins Publishers.

Atana and the Firebird
Copyright © 2023 by Vivian Zhou
Library of Congress Control Number: 2023933924
ISBN 978-0-06-307591-7 (pbk.) — ISBN 978-0-06-307592-4

The artist used Adobe Photoshop to create the digital illustrations for this book.
Design by Marisa Rother
23 24 25 26 27 GPS 10 9 8 7 6 5 4 3 2 1
First Edition